SELECTED

POETRY OF

BROWNING

SELECTED POETRY OF

Robert Browning

EDITED, WITH AN INTRODUCTION, BY

KENNETH L. KNICKERBOCKER

PROFESSOR OF ENGLISH, *University of Tennessee*

THE MODERN LIBRARY · NEW YORK

#19987115

Copyright, 1951, by Random House, Inc.

Library of Congress Catalog Card Number: 54-9972

Acknowledgment is made to the Thomas Y. Crowell
Company for their kind permission to use the text
of their complete edition of Browning's poetry by
Charlotte Porter and Helen A. Clarke in the prepa-
ration of this volume.

Random House IS THE PUBLISHER OF *The Modern Library*

BENNETT A. CERF · DONALD S. KLOPFER · ROBERT K. HAAS

Manufactured in the United States of America

By H. Wolff

CONTENTS

v

INTRODUCTION

by Kenneth L. Knickerbocker

Browning used to complain that his critics spent so much time reviewing—and condemning—his early work that they left themselves insufficient time and space to judge the quality of his later poems. Now that the complete evidence has long been in, Browning fares best if the critic slights both his early and his late poems. Black charges that he was willfully obscure, deliberately unmusical and arrogantly learned fade, at worst, to light gray and, at best, vanish altogether if one considers only the poems published during the poet's middle years.

Browning's literary career may be trisected, somewhat arbitrarily, as follows: Immaturity, 1832–1840; Maturity, 1841–1869; Senescence, 1870–1889. Some of the poems published during the early part of the second period were actually composed during the first period. There is much less overlapping between the second and the third period.

IMMATURITY: 1832–1840

Four works reached print during this period: *Pauline* (1833); *Paracelsus* (1835); *Strafford* (1837); *Sordello* (1840). Literature would not be greatly impoverished by the loss of any one or all of these publications. The author would agree with this opinion as far as *Pauline* and *Strafford* are concerned, and the public, in spite of any protests from the author and his sturdiest disciples, would not and will not have anything to do with *Sordello*. Browning took some pride in *Paracelsus* and rightly, for it contains many anticipations of his best works.

Pauline, though expendable as a piece of literature, was important to Browning. It was a by-product of Browning's peculiarly informal education. After some desultory and apparently ineffective early schooling, he was entered at sixteen in the newly established University of London where he remained on the rolls for six months but in attendance for a much shorter period than that. Thenceforward he managed his own education with the assistance of a tutor in Italian, a music master, his father's fine library of some six thousand volumes and the Dulwich Art Gallery which lay a short woodland walk from his home and contained paintings by Andrea del Sarto, Raphael, Titian, de Lairesse, and others. The youthful Browning, who had both energy and curiosity in abundance, proceeded unsystematically but effectively to extract from these resources a fund of extraordinary knowledge.

That he contemplated taking all arts to be his province is evident from the panoramic scope of his first literary plan. He was to be successively poet, composer of opera, novelist, writer of speeches and master of other unspecified forms of artistic communication. He planned to issue these works anonymously or pseudonymously, then, darkling, listen to and chuckle at the world's gasps of astonishment and delight. *Pauline*, "the first work of the *Poet* of the batch," was the only part of this vast scheme to reach print.

It is the standard view to suppose that John Stuart Mill's review of *Pauline* stung Browning "into quite another style of writing." Mill had commented that the anonymous author of the poem was "possessed with a more intense and morbid self-consciousness" than he had ever observed "in any sane human being." No doubt such a remark did sting the young poet. Nevertheless, critics for the next thirty years were to say that much and more and receive for their pains increasing doses of the same medicine in the next volume Browning published. Mill's strictures were effective because Browning wanted them to be. He was ashamed of *Pauline* because it so obviously told a tale on him. He was ashamed of it for two other reasons: one, it was and must remain a fragment; two, it was an ineffaceable reminder of an overconfident scheme, other parts of which must have made the poet shudder.

Fragments were as abhorrent to Browning as a vacuum is supposed to be to Nature. In the poem "Waring," he imagines his friend protesting against a lack of public recognition. "True," replied Waring to the charge that he had been silent,

> *but there were sundry jottings,*
> *Stray-leaves, fragments, blurrs and blottings,*
> *Certain first steps were achieved*
> *Already which . . .*
> *Had well borne out whoe'er believed*
> *In more to come!*

Browning's answer is disdainful:

> *But who goes gleaning*
> *Hedgeside chance-blades. while full-sheaved*
> *Stand cornfields by him? Pride, o'erweening*
> *Pride alone, puts forth such claims*
> *O'er the day's distinguished names.*

Pauline was a fragment, and Browning, for all his philosophic admiration of Giotto's unfinished campanile and for all his doctrine of imperfection and incompleteness, looked upon the poem as an untimely abortion.

Then, too, *Pauline* reminded him of his wondrous plan. Of this scheme more than the fragment *Pauline* had probably been executed by 1833. For one thing, Browning allowed a pretentious preface to be printed with *Pauline,* an action from which he might have recoiled if more material had not been in readiness. Moreover, he said of the poem: "Only this crab *remains* of the shapely Tree of Life in this Fool's paradise of mine." I have italicized *remains,* for the word implies, I think, that other parts of the plan had been partly or completely executed. It implies, too, of course, that these other parts had now been destroyed. *Pauline* could not be destroyed, though the author did burn a bale of unbound sheets and create thereby, in strict innocence, a future half-million dollar market for the twenty-one copies of *Pauline* which escaped into our century. Was it a novel, an opera, a speech—all of these, or something else which Browning associated with the poem to cause him a life-long hatred of his first-born?

Of the remaining three works of this first period, only these remarks need be made: *Paracelsus* contains the outlines of Browning's own aspirations; *Strafford* is an unsuccessful imitation of Elizabethan drama and should have been but was not a warning to Browning that stage drama was not his forte; and *Sordello* is what Professor Lounsbury called it, "a colossal derelict upon the sea of literature, inflicting damage upon the strongest intellects which graze it even slightly, and hopelessly wrecking the frailer mental craft that come into full collision with it." Tactfully tacking, therefore, we may move quickly into safer and clearer waters.

MATURITY: 1841–1869

DURING this period Browning published twelve volumes of poems. These volumes contain almost exactly fifty thousand lines. It may be estimated, however, on the basis of Professor De Vane's dates for the composition of the poems, that about fifty-three hundred lines printed in 1841 or later were actually composed in 1840 or earlier. This still leaves a respectable total of lines composed and printed during this middle period, but for a professional poet the production pace was plodding. Averages are deceptive, and perhaps a bit boring, but it may be of interest to note that during his first period Browning composed at the rapid rate of more than two thousand lines a year; during his second period through 1864 his pace slowed down to less than a thousand lines a year.

Two observations may be based upon these statistics: one concerns Browning's artistry, the other, the effect of his marriage. In *The Inn Album* (1875), the poet, with an eye to a standard bit of criticism of his work, allows one of his characters to say:

> *That bard's a Browning; he neglects the form:*
> *But ah, the sense, ye gods, the weighty sense!*

Through the years of his maturity and before senescence brought in its touch of garrulity and "mere gray argument," Browning did not neglect the form but wrote slowly, carefully and with a high degree of concentration. For fifteen years of the middle period (1846–1861) Browning was married. To what effect on his work? Quantitatively the poet was slowed to a fastidious pace but in quality, except for *Christmas Eve and Easter Day,* the poet never succeeded better in decking out what he had to say in the most fitting form.

Naturally, this volume of selections from Browning concentrates on this middle period, which begins with *Pippa Passes* (1841)—but written earlier—and closes with *The Ring and the Book* (1868–1869).

As has been frequently observed, *Pippa Passes* introduced a new, fresh note into English literature. Yet, this play, more than a hundred years after its publication, has not been recognized for what it is. Although written as a closet drama, it may some day be hailed as the most actable of Browning's plays and, if that is faint praise, one may add that it is potentially a great play judged by any standard. As a motion picture *Pippa Passes* could be a triumph. For once, Browning manipulated the stage business with a finesse which is almost totally lacking in his other plays. This stage awareness is apparent in all the four episodes of the play. Ottima and Sebald in the gloomy garden house, blood on their hands, guilt in their consciences, enact one of the tensest scenes in all literature. The Jules–Phene episode contains both humor and pathos. The scene between Luigi and his mother exalts a selflessness into the heroic. In the final scene Pippa unwittingly sings her own salvation and thereby brings the play to a dramatically satisfactory close.

The inspiration for the idea in *Pippa Passes* may possibly have come, perhaps unconsciously, from Carlyle. Browning dramatized the notion that all people interact so sensitively that the idlest word will produce an effect on the moral structure of society. Carlyle, in *Sartor Resartus*, called these ties between men "organic filaments."

> Wondrous truly [he said] are the bonds that unite us one and all. . . . Such venous-arterial circulation, of Letters, verbal messages, paper and other Packages, going out from him [man] and coming in, are a blood-circulation, visible to the eye: but for the finer nervous circulation, by which all things, the minutest that he does, minutely influence all men, and the very look of his face blesses or curses whomso it lights on, and so generates ever new blessing or cursing: all this you cannot see but only imagine.

Pippa Passes contains Browning's high imagining of effects produced by "one apparently too obscure to leave a trace . . . of her passage, yet exercising a lasting though unconscious influence at every step." (Mrs. Orr, *Handbook*, p. 55.) After the death of Carlyle, Browning estimated his debt to him. He recalled their first meeting and then commented: "If then and there had begun and ended our acquaintanceship, very likely I had figured in some corner of a page as a poor scribbling-man with proclivities for the turf and scamphood. What then? He wrote *Sartor*—and such letters to me in those old days! No, I am his devotedly." (*New Letters of Robert Browning*, ed. Wm. C. De Vane and K. L. Knickerbocker, New Haven, 1950, p. 263.) Perhaps Browning's special debt to *Sartor Resartus* is reflected in *Pippa Passes*.

There is perhaps such a thing as knowing too much about a poet. For example Browning may have believed the doctrine which he dramatized in *Pippa*. Undoubtedly poetic determinism is inescapable. What Browning was would appear inevitably in his poetry. Yet Shakespeare's universality *plus* the lack of any directives, or few, in the way of prefaces, portraits, personal letters, diaries, journals, contemporary reviews of his poems and plays, contemporary accounts of his actions and conversation, has created the impression that his pen flowed wondrously, impelled to its mission by one disembodied, by one serenely free from personal belief or philosophy. Consequently, Shakespeare can be and is all things to all men. Too much is known of the writers of the nineteenth century. Their beliefs, prejudices, philosophy, religion, daily life, love affairs are known with startling minuteness and exactness. Pigeonholes are found for every author. Browning, for example, is supposed to fit the well-padded pigeonhole reserved for robust optimists. If all we know of Browning had to be deduced exclusively from his poetry, we would know much; we might even know that he was a robust optimist, but there would be long stretches of his poetry to disturb our confidence.

All *is* a bit righter with the world at the end of Pippa's day, and perhaps only an optimist would have thought this possible. But the rightness is not a simple matter of happy endings. By suicide Ottima and Sebald have quenched their passion, and Luigi has gone to his triumph and doom. Jules has married and will cherish Phene, and Monsignor is arranging a secure future for Pippa. Thus two happy and two unhappy endings were created by Pippa's songs. This may be an optimistic view of life's chances, but it can hardly be called flagrant Pollyannaism.

But is it not childlike—not to say fatuously blind—for a poet to allow even a child character to sing,

> *God's in his heaven—*
> *All's right with the world?*

These lines are without question dramatic, but Browning, I think, would accept them as expressing his basic view of man's relation with the universe. Philosophy's chief problem is to account for everything in the universe. No one has yet been able to do this by restricting speculation to things seen. Even science puzzles daily over things unseen. Browning's hypothesis is that under an omnipotent, benevolent God, all must, at least in a cosmic sense, be right with the world. It could not be otherwise.

From the fundamental assumption of Pippa's song stemmed all the poet's other beliefs, the accounting for imperfection and frustration, for example. Birds sing and frogs croak. The song is perfect and a croak is a croak and nothing much can be done about it. But man constantly reaches for the unattainable. A poet sings, but the song, unlike the song of the bird, only approximates faintly what the poet feels. Why, he may ask himself, as Browning did ask himself, this hoarse whisper instead of the spheral music which I feel? Well, if God is in His heaven with perfection and completeness in His hands, there may be logic in this one of many human frustrations. "A man's reach should exceed his grasp/ Or what's a heaven for?" Life, then, becomes a divine titillation. Many of Browning's best known poems contain expressions of this idea, particularly "Andrea del Sarto," "Old Pictures in Florence," "A Grammarian's Funeral," "Abt Vogler," and "Rabbi Ben Ezra."

Browning thought that man could look within himself for other evidences of God's plan and God's nature. Man, for example, can and does love with an overwhelming devotion and passion. The feeling is wholly irrational and is as puzzling to philosophy as the problem of evil. Whence comes it? It expresses itself in the hot passions of an Ottima and Sebald, in the hopeless enthrallment of Andrea del Sarto and the speaker in "Time's Revenges," in the purer devotion of a Pompilia and a Caponsacchi, of a Robert Browning and a spinster-aged Miss Barrett. Whence comes it? It may shift from concern for persons to concern for causes and ideals. Karshish, the Arab physician, felt its touch; Cleon, the intellectual Greek, felt its absence. But David, the Hebrew boy, knew the full answer:

I believe it! 'Tis thou, God, that givest, 'tis I who receive. . . .
Would I suffer for him that I love? So wouldst thou—so wilt
thou.

Man in his capacity for love touches divinity.

But if man can love, he can also hate. If man can believe, he can also doubt. As Browning observed, "A scientific faith's absurd" (*Christmas Eve*). A clear-cut miracle would destroy faith by substituting certainty. Doubt, therefore, is an ingredient of faith. Why this should be the Divine Plan the poet does not say. He simply is aware that in coldly rational moments, man doubts; but man does not settle back comfortably into this state of negative certainty.

Just when we are safest, there's a sunset-touch,
A fancy from a flower-bell, some one's death,
A chorus-ending from Euripides,—
And that's enough for fifty hopes and fears
As old and new at once as nature's self,

> *To rap and knock and enter in our soul,*
> *Take hands and dance there, a fantastic ring,*
> *Round the ancient idol, on his base again,—*
> *The grand Perhaps!*
>
> ("Bishop Blougram's Apology")

Browning makes it clear that not for him nor for any man can there be a grand certainty. Yet, when reason balked, he was willing to plunge ahead under the guidance of his feelings. Among the poems in which doubt and faith are discussed are included "The Boy and the Angel," *Christmas Eve and Easter Day,* "Master Hugues of Saxe-Gotha," "Bishop Blougram's Apology," "Abt Vogler," "Rabbi Ben Ezra"; and from his third period, such poems as *La Saisiaz* and "Fears and Scruples."

Although Browning placed Johannes Agricola in a madhouse cell for his extreme antinomianism, the poet was more than a little touched with this doctrine himself. In "Apparent Failure" he gazes upon three men who have committed suicide and are awaiting identification in a Paris morgue. He speculates that one of these "Poor men, God made . . . wanted to be Buona-parte"; another wanted a classless society; and the third a gay and lustful life. All were frustrated. To these men, the smugly righteous would say:

> *It's wiser being good than bad;*
> *It's safer being meek than fierce:*
> *It's fitter being sane than mad.*

But if there is an all-loving God who created these men, what then? The poet answers that his own hope is

> *That what began best, can't end worst,*
> *Nor what God blessed once, prove accurst.*

This is surely a one-sided antinomianism which implies that man has "God's warrant" to protect him from any ultimate responsi-bility for his own actions. Here, I think, is the best evidence of Browning's confirmed optimism.

Although man cannot be ultimately cursed for his way of life, no matter how evil, he can damn himself within his own life span. The one best way of doing this is by ignoring the prompt-ings of love, which to Browning were never dubious murmur-ings but sudden alarums loud enough to awaken the sleepiest heart. When, in 1845, the alarum had sounded for him, he had sprung into action. He expected others to do likewise and reserved his keenest scorn for the laggards in love. This conviction stems, too, I think, from the premise that God is all-loving and man, if he would understand this characteristic, must be expanded and made generous by this Godlike quality. The poet, therefore, asks society to stand aside for men and women in love. Is one of the lovers in the poem "In a Gondola" married? Yes, but that fact is unimportant. Is the bride of the Riccardi ("The Statue and the Bust") to allow her marriage to interfere with her sudden love for the Duke? She does, but, says the poet with emphatic disapproval, she should not have. "The world's honours" blinded Cristina to a love which could have saved her from such secondary concerns. And the feminine speaker in "Dîs Aliter Visum" pours out her pent-up scorn on the venerable poet who, ten years before, had refused to say,

> Let me get
> Her for myself, and what's the earth
> With all its art, verse, music, worth—
> Compared with love, found, gained, and kept?

I have scanned rapidly Browning's central belief and some of the doctrines that radiated from this hub. It is a legitimate concern of the reader to ferret out a poet's system of thought, but it should not be his only, or even his chief, concern. Browning's greatness does not lie in what he believed. It does lie in his creative sensitivity to life direct and to life recorded. It lies, too, in his perfecting of a form, the dramatic monologue, through which he could best display this creative sensitivity. On each of these points a word should be said.

Browning created two kinds of characters: those cut, as far as we know, from the whole cloth of his imagination and those based upon historical persons. He managed to allow many of his imagined persons to be pretty much themselves. The speaker in the "Soliloquy of the Spanish Cloister," the Bishop of St. Praxed's, the lover of Porphyria, the girls of "The Laboratory" and "The Confessional," and a considerable number of other characters say *their* say, not Browning's. It was different for the historical characters. One example will suffice. In writing "Andrea del Sarto," the poet was more than usually faithful to his sources, Vasari and Baldinucci, and the result is a triumphant portrait of the love-bemused painter. Andrea says what the reader is convinced he would say. Unfortunately, he says more. He accepts the doctrine of compensation: if things do not go well in this world, things will be proportionately better in the next. Moreover, he accounts for his failure as growing out of the mean goal he had set himself, the goal of mere mechanical perfection. Both these ideas are certainly Browning's; whether they were Andrea's is open to question. Nevertheless, Andrea lives within the framework of the poet's conception, and perhaps only scholars are concerned with Browning's intrusions. Certain it is that if one objects to this procedure, he will object to much of Browning's work. When his characters are being most themselves, up comes Browning. Indeed, to describe the poet's intrusive behavior one may paraphrase the lines of Fra Lippo Lippi:

> *Well, all these*
> *Secured at their devotions, up shall come*
> *Out of a corner when you least expect,*
> *As one by a dark stair into a great light,*
> *Music and talking, who but Browning!*

Why, then, has Browning long been regarded, except by latter-day initiates, as one of the most objective poets since Shakespeare? For one thing, Browning said so: he vowed that his poems were "so many utterances of so many imaginary persons, not mine." For another thing, many of his best short poems *are* objective. Moreover, earlier critics and readers with only a fragmentary knowledge of Browning the man could not be certain about the extent of the subjectivity in the poems. Finally, and most important, the dramatic monologue is a magnificently deceptive device which seemed—and still seems—to guarantee objectivity.

If, as is contended in "Old Pictures in Florence," "what's come to perfection perishes," then Browning himself put the poetic form of the dramatic monologue in jeopardy, a jeopardy as serious as that visited on heroic couplets by Alexander Pope. The dramatic monologue is a literary trick, a deliberate use of one hand, so to speak, when two are available. But it is a neat trick, a thorough test of artistry, a confining, demanding form, and not one to be lightly self-imposed. Browning, however, apparently reveled in the restrictions.

Each monologue presented its own set of problems. Who was to speak? On what subject? To whom? Where? When? For how long? During his period of maturity, Browning integrated the answers to these and other questions with exquisite skill to produce his greatest poems. Since the requirements of the dramatic monologue and its related form, the soliloquy, have been much discussed elsewhere, I shall restrict myself to brief comments on Browning's handling of the answers to the questions: To whom? and For how long?

Upon choice of the listener depends much of the effectiveness and realism of the monologues. Two examples will demonstrate the importance of this choice. The listener in "My Last Duchess" is the emissary of a count whose daughter may become the next Duchess of Ferrara. The Duke of Ferrara in describing his relationship with his last Duchess was not deliberately preening himself on his arrogance and cruelty. He was issuing a sober warning to his prospective wife. Once the count's daughter linked herself with his "nine-hundred-years-old name," she would be given no further hint concerning conduct becoming a duchess. To this particular listener, therefore, the Duke would make such a speech. Would, however, Bishop Blougram speak as he did to Gigadibs in "Bishop Blougram's Apology"? One may be sure that Browning thought carefully before selecting the atheistic journalist as the listener in this poem. He did not pit the Bishop against an Anglican nor a Dissenter, against a Jew nor even a Higher Critic. Instead he gave to the loquacious prelate a straw man for opponent. In spite of this careful choice, Browning realized that the Bishop might not have been so indiscreet. Therefore, he has Blougram say that if Gigadibs dares print any part of the evening's talk, no one will believe the report. Even Blougram's enemies will sneer:

> *the bishop's an arch-hypocrite*
> *And knave perhaps, but not so frank a fool.*

Dramatically, these lines are sound enough. The Bishop's pride and confidence in his power make such a challenge fairly plausible—but only against an opponent of Gigadibs' stamp. A slightly more astute antagonist would have known that anyone who thought the Bishop an arch-hypocrite and knave would already be aware of what the Bishop had been confessing to Gigadibs. Why, then, would they disbelieve a report which substantiated their judgment? They would not. Instead, they would say: "The Bishop, as we suspected, is an arch-hypocrite, a knave, *and* a frank fool besides." In choosing Gigadibs, Browning obviously stacked the cards.

A monologue should be short. Browning was apparently aware of this restriction and in most of the monologues published between 1842 and 1864 was sufficiently terse. Notable exceptions are "Bishop Blougram's Apology" and "Mr. Sludge, 'The Medium.'" Browning estimates that the Bishop "talked his hour." One does not have to test this estimate nor call in question the naturalness of a bishop's talking so long to say that the poem is wordy. Gigadibs, overawed, stayed through the performance but, wisely, "did not sit five minutes" once it was done. Mr. Sludge's speech, more than half again as long as the Bishop's, must have taken over an hour and a half to deliver. Mr. Sludge was desperate and perhaps Mr. Horsefall, his listener, was, too, before "The Medium's" apologia ended.

In *The Ring and the Book* each speaker simply talks himself out. Guido, for example, speaks twice for a total of over forty-five hundred lines; his second speech would have taken perhaps two hours and a half to deliver. Browning had come to ignore the question: For how long? For the sake of the great things in this gargantuan murder story, the reader, too, may be willing to ignore this question. But the floodgates were down when Browning entered his period of senescence and seldom after *The Ring and the Book* did he strive for dramatically appropriate length for his monologues.

SENESCENCE: 1869–1889

During the last twenty years of his life, Browning published fifteen volumes of poems. Because of this large output, it has been said that criticism toiled after him in vain. Willing toilers appeared in the persons of Browning Society members who, in 1881, had banded themselves together for the sole purpose of studying minutely the every utterance of the sage of Warwick Crescent. The personal good to Browning was tremendous and tangible, as the sale of his books, which had been good since 1863, picked up considerably. There were penalties too. Sober, objective studies of the poet were caught in a wash—a gush, one might say—of sentimental interpretations. One still must pick his way carefully if he goes back very far into "scholarship" on Browning.

The present volume includes poems from seven of the poet's late volumes. One can point to few things new. *Pacchiarotto, with Other Poems* did contain some doggerel verses attacking critics. That was new. New, too, was Browning's poetic insistence, in "House" and several other poems of the *Pacchiarotto* volume, that he disdained to write his life into his poetry. Yet,

"Fears and Scruples" and "St. Martin's Summer" from this same volume are laden with autobiography. The *Dramatic Idyls* of 1879 and 1880 contain some remarkably vigorous narratives and the "Parleying with Daniel Bartoli" (1887) demonstrates that this vigor remained unabated. *Asolando* (1889), the final volume, though filled with poetic niblets and thrice-told ideas, is no weak valedictory to a career which measured almost exactly fifty-seven years from the conception of *Pauline* to the final battle cry:

> "*Strive and thrive!*" cry "*Speed,—fight on,*
> *There as here!*"

This sort of muscular challenge to life and death falls on cynical ears these days. Yet it is doubtful that Browning really very gravely misjudged man's essentially indomitable spirit. From the dust and shadows men "may seek to escape, and yet they cannot . . . they are condemned to some nobility their lives long, the desire of good is at their heels, the implacable hunter."

SELECTED BIBLIOGRAPHY

WORKS

The Complete Works of Robert Browning, ed. with introduction and notes by Charlotte Porter and Helen A. Clarke, 12 vols. New York, 1901.

The Poems and Plays of Robert Browning, with introduction by Saxe Commins. New York, 1934.

LETTERS

The Letters of Elizabeth Barrett Browning, ed. F. G. Kenyon, 2 vols. New York, 1897.

The Letters of Robert Browning and Elizabeth Barrett Barrett, 1845–1846, 2 vols. New York and London, 1899.

Robert Browning and Alfred Domett, ed. F. G. Kenyon. London, 1906.

Letters of Robert Browning to Miss Isa Blagden, arr. A. J. Armstrong. Waco, Texas, 1923.

Elizabeth Barrett Browning: Letters to her Sister, 1846–1859, ed. Leonard Huxley. London, 1929.

Letters of Robert Browning, Collected by T. J. Wise, ed. with introduction, notes, and appendix by T. L. Hood. New Haven, 1933.

Twenty-two Unpublished Letters of Elizabeth Barrett Browning and Robert Browning Addressed to Henrietta and Arabella Moulton-Barrett, with a foreword by J. A. S. Altham. New York, 1935.

Robert Browning and Julia Wedgwood, Their Letters, ed. Richard Curle. New York, 1937.

New Letters of Robert Browning, ed. with introduction, notes, and appendices by William C. De Vane and K. L. Knickerbocker. New Haven, 1950.

BIOGRAPHIES

Besier, Rudolph, *The Barretts of Wimpole Street.* New York, 1931.

Griffin, W. H. and Minchin, H. C., *The Life of Robert Browning*. London, 1910 (New ed., 1938).

Lounsbury, T. R., *The Early Literary Career of Robert Browning*. New York, 1911.

Orr, Mrs. Sutherland, *Life and Letters of Robert Browning*. Revised by F. G. Kenyon, New York, 1908.

Whiting, Lilian, *The Brownings; Their Life and Art*. Boston, 1911.

Winwar, Frances, *The Immortal Lovers*. New York, 1950.

WORKS OF REFERENCE

Berdoe, Edward, *The Browning Cyclopaedia*. London, 1891.

Broughton, L. N. and B. F. Stelter, *A Concordance to the Poems of Robert Browning*, 2 vols. New York, 1924–25.

Browning Collections, The. London, 1913. (Catalogue of Browning's library at the time of its sale by the auctioneers, Sotheby, Wilkinson, and Hodge.)

Browning Society Papers. London, 1881–1891.

Cooke, G. W., *A Guide-Book to the Poetic and Dramatic Works of Robert Browning*. Boston, 1891.

De Vane, William C., *A Browning Handbook*. New York, 1935.

Orr, Mrs. Sutherland, *A Handbook to the Works of Robert Browning*. London, 1886, with additions in successive issues.

Wise, T. J., *A Complete Bibliography of the Writings in Prose and Verse of Robert Browning*. London, 1897.

STUDIES

De Vane, William C., *Browning's Parleyings; The Autobiography of a Mind*. New Haven, 1927.

Duckworth, F. G. R., *Browning: Background and Conflict*. London, 1931.

Elliott, G. R., "Shakespeare's Significance for Browning," *Anglia*, XXXII (January–April, 1901), 90–162.

Grierson, H. J. C., "Tennyson, Browning and Some Others," *Lyrical Poetry of the Nineteenth Century*. New York, 1929.

Hatcher, Harlan H., *The Versification of Robert Browning*. Columbus, Ohio, 1928.

Inge, W. R., "The Mysticism of Robert Browning," *Studies of English Mystics*. London, 1907.

Jones, Henry, *Browning as a Philosophical and Religious Teacher*. Glasgow, London, New York, 1891.

Knickerbocker, K. L., "Browning and His Critics," *Sewanee Review*, XLIII (July-September, 1935), 283–291.

More, P. E., "Why Is Browning Popular?", *Shelburne Essays*, Third Series. New York, 1905.

Pater, Walter, "Robert Browning," *Essays from "The Guardian."* London, 1901.

Phelps, William Lyon, *Robert Browning*. Indianapolis, 1931.

Pottle, F. A., *Shelley and Browning: A Myth and Some Facts*. Chicago, 1923.

Raymond, William O., "Browning and the Higher Criticism," *PMLA*, XLIV (June, 1929), 590–621.

Russell, Frances T., *One Word More on Browning*. Stanford University, 1927.

Saintsbury, George, "Browning," *Corrected Impressions*. New York, 1895.

Santayana, George, "The Poetry of Barbarism," *Interpretations of Poetry and Religion*. New York, 1900.

Smalley, Donald, ed. *Browning's Essay on Chatterton*, with foreword by William C. De Vane, Cambridge, Mass., 1948.

Woodberry, G. E., "Late Victorian Verse," *Studies of a Littérateur*. New York, 1921.

SELECTED POETRY
OF BROWNING

PIPPA PASSES

A DRAMA

[1841]

I dedicate my best intentions, in this poem, admiringly to the author of "Ion," affectionately to Mr. Sergeant Talfourd.
R. B.

LONDON: 1841

PERSONS

Pippa	Jules
Ottima	Phene
Sebald	*Austrian Police*
Foreign Students	Bluphocks
Gottlieb	Luigi *and his* Mother
Schramm	*Poor Girls*
Monsignor *and his Attendants*	

INTRODUCTION

New Year's Day at Asolo in the Trevisan

SCENE—*A large mean airy chamber. A girl,* PIPPA, *from the Silk-mills, springing out of bed.*

DAY!
Faster and more fast,
O'er night's brim, day boils at last:
Boils, pure gold, o'er the cloud-cup's brim
Where spurting and suppressed it lay,
For not a froth-flake touched the rim
Of yonder gap in the solid gray
Of the eastern cloud, an hour away;
But forth one wavelet, then another, curled,
Till the whole sunrise, not to be suppressed,   10

Rose, reddened, and its seething breast
Flickered in bounds, grew gold, then overflowed the world.

Oh, Day, if I squander a wavelet of thee,
A mite of my twelve hours' treasure,
The least of thy gazes or glances,
(Be they grants thou art bound to or gifts above measure)
One of thy choices or one of thy chances,
(Be they tasks God imposed thee or freaks at thy pleasure)
—My Day, if I squander such labor or leisure,
Then shame fall on Asolo, mischief on me!   20

Thy long blue solemn hours serenely flowing,
Whence earth, we feel, gets steady help and good—
Thy fitful sunshine-minutes, coming, going,
As if earth turned from work in gamesome mood—
All shall be mine! But thou must treat me not
As prosperous ones are treated, those who live
At hand here, and enjoy the higher lot,
In readiness to take what thou wilt give,
And free to let alone what thou refusest;
For, Day, my holiday, if thou ill-usest   30
Me, who am only Pippa,—old-year's sorrow,
Cast off last night, will come again to-morrow:
Whereas, if thou prove gentle, I shall borrow
Sufficient strength of thee for new-year's sorrow.
All other men and women that this earth
Belongs to, who all days alike possess,
Make general plenty cure particular dearth,
Get more joy one way, if another, less;
Thou art my single day, God lends to leaven
What were all earth else, with a feel of heaven,—   40
Sole light that helps me through the year, thy sun's!
Try now! Take Asolo's Four Happiest Ones—
And let thy morning rain on that superb
Great haughty Ottima; can rain disturb
Her Sebald's homage? All the while thy rain
Beats fiercest on her shrub-house window-pane,
He will but press the closer, breathe more warm
Against her cheek; how should she mind the storm?
And, morning past, if mid-day shed a gloom
O'er Jules and Phene,—what care bride and groom   50
Save for their dear selves? 'Tis their marriage-day;

And while they leave church and go home their way,
Hand clasping hand, within each breast would be
Sunbeams and pleasant weather spite of thee.
Then, for another trial, obscure thy eve
With mist,—will Luigi and his mother grieve—
The lady and her child, unmatched, forsooth,
She in her age, as Luigi in his youth,
For true content? The cheerful town, warm, close
And safe, the sooner that thou art morose,   60
Receives them. And yet once again, outbreak
In storm at night on Monsignor, they make
Such stir about,—whom they expect from Rome
To visit Asolo, his brothers' home,
And say here masses proper to release
A soul from pain,—what storm dares hurt his peace?
Calm would he pray, with his own thoughts to ward
Thy thunder off, nor want the angels' guard.
But Pippa—just one such mischance would spoil
Her day that lightens the next twelvemonth's toil   70
At wearisome silk-winding, coil on coil!
    And here I let time slip for naught!
Aha, you foolhardy sunbeam, caught
With a single splash from my ewer!
You that would mock the best pursuer,
Was my basin over-deep?
One splash of water ruins you asleep,
And up, up, fleet your brilliant bits
Wheeling and counterwheeling,
Reeling, broken beyond healing: 80
Now grow together on the ceiling!
That will task your wits.
Whoever it was quenched fire first, hoped to see
Morsel after morsel flee
As merrily, as giddily . . .
Meantime, what lights my sunbeam on,
Where settles by degrees the radiant cripple?
Oh, is it surely blown, my martagon?
New-blown and ruddy as St. Agnes' nipple,
Plump as the flesh-bunch on some Turk bird's poll!   90
Be sure if corals, branching 'neath the ripple
Of ocean, bud there,—fairies watch unroll
Such turban-flowers; I say, such lamps disperse
Thick red flame through that dusk green universe!

I am queen of thee, floweret!
And each fleshy blossom
Preserve I not—(safer
Than leaves that embower it,
Or shells that embosom)
—From weevil and chafer?   100
Laugh through my pane then; solicit the bee;
Gibe him, be sure; and, in midst of thy glee,
Love thy queen, worship me!

—Worship whom else? For am I not, this day,
Whate'er I please? What shall I please to-day?
My morn, noon, eve and night—how spend my day?
To-morrow I must be Pippa who winds silk,
The whole year round, to earn just bread and milk:
But, this one day, I have leave to go,
And play out my fancy's fullest games;   110
I may fancy all day—and it shall be so—
That I taste of the pleasures, am called by the names
Of the Happiest Four in our Asolo!

See! Up the hill-side yonder, through the morning,
Some one shall love me, as the world calls love:
I am no less than Ottima, take warning!
The gardens, and the great stone house above,
And other house for shrubs, all glass in front,
Are mine; where Sebald steals, as he is wont,
To court me, while old Luca yet reposes: 120
And therefore, till the shrub-house door uncloses,
I . . . what now?—give abundant cause for prate
About me—Ottima, I mean—of late,
Too bold, too confident she'll still face down
The spitefullest of talkers in our town.
How we talk in the little town below!
    But love, love, love—there's better love, I know!
This foolish love was only day's first offer;
I choose my next love to defy the scoffer:
For do not our Bride and Bridegroom sally   130
Out of Possagno church at noon?
Their house looks over Orcana valley:
Why should not I be the bride as soon
As Ottima? For I saw, beside,
Arrive last night that little bride—

Saw, if you call it seeing her, one flash
Of the pale snow-pure cheek and black bright tresses,
Blacker than all except the black eyelash;
I wonder she contrives those lids no dresses!
—So strict was she, the veil   140
Should cover close her pale
Pure cheeks—a bride to look at and scarce touch,
Scarce touch, remember, Jules! For are not such
Used to be tended, flower-like, every feature,
As if one's breath would fray the lily of a creature?
A soft and easy life these ladies lead:
Whiteness in us were wonderful indeed.
Oh, save that brow its virgin dimness,
Keep that foot its lady primness,
Let those ankles never swerve   150
From their exquisite reserve,
Yet have to trip along the streets like me,
All but naked to the knee!
How will she ever grant her Jules a bliss
So startling as her real first infant kiss?
Oh, no—not envy, this!

—Not envy, sure!—for if you gave me
Leave to take or to refuse,
In earnest, do you think I'd choose
That sort of new love to enslave me?   160
Mine should have lapped me round from the beginning;
As little fear of losing it as winning:
Lovers grow cold, men learn to hate their wives,
And only parents' love can last our lives.
At eve the Son and Mother, gentle pair,
Commune inside our turret: what prevents
My being Luigi? While that mossy lair
Of lizards through the winter-time is stirred
With each to each imparting sweet intents
For this new-year, as brooding bird to bird—   170
(For I observe of late, the evening walk
Of Luigi and his mother, always ends
Inside our ruined turret, where they talk,
Calmer than lovers, yet more kind than friends)
—Let me be cared about, kept out of harm,
And schemed for, safe in love as with a charm;
Let me be Luigi! If I only knew

What was my mother's face—my father, too!
  Nay, if you come to that, best love of all
Is God's; then why not have God's love befall   180
Myself as, in the palace by the Dome,
Monsignor?—who to-night will bless the home
Of his dead brother; and God bless in turn
That heart which beats, those eyes which mildly burn
With love for all men! I, to-night at least,
Would be that holy and beloved priest.

Now wait!—even I already seem to share
In God's love: what does New-year's hymn declare?
What other meaning do these verses bear?

> All service ranks the same with God: 190
> If now, as formerly he trod
> Paradise, his presence fills
> Our earth, each only as God wills
> Can work—God's puppets, best and worst,
> Are we; there is no last nor first.
> Say not "a small event!" Why "small"?
> Costs it more pain that this, ye call
> A "great event," should come to pass,
> Than that? Untwine me from the mass
> Of deeds which make up life, one deed   200
> Power shall fall short in or exceed!

And more of it, and more of it!—oh yes—
I will pass each, and see their happiness,
And envy none—being just as great, no doubt,
Useful to men, and dear to God, as they!
A pretty thing to care about
So mightily, this single holiday!
But let the sun shine! Wherefore repine?
—With thee to lead me, O Day of mine,
Down the grass path gray with dew,   210
Under the pine-wood, blind with boughs
Where the swallow never flew
Nor yet cicala dared carouse—
No, dared carouse!   [*She enters the street.*

I—MORNING

SCENE—*Up the Hill-side, inside the Shrub-house.* LUCA'S *wife,* OTTIMA, *and her paramour, the German* SEBALD.

Sebald [*sings*].

> Let the watching lids wink!
> Day's a-blaze with eyes, think!
> Deep into the night, drink!

Ottima. Night? Such may be your Rhineland nights perhaps;
But this blood-red beam through the shutter's chink
—We call such light, the morning: let us see!
Mind how you grope your way, though! How these tall
Naked geraniums straggle! Push the lattice
Behind that frame!—Nay, do I bid you?—Sebald,
It shakes the dust down on me! Why, of course   10
The slide-bolt catches. Well, are you content,
Or must I find you something else to spoil?
Kiss and be friends, my Sebald! Is't full morning?
Oh, don't speak then!
    Sebald.   Ay, thus it used to be.
Ever your house was, I remember, shut
Till mid-day; I observed that, as I strolled
On mornings through the vale here; country girls
Were noisy, washing garments in the brook,
Hinds drove the slow white oxen up the hills:
But no, your house was mute, would ope no eye.   20
And wisely: you were plotting one thing there,
Nature, another outside. I looked up—
Rough white wood shutters, rusty iron bars,
Silent as death, blind in a flood of light.
Oh, I remember!—and the peasants laughed
And said, "The old man sleeps with the young wife."
This house was his, this chair, this window—his.
    Ottima. Ah, the clear morning! I can see St. Mark's;
That black streak is the belfry. Stop: Vicenza
Should lie . . . there's Padua, plain enough, that blue!   30
Look o'er my shoulder, follow my finger!
    Sebald.   Morning?

It seems to me a night with a sun added.
Where's dew, where's freshness? That bruised plant, I bruised
In getting through the lattice yestereve,
Droops as it did. See, here's my elbow's mark
I' the dust o' the sill.

    Ottima.   Oh, shut the lattice, pray!

    Sebald. Let me lean out. I cannot scent blood here,
Foul as the morn may be.

                    There, shut the world out!
How do you feel now, Ottima? There, curse
The world and all outside! Let us throw off   40
This mask: how do you bear yourself? Let's out
With all of it.

    Ottima.   Best never speak of it.

    Sebald. Best speak again and yet again of it,
Till words cease to be more than words. "His blood,"
For instance—let those two words mean "His blood"
And nothing more. Notice, I'll say them now,
"His blood."

    Ottima.   Assuredly if I repented
The deed—

    Sebald.   Repent? Who should repent, or why?
What puts that in your head? Did I once say
That I repented?

    Ottima.   No, I said the deed.   50

    Sebald. "The deed" and "the event"—just now it was
"Our passion's fruit"—the devil take such cant!
Say, once and always, Luca was a wittol,
I am his cut-throat, you are . . .

    Ottima.   Here's the wine;
I brought it when we left the house above,
And glasses too—wine of both sorts. Black? White then?

    Sebald. But am not I his cut-throat? What are you?

    Ottima. There trudges on his business from the Duomo
Benet the Capuchin, with his brown hood
And bare feet; always in one place at church,   60
Close under the stone wall by the south entry.
I used to take him for a brown cold piece
Of the wall's self, as out of it he rose
To let me pass—at first, I say, I used:
Now, so has that dumb figure fastened on me,
I rather should account the plastered wall
A piece of him, so chilly does it strike.

This, Sebald?
    Sebald.   No, the white wine—the white wine!
Well, Ottima, I promised no new year
Should rise on us the ancient shameful way;   70
Nor does it rise. Pour on! To your black eyes!
Do you remember last damned New Year's day?
    Ottima. You brought those foreign prints. We looked at them
Over the wine and fruit. I had to scheme
To get him from the fire. Nothing but saying
His own set wants the proof-mark, roused him up
To hunt them out.
    Sebald.   'Faith, he is not alive
To fondle you before my face.
    Ottima.   Do you
Fondle me then! Who means to take your life
For that, my Sebald?
    Sebald.   Hark you, Ottima!   80
One thing to guard against. We'll not make much
One of the other—that is, not make more
Parade of warmth, childish officious coil,
Than yesterday: as if, sweet, I supposed
Proof upon proof were needed now, now first,
To show I love you—yes, still love you—love you
In spite of Luca and what's come to him
—Sure sign we had him ever in our thoughts,
White sneering old reproachful face and all!
We'll even quarrel, love, at times, as if   90
We still could lose each other, were not tied
By this: conceive you?
    Ottima.   Love!
    Sebald.   Not tied so sure.
Because though I was wrought upon, have struck
His insolence back into him—am I
So surely yours?—therefore forever yours?
    Ottima. Love, to be wise, (one counsel pays another)
Should we have—months ago, when first we loved,
For instance that May morning we two stole
Under the green ascent of sycamores—
If we had come upon a thing like that   100
Suddenly . . .
    Sebald. "A thing"—there again—"a thing!"
    Ottima. Then, Venus' body, had we come upon
My husband Luca Gaddi's murdered corpse

Within there, at his couch-foot, covered close—
Would you have pored upon it? Why persist
In poring now upon it? For 'tis here
As much as there in the deserted house:
You cannot rid your eyes of it. For me,
Now he is dead I hate him worse: I hate . . .
Dare you stay here? I would go back and hold   110
His two dead hands, and say, "I hate you worse,
Luca, than . . ."
   Sebald.   Off, off—take your hands off mine,
'Tis the hot evening—off! oh, morning is it?
   Ottima. There's one thing must be done; you know what
     thing.
Come in and help to carry. We may sleep
Anywhere in the whole wide house to-night.
   Sebald. What would come, think you, if we let him lie
Just as he is? Let him lie there until
The angels take him! He is turned by this
Off from his face beside, as you will see.   120
   Ottima. This dusty pane might serve for looking-glass.
Three, four—four gray hairs! Is it so you said
A plait of hair should wave across my neck?
No—this way.
   Sebald.   Ottima, I would give your neck,
Each splendid shoulder, both those breasts of yours,
That this were undone! Killing! Kill the world
So Luca lives again!—ay, lives to sputter
His fulsome dotage on you—yes, and feign
Surprise that I return at eve to sup,
When all the morning I was loitering here—   130
Bid me despatch my business and begone.
I would . . .
   Ottima.   See!
   Sebald.   No, I'll finish. Do you think
I fear to speak the bare truth once for all?
All we have talked of, is, at bottom, fine
To suffer; there's a recompense in guilt;
One must be venturous and fortunate:
What is one young for, else? In age we'll sigh
O'er the wild reckless wicked days flown over;
Still, we have lived: the vice was in its place.
But to have eaten Luca's bread, have worn   140
His clothes, have felt his money swell my purse—

Do lovers in romances sin that way?
Why, I was starving when I used to call
And teach you music, starving while you plucked me
These flowers to smell!
    Ottima.   My poor lost friend!
    Sebald.   He gave me
Life, nothing less: what if he did reproach
My perfidy, and threaten, and do more—
Had he no right? What was to wonder at?
He sat by us at table quietly:
Why must you lean across till our cheeks touched?   15
Could he do less than make pretence to strike?
'Tis not the crime's sake—I'd commit ten crimes
Greater, to have this crime wiped out, undone!
And you—O how feel you? Feel you for me?
    Ottima. Well then, I love you better now than ever
And best (look at me while I speak to you)—
Best for the crime; nor do I grieve, in truth,
This mask, this simulated ignorance,
This affectation of simplicity,
Falls off our crime; this naked crime of ours   160
May not now be looked over: look it down!
Great? let it be great; but the joys it brought,
Pay they or no its price? Come: they or it!
Speak not! The past, would you give up the past
Such as it is, pleasure and crime together?
Give up that noon I owned my love for you?
The garden's silence: even the single bee
Persisting in his toil, suddenly stopped,
And where he hid you only could surmise
By some campanula chalice set a-swing.   170
Who stammered—"Yes, I love you"?
    Sebald.   And I drew
Back; put far back your face with both my hands
Lest you should grow too full of me—your face
So seemed athirst for my whole soul and body!
    Ottima. And when I ventured to receive you here,
Made you steal hither in the mornings—
    Sebald.   When
I used to look up 'neath the shrub-house here,
Till the red fire on its glazed windows spread
To a yellow haze?
    Ottima.   Ah—my sign was, the sun

Inflamed the sere side of yon chestnut-tree   180
Nipped by the first frost.

  Sebald.   You would always laugh
At my wet boots: I had to stride thro' grass
Over my ankles.

  Ottima.   Then our crowning night!

  Sebald. The July night?

  Ottima.   .The day of it too, Sebald!
When heaven's pillars seemed o'erbowed with heat,
Its black-blue canopy suffered descend
Close on us both, to weigh down each to each,
And smother up all life except our life.
So lay we till the storm came.

  Sebald.   How it came!

  Ottima. Buried in woods we lay, you recollect;   190
Swift ran the searching tempest overhead;
And ever and anon some bright white shaft
Burned thro' the pine-tree roof, here burned and there,
As if God's messenger thro' the close wood screen
Plunged and replunged his weapon at a venture,
Feeling for guilty thee and me: then broke
The thunder like a whole sea overhead—

  Sebald. Yes!

  Ottima. —While I stretched myself upon you, hands
To hands, my mouth to your hot mouth, and shook
All my locks loose, and covered you with them—   200
You, Sebald, the same you!

  Sebald.   Slower, Ottima!

  Ottima. And as we lay—

  Sebald.   Less vehemently! Love me!
Forgive me! Take not words, mere words, to heart!
Your breath is worse than wine! Breathe slow, speak slow!
Do not lean on me!

  Ottima.   Sebald, as we lay,
Rising and falling only with our pants,
Who said, "Let death come now! 'Tis right to die!
Right to be punished! Naught completes such bliss
But woe!" Who said that?

  Sebald.   How did we ever rise?
Was't that we slept? Why did it end?

  Ottima.   I felt you   210
Taper into a point the ruffled ends
Of my loose locks 'twixt both your humid lips.

My hair is fallen now: knot it again!
   Sebald. I kiss you now, dear Ottima, now and now!
This way? Will you forgive me—be once more
My great queen?
   Ottima.   Bind it thrice about my brow;
Crown me your queen, your spirit's arbitress,
Magnificent in sin. Say that!
   Sebald.   I crown you
My great white queen, my spirit's arbitress,
Magnificent . . .   220
        [From without is heard the voice of PIPPA, *singing—*

      The year's at the spring
      And day's at the morn;
      Morning's at seven;
      The hill-side's dew-pearled;
      The lark's on the wing;
      The snail's on the thorn:
      God's in his heaven—
      All's right with the world!   *[*PIPPA *passes.*

   Sebald. God's in his heaven! Do you hear that? Who spoke?
You, you spoke!
   Ottima.   Oh—that little ragged girl!   230
She must have rested on the step: we give them
But this one holiday the whole year round.
Did you ever see our silk-mills—their inside?
There are ten silk-mills now belong to you.
She stoops to pick my double heartsease . . . Sh!
She does not hear: call you out louder!
   Sebald.   Leave me!
Go, get your clothes on—dress those shoulders!
   Ottima.   Sebald?
   Sebald. Wipe off that paint! I hate you.
   Ottima.   Miserable!
   Sebald. My God, and she is emptied of it now!
Outright now!—how miraculously gone   240
All of the grace—had she not strange grace once?
Why, the blank cheek hangs listless as it likes,
No purpose holds the features up together,
Only the cloven brow and puckered chin
Stay in their places: and the very hair,

That seemed to have a sort of life in it,
Drops, a dead web!
    Ottima.   Speak to me—not of me!
    Sebald.—That round great full-orbed face, where not an
      angle
Broke the delicious indolence—all broken!
    Ottima. To me—not of me! Ungrateful, perjured cheat!   250
A coward too: but ingrate's worse than all.
Beggar—my slave—a fawning, cringing lie!
Leave me! Betray me! I can see your drift!
A lie that walks and eats and drinks!
    Sebald.   My God!
Those morbid olive faultless shoulder-blades—
I should have known there was no blood beneath!
    Ottima. You hate me then? You hate me then?
    Sebald.   To think
She would succeed in her absurd attempt,
And fascinate by sinning, show herself
Superior—guilt from its excess superior   260
To innocence! That little peasant's voice
Has righted all again. Though I be lost,
I know which is the better, never fear,
Of vice or virtue, purity or lust,
Nature or trick! I see what I have done,
Entirely now! Oh I am proud to feel
Such torments—let the world take credit thence—
I, having done my deed, pay too its price!
I hate, hate—curse you! God's in his heaven!
    Ottima.   —Me!
Me! no, no, Sebald, not yourself—kill me!   270
Mine is the whole crime. Do but kill me—then
Yourself—then—presently—first hear me speak!
I always meant to kill myself—wait, you!
Lean on my breast—not as a breast; don't love me
The more because you lean on me, my own
Heart's Sebald! There, there, both deaths presently!
    Sebald. My brain is drowned now—quite drowned: all I feel
Is . . . is, at swift-recurring intervals,
A hurry-down within me, as of waters
Loosened to smother up some ghastly pit: 280
There they go—whirls from a black fiery sea!
    Ottima. Not me—to him, O God, be merciful!

Talk by the way, while PIPPA *is passing from the hill-side to
    Orcana. Foreign Students of painting and sculpture, from
    Venice, assembled opposite the house of* JULES, *a young
    French statuary, at Possagno.*

1st Student. Attention! My own post is beneath this window,
but the pomegranate clump yonder will hide three or four of
you with a little squeezing, and Schramm and his pipe must lie
flat in the balcony. Four, five—who's a defaulter? We want
everybody, for Jules must not be suffered to hurt his bride when
the jest's found out.

2nd Student. All here! Only our poet's away—never having
much meant to be present, moonstrike him! The airs of   290
that fellow, that Giovacchino! He was in violent love with him-
self, and had a fair prospect of thriving in his suit, so unmolested
was it,—when suddenly a woman falls in love with him, too;
and out of pure jealousy he takes himself off to Trieste, immor-
tal poem and all: whereto is this prophetical epitaph appended
already, as Bluphocks assures me,—*"Here a mammoth-poem
lies, Fouled to death by butterflies."* His own fault, the simple-
ton! Instead of cramp couplets, each like a knife in your entrails,
he should write, says Bluphocks, both classically and intelligibly.
—Æsculapius, an Epic. Catalogue of the drugs: Hebe's   300
*plaister—One strip Cools your lip. Phœbus' emulsion—One bot-
tle Clears your throttle. Mercury's bolus—One box Cures* . . .

3rd student. Subside, my fine fellow! If the marriage was over
by ten o'clock, Jules will certainly be here in a minute with his
bride.

2nd Student. Good!—only, so should the poet's muse have been
universally acceptable, says Bluphocks, *et canibus nostris* . . .
and Delia not better known to our literary dogs than the boy
Giovacchino!

1st Student. To the point, now. Where's Gottlieb, the   310
new-comer? Oh,—listen, Gottlieb, to what has called down this
piece of friendly vengeance on Jules, of which we now assemble
to witness the winding-up. We are all agreed, all in a tale, ob-
serve, when Jules shall burst out on us in a fury by and by: I am
spokesman—the verses that are to undeceive Jules bear my name
of Lutwyche—but each professes himself alike insulted by this
strutting stone-squarer, who came alone from Paris to Munich,
and thence with a crowd of us to Venice and Possagno here, but
proceeds in a day or two alone again—oh, alone indubitably!—to

Rome and Florence. He, forsooth, take up his portion with   320
these dissolute, brutalized, heartless bunglers!—so he was heard
to call us all: now, is Schramm brutalized, I should like to know?
Am I heartless?

Gottlieb. Why, somewhat heartless; for, suppose Jules a cox·
comb as much as you choose, still, for this mere coxcombry, you
will have brushed off—what do folks style it?—the bloom of his
life. Is it too late to alter? These love-letters now, you call his—I
can't laugh at them.

4th Student. Because you never read the sham letters of our
inditing which drew forth these.   330

Gottlieb. His discovery of the truth will be frightful.

4th Student. That's the joke. But you should have joined us at
the beginning: there's no doubt he loves the girl—loves a model
he might hire by the hour!

Gottlieb. See here! "He has been accustomed," he writes, "to
have Canova's women about him, in stone, and the world's
women beside him, in flesh; these being as much below, as those
above, his soul's aspiration: but now he is to have the reality."
There you laugh again! I say, you wipe off the very dew of his
youth.   340

1st Student. Schramm! (Take the pipe out of his mouth, some-
body!) Will Jules lose the bloom of his youth?

Schramm. Nothing worth keeping is ever lost in this world:
look at a blossom,—it drops presently, having done its service and
lasted its time; but fruits succeed, and where would be the blos-
som's place could it continue? As well affirm that your eye is no
longer in your body, because its earliest favorite, whatever it may
have first loved to look on, is dead and done with—as that any
affection is lost to the soul when its first object, whatever hap-
pened first to satisfy it, is superseded in due course. Keep   350
but ever looking, whether with the body's eye or the mind's, and
you will soon find something to look on! Has a man done wonder-
ing at women?—there follow men, dead and alive, to wonder at.
Has he done wondering at men?—there's God to wonder at: and
the faculty of wonder may be, at the same time, old and tired
enough with respect to its first object, and yet young and fresh
sufficiently, so far as concerns its novel one. Thus . . .

1st Student. Put Schramm's pipe into his mouth again! There,
you see! Well, this Jules . . . a wretched fribble—oh, I watched
his disportings at Possagno, the other day! Canova's gallery   360
—you know: there he marches first resolvedly past great works
by the dozen without vouchsafing an eye: all at once he stops full!

at the *Psiche-fanciulla*—cannot pass that old acquaintance without a nod of encouragement—"In your new place, beauty? Then behave yourself as well here as at Munich—I see you!" Next he posts himself deliberately before the unfinished *Pietà* for half an hour without moving, till up he starts of a sudden, and thrusts his very nose into—I say, into—the group; by which gesture you are informed that precisely the sole point he had not fully mastered in Canova's practice was a certain method of using the drill 370 in the articulation of the knee-joint—and that, likewise, has he mastered at length! Good-bye, therefore, to poor Canova—whose gallery no longer needs detain his successor Jules, the predestinated novel thinker in marble!

5th Student. Tell him about the women: go on to the women!

1st Student. Why, on that matter he could never be supercilious enough. How should we be other (he said) than the poor devils you see, with those debasing habits we cherish? He was not to wallow in that mire, at least: he would wait, and love only at the proper time, and meanwhile put up with the *Psiche-fanci-* 380 *ulla.* Now, I happened to hear of a young Greek—real Greek girl at Malamocco; a true Islander, do you see, with Alciphron's "hair like sea-moss"—Schramm knows!—white and quiet as an apparition, and fourteen years old at farthest,—a daughter of Natalia, so she swears—that hag Natalia, who helps us to models at three *lire* an hour. We selected this girl for the heroine of our jest. So first, Jules received a scented letter—somebody had seen his Tydeus at the Academy, and my picture was nothing to it: a profound admirer bade him persevere—would make herself known to him ere long. (Paolina, my little friend of the *Fenice,* 390 transcribes divinely.) And in due time, the mysterious correspondent gave certain hints of her peculiar charms—the pale cheeks, the black hair—whatever, in short, had struck us in our Malamocco model: we retained her name, too—Phene, which is, by interpretation, sea-eagle. Now, think of Jules finding himself distinguished from the herd of us by such a creature! In his very first answer he proposed marrying his monitress: and fancy us over these letters, two, three times a day, to receive and despatch! I concocted the main of it: relations were in the way—secrecy must be observed—in fine, would he wed her on trust, and 400 only speak to her when they were indissolubly united? St—st— Here they come!

6th Student. Both of them! Heaven's love, speak softly, speak within yourselves!

5th Student. Look at the bridegroom! Half his hair in storm

and half in calm,—patted down over the left temple,—like a
frothy cup one blows on to cool it: and the same old blouse that
he murders the marble in.

2nd Student. Not a rich vest like yours, Hannibal Scratchy!—
rich, that your face may the better set it off.   410

6th Student. And the bride! Yes, sure enough, our Phene!
Should you have known her in her clothes? How magnificently
pale!

Gottlieb. She does not also take it for earnest, I hope?

1st Student. Oh, Natalia's concern, that is! We settle with
Natalia.

6th Student. She does not speak—has evidently let out no
word. The only thing is, will she equally remember the rest of her
lesson, and repeat correctly all those verses which are to break the
secret to Jules?   420

Gottlieb. How he gazes on her! Pity—pity!

1st Student. They go in: now, silence! You three,—not nearer
the window, mind, than that pomegranate: just where the little
girl, who a few minutes ago passed us singing, is seated!

II—NOON

SCENE—*Over Orcana. The house of* JULES, *who crosses its thresh-
old with* PHENE: *she is silent, on which* JULES *begins—*

Do not die, Phene! I am yours now, you
Are mine now; let fate reach me how she likes,
If you'll not die: so, never die! Sit here—
My work-room's single seat. I over-lean
This length of hair and lustrous front; they turn
Like an entire flower upward: eyes, lips, last
Your chin—no, last your throat turns: 'tis their scent
Pulls down my face upon you. Nay, look ever
This one way till I change, grow you—I could
Change into you, beloved!
                You by me,   10
And I by you; this is your hand in mine,
And side by side we sit: all's true. Thank God!
I have spoken: speak you!
                O my life to come!
My Tydeus must be carved that's there in clay;
Yet how be carved, with you about the room?

Where must I place you? When I think that once
This room-full of rough block-work seemed my heaven
Without you! Shall I ever work again,
Get fairly into my old ways again,
Bid each conception stand while, trait by trait,   20
My hand transfers its lineaments to stone?
Will my mere fancies live near you, their truth—
The live truth, passing and repassing me,
Sitting beside me?
                Now speak!
                          Only first,
See, all your letters! Was't not well contrived?
Their hiding-place is Psyche's robe; she keeps
Your letters next her skin: which drops out foremost?
Ah,—this that swam down like a first moonbeam
Into my world!
              Again those eyes complete
Their melancholy survey, sweet and slow,   30
Of all my room holds; to return and rest
On me, with pity, yet some wonder too:
As if God bade some spirit plague a world,
And this were the one moment of surprise
And sorrow while she took her station, pausing
O'er what she sees, finds good, and must destroy!
What gaze you at? Those? Books, I told you of;
Let your first word to me rejoice them, too:
This minion, a Coluthus, writ in red
Bistre and azure by Bessarion's scribe—   40
Read this line . . . no, shame—Homer's be the Greek
First breathed me from the lips of my Greek girl!
This Odyssey in coarse black vivid type
With faded yellow blossoms 'twixt page and page,
To mark great places with due gratitude;
"*He said, and on Antinous directed
A bitter shaft*" . . . a flower blots out the rest!
Again upon your search? My statues, then!
—Ah, do not mind that—better that will look
When cast in bronze—an Almaign Kaiser, that,   50
Swart-green and gold, with truncheon based on hip.
This, rather, turn to! What, unrecognized?
I thought you would have seen that here you sit
As I imagined you,—Hippolyta,
Naked upon her bright Numidian horse.

Recall you this then? "Carve in bold relief"—
So you commanded—"carve, against I come,
A Greek, in Athens, as our fashion was,
Feasting, bay-filleted and thunder-free,
Who rises 'neath the lifted myrtle-branch.   60
'Praise those who slew Hipparchus!' cry the guests,
'While o'er thy head the singer's myrtle waves
As erst above our champion: stand up, all!' "
See, I have labored to express your thought.
Quite round, a cluster of mere hands and arms,
(Thrust in all senses, all ways, from all sides,
Only consenting at the branch's end
They strain toward) serves for frame to a sole face,
The Praiser's, in the centre: who with eyes
Sightless, so bend they back to light inside   70
His brain where visionary forms throng up,
Sings, minding not that palpitating arch
Of hands and arms, nor the quick drip of wine
From the drenched leaves o'erhead, nor crowns cast off,
Violet and parsley crowns to trample on—
Sings, pausing as the patron-ghosts approve,
Devoutly their unconquerable hymn.
But you must say a "well" to that—say "well!"
Because you gaze—am I fantastic, sweet?
Gaze like my very life's-stuff, marble—marbly   80
Even to the silence! Why, before I found
The real flesh Phene, I inured myself
To see, throughout all nature, varied stuff
For better nature's birth by means of art:
With me, each substance tended to one form
Of beauty—to the human archetype.
On every side occurred suggestive germs
Of that—the tree, the flower—or take the fruit,—
Some rosy shape, continuing the peach,
Curved beewise o'er its bough; as rosy limbs,   90
Depending, nestled in the leaves; and just
From a cleft rose-peach the whole Dryad sprang.
But of the stuffs one can be master of,
How I divined their capabilities!
From the soft-rinded smoothening facile chalk
That yields your outline to the air's embrace,
Half-softened by a halo's pearly gloom;
Down to the crisp imperious steel, so sure

To cut its one confided thought clean out
Of all the world. But marble!—'neath my tools   100
More pliable than jelly—as it were
Some clear primordial creature dug from depths
In the earth's heart, where itself breeds itself,
And whence all baser substance may be worked;
Refine it off to air, you may,—condense it
Down to the diamond;—is not metal there,
When o'er the sudden speck my chisel trips?
—Not flesh, as flake off flake I scale, approach,
Lay bare those bluish veins of blood asleep?
Lurks flame in no strange windings where, surprised   110
By the swift implement sent home at once,
Flushes and glowings radiate and hover
About its track?
              Phene? what—why is this?
That whitening cheek, those still dilating eyes!
Ah, you will die—I knew that you would die!

PHENE *begins, on his having long remained silent.*

Now the end's coming; to be sure, it must
Have ended sometime! Tush, why need I speak
Their foolish speech? I cannot bring to mind
One half of it, beside; and do not care
For old Natalia now, nor any of them.   120
Oh, you—what are you?—if I do not try
To say the words Natalia made me learn,
To please your friends,—it is to keep myself
Where your voice lifted me, by letting that
Proceed: but can it? Even you, perhaps,
Cannot take up, now you have once let fall,
The music's life, and me along with that—
No, or you would! We'll stay, then, as we are:
Above the world.
              You creature with the eyes!
If I could look forever up to them,   130
As now you let me,—I believe, all sin,
All memory of wrong done, suffering borne,
Would drop down, low and lower, to the earth
Whence all that's low comes, and there touch and stay
—Never to overtake the rest of me,
All that, unspotted, reaches up to you,

Drawn by those eyes! What rises is myself,
Not me the shame and suffering; but they sink,
Are left, I rise above them. Keep me so,
Above the world!

          But you sink, for your eyes   140
Are altering—altered! Stay—"I love you, love" . . .
I could prevent it if I understood:
More of your words to me: was't in the tone
Or the words, your power?

               Or stay—I will repeat
Their speech, if that contents you! Only change
No more, and I shall find it presently
Far back here, in the brain yourself filled up.
Natalia threatened me that harm should follow
Unless I spoke their lesson to the end,
But harm to me, I thought she meant, not you.   150
Your friends,—Natalia said they were your friends
And meant you well,—because, I doubted it,
Observing (what was very strange to see)
On every face, so different in all else,
The same smile girls like me are used to bear,
But never men, men cannot stoop so low;
Yet your friends, speaking of you, used that smile,
That hateful smirk of boundless self-conceit
Which seems to take possession of the world
And make of God a tame confederate,   160
Purveyor to their appetites . . . you know!
But still Natalia said they were your friends,
And they assented though they smiled the more.
And all came round me,—that thin Englishman
With light lank hair seemed leader of the rest;
He held a paper—"What we want," said he,
Ending some explanation to his friends—
"Is something slow, involved and mystical,
To hold Jules long in doubt, yet take his taste
And lure him on until, at innermost   170
Where he seeks sweetness' soul, he may find—this!
—As in the apple's core, the noisome fly:
For insects on the rind are seen at once,
And brushed aside as soon, but this is found
Only when on the lips or loathing tongue."
And so he read what I have got by heart:
I'll speak it,—"Do not die, love! I am yours."

No—is not that, or like that, part of words
Yourself began by speaking? Strange to lose
What cost such pains to learn! Is this more right?   180

> *I am a painter who cannot paint;*
> *In my life, a devil rather than saint;*
> *In my brain, as poor a creature too:*
> *No end to all I cannot do!*
> *Yet do one thing at least I can—*
> *Love a man or hate a man*
> *Supremely: thus my lore began.*
> *Through the Valley of Love I went,*
> *In the lovingest spot to abide,*
> *And just on the verge where I pitched my tent,*   190
> *I found Hate dwelling beside.*
> *(Let the Bridegroom ask what the painter meant,*
> *Of his Bride, of the peerless Bride!)*
> *And further, I traversed Hate's grove,*
> *In the hatefullest nook to dwell;*
> *But lo, where I flung myself prone, couched Love*
> *Where the shadow threefold fell.*
> *(The meaning—those black bride's-eyes above,*
> *Not a painter's lip should tell!)*

"And here," said he, "Jules probably will ask,   200
'You have black eyes, Love,—you are, sure enough,
My peerless bride,—then do you tell indeed
What needs some explanation! What means this?' "
—And I am to go on, without a word—

> *So, I grew wise in Love and Hate,*
> *From simple that I was of late.*
> *Once, when I loved, I would enlace*
> *Breast, eyelids, hands, feet, form and face*
> *Of her I loved, in one embrace—*
> *As if by mere love I could love immensely!*   210
> *Once, when I hated, I would plunge*
> *My sword, and wipe with the first lunge*
> *My foe's whole life out like a sponge—*
> *As if by mere hate I could hate intensely!*
> *But now I am wiser, know better the fashion*
> *How passion seeks aid from its opposite passion:*
> *And if I see cause to love more, hate more*

Than ever man loved, ever hated before—
And seek in the Valley of Love,
The nest, or the nook in Hate's Grove,   220
Where my soul may surely reach
The essence, naught less, of each,
The Hate of all Hates, the Love
Of all Loves, in the Valley or Grove,—
I find them the very warders
Each of the other's borders.
When I love most, Love is disguised
In Hate; and when Hate is surprised
In Love, then I hate most: ask
How Love smiles through Hate's iron casque,   230
Hate grins through Love's rose-braided mask,—
And how, having hated thee,
I sought long and painfully
To reach thy heart, nor prick
The skin but pierce to the quick—
Ask this, my Jules, and be answered straight
By thy bride—how the painter Lutwyche can hate!

JULES *interposes.*

Lutwyche! Who else? But all of them, no doubt,
Hated me: they at Venice—presently
Their turn, however! You I shall not meet: 240
If I dreamed, saying this would wake me.
                                 Keep
What's here, the gold—we cannot meet again,
Consider! and the money was but meant
For two years' travel, which is over now,
All chance or hope or care or need of it.
This—and what comes from selling these, my casts
And books and medals, except . . . let them go
Together, so the produce keeps you safe
Out of Natalia's clutches! If by chance
(For all's chance here) I should survive the gang   250
At Venice, root out all fifteen of them,
We might meet somewhere, since the world is wide.
      [*From without is heard the voice of* PIPPA, *singing—*

Give her but at least excuse to love me!
When—where—
How—can this arm establish her above me,
If fortune fixed her as my lady there,
There already, to eternally reprove me?
　　("Hist!"—said Kate the Queen;
　　But "Oh!"—cried the maiden, binding her tresses,
　　" 'Tis only a page that carols unseen,　　　　　　　260
　　Crumbling your hounds their messes!")

Is she wronged?—To the rescue of her honor,
My heart!
Is she poor?—What costs it to be styled a donor?
Merely an earth to cleave, a sea to part.
But that fortune should have thrust all this upon her!
　　("Nay, list!"—bade Kate the Queen;
　　And still cried the maiden, binding her tresses,
　　" 'Tis only a page that carols unseen,
　　Fitting your hawks their jesses!")　　　　　　　270
　　　　　　　　　　　　　　　　[PIPPA *passes.*

JULES *resumes.*

What name was that the little girl sang forth?
Kate? The Cornaro, doubtless, who renounced
The crown of Cyprus to be lady here
At Asolo, where still her memory stays,
And peasants sing how once a certain page
Pined for the grace of her so far above
His power of doing good to, "Kate the Queen—
She never could be wronged, be poor," he sighed,
"Need him to help her!"
　　　　　　　　Yes, a bitter thing
To see our lady above all need of us;　　　　　　　280
Yet so we look ere we will love; not I,
But the world looks so. If whoever loves
Must be, in some sort, god or worshipper,
The blessing or the blest one, queen or page,
Why should we always choose the page's part?
Here is a woman with utter need of me,—
I find myself queen here, it seems!
　　　　　　　　　　　　How strange!

Look at the woman here with the new soul,
Like my own Psyche,—fresh upon her lips
Alit, the visionary butterfly,   290
Waiting my word to enter and make bright,
Or flutter off and leave all blank as first.
This body had no soul before, but slept
Or stirred, was beauteous or ungainly, free
From taint or foul with stain, as outward things
Fastened their image on its passiveness:
Now, it will wake, feel, live—or die again!
Shall to produce form out of unshaped stuff
Be Art—and further, to evoke a soul
From form be nothing? This new soul is mine!   300

Now, to kill Lutwyche, what would that do?—save
A wretched dauber, men will hoot to death
Without me, from their hooting. Oh, to hear
God's voice plain as I heard it first, before
They broke in with their laughter! I heard them
Henceforth, not God.
                 To Ancona—Greece—some isle!
I wanted silence only; there is clay
Everywhere. One may do whate'er one likes
In Art: the only thing is, to make sure
That one does like it—which takes pains to know.   310
   Scatter all this, my Phene—this mad dream!
Who, what is Lutwyche, what Natalia's friends,
What the whole world except our love—my own,
Own Phene? But I told you, did I not,
Ere night we travel for your land—some isle
With the sea's silence on it? Stand aside—
I do but break these paltry models up
To begin Art afresh. Meet Lutwyche, I—
And save him from my statue meeting him?
Some unsuspected isle in the far seas!   320
Like a god going through his world, there stands
One mountain for a moment in the dusk,
Whole brotherhoods of cedars on its brow:
And you are ever by me while I gaze
—Are in my arms as now—as now—as now!
Some unsuspected isle in the far seas!
Some unsuspected isle in far-off seas!

Talk by the way, while PIPPA *is passing from Orcana to the Turret. Two or three of the Austrian Police loitering with* BLUPHOCKS, *an English vagabond, just in view of the Turret.*

Bluphocks. So, that is your Pippa, the little girl who passed us singing? Well, your Bishop's Intendant's money shall be honestly earned:—now, don't make me that sour face because I bring   330 the Bishop's name into the business; we know he can have nothing to do with such horrors: we know that he is a saint and all that a bishop should be, who is a great man beside. *Oh were but every worm a maggot, Every fly a grig, Every bough a Christmas faggot, Every tune a jig!* In fact, I have abjured all religions; but the last I inclined to, was the Armenian: for I have travelled, do you see, and at Koenigsberg, Prussia Improper (so styled because there's a sort of bleak hungry sun there), you might remark over a venerable house-porch, a certain Chaldee inscription; and brief as it is, a mere glance at it used absolutely to change the   340 mood of every bearded passenger. In they turned, one and all; the young and lightsome, with no irreverent pause, the aged and decrepit, with a sensible alacrity: 'twas the Grand Rabbi's abode, in short. Struck with curiosity, I lost no time in learning Syriac— (these are vowels, you dogs,—follow my stick's end in the mud— *Celarent, Darii, Ferio!*) and one morning presented myself, spelling-book in hand, a, b, c,—I picked it out letter by letter, and what was the purport of this miraculous posy? Some cherished legend of the past, you'll say—"*How Moses hocuspocussed Egypt's land with fly and locust,*"—or, "*How to Jonah*   350 *sounded harshish, Get thee up and go to Tarshish,*"—or, "*How the angel meeting Balaam, Straight his ass returned a salaam.*" In no wise! "*Shackabrack—Boach—somebody or other—Isaach, Re-cei-ver, Pur-cha-ser and Ex-chan-ger of—Stolen Goods!*" So, talk to me of the religion of a bishop! I have renounced all bishops save Bishop Beveridge—mean to live so—and die—*As some Greek dog-sage, dead and merry, Hellward bound in Charon's wherry, With food for both worlds, under and upper, Lupine-seed and Hecate's supper, And never an obolus* . . . (Though thanks to you, or this Intendant through you, or this Bishop   360 through his Intendant—I possess a burning pocketful of *zwanzigers*) . . . *To pay the Stygian Ferry!*

1st *Policeman.* There is the girl, then; go and deserve them the moment you have pointed out to us Signor Luigi and his mother. [*To the rest.*] I have been noticing a house yonder, this long while: not a shutter unclosed since morning!

2nd Policeman. Old Luca Gaddi's, that owns the silk-mills here: he dozes by the hour, wakes up, sighs deeply, says he should like to be Prince Metternich, and then dozes again, after having bidden young Sebald, the foreigner, set his wife to 370 playing draughts. Never molest such a household, they mean well.

Bluphocks. Only, cannot you tell me something of this little Pippa, I must have to do with? One could make something of that name. Pippa—that is, short for Felippa—rhyming to *Panurge consults Hertrippa—Believest thou, King Agrippa?* Something might be done with that name.

2nd Policeman. Put into rhyme that your head and a ripe musk-melon would not be dear at half a *zwanziger!* Leave this fooling, and look out; the afternoon's over or nearly so.

3rd Policeman. Where in this passport of Signor Luigi 380 does our Principal instruct you to watch him so narrowly? There? What's there beside a simple signature? (That English fool's busy watching.)

2nd Policeman. Flourish all round—"Put all possible obstacles in his way;" oblong dot at the end—"Detain him till further advices reach you;" scratch at bottom—"Send him back on pretence of some informality in the above;" ink-spirt on right-hand side (which is the case here)—"Arrest him at once." Why and wherefore, I don't concern myself, but my instructions amount to this: if Signor Luigi leaves home to-night for Vienna— 390 well and good, the passport deposed with us for our *visa* is really for his own use, they have misinformed the Office, and he means well; but let him stay over to-night—there has been the pretence we suspect, the accounts of his corresponding and holding intelligence with the Carbonari are correct, we arrest him at once, to-morrow comes Venice, and presently Spielberg. Bluphocks makes the signal, sure enough! That is he, entering the turret with his mother, no doubt.

III—EVENING

SCENE—*Inside the Turret on the Hill above Asolo.* LUIGI *and his* Mother *entering.*

Mother. If there blew wind, you'd hear a long sigh, easing
The utmost heaviness of music's heart.
Luigi. Here in the archway?

Mother.   Oh no, no—in farther,
Where the echo is made, on the ridge.
   Luigi.   Here surely, then.
How plain the tap of my heel as I leaped up!
Hark—"Lucius Junius!" The very ghost of a voice
Whose body is caught and kept by . . . what are those?
Mere withered wallflowers, waving overhead?
They seem an elvish group with thin bleached hair
That lean out of their topmost fortress—look   10
And listen, mountain men, to what we say,
Hand under chin of each grave earthy face.
Up and show faces all of you!—"All of you!"
That's the king dwarf with the scarlet comb; old Franz,
Come down and meet your fate? Hark—"Meet your fate!"
   Mother. Let him not meet it, my Luigi—do not
Go to his City! Putting crime aside,
Half of these ills of Italy are feigned:
Your Pellicos and writers for effect,
Write for effect.
   Luigi.   Hush! Say A. writes, and B.   20
   Mother. These A.s and B.s write for effect, I say.
Then, evil is in its nature loud, while good
Is silent; you hear each petty injury,
None of his virtues; he is old beside,
Quiet and kind, and densely stupid. Why
Do A. and B. not kill him themselves?
   Luigi.   They teach
Others to kill him—me—and, if I fail,
Others to succeed; now, if A. tried and failed,
I could not teach that: mine's the lesser task.
Mother, they visit night by night . . .
   Mother.   —You, Luigi?   30
Ah, will you let me tell you what you are?
   Luigi. Why not? Oh, the one thing you fear to hint,
You may assure yourself I say and say
Ever to myself! At times—nay, even as now
We sit—I think my mind is touched, suspect
All is not sound: but is not knowing that,
What constitutes one sane or otherwise?
I know I am thus—so, all is right again.
I laugh at myself as through the town I walk,
And see men merry as if no Italy   40
Were suffering; then I ponder—"I am rich,

Young, healthy; why should this fact trouble me,
More than it troubles these?" But it does trouble.
No, trouble's a bad word: for as I walk
There's springing and melody and giddiness,
And old quaint turns and passages of my youth,
Dreams long forgotten, little in themselves,
Return to me—whatever may amuse me:
And earth seems in a truce with me, and heaven
Accords with me, all things suspend their strife,   50
The very cicala laughs "There goes he, and there!
Feast him, the time is short; he is on his way
For the world's sake: feast him this once, our friend!"
And in return for all this, I can trip
Cheerfully up the scaffold-steps. I go
This evening, mother!
    Mother.   But mistrust yourself—
Mistrust the judgment you pronounce on him!
    Luigi. Oh, there I feel—am sure that I am right!
    Mother. Mistrust your judgment then, of the mere means
To this wild enterprise. Say, you are right,—   60
How should one in your state e'er bring to pass
What would require a cool head, a cold heart,
And a calm hand? You never will escape.
    Luigi. Escape? To even wish that, would spoil all.
The dying is best part of it. Too much
Have I enjoyed these fifteen years of mine,
To leave myself excuse for longer life:
Was not life pressed down, running o'er with joy,
That I might finish with it ere my fellows
Who, sparelier feasted, make a longer stay?   70
I was put at the board-head, helped to all
At first; I rise up happy and content.
God must be glad one loves his world so much.
I can give news of earth to all the dead
Who ask me:—last year's sunsets, and great stars
Which had a right to come first and see ebb
The crimson wave that drifts the sun away—
Those crescent moons with notched and burning rims
That strengthened into sharp fire, and there stood,
Impatient of the azure—and that day   80
In March, a double rainbow stopped the storm—
May's warm slow yellow moonlit summer nights—
Gone are they, but I have them in my soul!

Mother. (He will not go!)
 Luigi.   You smile at me? 'Tis true,—
Voluptuousness, grotesqueness, ghastliness,
Environ my devotedness as quaintly
As round about some antique altar wreathe
The rose festoons, goats' horns, and oxen's skulls.
 Mother. See now: you reach the city, you must cross
His threshold—how?
 Luigi.   Oh, that's if we conspired!   90
Then would come pains in plenty, as you guess—
But guess not how the qualities most fit
For such an office, qualities I have,
Would little stead me, otherwise employed,
Yet prove of rarest merit only here.
Every one knows for what his excellence
Will serve, but no one ever will consider
For what his worst defect might serve: and yet
Have you not seen me range our coppice yonder
In search of a distorted ash?—I find   100
The wry spoilt branch a natural perfect bow.
Fancy the thrice-sage, thrice-precautioned man
Arriving at the palace on my errand!
No, no! I have a handsome dress packed up—
White satin here, to set off my black hair;
In I shall march—for you may watch your life out
Behind thick walls, make friends there to betray you;
More than one man spoils everything. March straight—
Only, no clumsy knife to fumble for.
Take the great gate, and walk (not saunter) on   110
Thro' guards and guards——I have rehearsed it all
Inside the turret here a hundred times.
Don't ask the way of whom you meet, observe!
But where they cluster thickliest is the door
Of doors; they'll let you pass—they'll never blab
Each to the other, he knows not the favorite,
Whence he is bound and what's his business now.
Walk in—straight up to him; you have no knife:
Be prompt, how should he scream? Then, out with you!
Italy, Italy, my Italy!   120
You're free, you're free! Oh mother, I could dream
They got about me—Andrea from his exile,
Pier from his dungeon, Gualtier from his grave!
 Mother. Well, you shall go. Yet seems this patriotism

The easiest virtue for a selfish man
To acquire: he loves himself—and next, the world—
If he must love beyond,—but naught between:
As a short-sighted man sees naught midway
His body and the sun above. But you
Are my adored Luigi, ever obedient   130
To my least wish, and running o'er with love:
I could not call you cruel or unkind.
Once more, your ground for killing him!—then go!
    Luigi. Now do you try me, or make sport of me?
How first the Austrians got these provinces . . .
(If that is all, I'll satisfy you soon)
—Never by conquest but by cunning, for
That treaty whereby . . .
    Mother.   Well?
    Luigi.   (Sure, he's arrived,
The tell-tale cuckoo: spring's his confidant,
And he lets out her April purposes!)   140
Or . . . better go at once to modern time,
He has . . . they have . . . in fact, I understand
But can't restate the matter; that's my boast:
Others could reason it out to you, and prove
Things they have made me feel.
    Mother.   Why go to-night?
Morn's for adventure. Jupiter is now
A morning-star. I cannot hear you, Luigi!
    Luigi. "I am the bright and morning-star," saith God—
And, "to such an one I give the morning-star,"
The gift of the morning-star! Have I God's gift   150
Of the morning-star?
    Mother.   Chiara will love to see
That Jupiter an evening-star next June.
    Luigi. True, mother. Well for those who live through June!
Great noontides, thunder-storms, all glaring pomps
That triumph at the heels of June the god
Leading his revel through our leafy world.
Yes, Chiara will be here.
    Mother.   In June: remember,
Yourself appointed that month for her coming.
    Luigi. Was that low noise the echo?
    Mother.   The night-wind.
She must be grown—with her blue eyes upturned   160
As if life were one long and sweet surprise:

In June she comes.
 Luigi.   We were to see together
The Titian at Treviso. There, again!
    [*From without is heard the voice of* PIPPA, *singing—*

  A king lived long ago,
  In the morning of the world,
  When earth was nigher heaven than now:
  And the king's locks curled,
  Disparting o'er a forehead full
  As the milk-white space 'twixt horn and horn
  Of some sacrificial bull—   170
  Only calm as a babe new-born:
  For he was got to a sleepy mood,
  So safe from all decrepitude,
  Age with its bane, so sure gone by,
  (The gods so loved him while he dreamed)
  That, having lived thus long, there seemed
  No need the king should ever die.

 Luigi. No need that sort of king should ever die!

  Among the rocks his city was:
  Before his palace, in the sun,   180
  He sat to see his people pass,
  And judge them every one
  From its threshold of smooth stone.
  They haled him many a valley-thief
  Caught in the sheep-pens, robber-chief
  Swarthy and shameless, beggar-cheat,
  Spy-prowler, or rough pirate found
  On the sea-sand left aground;
  And sometimes clung about his feet,
  With bleeding lip and burning cheek,   190
  A woman, bitterest wrong to speak
  Of one with sullen thickset brows:
  And sometimes from the prison-house
  The angry priests a pale wretch brought,
  Who through some chink had pushed and pressed
  On knees and elbows, belly and breast,
  Worm-like into the temple,—caught
  He was by the very god,

Who ever in the darkness strode
Backward and forward, keeping watch   200
O'er his brazen bowls, such rogues to catch!
These, all and every one,
The king judged, sitting in the sun.

Luigi. That king should still judge sitting in the sun!

His councillors, on left and right,
Looked anxious up,—but no surprise
Disturbed the king's old smiling eyes
Where the very blue had turned to white.
'Tis said, a Python scared one day
The breathless city, till he came,   210
With forky tongue and eyes on flame,
Where the old king sat to judge alway;
But when he saw the sweepy hair
Girt with a crown of berries rare
Which the god will hardly give to wear
To the maiden who singeth, dancing bare
In the altar-smoke by the pine-torch lights,
At his wondrous forest rites.—
Seeing this, he did not dare
Approach that threshold in the sun,   220
Assault the old king smiling there.
Such grace had kings when the world begun!

                                    [PIPPA *passes.*

Luigi. And such grace have they, now that the world ends!
The Python at the city, on the throne,
And brave men, God would crown for slaying him.
Lurk in bye-corners lest they fall his prey.
Are crowns yet to be won in this late time,
Which weakness makes me hesitate to reach?
'Tis God's voice calls: how could I stay? Farewell!

Talk by the way, while PIPPA *is passing from the Turret to the Bishop's Brother's House, close to the Duomo S. Maria. Poor Girls sitting on the steps.*

1st Girl. There goes a swallow to Venice—the stout sea-farer!   230
Seeing those birds fly, makes one wish for wings.

Let us all wish; you wish first!
   2nd Girl.   I? This sunset
To finish.
   3rd Girl. That old—somebody I know,
Grayer and older than my grandfather,
To give me the same treat he gave last week—
Feeding me on his knee with fig-peckers,
Lampreys and red Breganze-wine, and mumbling
The while some folly about how well I fare,
Let sit and eat my supper quietly:
Since had he not himself been late this morning   240
Detained at—never mind where,—had he not . . .
"Eh, baggage, had I not!"—
   2nd Girl.   How she can lie!
   3rd Girl. Look there—by the nails!
   2nd Girl.   What makes your fingers red!
   3rd Girl. Dipping them into wine to write bad words with
On the bright table: how he laughed!
   1st Girl.   My turn.
Spring's come and summer's coming. I would wear
A long loose gown, down to the feet and hands,
With plaits here, close about the throat, all day;
And all night lie, the cool long nights, in bed;
And have new milk to drink, apples to eat,   250
Deuzans and juneatings, leather-coats . . . ah, I should say,
This is away in the fields—miles!
   3rd Girl.   Say at once
You'd be at home: she'd always be at home!
Now comes the story of the farm among
The cherry orchards, and how April snowed
White blossoms on her as she ran. Why, fool,
They've rubbed the chalk-mark out, how tall you were,
Twisted your starling's neck, broken his cage,
Made a dung-hill of your garden!
   1st Girl.   They, destroy
My garden since I left them? well—perhaps!   260
I would have done so: so I hope they have!
A fig-tree curled out of our cottage wall;
They called it mine, I have forgotten why,
It must have been there long ere I was born:
Cric—cric—I think I hear the wasps o'erhead
Pricking the papers strung to flutter there
And keep off birds in fruit-time—coarse long papers,

And the wasps eat them, prick them through and through.

   3rd Girl. How her mouth twitches! Where was I?—before
She broke in with her wishes and long gowns   270
And wasps—would I be such a fool!—oh, here!
This is my way: I answer every one
Who asks me why I make so much of him—
(If you say, "you love him"—straight "he'll not be gulled!")
"He that seduced me when I was a girl
Thus high—had eyes like yours, or hair like yours,
Brown, red, white,"—as the case may be: that pleases!
See how that beetle burnishes in the path!
There sparkles he along the dust: and, there—
Your journey to that maize-tuft spoiled at least!   280

   1st Girl. When I was young, they said if you killed one
Of those sunshiny beetles, that his friend
Up there, would shine no more that day nor next.

   2nd Girl. When you were young? Nor are you young, that's
     true.
How your plump arms, that were, have dropped away!
Why, I can span them. Cecco beats you still?
No matter, so you keep your curious hair.
I wish they'd find a way to dye our hair
Your color—any lighter tint, indeed,
Than black: the men say they are sick of black,   290
Black eyes, black hair!

   4th Girl.   Sick of yours, like enough.
Do you pretend you ever tasted lampreys
And ortolans? Giovita, of the palace,
Engaged (but there's no trusting him) to slice me
Polenta with a knife that had cut up
An ortolan.

   2nd Girl. Why, there! Is not that Pippa
We are to talk to, under the window,—quick,—
Where the lights are?

   1st Girl.   That she? No, or she would sing,
For the Intendant said . . .

   3rd Girl.   Oh, you sing first!
Then, if she listens and comes close . . . I'll tell you,—   300
Sing that song the young English noble made,
Who took you for the purest of the pure,
And meant to leave the world for you—what fun!

2nd Girl [sings].
　　You'll love me yet!—and I can tarry
　　　　Your love's protracted growing:
　　June reared that bunch of flowers you carry,
　　　　From seeds of April's sowing.

　　I plant a heartful now: some seed
　　　　At least is sure to strike,
　　And yield—what you'll not pluck indeed,   310
　　　　Not love, but, may be, like.

　　You'll look at least on love's remains,
　　　　A grave's one violet:
　　Your look?—that pays a thousand pains.
　　　　What's death? You'll love me yet!

　3rd Girl [to PIPPA, who approaches]. Oh, you may come closer
—we shall not eat you! Why, you seem the very person that the
great rich handsome Englishman has fallen so violently in love
with. I'll tell you all about it.

IV—NIGHT

SCENE—*Inside the Palace by the Duomo.* MONSIGNOR, *dismissing
his* Attendants.

　Monsignor. Thanks, friends, many thanks! I chiefly desire life
now, that I may recompense every one of you. Most I know some-
thing of already. What, a repast prepared? *Benedicto bene-
dicatur* . . . ugh, ugh! Where was I? Oh, as you were remark-
ing, Ugo, the weather is mild, very unlike winter-weather: but
I am a Sicilian, you know, and shiver in your Julys here. To be
sure, when 'twas full summer at Messina, as we priests used to
cross in procession the great square on Assumption Day, you
might see our thickest yellow tapers twist suddenly in two, each
like a falling star, or sink down on themselves in a gore of   10
wax. But go, my friends, but go! [*To the* Intendant.] Not you,
Ugo! [*The others leave the apartment.*] I have long wanted to
converse with you, Ugo.
　Intendant. Uguccio—
　Monsignor. . . . 'guccio Stefani, man! of Ascoli, Fermo and
Fossombruno;—what I do need instructing about, are these
accounts of your administration of my poor brother's affairs. Ugh!

I shall never get through a third part of your accounts: take
some of these dainties before we attempt it, however. Are you
bashful to that degree? For me, a crust and water suffice.   20

Intendant. Do you choose this especial night to question me?

Monsignor. This night, Ugo. You have managed my late
brother's affairs since the death of our elder brother: fourteen
years and a month, all but three days. On the Third of December,
I find him . . .

Intendant. If you have so intimate an acquaintance with your
brother's affairs, you will be tender of turning so far back: they
will hardly bear looking into, so far back.

Monsignor. Ay, ay, ugh, ugh,—nothing but disappointments
here below! I remark a considerable payment made to your-   30
self on this Third of December. Talk of disappointments! There
was a young fellow here, Jules, a foreign sculptor I did my
utmost to advance, that the Church might be a gainer by us
both: he was going on hopefully enough, and of a sudden he
notifies to me some marvellous change that has happened in his
notions of Art. Here's his letter,—"He never had a clearly con-
ceived Ideal within his brain till to-day. Yet since his hand could
manage a chisel, he has practised expressing other men's Ideals;
and, in the very perfection he has attained to, he foresees an
ultimate failure: his unconscious hand will pursue its pre-   40
scribed course of old years, and will reproduce with a fatal
expertness the ancient types, let the novel one appear never so
palpably to his spirit. There is but one method of escape: con-
fiding the virgin type to as chaste a hand, he will turn painter
instead of sculptor, and paint, not carve, its characteristics,"—
strike out, I dare say, a school like Correggio: how think you,
Ugo?

Intendant. Is Correggio a painter?

Monsignor. Foolish Jules! and yet, after all, why foolish? He
may—probably will—fail egregiously; but if there should   50
arise a new painter, will it not be in some such way, by a poet
now, or a musician (spirits who have conceived and perfected
an Ideal through some other channel), transferring it to this,
and escaping our conventional roads by pure ignorance of them;
eh, Ugo? If you have no appetite, talk at least, Ugo!

Intendant. Sir, I can submit no longer to this course of yours.
First, you select the group of which I formed one,—next you
thin it gradually,—always retaining me with your smile,—and
so do you proceed till you have fairly got me alone with you

between four stone walls. And now then? Let this farce, this   60
chatter end now: what is it you want with me?

Monsignor. Ugo!

Intendant. From the instant you arrived, I felt your smile on
me as you questioned me about this and the other article in
those papers—why your brother should have given me this villa,
that *podere,*—and your nod at the end meant,—what?

Monsignor. Possibly that I wished for no loud talk here. If once
you set me coughing, Ugo!—

Intendant. I have your brother's hand and seal to all I pos-
sess: now ask me what for! what service I did him—ask me!   70

Monsignor. I would better not: I should rip up old disgraces,
let out my poor brother's weaknesses. By the way, Maffeo of
Forli (which, I forgot to observe, is your true name), was the
interdict ever taken off you, for robbing that church at Cesena?

Intendant. No, nor needs be: for when I murdered your
brother's friend, Pasquale, for him . . .

Monsignor. Ah, he employed you in that business, did he?
Well, I must let you keep, as you say, this villa and that *podere,*
for fear the world should find out my relations were of so indiffer-
ent a stamp? Maffeo, my family is the oldest in Messina,   80
and century after century have my progenitors gone on polluting
themselves with every wickedness under heaven: my own father
. . . rest his soul!—I have, I know, a chapel to support that it
may rest: my dear two dead brothers were,—what you know
tolerably well; I, the youngest, might have rivalled them in vice,
if not in wealth: but from my boyhood I came out from among
them, and so am not partaker of their plagues. My glory springs
from another source; or if from this, by contrast only,—for I, the
bishop, am the brother of your employers, Ugo. I hope to repair
some of their wrong, however; so far as my brother's ill-   90
gotten treasure reverts to me, I can stop the consequences of his
crime: and not one *soldo* shall escape me. Maffeo, the sword we
quiet men spurn away, you shrewd knaves pick up and commit
murders with; what opportunities the virtuous forego, the vil-
lanous seize. Because, to pleasure myself apart from other con-
siderations, my food would be millet-cake, my dress sackcloth,
and my couch straw,—am I therefore to let you, the offscouring
of the earth, seduce the poor and ignorant by appropriating a
pomp these will be sure to think lessens the abominations so
unaccountably and exclusively associated with it? Must I   100
let villas and *poderi* go to you, a murderer and thief, that you

may beget by means of them other murderers and thieves? No
—if my cough would but allow me to speak!

Intendant. What am I to expect? You are going to punish me?

Monsignor.—Must punish you, Maffeo. I cannot afford to cast
away a chance. I have whole centuries of sin to redeem, and only
a month or two of life to do it in. How should I dare to say . . .

Intendant. "Forgive us our trespasses"?

Monsignor. My friend, it is because I avow myself a very
worm, sinful beyond measure, that I reject a line of conduct   110
you would applaud perhaps. Shall I proceed, as it were, a-par-
doning?—I?—who have no symptom of reason to assume that
aught less than my strenuousest efforts will keep myself out of
mortal sin, much less keep others out. No: I do trespass, but will
not double that by allowing you to trespass.

Intendant. And suppose the villas are not your brother's to
give, nor yours to take? Oh, you are hasty enough just now!

Monsignor. 1, 2—N° 3!—ay, can you read the substance of a
letter, N° 3, I have received from Rome? It is precisely on the
ground there mentioned, of the suspicion I have that a cer-   120
tain child of my late elder brother, who would have succeeded to
his estates, was murdered in infancy by you, Maffeo, at the insti-
gation of my late younger brother—that the Pontiff enjoins on me
not merely the bringing that Maffeo to condign punishment, but
the taking all pains, as guardian of the infant's heritage for the
Church, to recover it parcel by parcel, howsoever, whensoever,
and wheresoever. While you are now gnawing those fingers, the
police are engaged in sealing up your papers, Maffeo, and the
mere raising my voice brings my people from the next room to
dispose of yourself. But I want you to confess quietly, and   130
save me raising my voice. Why, man, do I not know the old
story? The heir between the succeeding heir, and this heir's
ruffianly instrument, and their complot's effect, and the life of
fear and bribes and ominous smiling silence? Did you throttle
or stab my brother's infant? Come now!

Intendant. So old a story, and tell it no better? When did such
an instrument ever produce such an effect? Either the child smiles
in his face; or, most likely, he is not fool enough to put himself
in the employer's power so thoroughly: the child is always ready
to produce—as you say—howsoever, wheresoever, and   140
whensoever.

Monsignor. Liar!

Intendant. Strike me? Ah, so might a father chastise! I shall
sleep soundly to-night at least, though the gallows await me

to-morrow; for what a life did I lead! Carlo of Cesena reminds
me of his connivance, every time I pay his annuity; which hap-
pens commonly thrice a year. If I remonstrate, he will confess
all to the good bishop—you!

Monsignor. I see through the trick, caitiff! I would you spoke
truth for once. All shall be sifted, however—seven times   150
sifted.

Intendant. And how my absurd riches encumbered me! I
dared not lay claim to above half my possessions. Let me but
once unbosom myself, glorify Heaven, and die!

Sir, you are no brutal dastardly idiot like your brother I
frightened to death: let us understand one another. Sir, I will
make away with her for you—the girl—here close at hand; not
the stupid obvious kind of killing; do not speak—know nothing
of her nor of me! I see her every day—saw her this morn-
ing: of course there is to be no killing; but at Rome the   160
courtesans perish off every three years, and I can entice her
thither—have indeed begun operations already. There's a certain
lusty blue-eyed florid-complexioned English knave, I and the
Police employ occasionally. You assent, I perceive—no, that's
not it—assent I do not say—but you will let me convert my
present havings and holdings into cash, and give me time to
cross the Alps? 'Tis but a little black-eyed pretty singing Felippa,
gay silk-winding girl. I have kept her out of harm's way up to
this present; for I always intended to make your life a plague to
you with her. 'Tis as well settled once and forever. Some   170
women I have procured will pass Bluphocks, my handsome
scoundrel, off for somebody; and once Pippa entangled!—you
conceive? Through her singing? Is it a bargain?

   [*From without is heard the voice of* PIPPA, *singing*—

  Overhead the tree-tops meet,
  Flowers and grass spring 'neath one's feet;
  There was naught above me, naught below,
  My childhood had not learned to know:
  For, what are the voices of birds
  —Ay, and of beasts,—but words, our words,
  Only so much more sweet?   180
  The knowledge of that with my life begun.
  But I had so near made out the sun,
  And counted your stars, the seven and one,
  Like the fingers of my hand:
  Nay, I could all but understand

Wherefore through heaven the white moon ranges;
And just when out of her soft fifty changes
No unfamiliar face might overlook me—
Suddenly God took me.

[PIPPA *passes.*

Monsignor [*springing up*]. My people—one and all—   190
all—within there! Gag this villain—tie him hand and foot! He
dares . . . I know not half he dares—but remove him—quick!
Miserere mei, Domine! Quick, I say!

SCENE—PIPPA'S *chamber again. She enters it.*

The bee with his comb,
The mouse at her dray,
The grub in his tomb,
Wile winter away;
But the fire-fly and hedge-shrew and lob-worm, I pray,
How fare they?
Ha, ha, thanks for your counsel, my Zanze!   200
"Feast upon lampreys, quaff Breganze"—
The summer of life so easy to spend,
And care for to-morrow so soon put away!
But winter hastens at summer's end,
And fire-fly, hedge-shrew, lob-worm, pray,
How fare they?
No bidding me then to . . . what did Zanze say?
"Pare your nails pearlwise, get your small feet shoes
More like" . . . (what said she?)—"and less like canoes!"
How pert that girl was!—would I be those pert   210
Impudent staring women! It had done me,
However, surely no such mighty hurt
To learn his name who passed that jest upon me:
No foreigner, that I can recollect,
Came, as she says, a month since, to inspect
Our silk-mills—none with blue eyes and thick rings
Of raw-silk-colored hair, at all events.
Well, if old Luca keep his good intents,
We shall do better, see what next year brings.
I may buy shoes, my Zanze, not appear   220
More destitute than you perhaps next year!
Bluph . . . something! I had caught the uncouth name

But for Monsignor's people's sudden clatter
Above us—bound to spoil such idle chatter
As ours: it were indeed a serious matter
If silly talk like ours should put to shame
The pious man, the man devoid of blame,
The . . . ah but—ah but, all the same,
No mere mortal has a right
To carry that exalted air;   230
Best people are not angels quite:
While—not the worst of people's doings scare
The devil; so there's that proud look to spare!

    Which is mere counsel to myself, mind! for
I have just been the holy Monsignor:
And I was you too, Luigi's gentle mother,
And you too, Luigi!—how that Luigi started
Out of the turret—doubtlessly departed
On some good errand or another,
For he passed just now in a traveller's trim,   240
And the sullen company that prowled
About his path, I noticed, scowled
As if they had lost a prey in him,
And I was Jules the sculptor's bride,
And I was Ottima beside,
And now what am I?—tired of fooling.
Day for folly, night for schooling!
New Year's day is over and spent,
Ill or well, I must be content.
    Even my lily's asleep, I vow: 250
Wake up—here's a friend I've plucked you:
Call this flower a heart's-ease now!
Something rare, let me instruct you,
Is this, with petals triply swollen,
Three times spotted, thrice the pollen;
While the leaves and parts that witness
Old proportions and their fitness,
Here remain unchanged, unmoved now;
Call this pampered thing improved now!
Suppose there's a king of the flowers   260
And a girl-show held in his bowers—
"Look ye, buds, this growth of ours,"
Says he, "Zanze from the Brenta,
I have made her gorge polenta

Till both cheeks are near as bouncing
As her . . . name there's no pronouncing!
See this heightened color too,
For she swilled Breganze wine
Till her nose turned deep carmine;
'Twas but white when wild she grew.   270
And only by this Zanze's eyes
Of which we could not change the size,
The magnitude of all achieved
Otherwise, may be perceived."

Oh what a drear dark close to my poor day!
How could that red sun drop in that black cloud?
Ah Pippa, morning's rule is moved away,
Dispensed with, never more to be allowed!
Day's turn is over, now arrives the night's.
Oh lark, be day's apostle   280
To mavis, merle and throstle,
Bid them their betters jostle
From day and its delights!
But at night, brother howlet, over the woods,
Toll the world to thy chantry;
Sing to the bat's sleek sisterhoods
Full complines with gallantry:
Then, owls and bats,
Cowls and twats,
Monks and nuns, in a cloister's moods,   290
Adjourn to the oak-stumped pantry!
                    [*After she has begun to undress herself.*
Now, one thing I should like to really know:
How near I ever might approach all these
I only fancied being, this long day:
—Approach, I mean, so as to touch them, so
As to . . . in some way . . . move them—if you please,
Do good or evil to them some slight way.
For instance, if I wind
Silk to-morrow, my silk may bind
                              [*Sitting on the bedside.*
And border Ottima's cloak's hem.   300
Ah me, and my important part with them,
This morning's hymn half promised when I rose!

True in some sense or other, I suppose.

[*As she lies down.*

God bless me! I can pray no more to-night.
No doubt, some way or other, hymns say right.

> *All service ranks the same with God—*
> *With God, whose puppets, best and worst,*
> *Are we: there is not last nor first.*

[*She sleeps.*

DRAMATIC LYRICS [1842]

CAVALIER TUNES

1 MARCHING ALONG

I

KENTISH Sir Byng stood for his King,
Bidding the crop-headed Parliament swing:
And, pressing a troop unable to stoop
And see the rogues flourish and honest folk droop,
Marched them along, fifty-score strong,
Great-hearted gentlemen, singing this song.

II

God for King Charles! Pym and such carles
To the Devil that prompts 'em their treasonous parles!
Cavaliers, up! Lips from the cup,
Hands from the pasty, nor bite take nor sup
Till you're—
    CHORUS. *Marching along, fifty-score strong,*
            Great-hearted gentlemen, singing this song.

III

Hampden to hell, and his obsequies' knell
Serve Hazelrig, Fiennes, and young Harry as well!
England, good cheer! Rupert is near!
Kentish and loyalists, keep we not here
    CHORUS. *Marching along, fifty-score strong,*
            Great-hearted gentlemen, singing this song?

IV

Then, God for King Charles! Pym and his snarls
To the Devil that pricks on such pestilent carles!
Hold by the right, you double your might;
So, onward to Nottingham, fresh for the fight,
   Chorus. *March we along, fifty-score strong,*
            Great-hearted gentlemen, singing this song!

2. GIVE A ROUSE

I

King Charles, and who'll do him right now?
King Charles, and who's ripe for fight now?
Give a rouse: here's, in hell's despite now,
King Charles!

II

Who gave me the goods that went since?
Who raised me the house that sank once?
Who helped me to gold I spent since?
Who found me in wine you drank once?
     Chorus. *King Charles, and who'll do him right now?*
            King Charles, and who's ripe for fight now?
            Give a rouse: here's, in hell's despite now,
            King Charles!

III

To whom used my boy George quaff else,
By the old fool's side that begot him?
For whom did he cheer and laugh else,
While Noll's damned troopers shot him?
     Chorus. *King Charles, and who'll do him right now?*
            King Charles, and who's ripe for fight now?
            Give a rouse: here's, in hell's despite now,
            King Charles!

3   BOOT AND SADDLE

I

Boot, saddle, to horse, and away!
Rescue my castle before the hot day
Brightens to blue from its silvery gray,
    CHORUS. *Boot, saddle, to horse, and away!*

II

Ride past the suburbs, asleep as you'd say;
Many's the friend there, will listen and pray
"God's luck to gallants that strike up the lay—
    CHORUS. *"Boot, saddle, to horse, and away!"*

III

Forty miles off, like a roebuck at bay,
Flouts Castle Brancepeth the Roundheads' array:
Who laughs, "Good fellows ere this, by my fay,
    CHORUS. *"Boot, saddle, to horse, and away!"*

IV

Who? My wife Gertrude; that, honest and gay,
Laughs when you talk of surrendering, "Nay!
I've better counsellors; what counsel they?
    CHORUS. *"Boot, saddle, to horse, and away!"*

MY LAST DUCHESS

FERRARA

THAT's my last Duchess painted on the wall,
Looking as if she were alive. I call
That piece a wonder, now: Frà Pandolf's hands
Worked busily a day, and there she stands.
Will't please you sit and look at her? I said
"Frà Pandolf" by design, for never read

Strangers like you that pictured countenance,
The depth and passion of its earnest glance,
But to myself they turned (since none puts by
The curtain I have drawn for you, but I)   10
And seemed as they would ask me, if they durst,
How such a glance came there; so, not the first
Are you to turn and ask thus. Sir 'twas not
Her husband's presence only, called that spot
Of joy into the Duchess' cheek: perhaps
Frà Pandolf chanced to say "Her mantle laps
Over my lady's wrist too much," or "Paint
Must never hope to reproduce the faint
Half-flush that dies along her throat:" such stuff
Was courtesy, she thought, and cause enough   20
For calling up that spot of joy. She had
A heart—how shall I say?—too soon made glad,
Too easily impressed; she liked whate'er
She looked on, and her looks went everywhere.
Sir, 'twas all one! My favor at her breast,
The drooping of the daylight in the West,
The bough of cherries some officious fool
Broke in the orchard for her, the white mule
She rode with round the terrace—all and each
Would draw from her alike the approving speech,   30
Or blush, at least. She thanked men,—good! but thanked
Somehow—I know not how—as if she ranked
My gift of a nine-hundred-years-old name
With anybody's gift. Who'd stoop to blame
This sort of trifling? Even had you skill
In speech—(which I have not)—to make your will
Quite clear to such an one, and say, "Just this
Or that in you disgusts me; here you miss,
Or there exceed the mark"—and if she let
Herself be lessoned so, nor plainly set   40
Her wits to yours, forsooth, and made excuse,
—E'en then would be some stooping; and I choose
Never to stoop. Oh sir, she smiled, no doubt,
Whene'er I passed her; but who passed without
Much the same smile? This grew; I gave commands;
Then all smiles stopped together. There she stands
As if alive. Will't please you rise? We'll meet
The company below, then. I repeat,
The Count your master's known munificence

Is ample warrant that no just pretence
Of mine for dowry will be disallowed;
Though his fair daughter's self, as I avowed
At starting, is my object. Nay, we'll go
Together down, sir. Notice Neptune, though,
Taming a sea-horse, thought a rarity,
Which Claus of Innsbruck cast in bronze for me!

COUNT GISMOND

AIX IN PROVENCE

I

CHRIST God who savest man, save most
  Of men Count Gismond who saved me!
Count Gauthier, when he chose his post,
  Chose time and place and company
To suit it; when he struck at length
My honor, 'twas with all his strength.

II

And doubtlessly ere he could draw
  All points to one, he must have schemed!
That miserable morning saw
  Few half so happy as I seemed,
While being dressed in queen's array
To give our tourney prize away.

III

I thought they loved me, did me grace
  To please themselves: 'twas all their deed;
God makes, or fair or foul, our face;
  If showing mine so caused to bleed
My cousins' hearts, they should have dropped
A word, and straight the play had stopped.

IV

They, too, so beauteous! Each a queen
    By virtue of her brow and breast;   20
Not needing to be crowned, I mean,
    As I do. E'en when I was dressed,
Had either of them spoke, instead
Of glancing sideways with still head!

V

But no: they let me laugh, and sing
    My birthday song quite through, adjust
The last rose in my garland, fling
    A last look on the mirror, trust
My arms to each an arm of theirs,
And so descend the castle-stairs—   30

VI

And come out on the morning-troop
    Of merry friends who kissed my cheek,
And called me queen, and made me stoop
    Under the canopy—(a streak
That pierced it, of the outside sun,
Powdered with gold its gloom's soft dun)—

VII

And they could let me take my state
    And foolish throne amid applause
Of all come there to celebrate
    My queen's-day—Oh I think the cause   40
Of much was, they forgot no crowd
Makes up for parents in their shroud!

VIII

However that be, all eyes were bent
    Upon me, when my cousins cast
Theirs down; 'twas time I should present
    The victor's crown, but . . . there, 'twill last
No long time . . . the old mist again
Blinds me as it did. How vain!

IX

See! Gismond's at the gate, in talk
   With his two boys: I can proceed.   50
Well, at that moment, who should stalk
   Forth boldly—to my face, indeed—
But Gauthier, and he thundered "Stay!"
And all stayed. "Bring no crowns, I say!

X

"Bring torches! Wind the penance-sheet
   About her! Let her shun the chaste,
Or lay herself before their feet!
   Shall she whose body I embraced
A night long, queen it in the day?
For honor's sake no crowns, I say!"   60

XI

I? What I answered? As I live,
   I never fancied such a thing
As answer possible to give.
   What says the body when they spring
Some monstrous torture-engine's whole
Strength on it? No more says the soul.

XII

Till out strode Gismond; then I knew
   That I was saved. I never met
His face before, but, at first view,
   I felt quite sure that God had set   70
Himself to Satan; who would spend
A minute's mistrust on the end?

XIII

He strode to Gauthier, in his throat
   Gave him the lie, then struck his mouth
With one back-handed blow that wrote
   In blood men's verdict there. North, South,
East, West, I looked. The lie was dead,
And damned, and truth stood up instead.

XIV

This glads me most, that I enjoyed
   The heart of the joy, with my content
In watching Gismond unalloyed
   By any doubt of the event:
God took that on him—I was bid
Watch Gismond for my part: I did.

XV

Did I not watch him while he let
   His armorer just brace his greaves,
Rivet his hauberk, on the fret
   The while! His foot . . . my memory leaves
No least stamp out, nor how anon
He pulled his ringing gauntlets on.

XVI

And e'en before the trumpet's sound
   Was finished, prone lay the false knight,
Prone as his lie, upon the ground:
   Gismond flew at him, used no sleight
O' the sword, but open-breasted drove,
Cleaving till out the truth he clove.

XVII

Which done, he dragged him to my feet
   And said "Here die, but end thy breath
In full confession, lest thou fleet
   From my first, to God's second death!
Say, hast thou lied?" And, "I have lied
To God and her," he said, and died.

XVIII

Then Gismond, kneeling to me, asked
   —What safe my heart holds, though no word
Could I repeat now, if I tasked
   My powers forever, to a third
Dear even as you are. Pass the rest
Until I sank upon his breast.

XIX

Over my head his arm he flung
　Against the world; and scarce I felt
His sword (that dripped by me and swung)
　A little shifted in its belt:
For he began to say the while
How South our home lay many a mile.

XX

So 'mid the shouting multitude
　We two walked forth to never more
Return. My cousins have pursued
　Their life, untroubled as before
I vexed them. Gauthier's dwelling-place
God lighten! May his soul find grace!

XXI

Our elder boy has got the clear
　Great brow; tho' when his brother's black
Full eye shows scorn, it . . . Gismond here?
　And have you brought my tercel back?
I just was telling Adela
How many birds it struck since May.

INCIDENT OF THE FRENCH CAMP

I

You know, we French stormed Ratisbon:
　A mile or so away,
On a little mound, Napoleon
　Stood on our storming-day;
With neck out-thrust, you fancy how,
　Legs wide, arms locked behind,
As if to balance the prone brow
　Oppressive with its mind.

II

Just as perhaps he mused "My plans
 That soar, to earth may fall,
Let once my army-leader Lannes
 Waver at yonder wall,"—
Out 'twixt the battery-smokes there flew
 A rider, bound on bound
Full-galloping; nor bridle drew
 Until he reached the mound.

III

Then off there flung in smiling joy,
 And held himself erect
By just his horse's mane, a boy:
 You hardly could suspect—
(So tight he kept his lips compressed,
 Scarce any blood came through)
You looked twice ere you saw his breast
 Was all but shot in two.

IV

"Well," cried he, "Emperor, by God's grace
 We've got you Ratisbon!
The Marshal's in the market-place,
 And you'll be there anon
To see your flag-bird flap his vans
 Where I, to heart's desire,
Perched him!" The chief's eye flashed; his plans
 Soared up again like fire.

V

The chief's eye flashed; but presently
 Softened itself, as sheathes
A film the mother-eagle's eye
 When her bruised eaglet breathes;
"You're wounded!" "Nay," the soldier's pride
 Touched to the quick, he said:
"I'm killed, Sire!" And his chief beside
 Smiling the boy fell dead.

SOLILOQUY OF THE SPANISH CLOISTER

I

Gr-r-r—there go, my heart's abhorrence!
    Water your damned flower-pots, do!
If hate killed men, Brother Lawrence,
    God's blood, would not mine kill you!
What? your myrtle-bush wants trimming?
    Oh, that rose has prior claims—
Needs its leaden vase filled brimming?
    Hell dry you up with its flames!

II

At the meal we sit together:
    Salve tibi! I must hear
Wise talk of the kind of weather,
    Sort of season, time of year:
*Not a plenteous cork-crop: scarcely
    Dare we hope oak-galls, I doubt:
What's the Latin name for "parsley"?*
    What's the Greek name for Swine's Snout?

III

Whew! We'll have our platter burnished,
    Laid with care on our own shelf!
With a fire-new spoon we're furnished,
    And a goblet for ourself,
Rinsed like something sacrificial
    Ere 'tis fit to touch our chaps—
Marked with L. for our initial!
    (He-he! There his lily snaps!)

IV

Saint, forsooth! While brown Dolores
    Squats outside the Convent bank
With Sanchicha, telling stories,
    Steeping tresses in the tank,

Blue-black, lustrous, thick like horsehairs,
  —Can't I see his dead eye glow,
Bright as 'twere a Barbary corsair's?
  (That is, if he'd let it show!)

V

When he finishes refection,
  Knife and fork he never lays
Cross-wise, to my recollection,
  As do I, in Jesu's praise.
I the Trinity illustrate,
  Drinking watered orange-pulp—
In three sips the Arian frustrate;
  While he drains his at one gulp.

VI

Oh, those melons? If he's able
  We're to have a feast! so nice!
One goes to the Abbot's table,
  All of us get each a slice.
How go on your flowers? None double
  Not one fruit-sort can you spy?
Strange!—And I, too, at such trouble,
  Keep them close-nipped on the sly!

VII

There's a great text in Galatians,
  Once you trip on it, entails
Twenty-nine distinct damnations,
  One sure, if another fails:
If I trip him just a-dying,
  Sure of heaven as sure can be,
Spin him round and send him flying
  Off to hell, a Manichee?

VIII

Or, my scrofulous French novel
  On gray paper with blunt type!
Simply glance at it, you grovel
  Hand and foot in Belial's gripe:

If I double down its pages
    At the woful sixteenth print,
When he gathers his greengages,
    Ope a sieve and slip it in't?

IX

Or, there's Satan!—one might venture
    Pledge one's soul to him, yet leave
Such a flaw in the indenture
    As he'd miss till, past retrieve,
Blasted lay that rose-acacia
    We're so proud of! *Hy, Zy, Hine.*
'St, there's Vespers! *Plena gratiâ*
    Ave, Virgo! Gr-r-r—you swine!

IN A GONDOLA

He sings

I SEND my heart up to thee, all my heart
    In this my singing.
For the stars help me, and the sea bears part;
    The very night is clinging
Closer to Venice' streets to leave one space
    Above me, whence thy face
May light my joyous heart to thee its dwelling-place.

She speaks

Say after me, and try to say
My very words, as if each word
Came from you of your own accord,
In your own voice, in your own way:
"This woman's heart and soul and brain
Are mine as much as this gold chain
She bids me wear; which" (say again)
"I choose to make by cherishing
A precious thing, or choose to fling
Over the boat-side, ring by ring."

10

And yet once more say . . . no word more!
Since words are only words. Give o'er!

Unless you call me, all the same,   20
Familiarly by my pet name,
Which if the Three should hear you call,
And me reply to, would proclaim
At once our secret to them all.
Ask of me, too, command me, blame—
Do, break down the partition-wall
'Twixt us, the daylight world beholds
Curtained in dusk and splendid folds!
What's left but—all of me to take?
I am the Three's: prevent them, slake   30
Your thirst! 'Tis said, the Arab sage,
In practising with gems, can loose
Their subtle spirit in his cruce
And leave but ashes: so, sweet mage,
Leave them my ashes when thy use
Sucks out my soul, thy heritage!

He sings

I

Past we glide, and past, and past!
    What's that poor Agnese doing
Where they make the shutters fast?
    Gray Zanobi's just a-wooing   40
To his couch the purchased bride:
    Past we glide!

II

Past we glide, and past, and past!
    Why's the Pucci Palace flaring
Like a beacon to the blast?
    Guests by hundreds, not one caring
If the dear host's neck were wried:
    Past we glide!

She sings

I

The moth's kiss, first!
Kiss me as if you made believe   **50**
You were not sure, this eve,
How my face, your flower, had pursed
Its petals up; so, here and there
You brush it, till I grow aware
Who wants me, and wide ope I burst.

II

The bee's kiss, now!
Kiss me as if you entered gay
My heart at some noonday,
A bud that dares not disallow
The claim, so all is rendered up,   **60**
And passively its shattered cup
Over your head to sleep I bow.

He sings

I

What are we two?
I am a Jew,
And carry thee, farther than friends can pursue,
To a feast of our tribe;
Where they need thee to bribe
The devil that blasts them unless he imbibe
Thy . . . Scatter the vision forever! And now,
As of old, I am I, thou art thou!   **70**

II

Say again, what we are?
The sprite of a star,
I lure thee above where the destinies bar
My plumes their full play
Till a ruddier ray
Than my pale one announce there is withering away
Some . . . Scatter the vision forever! And now,
As of old, I am I, thou art thou!

He muses

Oh, which were best, to roam or rest?
The land's lap or the water's breast? 80
To sleep on yellow millet-sheaves,
Or swim in lucid shallows just
Eluding water-lily leaves,
An inch from Death's black fingers, thrust
To lock you, whom release he must;
Which life were best on Summer eves?

He speaks, musing

Lie back; could thought of mine improve you?
From this shoulder let there spring
A wing; from this, another wing;
Wings, not legs and feet, shall move you! 90
Snow-white must they spring, to blend
With your flesh, but I intend
They shall deepen to the end,
Broader, into burning gold,
Till both wings crescent-wise enfold
Your perfect self, from 'neath your feet
To o'er your head, where, lo, they meet
As if a million sword-blades hurled
Defiance from you to the world!

Rescue me thou, the only real! 100
And scare away this mad ideal
That came, nor motions to depart!
Thanks! Now, stay ever as thou art!

Still he muses

I

What if the Three should catch at last
Thy serenader? While there's cast
Paul's cloak about my head, and fast
Gian pinions me, Himself has past
His stylet thro' my back; I reel;
And . . . is it thou I feel?

II

They trail me, these three godless knaves,   110
Past every church that saints and saves,
Nor stop till, where the cold sea raves
By Lido's wet accursed graves,
They scoop mine, roll me to its brink,
And . . . on thy breast I sink!

She replies, musing

Dip your arm o'er the boat-side, elbow-deep,
As I do: thus: were death so unlike sleep,
Caught this way? Death's to fear from flame or steel,
Or poison doubtless; but from water—feel!
Go find the bottom! Would you stay me? There!   120
Now pluck a great blade of that ribbon-grass
To plait in where the foolish jewel was,
I flung away: since you have praised my hair,
'Tis proper to be choice in what I wear.

He speaks

Row home? must we row home? Too surely
Know I where its front's demurely
Over the Giudecca piled;
Window just with window mating,
Door on door exactly waiting,
All's the set face of a child: 130
But behind it, where's a trace
Of the staidness and reserve,
And formal lines without a curve,
In the same child's playing-face?
No two windows look one way
O'er the small sea-water thread
Below them. Ah, the autumn day
I, passing, saw you overhead!
First, out a cloud of curtain blew,
Then a sweet cry, and last came you—   140
To catch your lory that must needs
Escape just then, of all times then,
To peck a tall plant's fleecy seeds,
And make me happiest of men.

I scarce could breathe to see you reach
So far back o'er the balcony
To catch him ere he climbed too high
Above you in the Smyrna peach
That quick the round smooth cord of gold,
This coiled hair on your head, unrolled,   150
Fell down you like a gorgeous snake
The Roman girls were wont, of old,
When Rome there was, for coolness' sake
To let lie curling o'er their bosoms.
Dear lory, may his beak retain
Ever its delicate rose stain
As if the wounded lotus-blossoms
Had marked their thief to know again!

Stay longer yet, for others' sake
Than mine! What should your chamber do?   160
—With all its rarities that ache
In silence while day lasts, but wake
At night-time and their life renew,
Suspended just to pleasure you
Who brought against their will together
These objects, and, while day lasts, weave
Around them such a magic tether
That dumb they look: your harp, believe,
With all the sensitive tight strings
Which dare not speak, now to itself   170
Breathes slumberously, as if some elf
Went in and out the chords, his wings
Make murmur wheresoe'er they graze,
As an angel may, between the maze
Of midnight palace-pillars, on
And on, to sow God's plagues, have gone
Through guilty glorious Babylon.
And while such murmurs flow, the nymph
Bends o'er the harp-top from her shell
As the dry limpet for the lymph   180
Come with a tune he knows so well.
And how your statues' hearts must swell!
And how your pictures must descend
To see each other, friend with friend!
Oh, could you take them by surprise,
You'd find Schidone's eager Duke

Doing the quaintest courtesies
To that prim saint by Haste-thee-Luke!
And, deeper into her rock den,
Bold Castelfranco's Magdalen   190
You'd find retreated from the ken
Of that robed counsel-keeping Ser—
As if the Tizian thinks of her,
And is not, rather, gravely bent
On seeing for himself what toys
Are these, his progeny invent,
What litter now the board employs
Whereon he signed a document
That got him murdered! Each enjoys
Its night so well, you cannot break   200
The sport up, so, indeed must make
More stay with me, for others' sake.

                    She speaks

                      I

To-morrow, if a harp-string, say,
Is used to tie the jasmine back
That overfloods my room with sweets,
Contrive your Zorzi somehow meets
My Zanze! If the ribbon's black,
The Three are watching: keep away!

                      II

Your gondola—let Zorzi wreathe
A mesh of water-weeds about   210
Its prow, as if he unaware
Had struck some quay or bridge-foot stair!
That I may throw a paper out
As you and he go underneath.

There's Zanze's vigilant taper; safe are we.
Only one minute more to-night with me?
Resume your past self of a month ago!
Be you the bashful gallant, I will be
The lady with the colder breast than snow.
Now bow you, as becomes, nor touch my hand   220

More than I touch yours when I step to land,
And say, "All thanks, Siora!"—

                       Heart to heart
And lips to lips! Yet once more, ere we part,
Clasp me and make me thine, as mine thou art!
                [*He is surprised, and stabbed.*
It was ordained to be so, sweet!—and best
Comes now, beneath thine eyes, upon thy breast.
Still kiss me! Care not for the cowards! Care
Only to put aside thy beauteous hair
My blood will hurt! The Three, I do not scorn
To death, because they never lived: but I   230
Have lived indeed, and so—(yet one more kiss)—can die!

ARTEMIS PROLOGIZES

I AM a Goddess of the ambrosial courts,
And save by Here, Queen of Pride, surpassed
By none whose temples whiten this the world.
Through heaven I roll my lucid moon along;
I shed in hell o'er my pale people peace;
On earth I, caring for the creatures, guard
Each pregnant yellow wolf and fox-bitch sleek,
And every feathered mother's callow brood,
And all that love green haunts and loneliness.
Of men, the chaste adore me, hanging crowns   10
Of poppies red to blackness, bell and stem,
Upon my image at Athenai here;
And this dead Youth, Asclepios bends above,
Was dearest to me. He, my buskined step
To follow through the wild-wood leafy ways,
And chase the panting stag, or swift with darts
Stop the swift ounce, or lay the leopard low,
Neglected homage to another god:
Whence Aphrodite, by no midnight smoke
Of tapers lulled, in jealousy despatched   20
A noisome lust that, as the gadbee stings,
Possessed his stepdame Phaidra for himself
The son of Theseus her great absent spouse.
Hippolutos exclaiming in his rage
Against the fury of the Queen, she judged

Life insupportable; and, pricked at heart
An Amazonian stranger's race should dare
To scorn her, perished by the murderous cord:
Yet, ere she perished, blasted in a scroll
The fame of him her swerving made not swerve.   30
And Theseus, read, returning, and believed,
And exiled, in the blindness of his wrath,
The man without a crime who, last as first,
Loyal, divulged not to his sire the truth.
Now Theseus from Poseidon had obtained
That of his wishes should be granted three,
And one he imprecated straight—"Alive
May ne'er Hippolutos reach other lands!"
Poseidon heard, ai ai! And scarce the prince
Had stepped into the fixed boots of the car   40
That give the feet a stay against the strength
Of the Henetian horses, and around
His body flung the rein, and urged their speed
Along the rocks and shingles of the shore,
When from the gaping wave a monster flung
His obscene body in the coursers' path.
These, mad with terror, as the sea-bull sprawled
Wallowing about their feet, lost care of him
That reared them; and the master-chariot-pole
Snapping beneath their plunges like a reed,   50
Hippolutos, whose feet were trammelled fast,
Was yet dragged forward by the circling rein
Which either hand directed; nor they quenched
The frenzy of their flight before each trace,
Wheel-spoke and splinter of the woful car,
Each boulder-stone, sharp stub and spiny shell,
Huge fish-bone wrecked and wreathed amid the sands
On that detested beach, was bright with blood
And morsels of his flesh: then fell the steeds
Head foremost, crashing in their mooned fronts,   60
Shivering with sweat, each white eye horror-fixed.
His people, who had witnessed all afar,
Bore back the ruins of Hippolutos.
But when his sire, too swoln with pride, rejoiced
(Indomitable as a man foredoomed)
That vast Poseidon had fulfilled his prayer,
I, in a flood of glory visible,
Stood o'er my dying votary and, deed

By deed, revealed, as all took place, the truth.
Then Theseus lay the wofullest of men,   70
And worthily; but ere the death-veils hid
His face, the murdered prince full pardon breathed
To his rash sire. Whereat Athenai wails.
   So I, who ne'er forsake my votaries,
Lest in the cross-way none the honey-cake
Should tender, nor pour out the dog's hot life;
Lest at my fane the priests disconsolate
Should dress my image with some faded poor
Few crowns, made favors of, nor dare object
Such slackness to my worshippers who turn   80
Elsewhere the trusting heart and loaded hand,
As they had climbed Olumpos to report
Of Artemis and nowhere found her throne—
I interposed: and, this eventful night,—
(While round the funeral pyre the populace
Stood with fierce light on their black robes which bound
Each sobbing head, while yet their hair they clipped
O'er the dead body of their withered prince,
And, in his palace, Theseus prostrated
On the cold hearth, his brow cold as the slab   90
'Twas bruised on, groaned away the heavy grief—
As the pyre fell, and down the cross logs crashed
Sending a crowd of sparkles through the night,
And the gay fire, elate with mastery,
Towered like a serpent o'er the clotted jars
Of wine, dissolving oils and frankincense,
And splendid gums like gold),—my potency
Conveyed the perished man to my retreat
In the thrice-venerable forest here.
And this white-bearded sage who squeezes now   100
The berried plant, is Phoibos' son of fame,
Asclepios, whom my radiant brother taught
The doctrine of each herb and flower and root,
To know their secret'st virtue and express
The saving soul of all: who so has soothed
With lavers the torn brow and murdered cheeks,
Composed the hair and brought its gloss again,
And called the red bloom to the pale skin back,
And laid the strips and jagged ends of flesh
Even once more, and slacked the sinew's knot   110
Of every tortured limb—that now he lies

As if mere sleep possessed him underneath
These interwoven oaks and pines. Oh cheer,
Divine presenter of the healing rod,
Thy snake, with ardent throat and lulling eye,
Twines his lithe spires around! I say, much cheer!
Proceed thou with thy wisest pharmacies!
And ye, white crowd of woodland sister-nymphs,
Ply, as the sage directs, these buds and leaves
That strew the turf around the twain! While I   120
Await, in fitting silence, the event.

WARING

I

I

WHAT's become of Waring
Since he gave us all the slip,
Chose land-travel or seafaring,
Boots and chest or staff and scrip,
Rather than pace up and down
Any longer London town?

II

Who'd have guessed it from his lip
Or his brow's accustomed bearing,
On the night he thus took ship
Or started landward?—little caring   10
For us, it seems, who supped together
(Friends of his too, I remember)
And walked home thro' the merry weather,
The snowiest in all December.
I left his arm that night myself
For what's-his-name's, the new prose-poet
Who wrote the book there, on the shelf—
How, forsooth, was I to know it
If Waring meant to glide away
Like a ghost at break of day?   20
Never looked he half so gay!

III

He was prouder than the devil:
How he must have cursed our revel!
Ay and many other meetings,
Indoor visits, outdoor greetings,
As up and down he paced this London,
With no work done, but great works undone,
Where scarce twenty knew his name.
Why not, then, have earlier spoken,
Written, bustled? Who's to blame   30
If your silence kept unbroken?
"True, but there were sundry jottings,
Stray-leaves, fragments, blurrs and blottings,
Certain first steps were achieved
Already which"—(is that your meaning?)
"Had well borne out whoe'er believed
In more to come!" But who goes gleaning
Hedgside chance-glades, while full-sheaved
Stand cornfields by him? Pride, o'erweening
Pride alone, puts forth such claims   40
O'er the day's distinguished names.

IV

Meantime, how much I loved him,
I find out now I've lost him.
I who cared not if I moved him,
Who could so carelessly accost him,
Henceforth never shall get free
Of his ghostly company,
His eyes that just a little wink
As deep I go into the merit
Of this and that distinguished spirit—   50
His cheeks' raised color, soon to sink,
As long I dwell on some stupendous
And tremendous (Heaven defend us!)
Monstr'-inform'-ingens-horrend-ous
Demoniaco-seraphic
Penman's latest piece of graphic.
Nay, my very wrist grows warm
With his dragging weight of arm.

E'en so, swimmingly appears,
Through one's after-supper musings,   60
Some lost lady of old years
With her beauteous vain endeavor
And goodness unrepaid as ever;
The face, accustomed to refusings,
We, puppies that we were . . . Oh never
Surely, nice of conscience, scrupled
Being aught like false, forsooth, to?
Telling aught but honest truth to?
What a sin, had we centupled
Its possessor's grace and sweetness!   70
No! she heard in its completeness
Truth, for truth's a weighty matter,
And truth, at issue, we can't flatter!
Well, 'tis done with; she's exempt
From damning us thro' such a sally;
And so she glides, as down a valley,
Taking up with her contempt,
Past our reach; and in, the flowers
Shut her unregarded hours.

v

Oh, could I have him back once more,   80
This Waring, but one half-day more!
Back, with the quiet face of yore,
So hungry for acknowledgment
Like mine! I'd fool him to his bent.
Feed, should not he, to heart's content?
I'd say, "to only have conceived,
Planned your great works, apart from progress,
Surpasses little works achieved!"
I'd lie so, I should be believed.
I'd make such havoc of the claims   90
Of the day's distinguished names
To feast him with, as feasts an ogress
Her feverish sharp-toothed gold-crowned child!
Or as one feasts a creature rarely
Captured here, unreconciled
To capture; and completely gives
Its pettish humors license, barely
Requiring that it lives.

VI

Ichabod, Ichabod,
The glory is departed!   100
Travels Waring East away?
Who, of knowledge, by hearsay,
Reports a man upstarted
Somewhere as a god,
Hordes grown European-hearted,
Millions of the wild made tame
On a sudden at his fame?
In Vishnu-land what Avatar?
Or who in Moscow, toward the Czar,
With the demurest of footfalls   110
Over the Kremlin's pavement bright
With serpentine and syenite,
Steps, with five other Generals
That simultaneously take snuff,
For each to have pretext enough
And kerchiefwise unfold his sash
Which, softness' self, is yet the stuff
To hold fast where a steel chain snaps,
And leave the grand white neck no gash?
Waring in Moscow, to those rough   120
Cold northern natures born perhaps,
Like the lambwhite maiden dear
From the circle of mute kings
Unable to repress the tear,
Each as his sceptre down he flings,
To Diana's fane at Taurica,
Where now a captive priestess, she alway
Mingles her tender grave Hellenic speech
With theirs, tuned to the hailstone-beaten beach
As pours some pigeon, from the myrrhy lands   130
Rapt by the whirlblast to fierce Scythian strands
Where breed the swallows, her melodious cry
Amid their barbarous twitter!
In Russia? Never! Spain were fitter!
Ay, most likely 'tis in Spain
That we and Waring meet again
Now, while he turns down that cool narrow lane
Into the blackness, out of grave Madrid
All fire and shine, abrupt as when there's slid

Its stiff gold blazing pall 140
From some black coffin-lid.
Or, best of all,
I love to think
The leaving us was just a feint;
Back here to London did he slink,
And now works on without a wink
Of sleep, and we are on the brink
Of something great in fresco-paint:
Some garret's ceiling, walls and floor,
Up and down and o'er and o'er 150
He splashes, as none splashed before
Since great Caldera Polidore.
Or Music means this land of ours
Some favor yet, to pity won
By Purcell from his Rosy Bowers,—
"Give me my so-long promised son,
Let Waring end what I begun!"
Then down he creeps and out he steals
Only when the night conceals
His face; in Kent 'tis cherry-time, 160
Or hops are picking: or at prime
Of March he wanders as, too happy,
Years ago when he was young,
Some mild eve when woods grew sappy
And the early moths had sprung
To life from many a trembling sheath
Woven the warm boughs beneath;
While small birds said to themselves
What should soon be actual song,
And young gnats, by tens and twelves, 170
Made as if they were the throng
That crowd around and carry aloft
The sound they have nursed, so sweet and pure,
Out of a myriad noises soft,
Into a tone that can endure
Amid the noise of a July noon
When all God's creatures crave their boon,
All at once and all in tune,
And get it, happy as Waring then,
Having first within his ken 180
What a man might do with men:
And far too glad, in the even-glow,

To mix with the world he meant to take
Into his hand, he told you, so—
And out of it his world to make,
To contract and to expand
As he shut or oped his hand.
Oh Waring, what's to really be?
A clear stage and a crowd to see!
Some Garrick, say, out shall not he   190
The heart of Hamlet's mystery pluck?
Or, where most unclean beasts are rife,
Some Junius—am I right?—shall tuck
His sleeve, and forth with flaying-knife!
Some Chatterton shall have the luck
Of calling Rowley into life!
Some one shall somehow run a muck
With this old world for want of strife
Sound asleep. Contrive, contrive
To rouse us, Waring! Who's alive?   200
Our men scarce seem in earnest now.
Distinguished names!—but 'tis, somehow,
As if they played at being names
Still more distinguished, like the games
Of children. Turn our sport to earnest
With a visage of the sternest!
Bring the real times back, confessed
Still better than our very best!

II

I

"When I last saw Waring . . ."
(How all turned to him who spoke!   210
You saw Waring? Truth or joke?
In land-travel or sea-faring?)

II

"We were sailing by Triest
Where a day or two we harbored:
A sunset was in the West,
When, looking over the vessel's side,

One of our company espied
A sudden speck to larboard.
And as a sea-duck flies and swims
At once, so came the light craft up,   220
With its sole lateen sail that trims
And turns (the water round its rims
Dancing, as round a sinking cup)
And by us like a fish it curled,
And drew itself up close beside,
Its great sail on the instant furled,
And o'er its thwarts a shrill voice cried,
(A neck as bronzed as a Lascar's)
'Buy wine of us, you English Brig?
Or fruit, tobacco and cigars?   230
A pilot for you to Triest?
Without one, look you ne'er so big,
They'll never let you up the bay!
We natives should know best.'
I turned, and 'just those fellows' way,'
Our captain said, 'The 'long-shore thieves
Are laughing at us in their sleeves.'

III

"In truth, the boy leaned laughing back;
And one, half-hidden by his side
Under the furled sail, soon I spied,   240
With great grass hat and kerchief black,
Who looked up with his kingly throat,
Said somewhat, while the other shook
His hair back from his eyes to look
Their longest at us; then the boat,
I know not how, turned sharply round,
Laying her whole side on the sea
As a leaping fish does; from the lee
Into the weather, cut somehow
Her sparkling path beneath our bow   250
And so went off, as with a bound,
Into the rosy and golden half
O' the sky, to overtake the sun
And reach the shore, like the sea-calf
Its singing cave; yet I caught one
Glance ere away the boat quite passed,

And neither time nor toil could mar
Those features: so I saw the last
Of Waring!"—You? Oh, never star
Was lost here, but it rose afar!   260
Look East, where whole new thousands are!
In Vishnu-land what Avatar?

RUDEL TO THE LADY OF TRIPOLI

I

I KNOW a Mount, the gracious Sun perceives
First, when he visits, last, too, when he leaves
The world; and, vainly favored, it repays
The day-long glory of his steadfast gaze
By no change of its large calm front of snow.
And underneath the Mount, a Flower I know,
He cannot have perceived, that changes ever
At his approach; and, in the lost endeavor
To live his life, has parted, one by one,
With all a flower's true graces, for the grace   10
Of being but a foolish mimic sun,
With ray-like florets round a disk-like face.
Men nobly call by many a name the Mount
As over many a land of theirs its large
Calm front of snow like a triumphal targe
Is reared, and still with old names, fresh names vie,
Each to its proper praise and own account:
Men call the Flower, the Sunflower, sportively.

II

Oh, Angel of the East, one, one gold look
Across the waters to this twilight nook,   20
—The far sad waters, Angel, to this nook!

III

Dear Pilgrim, art thou for the East indeed?
Go!—saying ever as thou dost proceed,
That I, French Rudel, choose for my device

A sunflower outspread like a sacrifice
Before its idol. See! These inexpert
And hurried fingers could not fail to hurt
The woven picture; 'tis a woman's skill
Indeed; but nothing baffled me, so, ill
Or well, the work is finished. Say, men feed   30
On songs I sing, and therefore bask the bees
On my flower's breast as on a platform broad.
But, as the flower's concern is not for these
But solely for the sun, so men applaud
In vain this Rudel, he not looking here
But to the East—the East! Go, say this, Pilgrim dear!

CRISTINA

I

SHE should never have looked at me
    If she meant I should not love her!
There are plenty . . . men, you call such,
    I suppose . . . she may discover
All her soul to, if she pleases,
    And yet leave much as she found them:
But I'm not so, and she knew it
    When she fixed me, glancing round them.

II

What? To fix me thus meant nothing?
    But I can't tell (there's my weakness)
What her look said!—no vile cant, sure,
    About "need to strew the bleakness
Of some lone shore with its pearl-seed
    That the sea feels"—no "strange yearning
That such souls have, most to lavish
    Where there's chance of least returning."

III

Oh, we're sunk enough here, God knows!
    But not quite so sunk that moments,

Sure tho' seldom, are denied us,
   When the spirit's true endowments
Stand out plainly from its false ones,
   And apprise it if pursuing
Or the right way or the wrong way,
   To its triumph or undoing.

IV

There are flashes struck from midnights,
   There are fire-flames noondays kindle,
Whereby piled-up honors perish,
   Whereby swollen ambitions dwindle,
While just this or that poor impulse,
   Which for once had play unstifled,
Seems the sole work of a life-time
   That away the rest have trifled.

V

Doubt you if, in some such moment,
   As she fixed me, she felt clearly,
Ages past the soul existed,
   Here an age 'tis resting merely,
And hence fleets again for ages,
   While the true end, sole and single,
It stops here for is, this love-way,
   With some other soul to mingle?

VI

Else it loses what it lived for,
   And eternally must lose it;
Better ends may be in prospect,
   Deeper blisses (if you choose it),
But this life's end and this love-bliss
   Have been lost here. Doubt you whether
This she felt as, looking at me,
   Mine and her souls rushed together?

VII

Oh, observe! Of course, next moment,
  The world's honors, in derision,
Trampled out the light forever:
  Never fear but there's provision
Of the devil's to quench knowledge
  Lest we walk the earth in rapture!
—Making those who catch God's secret
  Just so much more prize their capture!

VIII

Such am I: the secret's mine now!
  She has lost me, I have gained her;
Her soul's mine: and thus, grown perfect,
  I shall pass my life's remainder.
Life will just hold out the proving
  Both our powers, alone and blended:
And then, come next life quickly!
  This world's use will have been ended.

JOHANNES AGRICOLA IN MEDITATION

There's heaven above, and night by night
  I look right through its gorgeous roof;
No suns and moons though e'er so bright
  Avail to stop me; splendor-proof
  I keep the broods of stars aloof:
For I intend to get to God,
  For 'tis to God I speed so fast,
For in God's breast, my own abode,
  Those shoals of dazzling glory, past,
  I lay my spirit down at last.
I lie where I have always lain,
  God smiles as he has always smiled;
Ere suns and moons could wax and wane,
  Ere stars were thundergirt, or piled
  The heavens, God thought on me his child;
Ordained a life for me, arrayed
  Its circumstances, every one

10

To the minutest; ay, God said
  This head this hand should rest upon
  Thus, ere he fashioned star or sun.   20
And having thus created me,
  Thus rooted me, he bade me grow,
Guiltless forever, like a tree
  That buds and blooms, nor seeks to know
  The law by which it prospers so:
But sure that thought and word and deed
  All go to swell his love for me,
Me, made because that love had need
  Of something irreversibly
  Pledged solely its content to be.   30
Yes, yes, a tree which must ascend,
  No poison-gourd foredoomed to stoop!
I have God's warrant, could I blend
  All hideous sins, as in a cup,
  To drink the mingled venoms up;
Secure my nature will convert
  The draught to blossoming gladness fast:
While sweet dews turn to the gourd's hurt,
  And bloat, and while they bloat it, blast,
  As from the first its lot was çast.   40
For as I lie, smiled on, full-fed
  By unexhausted power to bless,
I gaze below on hell's fierce bed,
  And those its waves of flame oppress,
  Swarming in ghastly wretchedness;
Whose life on earth aspired to be
  One altar-smoke, so pure!—to win
If not love like God's love for me,
  At least to keep his anger in;
  And all their striving turned to sin.   50
Priest, doctor, hermit, monk grown white
  With prayer, the broken-hearted nun,
The martyr, the wan acolyte,
  The incense-swinging child,—undone
  Before God fashioned star or sun!
God, whom I praise; how could I praise,
  If such as I might understand,
Make out and reckon on his ways,
  And bargain for his love, and stand,
Paying a price, at his right hand?   60

PORPHYRIA'S LOVER

THE rain set early in to-night,
    The sullen wind was soon awake,
It tore the elm-tops down for spite,
    And did its worst to vex the lake:
    I listened with heart fit to break.
When glided in Porphyria; straight
    She shut the cold out and the storm,
And kneeled and made the cheerless grate
    Blaze up, and all the cottage warm;
    Which done, she rose, and from her form   10
Withdrew the dripping cloak and shawl,
    And laid her soiled gloves by, untied
Her hat and let the damp hair fall,
    And, last, she sat down by my side
    And called me. When no voice replied,
She put my arm about her waist,
    And made her smooth white shoulder bare,
And all her yellow hair displaced,
    And, stooping, made my cheek lie there,
    And spread, o'er all, her yellow hair,   20
Murmuring how she loved me—she
    Too weak, for all her heart's endeavor,
To set its struggling passion free
    From pride, and vainer ties dissever,
    And give herself to me forever.
But passion sometimes would prevail,
    Nor could to-night's gay feast restrain
A sudden thought of one so pale
    For love of her, and all in vain:
    So, she was come through wind and rain.   30
Be sure I looked up at her eyes
    Happy and proud; at last I knew
Porphyria worshipped me: surprise
    Made my heart swell, and still it grew
    While I debated what to do.
That moment she was mine, mine, fair,
    Perfectly pure and good: I found
A thing to do, and all her hair
    In one long yellow string I wound
    Three times her little throat around,   40

And strangled her. No pain felt she;
   I am quite sure she felt no pain.
As a shut bud that holds a bee,
   I warily oped her lids: again
   Laughed the blue eyes without a stain.
And I untightened next the tress
   About her neck; her cheek once more
Blushed bright beneath my burning kiss:
   I propped her head up as before,
   Only, this time my shoulder bore   50
Her head, which droops upon it still:
   The smiling rosy little head,
So glad it has its utmost will,
   That all it scorned at once is fled,
   And I, its love, am gained instead!
Porphyria's love: she guessed not how
   Her darling one wish would be heard.
And thus we sit together now,
   And all night long we have not stirred,
   And yet God has not said a word!   60

THROUGH THE METIDJA TO ABD-EL-KADR

I

As I ride, as I ride,
With a full heart for my guide,
So its tide rocks my side,
As I ride, as I ride,
That, as I were double-eyed,
He, in whom our Tribes confide,
Is descried, ways untried
As I ride, as I ride.

II

As I ride, as I ride
To our Chief and his Allied,
Who dares chide my heart's pride
As I ride, as I ride?
Or are witnesses denied—

Through the desert waste and wide
Do I glide unespied
As I ride, as I ride?

III

As I ride, as I ride,
When an inner voice has cried,
The sands slide, nor abide
(As I ride, as I ride)
O'er each visioned homicide
That came vaunting (has he lied?)
To reside—where he died,
As I ride, as I ride.

IV

As I ride, as I ride,
Ne'er has spur my swift horse plied,
Yet his hide, streaked and pied,
As I ride, as I ride,
Shows where sweat has sprung and dried,
—Zebra-footed, ostrich-thighed—
How has vied stride with stride
As I ride, as I ride!

V

As I ride, as I ride,
Could I loose what Fate has tied,
Ere I pried, she should hide
(As I ride, as I ride)
All that's meant me—satisfied
When the Prophet and the Bride
Stop veins I'd have subside
As I ride, as I ride!

THE PIED PIPER OF HAMELIN;

A CHILD'S STORY

(Written for, and inscribed to, W. M. the Younger.)

I

HAMELIN TOWN's in Brunswick,
   By famous Hanover city;
The river Weser, deep and wide,
Washes its wall on the southern side;
A pleasanter spot you never spied;
   But, when begins my ditty,
Almost five hundred years ago,
To see the townsfolk suffer so
   From vermin, was a pity.

II

  Rats!   10
They fought the dogs and killed the cats,
   And bit the babies in the cradles,
And ate the cheeses out of the vats,
   And licked the soup from the cooks' own ladles,
Split open the kegs of salted sprats,
Made nests inside men's Sunday hats,
And even spoiled the women's chats
      By drowning their speaking
      With shrieking and squeaking
In fifty different sharps and flats.   20

III

At last the people in a body
     To the Town Hall came flocking:
" 'Tis clear," cried they, "our Mayor's a noddy;
     And as for our Corporation—shocking
To think we buy gowns lined with ermine
For dolts that can't or won't determine
What's best to rid us of our vermin!
You hope, because you're old and obese,
To find in the furry civic robe ease?

Rouse up, sirs! Give your brains a racking   30
To find the remedy we're lacking,
Or, sure as fate, we'll send you packing!"
At this the Mayor and Corporation
Quaked with a mighty consternation.

IV

An hour they sat in council,
    At length the Mayor broke silence:
"For a guilder I'd my ermine gown sell,
    I wish I were a mile hence!
It's easy to bid one rack one's brain—
I'm sure my poor head aches again,   40
I've scratched it so, and all in vain.
Oh for a trap, a trap, a trap!"
Just as he said this, what should hap
At the chamber door but a gentle tap?
"Bless us," cried the Mayor, "what's that?"
(With the Corporation as he sat,
Looking little though wondrous fat;
Nor brighter was his eye, nor moister
Than a too-long-opened oyster,
Save when at noon his paunch grew mutinous   50
For a plate of turtle green and glutinous)
"Only a scraping of shoes on the mat?
Anything like the sound of a rat
Makes my heart go pit-a-pat!"

V

"Come in!"—the Mayor cried, looking bigger:
And in did come the strangest figure!
His queer long coat from heel to head
Was half of yellow and half of red,
And he himself was tall and thin,
With sharp blue eyes, each like a pin,   60
And light loose hair, yet swarthy skin,
No tuft on cheek nor beard on chin,
But lips where smiles went out and in;
There was no guessing his kith and kin:
And nobody could enough admire
The tall man and his quaint attire.

Quoth one: "It's as my great-grandsire,
Starting up at the Trump of Doom's tone,
Had walked this way from his painted tombstone!"

VI

He advanced to the council-table: 70
And, "Please your honors," said he, "I'm able,
By means of a secret charm, to draw
   All creatures living beneath the sun,
   That creep or swim or fly or run,
After me so as you never saw!
And I chiefly use my charm
On creatures that do people harm,
The mole and toad and newt and viper;
And people call me the Pied Piper."
(And here they noticed round his neck   80
   A scarf of red and yellow stripe,
To match with his coat of the self-same cheque;
   And at the scarf's end hung a pipe;
And his fingers, they noticed, were ever straying
As if impatient to be playing
Upon this pipe, as low it dangled
Over his vesture so old-fangled.)
"Yet," said he, "poor piper as I am,
In Tartary I freed the Cham,
   Last June, from his huge swarms of gnats;   90
I eased in Asia the Nizam
   Of a monstrous brood of vampyre-bats:
And as for what your brain bewilders,
   If I can rid your town of rats
Will you give me a thousand guilders?"
"One? fifty thousand!"—was the exclamation
Of the astonished Mayor and Corporation.

VII

Into the street the Piper stept,
   Smiling first a little smile,
As if he knew what magic slept   100
   In his quiet pipe the while;
Then, like a musical adept,
To blow the pipe his lips he wrinkled,

And green and blue his sharp eyes twinkled,
Like a candle-flame where salt is sprinkled;
And ere three shrill notes the pipe uttered,
You heard as if an army muttered;
And the muttering grew to a grumbling;
And the grumbling grew to a mighty rumbling;
And out of the houses the rats came tumbling.   110
Great rats, small rats, lean rats, brawny rats,
Brown rats, black rats, gray rats, tawny rats,
Grave old plodders, gay young friskers,
   Fathers, mothers, uncles, cousins,
Cocking tails and pricking whiskers,
   Families by tens and dozens,
Brothers, sisters, husbands, wives—
Followed the Piper for their lives.
From street to street he piped advancing,
And step for step they followed dancing,   120
Until they came to the river Weser,
   Wherein all plunged and perished!
—Save one who, stout as Julius Cæsar,
Swam across and lived to carry
   (As he, the manuscript he cherished)
To Rat-land home his commentary:
Which was, "At the first shrill notes of the pipe,
I heard a sound as of scraping tripe,
And putting apples, wondrous ripe,
Into a cider-press's gripe: 130
And a moving away of pickle-tub-boards,
And a leaving ajar of conserve-cupboards,
And a drawing the corks of train-oil-flasks,
And a breaking the hoops of butter-casks:
And it seemed as if a voice
   (Sweeter far than bý harp or bý psaltery
Is breathed) called out, 'Oh rats, rejoice!
   The world is grown to one vast drysaltery!
So munch on, crunch on, take your nuncheon,
Breakfast, supper, dinner, luncheon!'   140
And just as a bulky sugar-puncheon,
All ready staved, like a great sun shone
Glorious scarce an inch before me,
Just as methought it said, 'Come, bore me!'
—I found the Weser rolling o'er me."

VIII

You should have heard the Hamelin people
Ringing the bells till they rocked the steeple.
"Go," cried the Mayor, "and get long poles,
Poke out the nests and block up the holes!
Consult with carpenters and builders,   150
And leave in our town not even a trace
Of the rats!"—when suddenly, up the face
Of the Piper perked in the market-place,
With a, "First, if you please, my thousand guilders!"

IX

A thousand guilders! The Mayor looked blue;
So did the Corporation too.
For council dinners made rare havoc
With Claret, Moselle, Vin-de-Grave, Hock;
And half the money would replenish
Their cellar's biggest butt with Rhenish.   160
To pay this sum to a wandering fellow
With a gipsy coat of red and yellow!
"Beside," quoth the Mayor with a knowing wink,
"Our business was done at the river's brink;
We saw with our eyes the vermin sink,
And what's dead can't come to life, I think.
So, friend, we're not the folks to shrink
From the duty of giving you something for drink,
And a matter of money to put in your poke;
But as for the guilders, what we spoke   170
Of them, as you very well know, was in joke.
Beside, our losses have made us thrifty.
A thousand guilders! Come, take fifty!"

X

The Piper's face fell, and he cried
"No trifling! I can't wait, beside!
I've promised to visit by dinnertime
Bagdat, and accept the prime
Of the Head-Cook's pottage, all he's rich in,
For having left, in the Caliph's kitchen,
Of a nest of scorpions no survivor: 180

With him I proved no bargain-driver,
With you, don't think I'll bate a stiver!
And folks who put me in a passion
May find me pipe after another fashion."

XI

"How?" cried the Mayor, "d'ye think I brook
Being worse treated than a Cook?
Insulted by a lazy ribald
With idle pipe and vesture piebald?
You threaten us, fellow? Do your worst,
Blow your pipe there till you burst!"   196

XII

Once more he stept into the street
    And to his lips again
    Laid his long pipe of smooth straight cane;
And ere he blew three notes (such sweet
Soft notes as yet musician's cunning
    Never gave the enraptured air)
There was a rustling that seemed like a bustling
Of merry crowds justling at pitching and hustling,
Small feet were pattering, wooden shoes clattering,
Little hands clapping and little tongues chattering,   200
And, like fowls in a farm-yard when barley is scattering,
Out came the children running.
All the little boys and girls,
With rosy cheeks and flaxen curls,
And sparkling eyes and teeth like pearls,
Tripping and skipping, ran merrily after
The wonderful music with shouting and laughter.

XIII

The Mayor was dumb, and the Council stood
As if they were changed into blocks of wood,
Unable to move a step, or cry   210
To the children merrily skipping by,
—Could only follow with the eye

That joyous crowd at the Piper's back.
But how the Mayor was on the rack,
And the wretched Council's bosoms beat,
As the Piper turned from the High Street
To where the Weser rolled its waters
Right in the way of their sons and daughters!
However he turned from South to West,
And to Koppelberg Hill his steps addressed, 220
And after him the children pressed;
Great was the joy in every breast.
"He never can cross that mighty top!
He's forced to let the piping drop,
And we shall see our children stop!"
When, lo, as they reached the mountain-side,
A wondrous portal opened wide,
As if a cavern was suddenly hollowed;
And the Piper advanced and the children followed,
And when all were in to the very last, 230
The door in the mountain-side shut fast.
Did I say, all? No! One was lame,
 And could not dance the whole of the way;
And in after years, if you would blame
 His sadness, he was used to say,—
"It's dull in our town since my playmates left!
I can't forget that I'm bereft
Of all the pleasant sights they see,
Which the Piper also promised me.
For he led us, he said, to a joyous land, 240
Joining the town and just at hand,
Where waters gushed and fruit-trees grew
And flowers put forth a fairer hue,
And everything was strange and new;
The sparrows were brighter than peacocks here,
And their dogs outran our fallow deer,
And honey-bees had lost their stings,
And horses were born with eagles' wings:
And just as I became assured
My lame foot would be speedily cured, 250
The music stopped and I stood still,
And found myself outside the hill,
Left alone against my will,
To go now limping as before,
And never hear of that country more!"

XIV

Alas, alas for Hamelin!
   There came into many a burgher's pate
   A text which says that heaven's gate
   Opes to the rich at as easy rate
As the needle's eye takes a camel in!   260
The mayor sent East, West, North and South,
To offer the Piper, by word of mouth,
   Wherever it was men's lot to find him,
Silver and gold to his heart's content,
If he'd only return the way he went,
   And bring the children behind him.
But when they saw 'twas a lost endeavor,
And Piper and dancers were gone forever,
They made a decree that lawyers never
   Should think their records dated duly   270
If, after the day of the month and year,
These words did not as well appear,
"And so long after what happened here
   On the Twenty-second of July,
Thirteen hundred and seventy-six:"
And the better in memory to fix
The place of the children's last retreat,
They called it, the Pied Piper's Street—
Where any one playing on pipe or tabor
Was sure for the future to lose his labor.   280
Nor suffered they hostelry or tavern
   To shock with mirth a street so solemn;
But opposite the place of the cavern
   They wrote the story on a column,
And on the great church-window painted
The same, to make the world acquainted
How their children were stolen away,
And there it stands to this very day.
And I must not omit to say
That in Transylvania there's a tribe   290
Of alien people who ascribe
The outlandish ways and dress
On which their neighbors lay such stress,
To their fathers and mothers having risen
Out of some subterraneous prison
Into which they were trepanned

Long time ago in a mighty band
Out of Hamelin town in Brunswick land,
But how or why, they don't understand.

XV

So, Willy, let me and you be wipers   300
Of scores out with all men—especially pipers!
And, whether they pipe us free fróm rats or fróm mice,
If we've promised them aught, let us keep our promise!

From DRAMATIC ROMANCES AND LYRICS [1845]

"HOW THEY BROUGHT THE GOOD NEWS FROM GHENT TO AIX"

[16—]

I

I SPRANG to the stirrup, and Joris, and he;
I galloped, Dirck galloped, we galloped all three;
"Good speed!" cried the watch, as the gate-bolts undrew;
"Speed!" echoed the wall to us galloping through;
Behind shut the postern, the lights sank to rest,
And into the midnight we galloped abreast.

II

Not a word to each other; we kept the great pace
Neck by neck, stride by stride, never changing our place;
I turned in my saddle and made its girths tight,
Then shortened each stirrup, and set the pique right,
Rebuckled the cheek-strap, chained slacker the bit,
Nor galloped less steadily Roland a whit.

III

'Twas moonset at starting; but while we drew near
Lokeren, the cocks crew and twilight dawned clear;
At Boom, a great yellow star came out to see;
At Düffeld, 'twas morning as plain as could be;
And from Mecheln church-steeple we heard the half-chime,
So, Joris broke silence with, "Yet there is time!"

IV

At Aershot, up leaped of a sudden the sun,
And against him the cattle stood black every one,
To stare thro' the mist at us galloping past,
And I saw my stout galloper Roland at last,
With resolute shoulders, each butting away
The haze, as some bluff river headland its spray:

V

And his low head and crest, just one sharp ear bent back
For my voice, and the other pricked out on his track;
And one eye's black intelligence,—ever that glance
O'er its white edge at me, his own master, askance!
And the thick heavy spume-flakes which aye and anon
His fierce lips shook upwards in galloping on.

VI

By Hasselt, Dirck groaned; and cried Joris, "Stay spur!
Your Roos galloped bravely, the fault's not in her,
We'll remember at Aix"—for one heard the quick wheeze
Of her chest, saw the stretched neck and staggering knees,
And sunk tail, and horrible heave of the flank,
As down on her haunches she shuddered and sank.

VII

So, we were left galloping, Joris and I,
Past Looz and past Tongres, no cloud in the sky;
The broad sun above laughed a pitiless laugh,
'Neath our feet broke the brittle bright stubble like chaff;
Till over by Dalhem a dome-spire sprang white,
And "Gallop," gasped Joris, "for Aix is in sight!"

VIII

"How they'll greet us!"—and all in a moment his roan
Rolled neck and croup over, lay dead as a stone;
And there was my Roland to bear the whole weight
Of the news which alone could save Aix from her fate,

With his nostrils like pits full of blood to the brim,
And with circles of red for his eye-sockets' rim.

IX

Then I cast loose my buffcoat, each holster let fall,
Shook off both my jack-boots, let go belt and all,
Stood up in the stirrup, leaned, patted his ear,
Called my Roland his pet-name, my horse without peer;
Clapped my hands, laughed and sang, any noise, bad or good,
Till at length into Aix Roland galloped and stood.

X

And all I remember is—friends flocking round
As I sat with his head 'twixt my knees on the ground;
And no voice but was praising this Roland of mine,
As I poured down his throat our last measure of wine,
Which (the burgesses voted by common consent)
Was no more than his due who brought good news from Ghent.

PICTOR IGNOTUS

FLORENCE, 15—

I COULD have painted pictures like that youth's
    Ye praise so. How my soul springs up! No bar
Stayed me—ah, thought which saddens while it soothes!
    —Never did fate forbid me, star by star,
To outburst on your night with all my gift
    Of fires from God: nor would my flesh have shrunk
From seconding my soul, with eyes uplift
    And wide to heaven, or, straight like thunder, sunk
To the centre, of an instant; or around
    Turned calmly and inquisitive, to scan   10
The license and the limit, space and bound,
    Allowed to truth made visible in man.
And, like that youth ye praise so, all I saw,
    Over the canvas could my hand have flung,
Each face obedient to its passion's law,
    Each passion clear proclaimed without a tongue;

Whether Hope rose at once in all the blood,
　　A-tiptoe for the blessing of embrace,
Or Rapture drooped the eyes, as when her brood
　　Pull down the nesting dove's heart to its place;　　20
Or Confidence lit swift the forehead up,
　　And locked the mouth fast, like a castle braved,—
O human faces, hath it spilt, my cup?
　　What did ye give me that I have not saved?
Nor will I say I have not dreamed (how well!)
　　Of going—I, in each new picture,—forth,
As, making new hearts beat and bosoms swell,
　　To Pope or Kaiser, East, West, South, or North,
Bound for the calmly-satisfied great State,
　　Or glad aspiring little burgh, it went,　　30
Flowers cast upon the car which bore the freight,
　　Through old streets named afresh from the event,
Till it reached home, where learned age should greet
　　My face, and youth, the star not yet distinct
Above his hair, lie learning at my feet!—
　　Oh, thus to live, I and my picture, linked
With love about, and praise, till life should end,
　　And then not go to heaven, but linger here,
Here on my earth, earth's every man my friend,—
　　The thought grew frightful, 'twas so wildly dear!　　40
But a voice changed it. Glimpses of such sights
　　Have scared me, like the revels through a door
Of some strange house of idols at its rites!
　　This world seemed not the world it was before:
Mixed with my loving trusting ones, there trooped
　　. . . Who summoned those cold faces that begun
To press on me and judge me? Though I stooped
　　Shrinking, as from the soldiery a nun,
They drew me forth, and spite of me . . . enough!
　　These buy and sell our pictures, take and give,　　50
Count them for garniture and household-stuff,
　　And where they live needs must our pictures live
And see their faces, listen to their prate,
　　Partakers of their daily pettiness,
Discussed of,—"This I love, or this I hate,
　　This likes me more, and this affects me less!"
Wherefore I chose my portion. If at whiles
　　My heart sinks, as monotonous I paint
These endless cloisters and eternal aisles

With the same series, Virgin, Babe and Saint,   60
With the same cold calm beautiful regard,—
    At least no merchant traffics in my heart;
The sanctuary's gloom at least shall ward
    Vain tongues from where my pictures stand apart:
Only prayer breaks the silence of the shrine
    While, blackening in the daily candle-smoke,
They moulder on the damp wall's travertine,
    'Mid echoes the light footstep never woke.
So, die my pictures! surely, gently die!
    O youth, men praise so,—holds their praise its worth?   70
Blown harshly, keeps the trump its golden cry?
    Tastes sweet the water with such specks of earth?

THE ITALIAN IN ENGLAND

THAT second time they hunted me
From hill to plain, from shore to sea,
And Austria, hounding far and wide
Her blood-hounds through the country-side,
Breathed hot and instant on my trace,—
I made six days a hiding-place
Of that dry green old aqueduct
Where I and Charles, when boys, have plucked
The fire-flies from the roof above,
Bright creeping thro' the moss they love: 10
—How long it seems since Charles was lost!
Six days the soldiers crossed and crossed
The country in my very sight;
And when that peril ceased at night,
The sky broke out in red dismay
With signal fires; well, there I lay
Close covered o'er in my recess,
Up to the neck in ferns and cress,
Thinking on Metternich our friend,
And Charles's miserable end,   20
And much beside, two days; the third,
Hunger o'ercame me when I heard
The peasants from the village go
To work among the maize; you know,
With us in Lombardy, they bring

Provisions packed on mules, a string
With little bells that cheer their task,
And casks, and boughs on every cask
To keep the sun's heat from the wine;
These I let pass in jingling line,   30
And, close on them, dear noisy crew,
The peasants from the village, too;
For at the very rear would troop
Their wives and sisters in a group
To help, I knew. When these had passed,
I threw my glove to strike the last,
Taking the chance: she did not start,
Much less cry out, but stooped apart,
One instant rapidly glanced round,
And saw me beckon from the ground.   40
A wild bush grows and hides my crypt;
She picked my glove up while she stripped
A branch off, then rejoined the rest
With that; my glove lay in her breast.
Then I drew breath; they disappeared:
It was for Italy I feared.

    An hour, and she returned alone
Exactly where my glove was thrown.
Meanwhile came many thoughts: on me
Rested the hopes of Italy.   50
I had devised a certain tale
Which, when 'twas told her, could not fail
Persuade a peasant of its truth;
I meant to call a freak of youth
This hiding, and give hopes of pay,
And no temptation to betray.
But when I saw that woman's face,
Its calm simplicity of grace,
Our Italy's own attitude
In which she walked thus far, and stood,   60
Planting each naked foot so firm,
To crush the snake and spare the worm—
At first sight of her eyes, I said,
"I am that man upon whose head
They fix the price, because I hate
The Austrians over us: the State

Will give you gold—oh, gold so much!—
If you betray me to their clutch,
And be your death, for aught I know,
If once they find you saved their foe.   70
Now, you must bring me food and drink,
And also paper, pen and ink,
And carry safe what I shall write
To Padua, which you'll reach at night
Before the duomo shuts; go in,
And wait till Tenebræ begin;
Walk to the third confessional,
Between the pillar and the wall,
And kneeling whisper, *Whence comes peace?*
Say it a second time, then cease;   80
And if the voice inside returns,
*From Christ and Freedom; what concerns
The cause of Peace?*—for answer, slip
My letter where you placed your lip;
Then come back happy we have done
Our mother service—I, the son,
As you the daughter of our land!"

Three mornings more, she took her stand
In the same place, with the same eyes:
I was no surer of sun-rise   90
Than of her coming. We conferred
Of her own prospects, and I heard
She had a lover—stout and tall,
She said—then let her eyelids fall,
"He could do much"—as if some doubt
Entered her heart,—then, passing out,
"She could not speak for others, who
Had other thoughts; herself she knew."
And so she brought me drink and food.
After four days, the scouts pursued   100
Another path; at last arrived
The help my Paduan friends contrived
To furnish me: she brought the news.
For the first time I could not choose
But kiss her hand, and lay my own
Upon her head—"This faith was shown
To Italy, our mother; she

Uses my hand and blesses thee."
She followed down to the sea-shore;
I left and never saw her more. 110

How very long since I have thought
Concerning—much less wished for—aught
Beside the good of Italy,
For which I live and mean to die!
I never was in love; and since
Charles proved false, what shall now convince
My inmost heart I have a friend?
However, if I pleased to spend
Real wishes on myself—say, three—
I know at least what one should be. 120
I would grasp Metternich until
I felt his red wet throat distil
In blood thro' these two hands. And next,
—Nor much for that am I perplexed—
Charles, perjured traitor, for his part,
Should die slow of a broken heart
Under his new employers. Last
—Ah, there, what should I wish? For fast
Do I grow old and out of strength.
If I resolved to seek at length 130
My father's house again, how scared
They all would look, and unprepared!
My brothers live in Austria's pay
—Disowned me long ago, men say;
And all my early mates who used
To praise me so—perhaps induced
More than one early step of mine—
Are turning wise: while some opine
"Freedom grows license," some suspect
"Haste breeds delay," and recollect 140
They always said, such premature
Beginnings never could endure!
So, with a sullen "All's for best,"
The land seems settling to its rest.
I think, then, I should wish to stand
This evening in that dear, lost land,
Over the sea the thousand miles,
And know if yet that woman smiles
With the calm smile; some little farm

She lives in there, no doubt; what harm   150
If I sat on the door-side bench,
And, while her spindle made a trench
Fantastically in the dust,
Inquired of all her fortunes—just
Her children's ages and their names,
And what may be the husband's aims
For each of them. I'd talk this out,
And sit there, for an hour about,
Then kiss her hand once more, and lay
Mine on her head, and go my way.   160

So much for idle wishing—how
It steals the time! To business now!

THE ENGLISHMAN IN ITALY

PIANO DI SORRENTO

Fortù, Fortù, my beloved one,
    Sit here by my side,
On my knees put up both little feet!
    I was sure, if I tried,
I could make you laugh spite of Scirocco.
    Now, open your eyes,
Let me keep you amused till he vanish
    In black from the skies,
With telling my memories over
    As you tell your beads;   10
All the Plain saw me gather, I garland
    —The flowers or the weeds.

Time for rain! for your long hot dry Autumn
    Had net-worked with brown
The white skin of each grape on the bunches,
    Marked like a quail's crown,
Those creatures you make such account of,
    Whose heads,—speckled white
Over brown like a great spider's back,
    As I told you last night,—   20

Your mother bites off for her supper.
    Red-ripe as could be,
Pomegranates were chapping and splitting
    In halves on the tree:
And betwixt the loose walls of great flint-stone,
    Or in the thick dust
On the path, or straight out of the rock-side,
    Wherever could thrust
Some burnt sprig of bold hardy rock-flower
    Its yellow face up,   30
For the prize were great butterflies fighting,
    Some five for one cup.
So, I guessed, ere I got up this morning,
    What change was in store,
By the quick rustle-down of the quail-nets
    Which woke me before
I could open my shutter, made fast
    With a bough and a stone,
And looked thro' the twisted dead vine-twigs,
    Sole lattice that's known.   40
Quick and sharp rang the rings down the net-poles,
    While, busy beneath,
Your priest and his brother tugged at them,
    The rain in their teeth.
And out upon all the flat house-roofs
    Where split figs lay drying,
The girls took the frails under cover:
    Nor use seemed in trying
To get out the boats and go fishing,
    For, under the cliff,   50
Fierce the black water frothed o'er the blind-rock.
    No seeing our skiff
Arrive about noon from Amalfi,
    —Our fisher arrive,
And pitch down his basket before us,
    All trembling alive
With pink and gray jellies, your sea-fruit;
    You touch the strange lumps,
And mouths gape there, eyes open, all manner
    Of horns and of humps,   60
Which only the fisher looks grave at,
    While round him like imps
Cling screaming the children as naked

And brown as his shrimps;
Himself too as bare to the middle
   —You see round his neck
The string and its brass coin suspended,
   That saves him from wreck.
But to-day not a boat reached Salerno,
   So back, to a man,   70
Came our friends, with whose help in the vineyards
   Grape-harvest began.
In the vat, halfway up in our house-side,
   Like blood the juice spins,
While your brother all bare-legged is dancing
   Till breathless he grins
Dead-beaten in effort on effort
   To keep the grapes under,
Since still when he seems all but master,
   In pours the fresh plunder   80
From girls who keep coming and going
   With basket on shoulder,
And eyes shut against the rain's driving;
   Your girls that are older,—
For under the hedges of aloe,
   And where, on its bed
Of the orchard's black mould, the love-apple
   Lies pulpy and red,
All the young ones are kneeling and filling
   Their laps with the snails   90
Tempted out by this first rainy weather,—
   Your best of regales,
As to-night will be proved to my sorrow,
   When, supping in state,
We shall feast our grape-gleaners (two dozen,
   Three over one plate)
With lasagne so tempting to swallow
   In slippery ropes,
And gourds fried in great purple slices,
   That color of popes.   100
Meantime, see the grape bunch they've brought you:
   The rain-water slips
O'er the heavy blue bloom on each globe
   Which the wasp to your lips
Still follows with fretful persistence:
   Nay, taste, while awake,

This half of a curd-white smooth cheese-ball
    That peels, flake by flake,
Like an onion, each smoother and whiter;
    Next, sip this weak wine   110
From the thin green glass flask, with its stopper,
    A leaf of the vine;
And end with the prickly-pear's red flesh
    That leaves thro' its juice
The stony black seeds on your pearl-teeth.
    Scirocco is loose!
Hark, the quick, whistling pelt of the olives
    Which, thick in one's track,
Tempt the stranger to pick up and bite them,
    Tho' not yet half black!   120
How the old twisted olive trunks shudder,
    The medlars let fall
Their hard fruit, and the brittle great fig-trees
    Snap off, figs and all,
For here comes the whole of the tempest!
    No refuge, but creep
Back again to my side and my shoulder,
    And listen or sleep.
O how will your country show next week,
    When all the vine-boughs   130
Have been stripped of their foliage to pasture
    The mules and the cows?
Last eve, I rode over the mountains:
    Your brother, my guide,
Soon left me, to feast on the myrtles
    That offered, each side,
Their fruit-balls, black, glossy and luscious,—
    Or strip from the sorbs
A treasure, or, rosy and wondrous,
    Those hairy gold orbs!   140
But my mule picked his sure sober path out,
    Just stopping to neigh
When he recognized down in the valley
    His mates on their way
With the faggots and barrels of water;
    And soon we emerged
From the plain, where the woods could scarce follow;
    And still as we urged
Our way, the woods wondered, and left us,

As up still we trudged   150
Though the wild path grew wilder each instant,
    And place was e'en grudged
'Mid the rock-chasms and piles of loose stones
    Like the loose broken teeth
Of some monster which climbed there to die
    From the ocean beneath—
Place was grudged to the silver-gray fume-weed
    That clung to the path,
And dark rosemary ever a-dying
    That, 'spite the wind's wrath,   160
So loves the salt rock's face to seaward,
    And lentisks as stanch
To the stone where they root and bear berries,
    And . . . what shows a branch
Coral-colored, transparent, with circlets
    Of pale seagreen leaves;
Over all trod my mule with the caution
    Of gleaners o'er sheaves,
Still, foot after foot like a lady,
    Till, round after round,   170
He climbed to the top of Calvano,
    And God's own profound
Was above me, and round me the mountains,
    And under, the sea,
And within me my heart to bear witness
    What was and shall be.
Oh, heaven and the terrible crystal!
    No rampart excludes
Your eye from the life to be lived
    In the blue solitudes.   180
Oh, those mountains, their infinite movement!
    Still moving with you;
For, ever some new head and breast of them
    Thrusts into view
To observe the intruder; you see it
    If quickly you turn
And, before they escape you surprise them.
    They grudge you should learn
How the soft plains they look on, lean over
    And love (they pretend)   190
—Cower beneath them, the flat sea-pine crouches,
    The wild fruit-trees bend,

E'en the myrtle-leaves curl, shrink and shut:
 All is silent and grave:
'Tis a sensual and timorous beauty,
 How fair! but a slave.
So, I turned to the sea; and there slumbered
 As greenly as ever
Those isles of the siren, your Galli;
 No ages can sever   200
The Three, nor enable their sister
 To join them,—halfway
On the voyage, she looked at Ulysses—
 No farther to-day,
Tho' the small one, just launched in the wave,
 Watches breast-high and steady
From under the rock, her bold sister
 Swum halfway already.
Fortù, shall we sail there together
 And see from the sides   210
Quite new rocks show their faces, new haunts
 Where the siren abides?
Shall we sail round and round them, close over
 The rocks, tho' unseen,
That ruffle the gray glassy water
 To glorious green?
Then scramble from splinter to splinter,
 Reach land and explore,
On the largest, the strange square black turret
 With never a door,   220
Just a loop to admit the quick lizards;
 Then, stand there and hear
The birds' quiet singing, that tells us
 What life is, so clear?
—The secret they sang to Ulysses
 When, ages ago,
He heard and he knew this life's secret
 I hear and I know.

Ah, see! The sun breaks o'er Calvano;
 He strikes the great gloom   230
And flutters it o'er the mount's summit
 In airy gold fume.
All is over. Look out, see the gipsy,
 Our tinker and smith,

Has arrived, set up bellows and forge,
    And down-squatted forthwith
To his hammering, under the wall there;
    One eye keeps aloof
The urchins that itch to be putting
    His jews'-harps to proof,   240
While the other, thro' locks of curled wire,
    Is watching how sleek
Shines the hog, come to share in the windfall
    —Chew, abbot's own cheek!
All is over. Wake up and come out now,
    And down let us go,
And see the fine things got in order
    At church for the show
Of the Sacrament, set forth this evening.
    To-morrow's the Feast   250
Of the Rosary's Virgin, by no means
    Of Virgins the least,
As you'll hear in the off-hand discourse
    Which (all nature, no art)
The Dominican brother, these three weeks,
    Was getting by heart.
Not a pillar nor post but is dizened
    With red and blue papers;
All the roof waves with ribbons, each altar
    A-blaze with long tapers;   260
But the great masterpiece is the scaffold
    Rigged glorious to hold
All the fiddlers and fifers and drummers
    And trumpeters bold,
Not afraid of Bellini nor Auber,
    Who, when the priest's hoarse,
Will strike us up something that's brisk
    For the feast's second course.
And then will the flaxen-wigged Image
    Be carried in pomp   270
Thro' the plain, while in gallant procession
    The priests mean to stomp.
All round the glad church lie old bottles
    With gunpowder stopped,
Which will be, when the Image re-enters,
    Religiously popped;
And at night from the crest of Calvano

Great bonfires will hang,
On the plain will the trumpets join chorus,
    And more poppers bang.   280
At all events, come—to the garden
    As far as the wall;
See me tap with a hoe on the plaster
    Till out there shall fall
A scorpion with wide angry nippers!

      —"Such trifles!" you say?
Fortù, in my England at home,
    Men meet gravely to-day
And debate, if abolishing Corn-laws
    Be righteous and wise   290
—If't were proper, Scirocco should vanish
    In black from the skies!

THE LOST LEADER

I

JUST for a handful of silver he left us,
    Just for a riband to stick in his coat—
Found the one gift of which fortune bereft us,
    Lost all the others she lets us devote;
They, with the gold to give, doled him out silver,
    So much was theirs who so little allowed:
How all our copper had gone for his service!
    Rags—were they purple, his heart had been proud!
We that had loved him so, followed him, honored him,
    Lived in his mild and magnificent eye,   10
Learned his great language, caught his clear accents,
    Made him our pattern to live and to die!
Shakespeare was of us, Milton was for us,
    Burns, Shelley, were with us,—they watch from their graves!
He alone breaks from the van and the freemen,
    He alone sinks to the rear and the slaves!

II

We shall march prospering,—not thro' his presence;
   Songs may inspirit us,—not from his lyre;
Deeds will be done,—while he boasts his quiescence,
   Still bidding crouch whom the rest bade aspire: 20
Blot out his name, then, record one lost soul more,
   One task more declined, one more footpath untrod,
One more devil's-triumph and sorrow for angels,
   One wrong more to man, one more insult to God!
Life's night begins: let him never come back to us!
   There would be doubt, hesitation and pain,
Forced praise on our part—the glimmer of twilight,
   Never glad confident morning again!
Best fight on well, for we taught him—strike gallantly,
   Menace our heart ere we master his own;   30
Then let him receive the new knowledge and wait us,
   Pardoned in heaven, the first by the throne!

HOME-THOUGHTS, FROM ABROAD

I

Oh, to be in England
Now that April's there,
And whoever wakes in England
Sees, some morning, unaware,
That the lowest boughs and the brushwood sheaf
Round the elm-tree bole are in tiny leaf,
While the chaffinch sings on the orchard bough
In England—now!

II

And after April, when May follows,
And the whitethroat builds, and all the swallows!
Hark, where my blossomed pear-tree in the hedge
Leans to the field and scatters on the clover
Blossoms and dewdrops—at the bent spray's edge—
That's the wise thrush; he sings each song twice over,

Lest you should think he never could recapture
The first fine careless rapture!
And though the fields look rough with hoary dew,
All will be gay when noontide wakes anew
The buttercups, the little children's dower
—Far brighter than this gaudy melon-flower!

HOME-THOUGHTS, FROM THE SEA

NOBLY, nobly Cape Saint Vincent to the North-west died away;
Sunset ran, one glorious blood-red, reeking into Cadiz Bay;
Bluish 'mid the burning water, full in face Trafalgar lay;
In the dimmest North-east distance dawned Gibraltar grand and
    gray;
"Here and here did England help me: how can I help England?"
    —say,
Whoso turns as I, this evening, turn to God to praise and pray,
While Jove's planet rises yonder, silent over Africa.

THE BISHOP ORDERS HIS TOMB AT
SAINT PRAXED'S CHURCH

ROME, 15—

VANITY, saith the preacher, vanity!
Draw round my bed: is Anselm keeping back?
Nephews—sons mine . . . ah God, I know not! Well—
She, men would have to be your mother once,
Old Gandolf envied me, so fair she was!
What's done is done, and she is dead beside,
Dead long ago, and I am Bishop since,
And as she died so must we die ourselves,
And thence ye may perceive the world's a dream.
Life, how and what is it? As here I lie   10
In this state-chamber, dying by degrees,
Hours and long hours in the dead night, I ask
"Do I live, am I dead?" Peace, peace seems all.
Saint Praxed's ever was the church for peace;
And so, about this tomb of mine. I fought
With tooth and nail to save my niche, ye know:

—Old Gandolf cozened me, despite my care;
Shrewd was that snatch from out the corner South
He graced his carrion with, God curse the same!
Yet still my niche is not so cramped but thence   20
One sees the pulpit o' the epistle-side,
And somewhat of the choir, those silent seats, ·
And up into the aery dome where live
The angels, and a sunbeam's sure to lurk:
And I shall fill my slab of basalt there,
And 'neath my tabernacle take my rest,
With those nine columns round me, two and two,
The odd one at my feet where Anselm stands:
Peach-blossom marble all, the rare, the ripe
As fresh-poured red wine of a mighty pulse.   30
—Old Gandolf with his paltry onion-stone,
Put me where I may look at him! True peach,
Rosy and flawless: how I earned the prize!
Draw close: that conflagration of my church
—What then? So much was saved if aught were missed!
My sons, ye would not be my death? Go dig
The white-grape vineyard where the oil-press stood,
Drop water gently till the surface sink,
And if ye find . . . Ah God, I know not, I! . . .
Bedded in store of rotten fig-leaves soft,   40
And corded up in a tight olive-frail,
Some lump, ah God, of *lapis lazuli,*
Big as a Jew's head cut off at the nape,
Blue as a vein o'er the Madonna's breast . . .
Sons, all have I bequeathed you, villas, all,
That brave Frascati villa with its bath,
So, let the blue lump poise between my knees,
Like God the Father's globe on both his hands
Ye worship in the Jesu Church so gay,
For Gandolf shall not choose but see and burst!   50
Swift as a weaver's shuttle fleet our years:
Man goeth to the grave, and where is he?
Did I say basalt for my slab, sons? Black—
'Twas ever antique-black I meant! How else
Shall ye contrast my frieze to come beneath?
The bas-relief in bronze ye promised me,
Those Pans and Nymphs ye wot of, and perchance
Some tripod, thyrsus, with a vase or so,
The Saviour at his sermon on the mount,

Saint Praxed in a glory, and one Pan   60
Ready to twitch the Nymph's last garment off,
And Moses with the tables . . . but I know
Ye mark me not! What do they whisper thee,
Child of my bowels, Anselm? Ah, ye hope
To revel down my villas while I gasp
Bricked o'er with beggar's mouldy travertine
Which Gandolf from his tomb-top chuckles at!
Nay, boys, ye love me—all of jasper, then!
'Tis jasper ye stand pledged to, lest I grieve
My bath must needs be left behind, alas!   70
One block, pure green as a pistachio-nut,
There's plenty jasper somewhere in the world—
And have I not Saint Praxed's ear to pray
Horses for ye, and brown Greek manuscripts,
And mistresses with great smooth marbly limbs?
—That's if ye carve my epitaph aright,
Choice Latin, picked phrase, Tully's every word,
No gaudy ware like Gandolf's second line—
Tully, my masters? Ulpian serves his need!
And then how I shall lie through centuries,   80
And hear the blessed mutter of the mass,
And see God made and eaten all day long,
And feel the steady candle-flame, and taste
Good strong thick stupefying incense-smoke!
For as I lie here, hours of the dead night,
Dying in state and by such slow degrees,
I fold my arms as if they clasped a crook,
And stretch my feet forth straight as stone can point,
And let the bedclothes, for a mortcloth, drop
Into great laps and folds of sculptor's-work: 90
And as yon tapers dwindle, and strange thoughts
Grow, with a certain humming in my ears,
About the life before I lived this life,
And this life too, popes, cardinals and priests,
Saint Praxed at his sermon on the mount,
Your tall pale mother with her talking eyes,
And new-found agate urns as fresh as day,
And marble's language, Latin pure, discreet,
—Aha, ELUCESCEBAT quoth our friend?
No Tully, said I, Ulpian at the best!   100
Evil and brief hath been my pilgrimage.
All *lapis*, all, sons! Else I give the Pope

My villas! Will ye ever eat my heart?
Ever your eyes were as a lizard's quick,
They glitter like your mother's for my soul,
Or ye would heighten my impoverished frieze,
Piece out its starved design, and fill my vase
With grapes, and add a vizor and a Term,
And to the tripod ye would tie a lynx
That in his struggle throws the thyrsus down,   110
To comfort me on my entablature
Whereon I am to lie till I must ask
"Do I live, am I dead?" There, leave me, there!
For ye have stabbed me with ingratitude
To death—ye wish it—God, ye wish it! Stone—
Gritstone, a-crumble! Clammy squares which sweat
As if the corpse they keep were oozing through—
And no more *lapis* to delight the world!
Well go! I bless ye. Fewer tapers there,
But in a row: and, going, turn your backs   120
—Ay, like departing altar-ministrants,
And leave me in my church, the church for peace,
That I may watch at leisure if he leers—
Old Gandolf, at me, from his onion-stone,
As still he envied me, so fair she was!

GARDEN FANCIES

1 THE FLOWER'S NAME

I

HERE's the garden she walked across,
    Arm in my arm, such a short while since:
Hark, now I push its wicket, the moss
    Hinders the hinges and makes them wince!
She must have reached this shrub ere she turned,
    As back with that murmur the wicket swung;
For she laid the poor snail, my chance foot spurned,
    To feed and forget it the leaves among.

II

Down this side of the gravel-walk
   She went while her robe's edge brushed the **box**
And here she paused in her gracious talk
   To point me a moth on the milk-white phlox.
Roses, ranged in valiant row,
   I will never think that she passed you by!
She loves you noble roses, I know;
   But yonder, see, where the rock-plants lie!

III

This flower she stopped at, finger on lip,
   Stooped over, in doubt, as settling its claim;
Till she gave me, with pride to make no slip,
   Its soft meandering Spanish name:
What a name! Was it love, or praise?
   Speech half-asleep or song half-awake?
I must learn Spanish, one of these days,
   Only for that slow sweet name's sake.

IV

Roses, if I live and do well,
   I may bring her, one of these days,
To fix you fast with as fine a spell,
   Fit you each with his Spanish phrase;
But do not detain me now; for she lingers
   There, like sunshine over the ground,
And ever I see her soft white fingers
   Searching after the bud she found.

V

Flower, you Spaniard, look that you grow **not**,
   Stay as you are and be loved for ever!
Bud, if I kiss you 'tis that you blow not:
   Mind, the shut pink mouth opens never!
For while it pouts, her fingers wrestle,
   Twinkling the audacious leaves between,
Till round they turn and down they nestle—
   Is not the dear mark still to be seen?

VI

Where I find her not, beauties vanish;
　　Whither I follow her, beauties flee;
Is there no method to tell her in Spanish
　　June's twice June since she breathed it with me?
Come, bud, show me the least of her traces,
　　Treasure my lady's lightest footfall!
—Ah, you may flout and turn up your faces—
　　Roses, you are not so fair after all!

2　SIBRANDUS SCHAFNABURGENSIS

I

Plague take all your pedants, say I!
　　He who wrote what I hold in my hand,
Centuries back was so good as to die,
　　Leaving this rubbish to cumber the land;
This, that was a book in its time,
　　Printed on paper and bound in leather,
Last month in the white of a matin-prime
　　Just when the birds sang all together.

II

Into the garden I brought it to read,
　　And under the arbute and laurustine
Read it, so help me grace in my need,
　　From title-page to closing line.
Chapter on chapter did I count,
　　As a curious traveller counts Stonehenge;
Added up the mortal amount;
　　And then proceeded to my revenge.

III

Yonder's a plum-tree with a crevice
　　An owl would build in, were he but sage;
For a lap of moss, like a fine pont-levis
　　In a castle of the Middle Age,
Joins to a lip of gum, pure amber;
　　When he'd be private, there might he spend

Hours alone in his lady's chamber:
　Into this crevice I dropped our friend.

IV

Splash, went he, as under he ducked,
　—At the bottom, I knew, rain-drippings stagnate:
Next, a handful of blossoms I plucked
　To bury him with, my bookshelf's magnate;
Then I went in-doors, brought out a loaf,
　Half a cheese, and a bottle of Chablis;
Lay on the grass and forgot the oaf
　Over a jolly chapter of Rabelais.

V

Now, this morning, betwixt the moss
　And gum that locked our friend in limbo,
A spider had spun his web across,
　And sat in the midst with arms akimbo:
So, I took pity, for learning's sake,
　And, *de profundis, accentibus lætis,*
Cantate! quoth I, as I got a rake;
　And up I fished his delectable treatise.

VI

Here you have it, dry in the sun,
　With all the binding all of a blister,
And great blue spots where the ink has run,
　And reddish streaks that wink and glister
O'er the page so beautifully yellow:
　Oh, well have the droppings played their tricks!
Did he guess how toadstools grow, this fellow?
　Here's one stuck in his chapter six!

VII

How did he like it when the live creatures
　Tickled and toused and browsed him all over,
And worm, slug, eft, with serious features,
　Came in, each one, for his right of trover?
—When the water-beetle with great blind deaf face

Made of her eggs the stately deposit
And the newt borrowed just so much of the preface
    As tiled in the top of his black wife's closet?

VIII

All that life and fun and romping,
    All that frisking and twisting and coupling,
While slowly our poor friend's leaves were swamping
    And clasps were cracking and covers suppling!
As if you had carried sour John Knox
    To the play-house at Paris, Vienna or Munich,
Fastened him into a front-row box,
    And danced off the ballet with trousers and tunic.

IX

Come, old martyr! What, torment enough is it?
    Back to my room shall you take your sweet self.
Good-bye, mother-beetle; husband-eft, *sufficit!*
    See the snug niche I have made on my shelf!
A.'s book shall prop you up, B.'s shall cover you,
    Here's C. to be grave with, or D. to be gay,
And with E. on each side, and F. right over you,
    Dry-rot at ease till the Judgment-day!

THE LABORATORY

ANCIEN RÉGIME

I

Now that I, tying thy glass mask tightly,
May gaze thro' these faint smokes curling whitely,
As thou pliest thy trade in this devil's-smithy—
Which is the poison to poison her, prithee?

II

He is with her, and they know that I know
Where they are, what they do: they believe my tears flow

While they laugh, laugh at me, at me fled to the drear
Empty church, to pray God in, for them!—I am here.

III

Grind away, moisten and mash up thy paste,
Pound at thy powder,—I am not in haste!
Better sit thus, and observe thy strange things,
Than go where men wait me and dance at the King's.

IV

That in the mortar—you call it a gum?
Ah, the brave tree whence such gold oozings come!
And yonder soft phial, the exquisite blue,
Sure to taste sweetly,—is that poison too?

V

Had I but all of them, thee and thy treasures,
What a wild crowd of invisible pleasures!
To carry pure death in an earring, a casket,
A signet, a fan-mount, a filigree basket!

VI

Soon, at the King's, a mere lozenge to give,
And Pauline should have just thirty minutes to live!
But to light a pastile, and Elise, with her head
And her breast and her arms and her hands, should drop dead!

VII

Quick—is it finished? The color's too grim!
Why not soft like the phial's, enticing and dim?
Let it brighten her drink, let her turn it and stir,
And try it and taste, ere she fix and prefer!

VIII

What a drop! She's not little, no minion like me!
That's why she ensnared him: this never will free

The soul from those masculine eyes,—say, "no!"
To that pulse's magnificent come-and-go.

IX

For only last night, as they whispered, I brought
My own eyes to bear on her so, that I thought
Could I keep them one half minute fixed, she would fall
Shrivelled; she fell not; yet this does it all!

X

Not that I bid you spare her the pain;
Let death be felt and the proof remain:
Brand, burn up, bite into its grace—
He is sure to remember her dying face!

XI

Is it done? Take my mask off! Nay, be not morose;
It kills her, and this prevents seeing it close:
The delicate droplet, my whole fortune's fee!
If it hurts her, beside, can it ever hurt me?

XII

Now, take all my jewels, gorge gold to your fill,
You may kiss me, old man, on my mouth if you will!
But brush this dust off me, lest horror it brings
Ere I know it—next moment I dance at the King's!

THE CONFESSIONAL

[SPAIN]

I

IT IS a lie—their Priests, their Pope,
Their Saints, their . . . all they fear or hope
Are lies, and lies—there! through my door
And ceiling, there! and walls and floor

There, lies, they lie—shall still be hurled
Till spite of them I reach the world!

II

You think Priests just and holy men!
Before they put me in this den
I was a human creature too,
With flesh and blood like one of you,
A girl that laughed in beauty's pride
Like lilies in your world outside.

III

I had a lover—shame avaunt!
This poor wrenched body, grim and gaunt,
Was kissed all over till it burned,
By lips the truest, love e'er turned
His heart's own tint: one night they kissed
My soul out in a burning mist.

IV

So, next day when the accustomed train
Of things grew round my sense again,
"That is a sin," I said: and slow
With downcast eyes to church I go,
And pass to the confession-chair,
And tell the old mild father there.

V

But when I falter Beltran's name,
"Ha?" quoth the father; "much I blame
The sin; yet wherefore idly grieve?
Despair not—strenuously retrieve!
Nay, I will turn this love of thine
To lawful love, almost divine;

VI

"For he is young, and led astray,
This Beltran, and he schemes, men say,

To change the laws of church and state;
So, thine shall be an angel's fate,
Who, ere the thunder breaks, should roll
Its cloud away and save his soul.

VII

"For, when he lies upon thy breast,
Thou mayst demand and be possessed
Of all his plans, and next day steal
To me, and all those plans reveal,
That I and every priest, to purge
His soul, may fast and use the scourge."

VIII

That father's beard was long and white,
With love and truth his brow seemed bright;
I went back, all on fire with joy,
And, that same evening, bade the boy
Tell me, as lovers should, heart-free,
Something to prove his love of me.

IX

He told me what he would not tell
For hope of heaven or fear of hell;
And I lay listening in such pride!
And, soon as he had left my side,
Tripped to the church by morning-light
To save his soul in his despite.

X

I told the father all his schemes,
Who were his comrades, what their dreams;
"And now make haste," I said, "to pray
The one spot from his soul away;
To-night he comes, but not the same
Will look!" At night he never came.

XI

Nor next night: on the after-morn,
I went forth with a strength new-born.
The church was empty; something drew
My steps into the street; I knew
It led me to the market-place:
Where, lo, on high, the father's face!

XII

That horrible black scaffold dressed,
That stapled block . . . God sink the rest!
That head strapped back, that blinding vest,
Those knotted hands and naked breast,
Till near one busy hangman pressed,
And, on the neck these arms caressed . . .

XIII

No part in aught they hope or fear!
No heaven with them, no hell!—and here,
No earth, not so much space as pens
My body in their worst of dens
But shall bear God and man my cry,
Lies—lies, again—and still, they lie!

THE FLIGHT OF THE DUCHESS

I

You're my friend:
    I was the man the Duke spoke to;
    I helped the Duchess to cast off his yoke, too;
So here's the tale from beginning to end,
    My friend!

II

Ours is a great wild country:
    If you climb to our castle's top,
    I don't see where your eye can stop;

For when you've passed the cornfield country,
Where vineyards leave off, flocks are packed,   10
And sheep-range leads to cattle-tract,
And cattle-tract to open-chase,
And open-chase to the very base
Of the mountain where, at a funeral pace,
Round about, solemn and slow,
One by one, row after row,
Up and up the pine-trees go,
So, like black priests up, and so
Down the other side again
    To another greater, wilder country,   20
That's one vast red drear burnt-up plain,
Branched through and through with many a vein
Whence iron's dug, and copper's dealt;
    Look right, look left, look straight before,—
Beneath they mine, above they smelt,
    Copper-ore and iron-ore,
And forge and furnace mould and melt,
    And so on, more and ever more,
Till at the last, for a bounding belt,
    Comes the salt sand hoar of the great sea-shore,   30
—And the whole is our Duke's country.

III

I was born the day this present Duke was—
    (And O, says the song, ere I was old!)
In the castle where the other Duke was—
    (When I was happy and young, not old!)
I in the kennel, he in the bower:
We are of like age to an hour.
My father was huntsman in that day;
Who has not heard my father say
That, when a boar was brought to bay,   40
Three times, four times out of five,
With his huntspear he'd contrive
To get the killing-place transfixed,
And pin him true, both eyes betwixt?
And that's why the old Duke would rather
He lost a salt-pit than my father,

And loved to have him ever in call;
That's why my father stood in the hall
When the old Duke brought his infant out
   To show the people, and while they passed   50
The wondrous bantling round about,
   Was first to start at the outside blast
As the Kaiser's courier blew his horn
Just a month after the babe was born.
"And," quoth the Kaiser's courier, "since
The Duke has got an heir, our Prince
   Needs the Duke's self at his side:"
The Duke looked down and seemed to wince,
   But he thought of wars o'er the world wide,
Castles a-fire, men on their march,   60
The toppling tower, the crashing arch;
   And up he looked, and awhile he eyed
The row of crests and shields and banners
Of all achievements after all manners,
   And "ay," said the Duke with a surly pride.
   The more was his comfort when he died
At next year's end, in a velvet suit,
With a gilt glove on his hand, his foot
In a silken shoe for a leather boot,
Petticoated like a herald,   70
   In a chamber next to an ante-room,
   Where he breathed the breath of page and groom,
   What he called stink, and they, perfume:
—They should have set him on red Berold
Mad with pride, like fire to manage!
They should have got his cheek fresh tannage
Such a day as to-day in the merry sunshine!
Had they stuck on his fist a rough-foot merlin!
(Hark, the wind's on the heath at its game!
Oh for a noble falcon-lanner   80
To flap each broad wing like a banner,
And turn in the wind, and dance like flame!)
Had they broached a white-beer cask from Berlin
—Or if you incline to prescribe mere wine
Put to his lips, when they saw him pine,
A cup of our own Moldavia fine,
Cotnar for instance, green as May sorrel
And ropy with sweet,—we shall not quarrel.

IV

So, at home, the sick tall yellow Duchess
Was left with the infant in her clutches, 90
She being the daughter of God knows who:
    And now was the time to revisit her tribe.
Abroad and afar they went, the two,
    And let our people rail and gibe
At the empty hall and extinguished fire,
    As loud as we liked, but ever in vain,
Till after long years we had our desire,
    And back came the Duke and his mother again.

V

And he came back the pertest little ape
That ever affronted human shape; 100
Full of his travel, struck at himself.
    You'd say, he despised our bluff old ways?
—Not he! For in Paris they told the elf
    Our rough North land was the Land of Lays,
    The one good thing left in evil days;
Since the Mid-Age was the Heroic Time,
    And only in wild nooks like ours
Could you taste of it yet as in its prime,
    And see true castles, with proper towers,
Young-hearted women, old-minded men, 110
And manners now as manners were then.
So, all that the old Dukes had been, without knowing it,
This Duke would fain know he was, without being it;
'Twas not for the joy's self, but the joy of his showing it,
Nor for the pride's self, but the pride of our seeing it,
He revived all usages thoroughly worn-out,
The souls of them fumed-forth, the hearts of them torn-out:
And chief in the chase his neck he perilled
On a lathy horse, all legs and length,
With blood for bone, all speed, no strength; 120
—They should have set him on red Berold
With the red eye slow consuming in fire,
And the thin stiff ear like an abbey-spire!

VI

Well, such as he was, he must marry, we heard:
And out of a convent, at the word,
Came the lady, in time of spring.
—Oh, old thoughts they cling, they cling!
That day, I know, with a dozen oaths
I clad myself in thick hunting-clothes
Fit for the chase of urochs or buffle   130
In winter-time when you need to muffle.
But the Duke had a mind we should cut a figure,
    And so we saw the lady arrive:
My friend, I have seen a white crane bigger!
    She was the smallest lady alive,
Made in a piece of nature's madness,
Too small, almost, for the life and gladness
    That over-filled her, as some hive
Out of the bears' reach on the high trees
Is crowded with its safe merry bees: 140
In truth, she was not hard to please!
Up she looked, down she looked, round at the mead,
Straight at the castle, that's best indeed
To look at from outside the walls:
As for us, styled the "serfs and thralls,"
She as much thanked me as if she had said it,
    (With her eyes, do you understand?)
Because I patted her horse while I led it;
    And Max, who rode on her other hand,
Said, no bird flew past but she inquired   150
What its true name was, nor ever seemed tired—
If that was an eagle she saw hover,
And the green and gray bird on the field was the plover.
When suddenly appeared the Duke:
    And as down she sprung, the small foot pointed
On to my hand,—as with a rebuke,
    And as if his backbone were not jointed,
The Duke stepped rather aside than forward,
    And welcomed her with his grandest smile;
    And, mind you, his mother all the while   160
Chilled in the rear, like a wind to Nor'ward;
And up, like a weary yawn, with its pulleys
Went, in a shriek, the rusty portcullis;

And, like a glad sky the north-wind sullies,
The lady's face stopped its play,
As if her first hair had grown gray;
For such things must begin some one day.

VII

In a day or two she was well again;
As who should say, "You labor in vain!
This is all a jest against God, who meant   170
I should ever be, as I am, content
And glad in his sight; therefore, glad I will be."
So, smiling as at first went she.

VIII

She was active, stirring, all fire—
Could not rest, could not tire—
To a stone she might have given life!
    (I myself loved once, in my day)
--For a shepherd's, miner's, huntsman's wife,
    (I had a wife, I know what I say)
Never in all the world such an one!   180
And here was plenty to be done,
And she that could do it, great or small,
She was to do nothing at all.
There was already this man in his post,
    This in his station, and that in his office,
And the Duke's plan admitted a wife, at most,
    To meet his eye, with the other trophies,
Now outside the hall, now in it,
    To sit thus, stand thus, see and be seen,
At the proper place in the proper minute,   190
    And die away the life between.
And it was amusing enough, each infraction
    Of rule—(but for after-sadness that came)
To hear the consummate self-satisfaction
    With which the young Duke and the old dame
Would let her advise, and criticise,
And, being a fool, instruct the wise,
    And, child-like, parcel out praise or blame:
They bore it all in complacent guise,
As though an artificer, after contriving   200

A wheel-work image as if it were living,
Should find with delight it could motion to strike him!
So found the Duke, and his mother like him:
The lady hardly got a rebuff—
That had not been contemptuous enough,
With his cursed smirk, as he nodded applause,
And kept off the old mother-cat's claws.

IX

So, the little lady grew silent and thin,
    Paling and ever paling,
As the way is with a hid chagrin;   210
    And the Duke perceived that she was ailing,
And said in his heart, " 'Tis done to spite me,
But I shall find in my power to right me!"
Don't swear, friend! The old one, many a year,
Is in hell, and the Duke's self . . . you shall hear.

X

Well, early in autumn, at first winter-warning,
When the stag had to break with his foot, of a morning,
A drinking-hole out of the fresh tender ice
That covered the pond till the sun, in a trice,
Loosening it, let out a ripple of gold,   220
    And another and another, and faster and faster,
Till, dimpling to blindness, the wide water rolled:
    Then it so chanced that the Duke our master
Asked himself what were the pleasures in season,
    And found, since the calendar bade him be hearty,
He should do the Middle Age no treason
    In resolving on a hunting-party.
Always provided, old books showed the way of it!
    What meant old poets by their strictures?
And when old poets had said their say of it,   230
    How taught old painters in their pictures?
We must revert to the proper channels,
Workings in tapestry, paintings on panels,
And gather up woodcraft's authentic traditions:
Here was food for our various ambitions,
As on each case, exactly stated—
    To encourage your dog, now, the properest chirrup,
    Or best prayer to Saint Hubert on mounting your stirrup—

We of the household took thought and debated.
Blessed was he whose back ached with the jerkin   240
His sire was wont to do forest-work in;
Blesseder he who nobly sunk "ohs"
And "ahs" while he tugged on his grandsire's trunk-hose;
What signified hats if they had no rims on,
    Each slouching before and behind like the scallop,
    And able to serve at sea for a shallop,
Loaded with lacquer and looped with crimson?
So that the deer now, to make a short rhyme on't,
    What with our Venerers, Prickers and Verderers,
    Might hope for real hunters at length and not murderers,   250
And oh the Duke's tailor, he had a hot time on't!

XI

Now you must know that when the first dizziness
    Of flap-hats and buff-coats and jack-boots subsided,
    The Duke put this question, "The Duke's part provided,
Had not the Duchess some share in the business?"
For out of the mouth of two or three witnesses
Did he establish all fit-or-unfitnesses:
And, after much laying of heads together,
Somebody's cap got a notable feather
By the announcement with proper unction   260
That he had discovered the lady's function;
Since ancient authors gave this tenet,
    "When horns wind a mort and the deer is at siege,
Let the dame of the castle prick forth on her jennet,
    And, with water to wash the hands of her liege
In a clean ewer with a fair toweling,
Let her preside at the disemboweling."
Now, my friend, if you had so little religion
    As to catch a hawk, some falcon-lanner,
    And thrust her broad wings like a banner   270
Into a coop for a vulgar pigeon;
And if day by day and week by week
    You cut her claws, and seeled her eyes,
And clipped her wings, and tied her beak,
    Would it cause you any great surprise
If, when you decided to give her an airing,
You found she needed a little preparing?
—I say, should you be such a curmudgeon,

If she clung to the perch, as to take it in dudgeon?
Yet when the Duke to his lady signified,   280
Just a day before, as he judged most dignified,
In what a pleasure she was to participate,—
    And, instead of leaping wide in flashes,
    Her eyes just lifted their long lashes,
As if pressed by fatigue even he could not dissipate,
And duly acknowledged the Duke's forethought,
But spoke of her health, if her health were worth aught,
Of the weight by day and the watch by night,
And much wrong now that used to be right,
So, thanking him, declined the hunting,—   290
Was conduct ever more affronting?
With all the ceremony settled—
    With the towel ready, and the sewer
    Polishing up his oldest ewer,
    And the jennet pitched upon, a piebald,
    Black-barred, cream-coated and pink eyeballed,—
No wonder if the Duke was nettled!
And when she persisted nevertheless,—
Well, I suppose here's the time to confess
That there ran half round our lady's chamber   300
A balcony none of the hardest to clamber;
And that Jacynth the tire-woman, ready in waiting,
Stayed in call outside, what need of relating?
And since Jacynth was like a June rose, why, a fervent
Adorer of Jacynth of course was your servant;
And if she had the habit to peep through the casement,
    How could I keep at any vast distance?
    And so, as I say, on the lady's persistence,
The Duke, dumb-stricken with amazement,
Stood for a while in a sultry smother,   310
    And then, with a smile that partook of the awful,
Turned her over to his yellow mother
    To learn what was held decorous and lawful;
And the mother smelt blood with a cat-like instinct,
As her cheek quick whitened thro' all its quince-tinct.
Oh, but the lady heard the whole truth at once!
    What meant she?—Who was she?—Her duty and station,
The wisdom of age and the folly of youth, at once,
    Its decent regard and its fitting relation—
In brief, my friend, set all the devils in hell free   320
And turn them out to carouse in a belfry,

And treat the priests to a fifty-part canon,
And then you may guess how that tongue of hers ran on!
Well, somehow or other it ended at last
And, licking her whiskers, out she passed;
And after her,—making (he hoped) a face
    Like Emperor Nero or Sultan Saladin,
Stalked the Duke's self with the austere grace
    Of ancient hero or modern paladin,
From door to staircase—oh such a solemn   330
Unbending of the vertebral column!

                    XII

However, at sunrise our company mustered;
    And here was the huntsman bidding unkennel,
And there 'neath his bonnet the pricker blustered,
    With feather dank as a bough of wet fennel;
For the court-yard walls were filled with fog
You might have cut as an axe chops a log—
Like so much wool for color and bulkiness;
And out rode the Duke in a perfect sulkiness,
Since, before breakfast, a man feels but queasily,   340
    And a sinking at the lower abdomen
    Begins the day with indifferent omen.
And lo, as he looked around uneasily,
The sun ploughed the fog up and drove it asunder
This way and that from the valley under;
    And, looking through the court-yard arch,
Down in the valley, what should meet him
    But a troop of Gipsies on their march?
No doubt with the annual gifts to greet him.

                    XIII

Now, in your land, Gipsies reach you, only   350
    After reaching all lands beside;
North they go, South they go, trooping or lonely,
    And still, as they travel far and wide,
Catch they and keep now a trace here, a trace there,
That puts you in mind of a place here, a place there.
But with us, I believe they rise out of the ground,
And nowhere else, I take it, are found
With the earth-tint yet so freshly embrowned:

Born, no doubt, like insects which breed on
The very fruit they are meant to feed on.   360
For the earth—not a use to which they don't turn it,
   The ore that grows in the mountain's womb,
   Or the sand in the pits like a honeycomb,
They sift and soften it, bake it and burn it—
Whether they weld you, for instance, a snaffle
With side-bars never a brute can baffle;
Or a lock that's a puzzle of wards within wards;
Or, if your colt's fore-foot inclines to curve inwards,
Horseshoes they hammer which turn on a swivel
And won't allow the hoof to shrivel.   370
Then they cast bells like the shell of the winkle
That keep a stout heart in the ram with their tinkle;
But the sand—they pinch and pound it like otters;
Commend me to Gipsy glass-makers and potters!
Glasses they'll blow you, crystal-clear,
Where just a faint cloud of rose shall appear,
As if in pure water you dropped and let die
A bruised black-blooded mulberry;
And that other sort, their crowning pride,
With long white threads distinct inside,   380
Like the lake-flower's fibrous roots which dangle
Loose such a length and never tangle,
Where the bold sword-lily cuts the clear waters,
And the cup-lily couches with all the white daughters:
Such are the works they put their hand to,
The uses they turn and twist iron and sand to.
And these made the troop, which our Duke saw sally
Toward his castle from out of the valley,
Men and women, like new-hatched spiders,
Come out with the morning to greet our riders.   390
And up they wound till they reached the ditch,
Whereat all stopped save one, a witch
That I knew, as she hobbled from the group,
By her gait directly and her stoop,
I, whom Jacynth was used to importune
To let that same witch tell us our fortune.
The oldest Gipsy then above ground;
And, sure as the autumn season came round,
She paid us a visit for profit or pastime,
And every time, as she swore, for the last time.   400
And presently she was seen to sidle

Up to the Duke till she touched his bridle,
So that the horse of a sudden reared up
As under its nose the old witch peered up
With her worn-out eyes, or rather eye-holes
    Of no use now but to gather brine,
    And began a kind of level whine
Such as they used to sing to their viols
When their ditties they go grinding
Up and down with nobody minding: 410
And then, as of old, at the end of the humming
Her usual presents were forthcoming
—A dog-whistle blowing the fiercest of trebles,
(Just a sea-shore stone holding a dozen fine pebbles,)
Or a porcelain mouth-piece to screw on a pipe-end,—
And so she awaited her annual stipend.
But this time, the Duke would scarcely vouchsafe
    A word in reply; and in vain she felt
    With twitching fingers at her belt
    For the purse of sleek pine-martin pelt   420
Ready to put what he gave in her pouch safe,—
Till, either to quicken his apprehension,
Or possibly with an after-intention,
She was come, she said, to pay her duty
To the new Duchess, the youthful beauty.
No sooner had she named his lady,
Than a shine lit up the face so shady,
And its smirk returned with a novel meaning—
For it struck him, the babe just wanted weaning;
If one gave her a taste of what life was and sorrow,   430
She, foolish to-day, would be wiser to-morrow;
And who so fit a teacher of trouble
As this sordid crone bent well-nigh double?
So, glancing at her wolf-skin vesture,
    (If such it was, for they grow so hirsute
    That their own fleece serves for natural fur-suit)
He was contrasting, 'twas plain from his gesture,
The life of the lady so flower-like and delicate
With the loathsome squalor of this helicat.
I, in brief, was the man the Duke beckoned   440
    From out of the throng, and while I drew near
He told the crone—as I since have reckoned
    By the way he bent and spoke into her ear
With circumspection and mystery—

The main of the lady's history,
Her frowardness and ingratitude:
And for all the crone's submissive attitude
I could see round her mouth the loose plaits tightening,
And her brow with assenting intelligence brightening,
   As though she engaged with hearty good-will   450
   Whatever he now might enjoin to fulful,
And promised the lady a thorough frightening.
And so, just giving her a glimpse
Of a purse, with the air of a man who imps
The wing of the hawk that shall fetch the hernshaw,
   He bade me take the Gipsy mother
   And set her telling some story or other
Of hill or dale, oak-wood or fernshaw,
To wile away a weary hour
For the lady left alone in her bower,   460
Whose mind and body craved exertion
And yet shrank from all better diversion.

XIV

Then clapping heel to his horse, the mere curveter,
   Out rode the Duke, and after his hollo
Horses and hounds swept, huntsman and servitor,
   And back I turned and bade the crone follow.
And what makes me confident what's to be told you
   Had all along been of this crone's devising,
Is, that, on looking round sharply, behold you,
   There was a novelty quick as surprising: 470
For first, she had shot up a full head in stature,
   And her step kept pace with mine nor faltered,
As if age had foregone its usurpature,
   And the ignoble mien was wholly altered,
And the face looked quite of another nature,
And the change reached too, whatever the change meant,
Her shaggy wolf-skin cloak's arrangement:
For where its tatters hung loose like sedges,
Gold coins were glittering on the edges,
Like the band-roll strung with tomans   480
Which proves the veil a Persian woman's:
And under her brow, like a snail's horns newly
   Come out as after the rain he paces,
Two unmistakable eye-points duly

Live and aware looked out of their places.
So, we went and found Jacynth at the entry
Of the lady's chamber standing sentry;
I told the command and produced my companion,
And Jacynth rejoiced to admit any one,
For since last night, by the same token,   490
Not a single word had the lady spoken:
They went in both to the presence together,
While I in the balcony watched the weather.

XV

And now, what took place at the very first of all,
I cannot tell, as I never could learn it:
Jacynth constantly wished a curse to fall
On that little head of hers and burn it
If she knew how she came to drop so soundly
    Asleep of a sudden and there continue
The whole time sleeping as profoundly   500
    As one of the boars my father would pin you
'Twixt the eyes where life holds garrison,
—Jacynth forgive me the comparison!
But where I begin my own narration
Is a little after I took my station
To breathe the fresh air from the balcony,
And, having in those days a falcon eye,
To follow the hunt thro' the open country,
    From where the bushes thinlier crested
The hillocks, to a plain where's not one tree.   510
    When, in a moment, my ear was arrested
By—was it singing, or was it saying,
Or a strange musical instrument playing
In the chamber?—and to be certain
I pushed the lattice, pulled the curtain,
And there lay Jacynth asleep,
Yet as if a watch she tried to keep,
In a rosy sleep along the floor
With her head against the door;
While in the midst, on the seat of state,   520
Was a queen—the Gipsy woman late,
With head and face downbent
On the lady's head and face intent:

For, coiled at her feet like a child at ease,
The lady sat between her knees
And o'er them the lady's clasped hands met,
And on those hands her chin was set,
And her upturned face met the face of the crone
Wherein the eyes had grown and grown
As if she could double and quadruple   530
At pleasure the play of either pupil
    —Very like, by her hands' slow fanning,
As up and down like a gor-crow's flappers
They moved to measure, or bell-clappers.
    I said "Is it blessing, is it banning,
Do they applaud you or burlesque you—
    Those hands and fingers with no flesh on?"
But, just as I thought to spring in to the rescue,
    At once I was stopped by the lady's expression:
For it was life her eyes were drinking   540
From the crone's wide pair above unwinking,
—Life's pure fire received without shrinking,
Into the heart and breast whose heaving
Told you no single drop they were leaving,
—Life, that filling her, passed redundant
    Into her very hair, back swerving
Over each shoulder, loose and abundant,
    As her head thrown back showed the white throat curving;
And the very tresses shared in the pleasure,
Moving to the mystic measure,   550
Bounding as the bosom bounded.
I stopped short, more and more confounded,
As still her cheeks burned and eyes glistened,
As she listened and she listened:
When all at once a hand detained me,
The selfsame contagion gained me,
And I kept time to the wondrous chime,
Making out words and prose and rhyme,
Till it seemed that the music furled
    Its wings like a task fulfilled, and dropped   560
    From under the words it first had propped,
And left them midway in the world:
Word took word as hand takes hand,
I could hear at last, and understand,
And when I held the unbroken thread,
The Gipsy said:—

"And so at last we find my tribe.
  And so I set thee in the midst,
And to one and all of them describe
  What thou saidst and what thou didst,   570
Our long and terrible journey through,
And all thou art ready to say and do
In the trials that remain:
I trace them the vein and the other vein
That meet on thy brow and part again,
Making our rapid mystic mark;
  And I bid my people prove and probe
  Each eye's profound and glorious globe
Till they detect the kindred spark
In those depths so dear and dark,   580
Like the spots that snap and burst and flee,
Circling over the midnight sea.
And on that round young cheek of thine
  I make them recognize the tinge,
As when of the costly scarlet wine
  They drip so much as will impinge
And spread in a thinnest scale afloat
One thick gold drop from the olive's coat
Over a silver plate whose sheen
Still thro' the mixture shall be seen.   590
For so I prove thee, to one and all,
  Fit, when my people ope their breast,
To see the sign, and hear the call,
  And take the vow, and stand the test
  Which adds one more child to the rest—
When the breast is bare and the arms are wide,
And the world is left outside.
For there is probation to decree,
And many and long must the trials be
Thou shalt victoriously endure,   600
If that brow is true and those eyes are sure;
Like a jewel-finder's fierce assay
  Of the prize he dug from its mountain-tomb—
Let once the vindicating ray
  Leap out amid the anxious gloom,
And steel and fire have done their part
And the prize falls on its finder's heart;
So, trial after trial past,
Wilt thou fall at the very last

Breathless, half in trance   610
With the thrill of the great deliverance,
    Into our arms for evermore;
And thou shalt know, those arms once curled
    About thee, what we knew before,
How love is the only good in the world.
Henceforth be loved as heart can love,
Or brain devise, or hand approve!
Stand up, look below,
It is our life at thy feet we throw
To step with into light and joy;   620
Not a power of life but we employ
To satisfy thy nature's want;
Art thou the tree that props the plant,
Or the climbing plant that seeks the tree—
Canst thou help us, must we help thee?
If any two creatures grew into one,
They would do more than the world has done:
Though each apart were never so weak,
Ye vainly through the world should seek
For the knowledge and the might   630
Which in such union grew their right:
So, to approach at least that end,
And blend,—as much as may be, blend
Thee with us or us with thee,—
As climbing plant or propping tree,
Shall some one deck thee, over and down,
    Up and about, with blossoms and leaves?
Fix his heart's fruit for thy garland-crown,
    Cling with his soul as the gourd-vine cleaves,
Die on thy boughs and disappear   640
While not a leaf of thine is sere?
Or is the other fate in store,
And art thou fitted to adore,
To give thy wondrous self away,
And take a stronger nature's sway?
I foresee and could foretell
Thy future portion, sure and well:
But those passionate eyes speak true, speak true,
Let them say what thou shalt do!
Only be sure thy daily life,   650
In its peace or in its strife,
Never shall be unobserved;

We pursue thy whole career,
  And hope for it, or doubt, or fear,—
Lo, hast thou kept thy path or swerved,
We are beside thee in all thy ways,
With our blame, with our praise,
Our shame to feel, our pride to show,
Glad, angry—but indifferent, no!
Whether it be thy lot to go,   660
For the good of us all, where the haters meet
In the crowded city's horrible street;
Or thou step alone through the morass
Where never sound yet was
Save the dry quick clap of the stork's bill,
For the air is still, and the water still,
When the blue breast of the dipping coot
Dives under, and all is mute.
So, at the last shall come old age,
Decrepit as befits that stage;   670
How else wouldst thou retire apart
With the hoarded memories of thy heart,
And gather all to the very least
Of the fragments of life's earlier feast,
Let fall through eagerness to find
The crowning dainties yet behind?
Ponder on the entire past
Laid together thus at last,
When the twilight helps to fuse
The first fresh with the faded hues,   680
And the outline of the whole,
As round eve's shades their framework roll,
Grandly fronts for once thy soul.
And then as, 'mid the dark, a gleam
  Of yet another morning breaks,
And like the hand which ends a dream,
Death, with the might of his sunbeam,
  Touches the flesh and the soul awakes,
Then——"
                Ay, then indeed something would happen!
  But what? For here her voice changed like a bird's;   690
  There grew more of the music and less of the words;
Had Jacynth only been by me to clap pen
To paper and put you down every syllable
  With those clever clerkly fingers,

All I've forgotten as well as what lingers
In this old brain of mine that's but ill able
To give you even this poor version
    Of the speech I spoil, as it were, with stammering
    —More fault of those who had the hammering
    Of prosody into me and syntax,   700
    And did it, not with hobnails but tintacks!
But to return from this excursion,—
Just, do you mark, when the song was sweetest,
The peace most deep and the charm completest,
There came, shall I say, a snap—
    And the charm vanished!
    And my sense returned, so strangely banished,
And, starting as from a nap,
I knew the crone was bewitching my lady,
With Jacynth asleep; and but one spring made I   710
Down from the casement, round to the portal,
    Another minute and I had entered,—
When the door opened, and more than mortal
    Stood, with a face where to my mind centred
All beauties I ever saw or shall see,
The Duchess: I stopped as if struck by palsy.
She was so different, happy and beautiful,
    I felt at once that all was best,
    And that I had nothing to do, for the rest,
But wait her commands, obey and be dutiful.   720
Not that, in fact, there was any commanding;
    I saw the glory of her eye,
And the brow's height and the breast's expanding,
    And I was hers to live or to die.
As for finding what she wanted,
You know God Almighty granted
Such little signs should serve wild creatures
    To tell one another all their desires,
    So that each knows what his friend requires,
And does its bidding without teachers.   730
I preceded her; the crone
Followed silent and alone;
I spoke to her, but she merely jabbered
    In the old style; both her eyes had slunk
    Back to their pits; her stature shrunk; ·
    In short, the soul in its body sunk
Like a blade sent home to its scabbard.

We descended, I preceding;
Crossed the court with nobody heeding;
All the world was at the chase, 740
The courtyard like a desert-place,
The stable emptied of its small fry;
I saddled myself the very palfrey
I remember patting while it carried her,
The day she arrived and the Duke married her,
And, do you know, though it's easy deceiving
Oneself in such matters, I can't help believing
The lady had not forgotten it either,
And knew the poor devil so much beneath her
Would have been only too glad for her service 750
To dance on hot ploughshares like a Turk dervise,
But, unable to pay proper duty where owing it,
Was reduced to that pitiful method of showing it:
For though the moment I began setting
His saddle on my own nag of Berold's begetting,
(Not that I meant to be obtrusive)
    She stopped me, while his rug was shifting,
    By a single rapid finger's lifting,
And, with a gesture kind but conclusive,
And a little shake of the head, refused me,— 760
I say, although she never used me,
Yet when she was mounted, the Gipsy behind her,
And I ventured to remind her,
I suppose with a voice of less steadiness
    Than usual, for my feeling exceeded me,
—Something to the effect that I was in readiness
    Whenever God should please she needed me,—
Then, do you know, her face looked down on me
With a look that placed a crown on me,
And she felt in her bosom,—mark, her bosom— 770
And, as a flower-tree drops its blossom,
Dropped me . . . ah, had it been a purse
Of silver, my friend, or gold that's worse,
Why, you see, as soon as I found myself
    So understood,—that a true heart so may gain
    Such a reward,—I should have gone home again,
Kissed Jacynth, and soberly drowned myself!
It was a little plait of hair
    Such as friends in a convent make
    To wear, each for the other's sake,— 780

This, see, which at my breast I wear,
Ever did (rather to Jacynth's grudgment),
And ever shall, till the Day of Judgment.
And then,—and then,—to cut short,—this is idle,
    These are feelings it is not good to foster,—
I pushed the gate wide, she shook the bridle,
    And the palfrey bounded,—and so we lost her.

XVI

When the liquor's out why clink the cannikin?
I did think to describe you the panic in
The redoubtable breast of our master the mannikin,   790
And what was the pitch of his mother's yellowness,
    How she turned as a shark to snap the spare-rib
    Clean off, sailors say, from a pearl-diving Carib,
When she heard, what she called the flight of the feloness
—But it seems such child's play,
What they said and did with the lady away!
And to dance on, when we've lost the music,
Always made me—and no doubt makes you—sick.
Nay, to my mind, the world's face looked so stern
As that sweet form disappeared through the postern,   800
She that kept it in constant good humor,
It ought to have stopped; there seemed nothing to do more.
But the world thought otherwise and went on,
And my head's one that its spite was spent on:
Thirty years are fled since that morning,
And with them all my head's adorning.
Nor did the old Duchess die outright,
As you expect, of suppressed spite,
The natural end of every adder
Not suffered to empty its poison-bladder: 810
But she and her son agreed, I take it,
That no one should touch on the story to wake it,
For the wound in the Duke's pride rankled fiery,
So, they made no search and small inquiry—
And when fresh Gipsies have paid us a visit, I've
Noticed the couple were never inquisitive,
But told them they're folks the Duke don't want here,
And bade them make haste and cross the frontier.
Brief, the Duchess was gone and the Duke was glad of it,
    And the old one was in the young one's stead,   820

And took, in her place, the household's head,
And a blessed time the household had of it!
And were I not, as a man may say, cautious
How I trench, more than needs, on the nauseous,
I could favor you with sundry touches
Of the paint-smutches with which the Duchess
Heightened the mellowness of her cheek's yellowness
(To get on faster) until at last her
Cheek grew to be one master-plaster
Of mucus and fucus from mere use of ceruse: 830
In short, she grew from scalp to udder
Just the object to make you shudder.

XVII

You're my friend—
What a thing friendship is, world without end!
How it gives the heart and soul a stir-up
    As if somebody broached you a glorious runlet,
    And poured out, all lovelily, sparklingly, sunlit,
Our green Moldavia, the streaky syrup,
Cotnar as old as the time of the Druids—
Friendship may match with that monarch of fluids;   840
Each supplies a dry brain, fills you its ins-and-outs,
Gives your life's hour-glass a shake when the thin sand doubts
Whether to run on or stop short, and guarantees
Age is not all made of stark sloth and arrant ease.
I have seen my little lady once more,
    Jacynth, the Gipsy, Berold, and the rest of it,
For to me spoke the Duke, as I told you before;
    I always wanted to make a clean breast of it:
And now it is made—why, my heart's blood, that went trickle,
    Trickle, but anon, in such muddy driblets,   850
Is pumped up brisk now, through the main ventricle,
    And genially floats me about the giblets.
I'll tell you what I intend to do:
I must see this fellow his sad life through—
He is our Duke, after all,
And I, as he says, but a serf and thrall.
My father was born here, and I inherit
    His fame, a chain he bound his son with;
Could I pay in a lump I should prefer it,
    But there's no mine to blow up and get done with: 860
So, I must stay till the end of the chapter.

For, as to our middle-age-manners-adapter,
Be it a thing to be glad on or sorry on,
Some day or other, his head in a morion
And breast in a hauberk, his heels he'll kick up,
Slain by an onslaught fierce of hiccup.
And then, when red doth the sword of our Duke rust,
And its leathern sheath lie o'ergrown with a blue crust,
Then I shall scrape together my earnings;
 For, you see, in the churchyard Jacynth reposes,   870
 And our children all went the way of the roses:
It's a long lane that knows no turnings.
One needs but little tackle to travel in;
 So, just one stout cloak shall I indue:
And for a staff, what beats the javelin
 With which his boars my father pinned you?
And then, for a purpose you shall hear presently,
 Taking some Cotnar, a tight plump skinful,
I shall go journeying, who but I, pleasantly!
 Sorrow is vain and despondency sinful.   880
What's a man's age? He must hurry more, that's all;
 Cram in a day, what his youth took a year to hold:
 When we mind labor, then only, we're too old—
What age had Methusalem when he begat Saul?
And at last, as its haven some buffeted ship sees,
 (Come all the way from the north-parts with sperm oil)
 I hope to get safely out of the turmoil
And arrive one day at the land of the Gipsies,
And find my lady, or hear the last news of her
From some old thief and son of Lucifer,   890
His forehead chapleted green with wreathy hop,
Sunburned all over like an Æthiop.
And when my Cotnar begins to operate
And the tongue of the rogue to run at a proper rate,
And our wine-skin, tight once, shows each flaccid dent,
I shall drop in with—as if by accident—
"You never knew, then, how it all ended,
What fortune good or bad attended
The little lady your Queen befriended?"
—And when that's told me, what's remaining?   90
This world's too hard for my explaining.
The same wise judge of matters equine
 Who still preferred some slim four-year-old
 To the big-boned stock of mighty Berold,

And, for strong Cotnar, drank French weak wine,
He also must be such a lady's scorner!
  Smooth Jacob still robs homely Esau:
  Now up, now down, the world's one see-saw.
—So, I shall find out some snug corner
Under a hedge, like Orson the wood-knight,
Turn myself round and bid the world good-night;
And sleep a sound sleep till the trumpet's blowing
  Wakes me (unless priests cheat us laymen)
To a world where will be no further throwing
  Pearls before swine that can't value them. Amen!

910

EARTH'S IMMORTALITIES

FAME

Sᴇᴇ, as the prettiest graves will do in time,
Our poet's wants the freshness of its prime;
Spite of the sexton's browsing horse, the sods
Have struggled through its binding osier rods;
Headstone and half-sunk footstone lean awry,
Wanting the brick-work promised by-and-by;
How the minute grey lichens, plate o'er plate,
Have softened down the crisp-cut name and date!

LOVE

So, the year's done with!
    (*Love me forever!*)
All March begun with,
    April's endeavor;
May-wreaths that bound me
    June needs must sever;
Now snows fall round me,
    Quenching June's fever—
    (*Love me forever!*)

SONG

I

NAY but you, who do not love her,
　　Is she not pure gold, my mistress?
Holds earth aught—speak truth—above her?
　　Aught like this tress, see, and this tress,
And this last fairest tress of all,
So fair, see, ere I let it fall?

II

Because, you spend your lives in praising;
　　To praise, you search the wide world over:
Then why not witness, calmly gazing,
　　If earth holds aught—speak truth—above her?
Above this tress, and this, I touch
But cannot praise, I love so much!

THE BOY AND THE ANGEL

MORNING, evening, noon and night,
"Praise God," sang Theocrite.

Then to his poor trade he turned,
Whereby the daily meal was earned.

Hard he labored, long and well;
O'er his work the boy's curls fell.

But ever, at each period,
He stopped and sang, "Praise God!"

Then back again his curls he threw,
And cheerful turned to work anew.　　　10

Said Blaise, the listening monk, "Well done;
I doubt not thou art heard, my son:

"As well as if thy voice to-day
Were praising God, the Pope's great way.

"This Easter Day, the Pope at Rome
Praises God from Peter's dome."

Said Theocrite, "Would God that I
Might praise him, that great way, and die!"

Night passed, day shone,
And Theocrite was gone.   20

With God a day endures alway,
A thousand years are but a day.

God said in heaven, "Nor day nor night
Now brings the voice of my delight."

Then Gabriel, like a rainbow's birth,
Spread his wings and sank to earth;

Entered, in flesh, the empty cell,
Lived there, and played the craftsman well;

And morning, evening, noon and night,
Praised God in place of Theocrite.   30

And from a boy, to youth he grew:
The man put off the stripling's hue:

The man matured and fell away
Into the season of decay:

And ever o'er the trade he bent,
And ever lived on earth content.

(He did God's will; to him, all one
If on the earth or in the sun.)

God said, "A praise is in mine ear;
There is no doubt in it, no fear: 40

"So sing old worlds, and so
New worlds that from my footstool go.

"Clearer loves sound other ways:
I miss my little human praise."

Then forth sprang Gabriel's wings, off fell
The flesh disguise, remained the cell.

'Twas Easter Day: he flew to Rome,
And paused above Saint Peter's dome.

In the tiring-room close by
The great outer gallery,   50

With his holy vestments dight,
Stood the new Pope, Theocrite:

And all his past career
Came back upon him clear,

Since when, a boy, he plied his trade,
Till on his life the sickness weighed;

And in his cell, when death drew near,
An angel in a dream brought cheer:

And rising from the sickness drear
He grew a priest, and now stood here.   60

To the East with praise he turned,
And on his sight the angel burned.

"I bore thee from thy craftsman's cell
And set thee here; I did not well.

"Vainly I left my angel-sphere,
Vain was thy dream of many a year.

"Thy voice's praise seemed weak; it dropped—
Creation's chorus stopped!

"Go back and praise again
The early way, while I remain.   70

"With that weak voice of our disdain,
Take up creation's pausing strain.

"Back to the cell and poor employ:
Resume the craftsman and the boy!"

Theocrite grew old at home;
A new Pope dwelt in Peter's dome.

One vanished as the other died:
They sought God side by side.

MEETING AT NIGHT

I

THE gray sea and the long black land;
And the yellow half-moon large and low;
And the startled little waves that leap
In fiery ringlets from their sleep,
As I gain the cove with pushing prow,
And quench its speed i' the slushy sand.

II

Then a mile of warm sea-scented beach;
Three fields to cross till a farm appears;
A tap at the pane, the quick sharp scratch
And blue spurt of a lighted match,
And a voice less loud, thro' its joys and fears,
Than the two hearts beating each to each!

PARTING AT MORNING

ROUND the cape of a sudden came the sea,
And the sun looked over the mountain's rim:
And straight was a path of gold for him,
And the need of a world of men for me.

NATIONALITY IN DRINKS

I

My heart sank with our Claret-flask,
   Just now, beneath the heavy sedges
That serve this pond's black face for mask
   And still at yonder broken edges
O' the hole, where up the bubbles glisten,
After my heart I look and listen.

II

Our laughing little flask, compelled
   Thro' depth to depth more bleak and shady;
As when, both arms beside her held,
   Feet straightened out, some gay French lady   10
Is caught up from life's light and motion,
And dropped into death's silent ocean!

Up jumped Tokay on our table,
Like a pygmy castle-warder,
Dwarfish to see, but stout and able,
Arms and accoutrements all in order;
And fierce he looked North, then, wheeling South,
Blew with his bugle a challenge to Drouth,
Cocked his flap-hat with the tosspot-feather,
Twisted his thumb in his red moustache,   20
Jingled his huge brass spurs together,
Tightened his waist with its Buda sash,
And then, with an impudence naught could abash
Shrugged his hump-shoulder, to tell the beholder,
For twenty such knaves he should laugh but the bolder
And so, with his sword-hilt gallantly jutting,
And dexter-hand on his haunch abutting,
Went the little man, Sir Ausbruch, strutting!

Here's to Nelson's memory!
'Tis the second time that I, at sea,   30
Right off Cape Trafalgar here,
Have drunk it deep in British Beer.
Nelson for ever—any time

Am I his to command in prose or rhyme!
Give me of Nelson only a touch,
And I save it, be it little or much:
Here's one our Captain gives, and so
Down at the word, by George, shall it go!
He says that at Greenwich they point the beholder
To Nelson's coat, "still with tar on the shoulder: 40
For he used to lean with one shoulder digging,
Jigging, as it were, and zig-zag-zigging
Up against the mizen-rigging!"

TIME'S REVENGES

I'VE a Friend, over the sea;
I like him, but he loves me.
It all grew out of the books I write;
They find such favor in his sight
That he slaughters you with savage looks
Because you don't admire my books.
He does himself though,—and if some vein
Were to snap to-night in this heavy brain,
To-morrow month, if I lived to try,
Round should I just turn quietly,   10
Or out of the bedclothes stretch my hand
Till I found him, come from his foreign land,
To be my nurse in this poor place,
And make my broth and wash my face
And light my fire, and, all the while,
Bear with his old good-humored smile
That I told him "Better have kept away
Than come and kill me, night and day,
With, worse than fever throbs and shoots,
The creaking of his clumsy boots."   20
I am as sure that this he would do,
As that Saint Paul's is striking two.
And I think I rather . . . woe is me!
—Yes, rather would see him than not see,
If lifting a hand could seat him there
Before me in the empty chair
To-night, when my head aches indeed,
And I can neither think nor read

Nor make these purple fingers hold
The pen; this garret's freezing cold!   30

And I've a Lady—there he wakes,
The laughing fiend and prince of snakes
Within me, at her name, to pray
Fate send some creature in the way
Of my love for her, to be down-torn,
Upthrust and outward-borne,
So I might prove myself that sea
Of passion which I needs must be!
Call my thoughts false and my fancies quaint
And my style infirm and its figures faint,   40
All the critics say, and more blame yet,
And not one angry word you get.
But, please you, wonder I would put
My cheek beneath that lady's foot
Rather than trample under mine
The laurels of the Florentine,
And you shall see how the devil spends
A fire God gave for other ends!
I tell you, I stride up and down
This garret, crowned with love's best crown,   50
And feasted with love's perfect feast,
To think I kill for her, at least,
Body and soul and peace and fame,
Alike youth's end and manhood's aim,
—So is my spirit, as flesh with sin,
Filled full, eaten out and in
With the face of her, the eyes of her,
The lips, the little chin, the stir
Of shadow round her mouth; and she
—I'll tell you,—calmly would decree   60
That I should roast at a slow fire,
If that would compass her desire
And make her one whom they invite
To the famous ball to-morrow night.

There may be heaven; there must be hell;
Meantime, there is our earth here—well!

THE GLOVE

(PETER RONSARD *loquitur*)

"HEIGHO!" yawned one day King Francis,
"Distance all value enhances!
When a man's busy, why, leisure
Strikes him as wonderful pleasure:
'Faith, and at leisure once is he?
Straightway he wants to be busy.
Here we've got peace; and aghast I'm
Caught thinking war the true pastime.
Is there a reason in metre?
Give us your speech, master Peter!"   10
I who, if mortal dare say so,
Ne'er am at loss with my Naso,
"Sire," I replied, "joys prove cloudlets:
Men are the merest Ixions"—
Here the King whistled aloud. "Let's
—Heigho—go look at our lions!"
Such are the sorrowful chances
If you talk fine to King Francis.

And so, to the courtyard proceeding,
Our company, Francis was leading,   20
Increased by new followers tenfold
Before he arrived at the penfold;
Lords, ladies, like clouds which bedizen
At sunset the western horizon.
And Sir De Lorge pressed 'mid the foremost
With the dame he professed to adore most.
Oh, what a face! One by fits eyed
Her, and the horrible pitside;
For the penfold surrounded a hollow
Which led where the eye scarce dared follow,   30
And shelved to the chamber secluded
Where Bluebeard, the great lion, brooded.
The King hailed his keeper, an Arab
As glossy and black as a scarab,
And bade him make sport and at once stir
Up and out of his den the old monster.
They opened a hole in the wire-work

Across it, and dropped there a firework,
And fled: one's heart's beating redoubled;
A pause, while the pit's mouth was troubled,   40
The blackness and silence so utter,
By the firework's slow sparkling and sputter;
Then earth in a sudden contortion
Gave out to our gaze her abortion.
Such a brute! Were I friend Clement Marot
(Whose experience of nature's but narrow,
And whose faculties move in no small mist
When he versifies David the Psalmist)
I should study that brute to describe you
Illum Juda Leonem de Tribu.   50
One's whole blood grew curdling and creepy
To see the black mane, vast and heapy,
The tail in the air stiff and straining,
The wide eyes, nor waxing nor waning,
As over the barrier which bounded
His platform, and us who surrounded
The barrier, they reached and they rested
On space that might stand him in best stead:
For who knew, he thought, what the amazement,
The eruption of clatter and blaze meant,   60
And if, in this minute of wonder,
No outlet, 'mid lightning and thunder,
Lay broad, and, his shackles all shivered,
The lion at last was delivered?
Ay, that was the open sky o'erhead!
And you saw by the flash on his forehead,
By the hope in those eyes wide and steady,
He was leagues in the desert already,
Driving the flocks up the mountain,
Or catlike couched hard by the fountain   70
To waylay the date-gathering negress:
So guarded he entrance or egress.
"How he stands!" quoth the King: "we may well swear,
(No novice, we've won our spurs elsewhere
And so can afford the confession,)
We exercise wholesome discretion
In keeping aloof from his threshold;
Once hold you, those jaws want no fresh hold,
Their first would too pleasantly purloin
The visitor's brisket or surloin: 80

But who's he would prove so fool-hardy?
Not the best man of Marignan, pardie!"

The sentence no sooner was uttered,
Than over the rails a glove fluttered,
Fell close to the lion, and rested:
The dame 'twas, who flung it and jested
With life so, De Lorge had been wooing
For months past; he sat there pursuing
His suit, weighing out with nonchalance
Fine speeches like gold from a balance.   90

Sound the trumpet, no true knight's a tarrier!
De Lorge made one leap at the barrier,
Walked straight to the glove,—while the lion
Ne'er moved, kept his far-reaching eye on
The palm-tree-edged desert-spring's sapphire,
And the musky oiled skin of the Kaffir,—
Picked it up, and as calmly retreated,
Leaped back where the lady was seated,
And full in the face of its owner
Flung the glove.

    "Your heart's queen, you dethrone her?   100
So should I!"—cried the King—"'twas mere vanity,
Not love, set that task to humanity!"
Lords and ladies alike turned with loathing
From such a proved wolf in sheep's clothing.

Not so, I; for I caught an expression
In her brow's undisturbed self-possession
Amid the Court's scoffing and merriment,—
As if from no pleasing experiment
She rose, yet of pain not much heedful
So long as the process was needful,—   110
As if she had tried in a crucible,
To what "speeches like gold" were reducible,
And, finding the finest prove copper,
Felt the smoke in her face was but proper;
To know what she had *not* to trust to,
Was worth all the ashes and dust too.
She went out 'mid hooting and laughter;
Clement Marot stayed: I followed after,

And asked, as a grace, what it all meant?
If she wished not the rash deed's recallment?   120
"For I"—so I spoke—"am a poet:
Human nature,—behoves that I know it!"

She told me, "Too long had I heard
Of the deed proved alone by the word:
For my love—what De Lorge would not dare!
With my scorn—what De Lorge could compare!
And the endless descriptions of death
He would brave when my lip formed a breath,
I must reckon as braved, or, of course,
Doubt his word—and moreover, perforce,   130
For such gifts as no lady could spurn,
Must offer my love in return.
When I looked on your lion, it brought
All the dangers at once to my thought,
Encountered by all sorts of men,
Before he was lodged in his den,—
From the poor slave whose club or bare hands
Dug the trap, set the snare on the sands,
With no King and no Court to applaud,
By no shame, should he shrink, overawed,   140
Yet to capture the creature made shift,
That his rude boys might laugh at the gift,
—To the page who last leaped o'er the fence
Of the pit, on no greater pretence
Than to get back the bonnet he dropped,
Lest his pay for a week should be stopped.
So, wiser I judged it to make
One trial what 'death for my sake'
Really meant, while the power was yet mine,
Than to wait until time should define   150
Such a phrase not so simply as I,
Who took it to mean just 'to die.'
The blow a glove gives is but weak:
Does the mark yet discolor my cheek?
But when the heart suffers a blow,
Will the pain pass so soon, do you know?"

I looked, as away she was sweeping,
And saw a youth eagerly keeping
As close as he dared to the doorway.

No doubt that a noble should more weigh   160
His life than befits a plebeian;
And yet, had our brute been Nemean—
(I judge by a certain calm fervor
The youth stepped with, forward to serve her)
—He'd have scarce thought you did him the worst turn
If you whispered "Friend, what you'd get, first earn!"
And when, shortly after, she carried
Her shame from the Court, and they married,
To that marriage some happiness, maugre
The voice of the Court, I dared augur.   170

For De Lorge, he made women with men vie,
Those in wonder and praise, these in envy;
And in short stood so plain a head taller
That he wooed and won . . . How do you call her?
The beauty, that rose in the sequel
To the King's love, who loved her a week well.
And 'twas noticed he never would honor
De Lorge (who looked daggers upon her)
With the easy commission of stretching
His legs in the service, and fetching   180
His wife, from her chamber, those straying
Sad gloves she was always mislaying,
While the King took the closet to chat in,—
But of course this adventure came pat in.
And never the King told the story,
How bringing a glove brought such glory,
But the wife smiled—"His nerves are grown firmer:
Mine he brings now and utters no murmur."

Venienti occurrite morbo!
With which moral I drop my theorbo.   190

A SOUL'S TRAGEDY [1846]

**ACT FIRST, BEING WHAT WAS CALLED THE POETRY OF
CHIAPPINO'S LIFE: AND ACT SECOND, ITS PROSE**

PERSONS

LUITOLFO *and* EULALIA, *betrothed lovers*
CHIAPPINO, *their friend*
OGNIBEN, *the Pope's Legate*
Citizens of Faenza
TIME, 15—   PLACE, *Faenza*

ACT I

SCENE—*Inside* LUITOLFO'S *house*.

CHIAPPINO, EULALIA

Eulalia. What is it keeps Luitolfo? Night's fast falling,
And 'twas scarce sunset . . . had the ave-bell
Sounded before he sought the Provost's house?
I think not: all he had to say would take
Few minutes, such a very few, to say!
How do you think, Chiappino? If our lord
The Provost were less friendly to your friend
Than everybody here professes him,
I should begin to tremble—should not you?
Why are you silent when so many times   10
I turn and speak to you?
   Chiappino.   That's good!
   Eulalia.   You laugh!
   Chiappino. Yes. I had fancied nothing that bears price
In the whole world was left to call my own;
And, may be, felt a little pride thereat.
Up to a single man's or woman's love,

161

Down to the right in my own flesh and blood,
There's nothing mine, I fancied,—till you spoke:
—Counting, you see, as "nothing" the permission
To study this peculiar lot of mine
In silence: well, go silence with the rest   20
Of the world's good! What can I say, shall serve?
 Eulalia. This,—lest you, even more than needs, embitter
Our parting: say your wrongs have cast, for once,
A cloud across your spirit!
 Chiappino.   How a cloud?
 Eulalia. No man nor woman loves you, did you say?
 Chiappino. My God, were't not for thee!
 Eulalia.   Ay, God remains,
Even did men forsake you.
 Chiappino.   Oh, not so!
Were't not for God, I mean, what hope of truth—
Speaking truth, hearing truth, would stay with man?
I, now—the homeless friendless penniless   30
Proscribed and exiled wretch who speak to you,—
Ought to speak truth, yet could not, for my death,
(The thing that tempts me most) help speaking lies
About your friendship and Luitolfo's courage
And all our townsfolk's equanimity—
Through sheer incompetence to rid myself
Of the old miserable lying trick
Caught from the liars I have lived with,—God,
Did I not turn to thee! It is thy prompting
I dare to be ashamed of, and thy counsel   40
Would die along my coward lip, I know.
But I do turn to thee. This craven tongue,
These features which refuse the soul its way,
Reclaim thou! Give me truth—truth, power to speak—
And after be sole present to approve
The spoken truth! Or, stay, that spoken truth,
Who knows but you, too, may approve?
 Eulalia.   Ah, well—
Keep silence then, Chiappino!
 Chiappino.   You would hear,
You shall now,—why the thing we please to style
My gratitude to you and all your friends   50
For service done me, is just gratitude
So much as yours was service: no whit more.

I was born here, so was Luitolfo; both
At one time, much with the same circumstance
Of rank and wealth; and both, up to this night
Of parting company, have side by side
Still fared, he in the sunshine—I, the shadow.
"Why?" asks the world. "Because," replies the world
To its complacent self, "these playfellows,
Who took at church the holy-water drop   60
Each from the other's finger, and so forth,—
Were of two moods: Luitolfo was the proper
Friend-making, everywhere friend-finding soul,
Fit for the sunshine, so, it followed him.
A happy-tempered bringer of the best
Out of the worst; who bears with what's past cure,
And puts so good a face on't—wisely passive
Where action's fruitless, while he remedies
In silence what the foolish rail against;
A man to smooth such natures as parade   70
Of opposition must exasperate;
No general gauntlet-gatherer for the weak
Against the strong, yet over-scrupulous
At lucky junctures; one who won't forego
The after-battle work of binding wounds,
Because, forsooth he'd have to bring himself
To side with wound-inflictors for their leave!"
—Why do you gaze, nor help me to repeat
What comes so glibly from the common mouth,
About Luitolfo and his so-styled friend?   80
    Eulalia. Because that friend's sense is obscured . . .
    Chiappino.   I thought
You would be readier with the other half
Of the world's story, my half! Yet, 'tis true,
For all the world does say it. Say your worst!
True, I thank God, I ever said "you sin,"
When a man did sin: if I could not say it,
I glared it at him; if I could not glare it,
I prayed against him; then my part seemed over.
God's may begin yet: so it will, I trust.
    Eulalia. If the world outraged you, did we?
    Chiappino.   What's "me"   90
That you use well or ill? It's man, in me,
All your successes are an outrage to,

You all, whom sunshine follows, as you say!
Here's our Faenza birthplace; they send here
A provost from Ravenna: how he rules,
You can at times be eloquent about.
"Then, end his rule!"—"Ah yes, one stroke does that!
But patience under wrong works slow and sure.
Must violence still bring peace forth? He, beside,
Returns so blandly one's obeisance! ah—   100
Some latent virtue may be lingering yet,
Some human sympathy which, once excite,
And all the lump were leavened quietly:
So, no more talk of striking, for this time!"
But I, as one of those he rules, won't bear
These pretty takings-up and layings-down
Our cause, just as you think occasion suits.
Enough of earnest, is there? You'll play, will you?
Diversify your tactics, give submission,
Obsequiousness and flattery a turn,   110
While we die in our misery patient deaths?
We all are outraged then, and I the first:
I, for mankind, resent each shrug and smirk,
Each beck and bend, each . . . all you do and are,
I hate!
   Eulalia. We share a common censure, then.
'Tis well you have not poor Luitolfo's part
Nor mine to point out in the wide offence.
   Chiappino. Oh, shall I let you so escape me, lady?
Come, on your own ground, lady,—from yourself,
(Leaving the people's wrong, which most is mine)   120
What have I got to be so grateful for?
These three last fines, no doubt, one on the other
Paid by Luitolfo?
   Eulalia.   Shame, Chiappino!
   Chiappino.   Shame
Fall presently on who deserves it most!
—Which is to see. He paid my fines—my friend,
Your prosperous smooth lover presently,
Then, scarce your wooer,—soon, your husband: well—
I loved you.
   Eulalia. Hold!
   Chiappino.   You knew it, years ago.
When my voice faltered and my eye grew dim
Because you gave me your silk mask to hold—   130

My voice that greatens when there's need to curse
The people's Provost to their heart's content,
—My eye, the Provost, who bears all men's eyes,
Banishes now because he cannot bear,—
You knew . . . but you do your parts—my part, I:
So be it! You flourish, I decay: all's well.
   Eulalia. I hear this for the first time.
   Chiappino.   The fault's there?
Then my days spoke not, and my nights of fire
Were voiceless? Then the very heart may burst,
Yet all prove naught, because no mincing speech   140
Tells leisurely that thus it is and thus?
Eulalia, truce with toying for this once!
A banished fool, who troubles you to-night
For the last time—why, what's to fear from me?
You knew I loved you!
   Eulalia.   Not so, on my faith!
You were my now-affianced lover's friend—
Came in, went out with him, could speak as he.
All praise your ready parts and pregnant wit;
See how your words come from you in a crowd!
Luitolfo's first to place you o'er himself   150
In all that challenges respect and love:
Yet you were silent then, who blame me now.
I say all this by fascination, sure:
I, all but wed to one I love, yet listen!
It must be, you are wronged, and that the wrongs
Luitolfo pities . . .
   Chiappino.   —You too pity? Do!
But hear first what my wrongs are; so began
This talk and so shall end this talk. I say,
Was't not enough that I must strive (I saw)
To grow so far familiar with your charms   160
As next contrive some way to win them—which
To do, an age seemed far too brief—for, see!
We all aspire to heaven; and there lies heaven
Above us: go there! Dare we go? no, surely!
How dare we go without a reverent pause,
A growing less unfit for heaven? Just so,
I dared not speak: the greater fool, it seems!
Was't not enough to struggle with such folly,
But I must have, beside, the very man
Whose slight free loose and incapacious soul   170

Gave his tongue scope to say whate'er he would
—Must have him load me with his benefits
—For fortune's fiercest stroke?

    Eulalia.   Justice to him
That's now entreating, at his risk perhaps,
Justice for you! Did he once call those acts
Of simple friendship—bounties, benefits?

    Chiappino. No: the straight course had been to call them thus.
Then, I had flung them back, and kept myself
Unhampered, free as he to win the prize
We both sought. But "the gold was dross," he said: 180
"He loved me, and I loved him not: why spurn
A trifle out of superfluity?
He had forgotten he had done as much."
So had not I! Henceforth, try as I could
To take him at his word, there stood by you
My benefactor; who might speak and laugh
And urge his nothings, even banter me
Before you—but my tongue was tied. A dream!
Let's wake: your husband . . . how you shake at that!
Good—my revenge!

    Eulalia.   Why should I shake? What forced   190
Or forces me to be Luitolfo's bride?

    Chiappino. There's my revenge, that nothing forces you.
No gratitude, no liking of the eye
Nor longing of the heart, but the poor bond
Of habit—here so many times he came,
So much he spoke,—all these compose the tie
That pulls you from me. Well, he paid my fines,
Nor missed a cloak from wardrobe, dish from table;
He spoke a good word to the Provost here,
Held me up when my fortunes fell away   200
—It had not looked so well to let me drop—
Men take pains to preserve a tree-stump, even,
Whose boughs they played beneath—much more a friend
But one grows tired of seeing, after the first,
Pains spent upon impracticable stuff
Like me. I could not change: you know the rest.
I've spoke my mind too fully out, by chance,
This morning to our Provost; so, ere night
I leave the city on pain of death. And now
On my account there's gallant intercession   210
Goes forward—that's so graceful!—and anon

He'll noisily come back: "the intercession
Was made and fails; all's over for us both;
'Tis vain contending; I would better go."
And I do go—and straight to you he turns
Light of a load; and ease of that permits
His visage to repair the natural bland
Œconomy, sore broken late to suit
My discontent. Thus, all are pleased—you, with him,
He with himself, and all of you with me   220
—"Who," say the citizens, "had done far better
In letting people sleep upon their woes,
If not possessed with talent to relieve them
When once awake;—but then I had," they'll say,
"Doubtless some unknown compensating pride
In what I did; and as I seem content
With ruining myself, why, so should they be."
And so they are, and so be with his prize
The devil, when he gets them speedily!
Why does not your Luitolfo come? I long   230
To don this cloak and take the Lugo path.
It seems you never loved me, then?
    Eulalia.   Chiappino!
    Chiappino. Never?
    Eulalia.   Never.
    Chiappino.   That's sad. Say what I might,
There was no help from being sure this while
You loved me. Love like mine must have return,
I thought: no river starts but to some sea.
And had you loved me, I could soon devise
Some specious reason why you stifled love,
Some fancied self-denial on your part,
Which made you choose Luitolfo; so, excepting   240
From the wide condemnation of all here,
One woman. Well, the other dream may break!
If I knew any heart, as mine loved you,
Loved me, though in the vilest breast 'twere lodged,
I should, I think, be forced to love again:
Else there's no right nor reason in the world.
    Eulalia. "If you knew," say you,—but I did not know.
That's where you're blind, Chiappino!—a disease
Which if I may remove, I'll not repent
The listening to. You cannot, will not, see   250
How, place you but in every circumstance

Of us, you are just now indignant at,
You'd be as we.
    Chiappino.   I should be? . . . that; again!
I, to my friend, my country and my love,
Be as Luitolfo and these Faentines?
    Eulalia. As we.
    Chiappino.   Now, I'll say something to remember.
I trust in nature for the stable laws
Of beauty and utility.—Spring shall plant,
And Autumn garner to the end of time:
I trust in God—the right shall be the right   260
And other than the wrong, while he endures:
I trust in my own soul, that can perceive
The outward and the inward, nature's good
And God's: so, seeing these men and myself,
Having a right to speak, thus do I speak.
I'll not curse—God bears with them, well may I—
But I—protest against their claiming me.
I simply say, if that's allowable,
I would not (broadly) do as they have done.
—God curse this townful of born slaves, bred slaves, 270
Branded into the blood and bone, slaves! Curse
Whoever loves, above his liberty,
House, land or life! and . . .   [*A knocking without.*
           —bless my hero-friend,
Luitolfo!
    Eulalia. How he knocks!
    Chiappino.   The peril, lady!
"Chiappino, I have run a risk—a risk!
For when I prayed the Provost (he's my friend)
To grant you a week's respite of the sentence
That confiscates your goods, exiles yourself,
He shrugged his shoulder—I say, shrugged it! Yes,
And fright of that drove all else from my head.   280
Here's a good purse of *scudi:* off with you,
Lest of that shrug come what God only knows!
The *scudi*—friend, they're trash—no thanks, I beg!
Take the north gate,—for San Vitale's suburb,
Whose double taxes you appealed against,
In discomposure at your ill-success
Is apt to stone you: there, there—only go!
Beside, Eulalia here looks sleepily.

Shake . . . oh, you hurt me, so you squeeze my wrist!"
—Is it not thus you'll speak, adventurous friend?   290

[*As he opens the door,* LUITOLFO *rushes in,
his garments disordered.*

   Eulalia. Luitolfo! Blood?
   Luitolfo.   There's more—and more of it!
Eulalia—take the garment! No—you, friend!
You take it and the blood from me—you dare!
   Eulalia. Oh, who has hurt you? where's the wound?
   Chiappino.   "Who," say you?
The man with many a touch of virtue yet!
The Provost's friend has proved too frank of speech,
And this comes of it. Miserable hound!
This comes of temporizing, as I said!
Here's fruit of your smooth speeches and soft looks!
Now see my way! As God lives, I go straight   300
To the palace and do justice, once for all!
   Luitolfo. What says he?
   Chiappino.   I'll do justice on him.
   Luitolfo.   Him?
   Chiappino. The Provost.
   Luitolfo.   I've just killed him.
   Eulalia.   Oh, my God!
   Luitolfo. My friend, they're on my trace; they'll have me—now!
They're round him, busy with him: soon they'll find
He's past their help, and then they'll be on me!
Chiappino, save Eulalia! I forget . . .
Were you not bound for . . .
   Chiappino.   Lugo?
   Luitolfo.   Ah—yes—yes!
That was the point I prayed of him to change.
Well, go—be happy! Is Eulalia safe?   310
They're on me!
   Chiappino. 'Tis through me they reach you, then!
Friend, seem the man you are! Lock arms—that's right!
Now tell me what you've done; explain how you
That still professed forbearance, still preached peace,
Could bring yourself . . .
   Luitolfo.   What was peace for, Chiappino?
I tried peace: did that promise, when peace failed,
Strife should not follow? All my peaceful days
Were just the prelude to a day like this.

I cried "You call me 'friend': save my true friend!
Save him, or lose me!"
 Chiappino.   But you never said   320
You meant to tell the Provost thus and thus.
  Luitolfo. Why should I say it? What else did I mean?
  Chiappino. Well? He persisted?
  Luitolfo.   —"Would so order it
You should not trouble him too soon again."
I saw a meaning in his eye and lip;
I poured my heart's store of indignant words
Out on him: then—I know not! He retorted,
And I . . . some staff lay there to hand—I think
He bade his servants thrust me out—I struck . . .
Ah, they come! Fly you, save yourselves, you two! 330
The dead back-weight of the beheading axe!
The glowing trip-hook, thumbscrews and the gadge!
  Eulalia. They do come! Torches in the Place! Farewell,
Chiappino! You can work no good to us—
Much to yourself; believe not, all the world
Must needs be cursed henceforth!
  Chiappino.   And you?
  Eulalia.   I stay.
  Chiappino. Ha, ha! Now, listen! I am master here!
This was my coarse disguise; this paper shows
My path of flight and place of refuge—see—
Lugo, Argenta, past San Nicolo,   340
Ferrara, then to Venice and all's safe!
Put on the cloak! His people have to fetch
A compass round about. There's time enough
Ere they can reach us, so you straightway make
For Lugo . . . nay, he hears not! On with it—
The cloak, Luitolfo, do you hear me? See—
He obeys he knows not how. Then, if I must—
Answer me! Do you know the Lugo gate?
  Eulalia. The north-west gate, over the bridge?
  Luitolfo.   I know.
  Chiappino. Well, there—you are not frightened? all my 350
  route
Is traced in that: at Venice you escape
Their power. Eulalia, I am master here!
     [*Shouts from without. He pushes out* LUITOLFO,
          who complies mechanically.
In time! Nay, help me with him—so! He's gone.

Eulalia. What have you done? On you, perchance, all know
The Provost's hater, will men's vengeance fall
As our accomplice.
    Chiappino.   Mere accomplice? See!
                                [*Putting on* LUITOLFO'S *vest.*
Now, lady, am I true to my profession,
Or one of these?
    Eulalia.   You take Luitolfo's place?
    Chiappino. Die for him.
    Eulalia.   Well done!
                                 [*Shouts increase.*
    Chiappino.   How the people tarry!
I can't be silent; I must speak: or sing—   360
How natural to sing now!
    Eulalia.   Hush and pray!
We are to die; but even I perceive
'Tis not a very hard thing so to die.
My cousin of the pale-blue tearful eyes,
Poor Cesca, suffers more from one day's life
With the stern husband; Tisbe's heart goes forth
Each evening after that wild son of hers,
To track his thoughtless footstep through the streets:
How easy for them both to die like this!
I am not sure that I could live as they.   370
    Chiappino. Here they come, crowds! They pass the gate? Yes!
—No!—
One torch is in the courtyard. Here flock all.
    Eulalia. At least Luitolfo has escaped. What cries!
    Chiappino. If they would drag one to the market-place,
One might speak there!
    Eulalia.   List, list!
    Chiappino.   They mount the steps.

Enter the Populace.

    Chiappino. I killed the Provost!
    The Populace [*speaking together*]. 'Twas Chiappino, friends!
Our savior! The best man at last as first!
He who first made us feel what chains we wore,
He also strikes the blow that shatters them,
He at last saves us—our best citizen!   380
—Oh, have you only courage to speak now?

My eldest son was christened a year since
"Cino" to keep Chiappino's name in mind—
Cino, for shortness merely, you observe!
The city's in our hands. The guards are fled.
Do you, the cause of all, come down—come up—
Come out to counsel us, our chief, our king,
Whate'er rewards you! Choose your own reward!
The peril over, its reward begins!
Come and harangue us in the market-place!   390
 Eulalia. Chiappino?
 Chiappino.   Yes—I understand your eyes!
You think I should have promptlier disowned
This deed with its strange unforeseen success,
In favor of Luitolfo. But the peril,
So far from ended, hardly seems begun.
To-morrow, rather, when a calm succeeds,
We easily shall make him full amends:
And meantime—if we save them as they pray,
And justify the deed by its effects?
 Eulalia. You would, for worlds, you had denied at once.   400
 Chiappino. I know my own intention, be assured!
All's well. Precede us, fellow-citizens!

ACT II

SCENE—*The market-place.* LUITOLFO *in disguise mingling with
the* Populace *assembled opposite the* Provost's *Palace.*

 1st Bystander [*to* LUITOLFO]. You, a friend of Luitolfo's? Then,
your friend is vanished,—in all probability killed on the night
that his patron the tyrannical Provost was loyally suppressed here,
exactly a month ago, by our illustrious fellow-citizen, thrice-noble
savior, and new Provost that is like to be, this very morning,—
Chiappino!
 Luitolfo. He the new Provost?
 2nd Bystander. Up those steps will he go, and beneath yonder
pillar stand, while Ogniben, the Pope's Legate from Ravenna,
reads the new dignitary's title to the people, according to   10
established custom: for which reason, there is the assemblage
you inquire about.
 Luitolfo. Chiappino—the late Provost's successor? Impossible!

But tell me of that presently. What I would know first of all is, wherefore Luitolfo must so necessarily have been killed on that memorable night?

3rd Bystander. You were Luitolfo's friend? So was I. Never, if you will credit me, did there exist so poor-spirited a milksop. He, with all the opportunities in the world, furnished by daily converse with our oppressor, would not stir a finger to help 20 us: and, when Chiappino rose in solitary majesty and . . . how does one go on saying? . . . dealt the godlike blow,—this Luitolfo, not unreasonably fearing the indignation of an aroused and liberated people, fled precipitately. He may have got trodden to death in the press at the south-east gate, when the Provost's guards fled through it to Ravenna, with their wounded master,— if he did not rather hang himself under some hedge.

Luitolfo. Or why not simply have lain perdue in some quiet corner,—such as San Cassiano, where his estate was,—receiving daily intelligence from some sure friend, meanwhile, as to 30 the turn matters were taking here—how, for instance, the Provost was not dead, after all, only wounded—or, as to-day's news would seem to prove, how Chiappino was not Brutus the Elder, after all, only the new Provost—and thus Luitolfo be enabled to watch a favorable opportunity for returning? Might it not have been so?

3rd Bystander. Why, he may have taken that care of himself, certainly, for he came of a cautious stock. I'll tell you how his uncle, just such another gingerly treader on tiptoes with finger on lip,—how he met his death in the great plague-year: 40 *dico vobis!* Hearing that the seventeenth house in a certain street was infected, he calculates to pass it in safety by taking plentiful breath, say, when he shall arrive at the eleventh house; then scouring by, holding that breath, till he be got so far on the other side as number twenty-three, and thus elude the danger.— And so did he begin; but, as he arrived at thirteen, we will say,— thinking to improve on his precaution by putting up a little prayer to St. Nepomucene of Prague, this exhausted so much of his lungs' reserve, that at sixteen it was clean spent,—conse- quently at the fatal seventeen he inhaled with a vigor and 50 persistence enough to suck you any latent venom out of the heart of a stone— Ha, ha!

Luitolfo [aside]. (If I had not lent that man the money he wanted last spring, I should fear this bitterness was attributable to me.) Luitolfo is dead then, one may conclude?

3rd Bystander. Why, he had a house here, and a woman to whom he was affianced; and as they both pass naturally to the new Provost, his friend and heir . . .

Luitolfo. Ah, I suspected you of imposing on me with your pleasantry! I know Chiappino better.   60

1st Bystander. (Our friend has the bile! After all, I do not dislike finding somebody vary a little this general gape of admiration at Chiappino's glorious qualities.) Pray, how much may you know of what has taken place in Faenza since that memorable night?

Luitolfo. It is most to the purpose, that I know Chiappino to have been by profession a hater of that very office of Provost, you now charge him with proposing to accept.

1st Bystander. Sir, I'll tell you. That night was indeed memorable. Up we rose, a mass of us, men, women, children; out   70
fled the guards with the body of the tyrant; we were to defy the world: but, next gray morning, "What will Rome say?" began everybody. You know we are governed by Ravenna, which is governed by Rome. And quietly into the town, by the Ravenna road, comes on muleback a portly personage, Ogniben by name, with the quality of Pontifical Legate; trots briskly through the streets humming a *"Cur fremuere gentes,"* and makes directly for the Provost's Palace—there it faces you. "One Messer Chiappino is your leader? I have known three-and-twenty leaders of revolts!" (laughing gently to himself)—"Give me the help of your   80
arm from my mule to yonder steps under the pillar— So! And now, my revolters and good friends, what do you want? The guards burst into Ravenna last night bearing your wounded Provost; and, having had a little talk with him, I take on myself to come and try appease the disorderliness, before Rome, hearing of it, resort to another method: 'tis I come, and not another, from a certain love I confess to, of composing differences. So, do you understand, you are about to experience this unheard-of tyranny from me, that there shall be no heading nor hanging, no confiscation nor exile: I insist on your simply pleasing   90
yourselves. And now, pray, what does please you? To live without any government at all? Or having decided for one, to see its minister murdered by the first of your body that chooses to find himself wronged, or disposed for reverting to first principles and a justice anterior to all institutions,—and so will you carry matters, that the rest of the world must at length unite and put down such a den of wild beasts? As for vengeance on what has just taken place,—once for all, the wounded man assures me he

cannot conjecture who struck him; and this so earnestly, that
one may be sure he knows perfectly well what intimate   100
acquaintance could find admission to speak with him late last
evening. I come not for vengeance therefore, but from pure
curiosity to hear what you will do next." And thus he ran on, on,
easily and volubly, till he seemed to arrive quite naturally at the
praise of law, order, and paternal government by somebody from
rather a distance. All our citizens were in the snare, and about
to be friends with so congenial an adviser; but that Chiappino
suddenly stood forth, spoke out indignantly, and set things right
again.

    Luitolfo. Do you see? I recognize him there!   110

    3rd Bystander. Ay but, mark you, at the end of Chiappino's
longest period in praise of a pure republic,—"And by whom do
I desire such a government should be administered, perhaps, but
by one like yourself?"—returns the Legate: thereupon speaking
for a quarter of an hour together, on the natural and only legiti-
mate government by the best and wisest. And it should seem
there was soon discovered to be no such vast discrepancy at
bottom between this and Chiappino's theory, place but each in
its proper light. "Oh, are you there?" quoth Chiappino: "Ay, in
that, I agree," returns Chiappino: and so on.   120

    Luitolfo. But did Chiappino cede at once to this?

    1st Bystander. Why, not altogether at once. For instance, he
said that the difference between him and all his fellows was,
that they seemed all wishing to be kings in one or another way,—
"whereas what right," asked he, "has any man to wish to be
superior to another?"—whereat, "Ah, sir," answers the Legate,
"this is the death of me, so often as I expect something is really
going to be revealed to us by you clearer-seers, deeper-thinkers
—this—that your right-hand (to speak by a figure) should be
found taking up the weapon it displayed so ostentatiously,   130
not to destroy any dragon in our path, as was prophesied, but
simply to cut off its own fellow left-hand: yourself set about at-
tacking yourself. For see now! Here are you who, I make sure,
glory exceedingly in knowing the noble nature of the soul, its
divine impulses, and so forth; and with such a knowledge you
stand, as it were, armed to encounter the natural doubts and
fears as to that same inherent nobility, which are apt to waylay
us, the weaker ones, in the road of life. And when we look
eagerly to see them fall before you, lo, round you wheel, only the
left-hand gets the blow; one proof of the soul's nobility de-   140
stroys simply another proof, quite as good, of the same, for you

are found delivering an opinion like this! Why, what is this perpetual yearning to exceed, to subdue, to be better than, and a king over, one's fellow,—all that you so disclaim,—but the very tendency yourself are most proud of, and under another form, would oppose to it,—only in a lower stage of manifestation? You don't want to be vulgarly superior to your fellows after their poor fashion—to have me hold solemnly up your gown's tail, or hand you an express of the last importance from the Pope, with all these bystanders noticing how unconcerned you look the 150 while: but neither does our gaping friend, the burgess yonder, want the other kind of kingship, that consists in understanding better than his fellows this and similar points of human nature, nor to roll under his tongue this sweeter morsel still,—the feeling that, through immense philosophy, he does *not* feel, he rather thinks, above you and me!" And so chatting, they glided off arm-in-arm.

Luitolfo. And the result is . . .

1st Bystander. Why that, a month having gone by, the indomitable Chiappino, marrying as he will Luitolfo's love—at all 160 events succeeding to Luitolfo's wealth—becomes the first inhabitant of Faenza, and a proper aspirant to the Provostship; which we assemble here to see conferred on him this morning. The Legate's Guard to clear the way! He will follow presently.

Luitolfo [withdrawing a little]. I understand the drift of Eulalia's communications less than ever. Yet she surely said, in so many words, that Chiappino was in urgent danger: wherefore, disregarding her injunction to continue in my retreat and await the result of—what she called, some experiment yet in process— I hastened here without her leave or knowledge: how could 170 I else? But if this they say be true—if it were for such a purpose, she and Chiappino kept me away . . . Oh, no, no! I must confront him and her before I believe this of them. And at the word, see!

Enter CHIAPPINO *and* EULALIA.

Eulalia. We part here, then? The change in your principles would seem to be complete.

Chiappino. Now, why refuse to see that in my present course I change no principles, only re-adapt them and more adroitly? I had despaired of, what you may call the material instrumentality of life; of ever being able to rightly operate on mankind 180 through such a deranged machinery as the existing modes of government: but now, if I suddenly discover how to inform these perverted institutions with fresh purpose, bring the functionary limbs once more into immediate communication with, and subjection to, the soul I am about to bestow on them—do you see? Why should one desire to invent, as long as it remains possible to renew and transform? When all further hope of the old organization shall be extinct, then, I grant you, it may be time to try and create another.

Eulalia. And there being discoverable some hope yet in   190 the hitherto much-abused old system of absolute government by a Provost here, you mean to take your time about endeavoring to realize those visions of a perfect State, we once heard of?

Chiappino. Say, I would fain realize my conception of a palace, for instance, and that there is, abstractedly, but a single way of erecting one perfectly. Here, in the market-place is my allotted building-ground; here I stand without a stone to lay, or a laborer to help me,—stand, too, during a short day of life, close on which the night comes. On the other hand, circumstances suddenly offer me (turn and see it!) the old Provost's house to experiment   200 upon—ruinous, if you please, wrongly constructed at the beginning, and ready to tumble now. But materials abound, a crowd of workmen offer their services; here, exists yet a Hall of Audience of orginally noble proportions, there a Guest-chamber of symmetrical design enough: and I may restore, enlarge, abolish or unite these to heart's content. Ought I not make the best of such an opportunity, rather than continue to gaze disconsolately with folded arms on the flat pavement here, while the sun goes slowly down, never to rise again? Since you cannot understand this nor me, it is better we should part as you desire.   210

Eulalia. So, the love breaks away too!

Chiappino. No, rather my soul's capacity for love widens— needs more than one object to content it,—and, being better instructed, will not persist in seeing all the component parts of love in what is only a single part,—nor in finding that so many and so various loves are all united in the love of a woman,— manifold uses in one instrument, as the savage has his sword, staff, sceptre and idol, all in one club-stick. Love is a very compound thing. The intellectual part of my love I shall give to men, the mighty dead or the illustrious living; and determine to   220 call a mere sensual instinct by as few fine names as possible. What do I lose?

Eulalia. Nay, I only think, what do I lose? and, one more word
—which shall complete my instruction—does friendship go too?
What of Luitolfo, the author of your present prosperity?

Chiappino. How the author?

Eulalia. That blow now called yours . . .

Chiappino. Struck without principle or purpose, as by a blind
natural operation: yet to which all my thought and life directly
and advisedly tended. I would have struck it, and could not: 230
he would have done his utmost to avoid striking it, yet did so. I
dispute his right to that deed of mine—a final action with him,
from the first effect of which he fled away,—a mere first step
with me, on which I base a whole mighty superstructure of good
to follow. Could he get good from it?

Eulalia. So we profess, so we perform!

Enter OGNIBEN. EULALIA *stands apart.*

Ogniben. I have seen three-and-twenty leaders of revolts. By
your leave, sir! Perform? What does the lady say of performing?

Chiappino. Only the trite saying, that we must not trust pro-
fession, only performance.   240

Ogniben. She'll not say that, sir, when she knows you longer;
you'll instruct her better. Ever judge of men by their professions!
For though the bright moment of promising is but a moment and
cannot be prolonged, yet, if sincere in its moment's extravagant
goodness, why, trust it and know the man by it, I say—not by
his performance; which is half the world's work, interfere as the
world needs must, with its accidents and circumstances: the pro-
fession was purely the man's own. I judge people by what they
might be,—not are, nor will be.

Chiappino. But have there not been found, too, perform-   250
ing natures, not merely promising?

Ogniben. Plenty. Little Bindo of our town, for instance,
promised his friend, great ugly Masaccio, once, "I will repay you!"
—for a favor done him. So, when his father came to die, and
Bindo succeeded to the inheritance, he sends straightway for
Masaccio and shares all with him—gives him half the land, half
the money, half the kegs of wine in the cellar. "Good," say you:
and it is good. But had little Bindo found himself possessor of all
this wealth some five years before—on the happy night when
Masaccio procured him that interview in the garden with his   260
pretty cousin Lisa—instead of being the beggar he then was,—I
am bound to believe that in the warm moment of promise he

would have given away all the wine-kegs and all the money and all the land, and only reserved to himself some hut on a hill-top hard by, whence he might spend his life in looking and seeing his friend enjoy himself: he meant fully that much, but the world interfered.—To our business! Did I understand you just now within-doors? You are not going to marry your old friend's love, after all?

Chiappino. I must have a woman that can sympathize 270 with, and appreciate me, I told you.

Ogniben. Oh, I remember! you, the greater nature, needs must have a lesser one (—avowedly lesser—contest with you on that score would never do)—such a nature must comprehend you, as the phrase is, accompany and testify of your greatness from point to point onward. Why, that were being not merely as great as yourself, but greater considerably! Meantime, might not the more bounded nature as reasonably count on your appreciation of it, rather?—on your keeping close by it, so far as you both go together, and then going on by yourself as far as you please? 280 Thus God serves us.

Chiappino. And yet a woman that could understand the whole of me, to whom I could reveal alike the strength and the weakness—

Ogniben. Ah, my friend, wish for nothing so foolish! Worship your love, give her the best of you to see; be to her like the western lands (they bring us such strange news of) to the Spanish Court; send her only your lumps of gold, fans of feathers, your spirit-like birds, and fruits and gems! So shall you, what is unseen of you, be supposed altogether a paradise by her,—as these 290 western lands by Spain: though I warrant there is filth, red baboons, ugly reptiles and squalor enough, which they bring Spain as few samples of as possible. Do you want your mistress to respect your body generally? Offer her your mouth to kiss: don't strip off your boot and put your foot to her lips! You understand my humor by this time? I help men to carry out their own principles: if they please to say two and two make five, I assent, so they will but go on and say, four and four make ten.

Chiappino. But these are my private affairs; what I desire you to occupy yourself about, is my public appearance presently: 300 for when the people hear that I am appointed Provost, though you and I may thoroughly discern—and easily, too—the right principle at bottom of such a movement, and how my republicanism remains thoroughly unaltered, only takes a form of expression hitherto commonly judged (and heretofore by myself) incompatible with its existence,—when thus I reconcile myself to an old form of government instead of proposing a new one . . .

Ogniben. Why, you must deal with people broadly. Begin at a distance from this matter and say,— New truths, old truths! sirs, there is nothing new possible to be revealed to us in the moral world; we know all we shall ever know: and it is for simply reminding us, by their various respective expedients, how we do know this and the other matter, that men get called prophets, poets and the like. A philosopher's life is spent in discovering that, of the half-dozen truths he knew when a child, such an one is a lie, as the world states it in set terms; and then, after a weary lapse of years, and plenty of hard-thinking, it becomes a truth again after all, as he happens to newly consider it and view it in a different relation with the others: and so he restates it, to the confusion of somebody else in good time. As for adding to the original stock of truths,—impossible! Thus, you see the expression of them is the grand business:—you have got a truth in your head about the right way of governing people, and you took a mode of expressing it which now you confess to be imperfect. But what then? There is truth in falsehood, falsehood in truth. No man ever told one great truth, that I know, without the help of a good dozen of lies at least, generally unconscious ones. And as when a child comes in breathlessly and relates a strange story, you try to conjecture from the very falsities in it, what the reality was,—do not conclude that he saw nothing in the sky, because he assuredly did not see a flying horse there as he says,—so, through the contradictory expression, do you see, men should look painfully for, and trust to arrive eventually at, what you call the true principle at bottom. Ah, what an answer is there! to what will it not prove applicable?—"Contradictions? Of course there were," say you!

Chiappino. Still, the world at large may call it inconsistency, and what shall I urge in reply?

Ogniben. Why, look you, when they tax you with tergiversation or duplicity, you may answer—you begin to perceive that, when all's done and said, both great parties in the State, the advocators of change in the present system of things, and the opponents of it, patriot and anti-patriot, are found working together for the common good; and that in the midst of their efforts for and against its progress, the world somehow or other still advances: to which result they contribute in equal proportions, those who spend their life in pushing it onward, as those who give theirs to the business of pulling it back. Now, if you found the world stand still between the opposite forces, and were glad, I should conceive you: but it steadily advances, you rejoice 350 to see! By the side of such a rejoicer, the man who only winks as he keeps cunning and quiet, and says, "Let yonder hot-headed fellow fight out my battle! I, for one, shall win in the end by the blows he gives, and which I ought to be giving"—even he seems graceful in his avowal, when one considers that he might say, "I shall win quite as much by the blows our antagonist gives him, blows from which he saves me—I thank the antagonist equally!" Moreover, you may enlarge on the loss of the edge of party-animosity with age and experience . . .

Chiappino. And naturally time must wear off such asperi- 360 ties: the bitterest adversaries get to discover certain points of similarity between each other, common sympathies—do they not?

Ogniben. Ay, had the young David but sat first to dine on his cheeses with the Philistine, he had soon discovered an abundance of such common sympathies. He of Gath, it is recorded, was born of a father and mother, had brothers and sisters like another man, —they, no more than the sons of Jesse, were used to eat each other. But, for the sake of one broad antipathy that had existed from the beginning, David slung the stone, cut off the giant's head, made a spoil of it, and after ate his cheeses alone, with 370 the better appetite, for all I can learn. My friend, as you, with a quickened eye-sight, go on discovering much good on the worse side, remember that the same process should proportionably mag- nify and demonstrate to you the much more good on the better side! And when I profess no sympathy for the Goliaths of our time, and you object that a large nature should sympathize with every form of intelligence, and see the good in it, however limited —I answer, "So I do; but preserve the proportions of my sym- pathy, however finelier or widelier I may extend its action." I desire to be able, with a quickened eye-sight, to descry 380 beauty in corruption where others see foulness only: but I hope I shall also continue to see a redoubled beauty in the higher forms of matter, where already everybody sees no foulness at all. I must retain, too, my old power of selection, and choice of appropri- ation, to apply to such new gifts; else they only dazzle instead of enlightening me. God has his archangels and consorts with them: though he made too, and intimately sees what is good in, the worm. Observe, I speak only as you profess to think and, so, ought to speak: I do justice to your own principles, that is all.

Chiappino. But you very well know that the two parties 390 do, on occasion, assume each other's characteristics. What more disgusting, for instance, than to see how promptly the newly emancipated slave will adopt, in his own favor, the very measures of precaution, which pressed soreliest on himself as institutions of the tyranny he has just escaped from? Do the classes, hitherto without opinion, get leave to express it? there follows a confederacy immediately, from which—exercise your individual right and dissent, and woe be to you!

Ogniben. And a journey over the sea to you! That is the generous way. Cry—"Emancipated slaves, the first excess, and off 400 I go!" The first time a poor devil, who has been bastinadoed steadily his whole life long, finds himself let alone and able to legislate, so, begins pettishly, while he rubs his soles, "Woe be to whoever brings anything in the shape of a stick this way!"—you, rather than give up the very innocent pleasure of carrying one to switch flies with,—you go away, to everybody's sorrow. Yet you were quite reconciled to staying at home while the governors used to pass, every now and then, some such edict as "Let no man indulge in owning a stick which is not thick enough to chastise our slaves, if need require!" Well, there are preordained 410 hierarchies among us, and a profane vulgar subjected to a different law altogether; yet I am rather sorry you should see it so clearly: for, do you know what is to—all but save you at the Day of Judgment, all you men of genius? It is this: that, while you generally began by pulling down God, and went on to the end of your life, in one effort at setting up your own genius in his place,—still, the last, bitterest concession wrung with the utmost unwillingness from the experience of the very loftiest of you, was invariably—would one think it?—that the rest of mankind, down to the lowest of the mass, stood not, nor ever could stand, 420 just on a level and equality with yourselves. That will be a point in the favor of all such, I hope and believe.

Chiappino. Why, men of genius are usually charged, I think, with doing just the reverse; and at once acknowledging the natural inequality of mankind, by themselves participating in the universal craving after, and deference to, the civil distinctions which represent it. You wonder they pay such undue respect to titles and badges of superior rank.

Ogniben. Not I (always on your own ground and showing, be it noted!) Who doubts that, with a weapon to brandish, a 430 man is the more formidable? Titles and badges are exercised as such a weapon, to which you and I look up wistfully. We could pin lions with it moreover, while in its present owner's hands it hardly prods rats. Nay, better than a mere weapon of easy mas-

tery and obvious use, it is a mysterious divining rod that may
serve us in undreamed-of ways. Beauty, strength, intellect—men
often have none of these, and yet conceive pretty accurately what
kind of advantages they would bestow on the possessor. We
know at least what it is we make up our mind to forego, and so
can apply the fittest substitute in our power. Wanting   440
beauty, we cultivate good humor; missing wit, we get riches: but
the mystic unimaginable operation of that gold collar and string
of Latin names which suddenly turned poor stupid little peevish
Cecco of our town into natural lord of the best of us—a Duke, he
is now—there indeed is a virtue to be reverenced!

Chiappino. Ay, by the vulgar: not by Messere Stiatta the poet,
who pays more assiduous court to him than anybody.

Ogniben. What else should Stiatta pay court to? He has talent,
not honor and riches: men naturally covet what they have not.

Chiappino. No, or Cecco would covet talent, which he   450
has not, whereas he covets more riches, of which he has plenty,
already.

Ogniben. Because a purse added to a purse makes the holder
twice as rich: but just such another talent as Stiatta's, added to
what he now possesses, what would that profit him? Give the
talent a purse indeed, to do something with! But lo, how we keep
the good people waiting! I only desired to do justice to the noble
sentiments which animate you and which you are too modest to
duly enforce. Come, to our main business: shall we ascend the
steps? I am going to propose you for Provost to the people;   460
they know your antecedents, and will accept you with a joyful
unanimity: whereon I confirm their choice. Rouse up! Are you
nerving yourself to an effort? Beware the disaster of Messere
Stiatta we were talking of! who, determining to keep an equal
mind and constant face on whatever might be the fortune of his
last new poem with our townsmen, heard too plainly "hiss, hiss,
hiss," increase every moment. Till at last the man fell senseless:
not perceiving that the portentous sounds had all the while been
issuing from between his own nobly clenched teeth, and nostrils
narrowed by resolve.   470

Chiappino. Do you begin to throw off the mask?—to jest with
me, having got me effectually into your trap?

Ogniben. Where is the trap, my friend? You hear what I en
gage to do, for my part: you, for yours, have only to fulfil your
promise made just now within doors, of professing unlimited
obedience to Rome's authority in my person. And I shall authorize
no more than the simple re-establishment of the Provostship and

the conferment of its privileges upon yourself: the only novel
stipulation being a birth of the peculiar circumstances of the time.

Chiappino. And that stipulation?   480

Ogniben. Just the obvious one—that in the event of the dis-
covery of the actual assailant of the late Provost . . .

Chiappino. Ha!

Ogniben. Why, he shall suffer the proper penalty, of course;
what did you expect?

Chiappino. Who heard of this?

Ogniben. Rather, who needed to hear of this?

Chiappino. Can it be, the popular rumor never reached
you . . .

Ogniben. Many more such rumors reach me, friend, than   490
I choose to receive; those which wait longest have best chance.
Has the present one sufficiently waited? Now is its time for entry
with effect. See the good people crowding about yonder palace-
steps—which we may not have to ascend, after all. My good
friends! (nay, two or three of you will answer every purpose)—
who was it fell upon and proved nearly the death of your late
Provost? His successor desires to hear, that his day of inaugura-
tion may be graced by the act of prompt bare justice we all antici-
pate. Who dealt the blow that night, does anybody know?

Luitolfo [coming forward]. I!   500

All. Luitolfo!

Luitolfo. I avow the deed, justify and approve it, and stand
forth now, to relieve my friend of an unearned responsibility.
Having taken thought, I am grown stronger: I shall shrink from
nothing that awaits me. Nay, Chiappino—we are friends still:
I dare say there is some proof of your superior nature in this start-
ing aside, strange as it seemed at first. So, they tell me, my horse
is of the right stock, because a shadow in the path frightens him
into a frenzy, makes him dash my brains out. I understand only
the dull mule's way of standing stockishly, plodding soberly,   510
suffering on occasion a blow or two with due patience.

Eulalia. I was determined to justify my choice, Chiappino,—
to let Luitolfo's nature vindicate itself. Henceforth we are un-
divided, whatever be our fortune.

Ogniben. Now, in these last ten minutes of silence, what have
I been doing, deem you? Putting the finishing stroke to a homily
of mine, I have long taken thought to perfect, on the text, "Let
whoso thinketh he standeth, take heed lest he fall." To your
house, Luitolfo! Still silent, my patriotic friend? Well, that is a
good sign however. And you will go aside for a time? That is   520

better still. I understand: it would be easy for you to die of re-
morse here on the spot and shock us all, but you mean to live and
grow worthy of coming back to us one day. There, I will tell
everybody; and you only do right to believe you must get better
as you get older. All men do so: they are worst in childhood, im-
prove in manhood, and get ready in old age for another world.
Youth, with its beauty and grace, would seem bestowed on us for
some such reason as to make us partly endurable till we have
time for really becoming so of ourselves, without their aid; when
they leave us. The sweetest child we all smile on for his   530
pleasant want of the whole world to break up, or suck in his
mouth, seeing no other good in it—would be rudely handled by
that world's inhabitants, if he retained those angelic infantine de-
sires when he had grown six feet high, black and bearded. But,
little by little, he sees fit to forego claim after claim on the world,
puts up with a less and less share of its good as his proper portion;
and when the octogenarian asks barely a sup of gruel and a fire
of dry sticks, and thanks you as for his full allowance and right
in the common good of life,—hoping nobody may murder him,—
he who began by asking and expecting the whole of us to   540
bow down in worship to him,—why, I say he is advanced, far
onward, very far, nearly out of sight like our friend Chiappino
yonder. And now—(ay, good-bye to you! He turns round the
north-west gate: going to Lugo again? Good-bye!)—and now
give thanks to God, the keys of the Provost's palace to me, and
yourselves to profitable meditation at home! I have known *Four*-
and-twenty leaders of revolts.

From CHRISTMAS-EVE AND EASTER-DAY [1850]

CHRISTMAS EVE

I

Out of the little chapel I burst
   Into the fresh night-air again.
Five minutes full, I waited first
   In the doorway, to escape the rain
That drove in gusts down the common's centre
   At the edge of which the chapel stands,
Before I plucked up heart to enter.
   Heaven knows how many sorts of hands
Reached past me, groping for the latch
Of the inner door that hung on catch   10
More obstinate the more they fumbled,
   Till, giving way at last with a scold
Of the crazy hinge, in squeezed or tumbled
   One sheep more to the rest in fold,
And left me irresolute, standing sentry
In the sheepfold's lath-and-plaster entry,
Six feet long by three feet wide,
Partitioned off from the vast inside—
   I blocked up half of it at least.
No remedy; the rain kept driving.   20
   They eyed me much as some wild beast,
That congregation, still arriving,
Some of them by the main road, white
A long way past me into the night,
Skirting the common, then diverging;
Not a few suddenly emerging
From the common's self thro' the paling-gaps,
—They house in the gravel-pits perhaps,
Where the road stops short with its safeguard border
Of lamps, as tired of such disorder;—   30
But the most turned in yet more abruptly
   From a certain squalid knot of alleys,
Where the town's bad blood once slept corruptly,

Which now the little chapel rallies
And leads into day again,—its priestliness
Lending itself to hide their beastliness
So cleverly (thanks in part to the mason),
And putting so cheery a whitewashed face on
Those neophytes too much in lack of it,
    That, where you cross the common as I did,   **40**
    And meet the party thus presided,
"Mount Zion" with Love-lane at the back of it,
They front you as little disconcerted
As, bound for the hills, her fate averted,
And her wicked people made to mind him,
Lot might have marched with Gomorrah behind him.

II

Well, from the road, the lanes or the common,
In came the flock: the fat weary woman,
Panting and bewildered, down-clapping
    Her umbrella with a mighty report,   **50**
Grounded it by me, wry and flapping,
    A wreck of whalebones; then, with a snort,
Like a startled horse, at the interloper
(Who humbly knew himself improper,
But could not shrink up small enough)
—Round to the door, and in,—the gruff
Hinge's invariable scold
Making my very blood run cold.
Prompt in the wake of her, up-pattered
On broken clogs, the many-tattered   **60**
Little old-faced peaking sister-turned-mother
Of the sickly babe she tried to smother
Somehow up, with its spotted face,
From the cold, on her breast, the one warm place;
She too must stop, wring the poor ends dry
Of a draggled shawl, and add thereby
Her tribute to the door-mat, sopping
Already from my own clothes' dropping,
Which yet she seemed to grudge I should stand on:
    Then, stooping down to take off her pattens,   **70**
She bore them defiantly, in each hand one,
Planted together before her breast
And its babe, as good as a lance in rest.

Close on her heels, the dingy satins
Of a female something, past me flitted,
   With lips as much too white, as a streak
   Lay far too red on each hollow cheek;
And it seemed the very door-hinge pitied
All that was left of a woman once,
Holding at least its tongue for the nonce.   80
Then a tall yellow man, like the Penitent Thief,
With his jaw bound up in a handkerchief,
And eyelids screwed together tight,
Led himself in by some inner light.
And, except from him, from each that entered,
   I got the same interrogation—
"What, you the alien, you have ventured
   To take with us, the elect, your station?
A carer for none of it, a Gallio!"—
   Thus, plain as print, I read the glance   90
   At a common prey, in each countenance
As of huntsman giving his hounds the tallyho.
And, when the door's cry drowned their wonder,
   The draught, it always sent in shutting,
Made the flame of the single tallow candle
In the cracked square lantern I stood under,
   Shoot its blue lip at me, rebutting
As it were, the luckless cause of scandal:
I verily fancied the zealous light
(In the chapel's secret, too!) for spite   100
Would shudder itself clean off the wick,
With the airs of a Saint John's Candlestick.
There was no standing it much longer.
"Good folks," thought I, as resolve grew stronger,
"This way you perform the Grand-Inquisitor
When the weather sends you a chance visitor?
You are the men, and wisdom shall die with you,
And none of the old Seven Churches vie with you!
But still, despite the pretty perfection
   To which you carry your trick of exclusiveness,   110
And, taking God's word under wise protection,
   Correct its tendency to diffusiveness,
And bid one reach it over hot ploughshares,—
   Still, as I say, though you've found salvation,
If I should choose to cry, as now, 'Shares!'—
   See if the best of you bars me my ration!

I prefer, if you please, for my expounder
Of the laws of the feast, the feast's own Founder;
Mine's the same right with your poorest and sickliest
    Supposing I don the marriage vestiment: 120
    So, shut your mouth and open your Testament,
And carve me my portion at your quickliest!"
Accordingly, as a shoemaker's lad
    With wizened face in want of soap,
    And wet apron wound round his waist like a rope,
(After stopping outside, for his cough was bad,
To get the fit over, poor gentle creature,
And so avoid disturbing the preacher)
—Passed in, I sent my elbow spikewise
At the shutting door, and entered likewise,   130
Received the hinge's accustomed greeting,
    And crossed the threshold's magic pentacle,
    And found myself in full conventicle,
—To wit, in Zion Chapel Meeting,
On the Christmas-Eve of 'Forty-nine,
    Which, calling its flock to their special clover,
    Found all assembled and one sheep over,
Whose lot, as the weather pleased, was mine.

III

I very soon had enough of it.
    The hot smell and the human noises,   140
And my neighbor's coat, the greasy cuff of it,
    Were a pebble-stone that a child's hand poises,
Compared with the pig-of-lead-like pressure
    Of the preaching man's immense stupidity,
As he poured his doctrine forth, full measure,
    To meet his audience's avidity.
You needed not the wit of the Sibyl
    To guess the cause of it all, in a twinkling:
    No sooner our friend had got an inkling
Of treasure hid in the Holy Bible,   150
(Whene'er 'twas the thought first struck him,
How death, at unawares, might duck him
Deeper than the grave, and quench
The gin-shop's light in hell's grim drench)
Than he handled it so, in fine irreverence,
    As to hug the book of books to pieces:

And, a patchwork of chapters and texts in severance,
　　Not improved by the private dog's-ears and creases,
Having clothed his own soul with, he'd fain see equipt yours,—
　So tossed you again your Holy Scriptures. 160
And you picked them up, in a sense, no doubt:
　　Nay, had but a single face of my neighbors
　　Appeared to suspect that the preacher's labors
Were help which the world could be saved without,
'Tis odds but I might have borne in quiet
A qualm or two at my spiritual diet,
Or (who can tell?) perchance even mustered
　　Somewhat to urge in behalf of the sermon:
But the flock sat on, divinely flustered,
　　Sniffing, methought, its dew of Hermon 170
With such content in every snuffle,
As the devil inside us loves to ruffle.
My old fat woman purred with pleasure,
　　And thumb round thumb went twirling faster,
While she, to his periods keeping measure,
　　Maternally devoured the pastor.
The man with the handkerchief untied it,
Showed us a horrible wen inside it,
Gave his eyelids yet another screwing,
And rocked himself as the woman was doing. 180
The shoemaker's lad, discreetly choking,
Kept down his cough. 'Twas too provoking!
My gorge rose at the nonsense and stuff of it;
　So, saying like Eve when she plucked the apple,
"I wanted a taste, and now there's enough of it,"
　I flung out of the little chapel.

IV

There was a lull in the rain, a lull
　　In the wind too; the moon was risen,
And would have shone out pure and full,
　　But for the ramparted cloud-prison, 190
Block on block built up in the West,
For what purpose the wind knows best,
Who changes his mind continually.
And the empty other half of the sky
Seemed in its silence as if it knew
What, any moment, might look through

A chance gap in that fortress massy:—
   Through its fissures you got hints
   Of the flying moon, by the shifting tints,
Now, a dull lion-color, now, brassy   200
Burning to yellow, and whitest yellow,
Like furnace-smoke just ere flames bellow,
All a-simmer with intense strain
To let her through,—then blank again,
At the hope of her appearance failing.
Just by the chapel, a break in the railing
Shows a narrow path directly across;
'Tis ever dry walking there, on the moss—
Besides, you go gently all the way uphill.
   I stooped under and soon felt better;   210
My head grew lighter, my limbs more supple,
   As I walked on, glad to have slipt the fetter.
My mind was full of the scene I had left,
   That placid flock, that pastor vociferant,
   —How this outside was pure and different!
The sermon, now—what a mingled weft
Of good and ill! Were either less,
   Its fellow had colored the whole distinctly;
But alas for the excellent earnestness,
   And the truths, quite true if stated succinctly,   220
But as surely false, in their quaint presentment,
However to pastor and flock's contentment!
Say rather, such truths looked false to your eyes,
   With his provings and parallels twisted and twined,
Till how could you know them, grown double their size
   In the natural fog of the good man's mind,
Like yonder spots of our roadside lamps,
Haloed about with the common's damps?
Truth remains true, the fault's in the prover;
   The zeal was good, and the aspiration;   230
And yet, and yet, yet, fifty times over,
   Pharaoh received no demonstration,
By his Baker's dream of Baskets Three,
Of the doctrine of the Trinity,—
Although, as our preacher thus embellished it,
Apparently his hearers relished it
With so unfeigned a gust—who knows if
They did not prefer our friend to Joseph?
But so it is everywhere, one way with all of them!

These people have really felt, no doubt,   240
A something, the motion they style the Call of them;
    And this is their method of bringing about,
By a mechanism of words and tones,
(So many texts in so many groans)
A sort of reviving and reproducing,
    More or less perfectly, (who can tell?)
The mood itself, which strengthens by using;
    And how that happens, I understand well.
A tune was born in my head last week,
Out of the thump-thump and shriek-shriek   250
    Of the train, as I came by it, up from Manchester;
And when, next week, I take it back again,
My head will sing to the engine's clack again,
    While it only makes my neighbor's haunches stir,
—Finding no dormant musical sprout
In him, as in me, to be jolted out.
'Tis the taught already that profits by teaching;
He gets no more from the railway's preaching
    Than, from this preacher who does the rail's office, I,
Whom therefore the flock cast a jealous eye on.   260
Still, why paint over their door "Mount Zion,"
    To which all flesh shall come, saith the prophecy?

                    v

But wherefore be harsh on a single case?
    After how many modes, this Christmas-Eve,
Does the self-same weary thing take place?
    The same endeavor to make you believe,
And with much the same effect, no more:
    Each method abundantly convincing,
As I say, to those convinced before,
    But scarce to be swallowed without wincing   270
By the not-as-yet-convinced. For me,
I have my own church equally:
And in this church my faith sprang first!
    (I said, as I reached the rising ground,
And the wind began again, with a burst
    Of rain in my face, and a glad rebound
From the heart beneath, as if, God speeding me,
I entered his church-door, nature leading me)
—In youth I looked to these very skies,

And probing their immensities,   280
I found God there, his visible power;
    Yet felt in my heart, amid all its sense
    Of the power, an equal evidence
That his love, there too, was the nobler dower.
For the loving worm within its clod,
'Were diviner than a loveless god
Amid his worlds, I will dare to say.
    You know what I mean: God's all, man's naught:
    But also, God, whose pleasure brought
Man into being, stands away   290
    As it were a handbreadth off, to give
Room for the newly-made to live,
And look at him from a place apart,
And use his gifts of brain and heart,
Given, indeed, but to keep forever.
Who speaks of man, then, must not sever
Man's very elements from man,
Saying, "But all is God's"—whose plan
Was to create man and then leave him
Able, his own word saith, to grieve him,   300
But able to glorify him too,
As a mere machine could never do,
That prayed or praised, all unaware
Of its fitness for aught but praise and prayer,
Made perfect as a thing of course.
Man, therefore, stands on his own stock
Of love and power as a pin-point rock:
And, looking to God who ordained divorce
Of the rock from his boundless continent,
Sees, in his power made evident,   310
Only excess by a million-fold
O'er the power God gave man in the mould.
For, note: man's hand, first formed to carry
A few pounds' weight, when taught to marry
Its strength with an engine's, lifts a mountain,
    —Advancing in power by one degree;
    And why count steps through eternity?
But love is the ever-springing fountain:
Man may enlarge or narrow his bed
For the water's play, but the water-head—   320
How can he multiply or reduce it?
    As easy create it, as cause it to cease;

He may profit by it, or abuse it,
　　But 'tis not a thing to bear increase
As power does: be love less or more
　　In the heart of man, he keeps it shut
　　Or opes it wide, as he pleases, but
Love's sum remains what it was before.
So, gazing up, in my youth, at love
As seen through power, ever above　　　　　　　330
All modes which make it manifest,
My soul brought all to a single test—
That he, the Eternal First and Last,
Who, in his power, had so surpassed
All man conceives of what is might,—
Whose wisdom, too, showed infinite,
—Would prove as infinitely good;
Would never, (my soul understood,)
With power to work all love desires,
Bestow e'en less than man requires;　　　　　　340
That he who endlessly was teaching,
Above my spirit's utmost reaching,
What love can do in the leaf or stone,
(So that to master this alone,
This done in the stone or leaf for me,
I must go on learning endlessly)
Would never need that I, in turn,
　　Should point him out defect unheeded,
And show that God had yet to learn
　　What the meanest human creature needed,　　350
—Not life, to wit, for a few short years,
Tracking his way through doubts and fears,
While the stupid earth on which I stay
　　Suffers no change, but passive adds
　　Its myriad years to myriads,
Though I, he gave it to, decay,
Seeing death come and choose about me,
And my dearest ones depart without me.
No: love which, on earth, amid all the shows of it,
　　Has ever been seen the sole good of life in it,　　360
　　The love, ever growing there, spite of the strife in it,
Shall arise, made perfect, from death's repose of it.
And I shall behold thee, face to face,
O God, and in thy light retrace
How in all I loved here, still wast thou!

Whom pressing to, then, as I fain would now,
I shall find as able to satiate
     The love, thy gift, as my spirit's wonder
Thou art able to quicken and sublimate,
     With this sky of thine, that I now walk under,   370
And glory in thee for, as I gaze
Thus, thus! Oh, let men keep their ways
Of seeking thee in a narrow shrine—
Be this my way! And this is mine!

VI

For lo, what think you? suddenly
The rain and the wind ceased, and the sky
Received at once the full fruition
Of the moon's consummate apparition.
The black cloud-barricade was riven,
Ruined beneath her feet, and driven   380
Deep in the West; while, bare and breathless,
     North and South and East lay ready
For a glorious thing that, dauntless, deathless,
     Sprang across them and stood steady.
'Twas a moon-rainbow, vast and perfect,
From heaven to heaven extending, perfect
As the mother-moon's self, full in face.
It rose, distinctly at the base
     With its seven proper colors chorded,
Which still, in the rising, were compressed,   390
Until at last they coalesced,
     And supreme the spectral creature lorded
In a triumph of whitest white,—
Above which intervened the night.
But above night too, like only the next,
     The second of a wondrous sequence,
     Reaching in rare and rarer frequence,
Till the heaven of heavens were circumflexed,
Another rainbow rose, a mightier,
Fainter, flushier and flightier,—   400
Rapture dying along its verge.
Oh, whose foot shall I see emerge,
Whose, from the straining topmost dark,
On to the keystone of that arc?

VII

This sight was shown me, there and then,—
Me, one out of a world of men,
Singled forth, as the chance might hap
To another if, in a thunderclap
Where I heard noise and you saw flame,
Some one man knew God called his name.   410
For me, I think I said, "Appear!
Good were it to be ever here.
If thou wilt, let me build to thee
Service-tabernacles three,
Where, forever in thy presence,
In ecstatic acquiescence,
Far alike from thriftless learning
And ignorance's undiscerning,
I may worship and remain!"
    Thus at the show above me, gazing   420
With upturned eyes, I felt my brain
    Glutted with the glory, blazing
Throughout its whole mass, over and under
Until at length it burst asunder
And out of it bodily there streamed,
The too-much glory, as it seemed,
Passing from out me to the ground,
Then palely serpentining round
Into the dark with mazy error.

VIII

All at once I looked up with terror.   430
He was there.
He himself with his human air.
On the narrow pathway, just before.
I saw the back of him, no more—
He had left the chapel, then, as I.
I forgot all about the sky.
No face: only the sight
Of a sweepy garment, vast and white,
With a hem that I could recognize.
I felt terror, no surprise;   440
My mind filled with the cataract,

At one bound of the mighty fact.
"I remember, he did say
  Doubtless that, to this world's end,
Where two or three should meet and pray,
  He would be in the midst, their friend;
Certainly he was there with them!"
  And my pulses leaped for joy
  Of the golden thought without alloy,
That I saw his very vesture's hem.   450
Then rushed the blood back, cold and clear,
With a fresh enhancing shiver of fear;
And I hastened, cried out while I pressed
To the salvation of the vest,
"But not so, Lord! It cannot be
That thou, indeed, art leaving me—
Me, that have despised thy friends!
Did my heart make no amends?
Thou art the love of God—above
His power, didst hear me place his love,   460
And that was leaving the world for thee.
Therefore thou must not turn from me
As I had chosen the other part!
Folly and pride o'ercame my heart.
Our best is bad, nor bears thy test;
Still, it should be our very best.
I thought it best that thou, the spirit,
  Be worshipped in spirit and in truth,
And in beauty, as even we require it—
  Not in the forms burlesque, uncouth,   470
I left but now, as scarcely fitted
For thee: I knew not what I pitied.
But, all I felt there, right or wrong,
  What is it to thee, who curest sinning?
Am I not weak as thou art strong?
  I have looked to thee from the beginning,
Straight up to thee through all the world
Which, like an idle scroll, lay furled
To nothingness on either side:
And since the time thou wast descried,   480
Spite of the weak heart, so have I
Lived ever, and so fain would die,
Living and dying, thee before!
But if thou leavest me——"

IX

                  Less or more,
I suppose that I spoke thus.
When,—have mercy, Lord, on us!
The whole face turned upon me full.
   And I spread myself beneath it,
   As when the bleacher spreads, to seethe it
In the cleansing sun, his wool,—   490
Steeps in the flood of noontide whiteness
   Some defiled, discolored web—
So lay I, saturate with brightness.
   And when the flood appeared to ebb,
Lo, I was walking, light and swift,
   With my senses settling fast and steadying,
But my body caught up in the whirl and drift
   Of the vesture's amplitude, still eddying
On, just before me, still to be followed,
   As it carried me after with its motion: 500
What shall I say?—as a path were hollowed
   And a man went weltering through the ocean,
Sucked along in the flying wake
Of the luminous water-snake.
Darkness and cold were cloven, as through
I passed, upborne yet walking too.
And I turned to myself at intervals,—
"So he said, so it befalls.
God who registers the cup
   Of mere cold water, for his sake   510
To a disciple rendered up,
   Disdains not his own thirst to slake
At the poorest love was ever offered:
And because my heart I proffered,
With true love trembling at the brim,
He suffers me to follow him
Forever, my own way,—dispensed
From seeking to be influenced
By all the less immediate ways
   That earth, in worships manifold,   520
Adopts to reach, by prayer and praise,
   The garment's hem, which, lo, I hold!"

X

And so we crossed the world and stopped.
  For where am I, in city or plain,
  Since I am 'ware of the world again?
And what is this that rises propped
With pillars of prodigious girth?
Is it really on the earth,
This miraculous Dome of God?
Has the angel's measuring-rod   530
Which numbered cubits, gem from gem,
'Twixt the gates of the New Jerusalem,
Meted it out,—and what he meted,
Have the sons of men completed?
—Binding, ever as he bade,
Columns in the colonnade
With arms wide open to embrace
The entry of the human race
To the breast of . . . what is it, yon building,
Ablaze in front, all paint and gilding,   540
With marble for brick, and stones of price
For garniture of the edifice?
Now I see; it is no dream;
It stands there and it does not seem;
For ever, in pictures, thus it looks,
And thus I have read of it in books
Often in England, leagues away,
And wondered how these fountains play,
Growing up eternally
Each to a musical water-tree,   550
Whose blossoms drop, a glittering boon,
Before my eyes, in the light of the moon,
To the granite lavers underneath.
Liar and dreamer in your teeth!
I, the sinner that speak to you,
Was in Rome this night, and stood, and knew
Both this and more. For see, for see,
The dark is rent, mine eye is free
To pierce the crust of the outer wall,
And I view inside, and all there, all,   560
As the swarming hollow of a hive,
The whole Basilica alive!
Men in the chancel, body and nave,

Men on the pillars' architrave,
Men on the statues, men on the tombs
With popes and kings in their porphyry wombs,
All famishing in expectation
Of the main-altar's consummation.
For see, for see, the rapturous moment
Approaches, and earth's best endowment   570
Blends with heaven's; the taper-fires
Pant up, the winding brazen spires
Heave loftier yet the baldachin;
The incense-gaspings, long kept in,
Suspire in clouds; the organ blatant
Holds his breath and grovels latent,
As if God's hushing finger grazed him,
(Like Behemoth when he praised him)
At the silver bell's shrill tinkling,
Quick cold drops of terror sprinkling   580
On the sudden pavement strewed
With faces of the multitude.
Earth breaks up, time drops away,
In flows heaven, with its new day
Of endless life, when He who trod,
Very man and very God,
This earth in weakness, shame and pain,
Dying the death whose signs remain
Up yonder on the accursed tree,—
Shall come again, no more to be   590
Of captivity the thrall,
But the one God, All in all,
King of kings, Lord of lords,
As His servant John received the words,
"I died, and live for evermore!"

XI

Yet I was left outside the door.
"Why sit I here on the threshold-stone
Left till He return, alone
Save for the garment's extreme fold
Abandoned still to bless my hold?"   600
My reason, to my doubt, replied,
As if a book were opened wide,
And at a certain page I traced

Every record undefaced,
Added by successive years,—
The harvestings of truth's stray ears
Singly gleaned, and in one sheaf
Bound together for belief.
Yes, I said—that he will go
And sit with these in turn, I know.   610
Their faith's heart beats, though her head swims
Too giddily to guide her limbs,
Disabled by their palsy-stroke
From propping mine. Though Rome's gross yoke
Drops off, no more to be endured,
Her teaching is not so obscured
By errors and perversities,
That no truth shines athwart the lies:
And he, whose eye detects a spark
Even where, to man's, the whole seems dark,   620
May well see flame where each beholder
Acknowledges the embers smoulder.
But I, a mere man, fear to quit
The clue God gave me as most fit
To guide my footsteps through life's maze,
Because himself discerns all ways
Open to reach him: I, a man
Able to mark where faith began
To swerve aside, till from its summit
Judgment drops her damning plummet,   630
Pronouncing such a fatal space
Departed from the founder's base:
He will not bid me enter too,
But rather sit, as now I do,
Awaiting his return outside.
—'Twas thus my reason straight replied
And joyously I turned, and pressed
The garment's skirt upon my breast,
Until, afresh its light suffusing me,
My heart cried—What has been abusing me   640
That I should wait here lonely and coldly,
Instead of rising, entering boldly,
Baring truth's face, and letting drift
Her veils of lies as they choose to shift?
Do these men praise him? I will raise

My voice up to their point of praise!
I see the error; but above
The scope of error, see the love.—
Oh, love of those first Christian days!
—Fanned so soon into a blaze,   650
From the spark preserved by the trampled sect,
That the antique sovereign Intellect
Which then sat ruling in the world,
Like a change in dreams, was hurled
From the throne he reigned upon:
You looked up and he was gone.
Gone, his glory of the pen!
—Love, with Greece and Rome in ken,
Bade her scribes abhor the trick
Of poetry and rhetoric,   660
And exult with hearts set free,
In blessed imbecility
Scrawled, perchance, on some torn sheet
Leaving Sallust incomplete.
Gone, his pride of sculptor, painter!
—Love, while able to acquaint her
While the thousand statues yet
Fresh from chisel, pictures wet
From brush, she saw on every side,
Chose rather with an infant's pride   670
To frame those portents which impart
Such unction to true Christian Art.
Gone, music too! The air was stirred
By happy wings: Terpander's bird
(That, when the cold came, fled away)
Would tarry not the wintry day,—
As more-enduring sculpture must,
Till filthy saints rebuked the gust
With which they chanced to get a sight
Of some dear naked Aphrodite   680
They glanced a thought above the toes of,
By breaking zealously her nose off.
Love, surely, from that music's lingering,
Might have filched her organ-fingering,
Nor chosen rather to set prayings
To hog-grunts, praises to horse-neighings.
Love was the startling thing, the new:

Love was the all-sufficient too;
And seeing that, you see the rest:
As a babe can find its mother's breast   690
As well in darkness as in light,
Love shut our eyes, and all seemed right.
True, the world's eyes are open now:
—Less need for me to disallow
Some few that keep Love's zone unbuckled,
Peevish as ever to be suckled,
Lulled by the same old baby-prattle
With intermixture of the rattle,
When she would have them creep, stand steady
Upon their feet, or walk already,   700
Not to speak of trying to climb.
I will be wise another time,
And not desire a wall between us,
   When next I see a church-roof cover
So many species of one genus,
   All with foreheads bearing *lover*
Written above the earnest eyes of them;
   All with breasts that beat for beauty,
Whether sublimed, to the surprise of them,
   In noble daring, steadfast duty,   710
The heroic in passion, or in action,—
Or, lowered for sense's satisfaction,
To the mere outside of human creatures,
Mere perfect form and faultless features.
What? with all Rome here, whence to levy
   Such contributions to their appetite,
With women and men in a gorgeous bevy,
   They take, as it were, a padlock, clap it tight
On their southern eyes, restrained from feeding
On the glories of their ancient reading,   720
On the beauties of their modern singing,
On the wonders of the builder's bringing,
On the majesties of Art around them,—
   And, all these loves, late struggling incessant,
When faith has at last united and bound them,
   They offer up to God for a present?
Why, I will, on the whole, be rather proud of it,—
   And, only taking the act in reference
To the other recipients who might have allowed it,
   I will rejoice that God had the preference.   730

XII

So I summed up my new resolves:
    Too much love there can never be.
And where the intellect devolves
    Its function on love exclusively,
I, a man who possesses both,
Will accept the provision, nothing loth,
—Will feast my love, then depart elsewhere,
That my intellect may find its share.
And ponder, O soul, the while thou departest,
And see thou applaud the great heart of the artist   740
Who, examining the capabilities
    Of the block of marble he has to fashion
    Into a type of thought or passion,—
Not always, using obvious facilities,
Shapes it, as any artist can,
Into a perfect symmetrical man,
Complete from head to foot of the life-size,
Such as old Adam stood in his wife's eyes,—
But, now and then, bravely aspires to consummate
A Colossus by no means so easy to come at,   750
And uses the whole of his block for the bust,
    Leaving the mind to the public to finish it,
Since cut it ruefully short he must:
On the face alone he expends his devotion,
    He rather would mar than resolve to diminish it,
—Saying, "Applaud me for this grand notion
Of what a face may be! As for completing it
    In breast and body and limbs, do that, you!"
All hail! I fancy how, happily meeting it,
    A trunk and legs would perfect the statue,   760
Could man carve so as to answer volition.
    And how much nobler than petty cavils,
    Were a hope to find, in my spirit-travels,
Some artist of another ambition,
Who having a block to carve, no bigger,
    Has spent his power on the opposite quest,
    And believed to begin at the feet was best—
For so may I see, ere I die, the whole figure!

XIII

No sooner said than out in the night!
My heart beat lighter and more light: 770
And still, as before, I was walking swift,
    With my senses settling fast and steadying,
But my body caught up in the whirl and drift
    Of the vesture's amplitude, still eddying
On just before me, still to be followed,
    As it carried me after with its motion,
—What shall I say?—as a path were hollowed,
    And a man went weltering through the ocean,
Sucked along in the flying wake
Of the luminous water-snake.   780

XIV

Alone! I am left alone once more—
    (Save for the garment's extreme fold
    Abandoned still to bless my hold)
Alone, beside the entrance-door
    Of a sort of temple,—perhaps a college,
—Like nothing I ever saw before
    At home in England, to my knowledge.
The tall old quaint irregular town!
    It may be . . . though which, I can't affirm . . . any
    Of the famous middle-age towns of Germany;   790
And this flight of stairs where I sit down,
Is it Halle, Weimar, Cassel, Frankfort
Or Göttingen, I have to thank for't?
It may be Göttingen,—most likely.
Through the open door I catch obliquely
Glimpses of a lecture-hall;
    And not a bad assembly neither,
Ranged decent and symmetrical
    On benches, waiting what's to see there;
Which, holding still by the vesture's hem,   800
I also resolve to see with them,
Cautious this time how I suffer to slip
The chance of joining in fellowship
With any that call themselves his friends;
    As these folk do, I have a notion.

But hist—a buzzing and emotion!
All settle themselves, the while ascends
By the creaking rail to the lecture-desk,
　　Step by step, deliberate
　　Because of his cranium's over-freight,　　　　810
Three parts sublime to one grotesque,
If I have proved an accurate guesser,
The hawk-nosed high-cheek-boned Professor.
I felt at once as if there ran
A shoot of love from my heart to the man—
That sallow virgin-minded studious
　　Martyr to mild enthusiasm,
As he uttered a kind of cough-preludious
　　That woke my sympathetic spasm,
(Beside some spitting that made me sorry)　　　820
And stood, surveying his auditory
With a wan pure look, well nigh celestial,—
　　Those blue eyes had survived so much!
　　While, under the foot they could not smutch,
Lay all the fleshly and the bestial.
Over he bowed, and arranged his notes,
Till the auditory's clearing of throats
Was done with, died into a silence;
　　And, when each glance was upward sent,
　　Each bearded mouth composed intent,　　　830
And a pin might be heard drop half a mile hence,—
He pushed back higher his spectacles,
Let the eyes stream out like lamps from cells,
And giving his head of hair—a hake
　　Of undressed tow, for color and quantity—
One rapid and impatient shake,
　　(As our own Young England adjusts a jaunty tie
When about to impart, on mature digestion,
Some thrilling view of the surplice-question)
—The Professor's grave voice, sweet though hoarse,　　840
Broke into his Christmas-Eve discourse.

XV

And he began it by observing
　　How reason dictated that men
Should rectify the natural swerving,
　　By a reversion, now and then,

To the well-heads of knowledge, few
And far away, whence rolling grew
The life-stream wide whereat we drink,
Commingled, as we needs must think,
With waters alien to the source;   850
To do which, aimed this eve's discourse;
Since, where could be a fitter time
For tracing backward to its prime
This Christianity, this lake,
This reservoir, whereat we slake,
From one or other bank, our thirst?
So, he proposed inquiring first
Into the various sources whence
    This Myth of Christ is derivable;
Demanding from the evidence,   860
    (Since plainly no such life was liveable)
How these phenomena should class?
Whether 'twere best opine Christ was,
Or never was at all, or whether
He was and was not, both together—
It matters little for the name,
So the idea be left the same.
Only, for practical purpose' sake,
'Twas obviously as well to take
The popular story,—understanding   870
    How the ineptitude of the time,
And the penman's prejudice, expanding
    Fact into fable fit for the clime,
Had, by slow and sure degrees, translated it
    Into this myth, this Individuum,—
Which, when reason had strained and abated it
    Of foreign matter, left, for residuum,
A Man!—a right true man, however,
Whose work was worthy a man's endeavor:
Work, that gave warrant almost sufficient   880
    To his disciples, for rather believing
He was just omnipotent and omniscient,
    As it gives to us, for as frankly receiving
His word, their tradition,—which, though it meant
Something entirely different
From all that those who only heard it,
In their simplicity thought and averred it,
Had yet a meaning quite as respectable:

For, among other doctrines delectable,
Was he not surely the first to insist on   890
    The natural sovereignty of our race?—
    Here the lecturer came to a pausing-place.
And while his cough, like a drouthy piston,
Tried to dislodge the husk that grew to him,
I seized the occasion of bidding adieu to him,
The vesture still within my hand.

XVI

I could interpret its command.
    This time he would not bid me enter
The exhausted air-bell of the Critic.
Truth's atmosphere may grow mephitic   900
    When Papist struggles with Dissenter,
Impregnating its pristine clarity,
—One, by his daily fare's vulgarity,
    Its gust of broken meat and garlic;
—One, by his soul's too-much presuming
To turn the frankincense's fuming
    And vapors of the candle starlike
Into the cloud her wings she buoys on.
    Each, that thus sets the pure air seething,
    May poison it for healthy breathing—   910
But the Critic leaves no air to poison;
Pumps out with ruthless ingenuity
Atom by atom, and leaves you—vacuity.
Thus much of Christ does he reject?
And what retain? His intellect?
What is it I must reverence duly?
Poor intellect for worship, truly,
Which tells me simply what was told
    (If mere morality, bereft
    Of the God in Christ, be all that's left)   920
Elsewhere by voices manifold;
With this advantage, that the stater
    Made nowise the important stumble
    Of adding, he, the sage and humble,
Was also one with the Creator.
You urge Christ's followers' simplicity:
    But how does shifting blame, evade it?
Have wisdom's words no more felicity?

The stumbling-block, his speech—who laid it?
How comes it that for one found able   930
To sift the truth of it from fable,
Millions believe it to the letter?
Christ's goodness, then—does that fare better?
Strange goodness, which upon the score
    Of being goodness, the mere due
Of man to fellow-man, much more
    To God,—should take another view
Of its possessor's privilege,
And bid him rule his race! You pledge
Your fealty to such rule? What, all—   940
From heavenly John and Attic Paul,
And that brave weather-battered Peter,
Whose stout faith only stood completer
For buffets, sinning to be pardoned,
As, more his hands hauled nets, they hardened,—
All, down to you, the man of men,
Professing here at Göttingen,
Compose Christ's flock! They, you and I,
Are sheep of a good man! And why?
The goodness,—how did he acquire it?   950
Was it self-gained, did God inspire it?
Choose which; then tell me, on what ground
Should its possessor dare propound
His claim to rise o'er us an inch?
    Were goodness all some man's invention,
    Who arbitrarily made mention
What we should follow, and whence flinch,—
What qualities might take the style
    Of right and wrong,—and had such guessing
    Met with as general acquiescing   960
As graced the alphabet erewhile,
When A got leave an Ox to be,
No Camel (quoth the Jews) like G,—
For thus inventing thing and title
Worship were that man's fit requital.
But if the common conscience must
Be ultimately judge, adjust
Its apt name to each quality
Already known,—I would decree
Worship for such mere demonstration   970
    And simple work of nomenclature,

Only the day I praised, not nature,
But Harvey, for the circulation.
I would praise such a Christ, with pride
And joy, that he, as none beside,
Had taught us how to keep the mind
God gave him, as God gave his kind,
Freer than they from fleshly taint:
I would call such a Christ our Saint,
As I declare our Poet, him   980
Whose insight makes all others dim:
A thousand poets pried at life,
And only one amid the strife
Rose to be Shakespeare: each shall take
His crown, I'd say, for the world's sake—
Though some objected—"Had we seen
The heart and head of each, what screen
Was broken there to give them light,
While in ourselves it shuts the sight,
We should no more admire, perchance,   990
That these found truth out at a glance,
Than marvel how the bat discerns
Some pitch-dark cavern's fifty turns,
Led by a finer tact, a gift
He boasts, which other birds must shift
Without, and grope as best they can."
No, freely I would praise the man,—
Nor one whit more, if he contended
That gift of his, from God descended.
Ah friend, what gift of man's does not?   1000
No nearer something, by a jot,
Rise an infinity of nothings
    Than one: take Euclid for your teacher:
Distinguish kinds: do crownings, clothings,
    Make that creator which was creature?
Multiply gifts upon man's head,
And what, when all's done, shall be said
But—the more gifted he, I ween!
    That one's made Christ, this other, Pilate,
And this might be all that has been,—   1010
    So what is there to frown or smile at?
What is left for us, save, in growth
Of soul, to rise up, far past both,
From the gift looking to the giver,

And from the cistern to the river,
And from the finite to infinity,
And from man's dust to God's divinity?

XVII

Take all in a word: the truth in God's breast
Lies trace for trace upon ours impressed:
Though he is so bright and we so dim,   1020
We are made in his image to witness him:
And were no eye in us to tell,
    Instructed by no inner sense,
The light of heaven from the dark of hell,
    That light would want its evidence,—
Though justice, good and truth were still
Divine, if, by some demon's will,
Hatred and wrong had been proclaimed
Law through the worlds, and right misnamed.
No mere exposition of morality   1030
Made or in part or in totality,
Should win you to give it worship, therefore:
And, if no better proof you will care for,
—Whom do you count the worst man upon earth?
    Be sure, he knows, in his conscience, more
Of what right is, than arrives at birth
    In the best man's acts that we bow before:
This last knows better—true, but my fact is,
'Tis one thing to know, and another to practise.
And thence I conclude that the real God-function   1040
Is to furnish a motive and injunction
    For practising what we know already.
And such an injunction and such a motive
    As the God in Christ, do you waive, and "heady,
High-minded," hang your tablet-votive
Outside the fane on a finger-post?
Morality to the uttermost,
Supreme in Christ as we all confess,
    Why need we prove would avail no jot
    To make him God, if God he were not?   1050
What is the point where himself lays stress?
Does the precept run "Believe in good,
In justice, truth, now understood
For the first time"?—or, "Believe in me,

Who lived and died, yet essentially
Am Lord of Life"? Whoever can take
The same to his heart and for mere love's sake
Conceive of the love,—that man obtains
A new truth; no conviction gains
Of an old one only, made intense   1060
By a fresh appeal to his faded sense.

XVIII

Can it be that he stays inside?
    Is the vesture left me to commune with?
    Could my soul find aught to sing in tune with
Even at this lecture, if she tried?
Oh, let me at lowest sympathize
With the lurking drop of blood that lies
In the desiccated brain's white roots
Without throb for Christ's attributes,
As the lecturer makes his special boast!   1070
If love's dead there, it has left a ghost.
Admire we, how from heart to brain
    (Though to say so strike the doctors dumb)
One instinct rises and falls again,
    Restoring the equilibrium.
And how when the Critic had done his best,
And the pearl of price, at reason's test,
Lay dust and ashes levigable
On the Professor's lecture-table,—
When we looked for the inference and monition   1080
That our faith, reduced to such condition,
Be swept forthwith to its natural dust-hole,—
    He bids us, when we least expect it,
Take back our faith,—if it be not just whole,
    Yet a pearl indeed, as his tests affect it,
Which fact pays damage done rewardingly,
So, prize we our dust and ashes accordingly!
"Go home and venerate the myth
I thus have experimented with—
This man, continue to adore him   1090
Rather than all who went before him,
And all who ever followed after!"—
    Surely for this I may praise you, my brother!
Will you take the praise in tears or laughter?

That's one point gained: can I compass another?
Unlearned love was safe from spurning—
Can't we respect your loveless learning?
Let us at least give learning honor!
What laurels had we showered upon her,
Girding her loins up to perturb   1100
Our theory of the Middle Verb;
Or Turk-like brandishing a scimitar
O'er anapæsts in comic-trimeter;
Or curing the halt and maimed Iketides,
While we lounged on at our indebted ease:
Instead of which, a tricksy demon
Sets her at Titus or Philemon!
When ignorance wags his ears of leather
And hates God's word, 'tis altogether;
Nor leaves he his congenial thistles   1110
To go and browse on Paul's Epistles.
—And you, the audience, who might ravage
The world wide, enviably savage,
Nor heed the cry of the retriever,
More than Herr Heine (before his fever),—
I do not tell a lie so arrant
    As say my passion's wings are furled up,
And, without plainest heavenly warrant,
    I were ready and glad to give the world up—
But still, when you rub brow meticulous,   1120
    And ponder the profit of turning holy
  - If not for God's, for your own sake solely,
  ,—God forbid I should find you ridiculous!
Deduce from this lecture all that eases you,
Nay, call yourselves, if the calling pleases you,
"Christians,"—abhor the deist's pravity,—
Go on, you shall no more move my gravity
Than, when I see boys ride a-cockhorse,
    I find it in my heart to embarrass them
By hinting that their stick's a mock horse,   1130
    And they really carry what they say carries them.

XIX

So sat I talking with my mind.
    I did not long to leave the door
    And find a new church, as before,

But rather was quiet and inclined
To prolong and enjoy the gentle resting
From further tracking and trying and testing.
"This tolerance is a genial mood!"
(Said I, and a little pause ensued).
"One trims the bark 'twixt shoal and shelf,   1140
   And sees, each side, the good effects of it,
A value for religion's self,
   A carelessness about the sects of it.
Let me enjoy my own conviction,
   Nor watch my neighbor's faith with fretfulness,
Still spying there some dereliction
   Of truth, perversity, forgetfulness!
Better a mild indifferentism,
   Teaching that both our faiths (though duller
His shine through a dull spirit's prism)   1150
   Originally had one color!
Better pursue a pilgrimage
   Through ancient and through modern times
   To many peoples, various climes,
Where I may see saint, savage, sage
Fuse their respective creeds in one
Before the general Father's throne!"

XX

—'Twas the horrible storm began afresh!
The black night caught me in his mesh,
Whirled me up, and flung me prone.   1160
I was left on the college-step alone.
I looked, and far there, ever fleeting
Far, far away, the receding gesture
And looming of the lessening vesture!—
Swept forward from my stupid hand,
While I watched my foolish heart expand
In the lazy glow of benevolence,
   O'er the various modes of man's belief.
I sprang up with fear's vehemence.
   Needs must there be one way, our chief   1170
Best way of worship: let me strive
To find it, and when found, contrive
My fellows also take their share!
This constitutes my earthly care:

God's is above it and distinct.
For I, a man, with men am linked
And not a brute with brutes; no gain
That I experience, must remain
Unshared: but should my best endeavor
To share it, fail—subsisteth ever   1180
God's care above, and I exult
That God, by God's own ways occult,
May—doth, I will believe—bring back
All wanderers to a single track.
Meantime, I can but testify
God's care for me—no more, can I—
It is but for myself I know;
  The world rolls witnessing around me
  Only to leave me as it found me;
Men cry there, but my ear is slow: 1190
Their races flourish or decay
—What boots it, while yon lucid way
Loaded with stars divides the vault?
But soon my soul repairs its fault
When, sharpening sense's hebetude,
She turns on my own life! So viewed,
No mere mote's-breadth but teems immense
With witnessings of providence:
And woe to me if when I look
Upon that record, the sole book   1200
Unsealed to me, I take no heed
Of any warning that I read!
Have I been sure, this Christmas-Eve,
God's own hand did the rainbow weave,
Whereby the truth from heaven slid
Into my soul?—I cannot bid
The world admit he stooped to heal
My soul, as if in a thunder-peal
Where one heard noise, and one saw flame,
I only knew he named my name: 1210
But what is the world to me, for sorrow
Or joy in its censure, when to-morrow
It drops the remark, with just-turned head
Then, on again, "That man is dead"?
Yes, but for me—my name called,—drawn
As a conscript's lot from the lap's black yawn,
He has dipt into on a battle-dawn:

Bid out of life by a nod, a glance,—
Stumbling, mute-mazed, at nature's chance,—
With a rapid finger circled round, 1220
Fixed to the first poor inch of ground
To fight from, where his foot was found;
Whose ear but a minute since lay free
To the wide camp's buzz and gossipry—
Summoned, a solitary man
To end his life where his life began,
From the safe glad rear, to the dreadful van!
Soul of mine, hadst thou caught and held
    By the hem of the vesture!—

XXI

                        And I caught
At the flying robe, and unrepelled 1230
    Was lapped again in its folds full-fraught
With warmth and wonder and delight,
God's mercy being infinite.
For scarce had the words escaped my tongue,
When, at a passionate bound, I sprung,
Out of the wandering world of rain,
Into the little chapel again.

XXII

How else was I found there, bolt upright
    On my bench, as if I had never left it?
—Never flung out on the common at night, 1240
    Nor met the storm and wedge-like cleft it,
Seen the raree-show of Peter's successor,
Or the laboratory of the Professor!
For the Vision, that was true, I wist,
True as that heaven and earth exist.
There sat my friend, the yellow and tall,
    With his neck and its wen in the selfsame place;
Yet my nearest neighbor's cheek showed gall.
    She had slid away a contemptuous space:
And the old fat woman, late so placable, 1250
Eyed me with symptoms, hardly mistakable,
Of her milk of kindness turning rancid.
In short, a spectator might have fancied

That I had nodded, betrayed by slumber,
   Yet kept my seat, a warning ghastly,
Through the heads of the sermon, nine in number,
   And woke up now at the tenth and lastly.
But again, could such disgrace have happened?
   Each friend at my elbow had surely nudged it;
And, as for the sermon, where did my nap end?   1260
   Unless I heard it, could I have judged it?
Could I report as I do at the close,
First, the preacher speaks through his nose:
Second, his gesture is too emphatic:
   Thirdly, to waive what's pedagogic,
   The subject-matter itself lacks logic:
Fourthly, the English is ungrammatic.
Great news! the preacher is found no Pascal,
Whom, if I pleased, I might to the task call
Of making square to a finite eye   1270
The circle of infinity,
And find so all-but-just-succeeding!
Great news! the sermon proves no reading
Where bee-like in the flowers I bury me,
Like Taylor's the immortal Jeremy!
And now that I know the very worst of him,
What was it I thought to obtain at first of him?
Ha! Is God mocked, as he asks?
Shall I take on me to change his tasks,
And dare, despatched to a river-head   1280
   For a simple draught of the element,
Neglect the thing for which he sent,
   And return with another thing instead?—
Saying, "Because the water found
Welling up from underground,
Is mingled with the taints of earth,
While thou, I know, dost laugh at dearth,
And couldst, at wink or word, convulse
The world with the leap of a river-pulse,—
Therefore I turned from the oozings muddy,   1290
   And bring thee a chalice I found, instead:
See the brave veins in the breccia ruddy!
   One would suppose that the marble bled.
What matters the water? A hope I have nursed:
The waterless cup will quench my thirst."
   —Better have knelt at the poorest stream

That trickles in pain from the straitest rift!
For the less or the more is all God's gift,
   Who blocks up or breaks wide the granite-seam.
And here, is there water or not, to drink?   1300
   I then, in ignorance and weakness,
Taking God's help, have attained to think
   My heart does best to receive in meekness
That mode of worship, as most to his mind,
Where earthly aids being cast behind,
His All in All appears serene
With the thinnest human veil between,
   Letting the mystic lamps, the seven,
   The many motions of his spirit,
Pass, as they list, to earth from heaven.   1310
   For the preacher's merit or demerit,
It were to be wished the flaws were fewer
   In the earthen vessel, holding treasure
Which lies as safe in a golden ewer;
   But the main thing is, does it hold good measure?
Heaven soon sets right all other matters!—
   Ask, else, these ruins of humanity,
This flesh worn out to rags and tatters,
   This soul at struggle with insanity,
Who thence take comfort—can I doubt?—   1320
Which an empire gained, were a loss without.
May it be mine! And let us hope
That no worse blessing befall the Pope,
Turned sick at last of to-day's buffoonery,
   Of posturings and petticoatings,
   Beside his Bourbon bully's gloatings
In the bloody orgies of drunk poltroonery!
Nor may the Professor forego its peace
   At Göttingen presently, when, in the dusk
Of his life, if his cough, as I fear, should increase,   1330
   Prophesied of by that horrible husk—
When thicker and thicker the darkness fills
The world through his misty spectacles,
And he gropes for something more substantial
   Than a fable, myth or personification,—
May Christ do for him what no mere man shall,
   And stand confessed as the God of salvation!
Meantime, in the still recurring fear
   Lest myself, at unawares, be found,

While attacking the choice of my neighbors round, 1340
With none of my own made—I choose here!
The giving out of the hymn reclaims me;
I have done: and if any blames me,
Thinking that merely to touch in brevity
   The topics I dwell on, were unlawful,—
Or worse, that I trench, with undue levity,
   On the bounds of the holy and the awful,—
I praise the heart, and pity the head of him,
And refer myself to THEE, instead of him,
Who head and heart alike discernest, 1350
   Looking below light speech we utter,
   When frothy spume and frequent sputter
Prove that the soul's depths boil in earnest!
May truth shine out, stand ever before us!
I put up pencil and join chorus
To Hepzibah Tune, without further apology,
   The last five verses of the third section
   Of the seventeenth hymn of Whitfield's Collection,
To conclude with the doxology.

MEN AND WOMEN [1855]

LOVE AMONG THE RUINS

I

Where the quiet-colored end of evening smiles,
      Miles and miles
On the solitary pastures where our sheep
      Half-asleep
Tinkle homeward thro' the twilight, stray or stop
      As they crop—
Was the site once of a city great and gay,
      (So they say)
Of our country's very capital, its prince
      Ages since
Held his court in, gathered councils, wielding far
      Peace or war.

II

Now,—the country does not even boast a tree,
      As you see,
To distinguish slopes of verdure, certain rills
      From the hills
Intersect and give a name to, (else they run
      Into one)
Where the domed and daring palace shot its spires
      Up like fires
O'er the hundred-gated circuit of a wall
      Bounding all,
Made of marble, men might march on nor be pressed,
      Twelve abreast.

III

And such plenty and perfection, see, of grass
         Never was!
Such a carpet as, this summer-time, o'erspreads
         And embeds
Every vestige of the city, guessed alone,
         Stock or stone—
Where a multitude of men breathed joy and woe
         Long ago;
Lust of glory pricked their hearts up, dread of shame
         Struck them tame;
And that glory and that shame alike, the gold
         Bought and sold.

IV

Now,—the single little turret that remains
         On the plains,
By the caper overrooted, by the gourd
         Overscored,
While the patching houseleek's head of blossom winks
         Through the chinks—
Marks the basement whence a tower in ancient time
         Sprang sublime,
And a burning ring, all round, the chariots traced
         As they raced,
And the monarch and his minions and his dames
         Viewed the games.

V

And I know, while thus the quiet-colored eve
         Smiles to leave
To their folding, all our many-tinkling fleece
         In such peace,
And the slopes and rills in undistinguished gray
         Melt away—
That a girl with eager eyes and yellow hair
         Waits me there
In the turret whence the charioteers caught soul
         For the goal,

When the king looked, where she looks now, breathless, dumb
    Till I come.

VI

But he looked upon the city, every side,
    Far and wide,
All the mountains topped with temples, all the glades'
    Colonnades,
All the causeys, bridges, aqueducts,—and then,
    All the men!
When I do come, she will speak not, she will stand,
    Either hand
On my shoulder, give her eyes the first embrace
    Of my face,
Ere we rush, ere we extinguish sight and speech
    Each on each.

VII

In one year they sent a million fighters forth
    South and North,
And they built their gods a brazen pillar high
    As the sky,
Yet reserved a thousand chariots in full force—
    Gold, of course.
Oh heart! oh blood that freezes, blood that burns!
    Earth's returns
For whole centuries of folly, noise and sin!
    Shut them in,
With their triumphs and their glories and the rest!
    Love is best.

A LOVERS' QUARREL

I

    OH, WHAT a dawn of day!
    How the March sun feels like May!
      All is blue again

After last night's rain,
And the South dries the hawthorn-spray.
    Only, my Love's away!
I'd as lief that the blue were gray.

                    II

Runnels, which rillets swell,
Must be dancing down the dell,
    With a foaming head
    On the beryl bed   10
Paven smooth as a hermit's cell;
    Each with a tale to tell,
Could my Love but attend as well.

                    III

Dearest, three months ago!
When we lived blocked-up with snow,—
    When the wind would edge
    In and in his wedge,
In, as far as the point could go—
    Not to our ingle, though,   20
Where we loved each the other so!

                    IV

Laughs with so little cause!
We devised games out of straws.
    We would try and trace
    One another's face
In the ash, as an artist draws;
    Free on each other's flaws,
How we chattered like two church daws!

                    V

What's in the "Times"?—a scold
At the Emperor deep and cold;   30
    He has taken a bride
    To his gruesome side,
That's as fair as himself is bold:

There they sit ermine-stoled,
And she powders her hair with gold.

VI

Fancy the Pampas' sheen!
Miles and miles of gold and green
   Where the sunflowers blow
   In a solid glow,
And—to break now and then the screen—   40
   Black neck and eyeballs keen,
Up a wild horse leaps between!

VII

Try, will our table turn?
Lay your hands there light, and yearn
   Till the yearning slips
   Thro' the finger-tips
In a fire which a few discern,
   And a very few feel burn,
And the rest, they may live and learn!

VIII

Then we would up and pace,   50
For a change, about the place,
   Each with arm o'er neck:
   'Tis our quarter-deck,
We are seamen in woful case.
   Help in the ocean-space!
Or, if no help, we'll embrace.

IX

See, how she looks now, dressed
In a sledging-cap and vest!
   'Tis a huge fur cloak—
   Like a reindeer's yoke   60
Falls the lappet along the breast:
   Sleeves for her arms to rest,
Or to hang, as my Love likes best.

X

Teach me to flirt a fan
As the Spanish ladies can,
    Or I tint your lip
    With a burnt stick's tip
And you turn into such a man!
    Just the two spots that span
Half the bill of the young male swan.   70

XI

Dearest, three months ago
When the mesmerizer Snow
    With his hand's first sweep
    Put the earth to sleep:
'Twas a time when the heart could show
    All—how was earth to know,
'Neath the mute hand's to-and-fro?

XII

Dearest, three months ago
When we loved each other so,
    Lived and loved the same   80
    Till an evening came
When a shaft from the devil's bow
    Pierced to our ingle-glow,
And the friends were friend and foe!

XIII

Not from the heart beneath—
'Twas a bubble born of breath,
    Neither sneer nor vaunt,
    Nor reproach nor taunt.
See a word, how it severeth!
    Oh, power of life and death   90
In the tongue, as the Preacher saith!

XIV

Woman, and will you cast
For a word, quite off at last
   Me, your own, your You,—
   Since, as truth is true,
I was You all the happy past—
   Me do you leave aghast
With the memories We amassed?

XV

Love, if you knew the light
That your soul casts in my sight,   100
   How I look to you
   For the pure and true
And the beauteous and the right,—
   Bear with a moment's spite
When a mere mote threats the white!

XVI

What of a hasty word?
Is the fleshly heart not stirred
   By a worm's pin-prick
   Where its roots are quick?
See the eye, by a fly's foot blurred—   110
   Ear, when a straw is heard
Scratch the brain's coat of curd!

XVII

Foul be the world or fair
More or less, how can I care?
   'Tis the world the same
   For my praise or blame,
And endurance is easy there.
   Wrong in the one thing rare—
Oh, it is hard to bear!

XVIII

Here's the spring back or close,   120
When the almond-blossom blows:
   We shall have the word
   In a minor third
There is none but the cuckoo knows:
   Heaps of the guelder-rose!
I must bear with it, I suppose.

XIX

Could but November come,
Were the noisy birds struck dumb
   At the warning slash
   Of his driver's-lash—   130
I would laugh like the valiant Thumb
   Facing the castle glum
And the giant's fee-faw-fum!

XX

Then, were the world well stripped
Of the gear wherein equipped
   We can stand apart,
   Heart dispense with heart
In the sun, with the flowers unnipped,
   Oh, the world's hangings ripped,
We were both in a bare-walled crypt!   140

XXI

Each in the crypt would cry
"But one freezes here! and why?
   When a heart, as chill,
   At my own would thrill
Back to life, and its fires out-fly?
   Heart, shall we live or die?
The rest, . . . settle by-and-by!"

XXII

So, she'd efface the score,
And forgive me as before.
　　It is twelve o'clock: 150
　　I shall hear her knock
In the worst of a storm's uproar,
　　I shall pull her through the door,
I shall have her for evermore!

EVELYN HOPE

ī

BEAUTIFUL Evelyn Hope is dead!
　　Sit and watch by her side an hour.
That is her book-shelf, this her bed;
　　She plucked that piece of geranium-flower,
Beginning to die too, in the glass;
　　Little has yet been changed, I think:
The shutters are shut, no light may pass
　　Save two long rays thro' the hinge's chink.

II

Sixteen years old when she died!
　　Perhaps she had scarcely heard my name;
It was not her time to love; beside,
　　Her life had many a hope and aim,
Duties enough and little cares,
　　And now was quiet, now astir,
Till God's hand beckoned unawares,—
　　And the sweet white brow is all of her.

III

Is it too late then, Evelyn Hope?
　　What, your soul was pure and true,
The good stars met in your horoscope,
　　Made you of spirit, fire and dew—
And, just because I was thrice as old

And our paths in the world diverged so wide,
Each was naught to each, must I be told?
　　We were fellow mortals, naught beside?

IV

No, indeed! for God above
　　Is great to grant, as mighty to make,
And creates the love to reward the love:
　　I claim you still, for my own love's sake!
Delayed it may be for more lives yet,
　　Through worlds I shall traverse, not a few:
Much is to learn, much to forget
　　Ere the time be come for taking you.

V

But the time will come,—at last it will,
　　When, Evelyn Hope, what meant (I shall say)
In the lower earth, in the years long still,
　　That body and soul so pure and gay?
Why your hair was amber, I shall divine,
　　And your mouth of your own geranium's red—
And what you would do with me, in fine,
　　In the new life come in the old one's stead.

VI

I have lived (I shall say) so much since then,
　　Given up myself so many times,
Gained me the gains of various men,
　　Ransacked the ages, spoiled the climes;
Yet one thing, one, in my soul's full scope,
　　Either I missed or itself missed me:
And I want and find you, Evelyn Hope!
　　What is the issue? let us see!

VII

I loved you, Evelyn, all the while.
　　My heart seemed full as it could hold?
There was place and to spare for the frank young smile,
　　And the red young mouth, and the hair's young gold.

So, hush,—I will give you this leaf to keep:
 See, I shut it inside the sweet cold hand!
There, that is our secret: go to sleep!
 You will wake, and remember, and understand.

UP AT A VILLA—DOWN IN THE CITY

(AS DISTINGUISHED BY AN ITALIAN PERSON OF QUALITY)

I

HAD I but plenty of money, money enough and to spare,
The house for me, no doubt, were a house in the city-square;
Ah, such a life, such a life, as one leads at the window there!

II

Something to see, by Bacchus, something to hear, at least!
There, the whole day long, one's life is a perfect feast;
While up at a villa one lives, I maintain it, no more than a beast.

III

Well now, look at our villa! stuck like the horn of a bull
Just on a mountain-edge as bare as the creature's skull,
Save a mere shag of a bush with hardly a leaf to pull!
—I scratch my own, sometimes, to see if the hair's turned
 wool.   10

IV

But the city, oh the city—the square with the houses! Why?
They are stone-faced, white as a curd, there's something to take
 the eye!
Houses in four straight lines, not a single front awry;
You watch who crosses and gossips, who saunters, who hurries by;
Green blinds, as a matter of course, to draw when the sun gets
 high;
And the shops with fanciful signs which are painted properly.

V

What of a villa? Though winter be over in March by rights,
'Tis May perhaps ere the snow shall have withered well off the
    heights:
You've the brown ploughed land before, where the oxen steam
    and wheeze,
And the hills over-smoked behind by the faint gray olive-
    trees.   20

VI

Is it better in May, I ask you? You've summer all at once;
In a day he leaps complete with a few strong April suns.
'Mid the sharp short emerald wheat, scarce risen three fingers
    well,
The wild tulip, at end of its tube, blows out its great red bell
Like a thin clear bubble of blood, for the children to pick and sell.

VII

Is it ever hot in the square? There's a fountain to spout and
    splash!
In the shade it sings and springs; in the shine such foam-bows
    flash
On the horses with curling fish-tails, that prance and paddle and
    pash
Round the lady atop in her conch—fifty gazers do not abash,
Though all that she wears is some weeds round her waist in a
    sort of sash.   30

VIII

All the year long at the villa, nothing to see though you linger,
Except yon cypress that points like death's lean lifted forefinger.
Some think fireflies pretty, when they mix i the corn and mingle,
Or thrid the stinking hemp till the stalks of it seem a-tingle.
Late August or early September, the stunning cicala is shrill,
And the bees keep their tiresome whine round the resinous firs
    on the hill.
Enough of the seasons,—I spare you the months of the fever and
    chill.

IX

Ere you open your eyes in the city, the blessed church-bells
    begin:
No sooner the bells leave off than the diligence rattles in:
You get the pick of the news, and it costs you never a pin.   40
By-and-by there's the travelling doctor gives pills, lets blood,
    draws teeth;
Or the Pulcinello-trumpet breaks up the market beneath.
At the post-office such a scene-picture—the new play, piping hot!
And a notice how, only this morning, three liberal thieves were
    shot.
Above it, behold the Archbishop's most fatherly of rebukes,
And beneath, with his crown and his lion, some little new law
    of the Duke's!
Or a sonnet with flowery marge, to the Reverend Don So-and-so
Who is Dante, Boccaccio, Petrarca, Saint Jerome and Cicero,
"And moreover," (the sonnet goes rhyming,) "the skirts of Saint
    Paul has reached,
Having preached us those six Lent-lectures more unctuous than
    ever he preached."   50
Noon strikes,—here sweeps the procession! our Lady borne smil-
    ing and smart
With a pink gauze gown all spangles, and seven swords stuck in
    her heart!
Bang-whang-whang goes the drum, *tootle-te-tootle* the fife;
No keeping one's haunches still: it's the greatest pleasure in life.

X

But bless you, it's dear—it's dear! fowls, wine, at double the rate.
They have clapped a new tax upon salt, and what oil pays pass-
    ing the gate
It's a horror to think of. And so, the villa for me, not the city!
Beggars can scarcely be choosers: but still—ah, the pity, the
    pity!
Look, two and two go the priests, then the monks with cowls
    and sandals,
And the penitents dressed in white shirts, a-holding the yellow
    candles;   60
One, he carries a flag up straight, and another a cross with
    handles,

And the Duke's guard brings up the rear, for the better preven-
    tion of scandals:
Bang-whang-whang goes the drum, *tootle-te-tootle* the fife.
Oh, a day in the city-square, there is no such pleasure in life!

A WOMAN'S LAST WORD

I

LET's contend no more, Love,
    Strive nor weep:
All be as before, Love,
    —Only sleep!

II

What so wild as words are?
    I and thou
In debate, as birds are,
    Hawk on bough!

III

See the creature stalking
    While we speak!
Hush and hide the talking,
    Cheek on cheek!

IV

What so false as truth is,
    False to thee?
Where the serpent's tooth is
    Shun the tree—

V

Where the apple reddens
    Never pry—
Lest we lose our Edens,
    Eve and I.

VI

Be a god and hold me
  With a charm!
Be a man and fold me
  With thine arm!

VII

Teach me, only teach, Love!
  As I ought
I will speak thy speech, Love,
  Think thy thought—

VIII

Meet, if thou require it,
  Both demands,
Laying flesh and spirit
  In thy hands.

IX

That shall be to-morrow
  Not to-night:
I must bury sorrow
  Out of sight:

X

—Must a little weep, Love,
  (Foolish me!)
And so fall asleep, Love,
  Loved by thee.

FRA LIPPO LIPPI

I AM poor brother Lippo, by your leave!
You need not clap your torches to my face.
Zooks, what's to blame? you think you see a monk!

What, 'tis past midnight, and you go the rounds,
And here you catch me at an alley's end
Where sportive ladies leave their doors ajar?
The Carmine's my cloister: hunt it up,
Do,—harry out, if you must show your zeal,
Whatever rat, there, haps on his wrong hole,
And nip each softling of a wee white mouse,
Weke, weke, that's crept to keep him company! 10
Aha, you know your betters! Then, you'll take
Your hand away that's fiddling on my throat,
And please to know me likewise. Who am I?
Why, one, sir, who is lodging with a friend
Three streets off—he's a certain . . . how d'ye call?
Master—a . . . Cosimo of the Medici,
I' the house that caps the corner. Boh! you were best!
Remember and tell me, the day you're hanged,
How you affected such a gullet's-gripe! 20
But you, sir, it concerns you that your knaves
Pick up a manner nor discredit you:
Zooks, are we pilchards, that they sweep the streets
And count fair prize what comes into their net?
He's Judas to a tittle, that man is!
Just such a face! Why, sir, you make amends.
Lord, I'm not angry! Bid your hangdogs go
Drink out this quarter-florin to the health
Of the munificent House that harbors me
(And many more beside, lads! more beside!) 30
And all's come square again. I'd like his face—
His, elbowing on his comrade in the door
With the pike and lantern,—for the slave that holds
John Baptist's head a-dangle by the hair
With one hand ("Look you, now," as who should say)
And his weapon in the other, yet unwiped!
It's not your chance to have a bit of chalk,
A wood-coal or the like? or you should see!
Yes, I'm the painter, since you style me so.
What, brother Lippo's doings, up and down, 40
You know them and they take you? like enough!
I saw the proper twinkle in your eye—
'Tell you, I liked your looks at very first.
Let's sit and set things straight now, hip to haunch.
Here's spring come, and the nights one makes up bands
To roam the town and sing out carnival,

And I've been three weeks shut within my mew,
A-painting for the great man, saints and saints
And saints again. I could not paint all night—
Ouf! I leaned out of window for fresh air.   50
There came a hurry of feet and little feet,
A sweep of lute-strings, laughs, and whifts of song,—
Flower o' the broom,
Take away love, and our earth is a tomb!
Flower o' the quince,
I let Lisa go, and what good in life since?
Flower o' the thyme—and so on. Round they went.
Scarce had they turned the corner when a titter
Like the skipping of rabbits by moonlight,—three slim shapes,
And a face that looked up . . . zooks, sir, flesh and blood,   60
That's all I'm made of! Into shreds it went,
Curtain and counterpane and coverlet,
All the bed-furniture—a dozen knots,
There was a ladder! Down I let myself,
Hands and feet, scrambling somehow, and so dropped,
And after them. I came up with the fun
Hard by Saint Laurence, hail fellow, well met,—
Flower o' the rose,
If I've been merry, what matter who knows?
And so as I was stealing back again   70
To get to bed and have a bit of sleep
Ere I rise up to-morrow and go work
On Jerome knocking at his poor old breast
With his great round stone to subdue the flesh,
You snap me of the sudden. Ah, I see!
Though your eye twinkles still, you shake your head—
Mine's shaved—a monk, you say—the sting's in that!
If Master Cosimo announced himself,
Mum's the word naturally; but a monk!
Come, what am I a beast for? tell us, now!   80
I was a baby when my mother died
And father died and left me in the street.
I starved there, God knows how, a year or two
On fig-skins, melon-parings, rinds and shucks,
Refuse and rubbish. One fine frosty day,
My stomach being empty as your hat,
The wind doubled me up and down I went.
Old Aunt Lapaccia trussed me with one hand,
(Its fellow was a stinger as I knew)

And so along the wall, over the bridge,   90
By the straight cut to the convent. Six words there,
While I stood munching my first bread that month:
"So, boy, you're minded," quoth the good fat father
Wiping his own mouth, 'twas refection-time,—
"To quit this very miserable world?
Will you renounce" . . . "the mouthful of bread?" thought I;
By no means! Brief, they made a monk of me;
I did renounce the world, its pride and greed,
Palace, farm, villa, shop and banking-house,
Trash, such as these poor devils of Medici   100
Have given their hearts to—all at eight years old.
Well, sir, I found in time, you may be sure,
'Twas not for nothing—the good bellyful,
The warm serge and the rope that goes all round,
And day-long blessed idleness beside!
"Let's see what the urchin's fit for"—that came next.
Not overmuch their way, I must confess.
Such a to-do! They tried me with their books:
Lord, they'd have taught me Latin in pure waste!
Flower o' the clove,   110
All the Latin I construe is, "amo" I love!
But, mind you, when a boy starves in the streets
Eight years together, as my fortune was,
Watching folk's faces to know who will fling
The bit of half-stripped grape-bunch he desires,
And who will curse or kick him for his pains,—
Which gentleman processional and fine,
Holding a candle to the Sacrament,
Will wink and let him lift a plate and catch
The droppings of the wax to sell again,   120
Or holla for the Eight and have him whipped,—
How say I?—nay, which dog bites, which lets drop
His bone from the heap of offal in the street,—
Why, soul and sense of him grow sharp alike,
He learns the look of things, and none the less
For admonition from the hunger-pinch.
I had a store of such remarks, be sure,
Which, after I found leisure, turned to use.
I drew men's faces on my copy-books,
Scrawled them within the antiphonary's marge,   130
Joined legs and arms to the long music-notes,
Found eyes and nose and chin for A's and B's,

And made a string of pictures of the world
Betwixt the ins and outs of verb and noun,
On the wall, the bench, the door. The monks looked black.
"Nay," quoth the Prior, "turn him out, d' ye say?
In no wise. Lose a crow and catch a lark.
What if at last we get our man of parts,
We Carmelites, like those Camaldolese
And Preaching Friars, to do our church up fine   140
And put the front on it that ought to be!"
And hereupon he bade me daub away.
Thank you! my head being crammed, the walls a blank,
Never was such prompt disemburdening.
First, every sort of monk, the black and white,
I drew them, fat and lean: then, folk at church,
From good old gossips waiting to confess
Their cribs of barrel-droppings, candle-ends,—
To the breathless fellow at the altar-foot,
Fresh from his murder, safe and sitting there   150
With the little children round him in a row
Of admiration, half for his beard and half
For that white anger of his victim's son
Shaking a fist at him with one fierce arm,
Signing himself with the other because of Christ
(Whose sad face on the cross sees only this
After the passion of a thousand years)
Till some poor girl, her apron o'er her head,
(Which the intense eyes looked through) came at eve
On tiptoe, said a word, dropped in a loaf,   160
Her pair of earrings and a bunch of flowers
(The brute took growling), prayed, and so was gone.
I painted all, then cried " 'Tis ask and have;
Choose, for more's ready!"—laid the ladder flat,
And showed my covered bit of cloister-wall.
The monks closed in a circle and praised loud
Till checked, taught what to see and not to see,
Being simple bodies,—"That's the very man!
Look at the boy who stoops to pat the dog!
That woman's like the Prior's niece who comes   170
To care about his asthma: it's the life!"
But there my trumph's straw-fire flared and funked;
Their betters took their turn to see and say:
The Prior and the learned pulled a face
And stopped all that in no time. "How? what's here?

Quite from the mark of painting, bless us all!
Faces, arms, legs and bodies like the true
As much as pea and pea! it's devil's-game!
Your business is not to catch men with show,
With homage to the perishable clay,   180
But lift them over it, ignore it all,
Make them forget there's such a thing as flesh.
Your business is to paint the souls of men—
Man's soul, and it's a fire, smoke . . . no, it's not . . .
It's vapor done up like a new-born babe—
(In that shape when you die it leaves your mouth)
It's . . . well, what matters talking, it's the soul!
Give us no more of body than shows soul!
Here's Giotto, with his Saint a-praising God,
That sets us praising,—why not stop with him?   190
Why put all thoughts of praise out of our head
With wonder at lines, colors, and what not?
Paint the soul, never mind the legs and arms!
Rub all out, try at it a second time.
Oh, that white smallish female with the breasts,
She's just my niece . . . Herodias, I would say,—
Who went and danced and got men's heads cut off!
Have it all out!" Now, is this sense, I ask?
A fine way to paint soul, by painting body
So ill, the eye can't stop there, must go further   200
And can't fare worse! Thus, yellow does for white
When what you put for yellow's simply black,
And any sort of meaning looks intense
When all beside itself means and looks naught.
Why can't a painter lift each foot in turn,
Left foot and right foot, go a double step,
Make his flesh liker and his soul more like,
Both in their order? Take the prettiest face,
The Prior's niece . . . patron-saint—is it so pretty
You can't discover if it means hope, fear,   210
Sorrow or joy? won't beauty go with these?
Suppose I've made her eyes all right and blue,
Can't I take breath and try to add life's flash,
And then add soul and heighten them three-fold?
Or say there's beauty with no soul at all—
(I never saw it—put the case the same—)
If you get simple beauty and naught else,
You get about the best thing God invents:

That's somewhat: and you'll find the soul you have missed,
Within yourself, when you return him thanks.   220
"Rub all out!" Well, well, there's my life, in short,
And so the thing has gone on ever since.
I'm grown a man no doubt, I've broken bounds:
You should not take a fellow eight years old
And make him swear to never kiss the girls.
I'm my own master, paint now as I please—
Having a friend, you see, in the Corner-house!
Lord, it's fast holding by the rings in front—
Those great rings serve more purposes than just
To paint a flag in, or tie up a horse!   230
And yet the old schooling sticks, the old grave eyes
Are peeping o'er my shoulder as I work,
The heads shake still—"It's art's decline, my son!
You're not of the true painters, great and old;
Brother Angelico's the man, you'll find;
Brother Lorenzo stands his single peer:
Fag on at flesh, you'll never make the third!"
Flower o' the pine,
You keep your mistr . . . manners, and I'll stick to mine!
I'm not the third, then: bless us, they must know!   240
Don't you think they're the likeliest to know,
They with their Latin? So, I swallow my rage,
Clench my teeth, suck my lips in tight, and paint
To please them—sometimes do and sometimes don't;
For, doing most, there's pretty sure to come
A turn, some warm eve finds me at my saints—
A laugh, a cry, the business of the world—
(*Flower o' the peach,*
Death for us all, and his own life for each!)
And my whole soul revolves, the cup runs over,   250
The world and life's too big to pass for a dream,
And I do these wild things in sheer despite,
And play the fooleries you catch me at,
In pure rage! The old mill-horse, out at grass
After hard years, throws up his stiff heels so,
Although the miller does not preach to him
The only good of grass is to make chaff.
What would men have? Do they like grass or no—
May they or mayn't they? all I want's the thing
Settled forever one way. As it is,   260
You tell too many lies and hurt yourself:

You don't like what you only like too much,
You do like what, if given you at your word,
You find abundantly detestable.
For me, I think I speak as I was taught;
I always see the garden and God there
A-making man's wife: and, my lesson learned,
The value and significance of flesh,
I can't unlearn ten minutes afterwards.

    You understand me: I'm a beast, I know.　　　270
But see, now—why, I see as certainly
As that the morning-star's about to shine,
What will hap some day. We've a youngster here
Comes to our convent, studies what I do,
Slouches and stares and lets no atom drop:
His name is Guidi—he'll not mind the monks—
They call him Hulking Tom, he lets them talk—
He picks my practice up—he'll paint apace,
I hope so—though I never live so long,
I know what's sure to follow. You be judge!　　　280
You speak no Latin more than I, belike;
However, you're my man, you've seen the world
—The beauty and the wonder and the power,
The shapes of things, their colors, lights and shades,
Changes, surprises,—and God made it all!
—For what? Do you feel thankful, ay or no,
For this fair town's face, yonder river's line,
The mountain round it and the sky above,
Much more the figures of man, woman, child,
These are the frame to? What's it all about?　　　290
To be passed over, despised? or dwelt upon,
Wondered at? oh, this last of course!—you say.
But why not do as well as say,—paint these
Just as they are, careless what comes of it?
God's works—paint any one, and count it crime
To let a truth slip. Don't object, "His works
Are here already; nature is complete:
Suppose you reproduce her—(which you can't)
There's no advantage! you must beat her, then."
For, don't you mark? we're made so that we love　　　300
First when we see them painted, things we have passed
Perhaps a hundred times nor cared to see;
And so they are better, painted—better to us,

Which is the same thing. Art was given for that;
God uses us to help each other so,
Lending our minds out. Have you noticed, now,
Your cullion's hanging face? A bit of chalk,
And trust me but you should, though! How much more,
If I drew higher things with the same truth!
That were to take the Prior's pulpit-place,   310
Interpret God to all of you! Oh, oh,
It makes me mad to see what men shall do
And we in our graves! This world's no blot for us,
Nor blank; it means intensely, and means good:
To find its meaning is my meat and drink.
"Ay, but you don't so instigate to prayer!"
Strikes in the Prior: "when your meaning's plain
It does not say to folk—remember matins,
Or, mind you fast next Friday!" Why, for this
What need of art at all? A skull and bones,   320
Two bits of stick nailed crosswise, or, what's best,
A bell to chime the hour with, does as well.
I painted a Saint Laurence six months since
At Prato, splashed the fresco in fine style:
"How looks my painting, now the scaffold's down?"
I ask a brother: "Hugely," he returns—
"Already not one phiz of your three slaves
Who turn the Deacon off his toasted side,
But's scratched and prodded to our heart's content,
The pious people have so eased their own   330
With coming to say prayers there in a rage:
We get on fast to see the bricks beneath.
Expect another job this time next year,
For pity and religion grow i' the crowd—
Your painting serves its purpose!" Hang the fools!

    —That is—you'll not mistake an idle word
Spoke in a huff by a poor monk, God wot,
Tasting the air this spicy night which turns
The unaccustomed head like Chianti wine!
Oh, the church knows! don't misreport me, now!   340
It's natural a poor monk out of bounds
Should have his apt word to excuse himself:
And hearken how I plot to make amends.
I have bethought me: I shall paint a piece
. . . There's for you! Give me six months, then go, see

Something in Sant' Ambrogio's! Bless the nuns!
They want a cast o' my office. I shall paint
God in the midst, Madonna and her babe,
Ringed by a bowery flowery angel-brood,
Lilies and vestments and white faces, sweet   350
As puff on puff of grated orris-root
When ladies crowd to Church at midsummer.
And then i' the front, of course a saint or two—
Saint John, because he saves the Florentines,
Saint Ambrose, who puts down in black and white
The convent's friends and gives them a long day,
And Job, I must have him there past mistake,
The man of Uz (and Us without the z,
Painters who need his patience). Well, all these
Secured at their devotions, up shall come   360
Out of a corner when you least expect,
As one by a dark stair into a great light,
Music and talking, who but Lippo! I!—
Mazed, motionless and moonstruck—I'm the man!
Back I shrink—what is this I see and hear?
I, caught up with my monk's-things by mistake,
My old serge gown and rope that goes all round,
I, in this presence, this pure company!
Where's a hole, where's a corner for escape?
Then steps a sweet angelic slip of a thing   370
Forward, puts out a soft palm—"Not so fast!"
—Addresses the celestial presence, "nay—
He made you and devised you, after all,
Though he's none of you! Could Saint John there draw—
His camel-hair make up a painting-brush?
We come to brother Lippo for all that,
Iste perfecit opus!" So, all smile—
I shuffle sideways with my blushing face
Under the cover of a hundred wings
Thrown like a spread of kirtles when you're gay   380
And play hot cockles, all the doors being shut,
Till, wholly unexpected, in there pops
The hothead husband! Thus I scuttle off
To some safe bench behind, not letting go
The palm of her, the little lily thing
That spoke the good word for me in the nick,
Like the Prior's niece . . . Saint Lucy, I would say.
And so all's saved for me, and for the church

A pretty picture gained. Go, six months hence!
Your hand, sir, and good-bye: no lights, no lights!   390
The street's hushed, and I know my own way back,
Don't fear me! There's the gray beginning. Zooks!

A TOCCATA OF GALUPPI'S

I

OH, GALUPPI, Baldassaro, this is very sad to find!
I can hardly misconceive you; it would prove me deaf and blind;
But although I take your meaning, 'tis with such a heavy mind!

II

Here you come with your old music, and here's all the good it
    brings.
What, they lived once thus at Venice where the merchants were
    the kings,
Where Saint Mark's is, where the Doges used to wed the sea with
    rings?

III

Ay, because the sea's the street there; and 'tis arched by . . .
    what you call
. . . Shylock's bridge with houses on it, where they kept the car-
    nival:
I was never out of England—it's as if I saw it all.

IV

Did young people take their pleasure when the sea was warm in
    May?
Balls and masks begun at midnight, burning ever to mid-day,
When they made up fresh adventures for the morrow, do you say?

V

Was a lady such a lady, cheeks so round and lips so red,—
On her neck the small face buoyant, like a bell-flower on its bed,

O'er the breast's superb abundance where a man might base his
    head?

VI

Well, and it was graceful of them—they'd break talk off and
    afford
—She, to bite her mask's black velvet—he, to finger on his sword,
While you sat and played Toccatas, stately at the clavichord?

VII

What? Those lesser thirds so plaintive, sixths diminished, sigh on
    sigh,
Told them something? Those suspensions, those solutions—"Must
    we die?"
Those commiserating sevenths—"Life might last! we can but try!"

VIII

"Were you happy?"—"Yes."—"And are you still as happy?"—
    "Yes. And you?"
—"Then, more kisses!"—"Did *I* stop them, when a million seemed
    so few?"
Hark, the dominant's persistence till it must be answered to!

IX

So, an octave struck the answer. Oh, they praised you, I dare say!
"Brave Galuppi! that was music! good alike at grave and gay!
I can always leave off talking when I hear a master play!"

X

Then they left you for their pleasure: till in due time, one by one,
Some with lives that came to nothing, some with deeds as well
    undone,
Death stepped tacitly and took them where they never see the
    sun.

XI

But when I sit down to reason, think to take my stand nor swerve,
While I triumph o'er a secret wrung from nature's close reserve,
In you come with your cold music till I creep thro' every nerve.

XII

Yes, you, like a ghostly cricket, creaking where a house was
    burned:
"Dust and ashes, dead and done with, Venice spent what Venice
    earned.
The soul, doubtless, is immortal—where a soul can be discerned.

XIII

"Yours for instance: you know physics, something of geology,
Mathematics are your pastime; souls shall rise in their degree;
Butterflies may dread extinction,—you'll not die, it cannot be!

XIV

"As for Venice and her people, merely born to bloom and drop,
Here on earth they bore their fruitage, mirth and folly were the
    crop:
What of soul was left, I wonder, when the kissing had to stop?

XV

"Dust and ashes!" So you creak it, and I want the heart to scold.
Dear dead women, with such hair, too—what's become of all the
    gold
Used to hang and brush their bosoms? I feel chilly and grown
    old.

BY THE FIRE-SIDE

I

How well I know what I mean to do
    When the long dark autumn-evenings come:
And where, my soul, is thy pleasant hue?
    With the music of all thy voices, dumb
In life's November too!

II

I shall be found by the fire, suppose,
  O'er a great wise book as beseemeth age,
While the shutters flap as the cross-wind blows
  And I turn the page, and I turn the page,
Not verse now, only prose!   10

III

Till the young ones whisper, finger on lip,
  "There he is at it, deep in Greek:
Now then, or never, out we slip
  To cut from the hazels by the creek
A mainmast for our ship!"

IV

I shall be at it indeed, my friends:
  Greek puts already on either side
Such a branch-work forth as soon extends
  To a vista opening far and wide,
And I pass out where it ends.   20

V

The outside-frame, like your hazel-trees:
  But the inside-archway widens fast,
And a rarer sort succeeds to these,
  And we slope to Italy at last
And youth, by green degrees.

VI

I follow wherever I am led,
  Knowing so well the leader's hand:
Oh woman-country, wooed not wed,
  Loved all the more by earth's male-lands,
Laid to their hearts instead!   30

VII

Look at the ruined chapel again
    Half-way up in the Alpine gorge!
Is that a tower, I point you plain,
    Or is it a mill, or an iron-forge
Breaks solitude in vain?

VIII

A turn, and we stand in the heart of things;
    The woods are round us, heaped and dim;
From slab to slab how it slips and springs,
    The thread of water single and slim,
Through the ravage some torrent brings!   40

IX

Does it feed the little lake below?
    That speck of white just on its marge
Is Pella; see, in the evening-glow,
    How sharp the silver spear-heads charge
When Alp meets heaven in snow!

X

On our other side is the straight-up rock;
    And a path is kept 'twixt the gorge and it
By boulder-stones where lichens mock
    The marks on a moth, and small ferns fit
Their teeth to the polished block.   50

XI

Oh the sense of the yellow mountain-flowers,
    And thorny balls, each three in one,
The chestnuts throw on our path in showers!
    For the drop of the woodland fruit's begun,
These early November hours,

XII

That crimson the creeper's leaf across
   Like a splash of blood, intense, abrupt,
O'er a shield else gold from rim to boss,
   And lay it for show on the fairy-cupped
Elf-needled mat of moss,   60

XIII

By the rose-flesh mushrooms, undivulged
   Last evening—nay, in to-day's first dew
Yon sudden coral nipple bulged,
   Where a freaked fawn-colored flaky crew
Of toadstools peep indulged.

XIV

And yonder, at foot of the fronting ridge
   That takes the turn to a range beyond,
Is the chapel reached by the one-arched bridge
   Where the water is stopped in a stagnant pond
Danced over by the midge.   70

XV

The chapel and bridge are of stone alike,
   Blackish-gray and mostly wet;
Cut hemp-stalks steep in the narrow dyke.
   See here again, how the lichens fret
And the roots of the ivy strike!

XVI

Poor little place, where its one priest comes
   On a festa-day, if he comes at all,
To the dozen folk from their scattered homes,
   Gathered within that precinct small
By the dozen ways one roams—   80

XVII

To drop from the charcoal-burners' huts,
   Or climb from the hemp-dressers' low shed,
Leave the grange where the woodman stores his nuts,
   Or the wattled cote where the fowlers spread
Their gear on the rock's bare juts.

XVIII

It has some pretension too, this front,
   With its bit of fresco half-moon-wise
Set over the porch, Art's early wont:
   'Tis John in the Desert, I surmise,
But has borne the weather's brunt—   90

XIX

Not from the fault of the builder, though,
   For a penthouse properly projects
Where three carved beams make a certain show,
   Dating—good thought of our architect's—
'Five, six, nine, he lets you know.

XX

And all day long a bird sings there,
   And a stray sheep drinks at the pond at times;
The place is silent and aware;
   It has had its scenes, its joys and crimes,
But that is its own affair.   100

XXI

My perfect wife, my Leonor,
   Oh heart, my own, oh eyes, mine too,
Whom else could I dare look backward for,
   With whom beside should I dare pursue
The path gray heads abhor?

XXII

For it leads to a crag's sheer edge with them;
    Youth, flowery all the way, there stops—
Not they; age threatens and they contemn,
    Till they reach the gulf wherein youth drops,
One inch from life's safe hem!   110

XXIII

With me, youth led . . . I will speak now,
    No longer watch you as you sit
Reading by fire-light, that great brow
    And the spirit-small hand propping it,
Mutely, my heart knows how—

XXIV

When, if I think but deep enough,
    You are wont to answer, prompt as rhyme;
And you, too, find without rebuff
    Response your soul seeks many a time
Piercing its fine flesh-stuff.   120

XXV

My own, confirm me! If I tread
    This path back, is it not in pride
To think how little I dreamed it led
    To an age so blest that, by its side,
Youth seems the waste instead?

XXVI

My own, see where the years conduct!
    At first, 'twas something our two souls
Should mix as mists do; each is sucked
    In each now: on, the new stream rolls,
Whatever rocks obstruct.   130

XXVII

Think, when our one soul understands
   The great Word which makes all things new,
When earth breaks up and heaven expands,
   How will the change strike me and you
In the house not made with hands?

XXVIII

Oh I must feel your brain prompt mine,
   Your heart anticipate my heart,
You must be just before, in fine,
   See and make me see, for your part,
New depths of the divine!   140

XXIX

But who could have expected this
   When we two drew together first
Just for the obvious human bliss,
   To satisfy life's daily thirst
With a thing men seldom miss?

XXX

Come back with me to the first of all,
   Let us lean and love it over again,
Let us now forget and now recall,
   Break the rosary in a pearly rain,
And gather what we let fall!   150

XXXI

What did I say?—that a small bird sings
   All day long, save when a brown pair
Of hawks from the wood float with wide wings
   Strained to a bell: 'gainst noon-day glare
You count the streaks and rings.

XXXII

But at afternoon or almost eve
    'Tis better; then the silence grows
To that degree, you half believe
    It must get rid of what it knows,
Its bosom does so heave.   160

XXXIII

Hither we walked then, side by side,
    Arm in arm and cheek to cheek,
And still I questioned or replied,
    While my heart, convulsed to really speak,
Lay choking in its pride.

XXXIV

Silent the crumbling bridge we cross,
    And pity and praise the chapel sweet,
And care about the fresco's loss,
    And wish for our souls a like retreat,
And wonder at the moss.   170

XXXV

Stoop and kneel on the settle under,
    Look through the window's grated square:
Nothing to see! For fear of plunder,
    The cross is down and the altar bare,
As if thieves don't fear thunder.

XXXVI

We stoop and look in through the grate,
    See the little porch and rustic door,
Read duly the dead builder's date;
    Then cross the bridge that we crossed before,
Take the path again—but wait!   180

XXXVII

Oh moment, one and infinite!
    The water slips o'er stock and stone;
The West is tender, hardly bright:
    How gray at once is the evening grown—
One star, its chrysolite!

XXXVIII

We two stood there with never a third,
    But each by each, as each knew well:
The sights we saw and the sounds we heard,
    The lights and the shades made up a spell
Till the trouble grew and stirred.   190

XXXIX

Oh, the little more, and how much it is!
    And the little less, and what worlds away!
How a sound shall quicken content to bliss,
    Or a breath suspend the blood's best play,
And life be a proof of this!

XL

Had she willed it, still had stood the screen
    So slight, so sure, 'twixt my love and her:
I could fix her face with a guard between,
    And find her soul as when friends confer,
Friends—lovers that might have been.   200

XLI

For my heart had a touch of the woodland-time,
    Wanting to sleep now over its best.
Shake the whole tree in the summer-prime,
    But bring to the last leaf no such test!
"Hold the last fast!" runs the rhyme.

XLII

For a chance to make your little much,
    To gain a lover and lose a friend,
Venture the tree and a myriad such,
    When nothing you mar but the year can mend:
But a last leaf—fear to touch!   210

XLIII

Yet should it unfasten itself and fall
    Eddying down till it find your face
At some slight wind—best chance of all!
    Be your heart henceforth its dwelling-place
You trembled to forestall!

XLIV

Worth how well, those dark gray eyes,
    That hair so dark and dear, how worth
That a man should strive and agonize,
    And taste a veriest hell on earth
For the hope of such a prize!   220

XLV

You might have turned and tried a man,
    Set him a space to weary and wear,
And prove which suited more your plan,
    His best of hope or his worst despair,
Yet end as he began.

XLVI

But you spared me this, like the heart you are,
    And filled my empty heart at a word.
If two lives join, there is oft a scar,
    They are one and one, with a shadowy third;
One near one is too far.   230

XLVII

A moment after, and hands unseen
　　Were hanging the night around us fast;
But we knew that a bar was broken between
　　Life and life: we were mixed at last
In spite of the mortal screen.

XLVIII

The forests had done it; there they stood;
　　We caught for a moment the powers at play:
They had mingled us so, for once and good,
　　Their work was done—we might go or stay,
They relapsed to their ancient mood.　　　240

XLIX

How the world is made for each of us!
　　How all we perceive and know in it
Tends to some moment's product thus,
　　When a soul declares itself—to wit,
By its fruit, the thing it does!

L

Be hate that fruit or love that fruit,
　　It forwards the general deed of man,
And each of the Many helps to recruit
　　The life of the race by a general plan;
Each living his own, to boot.　　　250

LI

I am named and known by that moment's feat;
　　There took my station and degree;
So grew my own small life complete,
　　As nature obtained her best of me—
One born to love you, sweet!

LII

And to watch you sink by the fire-side now
    Back again, as you mutely sit
Musing by fire-light, that great brow
    And the spirit-small hand propping it,
Yonder, my heart knows how!   260

LIII

So, earth has gained by one man the more,
    And the gain of earth must be heaven's gain too;
And the whole is well worth thinking o'er
    When autumn comes: which I mean to do
One day, as I said before.

ANY WIFE TO ANY HUSBAND

I

My LOVE, this is the bitterest, that thou—
Who art all truth, and who dost love me now
    As thine eyes say, as thy voice breaks to say—
Shouldst love so truly, and couldst love me still
A whole long life through, had but love its will,
    Would death that leads me from thee brook delay.

II

I have but to be by thee, and thy hand
Will never let mine go, nor heart withstand
    The beating of my heart to reach its place.
When shall I look for thee and feel thee gone?   10
When cry for the old comfort and find none?
    Never, I know! Thy soul is in thy face.

III

Oh, I should fade—'tis willed so! Might I save,
Gladly I would, whatever beauty gave
    Joy to thy sense, for that was precious too.
It is not to be granted. But the soul
Whence the love comes, all ravage leaves that whole;
    Vainly the flesh fades; soul makes all things new.

IV

It would not be because my eye grew dim
Thou couldst not find the love there, thanks to Him 20
   Who never is dishonored in the spark
He gave us from his fire of fires, and bade
Remember whence it sprang, nor be afraid
   While that burns on, though all the rest grow dark.

V

So, how thou wouldst be perfect, white and clean
Outside as inside, soul and soul's demesne
   Alike, this body given to show it by!
Oh, three-parts through the worst of life's abyss,
What plaudits from the next world after this,
   Couldst thou repeat a stroke and gain the sky! 30

VI

And is it not the bitterer to think
That, disengage our hands and thou wilt sink
   Although thy love was love in very deed?
I know that nature! Pass a festive day,
Thou dost not throw its relic-flower away
   Nor bid its music's loitering echo speed.

VII

Thou let'st the stranger's glove lie where it fell;
If old things remain old things all is well,
   For thou art grateful as becomes man best:
And hadst thou only heard me play one tune, 40
Or viewed me from a window, not so soon
   With thee would such things fade as with the rest.

VIII

I seem to see! We meet and part; 'tis brief;
The book I opened keeps a folded leaf,
   The very chair I sat on, breaks the rank;
That is a portrait of me on the wall—

Three lines, my face comes at so slight a call:
 And for all this, one little hour to thank!

IX

But now, because the hour through years was fixed,
Because our inmost beings met and mixed,   50
 Because thou once hast loved me—wilt thou dare
Say to thy soul and Who may list beside,
"Therefore she is immortally my bride;
 Chance cannot change my love, nor time impair.

X

"So, what if in the dusk of life that's left,
I, a tired traveller of my sun bereft,
 Look from my path when, mimicking the same,
The fire-fly glimpses past me, come and gone?
—Where was it till the sunset? where anon
 It will be at the sunrise! What's to blame?"   60

XI

Is it so helpful to thee? Canst thou take
The mimic up, nor, for the true thing's sake,
 Put gently by such efforts at a beam?
Is the remainder of the way so long,
Thou need'st the little solace, thou the strong?
 Watch out thy watch, let weak ones doze and dream!

XII

—Ah, but the fresher faces! "Is it true,"
Thou'lt ask, "some eyes are beautiful and new?
 Some hair,—how can one choose but grasp such wealth?
And if a man would press his lips to lips   70
Fresh as the wilding hedge-rose-cup there slips
 The dew-drop out of, must it be by stealth?

XIII

"It cannot change the love still kept for Her,
More than if such a picture I prefer

Passing a day with, to a room's bare side:
The painted form takes nothing she possessed,
Yet, while the Titian's Venus lies at rest,
    A man looks. Once more, what is there to chide?"

XIV

So must I see, from where I sit and watch,
My own self sell myself, my hand attach   80
    Its warrant to the very thefts from me—
Thy singleness of soul that made me proud,
Thy purity of heart I loved aloud,
    Thy man's-truth I was bold to bid God see!

XV

Love so, then, if thou wilt! Give all thou canst
Away to the new faces—disentranced,
    (Say it and think it) obdurate no more:
Re-issue looks and words from the old mint,
Pass them afresh, no matter whose the print
    Image and superscription once they bore!   90

XVI

Re-coin thyself and give it them to spend,—
It all comes to the same thing at the end,
    Since mine thou wast, mine art and mine shalt be,
Faithful or faithless, sealing up the sum
Or lavish of my treasure, thou must come
    Back to the heart's place here I keep for thee!

XVII

Only, why should it be with stain at all?
Why must I, 'twixt the leaves of coronal,
    Put any kiss of pardon on thy brow?
Why need the other women know so much,   100
And talk together, "Such the look and such
    The smile he used to love with, then as now!"

XVIII

Might I die last and show thee! Should I find
Such hardship in the few years left behind,
　　If free to take and light my lamp, and go
Into thy tomb, and shut the door and sit,
Seeing thy face on those four sides of it
　　The better that they are so blank, I know!

XIX

Why, time was what I wanted, to turn o'er
Within my mind each look, get more and more   110
　　By heart each word, too much to learn at first;
And join thee all the fitter for the pause
'Neath the low doorway's lintel. That were cause
　　For lingering, though thou calledst, if I durst!

XX

And yet thou art the nobler of us two:
What dare I dream of, that thou canst not do,
　　Outstripping my ten small steps with one stride?
I'll say then, here's a trial and a task—
Is it to bear?—if easy, I'll not ask:
　　Though love fail, I can trust on in thy pride.   120

XXI

Pride?—when those eyes forestall the life behind
The death I have to go through!—when I find,
　　Now that I want thy help most, all of thee!
What did I fear? Thy love shall hold me fast
Until the little minute's sleep is past
　　And I wake saved.—And yet it will not be!

AN EPISTLE

Containing the Strange Medical Experience of Karshish,
The Arab Physician

KARSHISH, the picker-up of learning's crumbs,
The not-incurious in God's handiwork
(This man's-flesh he hath admirably made,
Blown like a bubble, kneaded like a paste,
To coop up and keep down on earth a space
That puff of vapor from his mouth, man's soul)
—To Abib, all-sagacious in our art,
Breeder in me of what poor skill I boast,
Like me inquisitive how pricks and cracks
Befall the flesh through too much stress and strain,   10
Whereby the wily vapor fain would slip
Back and rejoin its source before the term,—
And aptest in contrivance (under God)
To baffle it by deftly stopping such:—
The vagrant Scholar to his Sage at home
Sends greeting (health and knowledge, fame with peace)
Three samples of true snakestone—rarer still,
One of the other sort, the melon-shaped,
(But fitter, pounded fine, for charms than drugs)
And writeth now the twenty-second time.   20

My journeyings were brought to Jericho:
Thus I resume. Who studious in our art
Shall count a little labor unrepaid?
I have shed sweat enough, left flesh and bone
On many a flinty furlong of this land.
Also, the country-side is all on fire
With rumors of a marching hitherward:
Some say Vespasian cometh, some, his son.
A black lynx snarled and pricked a tufted ear;
Lust of my blood inflamed his yellow balls: 30
I cried and threw my staff and he was gone.
Twice have the robbers stripped and beaten me,
And once a town declared me for a spy;
But at the end, I reach Jerusalem,
Since this poor covert where I pass the night,

This Bethany, lies scarce the distance thence
A man with plague-sores at the third degree
Runs till he drops down dead. Thou laughest here!
'Sooth, it elates me, thus reposed and safe,
To void the stuffing of my travel-scrip   40
And share with thee whatever Jewry yields.
A viscid choler is observable
In tertians, I was nearly bold to say;
And falling-sickness hath a happier cure
Than our school wots of: there's a spider here
Weaves no web, watches on the ledge of tombs,
Sprinkled with mottles on an ash-gray back;
Take five and drop them . . . but who knows his mind,
The Syrian runagate I trust this to?
His service payeth me a sublimate   50
Blown up his nose to help the ailing eye.
Best wait: I reach Jerusalem at morn,
There set in order my experiences,
Gather what most deserves, and give thee all—
Or I might add, Judæa's gum-tragacanth
Scales off in purer flakes, shines clearer-grained,
Cracks 'twixt the pestle and the porphyry,
In fine exceeds our produce. Scalp-disease
Confounds me, crossing so with leprosy—
Thou hadst admired one sort I gained at Zoar—   60
But zeal outruns discretion. Here I end.

Yet stay: my Syrian blinketh gratefully,
Protesteth his devotion is my price—
Suppose I write what harms not, though he steal?
I half resolve to tell thee, yet I blush,
What set me off a-writing first of all.
An itch I had, a sting to write, a tang!
For, be it this town's barrenness—or else
The Man had something in the look of him—
His case has struck me far more than 'tis worth.   70
So, pardon if—(lest presently I lose
In the great press of novelty at hand
The care and pains this somehow stole from me)
I bid thee take the thing while fresh in mind,
Almost in sight—for, wilt thou have the truth?
The very man is gone from me but now,

Whose ailment is the subject of discourse.
Thus then, and let thy better wit help all!

   'Tis but a case of mania—subinduced
By epilepsy, at the turning-point   80
Of trance prolonged unduly some three days:
When, by the exhibition of some drug
Or spell, exorcisation, stroke of art
Unknown to me and which 'twere well to know,
The evil thing out-breaking all at once
Left the man whole and sound of body indeed,—
But, flinging (so to speak) life's gates too wide,
Making a clear house of it too suddenly,
The first conceit that entered might inscribe
Whatever it was minded on the wall   90
So plainly at that vantage, as it were,
(First come, first served) that nothing subsequent
Attaineth to erase those fancy-scrawls
The just-returned and new-established soul
Hath gotten now so thoroughly by heart
That henceforth she will read or these or none.
And first—the man's own firm conviction rests
That he was dead (in fact they buried him)
—That he was dead and then restored to life
By a Nazarene physician of his tribe: 100
—'Sayeth, the same bade "Rise," and he did rise.
"Such cases are diurnal," thou wilt cry.
Not so this figment!—not, that such a fume,
Instead of giving way to time and health,
Should eat itself into the life of life,
As saffron tingeth flesh, blood, bones and all!
For see, how he takes up the after-life.
The man—it is one Lazarus a Jew,
Sanguine, proportioned, fifty years of age,
The body's habit wholly laudable,   110
As much, indeed, beyond the common health
As he were made and put aside to show.
Think, could we penetrate by any drug
And bathe the wearied soul and worried flesh,
And bring it clear and fair, by three days' sleep!
Whence has the man the balm that brightens all?
This grown man eyes the world now like a child.

Some elders of his tribe, I should premise,
Led in their friend, obedient as a sheep,
To bear my inquisition. While they spoke,   120
Now sharply, now with sorrow,—told the case,—
He listened not except I spoke to him,
But folded his two hands and let them talk,
Watching the flies that buzzed: and yet no fool.
And that's a sample how his years must go.
Look, if a beggar, in fixed middle-life,
Should find a treasure,—can he use the same
With straitened habits and with tastes starved small,
And take at once to his impoverished brain
The sudden element that changes things,   130
That sets the undreamed-of rapture at his hand
And puts the cheap old joy in the scorned dust?
Is he not such an one as moves to mirth—
Warily parsimonious, when no need,
Wasteful as drunkenness at undue times?
All prudent counsel as to what befits
The golden mean, is lost on such an one:
The man's fantastic will is the man's law.
So here—we call the treasure knowledge, say,
Increased beyond the fleshly faculty—   140
Heaven opened to a soul while yet on earth,
Earth forced on a soul's use while seeing heaven:
The man is witless of the size, the sum,
The value in proportion of all things,
Or whether it be little or be much.
Discourse to him of prodigious armaments
Assembled to besiege his city now,
And of the passing of a mule with gourds—
'Tis one! Then take it on the other side,
Speak of some trifling fact,—he will gaze rapt   150
With stupor at its very littleness,
(Far as I see) as if in that indeed
He caught prodigious import, whole results;
And so will turn to us the bystanders
In ever the same stupor (note this point)
That we too see not with his opened eyes.
Wonder and doubt come wrongly into play,
Preposterously, at cross purposes.
Should his child sicken unto death,—why, look
For scarce abatement of his cheerfulness,   160

Or pretermission of the daily craft!
While a word, gesture, glance from that same child
At play or in the school or laid asleep,
Will startle him to an agony of fear,
Exasperation, just as like. Demand
The reason why—" 'tis but a word," object—
"A gesture"—he regards thee as our lord
Who lived there in the pyramid alone,
Looked at us (dost thou mind?) when, being young,
We both would unadvisedly recite   170
Some charm's beginning, from that book of his,
Able to bid the sun throb wide and burst
All into stars, as suns grown old are wont.
Thou and the child have each a veil alike
Thrown o'er your heads, from under which ye both
Stretch your blind hands and trifle with a match
Over a mine of Greek fire, did ye know!
He holds on firmly to some thread of life—
(It is the life to lead perforcedly)
Which runs across some vast distracting orb   180
Of glory on either side that meagre thread,
Which, conscious of, he must not enter yet—
The spiritual life around the earthly life:
The law of that is known to him as this,
His heart and brain move there, his feet stay here.
So is the man perplext with impulses
Sudden to start off crosswise, not straight on,
Proclaiming what is right and wrong across,
And not along, this black thread through the blaze—
"It should be" balked by "here it cannot be."   190
And oft the man's soul springs into his face
As if he saw again and heard again
His sage that bade him "Rise" and he did rise.
Something, a word, a tick o' the blood within
Admonishes: then back he sinks at once
To ashes, who was very fire before,
In sedulous recurrence to his trade
Whereby he earneth him the daily bread;
And studiously the humbler for that pride,
Professedly the faultier that he knows   200
God's secret, while he holds the thread of life.
Indeed the especial marking of the man
Is prone submission to the heavenly will—

Seeing it, what it is, and why it is.
'Sayeth, he will wait patient to the last
For that same death which must restore his being
To equilibrium, body loosening soul
Divorced even now by premature full growth:
He will live, nay, it pleaseth him to live
So long as God please, and just how God please.   210
He even seeketh not to please God more
(Which meaneth, otherwise) than as God please.
Hence, I perceive not he affects to preach
The doctrine of his sect whate'er it be,
Make proselytes as madmen thirst to do:
How can he give his neighbor the real ground,
His own conviction? Ardent as he is—
Call his great truth a lie, why, still the old
"Be it as God please" reassureth him.
I probed the sore as thy disciple should: 220
"How, beast," said I, "this stolid carelessness
Sufficeth thee, when Rome is on her march
To stamp out like a little spark thy town,
Thy tribe, thy crazy tale and thee at once?"
He merely looked with his large eyes on me.
The man is apathetic, you deduce?
Contrariwise, he loves both old and young,
Able and weak, affects the very brutes
And birds—how say I? flowers of the field—
As a wise workman recognizes tools   230
In a master's workshop, loving what they make.
Thus is the man as harmless as a lamb:
Only impatient, let him do his best,
At ignorance and carelessness and sin—
An indignation which is promptly curbed:
As when in certain travel I have feigned
To be an ignoramus in our art
According to some preconceived design,
And happed to hear the land's practitioners
Steeped in conceit sublimed by ignorance,   240
Prattle fantastically on disease,
Its cause and cure—and I must hold my peace!

Thou wilt object—Why have I not ere this
Sought out the sage himself, the Nazarene
Who wrought this cure, inquiring at the source,

Conferring with the frankness that befits?
Alas! it grieveth me, the learned leech
Perished in a tumult many years ago,
Accused,—our learning's fate,—of wizardry,
Rebellion, to the setting up a rule   250
And creed prodigious as described to me.
His death, which happened when the earthquake fell
(Prefiguring, as soon appeared, the loss
To occult learning in our lord the sage
Who lived there in the pyramid alone)
Was wrought by the mad people—that's their wont!
On vain recourse, as I conjecture it,
To his tried virtue, for miraculous help—
How could he stop the earthquake? That's their way!
The other imputations must be lies;   260
But take one, though I loathe to give it thee,
In mere respect for any good man's fame.
(And after all, our patient Lazarus
Is stark mad; should we count on what he says?
Perhaps not: though in writing to a leech
'Tis well to keep back nothing of a case.)
This man so cured regards the curer, then,
As—God forgive me! who but God himself,
Creator and sustainer of the world,
That came and dwelt in flesh on it awhile!   270
—'Sayeth that such an one was born and lived,
Taught, healed the sick, broke bread at his own house,
Then died, with Lazarus by, for aught I know,
And yet was . . . what I said nor choose repeat,
And must have so avouched himself, in fact,
In hearing of this very Lazarus
Who saith—but why all this of what he saith?
Why write of trivial matters, things of price
Calling at every moment for remark?
I noticed on the margin of a pool   280
Blue-flowering borage, the Aleppo sort,
Aboundeth, very nitrous. It is strange!

Thy pardon for this long and tedious case,
Which, now that I review it, needs must seem
Unduly dwelt on, prolixly set forth!
Nor I myself discern in what is writ
Good cause for the peculiar interest

And awe indeed this man has touched me with.
Perhaps the journey's end, the weariness
Had wrought upon me first. I met him thus: 290
I crossed a ridge of short sharp broken hills
Like an old lion's cheek teeth. Out there came
A moon made like a face with certain spots
Multiform, manifold and menacing:
Then a wind rose behind me. So we met
In this old sleepy town at unaware,
The man and I. I send thee what is writ.
Regard it as a chance, a matter risked
To this ambiguous Syrian—he may lose,
Or steal, or give it thee with equal good.   300
Jerusalem's repose shall make amends
For time this letter wastes, thy time and mine;
Till when, once more thy pardon and farewell!

    The very God! think, Abib; dost thou think?
So, the All-Great, were the All-Loving too—
So, through the thunder comes a human voice
Saying, "O heart I made, a heart beats here!
Face, my hands fashioned, see it in myself!
Thou hast no power nor mayst conceive of mine,
But love I gave thee, with myself to love,   310
And thou must love me who have died for thee!"
The madman saith He said so: it is strange.

MESMERISM

I

    ALL I believed is true!
      I am able yet
      All I want to get
    By a method as strange as new:
    Dare I trust the same to you?

II

    If at night, when doors are shut,
      And the wood-worm picks,
      And the death-watch ticks,

And the bar has a flag of smut,
And a cat's in the water-butt—

10

III

And the socket floats and flares,
 And the house-beams groan,
 And a foot unknown
Is surmised on the garret-stairs,
And the locks slip unawares—

IV

And the spider, to serve his ends,
 By a sudden thread,
 Arms and legs outspread,
On the table's midst descends,
Comes to find, God knows what friends!—

20

V

If since eve drew in, I say,
 I have sat and brought
 (So to speak) my thought
To bear on the woman away,
Till I felt my hair turn gray—

VI

Till I seemed to have and hold,
 In the vacancy
 'Twixt the wall and me,
From the hair-plait's chestnut gold
To the foot in its muslin fold—

30

VII

Have and hold, then and there,
 Her, from head to foot,
 Breathing and mute,
Passive and yet aware,
In the grasp of my steady stare—

VIII

Hold and have, there and then,
    All her body and soul
    That completes my whole,
All that women add to men,
In the clutch of my steady ken—   40

IX

Having and holding, till
    I imprint her fast
    On the void at last
As the sun does whom he will
By the calotypist's skill—

X

Then,—if my heart's strength serve,
    And through all and each
    Of the veils I reach
To her soul and never swerve,
Knitting an iron nerve—   50

XI

Command her soul to advance
    And inform the shape
    Which has made escape
And before my countenance
Answers me glance for glance—

XII

I, still with a gesture fit
    Of my hands that best
    Do my soul's behest,
Pointing the power from it,
While myself do steadfast sit—   60

XIII

Steadfast and still the same
   On my object bent,
    While the hands give vent
To my ardor and my aim
And break into very flame—

XIV

Then I reach, I must believe,
   Not her soul in vain,
    For to me again
It reaches, and past retrieve
Is wound in the toils I weave;

70

XV

And must follow as I require,
   As befits a thrall,
    Bringing flesh and all,
Essence and earth-attire,
To the source of the tractile fire:

XVI

Till the house called hers, not mine,
   With a growing weight
    Seems to suffocate
If she break not its leaden line
And escape from its close confine.

80

XVII

Out of doors into the night!
   On to the maze
    Of the wild wood-ways,
Not turning to left nor right
From the pathway, blind with sight—

XVIII

Making thro' rain and wind
　　O'er the broken shrubs,
　　'Twixt the stems and stubs,
With a still, composed, strong mind,
Nor a care for the world behind—　　　　　　90

XIX

Swifter and still more swift,
　　As the crowding peace
　　Doth to joy increase
In the wide blind eyes uplift
Thro' the darkness and the drift!

XX

While I—to the shape, I too
　　Feel my soul dilate
　　Nor a whit abate,
And relax not a gesture due,
As I see my belief come true.　　　　　　100

XXI

For, there! have I drawn or no
　　Life to that lip?
　　Do my fingers dip
In a flame which again they throw
On the cheek that breaks a-glow?

XXII

Ha! was the hair so first?
　　What, unfilleted,
　　Made alive, and spread
Through the void with a rich outburst,
Chestnut gold-interspersed?　　　　　　110

XXIII

Like the doors of a casket-shrine,
　　See, on either side,
　　Her two arms divide
Till the heart betwixt makes sign,
Take me, for I am thine!

XXIV

"Now—now"—the door is heard!
　　Hark, the stairs! and near—
　　Nearer—and here—
"Now!" and at call the third
She enters without a word.   120

XXV

On doth she march and on
　　To the fancied shape;
　　It is, past escape,
Herself, now: the dream is done
And the shadow and she are one.

XXVI

First I will pray. Do Thou
　　That ownest the soul,
　　Yet wilt grant control
To another, nor disallow
For a time, restrain me now!   130

XXVII

I admonish me while I may,
　　Not to squander guilt,
　　Since require Thou wilt
At my hand its price one day!
What the price is, who can say?

A SERENADE AT THE VILLA

I

THAT was I, you heard last night,
    When there rose no moon at all,
Nor, to pierce the strained and tight
    Tent of heaven, a planet small:
Life was dead and so was light.

II

Not a twinkle from the fly,
    Not a glimmer from the worm;
When the crickets stopped their cry,
    When the owls forbore a term,
You heard music; that was I.

III

Earth turned in her sleep with pain,
    Sultrily suspired for proof:
In at heaven and out again,
    Lightning!—where it broke the roof,
Bloodlike, some few drops of rain.

IV

What they could my words expressed,
    O my love, my all, my one!
Singing helped the verses best,
    And when singing's best was done,
To my lute I left the rest.

V

So wore night; the East was gray,
    White the broad-faced hemlock-flowers:
There would be another day;
    Ere its first of heavy hours
Found me, I had passed away.

VI

What became of all the hopes,
　　Words and song and lute as well?
Say, this struck you—"When life gropes
　　Feebly for the path where fell
Light last on the evening slopes,

VII

"One friend in that path shall be,
　　To secure my step from wrong;
One to count night day for me,
　　Patient through the watches long,
Serving most with none to see."

VIII

Never say—as something bodes—
　　"So, the worst has yet a worse!
When life halts 'neath double loads,
　　Better the taskmaster's curse
Than such music on the roads!

IX

"When no moon succeeds the sun,
　　Nor can pierce the midnight's tent
Any star, the smallest one,
　　While some drops, where lightning rent,
Show the final storm begun—

X

"When the fire-fly hides its spot,
　　When the garden-voices fail
In the darkness thick and hot,—
　　Shall another voice avail,
That shape be where these are not?

XI

"Has some plague a longer lease,
    Proffering its help uncouth?
Can't one even die in peace?
    As one shuts one's eyes on youth,
Is that face the last one sees?"

XII

Oh, how dark your villa was,
    Windows fast and obdurate!
How the garden grudged me grass
    Where I stood—the iron gate
Ground its teeth to let me pass!

MY STAR

All that I know
    Of a certain star,
Is, it can throw
    (Like the angled spar)
Now a dart of red,
    Now a dart of blue;
Till my friends have said
    They would fain see, too,
My star that dartles the red and the blue!
Then it stops like a bird; like a flower, hangs furled:
    They must solace themselves with the Saturn above it.
What matter to me if their star is a world?
    Mine has opened its soul to me; therefore I love it.

INSTANS TYRANNUS

I

Of the million or two, more or less,
I rule and possess,

One man, for some cause undefined,
Was least to my mind.

II

I struck him, he grovelled of course—
For, what was his force?
I pinned him to earth with my weight
And persistence of hate:
And he lay, would not moan, would not curse,
As his lot might be worse.   10

III

"Were the object less mean, would he stand
At the swing of my hand!
For obscurity helps him and blots
The hole where he squats."
So, I set my five wits on the stretch
To inveigle the wretch.
All in vain! Gold and jewels I threw,
Still he couched there perdue.
I tempted his blood and his flesh,
Hid in roses my mesh,   20
Choicest cates and the flagon's best spilth:
Still he kept to his filth!

IV

Had he kith now or kin, were access
To his heart, did I press:
Just a son or a mother to seize!
No such booty as these.
Were it simply a friend to pursue
'Mid my million or two,
Who could pay me in person or pelf
What he owes me himself!   30
No: I could not but smile through my chafe:
For the fellow lay safe
As his mates do, the midge and the nit,
—Through minuteness, to wit.

V

Then a humor more great took its place
At the thought of his face,
The droop, the low cares of the mouth,
The trouble uncouth
'Twixt the brows, all that air one is fain
To put out of its pain.   40
And, "no!" I admonished myself,
"Is one mocked by an elf,
Is one baffled by toad or by rat?
The gravamen's in that!
How the lion, who crouches to suit
His back to my foot,
Would admire that I stand in debate!
But the small turns the great
If it vexes you,—that is the thing!
Toad or rat vex the king?   50
Though I waste half my realm to unearth
Toad or rat, 'tis well worth!"

VI

So, I soberly laid my last plan
To extinguish the man.
Round his creep-hole, with never a break
Ran my fires for his sake;
Over-head, did my thunder combine
With my underground mine:
Till I looked from my labor content
To enjoy the event.   60

VII

When sudden . . . how think ye, the end?
Did I say "without friend"?
Say rather, from marge to blue marge
The whole sky grew his targe
With the sun's self for visible boss,
While an Arm ran across
Which the earth heaved beneath like a breast
Where the wretch was safe prest!

Do you see? Just my vengeance complete,
The man sprang to his feet, 70
Stood erect, caught at God's skirts, and prayed!
—So, *I* was afraid!

A PRETTY WOMAN

I

THAT fawn-skin-dappled hair of hers,
  And the blue eye
  Dear and dewy,
And that infantine fresh air of hers!

II

To think men cannot take you, Sweet,
  And enfold you,
  Ay, and hold you,
And so keep you what they make you, Sweet!

III

You like us for a glance, you know—
  For a word's sake,
  Or a sword's sake,
All's the same, whate'er the chance, you know.

IV

And in turn we make you ours, we say—
  You and youth too,
  Eyes and mouth too,
All the face composed of flowers, we say.

V

All's our own, to make the most of, Sweet—
  Sing and say for,
  Watch and pray for,
Keep a secret or go boast of, Sweet!

VI

But for loving, why, you would not, Sweet,
    Though we prayed you,
    Paid you, brayed you
In a mortar—for you could not, Sweet!

VII

So, we leave the sweet face fondly there:
    Be its beauty
    Its sole duty!
Let all hope of grace beyond, lie there!

VIII

And while the face lies quiet there,
    Who shall wonder
    That I ponder
A conclusion? I will try it there.

IX

As,—why must one, for the love foregone,
    Scout mere liking?
    Thunder-striking
Earth,—the heaven, we looked above for, gone!

X

Why, with beauty, needs there money be,
    Love with liking?
    Crush the fly-king
In his gauze, because no honey-bee?

XI

May not liking be so simple-sweet,
    If love grew there
    'Twould undo there
All that breaks the cheek to dimples sweet?

XII

Is the creature too imperfect, say?
    Would you mend it
    And so end it?
Since not all addition perfects aye!

XIII

Or is it of its kind, perhaps,
    Just perfection—
    Whence, rejection
Of a grace not to its mind, perhaps?

XIV

Shall we burn up, tread that face at once
    Into tinder,
    And so hinder
Sparks from kindling all the place at once?

XV

Or else kiss away one's soul on her?
    Your love-fancies!
    —A sick man sees
Truer, when his hot eyes roll on her!

XVI

Thus the craftsman thinks to grace the rose,—
    Plucks a mould-flower
    For his gold flower,
Uses fine things that efface the rose:

XVII

Rosy rubies make its cup more rose,
    Precious metals
    Ape the petals,—
Last, some old king locks it up, morose!

XVIII

Then, how grace a rose? I know a way!
    Leave it, rather.
    Must you gather?
Smell, kiss, wear it—at last, throw away!

"CHILDE ROLAND TO THE DARK TOWER CAME"

*(See Edgar's song in "*LEAR*")*

I

My FIRST thought was, he lied in every word,
    That hoary cripple, with malicious eye
    Askance to watch the working of his lie
On mine, and mouth scarce able to afford
Suppression of the glee, that pursed and scored
    Its edge, at one more victim gained thereby.

II

What else should he be set for, with his staff?
    What, save to waylay with his lies, ensnare
    All travellers who might find him posted there,
And ask the road? I guessed what skull-like laugh   10
Would break, what crutch 'gin write my epitaph
    For pastime in the dusty thoroughfare,

III

If at his counsel I should turn aside
    Into that ominous tract which, all agree,
    Hides the Dark Tower. Yet acquiescingly
I did turn as he pointed: neither pride
Nor hope rekindling at the end descried,
    So much as gladness that some end might be.

IV

For, what with my whole world-wide wandering,
  What with my search drawn out thro' years, my hope   20
    Dwindled into a ghost not fit to cope
With that obstreperous joy success would bring,
I hardly tried now to rebuke the spring
  My heart made, finding failure in its scope.

V

As when a sick man very near to death
  Seems dead indeed, and feels begin and end
    The tears and takes the farewell of each friend,
And hears one bid the other go, draw breath
Freelier outside, ("since all is o'er," he saith,
  "And the blow fallen no grieving can amend;")   30

VI

While some discuss if near the other graves
  Be room enough for this, and when a day
    Suits best for carrying the corpse away,
With care about the banners, scarves and staves:
And still the man hears all, and only craves
  He may not shame such tender love and stay.

VII

Thus, I had so long suffered in this quest,
  Heard failure prophesied so oft, been writ
    So many times among "The Band"—to wit,
The knights who to the Dark Tower's search addressed   40
Their steps—that just to fail as they, seemed best,
  And all the doubt was now—should I be fit?

VIII

So, quiet as despair, I turned from him,
  That hateful cripple, out of his highway
    Into the path he pointed. All the day

Had been a dreary one at best, and dim
Was settling to its close, yet shot one grim
    Red leer to see the plain catch its estray.

IX

For mark! no sooner was I fairly found
    Pledged to the plain, after a pace or two,   50
    Than, pausing to throw backward a last view
O'er the safe road, 'twas gone; gray plain all round:
Nothing but plain to the horizon's bound.
    I might go on; naught else remained to do.

X

So, on I went. I think I never saw
    Such starved ignoble nature; nothing throve:
    For flowers—as well expect a cedar grove!
But cockle, spurge, according to their law
Might propagate their kind, with none to awe,
    You'd think; a burr had been a treasure-trove.   60

XI

No! penury, inertness and grimace,
    In some strange sort, were the land's portion. "See
    Or shut your eyes," said Nature peevishly,
"It nothing skills: I cannot help my case:
'Tis the Last Judgment's fire must cure this place,
    Calcine its clods and set my prisoners free."

XII

If there pushed any ragged thistle-stalk
    Above its mates, the head was chopped; the bents
    Were jealous else. What made those holes and rents
In the dock's harsh swarth leaves, bruised as to balk   70
All hope of greenness? 'tis a brute must walk
    Pashing their life out, with a brute's intents.

XIII

As for the grass, it grew as scant as hair
   In leprosy; thin dry blades pricked the mud
   Which underneath looked kneaded up with blood.
One stiff blind horse, his every bone a-stare,
Stood stupefied, however he came there:
   Thrust out past service from the devil's stud!

XIV

Alive? he might be dead for aught I know,
   With that red gaunt and colloped neck a-strain,   80
   And shut eyes underneath the rusty mane;
Seldom went such grotesqueness with such woe;
I never saw a brute I hated so;
   He must be wicked to deserve such pain.

XV

I shut my eyes and turned them on my heart.
   As a man calls for wine before he fights,
   I asked one draught of earlier, happier sights,
Ere fitly I could hope to play my part.
Think first, fight afterwards—the soldier's art:
   One taste of the old time sets all to rights.   90

XVI

Not it! I fancied Cuthbert's reddening face
   Beneath its garniture of curly gold,
   Dear fellow, till I almost felt him fold
An arm in mine to fix me to the place,
That way he used. Alas, one night's disgrace!
   Out went my heart's new fire and left it cold.

XVII

Giles then, the soul of honour—there he stands
   Frank as ten years ago when knighted first.
   What honest man should dare (he said) he durst.

Good—but the scene shifts—faugh! what hangman
      hands   100
Pin to his breast a parchment? His own bands
    Read it. Poor traitor, spit upon the curst!

XVIII

Better this present than a past like that;
    Back therefore to my darkening path again!
    No sound, no sight as far as eye could strain.
Will the night send a howlet or a bat?
I asked: when something on the dismal flat
    Came to arrest my thoughts and change their train.

XIX

A sudden little river crossed my path
    As unexpected as a serpent comes.   110
    No sluggish tide congenial to the glooms;
This, as it frothed by, might have been a bath
For the fiend's glowing hoof—to see the wrath
    Of its black eddy bespate with flakes and spumes.

XX

So petty yet so spiteful! All along,
    Low scrubby alders kneeled down over it;
    Drenched willows flung them headlong in a fit
Of mute despair, a suicidal throng:
The river which had done them all the wrong,
    Whate'er that was, rolled by, deterred no whit.   120

XXI

Which, while I forded,—good saints, how I feared
    To set my foot upon a dead man's cheek,
    Each step, or feel the spear I thrust to seek
For hollows, tangled in his hair or beard!
—It may have been a water-rat I speared,
    But, ugh! it sounded like a baby's shriek.

XXII

Glad was I when I reached the other bank.
   Now for a better country. Vain presage!
   Who were the strugglers, what war did they wage,
Whose savage trample thus could pad the dank   130
Soil to a plash? Toads in a poisoned tank,
   Or wild cats in a red-hot iron cage—

XXIII

The fight must so have seemed in that fell cirque.
   What penned them there, with all the plain to choose?
   No foot-print leading to that horrid mews,
None out of it. Mad brewage set to work
Their brains, no doubt, like galley-slaves the Turk
   Pits for his pastime, Christians against Jews.

XXIV

And more than that—a furlong on—why, there!
   What bad use was that engine for, that wheel,   140
   Or brake, not wheel—that harrow fit to reel
Men's bodies out like silk? with all the air
Of Tophet's tool, on earth left unaware,
   Or brought to sharpen its rusty teeth of steel.

XXV

Then came a bit of stubbed ground, once a wood,
   Next a marsh, it would seem, and now mere earth
   Desperate and done with; (so a fool finds mirth,
Makes a thing and then mars it, till his mood
Changes and off he goes!) within a rood—
   Bog, clay and rubble, sand and stark black dearth.   150

XXVI

Now blotches rankling, colored gay and grim,
   Now patches where some leanness of the soil's
   Broke into moss or substances like boils;
Then came some palsied oak, a cleft in him

Like a distorted mouth that splits its rim
　　Gaping at death, and dies while it recoils.

XXVII

And just as far as ever from the end!
　　Naught in the distance but the evening, naught
　　To point my footstep further! At the thought,
A great black bird, Apollyon's bosom-friend,　　　　160
Sailed past, nor beat his wide wing dragon-penned
　　That brushed my cap—perchance the guide I sought.

XXVIII

For, looking up, aware I somehow grew,
　　'Spite of the dusk, the plain had given place
　　All round to mountains—with such name to grace
Mere ugly heights and heaps now stolen in view.
How thus they had surprised me,—solve it, you!
　　How to get from them was no clearer case.

XXIX

Yet half I seemed to recognize some trick
　　Of mischief happened to me, God knows when—　　　　170
　　In a bad dream perhaps. Here ended, then,
Progress this way. When, in the very nick
Of giving up, one time more, came a click
　　As when a trap shuts—you're inside the den!

XXX

Burningly it came on me all at once,
　　This was the place! those two hills on the right,
　　Crouched like two bulls locked horn in horn in fight;
While to the left, a tall scalped mountain . . . Dunce,
Dotard, a-dozing at the very nonce,
　　After a life spent training for the sight!　　　　180

XXXI

What in the midst lay but the Tower itself?
　　The round squat turret, blind as the fool's heart,

Built of brown stone, without a counterpart
In the whole world. The tempest's mocking elf
Points to the shipman thus the unseen shelf
  He strikes on, only when the timbers start.

XXXII

Not see? because of night perhaps?—why, day
  Came back again for that! before it left,
  The dying sunset kindled through a cleft:
The hills, like giants at a hunting, lay,   190
Chin upon hand, to see the game at bay,—
  "Now stab and end the creature—to the heft!"

XXXIII

Not hear? when noise was everywhere! it tolled
  Increasing like a bell. Names in my ears
  Of all the lost adventurers my peers,—
How such a one was strong, and such was bold,
And such was fortunate, yet each of old
  Lost, lost! one moment knelled the woe of years.

XXXIV

There they stood, ranged along the hill-sides, met
  To view the last of me, a living frame   200
  For one more picture! in a sheet of flame
I saw them and I knew them all. And yet
Dauntless the slug-horn to my lips I set,
  And blew. *"Childe Roland to the Dark Tower came."*

RESPECTABILITY

I

DEAR, had the world in its caprice
  Deigned to proclaim "I know you both,
  Have recognized your plighted troth,
Am sponsor for you: live in peace!"—

How many precious months and years
   Of youth had passed, that speed so fast,
   Before we found it out at last,
The world, and what it fears?

II

How much of priceless life were spent
   With men that every virtue decks,
   And women models of their sex,
Society's true ornament,—
   Ere we dared wander, nights like this,
   Thro' wind and rain, and watch the Seine,
   And feel the Boulevart break again
To warmth and light and bliss?

III

I know! the world proscribes not love;
   Allows my finger to caress
   Your lips' contour and downiness,
Provided it supply a glove.
The world's good word!—the Institute!
   Guizot receives Montalembert!
   Eh? Down the court three lampions flare:
Put forward your best foot!

A LIGHT WOMAN

I

So FAR as our story approaches the end,
   Which do you pity the most of us three?—
My friend, or the mistress of my friend
   With her wanton eyes, or me?

II

My friend was already too good to lose,
   And seemed in the way of improvement yet,

When she crossed his path with her hunting-noose
  And over him drew her net.

III

When I saw him tangled in her toils,
  A shame, said I, if she adds just him
To her nine-and-ninety other spoils,
  The hundredth for a whim!

IV

And before my friend be wholly hers,
  How easy to prove to him, I said,
An eagle's the game her pride prefers,
  Though she snaps at a wren instead!

V

So, I gave her eyes my own eyes to take,
  My hand sought hers as in earnest need,
And round she turned for my noble sake,
  And gave me herself indeed.

VI

The eagle am I, with my fame in the world,
  The wren is he, with his maiden face.
—You look away and your lip is curled?
  Patience, a moment's space!

VII

For see, my friend goes shaking and white;
  He eyes me as the basilisk:
I have turned, it appears, his day to night,
  Eclipsing his sun's disk.

VIII

And I did it, he thinks, as a very thief:
  "Though I love her—that, he comprehends—

One should master one's passions, (love, in chief)
   And be loyal to one's friends!"

IX

And she,—she lies in my hand as tame
   As a pear late basking over a wall;
Just a touch to try and off it came;
   'Tis mine,—can I let it fall?

X

With no mind to eat it, that's the worst!
   Were it thrown in the road, would the case assist?
'Twas quenching a dozen blue-flies' thirst
   When I gave its stalk a twist.

XI

And I,—what I seem to my friend, you see:
   What I soon shall seem to his love, you guess:
What I seem to myself, do you ask of me?
   No hero, I confess.

XII

'Tis an awkward thing to play with souls,
   And matter enough to save one's own:
Yet think of my friend, and the burning coals
   He played with for bits of stone!

XIII

One likes to show the truth for the truth;
   That the woman was light is very true:
But suppose she says,—Never mind that youth!
   What wrong have I done to you?

XIV

Well, anyhow, here the story stays,
   So far at least as I understand;

And, Robert Browning, you writer of plays,
  Here's a subject made to your hand!

THE STATUE AND THE BUST

THERE'S a palace in Florence, the world knows well,
And a statue watches it from the square,
And this story of both do our townsmen tell.

Ages ago, a lady there,
At the farthest window facing the East
Asked, "Who rides by with the royal air?"

The bridesmaids' prattle around her ceased;
She leaned forth, one on either hand;
They saw how the blush of the bride increased—

They felt by its beats her heart expand—   10
As one at each ear and both in a breath
Whispered, "The Great-Duke Ferdinand."

That selfsame instant, underneath,
The Duke rode past in his idle way,
Empty and fine like a swordless sheath.

Gay he rode, with a friend as gay,
Till he threw his head back—"Who is she?"
—"A bride the Riccardi brings home to-day."

Hair in heaps lay heavily
Over a pale brow spirit-pure—   20
Carved like the heart of a coal-black tree,

Crisped like a war-steed's encolure—
And vainly sought to dissemble her eyes
Of the blackest black our eyes endure.

And lo, a blade for a knight's emprise
Filled the fine empty sheath of a man,—
The Duke grew straightway brave and wise.

He looked at her, as a lover can;
She looked at him, as one who awakes:
The past was a sleep, and her life began.   30

Now, love so ordered for both their sakes,
A feast was held that selfsame night
In the pile which the mighty shadow makes.

(For Via Larga is three-parts light,
But the palace overshadows one,
Because of a crime which may God requite!

To Florence and God the wrong was done,
Through the first republic's murder there
By Cosimo and his cursed son.)

The Duke (with the statue's face in the square)   40
Turned in the midst of his multitude
At the bright approach of the bridal pair.

Face to face the lovers stood
A single minute and no more,
While the bridegroom bent as a man subdued—

Bowed till his bonnet brushed the floor—
For the Duke on the lady a kiss conferred,
As the courtly custom was of yore.

In a minute can lovers exchange a word?
If a word did pass, which I do not think,   50
Only one out of the thousand heard.

That was the bridegroom. At day's brink
He and his bride were alone at last
In a bedchamber by a taper's blink.

Calmly he said that her lot was cast,
That the door she had passed was shut on her
Till the final catafalk repassed.

The world meanwhile, its noise and stir,
Through a certain window facing the East,
She could watch like a convent's chronicler.   60

Since passing the door might lead to a feast,
And a feast might lead to so much beside,
He, of many evils, chose the least.

"Freely I choose too," said the bride—
"Your window and its world suffice,"
Replied the tongue, while the heart replied—

"If I spend the night with that devil twice,
May his window serve as my loop of hell
Whence a damned soul looks on paradise!

"I fly to the Duke who loves me well,   70
Sit by his side and laugh at sorrow
Ere I count another ave-bell.

" 'Tis only the coat of a page to borrow,
And tie my hair in a horse-boy's trim,
And I save my soul—but not to-morrow"—

(She checked herself and her eye grew dim)
"My father tarries to bless my state:
I must keep it one day more for him.

"Is one day more so long to wait?
Moreover the Duke rides past, I know;   80
We shall see each other, sure as fate."

She turned on her side and slept. Just so!
So we resolve on a thing and sleep:
So did the lady, ages ago.

That night the Duke said, "Dear or cheap
As the cost of this cup of bliss may prove
To body or soul, I will drain it deep."

And on the morrow, bold with love,
He beckoned the bridegroom (close on call,
As his duty bade, by the Duke's alcove)   90

And smiled " 'Twas a very funeral,
Your lady will think, this feast of ours,—
A shame to efface, whate'er befall!

"What if we break from the Arno bowers,
And try if Petraja, cool and green,
Cure last night's fault with this morning's flowers?"

The bridegroom, not a thought to be seen
On his steady brow and quiet mouth,
Said, "Too much favor for me so mean!

"But, alas! my lady leaves the South;   100
Each wind that comes from the Apennine
Is a menace to her tender youth:

"Nor a way exists, the wise opine,
If she quits her palace twice this year,
To avert the flower of life's decline."

Quoth the Duke, "A sage and a kindly fear.
Moreover Petraja is cold this spring:
Be our feast to-night as usual here!"

And then to himself—"Which night shall bring
Thy bride to her lover's embraces, fool—   110
Or I am the fool, and thou art the king!

"Yet my passion must wait a night, nor cool—
For to-night the Envoy arrives from France
Whose heart I unlock with thyself, my tool.

"I need thee still and might miss perchance.
To-day is not wholly lost, beside,
With its hope of my lady's countenance:

"For I ride—what should I do but ride?
And passing her palace, if I list,
May glance at its window—well betide!"   120

So said, so done: nor the lady missed
One ray that broke from the ardent brow,
Nor a curl of the lips where the spirit kissed.

Be sure that each renewed the vow,
No morrow's sun should arise and set
And leave them then as it left them now.

But next day passed, and next day yet,
With still fresh cause to wait one day more
Ere each leaped over the parapet.

And still, as love's brief morning wore,   130
With a gentle start, half smile, half sigh,
They found love not as it seemed before.

They thought it would work infallibly,
But not in despite of heaven and earth:
The rose would blow when the storm passed by.

Meantime they could profit in winter's dearth
By store of fruits that supplant the rose:
The world and its ways have a certain worth:

And to press a point while these oppose
Were simple policy; better wait: 140
We lose no friends and we gain no foes.

Meantime, worse fates than a lover's fate,
Who daily may ride and pass and look
Where his lady watches behind the grate!

And she—she watched the square like a book
Holding one picture and only one,
Which daily to find she undertook:

When the picture was reached the book was done,
And she turned from the picture at night to scheme
Of tearing it out for herself next sun.   150

So weeks grew months, years; gleam by gleam
The glory dropped from their youth and love,
And both perceived they had dreamed a dream;

Which hovered as dreams do, still above:
But who can take a dream for a truth?
Oh, hide our eyes from the next remove!

One day as the lady saw her youth
Depart, and the silver thread that streaked
Her hair, and, worn by the serpent's tooth,

The brow so puckered, the chin so peaked,—   160
And wondered who the woman was,
Hollow-eyed and haggard-cheeked,

Fronting her silent in the glass—
"Summon here," she suddenly said,
"Before the rest of my old self pass,

"Him, the Carver, a hand to aid,
Who fashions the clay no love will change,
And fixes a beauty never to fade.

"Let Robbia's craft so apt and strange   170
Arrest the remains of young and fair,
And rivet them while the seasons range.

"Make me a face on the window there,
Waiting as ever, mute the while,
My love to pass below in the square!

"And let me think that it may beguile
Dreary days which the dead must spend
Down in their darkness under the aisle,

"To say, 'What matters it at the end?
I did no more while my heart was warm
Than does that image, my pale-faced friend.'   180

"Where is the use of the lip's red charm,
The heaven of hair, the pride of the brow,
And the blood that blues the inside arm—

"Unless we turn, as the soul knows how,
The earthly gift to an end divine?
A lady of clay is as good, I trow."

But long ere Robbia's cornice, fine,
With flowers and fruits which leaves enlace,
Was set where now is the empty shrine—

(And, leaning out of a bright blue space,   190
As a ghost might lean from a chink of sky,
The passionate pale lady's face—

Eyeing ever, with earnest eye
And quick-turned neck at its breathless stretch,
Some one who ever is passing by—)

The Duke had sighed like the simplest wretch
In Florence, "Youth—my dream escapes!
Will its record stay?" And he bade them fetch

Some subtle moulder of brazen shapes—
"Can the soul, the will, die out of a man   200
Ere his body find the grave that gapes?

"John of Douay shall effect my plan,
Set me on horseback here aloft,
Alive, as the crafty sculptor can,

"In the very square I have crossed so oft:
That men may admire, when future suns
Shall touch the eyes to a purpose soft,

"While the mouth and the brow stay brave in bronze—
Admire and say, 'When he was alive
How he would take his pleasure once!'   210

"And it shall go hard but I contrive
To listen the while, and laugh in my tomb
At idleness which aspires to strive."

So! While these wait the trump of doom,
How do their spirits pass, I wonder,
Nights and days in the narrow room?

Still, I suppose, they sit and ponder
What a gift life was, ages ago,
Six steps out of the chapel yonder.

Only they see not God, I know,   220
Nor all that chivalry of his,
The soldier-saints who, row on row,

Burn upward each to his point of bliss—
Since, the end of life being manifest,
He had burned his way thro' the world to this.

I hear you reproach, "But delay was best,
For their end was a crime."—Oh, a crime will do
As well, I reply, to serve for a test,

As a virtue golden through and through,
Sufficient to vindicate itself   230
And prove its worth at a moment's view!

Must a game be played for the sake of pelf?
Where a button goes, 'twere an epigram
To offer the stamp of the very Guelph.

The true has no value beyond the sham:
As well the counter as coin, I submit,
When your table's a hat, and your prize a dram.

Stake your counter as boldly every whit,
Venture as warily, use the same skill,
Do your best, whether winning or losing it,   240

If you choose to play!—is my principle.
Let a man contend to the uttermost
For his life's set prize, be it what it will!

The counter our lovers staked was lost
As surely as if it were lawful coin:
And the sin I impute to each frustrate ghost

Is—the unlit lamp and the ungirt loin,
Though the end in sight was a vice, I say.
You of the virtue (we issue join)
How strive you? *De te, fabula!*   250

LOVE IN A LIFE

I

Room after room,
I hunt the house through
We inhabit together.
Heart, fear nothing, for, heart, thou shalt find her—

Next time, herself!—not the trouble behind her
Left in the curtain, the couch's perfume!
As she brushed it, the cornice-wreath blossomed anew:
Yon looking-glass gleamed at the wave of her feather.

II

Yet the day wears,
And door succeeds door;
I try the fresh fortune—
Range the wide house from the wing to the centre.
Still the same chance! she goes out as I enter.
Spend my whole day in the quest,—who cares?
But 'tis twilight, you see,—with such suites to explore,
Such closets to search, such alcoves to importune!

LIFE IN A LOVE

ESCAPE me?
Never—
Beloved!
While I am I, and you are you,
   So long as the world contains us both,
   Me the loving and you the loth,
While the one eludes, must the other pursue.
My life is a fault at last, I fear:
   It seems too much like a fate, indeed!
   Though I do my best I shall scarce succeed.
But what if I fail of my purpose here?
It is but to keep the nerves at strain,
   To dry one's eyes and laugh at a fall,
And baffled, get up and begin again,—
   So the chace takes up one's life, that's all.
While, look but once from your farthest bound
   At me so deep in the dust and dark,
No sooner the old hope goes to ground
   Than a new one, straight to the self-same mark,
I shape me—
Ever
Removed!

HOW IT STRIKES A CONTEMPORARY

I ONLY knew one poet in my life:
And this, or something like it, was his way.

You saw go up and down Valladolid,
A man of mark, to know next time you saw.
His very serviceable suit of black
Was courtly once and conscientious still,
And many might have worn it, though none did:
The cloak, that somewhat shone and showed the threads,
Had purpose, and the ruff, significance.
He walked and tapped the pavement with his cane,   10
Scenting the world, looking it full in face,
An old dog, bald and blindish, at his heels.
They turned up, now, the alley by the church,
That leads nowhither; now, they breathed themselves
On the main promenade just at the wrong time:
You'd come upon his scrutinizing hat,
Making a peaked shade blacker than itself
Against the single window spared some house
Intact yet with its mouldered Moorish work,—
Or else surprise the ferrel of his stick   20
Trying the mortar's temper 'tween the chinks
Of some new shop a-building, French and fine.
He stood and watched the cobbler at his trade,
The man who slices lemons into drink,
The coffee-roaster's brazier, and the boys
That volunteer to help him turn its winch.
He glanced o'er books on stalls with half an eye,
And fly-leaf ballads on the vendor's string,
And broad-edge bold-print posters by the wall.
He took such cognizance of men and things,   30
If any beat a horse, you felt he saw;
If any cursed a woman, he took note;
Yet stared at nobody,—you stared at him,
And found, less to your pleasure than surprise,
He seemed to know you and expect as much.
So, next time that a neighbor's tongue was loosed,
It marked the shameful and notorious fact,

We had among us, not so much a spy,
As a recording chief-inquisitor,
The town's true master if the town but knew!   40
We merely kept a governor for form,
While this man walked about and took account
Of all thought, said and acted, then went home,
And wrote it fully to our Lord the King
Who has an itch to know things, he knows why,
And reads them in his bedroom of a night.
Oh, you might smile! there wanted not a touch,
A tang of . . . well, it was not wholly ease
As back into your mind the man's look came.
Stricken in years a little,—such a brow   50
His eyes had to live under!—clear as flint
On either side the formidable nose
Curved, cut and colored like an eagle's claw.
Had he to do with A.'s surprising fate?
When altogether old B. disappeared
And young C. got his mistress,—was't our friend,
His letter to the King, that did it all?
What paid the bloodless man for so much pains?
Our Lord the King has favorites manifold,
And shifts his ministry some once a month;   60
Our city gets new governors at whiles,—
But never word or sign, that I could hear,
Notified to this man about the streets
The King's approval of those letters conned
The last thing duly at the dead of night.
Did the man love his office? Frowned our Lord,
Exhorting when none heard—"Beseech me not!
Too far above my people,—beneath me!
I set the watch,—how should the people know?
Forget them, keep me all the more in mind!"   70
Was some such understanding 'twixt the two?

I found no truth in one report at least—
That if you tracked him to his home, down lanes
Beyond the Jewry, and as clean to pace,
You found he ate his supper in a room
Blazing with lights, four Titians on the wall,
And twenty naked girls to change his plate!
Poor man, he lived another kind of life

In that new stuccoed third house by the bridge,
Fresh-painted, rather smart than otherwise!   80
The whole street might o'erlook him as he sat,
Leg crossing leg, one foot on the dog's back,
Playing a decent cribbage with his maid
(Jacynth, you're sure her name was) o'er the cheese
And fruit, three red halves of starved winter-pears,
Or treat of radishes in April. Nine,
Ten, struck the church clock, straight to bed went he.

My father, like the man of sense he was,
Would point him out to me a dozen times;
" 'St—'St," he'd whisper, "the Corregidor!"   90
I had been used to think that personage
Was one with lacquered breeches, lustrous belt,
And feathers like a forest in his hat,
Who blew a trumpet and proclaimed the news,
Announced the bull-fights, gave each church its turn,
And memorized the miracle in vogue!
He had a great observance from us boys;
We were in error; that was not the man.

I'd like now, yet had haply been afraid,
To have just looked, when this man came to die,   100
And seen who lined the clean gay garret-sides
And stood about the neat low truckle-bed,
With the heavenly manner of relieving guard.
Here had been, mark, the general-in-chief,
Thro' a whole campaign of the world's life and death,
Doing the King's work all the dim day long,
In his old coat and up to knees in mud,
Smoked like a herring, dining on a crust,—
And, now the day was won, relieved at once!
No further show or need for that old coat,   110
You are sure, for one thing! Bless us, all the while
How sprucely we are dressed out, you and I!
A second, and the angels alter that.
Well, I could never write a verse,—could you?
Let's to the Prado and make the most of time.

THE LAST RIDE TOGETHER

I

I SAID—Then, dearest, since 'tis so,
Since now at length my fate I know,
Since nothing all my love avails,
Since all, my life seemed meant for, fails,
    Since this was written and needs must be—
My whole heart rises up to bless
Your name in pride and thankfulness!
Take back the hope you gave,—I claim
Only a memory of the same,
—And this beside, if you will not blame,   10
    Your leave for one more last ride with me.

II

My mistress bent that brow of hers;
Those deep dark eyes where pride demurs
When pity would be softening through,
Fixed me a breathing-while or two
    With life or death in the balance: right!
The blood replenished me again;
My last thought was at least not vain:
I and my mistress, side by side
Shall be together, breathe and ride,   20
So, one day more am I deified.
    Who knows but the world may end to-night?

III

Hush! if you saw some western cloud
All billowy-bosomed, over-bowed
By many benedictions—sun's
And moon's and evening-stars at once—
    And so, you, looking and loving best,
Conscious grew, your passion drew
Cloud, sunset, moonrise, star-shine too,
Down on you, near and yet more near,   30

Till flesh must fade for heaven was here!—
Thus leant she and lingered—joy and fear!
   Thus lay she a moment on my breast.

IV

Then we began to ride. My soul
Smoothed itself out, a long-cramped scroll
Freshening and fluttering in the wind.
Past hopes already lay behind.
   What need to strive with a life awry?
Had I said that, had I done this,
So might I gain, so might I miss.   40
Might she have loved me? just as well
She might have hated, who can tell!
Where had I been now if the worst befell?
   And here we are riding, she and I.

V

Fail I alone, in words and deeds?
Why, all men strive and who succeeds?
We rode; it seemed my spirit flew,
Saw other regions, cities new,
   As the world rushed by on either side.
I thought,—All labor, yet no less   50
Bear up beneath their unsuccess.
Look at the end of work, contrast
The petty done, the undone vast,
This present of theirs with the hopeful past!
   I hoped she would love me; here we ride.

VI

What hand and brain went ever paired?
What heart alike conceived and dared?
What act proved all its thought had been?
What will but felt the fleshly screen?
   We ride and I see her bosom heave.   60
There's many a crown for who can reach.
Ten lines, a statesman's life in each!
The flag stuck on a heap of bones,

A soldier's doing! what atones?
They scratch his name on the Abbey-stones.
    My riding is better, by their leave.

VII

What does it all mean, poet? Well,
Your brains beat into rhythm, you tell ·
What we felt only; you expressed
You hold things beautiful the best,   70
    And pace them in rhyme so, side by side.
'Tis something, nay 'tis much: but then,
Have you yourself what's best for men?
Are you—poor, sick, old ere your time—
Nearer one whit your own sublime
Than we who never have turned a rhyme?
    Sing, riding's a joy! For me, I ride.

VIII

And you, great sculptor—so, you gave
A score of years to Art, her slave,
And that's your Venus, whence we turn   80
To yonder girl that fords the burn!
    You acquiesce, and shall I repine?
What, man of music, you grown gray
With notes and nothing else to say,
Is this your sole praise from a friend,
"Greatly his opera's strains intend,
But in music we know how fashions end!"
    I gave my youth; but we ride, in fine.

IX

Who knows what's fit for us? Had fate
Proposed bliss here should sublimate   90
My being—had I signed the bond—
Still one must lead some life beyond,
    Have a bliss to die with, dim-descried.
This foot once planted on the goal,
This glory-garland round my soul,

Could I descry such? Try and test!
I sink back shuddering from the quest.
Earth being so good, would Heaven seem best?
   Now, Heaven and she are beyond this ride.

X

And yet—she has not spoke so long!   100
What if heaven be that, fair and strong
At life's best, with our eyes upturned
Whither life's flower is first discerned,
   We, fixed so, ever should so abide?
What if we still ride on, we two
With life for ever old yet new,
Changed not in kind but in degree,
The instant made eternity,—
And heaven just prove that I and she
   Ride, ride together, forever ride?   110

THE PATRIOT

AN OLD STORY

I

It was roses, roses, all the way,
   With myrtle mixed in my path like mad:
The house-roofs seemed to heave and sway,
   The church-spires flamed, such flags they had,
A year ago on this very day.

II

The air broke into a mist with bells,
   The old walls rocked with the crowd and cries.
Had I said, "Good folk, mere noise repels—
   But give me your sun from yonder skies!"
They had answered, "And afterward, what else?"

III

Alack, it was I who leaped at the sun
    To give it my loving friends to keep!
Naught man could do, have I left undone:
    And you see my harvest, what I reap
This very day, now a year is run.

IV

There's nobody on the house-tops now—
    Just a palsied few at the windows set;
For the best of the sight is, all allow,
    At the Shambles' Gate—or, better yet,
By the very scaffold's foot, I trow.

V

I go in the rain, and, more than needs,
    A rope cuts both my wrists behind;
And I think, by the feel, my forehead bleeds,
    For they fling, whoever has a mind,
Stones at me for my year's misdeeds.

VI

Thus I entered, and thus I go!
    In triumphs, people have dropped down dead.
"Paid by the world, what dost thou owe
    Me?" God might question; now instead,
'Tis God shall repay: I am safer so.

MASTER HUGUES OF SAXE-GOTHA

I

Hist, but a word, fair and soft!
    Forth and be judged, Master Hugues!
Answer the question I've put you so oft:

What do you mean by your mountainous fugues?
See, we're alone in the loft,—

II

I, the poor organist here,
   Hugues, the composer of note,
Dead though, and done with, this many a year:
   Let's have a colloquy, something to quote,
Make the world prick up its ear!   10

III

See, the church empties apace:
   Fast they extinguish the lights.
Hallo there, sacristan! Five minutes' grace!
   Here's a crank pedal wants setting to rights,
Balks one of holding the base.

IV

See, our huge house of the sounds,
   Hushing its hundreds at once,
Bids the last loiterer back to his bounds!
   —O you may challenge them, not a response
Get the church-saints on their rounds!   20

V

(Saints go their rounds, who shall doubt?
   —March, with the moon to admire,
Up nave, down chancel, turn transept about,
   Supervise all betwixt pavement and spire,
Put rats and mice to the rout—

VI

Aloys and Jurien and Just—
   Order things back to their place,
Have a sharp eye lest the candlesticks rust,
   Rub the church-plate, darn the sacrament-lace,
Clear the desk-velvet of dust.)   30

VII

Here's your book, younger folks shelve!
  Played I not off-hand and runningly,
Just now, your masterpiece, hard number twelve?
  Here's what should strike, could one handle it cunningly:
Help the axe, give it a helve!

VIII

Page after page as I played,
  Every bar's rest, where one wipes
Sweat from one's brow, I looked up and surveyed,
  O'er my three claviers, yon forest of pipes
Whence you still peeped in the shade.   40

IX

Sure you were wishful to speak?
  You, with brow ruled like a score,
Yes, and eyes buried in pits on each cheek,
  Like two great breves, as they wrote them of yore,
Each side that bar, your straight beak!

X

Sure you said—"Good, the mere notes!
  Still, couldst thou take my intent,
Know what procured me our Company's votes—
  A master were lauded and sciolists shent,
Parted the sheep from the goats!"   50

XI

Well then, speak up, never flinch!
  Quick, ere my candle's a snuff
—Burnt, do you see? to its uttermost inch—
  I believe in you, but that's not enough:
Give my conviction a clinch!

XII

First you deliver your phrase
   —Nothing propound, that I see,
Fit in itself for much blame or much praise—
   Answered no less, where no answer needs be:
Off start the Two on their ways.   60

XIII

Straight must a Third interpose,
   Volunteer needlessly help;
In strikes a Fourth, a Fifth thrusts in his nose,
   So the cry's open, the kennel's a-yelp,
Argument's hot to the close.

XIV

One dissertates, he is candid;
   Two must discept,—has distinguished;
Three helps the couple, if ever yet man did;
   Four protests; Five makes a dart at the thing wished:
Back to One, goes the case bandied.   70

XV

One says his say with a difference;
   More of expounding, explaining!
All now is wrangle, abuse, and vociferance;
   Now there's a truce, all's subdued, self-restraining:
Five, though, stands out all the stiffer hence.

XVI

One is incisive, corrosive;
   Two retorts, nettled, curt, crepitant;
Three makes rejoinder, expansive, explosive;
   Four overbears them all, strident and strepitant:
Five . . . O Danaides, O Sieve!

XVII

Now, they ply axes and crowbars;
   Now, they prick pins at a tissue
Fine as a skein of the casuist Escobar's
   Worked on the bone of a lie. To what issue?
Where is our gain at the Two-bars?

XVIII

Est fuga, volvitur rota.
   On we drift: where looms the dim port?
One, Two, Three, Four, Five, contribute their quota;
   Something is gained, if one caught but the import—
Show it us, Hugues of Saxe-Gotha!   90

XIX

What with affirming, denying,
   Holding, risposting, subjoining,
All's like . . . it's like . . . for an instance I'm trying . . .
   There! See our roof, its gilt moulding and groining
Under those spider-webs lying!

XX

So your fugue broadens and thickens,
   Greatens and deepens and lengthens,
Till we exclaim—"But where's music, the dickens?
   Blot ye the gold, while your spider-web strengthens
—Blacked to the stoutest of tickens?"   100

XXI

I for man's effort am zealous:
   Prove me such censure unfounded!
Seems it surprising a lover grows jealous—
   Hopes 'twas for something, his organ-pipes sounded,
Tiring three boys at the bellows?

XXII

Is it your moral of Life?
  Such a web, simple and subtle,
Weave we on earth here in impotent strife,
  Backward and forward each throwing his shuttle,
Death ending all with a knife?   110

XXIII

Over our heads truth and nature—
  Still our life's zigzags and dodges,
Ins and outs, weaving a new legislature—
  God's gold just shining its last where that lodges,
Palled beneath man's usurpature.

XXIV

So we o'ershroud stars and roses,
  Cherub and trophy and garland;
Nothings grow something which quietly closes
  Heaven's earnest eye: not a glimpse of the far land
Gets through our comments and glozes.   120

XXV

Ah but traditions, inventions,
  (Say we and make up a visage)
So many men with such various intentions,
  Down the past ages, must know more than this age!
Leave we the web its dimensions!

XXVI

Who thinks Hugues wrote for the deaf,
  Proved a mere mountain in labor?
Better submit; try again; what's the clef?
  'Faith, 'tis no trifle for pipe and for tabor—
Four flats, the minor in F.   130

XXVII

Friend, your fugue taxes the finger:
    Learning it once, who would lose it?
Yet all the while a misgiving will linger,
    Truth's golden o'er us although we refuse it—
Nature, thro' cobwebs we string her!

XXVIII

Hugues! I advise *meâ pœnâ*
    (Counterpoint glares like a Gorgon)
Bid One, Two, Three, Four, Five, clear the arena!
    Say the word, straight I unstop the full-organ,
Blare out the *mode Palestrina*.   140

XXIX

While in the roof, if I'm right there,
    . . . Lo, you, the wick in the socket!
Hallo, you sacristan, show us a light there!
    Down it dips, gone like a rocket!
What, you want, do you, to come unawares,
Sweeping the church up for first morning-prayers,
And find a poor devil has ended his cares
At the foot of your rotten-runged rat-riddled stairs?
    Do I carry the moon in my pocket?

BISHOP BLOUGRAM'S APOLOGY

No more wine? then we'll push back chairs and talk.
A final glass for me, though: cool, i' faith!
We ought to have our Abbey back, you see.
It's different, preaching in basilicas,
And doing duty in some masterpiece
Like this of brother Pugin's, bless his heart!
I doubt if they're half baked, those chalk rosettes,
Ciphers and stucco-twiddlings everywhere;
It's just like breathing in a lime-kiln: eh?

These hot long ceremonies of our church   10
Cost us a little—oh, they pay the price,
You take me—amply pay it! Now, we'll talk.

So, you despise me, Mr. Gigadibs.
No deprecation,—nay, I beg you, sir!
Beside 'tis our engagement: don't you know,
I promised, if you'd watch a dinner out,
We'd see truth dawn together?—truth that peeps
Over the glasses' edge when dinner's done,
And body gets its sop and holds its noise
And leaves soul free a little. Now's the time: 20
Truth's break of day! You do despise me then.
And if I say, "despise me,"—never fear!
I know you do not in a certain sense—
Not in my arm-chair, for example: here,
I well imagine you respect my place
(*Status, entourage,* worldly circumstance)
Quite to its value—very much indeed:
—Are up to the protesting eyes of you
In pride at being seated here for once—
You'll turn it to such capital account!   30
When somebody, through years and years to come,
Hints of the bishop,—names me—that's enough:
"Blougram? I knew him"—(into it you slide)
"Dined with him once, a Corpus Christi Day,
All alone, we two; he's a clever man:
And after dinner,—why, the wine you know,—
Oh, there was wine, and good!—what with the wine . . .
'Faith, we began upon all sorts of talk!
He's no bad fellow, Blougram; he had seen
Something of mine he relished, some review: 40
He's quite above their humbug in his heart,
Half-said as much, indeed—the thing's his trade.
I warrant, Blougram's sceptical at times:
How otherwise? I liked him, I confess!"
Che che, my dear sir, as we say at Rome,
Don't you protest now! It's fair give and take;
You have had your turn and spoken your home-truths:
The hand's mine now, and here you follow suit.

Thus much conceded, still the first fact stays—
You do despise me; your ideal of life   50

Is not the bishop's: you would not be I.
You would like better to be Goethe, now,
Or Buonaparte, or, bless me, lower still,
Count D'Orsay,—so you did what you preferred,
Spoke as you thought, and, as you cannot help,
Believed or disbelieved, no matter what,
So long as on that point, whate'er it was,
You loosed your mind, were whole and sole yourself.
—That, my ideal never can include,
Upon that element of truth and worth
Never be based! for say they make me Pope— 60
(They can't—suppose it for our argument!)
Why, there I'm at my tether's end, I've reached
My height, and not a height which pleases you:
An unbelieving Pope won't do, you say.
It's like those eerie stories nurses tell,
Of how some actor on a stage played Death,
With pasteboard crown, sham orb and tinselled dart,
And called himself the monarch of the world;
Then, going in the tire-room afterward,
Because the play was done, to shift himself, 70
Got touched upon the sleeve familiarly,
The moment he had shut the closet door,
By Death himself. Thus God might touch a Pope
At unawares, ask what his baubles mean,
And whose part he presumed to play just now.
Best be yourself, imperial, plain and true!

So, drawing comfortable breath again,
You weigh and find, whatever more or less
I boast of my ideal realized
Is nothing in the balance when opposed 80
To your ideal, your grand simple life,
Of which you will not realize one jot.
I am much, you are nothing; you would be all,
I would be merely much: you beat me there.

No, friend, you do not beat me: hearken why!
The common problem, yours, mine, every one's,
Is—not to fancy what were fair in life
Provided it could be,—but, finding first
What may be, then find how to make it fair 90
Up to our means: a very different thing!

No abstract intellectual plan of life
Quite irrespective of life's plainest laws,
But one, a man, who is man and nothing more,
May lead within a world which (by your leave)
Is Rome or London, not Fool's-paradise.
Embellish Rome, idealize away,
Make paradise of London if you can,
You're welcome, nay, you're wise.

                     A simile!
We mortals cross the ocean of this world   100
Each in his average cabin of a life;
The best's not big, the worst yields elbow-room.
Now for our six months' voyage—how prepare?
You come on shipboard with a landsman's list
Of things he calls convenient: so they are!
An India screen is pretty furniture,
A piano-forte is a fine resource,
All Balzac's novels occupy one shelf,
The new edition fifty volumes long;
And little Greek books, with the funny type   110
They get up well at Leipsic, fill the next:
Go on! slabbed marble, what a bath it makes!
And Parma's pride, the Jerome, let us add!
'Twere pleasant could Correggio's fleeting glow
Hang full in face of one where'er one roams,
Since he more than the others brings with him
Italy's self,—the marvellous Modenese!—
Yet was not on your list before, perhaps.
—Alas, friend, here's the agent . . . is't the name?
The captain, or whoever's master here—   120
You see him screw his face up; what's his cry
Ere you set foot on shipboard? "Six feet square!"
If you won't understand what six feet mean,
Compute and purchase stores accordingly—
And if, in pique because he overhauls
Your Jerome, piano, bath, you come on board
Bare—why, you cut a figure at the first
While sympathetic landsmen see you off;
Not afterward, when long ere half seas over,
You peep up from your utterly naked boards   130
Into some snug and well-appointed berth,
Like mine for instance (try the cooler jug—

Put back the other, but don't jog the ice!)
And mortified you mutter "Well and good;
He sits enjoying his sea-furniture;
'Tis stout and proper, and there's store of it:
Though I've the better notion, all agree,
Of fitting rooms up. Hang the carpenter,
Neat ship-shape fixings and contrivances—
I would have brought my Jerome, frame and all!"   140
And meantime you bring nothing: never mind—
You've proved your artist-nature: what you don't
You might bring, so despise me, as I say.

Now come, let's backward to the starting-place.
See my way: we're two college friends, suppose.
Prepare together for our voyage, then;
Each note and check the other in his work,—
Here's mine, a bishop's outfit; criticise!
What's wrong? why won't you be a bishop too?

Why first, you don't believe, you don't and can't,   150
(Not statedly, that is, and fixedly
And absolutely and exclusively)
In any revelation called divine.
No dogmas nail your faith; and what remains
But say so, like the honest man you are?
First, therefore, overhaul theology!
Nay, I too, not a fool, you please to think,
Must find believing every whit as hard:
And if I do not frankly say as much,
The ugly consequence is clear enough.   160

Now wait, my friend: well, I do not believe—
If you'll accept no faith that is not fixed,
Absolute and exclusive, as you say.
You're wrong—I mean to prove it in due time.
Meanwhile, I know where difficulties lie
I could not, cannot solve, nor ever shall,
So give up hope accordingly to solve—
(To you, and over the wine). Our dogmas then
With both of us, though in unlike degree,
Missing full credence—overboard with them!   170
I mean to meet you on your own premise:
Good, there go mine in company with yours!

And now what are we? unbelievers both,
Calm and complete, determinately fixed
To-day, to-morrow and forever, pray?
You'll guarantee me that? Not so, I think!
In no wise! all we've gained is, that belief,
As unbelief before, shakes us by fits,
Confounds us like its predecessor. Where's
The gain? how can we guard our unbelief,   180
Make it bear fruit to us?—the problem here.
Just when we are safest, there's a sunset-touch,
A fancy from a flower-bell, some one's death,
A chorus-ending from Euripides,—
And that's enough for fifty hopes and fears
As old and new at once as nature's self,
To rap and knock and enter in our soul,
Take hands and dance there, a fantastic ring,
Round the ancient idol, on his base again,—
The grand Perhaps! We look on helplessly.   190
There the old misgivings, crooked questions are—
This good God,—what he could do, if he would,
Would, if he could—then must have done long since:
If so, when, where and how? some way must be,—
Once feel about, and soon or late you hit
Some sense, in which it might be, after all.
Why not, "The Way, the Truth, the Life?"

                                    —That way

Over the mountain, which who stands upon
Is apt to doubt if it be meant for a road;
While, if he views it from the waste itself,   200
Up goes the line there, plain from base to brow,
Not vague, mistakable! what's a break or two
Seen from the unbroken desert either side?
And then (to bring in fresh philosophy)
What if the breaks themselves should prove at last
The most consummate of contrivances
To train a man's eye, teach him what is faith?
And so we stumble at truth's very test!
All we have gained then by our unbelief
Is a life of doubt diversified by faith,   210
For one of faith diversified by doubt:
We called the chess-board white,—we call it black.

"Well," you rejoin, "the end's no worse, at least;
We've reason for both colors on the board:
Why not confess then, where I drop the faith
And you the doubt, that I'm as right as you?"

Because, friend, in the next place, this being so,
And both things even,—faith and unbelief
Left to a man's choice,—we'll proceed a step,
Returning to our image, which I like.   220

A man's choice, yes—but a cabin-passenger's—
The man made for the special life o' the world—
Do you forget him? I remember though!
Consult our ship's conditions and you find
One and but one choice suitable to all;
The choice, that you unluckily prefer,
Turning things topsy-turvy—they or it
Going to the ground. Belief or unbelief
Bears upon life, determines its whole course,
Begins at its beginning. See the world   230
Such as it is,—you made it not, nor I;
I mean to take it as it is,—and you,
Not so you'll take it,—though you get naught else.
I know the special kind of life I like,
What suits the most my idiosyncrasy,
Brings out the best of me and bears me fruit
In power, peace, pleasantness and length of days.
I find that positive belief does this
For me, and unbelief, no whit of this.
—For you, it does, however?—that, we'll try!   240
'Tis clear, I cannot lead my life, at least,
Induce the world to let me peaceably,
Without declaring at the outset, "Friends,
I absolutely and peremptorily
Believe!"—I say, faith is my waking life:
One sleeps, indeed, and dreams at intervals,
We know, but waking's the main point with us,
And my provision's for life's waking part.
Accordingly, I use heart, head and hand
All day, I build, scheme, study, and make friends;   250
And when night overtakes me, down I lie,
Sleep, dream a little, and get done with it.

The sooner the better, to begin afresh.
What's midnight doubt before the dayspring's faith?
You, the philosopher, that disbelieve,
That recognize the night, give dreams their weight—
To be consistent you should keep your bed,
Abstain from healthy acts that prove you man,
For fear you drowse perhaps at unawares!
And certainly at night you'll sleep and dream,   260
Live through the day and bustle as you please.
And so you live to sleep as I to wake,
To unbelieve as I to still believe?
Well, and the common sense o' the world calls you
Bed-ridden,—and its good things come to me.
Its estimation, which is half the fight,
That's the first-cabin comfort I secure:
The next . . . but you perceive with half an eye!
Come, come, it's best believing, if we may;
You can't but own that!

                    Next, concede again,   270
If once we choose belief, on all accounts
We can't be too decisive in our faith,
Conclusive and exclusive in its terms,
To suit the world which gives us the good things.
In every man's career are certain points
Whereon he dares not be indifferent;
The world detects him clearly, if he dare,
As baffled at the game, and losing life.
He may care little or he may care much
For riches, honor, pleasure, work, repose,   280
Since various theories of life and life's
Success are extant which might easily
Comport with either estimate of these;
And whoso chooses wealth or poverty,
Labor or quiet, is not judged a fool
Because his fellow would choose otherwise:
We let him choose upon his own account
So long as he's consistent with his choice.
But certain points, left wholly to himself,
When once a man has arbitrated on,   290
We say he must succeed there or go hang.
Thus, he should wed the woman he loves most
Or needs most, whatsoe'er the love or need—

For he can't wed twice. Then, he must avouch,
Or follow, at the least, sufficiently,
The form of faith his conscience holds the best,
Whate'er the process of conviction was:
For nothing can compensate his mistake
On such a point, the man himself being judge:
He cannot wed twice, nor twice lose his soul. 300

Well now, there's one great form of Christian faith
I happened to be born in—which to teach
Was given me as I grew up, on all hands,
As best and readiest means of living by;
The same on examination being proved
The most pronounced moreover, fixed, precise
And absolute form of faith in the whole world—
Accordingly, most potent of all forms
For working on the world. Observe, my friend!
Such as you know me, I am free to say, 310
In these hard latter days which hamper one,
Myself—by no immoderate exercise
Of intellect and learning, but the tact
To let external forces work for me,
—Bid the street's stones be bread and they are bread;
Bid Peter's creed, or rather, Hildebrand's,
Exalt me o'er my fellows in the world
And make my life an ease and joy and pride;
It does so,—which for me's a great point gained,
Who have a soul and body that exact 320
A comfortable care in many ways.
There's power in me and will to dominate
Which I must exercise, they hurt me else:
In many ways I need mankind's respect,
Obedience, and the love that's born of fear:
While at the same time, there's a taste I have,
A toy of soul, a titillating thing,
Refuses to digest these dainties crude.
The naked life is gross till clothed upon:
I must take what men offer, with a grace 330
As though I would not, could I help it, take!
An uniform I wear though over-rich—
Something imposed on me, no choice of mine;
No fancy-dress worn for pure fancy's sake
And despicable therefore! now folk kneel

And kiss my hand—of course the Church's hand.
Thus I am made, thus life is best for me,
And thus that it should be I have procured;
And thus it could not be another way,
I venture to imagine.

You'll reply,   340
So far my choice, no doubt, is a success;
But were I made of better elements,
With nobler instincts, purer tastes, like you,
I hardly would account the thing success
Though it did all for me I say.

But, friend.
We speak of what is; not of what might be,
And how 'twere better if 'twere otherwise.
I am the man you see here plain enough:
Grant I'm a beast, why, beasts must lead beasts' lives!
Suppose I own at once to tail and claws;   350
The tailless man exceeds me: but being tailed
I'll lash out lion fashion, and leave apes
To dock their stump and dress their haunches up.
My business is not to remake myself,
But make the absolute best of what God made.
Or—our first simile—though you prove me doomed
To a viler berth still, to the steerage-hole,
The sheep-pen or the pig-stye, I should strive
To make what use of each were possible;
And as this cabin gets upholstery,   360
That hutch should rustle with sufficient straw.

But, friend, I don't acknowledge quite so fast
I fail of all your manhood's lofty tastes
Enumerated so complacently,
On the mere ground that you forsooth can find
In this particular life I choose to lead
No fit provision for them. Can you not?
Say you, my fault is I address myself
To grosser estimators than should judge?
And that's no way of holding up the soul,   370
Which, nobler, needs men's praise perhaps, yet knows
One wise man's verdict outweighs all the fools'—
Would like the two, but, forced to choose, takes that.

I pine among my million imbeciles
(You think) aware some dozen men of sense
Eye me and know me, whether I believe
In the last winking Virgin, as I vow,
And am a fool, or disbelieve in her
And am a knave,—approve in neither case,
Withhold their voices though I look their way: 380
Like Verdi when, at his worst opera's end
(The thing they gave at Florence,—what's its name?)
While the mad houseful's plaudits near outbang
His orchestra of salt-box, tongs and bones,
He looks through all the roaring and the wreaths
Where sits Rossini patient in his stall.

   Nay, friend, I meet you with an answer here—
That even your prime men who appraise their kind
Are men still, catch a wheel within a wheel,
See more in a truth than the truth's simple self,   390
Confuse themselves. You see lads walk the street
Sixty the minute; what's to note in that?
You see one lad o'erstride a chimney-stack;
Him you must watch—he's sure to fall, yet stands!
Our interest's on the dangerous edge of things.
The honest thief, the tender murderer,
The superstitious atheist, demirep
That loves and saves her soul in new French books—
We watch while these in equilibrium keep
The giddy line midway: one step aside,   400
They're classed and done with. I, then, keep the line
Before your sages,—just the men to shrink
From the gross weights, coarse scales and labels broad
You offer their refinement. Fool or knave?
Why needs a bishop be a fool or knave
When there's a thousand diamond weights between?
So, I enlist them. Your picked twelve, you'll find,
Profess themselves indignant, scandalized
At thus being held unable to explain
How a superior man who disbelieves   410
May not believe as well: that's Schelling's way!
It's through my coming in the tail of time,
Nicking the minute with a happy tact.
Had I been born three hundred years ago
They'd say, "What's strange? Blougram of course believes;"

And, seventy years since, "disbelieves of course."
But now, "He may believe; and yet, and yet
How can he?" All eyes turn with interest.
Whereas, step off the line on either side—
You, for example, clever to a fault,   420
The rough and ready man who write apace,
Read somewhat seldomer, think perhaps even less—
You disbelieve! Who wonders and who cares?
Lord So-and-so—his coat bedropped with wax,
All Peter's chains about his waist, his back
Brave with the needlework of Noodledom—
Believes! Again, who wonders and who cares?
But I, the man of sense and learning too,
The able to think yet act, the this, the that,
I, to believe at this late time of day!   430
Enough; you see, I need not fear contempt.

   —Except it's yours! Admire me as these may,
You don't. But whom at least do you admire?
Present your own perfection, your ideal,
Your pattern man for a minute—oh, make haste,
Is it Napoleon you would have us grow?
Concede the means; allow his head and hand,
(A large concession, clever as you are)
Good! In our common primal element
Of unbelief (we can't believe, you know—   440
We're still at that admission, recollect!)
Where do you find—apart from, towering o'er
The secondary temporary aims
Which satisfy the gross taste you despise—
Where do you find his star?—his crazy trust
God knows through what or in what? it's alive
And shines and leads him, and that's all we want.
Have we aught in our sober night shall point
Such ends as his were, and direct the means
Of working out our purpose straight as his,   450
Nor bring a moment's trouble on success
With after-care to justify the same?
—Be a Napoleon, and yet disbelieve—
Why, the man's mad, friend, take his light away!
What's the vague good o' the world, for which you dare
With comfort to yourself blow millions up?
We neither of us see it! we do see

The blown-up millions—spatter of their brains
And writhing of their bowels and so forth,
In that bewildering entanglement   460
Of horrible eventualities
Past calculation to the end of time!
Can I mistake for some clear word of God
(Which were my ample warrant for it all)
His puff of hazy instinct, idle talk,
"The State, that's I," quack-nonsense about crowns,
And (when one beats the man to his last hold)
A vague idea of setting things to rights,
Policing people efficaciously,
More to their profit, most of all to his own;   470
The whole to end that dismallest of ends
By an Austrian marriage, cant to us the Church,
And resurrection of the old *régime?*
Would I, who hope to live a dozen years,
Fight Austerlitz for reasons such and such?
No: for, concede me but the merest chance
Doubt may be wrong—there's judgment, life to come!
With just that chance, I dare not. Doubt proves right?
This present life is all?—you offer me
Its dozen noisy years, without a chance   480
That wedding an archduchess, wearing lace,
And getting called by divers new-coined names,
Will drive off ugly thoughts and let me dine,
Sleep, read and chat in quiet as I like!
Therefore I will not.

               Take another case;
Fit up the cabin yet another way.
What say you to the poets? shall we write
Hamlet, Othello—make the world our own,
Without a risk to run of either sort?
I can't!—to put the strongest reason first.   490
"But try," you urge, "the trying shall suffice;
The aim, if reached or not, makes great the life:
Try to be Shakespeare, leave the rest to fate!"
Spare my self-knowledge—there's no fooling me!
If I prefer remaining my poor self,
I say so not in self-dispraise but praise.
If I'm a Shakespeare, let the well alone;
Why should I try to be what now I am?

If I'm no Shakespeare, as too probable,—
His power and consciousness and self-delight　　　　　　500
And all we want in common, shall I find—
Trying forever? while on points of taste
Wherewith, to speak it humbly, he and I
Are dowered alike—I'll ask you, I or he,
Which in our two lives realizes most?
Much, he imagined—somewhat, I possess.
He had the imagination; stick to that!
Let him say, "In the face of my soul's works
Your world is worthless and I touch it not
Lest I should wrong them"—I'll withdraw my plea.　　　　510
But does he say so? look upon his life!
Himself, who only can, gives judgment there.
He leaves his towers and gorgeous palaces
To build the trimmest house in Stratford town;
Saves money, spends it, owns the worth of things,
Giulio Romano's pictures, Dowland's lute;
Enjoys a show, respects the puppets, too,
And none more, had he seen its entry once,
Than "Pandulph, of fair Milan cardinal."
Why then should I who play that personage,　　　　　　520
The very Pandulph Shakespeare's fancy made,
Be told that had the poet chanced to start
From where I stand now (some degree like mine
Being just the goal he ran his race to reach)
He would have run the whole race back, forsooth,
And left being Pandulph, to begin write plays?
Ah, the earth's best can be but the earth's best!
Did Shakespeare live, he could but sit at home
And get himself in dreams the Vatican,
Greek busts, Venetian paintings, Roman walls,　　　　　530
And English books, none equal to his own,
Which I read, bound in gold (he never did).
—Terni's fall, Naples' bay and Gothard's top—
Eh, friend? I could not fancy one of these;
But, as I pour this claret, there they are:
I've gained them—crossed St. Gothard last July
With ten mules to the carriage and a bed
Slung inside; is my hap the worse for that?
We want the same things, Shakespeare and myself,
And what I want, I have: he, gifted more,　　　　　　540
Could fancy he too had them when he liked,

But not so thoroughly that, if fate allowed,
He would not have them also in my sense.
We play one game; I send the ball aloft
No less adroitly that of fifty strokes
Scarce five go o'er the wall so wide and high
Which sends them back to me: I wish and get.
He struck balls higher and with better skill,
But at a poor fence level with his head,
And hit—his Stratford house, a coat of arms,   550
Successful dealings in his grain and wool,—
While I receive heaven's incense in my nose
And style myself the cousin of Queen Bess.
Ask him, if this life's all, who wins the game?

Believe—and our whole argument breaks up.
Enthusiasm's the best thing, I repeat;
Only, we can't command it; fire and life
Are all, dead matter's nothing, we agree:
And be it a mad dream or God's very breath,
The fact's the same,—belief's fire, once in us,   560
Makes of all else mere stuff to show itself:
We penetrate our life with such a glow
As fire lends wood and iron—this turns steel,
That burns to ash—all's one, fire proves its power
For good or ill, since men call flare success.
But paint a fire, it will not therefore burn.
Light one in me, I'll find it food enough!
Why, to be Luther—that's a life to lead,
Incomparably better than my own.
He comes, reclaims God's earth for God, he says,   570
Sets up God's rule again by simple means,
Re-opens a shut book, and all is done.
He flared out in the flaring of mankind;
Such Luther's luck was: how shall such be mine?
If he succeeded, nothing's left to do:
And if he did not altogether—well,
Strauss is the next advance. All Strauss should be
I might be also. But to what result?
He looks upon no future: Luther did.
What can I gain on the denying side?   580
Ice makes no conflagration. State the facts,
Read the text right, emancipate the world—
The emancipated world enjoys itself

With scarce a thank-you: Blougram told it first
It could not owe a farthing,—not to him
More than Saint Paul! 'twould press its pay, you think?
Then add there's still that plaguy hundredth chance
Strauss may be wrong. And so a risk is run—
For what gain? not for Luther's, who secured
A real heaven in his heart throughout his life,   590
Supposing death a little altered things.

   "Ay, but since really you lack faith," you cry,
"You run the same risk really on all sides,
In cool indifference as bold unbelief.
As well be Strauss as swing 'twixt Paul and him.
It's not worth having, such imperfect faith,
No more available to do faith's work
Than unbelief like mine. Whole faith, or none!"

   Softly, my friend! I must dispute that point.
Once own the use of faith, I'll find you faith.   600
We're back on Christian ground. You call for faith:
I show you doubt, to prove that faith exists.
The more of doubt, the stronger faith, I say,
If faith o'ercomes doubt. How I know it does?
By life and man's free will, God gave for that!
To mould life as we choose it, shows our choice:
That's our one act, the previous work's his own.
You criticise the soul? it reared this tree—
This broad life and whatever fruit it bears!
What matter though I doubt at every pore,   610
Head-doubts, heart-doubts, doubts at my fingers' ends,
Doubts in the trivial work of every day,
Doubts at the very bases of my soul
In the grand moments when she probes herself—
If finally I have a life to show,
The thing I did, brought out in evidence
Against the thing done to me underground
By hell and all its brood, for aught I know?
I say, whence sprang this? shows it faith or doubt?
All's doubt in me; where's break of faith in this?   620
It is the idea, the feeling and the love,
God means mankind should strive for and show forth
Whatever be the process to that end,—
And not historic knowledge, logic sound,

And metaphysical acumen, sure!
"What think ye of Christ," friend? when all's done and said,
Like you this Christianity or not?
It may be false, but will you wish it true?
Has it your vote to be so if it can?
Trust you an instinct silenced long ago   630
That will break silence and enjoin you love
What mortified philosophy is hoarse,
And all in vain, with bidding you despise?
If you desire faith—then you've faith enough:
What else seeks God—nay, what else seek ourselves?
You form a notion of me, we'll suppose,
On hearsay; it's a favorable one:
"But still" (you add), "there was no such good man,
Because of contradiction in the facts.
One proves, for instance, he was born in Rome,   640
This Blougram; yet throughout the tales of him
I see he figures as an Englishman."
Well, the two things are reconcilable.
But would I rather you discover that,
Subjoining—"Still, what matter though they be?
Blougram concerns me naught, born here or there."

    Pure faith indeed—you know not what you ask!
Naked belief in God the Omnipotent,
Omniscient, Omnipresent, sears too much
The sense of conscious creatures to be borne.   650
It were the seeing him, no flesh shall dare.
Some think, Creation's meant to show him forth:
I say it's meant to hide him all it can,
And that's what all the blessed evil's for.
Its use in Time is to environ us,
Our breath, our drop of dew, with shield enough
Against that sight till we can bear its stress.
Under a vertical sun, the exposed brain
And lidless eye and disemprisoned heart
Less certainly would wither up at once   660
Than mind, confronted with the truth of him.
But time and earth case-harden us to live;
The feeblest sense is trusted most; the child
Feels God a moment, ichors o'er the place,
Plays on and grows to be a man like us.
With me, faith means perpetual unbelief

Kept quiet like the snake 'neath Michael's foot
Who stands calm just because he feels it writhe.
Or, if that's too ambitious,—here's my box—
I need the excitation of a pinch   670
Threatening the torpor of the inside-nose
Nigh on the imminent sneeze that never comes.
"Leave it in peace" advise the simple folk:
Make it aware of peace by itching-fits,
Say I—let doubt occasion still more faith!

   You'll say, once all believed, man, woman, child,
In that dear middle-age these noodles praise.
How you'd exult if I could put you back
Six hundred years, blot out cosmogony,
Geology, ethnology, what not,   680
(Greek endings, each the little passing-bell
That signifies some faith's about to die),
And set you square with Genesis again,—
When such a traveller told you his last news,
He saw the ark a-top of Ararat
But did not climb there since 'twas getting dusk
And robber-bands infest the mountain's foot!
How should you feel, I ask, in such an age,
How act? As other people felt and did;
With soul more blank than this decanter's knob,   690
Believe—and yet lie, kill, rob, fornicate
Full in belief's face, like the beast you'd be!

   No, when the fight begins within himself,
A man's worth something. God stoops o'er his head,
Satan looks up between his feet—both tug—
He's left, himself, i' the middle: the soul wakes
And grows. Prolong that battle through his life!
Never leave growing till the life to come!
Here, we've got callous to the Virgin's winks
That used to puzzle people wholesomely: 700
Men have outgrown the shame of being fools.
What are the laws of nature, not to bend
If the Church bid them?—brother Newman asks.
Up with the Immaculate Conception, then—
On to the rack with faith!—is my advice.
Will not that hurry us upon our knees,
Knocking our breasts, "It can't be—yet it shall!

Who am I, the worm, to argue with my Pope?
Low things confound the high things!" and so forth.
That's better than acquitting God with grace   710
As some folk do. He's tried—no case is proved,
Philosophy is lenient—he may go!

    You'll say, the old system's not so obsolete
But men believe still: ay, but who and where?
King Bomba's lazzaroni foster yet
The sacred flame, so Antonelli writes;
But even of these, what ragamuffin-saint
Believes God watches him continually,
As he believes in fire that it will burn,
Or rain that it will drench him? Break fire's law,   720
Sin against rain, although the penalty
Be just a singe or soaking? "No," he smiles;
"Those laws are laws that can enforce themselves."

    The sum of all is—yes, my doubt is great,
My faith's still greater, then my faith's enough.
I have read much, thought much, experienced much,
Yet would die rather than avow my fear
The Naples' liquefaction may be false,
When set to happen by the palace-clock
According to the clouds or dinner-time.   730
I hear you recommend, I might at least
Eliminate, decrassify my faith
Since I adopt it; keeping what I must
And leaving what I can—such points as this.
I won't—that is, I can't throw one away.
Supposing there's no truth in what I hold
About the need of trial to man's faith,
Still, when you bid me purify the same,
To such a process I discern no end.
Clearing off one excrescence to see two,   740
There's ever a next in size, now grown as big,
That meets the knife: I cut and cut again!
First cut the Liquefaction, what comes last
But Fichte's clever cut at God himself?
Experimentalize on sacred things!
I trust nor hand nor eye nor heart nor brain
To stop betimes: they all get drunk alike.
The first step, I am master not to take.

You'd find the cutting-process to your taste
As much as leaving growths of lies unpruned,   750
Nor see more danger in it,—you retort.
Your taste's worth mine; but my taste proves more wise
When we consider that the steadfast hold
On the extreme end of the chain of faith
Gives all the advantage, makes the difference
With the rough purblind mass we seek to rule:
We are their lords, or they are free of us,
Just as we tighten or relax our hold.
So, other matters equal, we'll revert
To the first problem—which, if solved my way   760
And thrown into the balance, turns the scale—
How we may lead a comfortable life,
How suit our luggage to the cabin's size.

Of course you are remarking all this time
How narrowly and grossly I view life,
Respect the creature-comforts, care to rule
The masses, and regard complacently
"The cabin," in our old phrase. Well, I do.
I act for, talk for, live for this world now,
As this world prizes action, life and talk: 770
No prejudice to what next world may prove,
Whose new laws and requirements, my best pledge
To observe then, is that I observe these now,
Shall do hereafter what I do meanwhile.
Let us concede (gratuitously though)
Next life relieves the soul of body, yields
Pure spiritual enjoyment: well, my friend,
Why lose this life i' the meantime, since its use
May be to make the next life more intense?

Do you know, I have often had a dream   780
(Work it up in your next month's article)
Of man's poor spirit in its progress, still
Losing true life forever and a day
Through ever trying to be and ever being—
In the evolution of successive spheres—
Before its actual sphere and place of life,
Halfway into the next, which having reached,
It shoots with corresponding foolery

Halfway into the next still, on and off!
As when a traveller, bound from North to South,   790
Scouts fur in Russia: what's its use in France?
In France spurns flannel: where's its need in Spain?
In Spain drops cloth, too cumbrous for Algiers!
Linen goes next, and last the skin itself,
A superfluity at Timbuctoo.
When, through his journey, was the fool at ease?
I'm at ease now, friend; worldly in this world,
I take and like its way of life; I think
My brothers, who administer the means,
Live better for my comfort—that's good too;   800
And God, if he pronounce upon such life,
Approves my service, which is better still.
If he keep silence,—why, for you or me
Or that brute beast pulled-up in to-day's "Times,"
What odds is 't, save to ourselves, what life we lead?

    You meet me at this issue: you declare,—
All special-pleading done with—truth is truth,
And justifies itself by undreamed ways.
You don't fear but it's better, if we doubt,
To say so, act up to our truth perceived   810
However feebly. Do then,—act away!
'Tis there I'm on the watch for you. How one acts
Is, both of us agree, our chief concern:
And how you'll act is what I fain would see
If, like the candid person you appear,
You dare to make the most of your life's scheme
As I of mine, live up to its full law
Since there's no higher law that counterchecks.
Put natural religion to the test
You've just demolished the revealed with—quick,   820
Down to the root of all that checks your will,
All prohibition to lie, kill and thieve,
Or even to be an atheistic priest!
Suppose a pricking to incontinence—
Philosophers deduce you chastity
Or shame, from just the fact that at the first
Whoso embraced a woman in the field,
Threw club down and forewent his brains beside,
So, stood a ready victim in the reach

Of any brother savage, club in hand;   830
Hence saw the use of going out of sight
In wood or cave to prosecute his loves:
I read this in a French book t' other day.
Does law so analyzed coerce you much?
Oh, men spin clouds of fuzz where matters end,
But you who reach where the first thread begins,
You'll soon cut that!—which means you can, but won't,
Through certain instincts, blind, unreasoned-out,
You dare not set aside, you can't tell why,
But there they are, and so you let them rule.   840
Then, friend, you seem as much a slave as I,
A liar, conscious coward and hypocrite,
Without the good the slave expects to get,
In case he has a master after all!
You own your instincts? why, what else do I,
Who want, am made for, and must have a God
Ere I can be aught, do aught?—no mere name
Want, but the true thing with what proves its truth,
To wit, a relation from that thing to me,
Touching from head to foot—which touch I feel,   850
And with it take the rest, this life of ours!
I live my life here; yours you dare not live.

    —Not as I state it, who (you please subjoin)
Disfigure such a life and call it names.
While, to your mind, remains another way
For simple men: knowledge and power have rights,
But ignorance and weakness have rights too.
There needs no crucial effort to find truth
If here or there or anywhere about:
We ought to turn each side, try hard and see,   860
And if we can't, be glad we've earned at least
The right, by one laborious proof the more,
To graze in peace earth's pleasant pasturage.
Men are not angels, neither are they brutes:
Something we may see, all we cannot see.
What need of lying? I say, I see all,
And swear to each detail the most minute
In what I think a Pan's face—you, mere cloud:
I swear I hear him speak and see him wink,
For fear, if once I drop the emphasis,   870

Mankind may doubt there's any cloud at all.
You take the simple life—ready to see,
Willing to see (for no cloud's worth a face)—
And leaving quiet what no strength can move,
And which, who bids you move? who has the right?
I bid you; but you are God's sheep, not mine:
"*Pastor est tui Dominus.*" You find
In this the pleasant pasture of our life
Much you may eat without the least offence,
Much you don't eat because your maw objects, 880
Much you would eat but that your fellow-flock
Open great eyes at you and even butt,
And thereupon you like your mates so well
You cannot please yourself, offending them;
Though when they seem exorbitantly sheep,
You weigh your pleasure with their butts and bleats
And strike the balance. Sometimes certain fears
Restrain you, real checks since you find them so;
Sometimes you please yourself and nothing checks:
And thus you graze through life with not one lie, 890
And like it best.
                    But do you, in truth's name?
If so, you beat—which means you are not I—
Who needs must make earth mine and feed my fill
Not simply unbutted at, unbickered with,
But motioned to the velvet of the sward
By those obsequious wethers' very selves.
Look at me, sir; my age is double yours:
At yours, I knew beforehand, so enjoyed,
What now I should be—as, permit the word,
I pretty well imagine your whole range 900
And stretch of tether twenty years to come.
We both have minds and bodies much alike:
In truth's name, don't you want my bishopric,
My daily bread, my influence and my state?
You're young. I'm old; you must be old one day;
Will you find then, as I do hour by hour,
Women their lovers kneel to, who cut curls
From your fat lap-dog's ear to grace a brooch—
Dukes, who petition just to kiss your ring—
With much beside you know or may conceive? 910
Suppose we die to-night: well, here am I,

Such were my gains, life bore this fruit to me,
While writing all the same my articles
On music, poetry, the fictile vase
Found at Albano, chess, Anacreon's Greek.
But you—the highest honor in your life,
The thing you'll crown yourself with, all your days,
Is—dining here and drinking this last glass
I pour you out in sign of amity
Before we part forever. Of your power   920
And social influence, worldly worth in short,
Judge what's my estimation by the fact,
I do not condescend to enjoin, beseech,
Hint secrecy on one of all these words!
You're shrewd and know that should you publish one
The world would brand the lie—my enemies first,
Who'd sneer—"the bishop's an arch-hypocrite
And knave perhaps, but not so frank a fool."
Whereas I should not dare for both my ears
Breathe one such syllable, smile one such smile,   930
Before the chaplain who reflects myself—
My shade's so much more potent than your flesh.
What's your reward, self-abnegating friend?
Stood you confessed of those exceptional
And privileged great natures that dwarf mine—
A zealot with a mad ideal in reach,
A poet just about to print his ode,
A statesman with a scheme to stop this war,
An artist whose religion is his art—
I should have nothing to object: such men   940
Carry the fire, all things grow warm to them,
Their drugget's worth my purple, they beat me.
But you,—you're just as little those as I—
You, Gigadibs, who, thirty years of age,
Write stately for Blackwood's Magazine,
Believe you see two points in Hamlet's soul
Unseized by the Germans yet—which view you'll print—
Meantime the best you have to show being still
That lively lightsome article we took
Almost for the true Dickens,—what's its name?   950
"The slum and Cellar, or Whitechapel life
Limned after dark!" it made me laugh, I know,
And pleased a month, and brought you in ten pounds.

—Success I recognize and compliment,
And therefore give you, if you choose, three words
(The card and pencil-scratch is quite enough)
Which whether here, in Dublin or New York,
Will get you, prompt as at my eyebrow's wink,
Such terms as never you aspired to get
In all our own reviews and some not ours. 960
Go write your lively sketches! be the first
"Blougram, or The Eccentric Confidence"—
Or better simply say, "The Outward-bound."
Why, men as soon would throw it in my teeth
As copy and quote the infamy chalked broad
About me on the church-door opposite.
You will not wait for that experience though,
I fancy, howsoever you decide,
To discontinue—not detesting, not
Defaming, but at least—despising me! 970

Over his wine so smiled and talked his hour
Sylvester Blougram, styled *in partibus
Episcopus, nec non*—(the deuce knows what
It's changed to by our novel hierarchy)
With Gigadibs the literary man,
Who played with spoons, explored his plate's design,
And ranged the olive-stones about its edge,
While the great bishop rolled him out a mind
Long crumpled, till creased consciousness lay smooth.

For Blougram, he believed, say, half he spoke. 980
The other portion, as he shaped it thus
For argumentatory purposes,
He felt his foe was foolish to dispute.
Some arbitrary accidental thoughts
That crossed his mind, amusing because new,
He chose to represent as fixtures there,
Invariable convictions (such they seemed
Beside his interlocutor's loose cards
Flung daily down, and not the same way twice)
While certain hell-deep instincts, man's weak tongue 990
Is never bold to utter in their truth
Because styled hell-deep ('tis an old mistake
To place hell at the bottom of the earth)

He ignored these,—not having in readiness
Their nomenclature and philosophy:
He said true things, but called them by wrong names.
"On the whole," he thought, "I justify myself
On every point where cavillers like this
Oppugn my life: he tries one kind of fence,
I close, he's worsted, that's enough for him.   1000
He's on the ground: if ground should break away
I take my stand on, there's a firmer yet
Beneath it, both of us may sink and reach.
His ground was over mine and broke the first:
So, let him sit with me this many a year!"

He did not sit five minutes. Just a week
Sufficed his sudden healthy vehemence.
Something had struck him in the "Outward-bound"
Another way than Blougram's purpose was:
And having bought, not cabin-furniture   1010
But settler's-implements (enough for three)
And started for Australia—there, I hope,
By this time he has tested his first plough,
And studied his last chapter of St. John.

MEMORABILIA

I

Ah, did you once see Shelley plain,
    And did he stop and speak to you
And did you speak to him again?
    How strange it seems and new!

II

But you were living before that,
    And also you are living after;
And the memory I started at—
    My starting moves your laughter.

III

I crossed a moor, with a name of its own
    And a certain use in the world no doubt,
Yet a hand's-breadth of it shines alone
    'Mid the blank miles round about:

IV

For there I picked up on the heather
    And there I put inside my breast
A moulted feather, an eagle-feather!
    Well, I forget the rest.

ANDREA DEL SARTO

(CALLED "THE FAULTLESS PAINTER")

But do not let us quarrel any more,
No, my Lucrezia; bear with me for once:
Sit down and all shall happen as you wish.
You turn your face, but does it bring your heart?
I'll work then for your friend's friend, never fear,
Treat his own subject after his own way,
Fix his own time, accept too his own price,
And shut the money into this small hand
When next it takes mine. Will it? tenderly?
Oh, I'll content him,—but to-morrow, Love!   10
I often am much wearier than you think,
This evening more than usual, and it seems
As if—forgive now—should you let me sit
Here by the window with your hand in mine
And look a half-hour forth on Fiesole,
Both of one mind, as married people use,
Quietly, quietly the evening through,
I might get up to-morrow to my work
Cheerful and fresh as ever. Let us try.
To-morrow, how you shall be glad for this!   20

Your soft hand is a woman of itself,
And mine the man's bared breast she curls inside.
Don't count the time lost, neither; you must serve
For each of the five pictures we require:
It saves a model. So! keep looking so—
My serpentining beauty, rounds on rounds!
—How could you ever prick those perfect ears,
Even to put the pearl there! oh, so sweet—
My face, my moon, my everybody's moon,
Which everybody looks on and calls his,   30
And, I suppose, is looked on by in turn,
While she looks—no one's: very dear, no less.
You smile? why, there's my picture ready made,
There's what we painters call our harmony!
A common grayness silvers everything,—
All in a twilight, you and I alike
—You, at the point of your first pride in me
(That's gone you know),—but I, at every point;
My youth, my hope, my art, being all toned down
To yonder sober pleasant Fiesole.   40
There's the bell clinking from the chapel-top;
That length of convent-wall across the way
Holds the trees safer, huddled more inside;
The last monk leaves the garden; days decrease,
And autumn grows, autumn in everything.
Eh? the whole seems to fall into a shape
As if I saw alike my work and self
And all that I was born to be and do,
A twilight-piece. Love, we are in God's hand.
How strange now, looks the life he makes us lead;   50
So free we seem, so fettered fast we are!
I feel he laid the fetter: let it lie!
This chamber for example—turn your head—
All that's behind us! You don't understand
Nor care to understand about my art,
But you can hear at least when people speak:
And that cartoon, the second from the door
—It is the thing, Love! so such things should be—
Behold Madonna!—I am bold to say.
I can do with my pencil what I know,   60
What I see, what at bottom of my heart
I wish for, if I ever wish so deep—
Do easily, too—when I say, perfectly,

I do not boast, perhaps: yourself are judge,
Who listened to the Legate's talk last week,
And just as much they used to say in France.
At any rate 'tis easy, all of it!
No sketches first, no studies, that's long past:
I do what many dream of, all their lives,
—Dream? strive to do, and agonize to do,   70
And fail in doing. I could count twenty such
On twice your fingers, and not leave this town,
Who strive—you don't know how the others strive
To paint a little thing like that you smeared
Carelessly passing with your robes afloat,—
Yet do much less, so much less, Someone says,
(I know his name, no matter)—so much less!
Well, less is more, Lucrezia: I am judged.
There burns a truer light of God in them,
In their vexed beating stuffed and stopped-up brain,   80
Heart, or whate'er else, than goes on to prompt
This low-pulsed forthright craftsman's hand of mine.
Their works drop groundward, but themselves, I know,
Reach many a time a heaven that's shut to me,
Enter and take their place there sure enough,
Though they come back and cannot tell the world.
My works are nearer heaven, but I sit here.
The sudden blood of these men! at a word—
Praise them, it boils, or blame them, it boils too.
I, painting from myself and to myself,   90
Know what I do, am unmoved by men's blame
Or their praise either. Somebody remarks
Morello's outline there is wrongly traced,
His hue mistaken; what of that? or else,
Rightly traced and well ordered; what of that?
Speak as they please, what does the mountain care?
Ah, but a man's reach should exceed his grasp,
Or what's a heaven for? All is silver-gray
Placid and perfect with my art: the worse!
I know both what I want and what might gain,   100
And yet how profitless to know, to sigh
"Had I been two, another and myself,
Our head would have o'erlooked the world!" No doubt.
Yonder's a work now, of that famous youth
The Urbinate who died five years ago.
('Tis copied, George Vasari sent it me.)

Well, I can fancy how he did it all,
Pouring his soul, with kings and popes to see,
Reaching, that heaven might so replenish him,
Above and through his art—for it gives way;   110
That arm is wrongly put—and there again—
A fault to pardon in the drawing's lines,
Its body, so to speak: its soul is right,
He means right—that, a child may understand.
Still, what an arm! and I could alter it:
But all the play, the insight and the stretch—
Out of me, out of me! And wherefore out?
Had you enjoined them on me, given me soul,
We might have risen to Rafael, I and you!
Nay, Love, you did give all I asked, I think—   120
More than I merit, yes, by many times.
But had you—oh, with the same perfect brow,
And perfect eyes, and more than perfect mouth,
And the low voice my soul hears, as a bird
The fowler's pipe, and follows to the snare—
Had you, with these the same, but brought a mind!
Some women do so. Had the mouth there urged
"God and the glory! never care for gain.
The present by the future, what is that?
Live for fame, side by side with Agnolo!   130
Rafael is waiting: up to God, all three!"
I might have done it for you. So it seems:
Perhaps not. All is as God over-rules.
Beside, incentives come from the soul's self;
The rest avail not. Why do I need you?
What wife had Rafael, or has Agnolo?
In this world, who can do a thing, will not;
And who would do it, cannot, I perceive:
Yet the will's somewhat—somewhat, too, the power—
And thus we half-men struggle. At the end,   140
God, I conclude, compensates, punishes.
'Tis safer for me, if the award be strict,
That I am something underrated here,
Poor this long while, despised, to speak the truth.
I dared not, do you know, leave home all day,
For fear of chancing on the Paris lords.
The best is when they pass and look aside;
But they speak sometimes; I must bear it all.
Well may they speak! That Francis, that first time,

And that long festal year at Fontainebleau!   150
I surely then could sometimes leave the ground,
Put on the glory, Rafael's daily wear,
In that humane great monarch's golden look,—
One finger in his beard or twisted curl
Over his mouth's good mark that made the smile,
One arm about my shoulder, round my neck,
The jingle of his gold chain in my ear,
I painting proudly with his breath on me,
All his court round him, seeing with his eyes,
Such frank French eyes, and such a fire of souls   160
Profuse, my hand kept plying by those hearts,—
And, best of all, this, this, this face beyond,
This in the background, waiting on my work,
To crown the issue with a last reward!
A good time, was it not, my kingly days?
And had you not grown restless . . . but I know—
'Tis done and past; 'twas right, my instinct said;
Too live the life grew, golden and not gray,
And I'm the weak-eyed bat no sun should tempt
Out of the grange whose four walls make his world.   170
How could it end in any other way?
You called me, and I came home to your heart.
The triumph was—to reach and stay there; since
I reached it ere the triumph, what is lost?
Let my hands frame your face in your hair's gold,
You beautiful Lucrezia that are mine!
"Rafael did this, Andrea painted that;
The Roman's is the better when you pray,
But still the other's Virgin was his wife—"
Men will excuse me. I am glad to judge   180
Both pictures in your presence; clearer grows
My better fortune, I resolve to think.
For, do you know, Lucrezia, as God lives,
Said one day Agnolo, his very self,
To Rafael . . . I have known it all these years . . .
(When the young man was flaming out his thoughts
Upon a palace-wall for Rome to see,
Too lifted up in heart because of it)
"Friend, there's a certain sorry little scrub
Goes up and down our Florence, none cares how,   190
Who, were he set to plan and execute
As you are, pricked on by your popes and kings,

Would bring the sweat into that brow of yours!"
To Rafael's—And indeed the arm is wrong.
I hardly dare . . . yet, only you to see,
Give the chalk here—quick, thus the line should go!
Ay, but the soul! he's Rafael! rub it out!
Still, all I care for, if he spoke the truth,
(What he? why, who but Michel Agnolo?
Do you forget already words like those?)   200
If really there was such a chance, so lost,—
Is, whether you're—not grateful—but more pleased.
Well, let me think so. And you smile indeed!
This hour has been an hour! Another smile?
If you would sit thus by me every night
I should work better, do you comprehend?
I mean that I should earn more, give you more.
See, it is settled dusk now; there's a star;
Morello's gone, the watch-lights show the wall,
The cue-owls speak the name we call them by.   210
Come from the window, love,—come in, at last,
Inside the melancholy little house
We built to be so gay with. God is just.
King Francis may forgive me: oft at nights
When I look up from painting, eyes tired out,
The walls become illumined, brick from brick
Distinct, instead of mortar, fierce bright gold,
That gold of his I did cement them with!
Let us but love each other. Must you go?
That Cousin here again? he waits outside?   220
Must see you—you, and not with me? Those loans?
More gaming debts to pay? you smiled for that?
Well, let smiles buy me! have you more to spend?
While hand and eye and something of a heart
Are left me, work's my ware, and what's it worth?
I'll pay my fancy. Only let me sit
The gray remainder of the evening out,
Idle, you call it, and muse perfectly
How I could paint, were I but back in France,
One picture, just one more—the Virgin's face,   230
Not yours this time! I want you at my side
To hear them—that is, Michel Agnolo—
Judge all I do and tell you of its worth.
Will you? To-morrow, satisfy your friend.
I take the subjects for his corridor,

Finish the portrait out of hand—there, there,
And throw him in another thing or two
If he demurs; the whole should prove enough
To pay for this same Cousin's freak. Beside,
What's better and what's all I care about,   240
Get you the thirteen scudi for the ruff!
Love, does that please you? Ah, but what does he,
The Cousin! What does he to please you more?

    I am grown peaceful as old age to-night.
I regret little, I would change still less.
Since there my past life lies, why alter it?
The very wrong to Francis!—it is true
I took his coin, was tempted and complied,
And built this house and sinned, and all is said.
My father and my mother died of want.   250
Well, had I riches of my own? you see
How one gets rich! Let each one bear his lot.
They were born poor, lived poor, and poor they died:
And I have labored somewhat in my time
And not been paid profusely. Some good son
Paint my two hundred pictures—let him try!
No doubt, there's something strikes a balance. Yes,
You loved me quite enough, it seems to-night.
This must suffice me here. What would one have?
In heaven, perhaps, new chances, one more chance—   260
Four great walls in the New Jerusalem,
Meted on each side by the angel's reed,
For Leonard, Rafael, Agnolo and me
To cover—the three first without a wife,
While I have mine! So—still they overcome
Because there's still Lucrezia,—as I choose.

Again the Cousin's whistle! Go, my Love.

BEFORE

I

LET them fight it out, friend! things have gone too far.
God must judge the couple: leave them as they are

—Whichever one's the guiltless, to his glory,
And whichever one the guilt's with, to my story!

II

Why, you would not bid men, sunk in such a slough,
Strike no arm out further, stick and stink as now,
Leaving right and wrong to settle the embroilment,
Heaven with snaky hell, in torture and entoilment?

III

Who's the culprit of them? How must he conceive
God—the queen he caps to, laughing in his sleeve,
" 'Tis but decent to profess oneself beneath her:
Still, one must not be too much in earnest, either!"

IV

Better sin the whole sin, sure that God observes;
Then go live his life out! Life will try his nerves,
When the sky, which noticed all, makes no disclosure,
And the earth keeps up her terrible composure.

V

Let him pace at pleasure, past the walls of rose,
Pluck their fruits when grape-trees graze him as he goes!
For he 'gins to guess the purpose of the garden,
With the sly mute thing, beside there, for a warden.

VI

What's the leopard-dog-thing, constant at his side,
A leer and lie in every eye of its obsequious hide?
When will come an end to all the mock obeisance,
And the price appear that pays for the misfeasance?

VII

So much for the culprit. Who's the martyred man?
Let him bear one stroke more, for be sure he can!

He that strove thus evil's lump with good to leaven,
Let him give his blood at last and get his heaven!

VIII

All or nothing, stake it! Trusts he God or no?
Thus far and no farther? farther? be it so!
Now, enough of your chicane of prudent pauses,
Sage provisos, sub-intents and saving-clauses!

IX

Ah, "forgive" you bid him? While God's champion lives,
Wrong shall be resisted: dead, why, he forgives.
But you must not end my friend ere you begin him;
Evil stands not crowned on earth, while breath is in him.

X

Once more—Will the wronger, at this last of all,
Dare to say, "I did wrong," rising in his fall?
No?—Let go, then! Both the fighters to their places!
While I count three, step you back as many paces!

AFTER

TAKE the cloak from his face, and at first
    Let the corpse do its worst!

How he lies in his rights of a man!
    Death has done all death can.
And, absorbed in the new life he leads,
    He recks not, he heeds
Nor his wrong nor my vengeance; both strike
    On his senses alike,
And are lost in the solemn and strange
    Surprise of the change.
Ha, what avails death to erase
    His offence, my disgrace?
I would we were boys as of old
    In the field, by the fold:

His outrage, God's patience, man's scorn
  Were so easily borne!

I stand here now, he lies in his place:
  Cover the face!

IN THREE DAYS

I

So, I shall see her in three days
And just one night, but nights are short,
Then two long hours, and that is morn.
See how I come, unchanged, unworn!
Feel, where my life broke off from thine,
How fresh the splinters keep and fine,—
Only a touch and we combine!

II

Too long, this time of year, the days!
But nights, at least the nights are short.
As night shows where her one moon is,
A hand's-breadth of pure light and bliss,
So life's night gives my lady birth
And my eyes hold her! What is worth
The rest of heaven, the rest of earth?

III

O loaded curls, release your store
Of warmth and scent, as once before
The tingling hair did, lights and darks
Outbreaking into fairy sparks,
When under curl and curl I pried
After the warmth and scent inside,
Thro' lights and darks how manifold—
The dark inspired, the light controlled!
As early Art embrowns the gold.

IV

What great fear, should one say, "Three days
That change the world might change as well
Your fortune; and if joy delays,
Be happy that no worse befell!"
What small fear, if another says,
"Three days and one short night beside
May throw no shadow on your ways;
But years must teem with change untried,
With chance not easily defied,
With an end somewhere undescried."
No fear!—or if a fear be born
This minute, it dies out in scorn.
Fear? I shall see her in three days
And one night, now the nights are short,
Then just two hours, and that is morn.

IN A YEAR

I

Never any more,
    While I live,
Need I hope to see his face
    As before.
Once his love grown chill,
    Mine may strive:
Bitterly we re-embrace,
    Single still.

II

Was it something said,
    Something done,
Vexed him? was it touch of hand,
    Turn of head?
Strange! that very way
    Love begun:

I as little understand
  Love's decay.

III

When I sewed or drew,
  I recall
How he looked as if I sung,
  —Sweetly too.
If I spoke a word,
  First of all
Up his cheek the color sprung,
  Then he heard.

IV

Sitting by my side,
  At my feet,
So he breathed but air I breathed,
  Satisfied!
I, too, at love's brim
  Touched the sweet:
I would die if death bequeathed
  Sweet to him.

V

"Speak, I love thee best!"
  He exclaimed:
"Let thy love my own foretell!"
  I confessed:
"Clasp my heart on thine
  Now unblamed,
Since upon thy soul as well
  Hangeth mine!"

VI

Was it wrong to own,
  Being truth?
Why should all the giving prove
  His alone?

I had wealth and ease,
  Beauty, youth:
Since my lover gave me love
  I gave these.

VII

That was all I meant,
  —To be just,
And the passion I had raised,
  To content.
Since he chose to change
  Gold for dust,
If I gave him what he praised
  Was it strange?

VIII

Would he loved me yet,
  On and on,
While I found some way undreamed
  —Paid my debt!
Gave more life and more,
  Till, all gone,
He should smile "She never seemed
  Mine before.

IX

"What, she felt the while,
  Must I think?
Love's so different with us men!"
  He should smile:
"Dying for my sake—
  White and pink!
Can't we touch these bubbles then
  But they break?"

X

Dear, the pang is brief,
  Do thy part,

Have thy pleasure! How perplexed
    Grows belief!
Well, this cold clay clod
    Was man's heart:
Crumble it, and what comes next?
    Is it God?

OLD PICTURES IN FLORENCE

I

THE morn when first it thunders in March,
    The eel in the pond gives a leap, they say:
As I leaned and looked over the aloed arch
    Of the villa-gate this warm March day,
No flash snapped, no dumb thunder rolled
    In the valley beneath where, white and wide
And washed by the morning water-gold,
    Florence lay out on the mountain-side.

II

River and bridge and street and square
    Lay mine, as much at my beck and call,   10
Through the live translucent bath of air,
    As the sights in a magic crystal ball.
And of all I saw and of all I praised,
    The most to praise and the best to see
Was the startling bell-tower Giotto raised:
    But why did it more than startle me?

III

Giotto, how, with that soul of yours,
    Could you play me false who loved you so?
Some slights if a certain heart endures
    Yet it feels, I would have your fellows know!   20
I' faith, I perceive not why I should care
    To break a silence that suits them best,

But the thing grows somewhat hard to bear
   When I find a Giotto join the rest.

IV

On the arch where olives overhead
   Print the blue sky with twig and leaf,
(That sharp-curled leaf which they never shed)
   'Twixt the aloes, I used to lean in chief,
And mark through the winter afternoons,
   By a gift God grants me now and then,   34
In the mild decline of those suns like moons,
   Who walked in Florence, besides her men.

V

They might chirp and chaffer, come and go
   For pleasure or profit, her men alive—
My business was hardly with them, I trow,
   But with empty cells of the human hive;
—With the chapter-room, the cloister-porch,
   The church's apsis, aisle or nave,
Its crypt, one fingers along with a torch,
   Its face set full for the sun to shave.   46

VI

Wherever a fresco peels and drops,
   Wherever an outline weakens and wanes
Till the latest life in the painting stops,
   Stands One whom each fainter pulse-tick pains:
One, wishful each scrap should clutch the brick,
   Each tinge not wholly escape the plaster,
—A lion who dies of an ass's kick,
   The wronged great soul of an ancient Master.

VII

For oh, this world and the wrong it does!
   They are safe in heaven with their backs to it,   50
The Michaels and Rafaels, you hum and buzz
   Round the works of, you of the little wit!

Do their eyes contract to the earth's old scope,
　　Now that they see God face to face,
And have all attained to be poets, I hope?
　　'Tis their holiday now, in any case.

VIII

Much they reck of your praise and you!
　　But the wronged great souls—can they be quit
Of a world where their work is all to do,
　　Where you style them, you of the little wit,   60
Old Master This and Early the Other,
　　Not dreaming that Old and New are fellows:
A younger succeeds to an elder brother,
　　Da Vincis derive in good time from Dellos.

IX

And here where your praise might yield returns,
　　And a handsome word or two give help,
Here, after your kind, the mastiff girns
　　And the puppy pack of poodles yelp.
What, not a word for Stefano there,
　　Of brow once prominent and starry,   70
Called Nature's Ape and the world's despair
　　For his peerless painting? (See Vasari.)

X

There stands the Master. Study, my friends,
　　What a man's work comes to! So he plans it,
Performs it, perfects it, makes amends
　　For the toiling and moiling, and then, *sic transit!*
Happier the thrifty blind-folk labor,
　　With upturned eye while the hand is busy,
Not sidling a glance at the coin of their neighbor!
　　'Tis looking downward that makes one dizzy.   80

XI

"If you knew their work you would deal your dole."
　　May I take upon me to instruct you?
When Greek Art ran and reached the goal,

Thus much had the world to boast *in fructu*—
The Truth of Man, as by God first spoken,
　　Which the actual generations garble,
Was re-uttered, and Soul (which Limbs betoken)
　　And Limbs (Soul informs) made new in marble.

XII

So, you saw yourself as you wished you were,
　　As you might have been, as you cannot be;　　**90**
Earth here, rebuked by Olympus there:
　　And grew content in your poor degree
With your little power, by those statues' godhead,
　　And your little scope, by their eyes' full sway,
And your little grace, by their grace embodied,
　　And your little date, by their forms that stay.

XIII

You would fain be kinglier, say, than I am?
　　Even so, you will not sit like Theseus.
You would prove a model? The Son of Priam
　　Has yet the advantage in arms' and knees' use.　　100
You're wroth—can you slay your snake like Apollo?
　　You're grieved—still Niobe's the grander!
You live—there's the Racers' frieze to follow:
　　You die—there's the dying Alexander.

XIV

So, testing your weakness by their strength,
　　Your meagre charms by their rounded beauty,
Measured by Art in your breadth and length,
　　You learned—to submit is a mortal's duty.
—When I say "you" 'tis the common soul,
　　The collective, I mean: the race of Man　　110
That receives life in parts to live in a whole,
　　And grow here according to God's clear plan.

XV

Growth came when, looking your last on them all,
　　You turned your eyes inwardly one fine day

And cried with a start—What if we so small
    Be greater and grander the while than they?
Are they perfect of lineament, perfect of stature?
    In both, of such lower types are we
Precisely because of our wider nature;
    For time, theirs—ours, for eternity.   120

XVI

To-day's brief passion limits their range;
    It seethes with the morrow for us and more.
They are perfect—how else? they shall never change:
    We are faulty—why not? we have time in store.
The Artificer's hand is not arrested
    With us; we are rough-hewn, nowise polished:
They stand for our copy, and, once invested
    With all they can teach, we shall see them abolished.

XVII

'Tis a life-long toil till our lump be leaven—
    The better! What's come to perfection perishes.   130
Things learned on earth, we shall practise in heaven:
    Works done least rapidly, Art most cherishes.
Thyself shalt afford the example, Giotto!
    Thy one work, not to decrease or diminish,
Done at a stroke, was just (was it not?) "O!"
    Thy great Campanile is still to finish.

XVIII

Is it true that we are now, and shall be hereafter,
    But what and where depend on life's minute?
Hails heavenly cheer or infernal laughter
    Our first step out of the gulf or in it?   140
Shall Man, such step within his endeavor,
    Man's face, have no more play and action
Than joy which is crystallized forever,
    Or grief, an eternal petrifaction?

XIX

On which I conclude, that the early painters,
    To cries of "Greek Art and what more wish you?"—

Replied, "To become now self-acquainters,
    And paint man man, whatever the issue!
Make new hopes shine through the flesh they fray,
    New fears aggrandize the rags and tatters: 150
To bring the invisible full into play!
    Let the visible go to the dogs—what matters?"

XX

Give these, I exhort you, their guerdon and glory
    For daring so much, before they well did it.
The first of the new, in our race's story,
    Beats the last of the old; 'tis no idle quiddit.
The worthies began a revolution,
    Which if on earth you intend to acknowledge,
Why, honor them now! (ends my allocution)
    Nor confer your degree when the folk leave college.   160

XXI

There's a fancy some lean to and others hate—
    That, when this life is ended, begins
New work for the soul in another state,
    Where it strives and gets weary, loses and wins:
Where the strong and the weak, this world's congeries,
    Repeat in large what they practised in small,
Through life after life in unlimited series;
    Only the scale's to be changed, that's all.

XXII

Yet I hardly know. When a soul has seen
    By the means of Evil that Good is best,   170
And, through earth and its noise, what is heaven's serene,—
    When our faith in the same has stood the test—
Why, the child grown man, you burn the rod,
    The uses of labor are surely done;
There remaineth a rest for the people of God:
    And I have had troubles enough, for one.

XXIII

But at any rate I have loved the season
   Of Art's spring-birth so dim and dewy;
My sculptor is Nicolo the Pisan,
   My painter—who but Cimabue?   180
Nor ever was man of them all indeed,
   From these to Ghiberti and Ghirlandajo,
Could say that he missed my critic-meed.
   So, now to my special grievance—heigh ho!

XXIV

Their ghosts still stand, as I said before,
   Watching each fresco flaked and rasped,
Blocked up, knocked out, or whitewashed o'er:
   —No getting again what the church has grasped!
The works on the wall must take their chance;
   "Works never conceded to England's thick clime!"   190
(I hope they prefer their inheritance
   Of a bucketful of Italian quick-lime.)

XXV

When they go at length, with such a shaking
   Of heads o'er the old delusion, sadly
Each master his way through the black streets taking,
   Where many a lost work breathes though badly—
Why don't they bethink them of who has merited?
   Why not reveal, while their pictures dree
Such doom, how a captive might be out-ferreted?
   Why is it they never remember me?   200

XXVI

Not that I expect the great Bigordi,
   Nor Sandro to hear me, chivalric, bellicose;
Nor the wronged Lippino; and not a word I
   Say of a scrap of Frà Angelico's:
But are you too fine, Taddeo Gaddi,
   To grant me a taste of your intonaco,

Some Jerome that seeks the heaven with a sad eye?
    Not a churlish saint, Lorenzo Monaco?

XXVII

Could not the ghost with the close red cap,
    My Pollajolo, the twice a craftsman,   210
Save me a sample, give me the hap
    Of a muscular Christ that shows the draughtsman?
No Virgin by him the somewhat petty,
    Of finical touch and tempera crumbly—
Could not Alesso Baldovinetti
    Contribute so much, I ask him humbly?

XXVIII

Margheritone of Arezzo,
    With the grave-clothes garb and swaddling barret
(Why purse up mouth and beak in a pet so,
    You bald old saturnine poll-clawed parrot?)   220
Not a poor glimmering Crucifixion,
    Where in the foreground kneels the donor?
If such remain, as is my conviction,
    The hoarding it does you but little honor.

XXIX

They pass; for them the panels may thrill,
    The tempera grow alive and tinglish;
Their pictures are left to the mercies still
    Of dealers and stealers, Jews and the English,
Who, seeing mere money's worth in their prize,
    Will sell it to somebody calm as Zeno   230
At naked High Art, and in ecstasies
    Before some clay-cold vile Carlino!

XXX

No matter for these! But Giotto, you,
    Have you allowed, as the town-tongues babble it,—
Oh, never! it shall not be counted true—
    That a certain precious little tablet
Which Buonarotti eyed like a lover,—

Was buried so long in oblivion's womb
And, left for another than I to discover,
   Turns up at last! and to whom?—to whom?   240

XXXI

I, that have haunted the dim San Spirito,
   (Or was it rather the Ognissanti?)
Patient on altar-step planting a weary toe!
   Nay, I shall have it yet! *Detur amanti!*
My Koh-i-noor—or (if that's a platitude)
   Jewel of Giamschid, the Persian Sofi's eye;
So, in anticipative gratitude,
   What if I take up my hope and prophesy?

XXXII

When the hour grows ripe, and a certain dotard
   Is pitched, no parcel that needs invoicing,   250
To the worse side of the Mont Saint Gothard,
   We shall begin by way of rejoicing;
None of that shooting the sky (blank cartridge),
   Nor a civic guard, all plumes and lacquer,
Hunting Radetzky's soul like a partridge
   Over Morello with squib and cracker.

XXXIII

This time we'll shoot better game and bag 'em hot—
   No mere display at the stone of Dante,
But a kind of sober Witanagemot
   (Ex: "Casa Guidi," *quod videas ante*)   260
Shall ponder, once Freedom restored to Florence,
   How Art may return that departed with her.
Go, hated house, go each trace of the Loraine's,
   And bring us the days of Orgagna hither!

XXXIV

How we shall prologize, how we shall perorate,
   Utter fit things upon art and history,
Feel truth at blood-heat and falsehood at zero rate,

Make of the want of the age no mystery;
Contrast the fructuous and sterile eras,
   Show—monarchy ever its uncouth cub licks   270
Out of the bear's shape into Chimæra's,
   While Pure Art's birth is still the republic's.

XXXV

Then one shall propose in a speech (curt Tuscan,
   Expurgate and sober, with scarcely an *"issimo,"*)
To end now our half-told tale of Cambuscan,
   And turn the bell-tower's *alt* to *altissimo:*
And fine as the beak of a young beccaccia
   The Campanile, the Duomo's fit ally,
Shall soar up in gold full fifty braccia,
   Completing Florence, as Florence Italy.   280

XXXVI

Shall I be alive that morning the scaffold
   Is broken away, and the long-pent fire,
Like the golden hope of the world, unbaffled
   Springs from its sleep, and up goes the spire
While, "God and the People" plain for its motto,
   Thence the new tricolor flaps at the sky?
At least to foresee that glory of Giotto
   And Florence together, the first am I!

IN A BALCONY

PERSONS

Norbert
Constance
The Queen

CONSTANCE *and* NORBERT

Norbert. Now!
Constance.   Not now!
Norbert.   Give me them again, those hands:
Put them upon my forehead, how it throbs!
Press them before my eyes, the fire comes through!

You cruellest, you dearest in the world,
Let me! The Queen must grant whate'er I ask—
How can I gain you and not ask the Queen?
There she stays waiting for me, here stand you;
Some time or other this was to be asked;
Now is the one time—what I ask, I gain:
Let me ask now, Love!

    Constance.   Do, and ruin us.   10

    Norbert. Let it be now, Love! All my soul breaks forth.
How I do love you! Give my love its way!
A man can have but one life and one death,
One heaven, one hell. Let me fulfil my fate—
Grant me my heaven now! Let me know you mine,
Prove you mine, write my name upon your brow,
Hold you and have you, and then die away,
If God please, with completion in my soul!

    Constance. I am not yours then? How content this man!
I am not his—who change into himself,   20
Have passed into his heart and beat its beats,
Who give my hands to him, my eyes, my hair,
Give all that was of me away to him—
So well, that now, my spirit turned his own,
Takes part with him against the woman here,
Bids him not stumble at so mere a straw
As caring that the world be cognizant
How he loves her and how she worships him.
You have this woman, not as yet that world.
Go on, I bid, nor stop to care for me   30
By saving what I cease to care about,
The courtly name and pride of circumstance—
The name you'll pick up and be cumbered with
Just for the poor parade's sake, nothing more;
Just that the world may slip from under you—
Just that the world may cry "So much for him—
The man predestined to the heap of crowns:
There goes his chance of winning one, at least!"

    Norbert. The world!

    Constance.   You love it. Love me quite as well,
And see if I shall pray for this in vain!   40
Why must you ponder what it knows or thinks?

    Norbert. You pray for—what, in vain?

    Constance.   Oh my heart's heart,
How I do love you, Norbert! That is right:

But listen, or I take my hands away!
You say, "let it be now": you would go now
And tell the Queen, perhaps six steps from us,
You love me—so you do, thank God!
   Norbert.   Thank God!
   Constance. Yes, Norbert,—but you fain would tell your love,
And, what succeeds the telling, ask of her
My hand. Now take this rose and look at it,   **5(**
Listening to me. You are the minister,
The Queen's first favorite, nor without a cause.
To-night completes your wonderful year's-work
(This palace-feast is held to celebrate)
Made memorable by her life's success,
The junction of two crowns, on her sole head,
Her house had only dreamed of anciently:
That this mere dream is grown a stable truth,
To-night's feast makes authentic. Whose the praise?
Whose genius, patience, energy, achieved   **60**
What turned the many heads and broke the hearts?
You are the fate, your minute's in the heaven.
Next comes the Queen's turn. "Name your own reward!"
With leave to clench the past, chain the to-come,
Put out an arm and touch and take the sun
And fix it ever full-faced on your earth,
Possess yourself supremely of her life,—
You choose the single thing she will not grant;
Nay, very declaration of which choice
Will turn the scale and neutralize your work: **70**
At best she will forgive you, if she can.
You think I'll let you choose—her cousin's hand?
   Norbert. Wait. First, do you retain your old belief
The Queen is generous,—nay, is just?
   Constance.   There, there!
So men make women love them, while they know
No more of women's hearts than . . . look you here,
You that are just and generous beside,
Make it your own case! For example now,
I'll say—I let you kiss me, hold my hands—
Why? do you know why? I'll instruct you, then—   **80**
The kiss, because you have a name at court;
This hand and this, that you may shut in each
A jewel, if you please to pick up such.
That's horrible? Apply it to the Queen—

Suppose I am the Queen to whom you speak:
"I was a nameless man; you needed me:
Why did I proffer you my aid? there stood
A certain pretty cousin at your side.
Why did I make such common cause with you?
Access to her had not been easy else.   90
You give my labor here abundant praise?
'Faith, labor, which she overlooked, grew play.
How shall your gratitude discharge itself?
Give me her hand!"
    Norbert.   And still I urge the same.
Is the Queen just? just—generous or no!
    Constance. Yes, just. You love a rose; no harm in that:
But was it for the rose's sake or mine
You put it in your bosom? mine, you said—
Then, mine you still must say or else be false.
You told the Queen you served her for herself;   100
If so, to serve her was to serve yourself,
She thinks, for all your unbelieving face!
I know her. In the hall, six steps from us,
One sees the twenty pictures; there's a life
Better than life, and yet no life at all.
Conceive her born in such a magic dome,
Pictures all round her! why, she sees the world,
Can recognize its given things and facts,
The fight of giants or the feast of gods,
Sages in senate, beauties at the bath,   110
Chases and battles, the whole earth's display,
Landscape and sea-piece, down to flowers and fruit—
And who shall question that she knows them all,
In better semblance than the things outside?
Yet bring into the silent gallery
Some live thing to contrast in breath and blood,
Some lion, with the painted lion there—
You think she'll understand composedly?
—Say, "that's his fellow in the hunting-piece
Yonder, I've turned to praise a hundred times"?   120
Not so. Her knowledge of our actual earth,
Its hopes and fears, concerns and sympathies,
Must be too far, too mediate, too unreal.
The real exists for us outside, not her:
How should it, with that life in these four walls—
That father and that mother, first to last

No father and no mother—friends, a heap,
Lovers, no lack—a husband in due time,
And every one of them alike a lie!
Things painted by a Rubens out of naught   130
Into what kindness, friendship, love should be;
All better, all more grandiose than the life,
Only no life; mere cloth and surface-paint,
You feel, while you admire. How should she feel?
Yet now that she has stood thus fifty years
The sole spectator in that gallery,
You think to bring this warm real struggling love
In to her of a sudden, and suppose
She'll keep her state untroubled? Here's the truth—
She'll apprehend truth's value at a glance,   140
Prefer it to the pictured loyalty?
You only have to say, "so men are made,
For this they act; the thing has many names,
But this the right one: and now, Queen, be just!"
Your life slips back; you lose her at the word:
You do not even for amends gain me.
He will not understand; oh, Norbert, Norbert,
Do you not understand?
    Norbert.   The Queen's the Queen:
I am myself—no picture, but alive
In every nerve and every muscle, here   150
At the palace-window o'er the people's street,
As she in the gallery where the pictures glow:
The good of life is precious to us both.
She cannot love; what do I want with rule?
When first I saw your face a year ago
I knew my life's good, my soul heard one voice—
"The woman yonder, there's no use of life
But just to obtain her! heap earth's woes in one
And bear them—make a pile of all earth's joys
And spurn them, as they help or help not this;   160
Only, obtain her!" How was it to be?
I found you were the cousin of the Queen;
I must then serve the Queen to get to you.
No other way. Suppose there had been one,
And I, by saying prayers to some white star
With promise of my body and my soul,
Might gain you,—should I pray the star or no?
Instead, there was the Queen to serve! I served,

Helped, did what other servants failed to do.
Neither she sought nor I declared my end.   170
Her good is hers, my recompense be mine,—
I therefore name you as that recompense.
She dreamed that such a thing could never be?
Let her wake now. She thinks there was more cause
In love of power, high fame, pure loyalty?
Perhaps she fancies men wear out their lives
Chasing such shades. Then, I've a fancy too;
I worked because I want you with my soul:
I therefore ask your hand. Let it be now!
    Constance. Had I not loved you from the very first,   180
Were I not yours, could we not steal out thus
So wickedly, so wildly, and so well,
You might become impatient. What's conceived
Of us without here, by the folk within?
Where are you now? immersed in cares of state—
Where am I now? intent on festal robes—
We two, embracing under death's spread hand!
What was this thought for, what that scruple of yours
Which broke the council up?—to bring about
One minute's meeting in the corridor!   190
And then the sudden sleights, strange secrecies,
Complots inscrutable, deep telegraphs,
Long-planned chance-meetings, hazards of a look,
"Does she know? does she not know? saved or lost?"
A year of this compression's ecstasy
All goes for nothing! you would give this up
For the old way, the open way, the world's,
His way who beats, and his who sells his wife!
What tempts you?—their notorious happiness
Makes you ashamed of ours? The best you'll gain   200
Will be—the Queen grants all that you require,
Concedes the cousin, rids herself of you
And me at once, and gives us ample leave
To live like our five hundred happy friends.
The world will show us with officious hand
Our chamber-entry, and stand sentinel
Where we so oft have stolen across its traps!
Get the world's warrant, ring the falcons' feet,
And make it duty to be bold and swift,
Which long ago was nature. Have it so!   210
We never hawked by rights till flung from fist?

Oh, the man's thought! no woman's such a fool.

   Norbert. Yes, the man's thought and my thought, which is
     more—
One made to love you, let the world take note!
Have I done worthy work? be love's the praise,
Though hampered by restrictions, barred against
By set forms, blinded by forced secrecies!
Set free my love, and see what love can do
Shown in my life—what work will spring from that!
The world is used to have its business done   220
On other grounds, find great effects produced
For power's sake, fame's sake, motives in men's mouth.
So, good: but let my low ground shame their high!
Truth is the strong thing. Let man's life be true!
And love's the truth of mine. Time prove the rest!
I choose to wear you stamped all over me,
Your name upon my forehead and my breast,
You, from the sword's blade to the ribbon's edge,
That men may see, all over, you in me—
That pale loves may die out of their pretence   230
In face of mine, shames thrown on love fall off.
Permit this, Constance! Love has been so long
Subdued in me, eating me through and through,
That now 'tis all of me and must have way.
Think of my work, that chaos of intrigues,
Those hopes and fears, surprises and delays,
That long endeavor, earnest, patient, slow,
Trembling at last to its assured result:
Then think of this revulsion! I resume
Life after death, (it is no less than life,   240
After such long unlovely laboring days)
And liberate to beauty life's great need
O' the beautiful, which, while it prompted work,
Suppressed itself erewhile. This eve's the time,
This eve intense with yon first trembling star
We seem to pant and reach; scarce aught between
The earth that rises and the heaven that bends;
All nature self-abandoned, every tree
Flung as it will, pursuing its own thoughts
And fixed so, every flower and every weed,   250
No pride, no shame, no victory, no defeat;
All under God, each measured by itself.
These statues round us stand abrupt, distinct,

The strong in strength, the weak in weakness fixed,
The Muse forever wedded to her lyre,
Nymph to her fawn, and Silence to her rose:
See God's approval on his universe!
Let us do so—aspire to live as these
In harmony with truth, ourselves being true!
Take the first way, and let the second come!   260
My first is to possess myself of you;
The music sets the march-step—forward, then!
And there's the Queen, I go to claim you of,
The world to witness, wonder and applaud.
Our flower of life breaks open. No delay!
    Constance. And so shall we be ruined, both of us.
Norbert, I know her to the skin and bone:
You do not know her, were not born to it,
To feel what she can see or cannot see.
Love, she is generous,—ay, despite your smile,   270
Generous as you are: for, in that thin frame
Pain-twisted, punctured through and through with cares,
There lived a lavish soul until it starved,
Debarred of healthy food. Look to the soul—
Pity that, stoop to that, ere you begin
(The true man's-way) on justice and your rights,
Exactions and acquittance of the past!
Begin so—see what justice she will deal!
We women hate a debt as men a gift.
Suppose her some poor keeper of a school   280
Whose business is to sit thro' summer months
And dole out children leave to go and play,
Herself superior to such lightness—she
In the arm-chair's state and pædagogic pomp—
To the life, the laughter, sun and youth outside:
We wonder such a face looks black on us?
I do not bid you wake her tenderness,
(That were vain truly—none is left to wake)
But let her think her justice is engaged
To take the shape of tenderness, and mark   290
If she'll not coldly pay its warmest debt!
Does she love me, I ask you? not a whit:
Yet, thinking that her justice was engaged
To help a kinswoman, she took me up—
Did more on that bare ground than other loves
Would do on greater argument. For me,

I have no equivalent of such cold kind
To pay her with, but love alone to give
If I give anything. I give her love:
I feel I ought to help her, and I will. 300
So, for her sake, as yours, I tell you twice
That women hate a debt as men a gift.
If I were you, I could obtain this grace—
Could lay the whole I did to love's account,
Nor yet be very false as courtiers go—
Declaring my success was recompense;
It would be so, in fact: what were it else?
And then, once loose her generosity,—
Oh, how I see it!—then, were I but you,
To turn it, let it seem to move itself, 310
And make it offer what I really take,
Accepting just, in the poor cousin's hand,
Her value as the next thing to the Queen's—
Since none love Queens directly, none dare that,
And a thing's shadow or a name's mere echo
Suffices those who miss the name and thing!
You pick up just a ribbon she has worn,
To keep in proof how near her breath you came.
Say, I'm so near I seem a piece of her—
Ask for me that way—(oh, you understand) 320
You'd find the same gift yielded with a grace,
Which, if you make the least show to extort . . .
—You'll see! and when you have ruined both of us,
Dissertate on the Queen's ingratitude!
    Norbert. Then, if I turn it that way, you consent?
'Tis not my way; I have more hope in truth:
Still, if you won't have truth—why, this indeed,
Were scarcely false, as I'd express the sense.
Will you remain here?
    Constance.   O best heart of mine,
How I have loved you! then, you take my way? 330
Are mine as you have been her minister,
Work out my thought, give it effect for me,
Paint plain my poor conceit and make it serve?
I owe that withered woman everything—
Life, fortune, you, remember! Take my part—
Help me to pay her! Stand upon your rights?
You, with my rose, my hands, my heart on you?
Your rights are mine—you have no rights but mine.

Norbert. Remain here. How you know me!
Constance.   Ah, but still——
          [*He breaks from her: she remains. Dance-music from within.*

Enter the QUEEN

Queen. Constance? She is here as he said. Speak quick!   340
Is it so? Is it true or false? One word!
    Constance. True.
    Queen.   Mercifullest Mother, thanks to thee!
    Constance. Madam?
    Queen.   I love you, Constance, from my soul.
Now say once more, with any words you will,
'Tis true, all true, as true as that I speak.
    Constance. Why should you doubt it?
    Queen.   Ah, why doubt? why doubt?
Dear, make me see it! Do you see it so?
None see themselves; another sees them best.
You say "why doubt it?"—you see him and me.
It is because the Mother has such grace   350
That if we had but faith—wherein we fail—
Whate'er we yearn for would be granted us;
Yet still we let our whims prescribe despair,
Our fancies thwart and cramp our will and power,
And, while accepting life, abjure its use.
Constance, I had abjured the hope of love
And being loved, as truly as yon palm
The hope of seeing Egypt from that plot.
    Constance. Heaven!
    Queen.   But it was so, Constance, it was so!
Men say—or do men say it? fancies say—   360
"Stop here, your life is set, you are grown old.
Too late—no love for you, too late for love—
Leave love to girls. Be queen: let Constance love."
One takes the hint—half meets it like a child,
Ashamed at any feelings that oppose.
"Oh love, true, never think of love again!
I am a queen: I rule, not love forsooth."
So it goes on; so a face grows like this,
Hair like this hair, poor arms as lean as these,
Till,—nay, it does not end so, I thank God!   370
    Constance. I cannot understand——
    Queen.   The happier you!

Constance, I know not how it is with men:
For women (I am a woman now like you)
There is no good of life but love—but love!
What else looks good, is some shade flung from love;
Love gilds it, gives it worth. Be warned by me,
Never you cheat yourself one instant! Love,
Give love, ask only love, and leave the rest!
O Constance, how I love you!
  Constance.   I love you.
  Queen. I do believe that all is come through you. 380
I took you to my heart to keep it warm
When the last chance of love seemed dead in me;
I thought your fresh youth warmed my withered heart.
Oh, I am very old now, am I not?
Not so! it is true and it shall be true!
  Constance. Tell it me: let me judge if true or false.
  Queen. Ah, but I fear you! you will look at me
And say, "she's old, she's grown unlovely quite
Who ne'er was beauteous: men want beauty still."
Well, so I feared—the curse! so I felt sure! 390
  Constance. Be calm. And now you feel not sure, you say?
  Queen. Constance, he came,—the coming was not strange—
Do not I stand and see men come and go?
I turned a half-look from my pedestal
Where I grow marble—"one young man the more!
He will love some one; that is naught to me:
What would he with my marble stateliness?"
Yet this seemed somewhat worse than heretofore;
The man more gracious, youthful, like a god,
And I still older, with less flesh to change— 400
We two those dear extremes that long to touch.
It seemed still harder when he first began
To labor at those state-affairs, absorbed
The old way for the old end—interest.
Oh, to live with a thousand beating hearts
Around you, swift eyes, serviceable hands,
Professing they've no care but for your cause,
Thought but to help you, love but for yourself,—
And you the marble statue all the time
They praise and point at as preferred to life, 410
Yet leave for the first breathing woman's smile,
First dancer's, gipsy's or street baladine's!
Why, how I have ground my teeth to hear men's speech

Stifled for fear it should alarm my ear,
Their gait subdued lest step should startle me,
Their eyes declined, such queendom to respect,
Their hands alert, such treasure to preserve,
While not a man of them broke rank and spoke,
Wrote me a vulgar letter all of love,
Or caught my hand and pressed it like a hand!   420
There have been moments, if the sentinel
Lowering his halbert to salute the queen,
Had flung it brutally and clasped my knees,
I would have stooped and kissed him with my soul.
    Constance. Who could have comprehended?
    Queen.   Ay, who—who?
Why, no one, Constance, but this one who did.
Not they, not you, not I. Even now perhaps
It comes too late—would you but tell the truth.
    Constance. I wait to tell it.
    Queen.   Well, you see, he came,
Outfaced the others, did a work this year   430
Exceeds in value all was ever done,
You know—it is not I who say it—all
Say it. And so (a second pang and worse)
I grew aware not only of what he did,
But why so wondrously. Oh, never work
Like his was done for work's ignoble sake—
Souls need a finer aim to light and lure!
I felt, I saw, he loved—loved somebody.
And Constance, my dear Constance, do you know,
I did believe this while 'twas you he loved.   440
    Constance. Me, madam?
    Queen.   It did seem to me, your face
Met him where'er he looked: and whom but you
Was such a man to love? It seemed to me,
You saw he loved you, and approved his love,
And both of you were in intelligence.
You could not loiter in that garden, step
Into this balcony, but I straight was stung
And forced to understand. It seemed so true,
So right, so beautiful, so like you both,
That all this work should have been done by him   450
Not for the vulgar hope of recompense,
But that at last—suppose, some night like this—
Borne on to claim his due reward of me,

He might say "Give her hand and pay me so."
And I (O Constance, you shall love me now!)
I thought, surmounting all the bitterness,
—"And he shall have it. I will make her blest,
My flower of youth, my woman's self that was,
My happiest woman's self that might have been!
These two shall have their joy and leave me here." 460
Yes—yes!

   Constance. Thanks!

   Queen.   And the word was on my lips
When he burst in upon me. I looked to hear
A mere calm statement of his just desire
For payment of his labor. When—O heaven,
How can I tell you? lightning on my eyes
And thunder in my ears proved that first word
Which told 'twas love of me, of me, did all—
He loved me—from the first step to the last,
Loved me!

   Constance. You hardly saw, scarce heard him speak
Of love: what if you should mistake?

   Queen.   No, no— 470
No mistake! Ha, there shall be no mistake!
He had not dared to hint the love he felt—
You were my reflex—(how I understood!)
He said you were the ribbon I had worn,
He kissed my hand, he looked into my eyes,
And love, love came at end of every phrase.
Love is begun; this much is come to pass:
The rest is easy. Constance, I am yours!
I will learn, I will place my life on you,
Teach me but how to keep what I have won! 480
Am I so old? This hair was early gray;
But joy ere now has brought hair brown again,
And joy will bring the cheek's red back, I feel.
I could sing once too; that was in my youth.
Still, when men paint me, they declare me . . . yes,
Beautiful—for the last French painter did!
I know they flatter somewhat; you are frank—
I trust you. How I loved you from the first!
Some queens would hardly seek a cousin out
And set her by their side to take the eye: 490
I must have felt that good would come from you.
I am not generous—like him—like you!

But he is not your lover after all:
It was not you he looked at. Saw you him?
You have not been mistaking words or looks?
He said you were the reflex of myself.
And yet he is not such a paragon
To you, to younger women who may choose
Among a thousand Norberts. Speak the truth!
You know you never named his name to me: 500
You know, I cannot give him up—ah God,
Not up now, even to you!
    Constance.   Then calm yourself.
    Queen. See, I am old—look here, you happy girl!
I will not play the fool, deceive—ah, whom?
'Tis all gone: put your cheek beside my cheek
And what a contrast does the moon behold!
But then I set my life upon one chance,
The last chance and the best—am *I* not left,
My soul, myself? All women love great men
If young or old; it is in all the tales: 510
Young beauties love old poets who can love—
Why should not he, the poems in my soul,
The passionate faith, the pride of sacrifice,
Life-long, death-long? I throw them at his feet.
Who cares to see the fountain's very shape,
Whether it be a Triton's or a Nymph's
That pours the foam, makes rainbows all around?
You could not praise indeed the empty conch;
But I'll pour floods of love and hide myself.
How I will love him! Cannot men love love?   520
Who was a queen and loved a poet once
Humpbacked, a dwarf? ah, women can do that!
Well, but men too; at least, they tell you so.
They love so many women in their youth,
And even in age they all love whom they please;
And yet the best of them confide to friends
That 'tis not beauty makes the lasting love—
They spend a day with such and tire the next:
They like soul,—well then, they like phantasy,
Novelty even. Let us confess the truth,   530
Horrible though it be, that prejudice,
Prescription . . . curses! they will love a queen.
They will, they do: and will not, does not—he?
    Constance. How can he? You are wedded: 'tis a name

We know, but still a bond. Your rank remains,
His rank remains. How can he, nobly souled
As you believe and I incline to think,
Aspire to be your favorite, shame and all?

    Queen. Hear her! There, there now—could she love like me? 540
What did I say of smooth-cheeked youth and grace?
See all it does or could do! so youth loves!
Oh, tell him, Constance, you could never do
What I will—you, it was not born in! I
Will drive these difficulties far and fast
As yonder mists curdling before the moon.
I'll use my light too, gloriously retrieve
My youth from its enforced calamity,
Dissolve that hateful marriage, and be his,
His own in the eyes alike of God and man.

    Constance. You will do—dare do . . . pause on what
      you say! 550

    Queen. Hear her! I thank you, sweet, for that surprise.
You have the fair face: for the soul, see mine!
I have the strong soul: let me teach you, here.
I think I have borne enough and long enough,
And patiently enough, the world remarks,
To have my own way now, unblamed by all.
It does so happen (I rejoice for it)
This most unhoped-for issue cuts the knot.
There's not a better way of settling claims
Than this; God sends the accident express: 560
And were it for my subjects' good, no more,
'Twere best thus ordered. I am thankful now,
Mute, passive, acquiescent. I receive,
And bless God simply, or should almost fear
To walk so smoothly to my ends at last.
Why, how I baffle obstacles, spurn fate!
How strong I am! Could Norbert see me now!

    Constance. Let me consider. It is all too strange.

    Queen. You, Constance, learn of me; do you, like me!
You are young, beautiful: my own, best girl, 570
You will have many lovers, and love one—
Light hair, not hair like Norbert's, to suit yours:
Taller than he is, since yourself are tall.
Love him, like me! Give all away to him;
Think never of yourself; throw by your pride,
Hope, fear,—your own good as you saw it once,

And love him simply for his very self.
Remember, I (and what am I to you?)
Would give up all for one, leave throne, lose life,
Do all but just unlove him! He loves me.   580
   Constance. He shall.
   Queen.   You, step inside my inmost heart!
Give me your own heart: let us have one heart!
I'll come to you for counsel; "this he says,
This he does; what should this amount to, pray?
Beseech you, change it into current coin!
Is that worth kisses? Shall I please him there?"
And then we'll speak in turn of you—what else?
Your love, according to your beauty's worth,
For you shall have some noble love, all gold:
Whom choose you? we will get him at your choice.   590
—Constance, I leave you. Just a minute since,
I felt as I must die or be alone
Breathing my soul into an ear like yours:
Now, I would face the world with my new life,
Wear my new crown. I'll walk around the rooms,
And then come back and tell you how it feels.
How soon a smile of God can change the world!
How we are made for happiness—how work
Grows play, adversity a winning fight!
True, I have lost so many years: what then?   600
Many remain: God has been very good.
You, stay here! 'Tis as different from dreams,
From the mind's cold calm estimate of bliss,
As these stone statues from the flesh and blood.
The comfort thou hast caused mankind, God's moon!
   [*She goes out, leaving* CONSTANCE. *Dance-music from within.*

NORBERT *enters*

   Norbert. Well? we have but one minute and one word!
   Constance. I am yours, Norbert!
   Norbert.   Yes, mine.
   Constance.   Not till now!
You were mine. Now I give myself to you.
   Norbert. Constance?
   Constance.   Your own! I know the thriftier way
Of giving—haply, 'tis the wiser way.   610
Meaning to give a treasure, I might dole

Coin after coin out (each, as that were all,
With a new largess still at each despair)
And force you keep in sight the deed, preserve
Exhaustless till the end my part and yours,
My giving and your taking; both our joys
Dying together. Is it the wiser way?
I choose the simpler; I give all at once.
Know what you have to trust to, trade upon!
Use it, abuse it,—anything but think   620
Hereafter, "Had I known she loved me so,
And what my means, I might have thriven with it."
This is your means. I give you all myself.

    Norbert. I take you and thank God.

    Constance.   Look on through years!
We cannot kiss, a second day like this;
Else were this earth no earth.

    Norbert.   With this day's heat
We shall go on through years of cold.

    Constance.   So, best!
—I try to see those years—I think I see.
You walk quick and new warmth comes; you look back
And lay all to the first glow—not sit down   630
Forever brooding on a day like this
While seeing embers whiten and love die.
Yes, love lives best in its effect; and mine,
Full in its own life, yearns to live in yours.

    Norbert. Just so. I take and know you all at once.
Your soul is disengaged so easily,
Your face is there, I know you; give me time,
Let me be proud and think you shall know me.
My soul is slower: in a life I roll
The minute out whereto you condense yours—   640
The whole slow circle round you I must move,
To be just you. I look to a long life
To decompose this minute, prove its worth.
'Tis the sparks' long succession one by one
Shall show you, in the end, what fire was crammed
In that mere stone you struck: how could you know,
If it lay ever unproved in your sight,
As now my heart lies? your own warmth would hide
Its coldness, were it cold.

    Constance.   But how prove, how?

    Norbert. Prove in my life, you ask?   650

Constance.   Quick, Norbert—how?

Norbert. That's easy told. I count life just a stuff
To try the soul's strength on, educe the man.
Who keeps one end in view makes all things serve.
As with the body—he who hurls a lance
Or heaps up stone on stone, shows strength alike:
So must I seize and task all means to prove
And show this soul of mine, you crown as yours,
And justify us both.

Constance.   Could you write books,
Paint pictures! One sits down in poverty
And writes or paints, with pity for the rich.   660

Norbert. And loves one's painting and one's writing, then,
And not one's mistress! All is best, believe,
And we best as no other than we are.
We live, and they experiment on life—
Those poets, painters, all who stand aloof
To overlook the farther. Let us be
The thing they look at! I might take your face
And write of it and paint it—to what end?
For whom? what pale dictatress in the air
Feeds, smiling sadly, her fine ghost-like form   670
With earth's real blood and breath, the beauteous life
She makes despised forever? You are mine,
Made for me, not for others in the world,
Nor yet for that which I should call my art,
The cold calm power to see how fair you look.
I come to you; I leave you not, to write
Or paint. You are, I am: let Rubens there
Paint us!

Constance. So, best!

Norbert.   I understand your soul.
You live, and rightly sympathize with life,
With action, power, success. This way is straight;   680
And time were short beside, to let me change
The craft my childhood learnt: my craft shall serve.
Men set me here to subjugate, enclose,
Manure their barren lives, and force thence fruit
First for themselves, and afterward for me
In the due tithe; the task of some one soul,
Through ways of work appointed by the world.
I am not bid create—men see no star
Transfiguring my brow to warrant that—

But find and bind and bring to bear their wills.   690
So I began: to-night sees how I end.
What if it see, too, power's first outbreak here
Amid the warmth, surprise and sympathy,
And instincts of the heart that teach the head?
What if the people have discerned at length
The dawn of the next nature, novel brain
Whose will they venture in the place of theirs,
Whose work, they trust, shall find them as novel ways
To untried heights which yet he only sees?
I felt it when you kissed me. See this Queen,   700
This people—in our phrase, this mass of men—
See how the mass lies passive to my hand
Now that my hand is plastic, with you by
To make the muscles iron! Oh, an end
Shall crown this issue as this crowns the first!
My will be on this people! then, the strain,
The grappling of the potter with his clay,
The long uncertain struggle,—the success
And consummation of the spirit-work,
Some vase shaped to the curl of the god's lip,   710
While rounded fair for human sense to see
The Graces in a dance men recognize
With turbulent applause and laughs of heart!
So triumph ever shall renew itself;
Ever shall end in efforts higher yet,
Ever begin . . .
    Constance.   I ever helping?
    Norbert.   Thus!
                [*As he embraces her, the* QUEEN *enters*
    Constance. Hist, madam! So have I performed my part.
You see your gratitude's true decency,
Norbert? A little slow in seeing it!
Begin, to end the sooner! What's a kiss?   72?
    Norbert. Constance?
    Constance.   Why, must I teach it you again:
You want a witness to your dulness, sir?
What was I saying these ten minutes long?
Then I repeat—when some young handsome man
Like you has acted out a part like yours,
Is pleased to fall in love with one beyond,
So very far beyond him, as he says—
So hopelessly in love that but to speak

Would prove him mad,—he thinks judiciously,
And makes some insignificant good soul,   730
Like me, his friend, adviser, confidant,
And very stalking-horse to cover him
In following after what he dares not face.
When his end's gained—(sir, do you understand?)
When she, he dares not face, has loved him first,
—May I not say so, madam?—tops his hope,
And overpasses so his wildest dream,
With glad consent of all, and most of her
The confidant who brought the same about—
Why, in the moment when such joy explodes,   740
I do hold that the merest gentleman
Will not start rudely from the stalking-horse,
Dismiss it with a "There, enough of you!"
Forget it, show his back unmannerly:
But like a liberal heart will rather turn
And say, "A tingling time of hope was ours;
Betwixt the fears and falterings, we two lived
A chanceful time in waiting for the prize:
The confidant, the Constance, served not ill.
And though I shall forget her in due time,   750
Her use being answered now, as reason bids,
Nay as herself bids from her heart of hearts,—
Still, she has rights, the first thanks go to her,
The first good praise goes to the prosperous tool,
And the first—which is the last—rewarding kiss."
    Norbert. Constance, it is a dream—ah, see, you smile!
    Constance. So, now his part being properly performed,
Madam, I turn to you and finish mine
As duly; I do justice in my turn.
Yes, madam, he has loved you—long and well;   760
He could not hope to tell you so—'twas I
Who served to prove your soul accessible,
I led his thoughts on, drew them to their place
When they had wandered else into despair,
And kept love constant toward its natural aim.
Enough, my part is played; you stoop half-way
And meet us royally and spare our fears:
'Tis like yourself. He thanks you, so do I.
Take him—with my full heart! my work is praised
By what comes of it. Be you both happy, both!   770
Yourself—the only one on earth who can—

Do all for him, much more than a mere heart
Which though warm is not useful in its warmth
As the silk vesture of a queen! fold that
Around him gently, tenderly. For him—
For him,—he knows his own part!
 Norbert.   Have you done?
I take the jest at last. Should I speak now?
Was yours the wager, Constance, foolish child;
Or did you but accept it? Well—at least
You lose by it.
 Constance. Nay, madam, 'tis your turn!   780
Restrain him still from speech a little more,
And make him happier as more confident!
Pity him, madam, he is timid yet!
Mark, Norbert! Do not shrink now! Here I yield
My whole right in you to the Queen, observe!
With her go put in practice the great schemes
You teem with, follow the career else closed—
Be all you cannot be except by her!
Behold her!—Madam, say for pity's sake
Anything—frankly say you love him! Else   790
He'll not believe it: there's more earnest in
His fear than you conceive: I know the man!
 Norbert. I know the woman somewhat, and confess
I thought she had jested better: she begins
To overcharge her part. I gravely wait
Your pleasure, madam: where is my reward?
 Queen. Norbert, this wild girl (whom I recognize
Scarce more than you do, in her fancy-fit,
Eccentric speech and variable mirth,
Not very wise perhaps and somewhat bold,   800
Yet suitable, the whole night's work being strange)
—May still be right: I may do well to speak
And make authentic what appears a dream
To even myself. For, what she says, is true:
Yes, Norbert—what you spoke just now of love,
Devotion, stirred no novel sense in me,
But justified a warmth felt long before.
Yes, from the first—I loved you, I shall say:
Strange! but I do grow stronger, now 'tis said.
Your courage helps mine: you did well to speak   810
To-night, the night that crowns your twelvemonths' toil:
But still I had not waited to discern

Your heart so long, believe me! From the first
The source of so much zeal was almost plain,
In absence even of your own words just now
Which hazarded the truth. 'Tis very strange,
But takes a happy ending—in your love
Which mine meets: be it so! as you chose me,
So I choose you.

    Norbert.   And worthily you choose.
I will not be unworthy your esteem, 820
No, madam. I do love you; I will meet
Your nature, now I know it. This was well:
I see,—you dare and you are justified:
But none had ventured such experiment,
Less versed than you in nobleness of heart,
Less confident of finding such in me.
I joy that thus you test me ere you grant
The dearest richest beauteousest and best
Of women to my arms: 'tis like yourself.
So—back again into my part's set words— 830
Devotion to the uttermost is yours,
But no, you cannot, madam, even you,
Create in me the love our Constance does.
Or—something truer to the tragic phrase—
Not yon magnolia-bell superb with scent
Invites a certain insect—that's myself—
But the small eye-flower nearer to the ground.
I take this lady.

    Constance. Stay—not hers, the trap—
Stay, Norbert—that mistake were worst of all!
He is too cunning, madam! It was I, 840
I, Norbert, who . . .

    Norbert. ·   You, was it, Constance? Then,
But for the grace of this divinest hour
Which gives me you, I might not pardon here!
I am the Queen's; she only knows my brain:
She may experiment upon my heart
And I instruct her too by the result.
But you, sweet, you who know me, who so long
Have told my heart-beats over, held my life
In those white hands of yours,—it is not well!

    Constance. Tush! I have said it, did I not say it all? 850
The life, for her—the heart-beats, for her sake!

    Norbert. Enough! my cheek grows red, I think. Your test?

There's not the meanest woman in the world,
Not she I least could love in all the world,
Whom, did she love me, had love proved itself,
I dare insult as you insult me now.
Constance, I could say, if it must be said,
"Take back the soul you offer, I keep mine!"
But— "Take the soul still quivering on your hand,
The soul so offered, which I cannot use,   860
And, please you, give it to some playful friend,
For—what's the trifle he requites me with?"
I, tempt a woman, to amuse a man,
That two may mock her heart if it succumb?
No: fearing God and standing 'neath his heaven,
I would not dare insult a woman so,
Were she the meanest woman in the world,
And he, I cared to please, ten emperors!
   Constance. Norbert!
   Norbert.   I loved once as I live but once.
What case is this to think or talk about?   870
I love you. Would it mend the case at all
If such a step as this killed love in me?
Your part were done: account to God for it!
But mine—could murdered love get up again,
And kneel to whom you please to designate,
And make you mirth? It is too horrible.
You did not know this, Constance? now you know
That body and soul have each one life, but one:
And here's my love, here, living, at your feet.
   Constance. See the Queen! Norbert—this one more last
     word—   880
If thus you have taken jest for earnest—thus
Loved me in earnest . . .
   Norbert.   Ah, no jest holds here!
Where is the laughter in which jests break up,
And what this horror that grows palpable?
Madam—why grasp you thus the balcony?
Have I done ill? Have I not spoken truth?
How could I other? Was it not your test,
To try me, what my love for Constance meant?
Madam, your royal soul itself approves,
The first, that I should choose thus! so one takes   890
A beggar,—asks him, what would buy his child?
And then approves the expected laugh of scorn

Returned as something noble from the rags.
Speak, Constance, I'm the beggar! Ha, what's this?
You two glare each at each like panthers now.
Constance, the world fades; only you stand there!
You did not, in to-night's wild whirl of things,
Sell me—your soul of souls for any price?
No—no—'tis easy to believe in you!
Was it your love's mad trial to o'ertop   900
Mine by this vain self-sacrifice? well, still—
Though I might curse, I love you. I am love
And cannot change: love's self is at your feet!

                                         [*The* QUEEN *goes out.*

   Constance. Feel my heart; let it die against your own!
   Norbert. Against my own. Explain not; let this be!
This is life's height.
   Constance.   Yours, yours, yours!
   Norbert.   You and I—
Why care by what meanders we are here
I' the centre of the labyrinth? Men have died
Trying to find this place, which we have found.
   Constance. Found, found!
   Norbert.   Sweet, never fear what she can do!   91(
We are past harm now.
   Constance.   On the breast of God.
I thought of men—as if you were a man.
Tempting him with a crown!
   Norbert.   This must end here:
It is too perfect.
   Constance.   There's the music stopped.
What measured heavy tread? It is one blaze
About me and within me.
   Norbert.   Oh, some death
Will run its sudden finger round this spark
And sever us from the rest!
   Constance.   And so do well.
Now the doors open.
   Norbert.   'Tis the guard comes.
   Constance.   Kiss!

SAUL

I

Said Abner, "At last thou art come! Ere I tell, ere thou speak,
Kiss my cheek, wish me well!" Then I wished it, and did kiss his
cheek.
And he, "Since the King, O my friend, for thy countenance sent,
Neither drunken nor eaten have we; nor until from his tent
Thou return with the joyful assurance the King liveth yet,
Shall our lip with the honey be bright, with the water be wet.
For out of the black mid-tent's silence, a space of three days,
Not a sound hath escaped to thy servants, of prayer nor of praise,
To betoken that Saul and the Spirit have ended their strife,
And that, faint in his triumph, the monarch sinks back upon
life.   10

II

"Yet now my heart leaps, O beloved! God's child with his dew
On thy gracious gold hair, and those lilies still living and blue
Just broken to twine round thy harp-strings, as if no wild heat
Were now raging to torture the desert!"

III

                                    Then I, as was meet,
Knelt down to the God of my fathers, and rose on my feet,
And ran o'er the sand burnt to powder. The tent was unlooped;
I pulled up the spear that obstructed, and under I stooped;
Hands and knees on the slippery grass-patch, all withered and
gone,
That extends to the second enclosure, I groped my way on
Till I felt where the foldskirts fly open. Then once more I
prayed,   20
And opened the foldskirts and entered, and was not afraid
But spoke, "Here is David, thy servant!" And no voice replied.
At the first I saw naught but the blackness; but soon I descried
A something more black than the blackness—the vast, the up-
right
Main prop which sustains the pavilion: and slow into sight

Grew a figure against it, gigantic and blackest of all.
Then a sunbeam, that burst thro' the tent-roof, showed Saul.

IV

He stood as erect as that tent-prop, both arms stretched out wide
On the great cross-support in the centre, that goes to each side;
He relaxed not a muscle, but hung there as, caught in his
      pangs   30
And waiting his change, the king-serpent all heavily hangs,
Far away from his kind, in the pine, till deliverance come
With the spring-time,—so agonized Saul, drear and stark, blind
      and dumb.

V

Then I tuned my harp,—took off the lilies we twine round its
      chords
Lest they snap 'neath the stress of the noon-tide—those sun-
      beams like swords!
And I first played the tune all our sheep know, as, one after one,
So docile they come to the pen-door till folding be done.
They are white and untorn by the bushes, for lo, they have fed
Where the long grasses stifle the water within the stream's bed;
And now one after one seeks its lodging, as star follows star   40
Into eve and the blue far above us,—so blue and so far!

VI

—Then the tune, for which quails on the cornland will each
      leave his mate
To fly after the player; then, what makes the crickets elate
Till for boldness they fight one another; and then, what has
      weight
To set the quick jerboa a-musing outside his sand house—
There are none such as he for a wonder, half bird and half mouse!
God made all the creatures and gave them our love and our fear,
To give sign, we and they are his children, one family here.

VII

Then I played the help-tune of our reapers, their wine-song,
      when hand

Grasps at hand, eye lights eye in good friendship, and great
    hearts expand   50
And grow one in the sense of this world's life.—And then, the
    last song
When the dead man is praised on his journey—"Bear, bear him
    along
With his few faults shut up like dead flowerets! Are balm-seeds
    not here
To console us? The land has none left such as he on the bier.
Oh, would we might keep thee, my brother!"—And then, the
    glad chaunt
Of the marriage,—first go the young maidens, next, she whom
    we vaunt
As the beauty, the pride of our dwelling.—And then, the great
    march
Wherein man runs to man to assist him and buttress an arch
Naught can break; who shall harm them, our friends?—Then,
    the chorus intoned
As the Levites go up to the altar in glory enthroned.   60
But I stopped here: for here in the darkness Saul groaned.

VIII

And I paused, held my breath in such silence, and listened apart;
And the tent shook, for mighty Saul shuddered: and sparkles
    'gan dart
From the jewels that woke in his turban, at once with a start,
All its lordly male-sapphires, and rubies courageous at heart.
So the head: but the body still moved not, still hung there erect.
And I bent once again to my playing, pursued it unchecked,
As I sang,—

IX

        "Oh, our manhood's prime vigor! No spirit feels waste,
Not a muscle is stopped in its playing nor sinew unbraced.
Oh, the wild joys of living! the leaping from rock up to rock,   70
The strong rending of boughs from the fir-tree, the cool silver
    shock
Of the plunge in a pool's living water, the hunt of the bear,
And the sultriness showing the lion is couched in his lair.
And the meal, the rich dates yellowed over with gold dust divine,

And the locust-flesh steeped in the pitcher, the full draught of
    wine,
And the sleep in the dried river-channel where bulrushes tell
That the water was wont to go warbling so softly and well.
How good is man's life, the mere living! how fit to employ
All the heart and the soul and the senses forever in joy!
Hast thou loved the white locks of thy father, whose sword thou
    didst guard   80
When he trusted thee forth with the armies, for glorious reward?
Didst thou see the thin hands of thy mother, held up as men
    sung
The low song of the nearly-departed, and hear her faint tongue
Joining in while it could to the witness, 'Let one more attest,
I have lived, seen God's hand thro' a lifetime, and all was for
    best'?
Then they sung thro' their tears in strong triumph, not much,
    but the rest.
And thy brothers, the help and the contest, the working whence
    grew
Such result as, from seething grape-bundles, the spirit strained
    true:
And the friends of thy boyhood—that boyhood of wonder and
    hope,
Present promise and wealth of the future beyond the eye's
    scope,—   90
Till lo, thou art grown to a monarch; a people is thine;
And all gifts, which the world offers singly, on one head com-
    bine!
On one head, all the beauty and strength, love and rage (like
    the throe
That, a-work in the rock, helps its labor and lets the gold go)
High ambition and deeds which surpass it, fame crowning them,
    —all
Brought to blaze on the head of one creature—King Saul!"

X

And lo, with that leap of my spirit,—heart, hand, harp and voice,
Each lifting Saul's name out of sorrow, each bidding rejoice
Saul's fame in the light it was made for—as when, dare I say,
The Lord's army, in rapture of service, strains through its
    array,   100

And upsoareth the cherubim-chariot—"Saul!" cried I, and
    stopped,
And waited the thing that should follow. Then Saul, who hung
    propped
By the tent's cross-support in the centre, was struck by his name.
Have ye seen when Spring's arrowy summons goes right to the
    aim,
And some mountain, the last to withstand her, that held (he
    alone,
While the vale laughed in freedom and flowers) on a broad bust
    of stone
A year's snow bound about for a breastplate,—leaves grasp of
    the sheet?
Fold on fold all at once it crowds thunderously down to his feet,
And there fronts you, stark, black, but alive yet, your mountain
    of old,
With his rents, the successive bequeathings of ages untold—   110
Yea, each harm got in fighting your battles, each furrow and scar
Of his head thrust 'twixt you and the tempest—all hail, there
    they are!
—Now again to be softened with verdure, again hold the nest
Of the dove, tempt the goat and its young to the green on his
    crest
For their food in the ardors of summer. One long shudder
    thrilled
All the tent till the very air tingled, then sank and was stilled
At the King's self left standing before me, released and aware.
What was gone, what remained? All to traverse, 'twixt hope and
    despair;
Death was past, life not come: so he waited. Awhile his right
    hand
Held the brow, helped the eyes left too vacant forthwith to re-
    mand   120
To their place what new objects should enter: 'twas Saul as be-
    fore.
I looked up and dared gaze at those eyes, nor was hurt any more
Than by slow pallid sunsets in autumn, ye watch from the shore,
At their sad level gaze o'er the ocean—a sun's slow decline
Over hills which, resolved in stern silence, o'erlap and entwine
Base with base to knit strength more intensely: so, arm folded
    arm
O'er the chest whose slow heavings subsided.

XI

What spell or what charm,
(For, awhile there was trouble within me) what next should I
    urge
To sustain him where song had restored him?—Song filled to the
    verge
His cup with the wine of this life, pressing all that it yields   130
Of mere fruitage, the strength and the beauty: beyond, on what
    fields,
Glean a vintage more potent and perfect to brighten the eye
And bring blood to the lip, and commend them the cup they put
    by?
He saith, "It is good;" still he drinks not: he lets me praise life,
Gives assent, yet would die for his own part.

XII

Then fancies grew rife
Which had come long ago on the pasture, when round me the
    sheep
Fed in silence—above, the one eagle wheeled slow as in sleep;
And I lay in my hollow and mused on the world that might lie
'Neath his ken, though I saw but the strip 'twixt the hill and
    the sky:
And I laughed—"Since my days are ordained to be passed with
    my flocks,   140
Let me people at least, with my fancies, the plains and the rocks,
Dream the life I am never to mix with, and image the show
Of mankind as they live in those fashions I hardly shall know!
Schemes of life, its best rules and right uses, the courage that
    gains,
And the prudence that keeps what men strive for." And now
    these old trains
Of vague thought came again; I grew surer; so, once more the
    string
Of my harp made response to my spirit, as thus—

XIII

"Yea, my King,"
I began—"thou dost well in rejecting mere comforts that spring

From the mere mortal life held in common by man and by brute:
In our flesh grows the branch of this life, in our soul it bears
    fruit. 150
Thou hast marked the slow rise of the tree,—how its stem trem-
    bled first
Till it passed the kid's lip, the stag's antler; then safely outburst
The fan-branches all round; and thou mindest when these too,
    in turn
Broke a-bloom and the palm-tree seemed perfect: yet more was
    to learn,
E'en the good that comes in with the palm-fruit. Our dates shall
    we slight,
When their juice brings a cure for all sorrow? or care for the
    plight
Of the palm's self whose slow growth produced them? Not so!
    stem and branch
Shall decay, nor be known in their place, while the palm-wine
    shall staunch
Every wound of man's spirit in winter. I pour thee such wine.
Leave the flesh to the fate it was fit for! the spirit be thine! 160
By the spirit, when age shall o'ercome thee, thou still shalt enjoy
More indeed, than at first when inconscious, the life of a boy.
Crush that life, and behold its wine running! Each deed thou
    hast done
Dies, revives, goes to work in the world; until e'en as the sun
Looking down on the earth, though clouds spoil him, though
    tempests efface,
Can find nothing his own deed produced not, must everywhere
    trace
The results of his past summer-prime,—so, each ray of thy will,
Every flash of thy passion and prowess, long over, shall thrill
Thy whole people, the countless, with ardor, till they too give
    forth
A like cheer to their sons, who in turn, fill the South and the
    North 170
With the radiance thy deed was the germ of. Carouse in the past!
But the license of age has its limit; thou diest at last:
As the lion when age dims his eyeball, the rose at her height,
So with man—so his power and his beauty forever take flight.
No! Again a long draught of my soul-wine! Look forth o'er the
    years!
Thou hast done now with eyes for the actual; begin with the
    seer's!

Is Saul dead? In the depth of the vale make his tomb—bid arise
A gray mountain of marble heaped four-square, till, built to the
    skies,
Let it mark where the great First King slumbers: whose fame
    would ye know?
Up above see the rock's naked face, where the record shall
    go   180
In great characters cut by the scribe,—Such was Saul, so he did;
With the sages directing the work, by the populace chid,—
For not half, they'll affirm, is comprised there! Which fault to
    amend,
In the grove with his kind grows the cedar, whereon they shall
    spend
(See, in tablets 'tis level before them) their praise, and record
With the gold of the graver, Saul's story,—the statesman's great
    word
Side by side with the poet's sweet comment. The river's a-wave
With smooth paper-reeds grazing each other when prophet-winds
    rave:
So the pen gives unborn generations their due and their part
In thy being! Then, first of the mighty, thank God that thou
    art!"   190

XIV

And behold while I sang . . . but O Thou who didst grant me
    that day,
And before it not seldom hast granted thy help to essay,
Carry on and complete an adventure,—my shield and my sword
In that act where my soul was thy servant, thy word was my
    word,—
Still be with me, who then at the summit of human endeavor
And scaling the highest, man's thought could, gazed hopeless as
    ever
On the new stretch of heaven above me—till, mighty to save,
Just one lift of thy hand cleared that distance—God's throne
    from man's grave!
Let me tell out my tale to its ending—my voice to my heart
Which can scarce dare believe in what marvels last night I took
    part,   200
As this morning I gather the fragments, alone with my sheep,
And still fear lest the terrible glory evanish like sleep!
For I wake in the gray dewy covert, while Hebron upheaves

The dawn struggling with night on his shoulder, and Kidron re-
    trieves
Slow the damage of yesterday's sunshine.

XV

                          I say then,—my song
While I sang thus, assuring the monarch, and ever more strong
Made a proffer of good to console him—he slowly resumed
His old motions and habitudes kingly. The right-hand replumed
His black locks to their wonted composure, adjusted the swathes
Of his turban, and see—the huge sweat that his countenance
    bathes,   210
He wipes off with the robe; and he girds now his loins as of yore,
And feels slow for the armlets of price, with the clasp set before.
He is Saul, ye remember in glory,—ere error had bent
The broad brow from the daily communion; and still, though
    much spent
Be the life and the bearing that front you, the same, God did
    choose,
To receive what a man may waste, desecrate, never quite lose.
So sank he along by the tent-prop till, stayed by the pile
Of his armor and war-cloak and garments, he leaned there awhile,
And sat out my singing,—one arm round the tent-prop, to raise
His bent head, and the other hung slack—till I touched on the
    praise   220
I foresaw from all men in all time, to the man patient there;
And thus ended, the harp falling forward. Then first I was 'ware
That he sat, as I say, with my head just above his vast knees
Which were thrust out on each side around me, like oak-roots
    which please
To encircle a lamb when it slumbers. I looked up to know
If the best I could do had brought solace: he spoke not, but slow
Lifted up the hand slack at his side, till he laid it with care
Soft and grave, but in mild settled will, on my brow: thro' my
    hair
The large fingers were pushed, and he bent back my head, with
    kind power—
All my face back, intent to peruse it, as men do a flower.   230
Thus held he me there with his great eyes that scrutinized mine—
And oh, all my heart how it loved him! but where was the sign?
I yearned—"Could I help thee, my father, inventing a bliss,
I would add, to that life of the past, both the future and this;

I would give thee new life altogether, as good, ages hence,
As this moment,—had love but the warrant, love's heart to dis-
    pense!"

XVI

Then the truth came upon me. No harp more—no song more!
    outbroke—

XVII

"I have gone the whole round of creation: I saw and I spoke:
I, a work of God's hand for that purpose, received in my brain
And pronounced on the rest of his handwork—returned him
    again   240
His creation's approval or censure: I spoke as I saw:
I report, as a man may of God's work—all's love, yet all's law.
Now I lay down the judgeship he lent me. Each faculty tasked
To perceive him, has gained an abyss, where a dewdrop was
    asked.
Have I knowledge? confounded it shrivels at Wisdom laid bare.
Have I forethought? how purblind, how blank, to the Infinite
    Care!
Do I task any faculty highest, to image success?
I but open my eyes,—and perfection, no more and no less,
In the kind I imagined, full-fronts me, and God is seen God
In the star, in the stone, in the flesh, in the soul and the clod. 250
And thus looking within and around me, I ever renew
(With that stoop of the soul which in bending upraises it too)
The submission of man's nothing-perfect to God's all-complete,
As by each new obeisance in spirit, I climb to his feet.
Yet with all this abounding experience, this deity known,
I shall dare to discover some province, some gift of my own.
There's a faculty pleasant to exercise, hard to hoodwink,
I am fain to keep still in abeyance, (I laugh as I think)
Lest, insisting to claim and parade in it, wot ye, I worst
E'en the Giver in one gift.—Behold, I could love if I durst! 260
But I sink the pretension as fearing a man may o'ertake
God's own speed in the one way of love: I abstain for love's sake.
—What, my soul? see thus far and no farther? when doors great
    and small,
Nine-and-ninety flew ope at our touch, should the hundredth
    appall?

In the least things have faith, yet distrust in the greatest of all?
Do I find love so full in my nature, God's ultimate gift,
That I doubt his own love can compete with it? Here, the parts
　　shift?
Here, the creature surpass the Creator,—the end, what Began?
Would I fain in my impotent yearning do all for this man,
And dare doubt he alone shall not help him, who yet alone
　　can?　　　　　　　　　　　　　　　　　　　　　　　270
Would it ever have entered my mind, the bare will, much less
　　power,
To bestow on this Saul what I sang of, the marvellous dower
Of the life he was gifted and filled with? to make such a soul,
Such a body, and then such an earth for insphering the whole?
And doth it not enter my mind (as my warm tears attest)
These good things being given, to go on, and give one more, the
　　best?
Ay, to save and redeem and restore him, maintain at the height
This perfection,—succeed with life's day-spring, death's minute
　　of night?
Interpose at the difficult minute, snatch Saul the mistake,
Saul the failure, the ruin he seems now,—and bid him awake　280
From the dream, the probation, the prelude, to find himself set
Clear and safe in new light and new life,—a new harmony yet
To be run, and continued, and ended—who knows?—or endure!
The man taught enough, by life's dream, of the rest to make sure;
By the pain-throb, triumphantly winning intensified bliss,
And the next world's reward and repose, by the struggles in this.

XVIII

"I believe it! 'Tis thou, God, that givest, 'tis I who receive:
In the first is the last, in thy will is my power to believe.
All's one gift: thou canst grant it moreover, as prompt to my
　　prayer
As I breathe out this breath, as I open these arms to the air.　290
From thy will, stream the worlds, life and nature, thy dread
　　Sabaoth:
I will?—the mere atoms despise me! Why am I not loth
To look that, even that in the face too? Why is it I dare
Think but lightly of such impuissance? What stops my despair?
This;—'tis not what man Does which exalts him, but what man
　　Would do!

See the King—I would help him but cannot, the wishes fall
    through.
Could I wrestle to raise him from sorrow, grow poor to enrich,
To fill up his life, starve my own out, I would—knowing which,
I know that my service is perfect. Oh, speak through me now!
Would I suffer for him that I love? So wouldst thou—so wilt
    thou!   300
So shall crown thee the topmost, ineffablest, uttermost crown—
And thy love fill infinitude wholly, nor leave up nor down
One spot for the creature to stand in! It is by no breath,
Turn of eye, wave of hand, that salvation joins issue with death!
As thy Love is discovered almighty, almighty be proved
Thy power, that exists with and for it, of being Beloved!
He who did most, shall bear most; the strongest shall stand the
    most weak.
'Tis the weakness in strength, that I cry for! my flesh, that I seek
In the Godhead! I seek and I find it. O Saul, it shall be
A Face like my face that receives thee; a Man like to me,   310
Thou shalt love and be loved by, forever: a Hand like this hand
Shall throw open the gates of new life to thee! See the Christ
    stand!"

                            XIX

I know not too well how I found my way home in the night.
There were witnesses, cohorts about me, to left and to right,
Angels, powers, the unuttered, unseen, the alive, the aware:
I repressed, I got through them as hardly, as strugglingly there,
As a runner beset by the populace famished for news—
Life or death. The whole earth was awakened, hell loosed with
    her crews;
And the stars of night beat with emotion, and tingled and shot
Out in fire the strong pain of pent knowledge: but I fainted
    not,   320
For the Hand still impelled me at once and supported, sup-
    pressed
All the tumult, and quenched it with quiet, and holy behest,
Till the rapture was shut in itself, and the earth sank to rest.
Anon at the dawn, all that trouble had withered from earth—
Not so much, but I saw it die out in the day's tender birth;
In the gathered intensity brought to the gray of the hills;
In the shuddering forests' held breath; in the sudden wind-thrills;
In the startled wild beasts that bore off, each with eye sidling still

Though averted with wonder and dread; in the birds stiff and
    chill
That rose heavily, as I approached them, made stupid with
    awe: 330
E'en the serpent that slid away silent,—he felt the new law.
The same stared in the white humid faces upturned by the
    flowers;
The same worked in the heart of the cedar and moved the vine-
    bowers:
And the little brooks witnessing murmured, persistent and low,
With their obstinate, all but hushed voices—"E'en so, it is so!"

"DE GUSTIBUS—"

I

Your ghost will walk, you lover of trees,
      (If our loves remain)
      In an English lane,
By a cornfield-side a-flutter with poppies.
Hark, those two in the hazel coppice—
A boy and a girl, if the good fates please,
      Making love, say,—
      The happier they!
Draw yourself up from the light of the moon,
And let them pass, as they will too soon,
      With the bean-flowers' boon,
      And the blackbird's tune,
      And May, and June!

II

What I love best in all the world
Is a castle, precipice-encurled,
In a gash of the wind-grieved Apennine
Or look for me, old fellow of mine,
(If I get my head from out the mouth
O' the grave, and loose my spirit's bands,
And come again to the land of lands)—
In a sea-side house to the farther South,
Where the baked cicala dies of drouth,

And one sharp tree—'tis a cypress—stands,
By the many hundred years red-rusted,
Rough iron-spiked, ripe fruit-o'ercrusted,
My sentinel to guard the sands
To the water's edge. For, what expands
Before the house, but the great opaque
Blue breadth of sea without a break?
While, in the house, for ever crumbles
Some fragment of the frescoed walls,
From blisters where a scorpion sprawls.
A girl bare-footed brings, and tumbles
Down on the pavement, green-flesh melons,
And says there's news to-day—the king
Was shot at, touched in the liver-wing,
Goes with his Bourbon arm in a sling:
—She hopes they have not caught the felons.
Italy, my Italy!
Queen Mary's saying serves for me—
     (When fortune's malice
     Lost her—Calais)—
Open my heart and you will see
Graved inside of it, "Italy."
Such lovers old are I and she:
So it always was, so shall ever be!

WOMEN AND ROSES

I

I DREAM of a red-rose tree.
And which of its roses three
Is the dearest rose to me?

II

Round and round, like a dance of snow
In a dazzling drift, as its guardians, go
Floating the women faded for ages,
Sculptured in stone, on the poet's pages.
Then follow women fresh and gay,

Living and loving and loved to-day.
Last, in the rear, flee the multitude of maidens,
Beauties yet unborn. And all, to one cadence,
They circle their rose on my rose tree.

III

Dear rose, thy term is reached,
Thy leaf hangs loose and bleached:
Bees pass it unimpeached.

IV

Stay then, stoop, since I cannot climb,
You, great shapes of the antique time!
How shall I fix you, fire you, freeze you,
Break my heart at your feet to please you?
Oh, to possess and be possessed!
Hearts that beat 'neath each pallid breast!
Once but of love, the poesy, the passion,
Drink but once and die!—In vain, the same fashion,
They circle their rose on my rose tree.

V

Dear rose, thy joy's undimmed,
Thy cup is ruby-rimmed,
Thy cup's heart nectar-brimmed.

VI

Deep, as drops from a statue's plinth
The bee sucked in by the hyacinth,
So will I bury me while burning,
Quench like him at a plunge my yearning,
Eyes in your eyes, lips on your lips!
Fold me fast where the cincture slips,
Prison all my soul in eternities of pleasure,
Girdle me for once! But no—the old measure,
They circle their rose on my rose tree.

VII

Dear rose without a thorn,
Thy bud's the babe unborn:
First streak of a new morn.

VIII

Wings, lend wings for the cold, the clear!
What is far conquers what is near.
Roses will bloom nor want beholders,
Sprung from the dust where our flesh moulders.
What shall arrive with the cycle's change?
A novel grace and a beauty strange.
I will make an Eve be the artist that began her,
Shaped her to his mind!—Alas! in like manner
They circle their rose on my rose tree.

PROTUS

AMONG these latter busts we count by scores,
Half-emperors and quarter-emperors,
Each with his bay-leaf fillet, loose-thonged vest,
Loric and low-browed Gorgon on the breast,—
One loves a baby face, with violets there,
Violets instead of laurel in the hair,
As those were all the little locks could bear.

Now read here. "Protus ends a period
Of empery beginning with a god;
Born in the porphyry chamber at Byzant,   **10**
Queens by his cradle, proud and ministrant:
And if he quickened breath there, 'twould like fire
Pantingly through the dim vast realm transpire.
A fame that he was missing spread afar:
The world from its four corners, rose in war,
Till he was borne out on a balcony
To pacify the world when it should see.

The captains ranged before him, one, his hand
Made baby points at, gained the chief command.
And day by day more beautiful he grew   20
In shape, all said, in feature and in hue,
While young Greek sculptors, gazing on the child,
Became with old Greek sculpture reconciled.
Already sages labored to condense
In easy tones a life's experience:
And artists took grave counsel to impart
In one breath and one hand-sweep, all their art—
To make his graces prompt as blossoming
Of plentifully-watered palms in spring:
Since well beseems it, whoso mounts the throne,   30
For beauty, knowledge, strength, should stand alone,
And mortals love the letters of his name."

—Stop! Have you turned two pages? Still the same.
New reign, same date. The scribe goes on to say
How that same year, on such a month and day,
"John the Pannonian, groundedly believed
A blacksmith's bastard, whose hard hand reprieved
The Empire from its fate the year before,—
Came, had a mind to take the crown, and wore
The same for six years (during which the Huns   40
Kept off their fingers from us), till his sons
Put something in his liquor"—and so forth.
Then a new reign. Stay—"Take at its just worth"
(Subjoins an annotator) "what I give
As hearsay. Some think, John let Protus live
And slip away. 'Tis said, he reached man's age
At some blind northern court; made, first a page,
Then tutor to the children; last, of use
About the hunting-stables. I deduce
He wrote the little tract 'On worming dogs,'   50
Whereof the name in sundry catalogues
Is extant yet. A Protus of the race
Is rumored to have died a monk in Thrace,—
And if the same, he reached senility."

Here's John the Smith's rough-hammered head. Great eye,
Gross jaw and griped lips do what granite can
To give you the crown-grasper. What a man!

HOLY-CROSS DAY

*On which the Jews were forced to attend an
annual Christian sermon in Rome*

["Now was come about Holy-Cross Day, and now must my
lord preach his first sermon to the Jews: as it was of old cared for
in the merciful bowels of the Church, that, so to speak, a crumb
at least from her conspicuous table here in Rome should be,
though but once yearly, cast to the famishing dogs, under-
trampled and bespitten-upon beneath the feet of the guests. And
a moving sight in truth, this, of so many of the besotted blind
restif and ready-to-perish Hebrews! now maternally brought—
nay (for He saith, 'Compel them to come in') haled, as it were,
by the head and hair, and against their obstinate hearts, to par-
take of the heavenly grace. What awakening, what striving with
tears, what working of a yeasty conscience! Nor was my lord
wanting to himself on so apt an occasion; witness the abundance
of conversions which did incontinently reward him: though not
to my lord be altogether the glory."—*Diary by the Bishop's
Secretary, 1600.*]

What the Jews really said, on thus being driven to church, was
rather to this effect:—

I

FEE, faw, fum! bubble and squeak!
Blessedest Thursday's the fat of the week.
Rumble and tumble, sleek and rough,
Stinking and savory, smug and gruff,
Take the church-road, for the bell's due chime
Gives us the summons—'tis sermon-time!

II

Boh, here's Barnabas! Job, that's you?
Up stumps Solomon—bustling too?
Shame, man! greedy beyond your years
To handsel the bishop's shaving-shears?   10

Fair play's a jewel! Leave friends in the lurch?
Stand on a line ere you start for the church!

III

Higgledy piggledy, packed we lie,
Rats in a hamper, swine in a stye,
Wasps in a bottle, frogs in a sieve,
Worms in a carcase, fleas in a sleeve.
Hist! square shoulders, settle your thumbs
And buzz for the bishop—here he comes.

IV

Bow, wow, wow—a bone for the dog!
I liken his Grace to an acorned hog.   20
What, a boy at his side, with the bloom of a lass,
To help and handle my lord's hour-glass!
Didst ever behold so lithe a chine?
His cheek hath laps like a fresh-singed swine.

V

Aaron's asleep—shove hip to haunch,
Or somebody deal him a dig in the paunch!
Look at the purse with the tassel and knob,
And the gown with the angel and thingumbob!
What's he at, quotha? reading his text!
Now you've his curtsey—and what comes next?   30

VI

See to our converts—you doomed black dozen—
No stealing away—nor cog nor cozen!
You five, that were thieves, deserve it fairly;
You seven, that were beggars, will live less sparely;
You took your turn and dipped in the hat,
Got fortune—and fortune gets you; mind that!

VII

Give your first groan—compunction's at work;
And soft! from a Jew you mount to a Turk.

Lo, Micah,—the selfsame beard on chin
He was four times already converted in! **40**
Here's a knife, clip quick—it's a sign of grace—
Or he ruins us all with his hanging-face.

VIII

Whom now is the bishop a-leering at?
I know a point where his text falls pat.
I'll tell him to-morrow, a word just now
Went to my heart and made me vow
I meddle no more with the worst of trades—
Let somebody else pay his serenades.

IX

Groan all together now, whee—hee—hee!
It's a-work, it's a-work, ah, woe is me! **50**
It began, when a herd of us, picked and placed,
Were spurred through the Corso, stripped to the waist;
Jew brutes, with sweat and blood well spent
To usher in worthily Christian Lent.

X

It grew, when the hangman entered our bounds,
Yelled, pricked us out to his church like hounds:
It got to a pitch, when the hand indeed
Which gutted my purse would throttle my creed:
And it overflows when, to even the odd,
Men I helped to their sins help me to their God. **60**

XI

But now, while the scapegoats leave our flock,
And the rest sit silent and count the clock,
Since forced to muse the appointed time
On these precious facts and truths sublime,—
Let us fitly employ it, under our breath,
In saying Ben Ezra's Song of Death.

XII

For Rabbi Ben Ezra, the night he died,
Called sons and sons' sons to his side,
And spoke, "This world has been harsh and strange;
Something is wrong: there needeth a change.   70
But what, or where? at the last or first?
In one point only we sinned, at worst.

XIII

"The Lord will have mercy on Jacob yet,
And again in his border see Israel set.
When Judah beholds Jerusalem,
The stranger-seed shall be joined to them:
To Jacob's House shall the Gentiles cleave.
So the Prophet saith and his sons believe.

XIV

"Ay, the children of the chosen race
Shall carry and bring them to their place: 80
In the land of the Lord shall lead the same,
Bondsmen and handmaids. Who shall blame,
When the slaves enslave, the oppressed ones o'er
The oppressor triumph for evermore?

XV

"God spoke, and gave us the word to keep,
Bade never fold the hands nor sleep
'Mid a faithless world,—at watch and ward,
Till Christ at the end relieve our guard.
By His servant Moses the watch was set:
Though near upon cock-crow, we keep it yet.   90

XVI

"Thou! if thou wast He, who at mid-watch came,
By the starlight, naming a dubious name!
And if, too heavy with sleep—too rash

With fear—O Thou, if that martyr-gash
Fell on Thee coming to take thine own,
And we gave the Cross, when we owed the Throne—

XVII

"Thou art the Judge. We are bruised thus.
But, the Judgment over, join sides with us!
Thine too is the cause! and not more thine
Than ours, is the work of these dogs and swine,   100
Whose life laughs through and spits at their creed!
Who maintain Thee in word, and defy Thee in deed!

XVIII

"We withstood Christ then? Be mindful how
At least we withstand Barabbas now!
Was our outrage sore? But the worst we spared,
To have called these—Christians, had we dared!
Let defiance to them pay mistrust of Thee,
And Rome make amends for Calvary!

XIX

"By the torture, prolonged from age to age,
By the infamy, Israel's heritage,   110
By the Ghetto's plague, by the garb's disgrace,
By the badge of shame, by the felon's place,
By the branding-tool, the bloody whip,
And the summons to Christian fellowship,—

XX

"We boast our proof that at least the Jew
Would wrest Christ's name from the Devil's crew.
Thy face took never so deep a shade
But we fought them in it, God our aid!
A trophy to bear, as we march, Thy band,
South, East, and on to the Pleasant Land!"   120

[*Pope Gregory XVI abolished this bad business of the sermon.*—R. B.]

THE GUARDIAN-ANGEL

A PICTURE AT FANO

I

Dear and great Angel, wouldst thou only leave
   That child, when thou hast done with him, for me!
Let me sit all the day here, that when eve
   Shall find performed thy special ministry,
And time come for departure, thou, suspending
Thy flight, mayst see another child for tending,
   Another still, to quiet and retrieve.

II

Then I shall feel thee step one step, no more,
   From where thou standest now, to where I gaze,
—And suddenly my head is covered o'er
   With those wings, white above the child who prays
Now on that tomb—and I shall feel thee guarding
Me, out of all the world; for me, discarding
   Yon heaven thy home, that waits and opes its door.

III

I would not look up thither past thy head
   Because the door opes, like that child, I know,
For I should have thy gracious face instead,
   Thou bird of God! And wilt thou bend me low
Like him, and lay, like his, my hands together,
And lift them up to pray, and gently tether
   Me, as thy lamb there, with thy garment's spread?

IV

If this was ever granted, I would rest
   My head beneath thine, while thy healing hands

Close-covered both my eyes beside thy breast,
  Pressing the brain, which too much thought expands,
Back to its proper size again, and smoothing
Distortion down till every nerve had soothing,
  And all lay quiet, happy and suppressed.

v

How soon all worldly wrong would be repaired!
  I think how I should view the earth and skies
And sea, when once again my brow was bared
  After thy healing, with such different eyes.
O world, as God has made it! All is beauty:
And knowing this, is love, and love is duty.
  What further may be sought for or declared?

VI

Guercino drew this angel I saw teach
  (Alfred, dear friend!)—that little child to pray,
Holding the little hands up, each to each
  Pressed gently,—with his own head turned away
Over the earth where so much lay before him
Of work to do, though heaven was opening o'er him,
  And he was left at Fano by the beach.

VII

We were at Fano, and three times we went
  To sit and see him in his chapel there,
And drink his beauty to our soul's content
  —My angel with me too: and since I care
For dear Guercino's fame (to which in power
And glory comes this picture for a dower,
  Fraught with a pathos so magnificent)—

VIII

And since he did not work thus earnestly
  At all times, and has else endured some wrong—

I took one thought his picture struck from me,
And spread it out, translating it to song.
My love is here. Where are you, dear old friend?
How rolls the Wairoa at your world's far end?
This is Ancona, yonder is the sea.

CLEON

'As certain also of your own poets have said'—

CLEON the poet, (from the sprinkled isles,
Lily on lily, that o'erlace the sea,
And laugh their pride when the light wave lisps "Greece")—
To Protos in his Tyranny: much health!

They give thy letter to me, even now:
I read and seem as if I heard thee speak.
The master of thy galley still unlades
Gift after gift; they block my court at last
And pile themselves along its portico
Royal with sunset, like a thought of thee: 10
And one white she-slave from the group dispersed
Of black and white slaves (like the chequer-work
Pavement, at once my nation's work and gift,
Now covered with this settle-down of doves),
One lyric woman, in her crocus vest
Woven of sea-wools, with her two white hands
Commends to me the strainer and the cup
Thy lip hath bettered ere it blesses mine.

Well-counselled, king, in thy munificence!
For so shall men remark, in such an act   20
Of love for him whose song gives life its joy,
Thy recognition of the use of life;
Nor call thy spirit barely adequate
To help on life in straight ways, broad enough
For vulgar souls, by ruling and the rest.
Thou, in the daily building of thy tower,—

Whether in fierce and sudden spasms of toil,
Or through dim lulls of unapparent growth,
Or when the general work 'mid good acclaim
Climbed with the eye to cheer the architect,—   30
Didst ne'er engage in work for mere work's sake—
Hadst ever in thy heart the luring hope
Of some eventual rest a-top of it,
Whence, all the tumult of the building hushed,
Thou first of men mightst look out to the East:
The vulgar saw thy tower, thou sawest the sun.
For this, I promise on thy festival
To pour libation, looking o'er the sea,
Making this slave narrate thy fortunes, speak
Thy great words, and describe thy royal face—   40
Wishing thee wholly where Zeus lives the most,
Within the eventual element of calm.

Thy letter's first requirement meets me here.
It is as thou hast heard: in one short life
I, Cleon, have effected all those things
Thou wonderingly dost enumerate.
That epos on thy hundred plates of gold
Is mine,—and also mine the little chant,
So sure to rise from every fishing-bark
When, lights at prow, the seamen haul their net.   50
The image of the sun-god on the phare,
Men turn from the sun's self to see, is mine;
The Pœcile, o'er-storied its whole length,
As thou didst hear, with painting, is mine too.
I know the true proportions of a man
And woman also, not observed before;
And I have written three books on the soul,
Proving absurd all written hitherto,
And putting us to ignorance again.
For music,—why, I have combined the moods,   60
Inventing one. In brief, all arts are mine;
Thus much the people know and recognize,
Throughout our seventeen islands. Marvel not.
We of these latter days, with greater mind
Than our forerunners, since more composite,
Look not so great, beside their simple way,
To a judge who only sees one way at once,

One mid-point and no other at a time,—
Compares the small part of a man of us
With some whole man of the heroic age,   70
Great in his way—not ours, nor meant for ours.
And ours is greater, had we skill to know:
For, what we call this life of men on earth,
This sequence of the soul's achievements here
Being, as I find much reason to conceive,
Intended to be viewed eventually
As a great whole, not analyzed to parts,
But each part having reference to all,—
How shall a certain part, pronounced complete,
Endure effacement by another part?   80
Was the thing done?—then, what's to do again?
See, in the chequered pavement opposite,
Suppose the artist made a perfect rhomb,
And next a lozenge, then a trapezoid—
He did not overlay them, superimpose
The new upon the old and blot it out,
But laid them on a level in his work,
Making at last a picture; there it lies.
So, first the perfect separate forms were made,
The portions of mankind; and after, so,   90
Occurred the combination of the same.
For where had been a progress, otherwise?
Mankind, made up of all the single men,—
In such a synthesis the labor ends.
Now mark me! those divine men of old time
Have reached, thou sayest well, each at one point
The outside verge that rounds our faculty;
And where they reached, who can do more than reach?
It takes but little water just to touch
At some one point the inside of a sphere,   100
And, as we turn the sphere, touch all the rest
In due succession: but the finer air
Which not so palpably nor obviously,
Though no less universally, can touch
The whole circumference of that emptied sphere,
Fills it more fully than the water did;
Holds thrice the weight of water in itself
Resolved into a subtler element.
And yet the vulgar call the sphere first full

Up to the visible height—and after, void;   110
Not knowing air's more hidden properties.
And thus our soul, misknown, cries out to Zeus
To vindicate his purpose in our life:
Why stay we on the earth unless to grow?
Long since, I imaged, wrote the fiction out,
That he or other god descended here
And, once for all, showed simultaneously
What, in its nature, never can be shown,
Piecemeal or in succession;—showed, I say,
The worth both absolute and relative   120
Of all his children from the birth of time,
His instruments for all appointed work.
I now go on to image,—might we hear
The judgment which should give the due to each,
Show where the labor lay and where the ease,
And prove Zeus' self, the latent everywhere!
This is a dream:—but no dream, let us hope,
That years and days, the summers and the springs,
Follow each other with unwaning powers.
The grapes which dye thy wine are richer far,   130
Through culture, than the wild wealth of the rock;
The suave plum than the savage-tasted drupe;
The pastured honey-bee drops choicer sweet;
The flowers turn double, and the leaves turn flowers;
That young and tender crescent-moon, thy slave,
Sleeping above her robe as buoyed by clouds,
Refines upon the women of my youth.
What, and the soul alone deteriorates?
I have not chanted verse like Homer, no—
Nor swept string like Terpander, no—nor carved   140
And painted men like Phidias and his friend:
I am not great as they are, point by point.
But I have entered into sympathy
With these four, running these into one soul,
Who, separate, ignored each other's art.
Say, is it nothing that I know them all?
The wild flower was the larger; I have dashed
Rose-blood upon its petals, pricked its cup's
Honey with wine, and driven its seed to fruit,
And show a better flower if not so large: 150
I stand myself. Refer this to the gods
Whose gift alone it is! which, shall I dare

(All pride apart) upon the absurd pretext
That such a gift by chance lay in my hand,
Discourse of lightly or depreciate?
It might have fallen to another's hand: what then?
I pass too surely: let at least truth stay!

   And next, of what thou followest on to ask.
This being with me as I declare, O king,
My works, in all these varicolored kinds,   160
So done by me, accepted so by men—
Thou askest, if (my soul thus in men's hearts)
I must not be accounted to attain
The very crown and proper end of life?
Inquiring thence how, now life closeth up,
I face death with success in my right hand:
Whether I fear death less than dost thyself
The fortunate of men? "For" (writest thou)
"Thou leavest much behind, while I leave naught.
Thy life stays in the poems men shall sing,   170
The pictures men shall study; while my life,
Complete and whole now in its power and joy,
Dies altogether with my brain and arm,
Is lost indeed; since, what survives myself?
The brazen statue to o'erlook my grave,
Set on the promontory which I named.
And that—some supple courtier of my heir
Shall use its robed and sceptred arm, perhaps,
To fix the rope to, which best drags it down.
I go then: triumph thou, who dost not go!"   180

   Nay, thou art worthy of hearing my whole mind.
Is this apparent, when thou turn'st to muse
Upon the scheme of earth and man in chief,
That admiration grows as knowledge grows?
That imperfection means perfection hid,
Reserved in part, to grace the after-time?
If, in the morning of philosophy,
Ere aught had been recorded, nay perceived,
Thou, with the light now in thee, couldst have looked
On all earth's tenantry, from worm to bird,   190
Ere man, her last, appeared upon the stage—
Thou wouldst have seen them perfect, and deduced

The perfectness of others yet unseen.
Conceding which,—had Zeus then questioned thee
"Shall I go on a step, improve on this,
Do more for visible creatures than is done?"
Thou wouldst have answered, "Ay, by making each
Grow conscious in himself—by that alone.
All's perfect else: the shell sucks fast the rock,
The fish strikes through the sea, the snake both swims   200
And slides, forth range the beasts, the birds take flight,
Till life's mechanics can no further go—
And all this joy in natural life is put
Like fire from off thy finger into each,
So exquisitely perfect is the same.
But 'tis pure fire, and they mere matter are;
It has them, not they it: and so I choose
For man, thy last premeditated work
(If I might add a glory to the scheme)
That a third thing should stand apart from both,   210
A quality arise within his soul,
Which, intro-active, made to supervise
And feel the force it has, may view itself,
And so be happy." Man might live at first
The animal life: but is there nothing more?
In due time, let him critically learn
How he lives; and, the more he gets to know
Of his own life's adaptabilities,
The more joy-giving will his life become.
Thus man, who hath this quality, is best.   220

    But thou, king, hadst more reasonably said:
"Let progress end at once,—man make no step
Beyond the natural man, the better beast,
Using his senses, not the sense of sense."
In man there's failure, only since he left
The lower and inconscious forms of life.
We called it an advance, the rendering plain
Man's spirit might grow conscious of man's life,
And, by new lore so added to the old,
Take each step higher over the brute's head.   230
This grew the only life, the pleasure-house,
Watch-tower and treasure-fortress of the soul,
Which whole surrounding flats of natural life
Seemed only fit to yield subsistence to;

A tower that crowns a country. But alas,
The soul now climbs it just to perish there!
For thence we have discovered ('tis no dream—
We know this, which we had not else perceived)
That there's a world of capability
For joy, spread round about us, meant for us,   240
Inviting us; and still the soul craves all,
And still the flesh replies, "Take no jot more
Than ere thou clombst the tower to look abroad!
Nay, so much less as that fatigue has brought
Deduction to it." We struggle, fain to enlarge
Our bounded physical recipiency,
Increase our power, supply fresh oil to life,
Repair the waste of age and sickness: no,
It skills not! life's inadequate to joy,
As the soul sees joy, tempting life to take.   250
They praise a fountain in my garden here
Wherein a Naiad sends the water-bow
Thin from her tube; she smiles to see it rise.
What if I told her, it is just a thread
From that great river which the hills shut up,
And mock her with my leave to take the same?
The artificer has given her one small tube
Past power to widen or exchange—what boots
To know she might spout oceans if she could?
She cannot lift beyond her first thin thread: 260
And so a man can use but a man's joy
While he sees God's. Is it for Zeus to boast,
"See, man, how happy I live, and despair—
That I may be still happier—for thy use!"
If this were so, we could not thank our Lord,
As hearts beat on to doing; 'tis not so—
Malice it is not. Is it carelessness?
Still, no. If care—where is the sign? I ask,
And get no answer, and agree in sum,
O king, with thy profound discouragement,   270
Who seest the wider but to sigh the more.
Most progress is most failure: thou sayest well.

   The last point now:—thou dost except a case—
Holding joy not impossible to one
With artist-gifts—to such a man as I
Who leave behind me living works indeed;

For, such a poem, such a painting lives.
What? dost thou verily trip upon a word,
Confound the accurate view of what joy is
(Caught somewhat clearer by my eyes than thine)   280
With feeling joy? confound the knowing how
And showing how to live (my faculty)
With actually living?—Otherwise
Where is the artist's vantage o'er the king?
Because in my great epos I display
How divers men young, strong, fair, wise, can act—
Is this as though I acted? if I paint,
Carve the young Phœbus, am I therefore young?
Methinks I'm older that I bowed myself
The many years of pain that taught me art!   290
Indeed, to know is something, and to prove
How all this beauty might be enjoyed, is more:
But, knowing naught, to enjoy is something too.
Yon rower, with the moulded muscles there,
Lowering the sail, is nearer it than I.
I can write love-odes: thy fair slave's an ode.
I get to sing of love, when grown too gray
For being beloved: she turns to that young man,
The muscles all a-ripple on his back.
I know the joy of kingship: well, thou art king!   300

    "But," sayest thou—(and I marvel, I repeat,
To find thee trip on such a mere word) "what
Thou writest, paintest, stays; that does not die:
Sappho survives, because we sing her songs,
And Æschylus, because we read his plays!"
Why, if they live still, let them come and take
Thy slave in my despite, drink from thy cup,
Speak in my place. Thou diest while I survive?
Say rather that my fate is deadlier still,
In this, that every day my sense of joy   310
Grows more acute, my soul (intensified
By power and insight) more enlarged, more keen;
While every day my hairs fall more and more,
My hand shakes, and the heavy years increase—
The horror quickening still from year to year,
The consummation coming past escape
When I shall know most, and yet least enjoy—
When all my works wherein I prove my worth,

Being present still to mock me in men's mouths,
Alive still, in the praise of such as thou,   320
I, I the feeling, thinking, acting man,
The man who loved his life so over-much,
Sleep in my urn. It is so horrible,
I dare at times imagine to my need
Some future state revealed to us by Zeus,
Unlimited in capability
For joy, as this is in desire for joy,
—To seek which, the joy-hunger forces us:
That, stung by straitness of our life, made strait
On purpose to make prized the life at large—   330
Freed by the throbbing impulse we call death,
We burst there as the worm into the fly,
Who, while a worm still, wants his wings. But no!
Zeus has not yet revealed it; and alas,
He must have done so, were it possible!

    Live long and happy, and in that thought die:
Glad for what was! Farewell. And for the rest,
I cannot tell thy messenger aright
Where to deliver what he bears of thine
To one called Paulus; we have heard his fame   340
Indeed, if Christus be not one with him—
I know not, nor am troubled much to know.
Thou canst not think a mere barbarian Jew,
As Paulus proves to be, one circumcised,
Hath access to a secret shut from us?
Thou wrongest our philosophy, O king,
In stooping to inquire of such an one,
As if his answer could impose at all!
He writeth, doth he? well, and he may write.
Oh, the Jew findeth scholars! certain slaves   350
Who touched on this same isle, preached him and Christ;
And (as I gathered from a bystander)
Their doctrine could be held by no sane man.

THE TWINS

"Give" and "It-shall-be-given-unto-you"

I

GRAND rough old Martin Luther
   Bloomed fables—flowers on furze,
The better the uncouther:
   Do roses stick like burrs?

II

A beggar asked an alms
   One day at an abbey-door,
Said Luther; but, seized with qualms,
   The Abbot replied, "We're poor!

III

"Poor, who had plenty once,
   When gifts fell thick as rain:
But they give us naught, for the nonce,
   And how should we give again?"

IV

Then the beggar, "See your sins!
   Of old, unless I err,
Ye had brothers for inmates, twins,
   Date and Dabitur.

V

"While Date was in good case
   Dabitur flourished too:
For Dabitur's lenten face
   No wonder if Date rue.

VI

"Would ye retrieve the one?
    Try and make plump the other!
When Date's penance is done,
    Dabitur helps his brother.

VII

"Only, beware relapse!"
    The Abbot hung his head.
This beggar might be perhaps
    An angel, Luther said.

POPULARITY

I

Stand still, true poet that you are!
    I know you; let me try and draw you.
Some night you'll fail us: when afar
    You rise, remember one man saw you,
Knew you, and named a star!

II

My star God's glow-worm! Why extend
    That loving hand of his which leads you,
Yet locks you safe from end to end
    Of this dark world, unless he needs you,
Just saves your light to spend?

III

His clenched hand shall unclose at last,
    I know, and let out all the beauty:
My poet holds the future fast,
    Accepts the coming ages' duty,
Their present for this past.

IV

That day, the earth's feast-master's brow
    Shall clear, to God the chalice raising;
"Others give best at first, but thou
    Forever set'st our table praising,
Keep'st the good wine till now!"

V

Meantime, I'll draw you as you stand,
    With few or none to watch and wonder:
I'll say—a fisher, on the sand
    By Tyre the old, with ocean-plunder,
A netful, brought to land.

VI

Who has not heard how Tyrian shells
    Enclosed the blue, that dye of dyes
Whereof one drop worked miracles,
    And colored like Astarte's eyes
Raw silk the merchant sells?

VII

And each bystander of them all
    Could criticise, and quote tradition
How depths of blue sublimed some pall
    —To get which, pricked a king's ambition;
Worth sceptre, crown and ball.

VIII

Yet there's the dye, in that rough mesh,
    The sea has only just o'erwhispered!
Live whelks, each lip's beard dripping fresh,
    As if they still the water's lisp heard
Through foam the rock-weeds thresh.

IX

Enough to furnish Solomon
  Such hangings for his cedar-house,
That, when gold-robed he took the throne
  In that abyss of blue, the Spouse
Might swear his presence shone

X

Most like the centre-spike of gold
  Which burns deep in the blue-bell's womb,
What time, with ardors manifold,
  The bee goes singing to her groom,
Drunken and overbold.

XI

Mere conchs! not fit for warp or woof!
  Till cunning come to pound and squeeze
And clarify,—refine to proof
  The liquor filtered by degrees,
While the world stands aloof.

XII

And there's the extract, flasked and fine,
  And priced and salable at last!
And Hobbs, Nobbs, Stokes and Nokes combine
  To paint the future from the past,
Put blue into their line.

XIII

Hobbs hints blue,—straight he turtle eats:
  Nobbs prints blue,—claret crowns his cup:
Nokes outdares Stokes in azure feats,—
  Both gorge. Who fished the murex up?
What porridge had John Keats?

THE HERETIC'S TRAGEDY

A MIDDLE-AGE INTERLUDE

ROSA MUNDI; SEU, FULCITE ME FLORIBUS. A CONCEIT OF MASTER
GYSBRECHT, CANON-REGULAR OF SAINT JODOCUS-BY-THE-BAR, YPRES
CITY. CANTUQUE, *Virgilius*. AND HATH OFTEN BEEN SUNG AT HOCK-
TIDE AND FESTIVALS. GAVISUS ERAM, *Jessides*.

(It would seem to be a glimpse from the burning of Jacques du
Bourg-Molay, at Paris, A.D. 1324; as distorted by the refraction from
Flemish brain to brain, during the course of a couple of centuries.)

[Molay was Grand Master of the Templars when that order was
suppressed in 1312.]

I

PREADMONISHETH THE ABBOT DEODAET

THE Lord, we look to once for all,
   Is the Lord we should look at, all at once:
He knows not to vary, saith Saint Paul,
   Nor the shadow of turning, for the nonce.
See him no other than as he is!
   Give both the infinitudes their due—
Infinite mercy, but, I wis,
   As infinite a justice too.

                        [Organ: plagal-cadence.

   As infinite a justice too.

II

ONE SINGETH

John, Master of the Temple of God,   10
   Falling to sin the Unknown Sin,
What he bought of Emperor Aldabrod,
   He sold it to Sultan Saladin:
Till, caught by Pope Clement, a-buzzing there,
   Hornet-prince of the mad wasps' hive,
And clipt of his wings in Paris square,

They bring him now to be burned alive.
    [*And wanteth there grace of lute or clavicithern, ye shall
                say to confirm him who singeth—*
We bring John now to be burned alive.

III

In the midst is a goodly gallows built;
  'Twixt fork and fork, a stake is stuck;   20
But first they set divers tumbrils a-tilt,
  Make a trench all round with the city muck;
Inside they pile log upon log, good store;
  Faggots no few, blocks great and small,
Reach a man's mid-thigh, no less, no more,—
  For they mean he should roast in the sight of all.

CHORUS

We mean he should roast in the sight of all.

IV

Good sappy bavins that kindle forthwith;
  Billets that blaze substantial and slow;
Pine-stump split deftly, dry as pith;   30
  Larch-heart that chars to a chalk-white glow:
Then up they hoist me John in a chafe,
  Sling him fast like a hog to scorch,
Spit in his face, then leap back safe,
  Sing "Laudes" and bid clap-to the torch.

CHORUS

Laus Deo—who bids clap-to the torch.

V

John of the Temple, whose fame so bragged,
  Is burning alive in Paris square!
How can he curse, if his mouth is gagged?
  Or wriggle his neck, with a collar there?   40
Or heave his chest. which a band goes round?

Or threat with his fist, since his arms are spliced?
Or kick with his feet, now his legs are bound?
—Thinks John, I will call upon Jesus Christ.

[*Here one crosseth himself.*

VI

Jesus Christ—John had bought and sold,
    Jesus Christ—John had eaten and drunk;
To him, the Flesh meant silver and gold.
    (*Salvâ reverentiâ.*)
Now it was, "Saviour, bountiful lamb,
    I have roasted thee Turks, though men roast me!   50
See thy servant, the plight wherein I am!
    Art thou a saviour? Save thou me!"

CHORUS

'Tis John the mocker cries, "Save thou me!"

VII

Who maketh God's menace an idle word?
    —Saith, it no more means what it proclaims,
Than a damsel's threat to her wanton bird?—
    For she too prattles of ugly names.
—Saith, he knoweth but one thing,—what he knows?
    That God is good and the rest is breath;
Why else is the same styled Sharon's rose?   60
    Once a rose, ever a rose, he saith.

CHORUS

O, John shall yet find a rose, he saith!

VIII

Alack, there be roses and roses, John!
    Some, honied of taste like your leman's tongue:
Some, bitter; for why? (roast gayly on!)
    Their tree struck root in devil's-dung.
When Paul once reasoned of righteousness
    And of temperance and of judgment to come,

Good Felix trembled, he could no less:
   John, snickering, crook'd his wicked thumb.   **70**

CHORUS

What cometh to John of the wicked thumb?

IX

Ha ha, John plucketh now at his rose
   To rid himself of a sorrow at heart!
Lo,—petal on petal, fierce rays unclose;
   Anther on anther, sharp spikes outstart;
And with blood for dew, the bosom boils;
   And a gust of sulphur is all its smell;
And lo, he is horribly in the toils
   Of a coal-black giant flower of hell!

CHORUS

What maketh heaven, That maketh hell.   *8 i*

X

So, as John called now, through the fire amain,
   On the Name, he had cursed with, all his life—
To the Person, he bought and sold again—
   For the Face, with its daily buffets rife—
Feature by feature It took its place:
   And his voice, like a mad dog's choking bark,
At the steady whole of the Judge's face—
   Died. Forth John's soul flared into the dark.

SUBJOINETH THE ABBOT DEODAET

God help all poor souls lost in the dark!

TWO IN THE CAMPAGNA

I

   I wonder do you feel to-day
     As I have felt since, hand in hand,

We sat down on the grass, to stray
　　In spirit better through the land,
This morn of Rome and May?

II

For me, I touched a thought, I know,
　　Has tantalized me many times,
(Like turns of thread the spiders throw
　　Mocking across our path) for rhymes
To catch at and let go.

III

Help me to hold it! First it left
　　The yellowing fennel, run to seed
There, branching from the brickwork's cleft,
　　Some old tomb's ruin: yonder weed
Took up the floating weft,

IV

Where one small orange cup amassed
　　Five beetles,—blind and green they grope
Among the honey-meal: and last,
　　Everywhere on the grassy slope
I traced it. Hold it fast!

V

The champaign with its endless fleece
　　Of feathery grasses everywhere!
Silence and passion, joy and peace,
　　An everlasting wash of air—
Rome's ghost since her decease.

VI

Such life here, through such lengths of hours,
　　Such miracles performed in play,
Such primal naked forms of flowers,
　　Such letting nature have her way
While heaven looks from its towers!

VII

How say you? Let us, O my dove,
   Let us be unashamed of soul,
As earth lies bare to heaven above!
   How is it under our control
To love or not to love?

VIII

I would that you were all to me,
   You that are just so much, no more.
Nor yours nor mine, nor slave nor free!
   Where does the fault lie? What the core
O' the wound, since wound must be?

IX

I would I could adopt your will,
   See with your eyes, and set my heart
Beating by yours, and drink my fill
   At your soul's springs,—your part my part
In life, for good and ill.

X

No. I yearn upward, touch you close,
   Then stand away. I kiss your cheek,
Catch your soul's warmth,—I pluck the rose
   And love it more than tongue can speak—
Then the good minute goes.

XI

Already how am I so far
   Out of that minute? Must I go
Still like the thistle-ball, no bar,
   Onward, whenever light winds blow,
Fixed by no friendly star?

XII

Just when I seemed about to learn!
    Where is the thread now? Off again!
The old trick! Only I discern—
    Infinite passion, and the pain
Of finite hearts that yearn.

A GRAMMARIAN'S FUNERAL

Shortly after the revival of learning in Europe

Let us begin and carry up this corpse,
    Singing together.
Leave we the common crofts, the vulgar thorpes,
    Each in its tether
Sleeping safe on the bosom of the plain,
    Cared-for till cock-crow:
Look out if yonder be not day again
    Rimming the rock-row!
That's the appropriate country; there, man's thought.
    Rarer, intenser,   10
Self-gathered for an outbreak, as it ought,
    Chafes in the censer.
Leave we the unlettered plain its herd and crop;
    Seek we sepulture
On a tall mountain, citied to the top,
    Crowded with culture!
All the peaks soar, but one the rest excels;
    Clouds overcome it;
No! yonder sparkle is the citadel's
    Circling its summit.   20
Thither our path lies; wind we up the heights:
    Wait ye the warning?
Our low life was the level's and the night's;
    He's for the morning.
Step to a tune, square chests, erect each head,
    'Ware the beholders!
This is our master, famous calm and dead,
    Borne on our shoulders.

Sleep, crop and herd! sleep, darkling thorpe and croft,
    Safe from the weather!   30
He, whom we convoy to his grave aloft,
    Singing together,
He was a man born with thy face and throat,
    Lyric Apollo!
Long he lived nameless: how should spring take note
    Winter would follow?
Till lo, the little touch, and youth was gone!
    Cramped and diminished,
Moaned he, "New measures, other feet anon!
    My dance is finished?"   40
No, that's the world's way: (keep the mountain-side,
    Make for the city!)
He knew the signal, and stepped on with pride
    Over men's pity;
Left play for work, and grappled with the world
    Bent on escaping:
"What's in the scroll," quoth he, "thou keepest furled?
    Show me their shaping,
Theirs who most studied man, the bard and sage,—
    Give!"—So, he gowned him,   50
Straight got by heart that book to its last page:
    Learned, we found him.
Yea, but we found him bald too, eyes like lead,
    Accents uncertain:
"Time to taste life," another would have said,
    "Up with the curtain!"
This man said rather, "Actual life comes next?
    Patience a moment!
Grant I have mastered learning's crabbed text,
    Still there's the comment.   60
Let me know all! Prate not of most or least,
    Painful or easy!
Even to the crumbs I'd fain eat up the feast,
    Ay, nor feel queasy."
Oh, such a life as he resolved to live,
    When he had learned it,
When he had gathered all books had to give!
    Sooner, he spurned it.
Image the whole, then execute the parts—
    Fancy the fabric   70

Quite, ere you build, ere steel strike fire from quartz,
  Ere mortar dab brick!

(Here's the town-gate reached: there's the market-place
  Gaping before us.)
Yea, this in him was the peculiar grace
  (Hearten our chorus!)
That before living he'd learn how to live—
  No end to learning:
Earn the means first—God surely will contrive
  Use for our earning.   80
Others mistrust and say, "But time escapes:
  Live now or never!"
He said, "What's time? Leave Now for dogs and apes!
  Man has Forever."
Back to his book then: deeper drooped his head:
  Calculus racked him:
Leaden before, his eyes grew dross of lead:
  Tussis attacked him.
"Now, master, take a little rest!"—not he!
  (Caution redoubled,   90
Step two abreast, the way winds narrowly!)
  Not a whit troubled
Back to his studies, fresher than at first,
  Fierce as a dragon
He (soul-hydroptic with a sacred thirst)
  Sucked at the flagon.
Oh, if we draw a circle premature,
  Heedless of far gain,
Greedy for quick returns of profit, sure
  Bad is our bargain!   100
Was it not great? did not he throw on God,
  (He loves the burthen)—
God's task to make the heavenly period
  Perfect the earthen?
Did not he magnify the mind, show clear
  Just what it all meant?
He would not discount life, as fools do here,
  Paid by instalment.
He ventured neck or nothing—heaven's success
  Found, or earth's failure: 110
"Wilt thou trust death or not?" He answered "Yes:
  Hence with life's pale lure!"

That low man seeks a little thing to do,
    Sees it and does it:
This high man, with a great thing to pursue,
    Dies ere he knows it.
That low man goes on adding one to one,
    His hundred's soon hit:
This high man, aiming at a million,
    Misses an unit.   120
That, has the world here—should he need the next,
    Let the world mind him!
This, throws himself on God, and unperplexed
    Seeking shall find him.
So, with the throttling hands of death at strife,
    Ground he at grammar;
Still, thro' the rattle, parts of speech were rife:
    While he could stammer
He settled *Hoti's* business—let it be!—
    Properly based *Oun*—   130
Gave us the doctrine of the enclitic *De*,
    Dead from the waist down.
Well, here's the platform, here's the proper place:
    Hail to your purlieus,
All ye highfliers of the feathered race,
    Swallows and curlews!
Here's the top-peak; the multitude below
    Live, for they can, there:
This man decided not to Live but Know—
    Bury this man there?   140
Here—here's his place, where meteors shoot, clouds form,
    Lightnings are loosened,
Stars come and go! Let joy break with the storm,
    Peace let the dew send!
Lofty designs must close in like effects:
    Loftily lying,
Leave him—still loftier than the world suspects,
    Living and dying.

ONE WAY OF LOVE

I

ALL June I bound the rose in sheaves.
Now, rose by rose, I strip the leaves
And strew them where Pauline may pass.
She will not turn aside? Alas!
Let them lie. Suppose they die?
The chance was they might take her eye.

II

How many a month I strove to suit
These stubborn fingers to the lute!
To-day I venture all I know.
She will not hear my music? So!
Break the string; fold music's wing:
Suppose Pauline had bade me sing!

III

My whole life long I learned to love.
This hour my utmost art I prove
And speak my passion—heaven or hell?
She will not give me heaven? 'Tis well!
Lose who may—I still can say,
Those who win heaven, blest are they!

ANOTHER WAY OF LOVE

I

JUNE was not over
  Though past the full,
And the best of her roses
  Had yet to blow,
  When a man I know

(But shall not discover,
    Since ears are dull,
    And time discloses)
Turned him and said with a man's true air,
Half sighing a smile in a yawn, as 'twere,—   10
"If I tire of your June, will she greatly care?"

II

Well, dear, in-doors with you!
    True! serene deadness
Tries a man's temper.
    What's in the blossom
    June wears on her bosom?
Can it clear scores with you?
    Sweetness and redness.
Eadem semper!
Go, let me care for it greatly or slightly!   20
If June mend her bower now, your hand left unsightly
By plucking the roses,—my June will do rightly.

III

And after, for pastime,
    If June be refulgent
With flowers in completeness,
    All petals, no prickles,
    Delicious as trickles
Of wine poured at mass-time,—
    And choose One indulgent
To redness and sweetness: 30
Or if, with experience of man and of spider,
June use my June-lightning, the strong insect-ridder,
And stop the fresh film-work,—why, June will consider.

"TRANSCENDENTALISM: A POEM IN TWELVE BOOKS"

STOP playing, poet! May a brother speak?
'Tis you speak, that's your error. Song's our art:
Whereas you please to speak these naked thoughts

Instead of draping them in sights and sounds.
—True thoughts, good thoughts, thoughts fit to treasure up!
But why such long prolusion and display,
Such turning and adjustment of the harp,
And taking it upon your breast, at length,
Only to speak dry words across its strings?
Stark-naked thought is in request enough: 10
Speak prose and hollo it till Europe hears!
The six-foot Swiss tube, braced about with bark,
Which helps the hunter's voice from Alp to Alp—
Exchange our harp for that,—who hinders you?

   But here's your fault; grown men want thought, you think;
Thought's what they mean by verse, and seek in verse.
Boys seek for images and melody,
Men must have reason—so, you aim at men.
Quite otherwise! Objects throng our youth, 'tis true;
We see and hear and do not wonder much: 20
If you could tell us what they mean, indeed!
As German Boehme never cared for plants
Until it happed, a-walking in the fields,
He noticed all at once that plants could speak,
Nay, turned with loosened tongue to talk with him.
That day the daisy had an eye indeed—
Colloquized with the cowslip on such themes!
We find them extant yet in Jacob's prose.
But by the time youth slips a stage or two
While reading prose in that tough book he wrote   30
(Collating and emendating the same
And settling on the sense most to our mind),
We shut the clasps and find life's summer past.
Then, who helps more, pray, to repair our loss—
Another Boehme with a tougher book
And subtler meanings of what roses say,—
Or some stout Mage like him of Halberstadt,
John, who made things Boehme wrote thoughts about?
He with a "look you!" vents a brace of rhymes,
And in there breaks the sudden rose herself,   40
Over us, under, round us every side,
Nay, in and out the tables and the chairs
And musty volumes, Boehme's book and all,—
Buries us with a glory, young once more,
Pouring heaven into this shut house of life.

So come, the harp back to your heart again!
You are a poem, though your poem's naught.
The best of all you showed before, believe,
Was your own boy-face o'er the finer chords
Bent, following the cherub at the top   50
That points to God with his paired half-moon wings.

MISCONCEPTIONS

I

This is a spray the Bird clung to,
    Making it blossom with pleasure,
Ere the high tree-top she sprung to,
    Fit for her nest and her treasure.
    Oh, what a hope beyond measure
Was the poor spray's, which the flying feet hung to,—
So to be singled out, built in, and sung to!

II

This is a heart the Queen leant on,
    Thrilled in a minute erratic,
Ere the true bosom she bent on,
    Meet for love's regal dalmatic.
    Oh, what a fancy ecstatic
Was the poor heart's, ere the wanderer went on—
Love to be saved for it, proffered to, spent on!

ONE WORD MORE

to E. B. B.

I

There they are, my fifty men and women
Naming me the fifty poems finished!
Take them, Love, the book and me together:
Where the heart lies, let the brain lie also.

II

Rafael made a century of sonnets,
Made and wrote them in a certain volume
Dinted with the silver-pointed pencil
Else he only used to draw Madonnas:
These, the world might view—but one, the volume.
Who that one, you ask? Your heart instructs you.   10
Did she live and love it all her life-time?
Did she drop, his lady of the sonnets,
Die, and let it drop beside her pillow
Where it lay in place of Rafael's glory,
Rafael's cheek so duteous and so loving—
Cheek, the world was wont to hail a painter's,
Rafael's cheek, her love had turned a poet's?

III

You and I would rather read that volume,
(Taken to his beating bosom by it)
Lean and list the bosom-beats of Rafael,   20
Would we not? than wonder at Madonnas—
Her, San Sisto names, and Her, Foligno,
Her, that visits Florence in a vision,
Her, that's left with lilies in the Louvre—
Seen by us and all the world in circle.

IV

You and I will never read that volume.
Guido Reni, like his own eye's apple
Guarded long the treasure-book and loved it.
Guido Reni dying, all Bologna
Cried, and the world cried too, "Ours, the treasure!"   30
Suddenly, as rare things will, it vanished.

V

Dante once prepared to paint an angel:
Whom to please? You whisper "Beatrice."
While he mused and traced it and retraced it,
(Peradventure with a pen corroded

Still by drops of that hot ink he dipped for,
When, his left-hand i' the hair o' the wicked,
Back he held the brow and pricked its stigma,
Bit into the live man's flesh for parchment,
Loosed him, laughed to see the writing rankle,   40
Let the wretch go festering through Florence)—
Dante, who loved well because he hated,
Hated wickedness that hinders loving,
Dante standing, studying his angel,—
In there broke the folk of his Inferno.
Says he—"Certain people of importance"
(Such he gave his daily dreadful line to)
"Entered and would seize, forsooth, the poet."
Says the poet—"Then I stopped my painting."

VI

You and I would rather see that angel,   50
Painted by the tenderness of Dante,
Would we not?—than read a fresh Inferno.

VII

You and I will never see that picture.
While he mused on love and Beatrice,
While he softened o'er his outlined angel,
In they broke, those "people of importance:"
We and Bice bear the loss forever.

VIII

What of Rafael's sonnets, Dante's picture?
This: no artist lives and loves, that longs not
Once, and only once, and for one only,   60
(Ah, the prize!) to find his love a language
Fit and fair and simple and sufficient—
Using nature that's an art to others,
Not, this time, art that's turned his nature.
Ay, of all the artists living, loving,
None but would forego his proper dowry,—
Does he paint? he fain would write a poem,—
Does he write? he fain would paint a picture,
Put to proof art alien to the artist's,

Once, and only once, and for one only,   70
So to be the man and leave the artist,
Gain the man's joy, miss the artist's sorrow.

IX

Wherefore? Heaven's gift takes earth's abatement!
He who smites the rock and spreads the water,
Bidding drink and live a crowd beneath him,
Even he, the minute makes immortal,
Proves, perchance, but mortal in the minute,
Desecrates, belike, the deed in doing.
While he smites, how can he but remember,
So he smote before, in such a peril,   80
When they stood and mocked—"Shall smiting help us?"
When they drank and sneered—"A stroke is easy!"
When they wiped their mouths and went their journey,
Throwing him for thanks—"But drought was pleasant."
Thus old memories mar the actual triumph;
Thus the doing savors of disrelish;
Thus achievement lacks a gracious somewhat;
O'er-importuned brows becloud the mandate,
Carelessness or consciousness—the gesture.
For he bears an ancient wrong about him,   90
Sees and knows again those phalanxed faces,
Hears, yet one time more, the 'customed prelude—
"How shouldst thou, of all men, smite, and save us?"
Guesses what is like to prove the sequel—
"Egypt's flesh-pots—nay, the drought was better."

X

Oh, the crowd must have emphatic warrant!
Theirs, the Sinai-forehead's cloven brilliance,
Right-arm's rod-sweep, tongue's imperial fiat.
Never dares the man put off the prophet.

XI

Did he love one face from out the thousands,   100
(Were she Jethro's daughter, white and wifely,
Were she but the Æthiopian bondslave,)
He would envy yon dumb patient camel,

Keeping a reserve of scanty water
Meant to save his own life in the desert;
Ready in the desert to deliver
(Kneeling down to let his breast be opened)
Hoard and life together for his mistress.

XII

I shall never, in the years remaining,
Paint you pictures, no, nor carve you statues,   110
Make you music that should all-express me;
So it seems: I stand on my attainment.
This of verse alone, one life allows me;
Verse and nothing else have I to give you.
Other heights in other lives, God willing:
All the gifts from all the heights, your own, Love!

XIII

Yet a semblance of resource avails us—
Shade so finely touched, love's sense must seize it.
Take these lines, look lovingly and nearly,
Lines I write the first time and the last time.   120
He who works in fresco, steals a hair brush,
Curbs the liberal hand, subservient proudly,
Cramps his spirit, crowds its all in little,
Makes a strange art of an art familiar,
Fills his lady's missal-marge with flowerets.
He who blows thro' bronze, may breathe thro' silver,
Fitly serenade a slumbrous princess.
He who writes, may write for once as I do.

XIV

Love, you saw me gather men and women,
Live or dead or fashioned by my fancy,   130
Enter each and all, and use their service,
Speak from every mouth,—the speech, a poem.
Hardly shall I tell my joys and sorrows,
Hopes and fears, belief and disbelieving:
I am mine and yours—the rest be all men's,
Karshish, Cleon, Norbert and the fifty.
Let me speak this once in my true person,

Not as Lippo, Roland or Andrea,
Though the fruit of speech be just this sentence:
Pray you, look on these my men and women,   140
Take and keep my fifty poems finished;
Where my heart lies, let my brain lie also!
Poor the speech; be how I speak, for all things.

XV

Not but that you know me! Lo, the moon's self!
Here in London, yonder late in Florence,
Still we find her face, the thrice-transfigured.
Curving on a sky imbrued with color,
Drifted over Fiesole by twilight,
Came she, our new crescent of a hair's-breadth.
Full she flared it, lamping Samminiato,   150
Rounder 'twixt the cypresses and rounder,
Perfect till the nightingales applauded.
Now, a piece of her old self, impoverished,
Hard to greet, she traverses the houseroofs,
Hurries with unhandsome thrift of silver,
Goes dispiritedly, glad to finish.

XVI

What, there's nothing in the moon noteworthy?
Nay: for if that moon could love a mortal,
Use, to charm him (so to fit a fancy),
All her magic ('tis the old sweet mythos),   160
She would turn a new side to her mortal,
Side unseen of herdsman, huntsman, steersman—
Blank to Zoroaster on his terrace,
Blind to Galileo on his turret,
Dumb to Homer, dumb to Keats—him, even!
Think, the wonder of the moonstruck mortal—
When she turns round, comes again in heaven,
Opens out anew for worse or better!
Proves she like some portent of an iceberg
Swimming full upon the ship it founders,   170
Hungry with huge teeth of splintered crystals?
Proves she as the paved work of a sapphire
Seen by Moses when he climbed the mountain?
Moses, Aaron, Nadab and Abihu

Climbed and saw the very God, the Highest,
Stand upon the paved work of a sapphire.
Like the bodied heaven in his clearness
Shone the stone, the sapphire of that paved work,
When they ate and drank and saw God also!

XVII

What were seen? None knows, none ever shall know.   189
Only this is sure—the sight were other,
Not the moon's same side, born late in Florence,
Dying now impoverished here in London.
God be thanked, the meanest of his creatures
Boasts two soul-sides, one to face the world with,
One to show a woman when he loves her!

XVIII

This I say of me, but think of you, Love!
This to you—yourself my moon of poets!
Ah, but that's the world's side, there's the wonder,
Thus they see you, praise you, think they know you!   190
There, in turn I stand with them and praise you—
Out of my own self, I dare to phrase it.
But the best is when I glide from out them,
Cross a step or two of dubious twilight,
Come out on the other side, the novel
Silent silver lights and darks undreamed of,
Where I hush and bless myself with silence.

XIX

Oh, their Rafael of the dear Madonnas,
Oh, their Dante of the dread Inferno,
Wrote one song—and in my brain I sing it,   200
Drew one angel—borne, see, on my bosom!

                                        R. B.

From DRAMATIS PERSONAE [1864]

JAMES LEE'S WIFE

1. JAMES LEE'S WIFE SPEAKS AT THE WINDOW

I

Ah, Love, but a day
   And the world has changed!
The sun's away,
   And the bird estranged;
The wind has dropped,
   And the sky's deranged:
Summer has stopped.

II

Look in my eyes!
   Wilt thou change too?
Should I fear surprise?
   Shall I find aught new
In the old and dear,
   In the good and true,
With the changing year?

III

Thou art a man,
   But I am thy love.
For the lake, its swan;
   For the dell, its dove;
And for thee—(oh, haste!)
   Me, to bend above,
Me, to hold embraced.

2. BY THE FIRESIDE

I

Is all our fire of shipwreck wood,
       Oak and pine?
Oh, for the ills half-understood,
       The dim dead woe
       Long ago
Befallen this bitter coast of France!
Well, poor sailors took their chance;
       I take mine.

II

A ruddy shaft our fire must shoot
       O'er the sea:
Do sailors eye the casement—mute,
       Drenched and stark,
       From their bark—
And envy, gnash their teeth for hate
O' the warm safe house and happy freight
       —Thee and me?

III

God help you, sailors, at your need!
       Spare the curse!
For some ships, safe in port indeed,
       Rot and rust,
       Run to dust,
All through worms i' the wood, which crept,
Gnawed our hearts out while we slept:
       That is worse.

IV

Who lived here before us two?
       Old-world pairs.
Did a woman ever—would I knew!—
       Watch the man
       With whom began

Love's voyage full-sail,—(now, gnash your teeth!)
When planks start, open hell beneath
        Unawares?

3. IN THE DOORWAY

I

THE swallow has set her six young on the rail,
        And looks sea-ward:
The water's in stripes like a snake, olive-pale
        To the leeward,—
On the weather-side, black, spotted white with the wind.
"Good fortune departs, and disaster's behind,"—
Hark, the wind with its wants and its infinite wail!

II

Our fig-tree, that leaned for the saltness, has furled
        Her five fingers,
Each leaf like a hand opened wide to the world
        Where there lingers
No glint of the gold, Summer sent for her sake:
How the vines writhe in rows, each impaled on its stake!
My heart shrivels up and my spirit shrinks curled.

III

Yet here are we two; we have love, house enough,
        With the field there,
This house of four rooms, that field red and rough,
        Though it yield there,
For the rabbit that robs, scarce a blade or a bent;
If a magpie alight now, it seems an event;
And they both will be gone at November's rebuff.

IV

But why must cold spread? but wherefore bring change
        To the spirit,
God meant should mate his with an infinite range,
        And inherit

His power to put life in the darkness and cold?
Oh, live and love worthily, bear and be bold!
Whom Summer made friends of, let Winter estrange!

4. ALONG THE BEACH

I

I WILL be quiet and talk with you,
   And reason why you are wrong.
You wanted my love—is that much true?
And so I did love, so I do:
   What has come of it all along?

II

I took you—how could I otherwise?
   For a world to me, and more;
For all, love greatens and glorifies
Till God's a-glow, to the loving eyes,
   In what was mere earth before.

III

Yes, earth—yes, mere ignoble earth!
   Now do I mis-state, mistake?
Do I wrong your weakness and call it worth?
Expect all harvest, dread no dearth,
   Seal my sense up for your sake?

IV

Oh, Love, Love, no, Love! not so, indeed!
   You were just weak earth, I knew:
With much in you waste, with many a weed,
And plenty of passions run to seed,
   But a little good grain too.

V

And such as you were, I took you for mine:
   Did not you find me yours,

To watch the olive and wait the vine,
And wonder when rivers of oil and wine
   Would flow, as the Book assures?

VI

Well, and if none of these good things came,
   What did the failure prove?
The man was my whole world, all the same,
With his flowers to praise or his weeds to blame,
   And, either or both, to love.

VII

Yet this turns now to a fault—there! there!
   That I do love, watch too long,
And wait too well, and weary and wear;
And 'tis all an old story, and my despair
   Fit subject for some new song:

VIII

"How the light, light love, he has wings to fly
   At suspicion of a bond:
My wisdom has bidden your pleasure good-bye,
Which will turn up next in a laughing eye,
   And why should you look beyond?"

5. ON THE CLIFF

I

I LEANED on the turf,
I looked at a rock
Left dry by the surf;
For the turf, to call it grass were to mock:
Dead to the roots, so deep was done
The work of the summer sun.

II

And the rock lay flat
As an anvil's face:
No iron like that!
Baked dry; of a weed, of a shell, no trace:
Sunshine outside, but ice at the core,
Death's altar by the lone shore.

III

On the turf, sprang gay
With his films of blue,
No cricket, I'll say,
But a warhorse, barded and chanfroned too,
The gift of a quixote-mage to his knight,
Real fairy, with wings all right.

IV

On the rock, they scorch
Like a drop of fire
From a brandished torch,
Fall two red fans of a butterfly:
No turf, no rock: in their ugly stead,
See, wonderful blue and red!

V

Is it not so
With the minds of men?
The level and low,
The burnt and bare, in themselves; but then
With such a blue and red grace, not theirs,—
Love settling unawares!

6. READING A BOOK, UNDER THE CLIFF

I

"STILL ailing, Wind? Wilt be appeased or no?
Which needs the other's office, thou or I?

Dost want to be disburthened of a woe,
　　And can, in truth, my voice untie
Its links, and let it go?

II

"Art thou a dumb wronged thing that would be righted,
　　Entrusting thus thy cause to me? Forbear!
No tongue can mend such pleadings; faith, requited
　　With falsehood,—love, at last aware
Of scorn,—hopes, early blighted,—

III

"We have them; but I know not any tone
　　So fit as thine to falter forth a sorrow:
Dost think men would go mad without a moan,
　　If they knew any way to borrow
A pathos like thy own?

IV

"Which sigh wouldst mock, of all the sighs? The one
　　So long escaping from lips starved and blue,
That lasts while on her pallet-bed the nun
　　Stretches her length; her foot comes through
The straw she shivers on;

V

"You had not thought she was so tall: and spent,
　　Her shrunk lids open, her lean fingers shut
Close, close, their sharp and livid nails indent
　　The clammy palm; then all is mute:
That way, the spirit went.

VI

"Or wouldst thou rather that I understand
　　Thy will to help me?—like the dog I found
Once, pacing sad this solitary strand,
　　Who would not take my food, poor hound,
But whined and licked my hand."

VII

All this, and more, comes from some young man's pride
    Of power to see,—in failure and mistake,
Relinquishment, disgrace, on every side,—
    Merely examples for his sake,
Helps to his path untried:

VIII

Instances he must—simply recognize?
    Oh, more than so!—must, with a learner's zeal,
Make doubly prominent, twice emphasize,
    By added touches that reveal
The god in babe's disguise.

IX

Oh, he knows what defeat means, and the rest!
    Himself the undefeated that shall be:
Failure, disgrace, he flings them you to test,—
    His triumph, in eternity
To plainly manifest!

X

Whence, judge if he learn forthwith what the wind
    Means in its moaning—by the happy prompt
Instinctive way of youth, I mean; for kind
    Calm years, exacting their accompt
Of pain, mature fhe mind:

XI

And some midsummer morning, at the lull
    Just about daybreak, as he looks across
A sparkling foreign country, wonderful
    To the sea's edge for gloom and gloss,
Next minute must annul,—

XII

Then, when the wind begins among the vines,
    So low, so low, what shall it say but this?
"Here is the change beginning, here the lines
    Circumscribe beauty, set to bliss
The limit time assigns."

XIII

Nothing can be as it has been before;
    Better, so call it, only not the same.
To draw one beauty into our hearts' core,
    And keep it changeless! such our claim;
So answered,—Never more!

XIV

Simple? Why, this is the old woe o' the world;
    Tune, to whose rise and fall we live and die.
Rise with it, then! Rejoice that man is hurled
    From change to change unceasingly,
His soul's wings never furled!

XV

That's a new question; still replies the fact,
    Nothing endures: the wind moans, saying so;
We moan in acquiescence: there's life's pact,
    Perhaps probation—do *I* know?
God does: endure his act!

XVI

Only, for man, how bitter not to grave
    On his soul's hands' palms one fair good wise thing
Just as he grasped it! For himself, death's wave;
    While time first washes—ah, the sting!—
O'er all he'd sink to save.

7. AMONG THE ROCKS

I

Oh, GOOD gigantic smile o' the brown old earth,
   This autumn morning! How he sets his bones
To bask i' the sun, and thrusts out knees and feet
For the ripple to run over in its mirth;
   Listening the while, where on the heap of stones
The white breast of the sea-lark twitters sweet.

II

That is the doctrine, simple, ancient, true;
   Such is life's trial, as old earth smiles and knows.
If you loved only what were worth your love,
Love were clear gain, and wholly well for you:
   Make the low nature better by your throes!
Give earth yourself, go up for gain above!

8. BESIDE THE DRAWING BOARD

I

"As like as a Hand to another Hand!"
   Whoever said that foolish thing,
Could not have studied to understand
   The counsels of God in fashioning,
Out of the infinite love of his heart,
This Hand, whose beauty I praise, apart
From the world of wonder left to praise,
.If I tried to learn the other ways
Of love in its skill, or love in its power.
   "As like as a Hand to another Hand":
   Who said that, never took his stand,
Found and followed, like me, an hour,
The beauty in this,—how free, how fine
To fear, almost,—of the limit-line!
As I looked at this, and learned and drew,
   Drew and learned, and looked again,

While fast the happy minutes flew,
    Its beauty mounted into my brain,
    And a fancy seized me; I was fain
To efface my work, begin anew,
Kiss what before I only drew;
Ay, laying the red chalk 'twixt my lips,
    With soul to help if the mere lips failed,
    I kissed all right where the drawing ailed,
Kissed fast the grace that somehow slips
Still from one's soulless finger-tips.

II

'Tis a clay cast, the perfect thing,
    From Hand live once, dead long ago:
Princess-like it wears the ring
    To fancy's eye, by which we know
That here at length a master found
    His match, a proud lone soul its mate,
As soaring genius sank to ground,
    And pencil could not emulate
The beauty in this,—how free, how fine
To fear almost!—of the limit-line.
Long ago the god, like me
The worm, learned, each in our degree:
Looked and loved, learned and drew,
    Drew and learned and loved again,
While fast the happy minutes flew,
    Till beauty mounted into his brain
And on the finger which outvied
    His art he placed the ring that's there,
Still by fancy's eye descried,
    In token of a marriage rare:
    For him on earth, his art's despair,
For him in heaven, his soul's fit bride.

III

Little girl with the poor coarse hand
    I turned from to a cold clay cast—
I have my lesson, understand
    The worth of flesh and blood at last.
Nothing but beauty in a Hand?

Because he could not change the hue,
Mend the lines and make them true
To this which met his soul's demand,—
Would Da Vinci turn from you?
I hear him laugh my woes to scorn—
"The fool forsooth is all forlorn
Because the beauty, she thinks best,
Lived long ago or was never born,—
Because no beauty bears the test
In this rough peasant Hand! Confessed!
'Art is null and study void!'
So sayest thou? So said not I,
Who threw the faulty pencil by,
And years instead of hours employed,
Learning the veritable use
Of flesh and bone and nerve beneath
Lines and hue of the outer sheath,
If haply I might reproduce
One motive of the powers profuse,
Flesh and bone and nerve that make
The poorest coarsest human hand
An object worthy to be scanned
A whole life long for their sole sake.
Shall earth and the cramped moment-space
Yield the heavenly crowning grace?
Now the parts and then the whole!
Who art thou, with stinted soul
And stunted body, thus to cry
'I love,—shall that be life's strait dole?
I must live beloved or die!'
This peasant hand that spins the wool
And bakes the bread, why lives it on,
Poor and coarse with beauty gone,—
What use survives the beauty?" Fool!

Go little girl with the poor coarse hand!
I have my lesson, shall understand.

9. ON DECK

I

THERE is nothing to remember in me,
   Nothing I ever said with a grace,
Nothing I did that you care to see,
   Nothing I was that deserves a place
In your mind, now I leave you, set you free.

II

Conceded! In turn, concede to me,
   Such things have been as a mutual flame.
Your soul's locked fast; but, love for a key,
   You might let it loose, till I grew the same
In your eyes, as in mine you stand: strange plea!

III

For then, then, what would it matter to me
   That I was the harsh ill-favored one?
We both should be like as pea and pea;
   It was ever so since the world begun:
So, let me proceed with my reverie.

IV

How strange it were if you had all me,
   As I have all you in my heart and brain,
You, whose least word brought gloom or glee,
   Who never lifted the hand in vain—
Will hold mine yet, from over the sea!

V

Strange, if a face, when you thought of me,
   Rose like your own face present now,
With eyes as dear in their due degree,
   Much such a mouth, and as bright a brow,
Till you saw yourself, while you cried " 'Tis She!"

VI

Well, you may, you must, set down to me
    Love that was life, life that was love;
A tenure of breath at your lips' decree,
    A passion to stand as your thoughts approve,
A rapture to fall where your foot might be.

VII

But did one touch of such love for me
    Come in a word or a look of yours,
Whose words and looks will, circling, flee
    Round me and round while life endures,—
Could I fancy "As I feel, thus feels he";

VIII

Why, fade you might to a thing like me,
    And your hair grow these coarse hanks of hair,
Your skin, this bark of a gnarled tree,—
    You might turn myself!—should I know or care
When I should be dead of joy, James Lee?

THE WORST OF IT

I

WOULD it were I had been false, not you!
    I that am nothing, not you that are all:
I, never the worse for a touch or two
    On my speckled hide; not you, the pride
Of the day, my swan, that a first fleck's fall
    On her wonder of white must unswan, undo!

II

I had dipped in life's struggle and, out again,
    Bore specks of it here, there, easy to see,
When I found my swan and the cure was plain;
    The dull turned bright as I caught your white   10

On my bosom: you saved me—saved in vain
   If you ruined yourself, and all through me!

III

Yes, all through the speckled beast that I am,
   Who taught you to stoop; you gave me yourself,
And bound your soul by the vows that damn:
   Since on better thought you break, as you ought,
Vows—words, no angel set down, some elf
   Mistook,—for an oath, an epigram!

IV

Yes, might I judge you, here were my heart,
   And a hundred its like, to treat as you pleased!   20
I choose to be yours, for my proper part,
   Yours, leave or take, or mar me or make;
If I acquiesce, why should you be teased
   With the conscience-prick and the memory-smart?

V

But what will God say? Oh, my sweet,
   Think, and be sorry you did this thing!
Though earth were unworthy to feel your feet,
   There's a heaven above may deserve your love:
Should you forfeit heaven for a snapt gold ring
   And a promise broke, were it just or meet?   30

VI

And I to have tempted you! I, who tried
   Your soul, no doubt, till it sank! Unwise,
I loved and was lowly, loved and aspired,
   Loved, grieving or glad, till I made you mad,
And you meant to have hated and despised—
   Whereas, you deceived me nor inquired!

VII

She, ruined? How? No heaven for her?
   Crowns to give, and none for the brow

That looked like marble and smelt like myrrh?
   Shall the robe be worn, and the palm-branch borne   40
And she go graceless, she graced now
   Beyond all saints, as themselves aver?

VIII

Hardly! That must be understood!
   The earth is your place of penance, then;
And what will it prove? I desire your good,
   But, plot as I may, I can find no way
How a blow should fall, such as falls on men,
   Nor prove too much for your womanhood.

IX

It will come, I suspect, at the end of life,
   When you walk alone, and review the past;   50
And I, who so long shall have done with strife,
   And journeyed my stage and earned my wage
And retired as was right,—I am called at last
   When the devil stabs you, to lend the knife.

X

He stabs for the minute of trivial wrong,
   Nor the other hours are able to save,
The happy, that lasted my whole life long:
   For a promise broke, not for first words spoke,
The true, the only, that turn my grave
   To a blaze of joy and a crash of song.   60

XI

Witness beforehand! Off I trip
   On a safe path gay through the flowers you flung:
My very name made great by your lip,
   And my heart a-glow with the good I know
Of a perfect year when we both were young,
   And I tasted the angels' fellowship.

XII

And witness, moreover . . . Ah, but wait!
   I spy the loop whence an arrow shoots!
It may be for yourself, when you meditate,
   That you grieve—for slain ruth, murdered truth.   70
"Though falsehood escape in the end, what boots?
   How truth would have triumphed!"—you sigh too late.

XIII

Ay, who would have triumphed like you, I say!
   Well, it is lost now; well, you must bear,
Abide and grow fit for a better day:
   You should hardly grudge, could I be your judge!
But hush! For you, can be no despair:
   There's amends: 'tis a secret: hope and pray!

XIV

For I was true at least—oh, true enough!
   And, Dear, truth is not as good as it seems!   80
Commend me to conscience! Idle stuff!
   Much help is in mine, as I mope and pine,
And skulk through day, and scowl in my dreams
   At my swan's obtaining the crow's rebuff.

XV

Men tell me of truth now—"False!" I cry:
   Of beauty—"A mask, friend! Look beneath!"
We take our own method, the devil and I,
   With pleasant and fair and wise and rare:
And the best we wish to what lives, is—death;
   Which even in wishing, perhaps we lie!   90

XVI

Far better commit a fault and have done—
   As you, Dear!—forever; and choose the pure,
And look where the healing waters run,
   And strive and strain to be good again,

And a place in the other world ensure,
  All glass and gold, with God for its sun.

XVII

Misery! What shall I say or do?
  I cannot advise, or, at least, persuade:
Most like, you are glad you deceived me—rue
  No whit of the wrong: you endured too long,　　　100
Have done no evil and want no aid,
  Will live the old life out and chance the new.

XVIII

And your sentence is written all the same,
  And I can do nothing,—pray, perhaps:
But somehow the world pursues its game,—
  If I pray, if I curse,—for better or worse:
And my faith is torn to a thousand scraps,
  And my heart feels ice while my words breathe flame.

XIX

Dear, I look from my hiding-place.
  Are you still so fair? Have you still the eyes?　　　110
Be happy! Add but the other grace,
  Be good! Why want what the angels vaunt?
I knew you once: but in Paradise,
  If we meet, I will pass nor turn my face.

DÎS ALITER VISUM; OR, LE BYRON DE NOS JOURS

I

STOP, let me have the truth of that!
  Is that all true? I say, the day
Ten years ago when both of us
  Met on a morning, friends—as thus
We meet this evening, friends or what?—

II

Did you—because I took your arm
   And sillily smiled, "A mass of brass
That sea looks, blazing underneath!"
   While up the cliff-road edged with heath,
We took the turns nor came to harm—   10

III

Did you consider "Now makes twice
   That I have seen her, walked and talked
With this poor pretty thoughtful thing,
   Whose worth I weigh: she tries to sing;
Draws, hopes in time the eye grows nice;

IV

"Reads verse and thinks she understands;
   Loves all, at any rate, that's great,
Good, beautiful; but much as we
   Down at the bath-house love the sea,
Who breathe its salt and bruise its sands: 20

V

"While . . . do but follow the fishing-gull
   That flaps and floats from wave to cave!
There's the sea-lover, fair my friend!
   What then? Be patient, mark and mend!
Had you the making of your skull?"

VI

And did you, when we faced the church
   With spire and sad slate roof, aloof
From human fellowship so far,
   Where a few graveyard crosses are,
And garlands for the swallows' perch,—   30

VII

Did you determine, as we stepped
    O'er the lone stone fence, "Let me get
Her for myself, and what's the earth
    With all its art, verse, music, worth—
Compared with love, found, gained, and kept?

VIII

"Schumann's our music-maker now;
    Has his march-movement youth and mouth?
Ingres's the modern man that paints;
    Which will lean on me, of his saints?
Heine for songs; for kisses, how?"   40

IX

And did you, when we entered, reached
    The votive frigate, soft aloft
Riding on air this hundred years,
    Safe-smiling at old hopes and fears,—
Did you draw profit while she preached?

X

Resolving, "Fools we wise men grow!
    Yes, I could easily blurt out curt
Some question that might find reply
    As prompt in her stopped lips, dropped eye,
And rush of red to cheek and brow: 50

XI

"Thus were a match made, sure and fast,
    'Mid the blue weed-flowers round the mound
Where, issuing, we shall stand and stay
    For one more look at baths and bay,
Sands, sea-gulls, and the old church last—

XII

"A match 'twixt me, bent, wigged and lamed,
   Famous, however, for verse and worse,
Sure of the Fortieth spare Arm-chair
   When gout and glory seat me there,
So, one whose love-freaks pass unblamed,—   60

XIII

"And this young beauty, round and sound
   As a mountain-apple, youth and truth
With loves and doves, at all events
   With money in the Three per Cents;
Whose choice of me would seem profound:—

XIV

"She might take me as I take her.
   Perfect the hour would pass, alas!
Climb high, love high, what matter? Still,
   Feet, feelings, must descend the hill:
An hour's perfection can't recur.   70

XV

"Then follows Paris and full time
   For both to reason: 'Thus with us!'
She'll sigh, 'Thus girls give body and soul
   At first word, think they gain the goal,
When 'tis the starting-place they climb!

XVI

" 'My friend makes verse and gets renown;
   Have they all fifty years, his peers?
He knows the world, firm, quiet and gay;
   Boys will become as much one day:
They're fools; he cheats, with beard less brown.   80

XVII

" 'For boys say, *Love me or I die!*
    He did not say, *The truth is, youth*
I want, who am old and know too much;
    I'd catch youth: lend me sight and touch!
Drop heart's blood where life's wheels grate dry!'

XVIII

"While I should make rejoinder"—(then
    It was, no doubt, you ceased that least
Light pressure of my arm in yours)
    " 'I can conceive of cheaper cures
For a yawning-fit o'er books and men.   90

XIX

" 'What? All I am, was, and might be,
    All, books taught, art brought, life's whole strife,
Painful results since precious, just
    Were fitly exchanged, in wise disgust,
For two cheeks freshened by youth and sea?

XX

" 'All for a nosegay!—what came first;
    With fields on flower, untried each side;
I rally, need my books and men,
    And find a nosegay': drop it, then,
No match yet made for best or worst!"   100

XXI

That ended me. You judged the porch
    We left by, Norman; took our look
At sea and sky; wondered so few
    Find out the place for air and view;
Remarked the sun began to scorch;

XXII

Descended, soon regained the baths,
  And then, good-bye! Years ten since then:
Ten years! We meet: you tell me, now,
  By a window-seat for that cliff-brow,
On carpet-stripes for those sand-paths.   110

XXIII

Now I may speak: you fool, for all
  Your lore! WHO made things plain in vain?
What was the sea for? What, the gray
  Sad church, that solitary day,
Crosses and graves and swallows' call?

XXIV

Was there naught better than to enjoy?
  No feat which, done, would make time break,
And let us pent-up creatures through
  Into eternity, our due?
No forcing earth teach heaven's employ?   120

XXV

No wise beginning, here and now,
  What cannot grow complete (earth's feat)
And heaven must finish, there and then?
  No tasting earth's true food for men,
Its sweet in sad, its sad in sweet?

XXVI

No grasping at love, gaining a share
  O' the sole spark from God's life at strife
With death, so, sure of range above
  The limits here? For us and love,
Failure; but, when God fails, despair.   130

XXVII

This you call wisdom? Thus you add
   Good unto good again, in vain?
You loved, with body worn and weak;
   I loved, with faculties to seek:
Were both loves worthless since ill-clad?

XXVIII

Let the mere star-fish in his vault
   Crawl in a wash of weed, indeed,
Rose-jacynth to the finger-tips:
   He, whole in body and soul, outstrips
Man, found with either in default.   140

XXIX

But what's whole, can increase no more,
   Is dwarfed and dies, since here's its sphere.
The devil laughed at you in his sleeve!
   You knew not? That I well believe;
Or you had saved two souls: nay, four.

XXX

For Stephanie sprained last night her wrist,
   Ankle or something. "Pooh," cry you?
At any rate she danced, all say,
   Vilely; her vogue has had its day.
Here comes my husband from his whist.   150

TOO LATE

I

HERE was I with my arm and heart
   And brain, all yours for a word, a want
Put into a look—just a look, your part,—
   While mine, to repay it . . . vainest vaunt,

Were the woman, that's dead, alive to hear,
   Had her lover, that's lost, love's proof to show!
But I cannot show it; you cannot speak
   From the churchyard neither, miles removed,
Though I feel by a pulse within my cheek,
   Which stabs and stops, that the woman I loved   10
Needs help in her grave and finds none near,
   Wants warmth from the heart which sends it—so!

II

Did I speak once angrily, all the drear days
   You lived, you woman I loved so well,
Who married the other? Blame or praise,
   Where was the use then? Time would tell,
And the end declare what man for you,
   What woman for me, was the choice of God.
But, Edith dead! no doubting more!
   I used to sit and look at my life   20
As it rippled and ran till, right before,
   A great stone stopped it: oh, the strife
Of waves at the stone some devil threw
   In my life's midcurrent, thwarting God!

III

But either I thought, "They may churn and chide
   Awhile, my waves which came for their joy
And found this horrible stone full-tide:
   Yet I see just a thread escape, deploy
Through the evening-country, silent and safe,
   And it suffers no more till it finds the sea."   30
Or else I would think, "Perhaps some night
   When new things happen, a meteor-ball
May slip through the sky in a line of light,
   And earth breathe hard, and landmae,
And my waves no longer champ nor place: let be!"
   Since a stone will have rolled fro

IV

              , who may,
But, dead! All's done with:r who will.
   Watch and wear and

Oh, my whole life that ends to-day!
 Oh, my soul's sentence, sounding still,   40
"The woman is dead that was none of his;
 And the man that was none of hers may go!"
There's only the past left: worry that!
 Wreak, like a bull, on the empty coat,
Rage, its late wearer is laughing at!
 Tear the collar to rags, having missed his throat;
Strike stupidly on—"This, this and this,
 Where I would that a bosom received the blow!"

V

I ought to have done more: once my speech,
 And once your answer, and there, the end,   50
And Edith was henceforth out of reach!
 Why, men do more to deserve a friend,
Be rid of a foe, get rich, grow wise,
 Nor, folding their arms, stare fate in the face.
Why, better even have burst like a thief
 And borne you away to a rock for us two,
In a moment's horror, bright, bloody and brief:
 Then changed to myself again—"I slew
Myself in that moment; a ruffian lies
 Somewhere: your slave, see, born in his place!"   60

VI

What did the other do? You be judge!
 Lo us, Edith! Here are we both!
 None is six whole years: I grudge
Myself the life with you, nay, loathe
 Of me who grudged his start in advance
But, as if he would overtake and pass.
 Nor any one you! No, not he,
Who ever heard in the world, 'tis plain:
 As I, young, proud, another, free
Poured life out, profits, sound and sane,   70
 Of those eyes of your—"Half a glance
  And I drop the glass!"

VII

Handsome, were you? 'Tis more than they held,
  More than they said; I was 'ware and watched:
I was the 'scapegrace, this rat belled
  The cat, this fool got his whiskers scratched:
The others? No head that was turned, no heart
  Broken, my lady, assure yourself!
Each soon made his mind up; so and so
  Married a dancer, such and such   80
Stole his friend's wife, stagnated slow,
  Or maundered, unable to do as much,
And muttered of peace where he had no part:
  While, hid in the closet, laid on the shelf,—

VIII

On the whole, you were let alone, I think!
  So, you looked to the other, who acquiesced;
My rival, the proud man,—prize your pink
  Of poets! A poet he was! I've guessed:
He rhymed you his rubbish nobody read,
  Loved you and doved you—did not I laugh!   90
There was a prize! But we both were tried.
  Oh, heart of mine, marked broad with her mark,
Tekel, found wanting, set aside,
  Scorned! See, I bleed these tears in the dark
Till comfort come and the last be bled:
  He? He is tagging your epitaph.

IX

If it would only come over again!
  —Time to be patient with me, and probe
This heart till you punctured the proper vein,
  Just to learn what blood is: twitch the robe   100
From that blank lay-figure your fancy draped,
  Prick the leathern heart till the—verses spirt!
And late it was easy; late, you walked
  Where a friend might meet you; Edith's name
Arose to one's lip if one laughed or talked;
  If I heard good news, you heard the same;

When I woke, I knew that your breath escaped;
I could bide my time, keep alive, alert.

X

And alive I shall keep and long, you will see!
I knew a man, was kicked like a dog   110
From gutter to cesspool; what cared he
So long as he picked from the filth his prog?
He saw youth, beauty and genius die,
And jollily lived to his hundredth year.
But I will live otherwise: none of such life!
At once I begin as I mean to end.
Go on with the world, get gold in its strife,
Give your spouse the slip and betray your friend!
There are two who decline, a woman and I,
And enjoy our death in the darkness here.   120

XI

I liked that way you.had with your curls
Wound to a ball in a net behind:
Your cheek was chaste as a quaker-girl's,
And your mouth—there was never, to my mind,
Such a funny mouth, for it would not shut;
And the dented chin too—what a chin!
There were certain ways when you spoke, some words
That you know you never could pronounce:
You were thin, however; like a bird's
Your hand seemed—some would say the pounce   130
Of a scaly-footed hawk—all but!
The world was right when it called you thin.

XII

But I turn my back on the world: I take
Your hand, and kneel, and lay to my lips.
Bid me live, Edith! Let me slake
Thirst at your presence! Fear no slips:
'Tis your slave shall pay, while his soul endures,
Full due, love's whole debt, *summum jus*.
My queen shall have high observance, planned
Courtship made perfect, no least line   140

Crossed without warrant. There you stand,
    Warm too, and white too: would this wine
Had washed all over that body of yours,
    Ere I drank it, and you down with it, thus!

ABT VOGLER

*(After he has been extemporizing upon the musical
instrument of his invention)*

I

WOULD that the structure brave, the manifold music I build,
    Bidding my organ obey, calling its keys to their work,
Claiming each slave of the sound, at a touch, as when Solomon
    willed
    Armies of angels that soar, legions of demons that lurk,
Man, brute, reptile, fly,—alien of end and of aim,
    Adverse, each from the other heaven-high, hell-deep re-
    moved,—
Should rush into sight at once as he named the ineffable Name,
    And pile him a palace straight, to pleasure the princess he
    loved!

II

Would it might tarry like his, the beautiful building of mine,
    This which my keys in a crowd pressed and importuned to
    raise!   10
Ah, one and all, how they helped, would dispart now and now
    combine,
    Zealous to hasten the work, heighten their master his praise!
And one would bury his brow with a blind plunge down to hell,
    Burrow awhile and build, broad on the roots of things,
Then up again swim into sight, having based me my palace well,
    Founded it, fearless of flame, flat on the nether springs.

III

And another would mount and march, like the excellent minion
    he was,
    Ay, another and yet another, one crowd but with many a crest,

Raising my rampired walls of gold as transparent as glass,
    Eager to do and die, yield each his place to the rest: 20
For higher still and higher (as a runner tips with fire,
    When a great illumination surprises a festal night—
Outlining round and round Rome's dome from space to spire)
    Up, the pinnacled glory reached, and the pride of my soul was
    in sight.

IV

In sight? Not half! for it seemed, it was certain, to match man's
    birth,
    Nature in turn conceived, obeying an impulse as I;
And the emulous heaven yearned down, made effort to reach the
    earth,
    As the earth had done her best, in my passion, to scale the sky:
Novel splendors burst forth, grew familiar and dwelt with mine,
    Not a point nor peak but found and fixed its wandering
    star;   30
Meteor-moons, balls of blaze: and they did not pale nor pine,
    For earth had attained to heaven, there was no more near nor
    far.

V

Nay more; for there wanted not who walked in the glare and
    glow,
    Presences plain in the place; or, fresh from the Protoplast,
Furnished for ages to come, when a kindlier wind should blow,
    Lured now to begin and live, in a house to their liking at last;
Or else the wonderful Dead who have passed through the body
    and gone,
    But were back once more to breathe in an old world worth
    their new:
What never had been, was now; what was, as it shall be anon;
    And what is,—shall I say, matched both? for I was made
    perfect too.   40

VI

All through my keys that gave their sounds to a wish of my soul,
    All through my soul that praised as its wish flowed visibly
    forth,
All through music and me! For think, had I painted the whole,
    Why, there it had stood, to see, nor the process so wonder-
    worth:

Had I written the same, made verse—still, effect proceeds from
  cause,
  Ye know why the forms are fair, ye hear how the tale is told;
It is all triumphant art, but art in obedience to laws,
  Painter and poet are proud in the artist-list enrolled:—

VII

But here is the finger of God, a flash of the will that can,
  Existent behind all laws, that made them and, lo, they
    are!   50
And I know not if, save in this, such gift be allowed to man,
  That out of three sounds he frame, not a fourth sound, but a
    star.
Consider it well: each tone of our scale in itself is naught;
  It is everywhere in the world—loud, soft, and all is said:
Give it to me to use! I mix it with two in my thought:
  And, there! Ye have heard and seen: consider and bow the
    head!

VIII

Well, it is gone at last, the palace of music I reared;
  Gone! and the good tears start, the praises that come too slow;
For one is assured at first, one scarce can say that he feared,
  That he even gave it a thought, the gone thing was to go.   60
Never to be again! But many more of the kind
  As good, nay, better perchance: is this your comfort to me?
To me, who must be saved because I cling with my mind
  To the same, same self, same love, same God: ay, what was,
    shall be.

IX

Therefore to whom turn I but to thee, the ineffable Name?
  Builder and maker, thou, of houses not made with hands!
What, have fear of change from thee who art ever the same?
  Doubt that thy power can fill the heart that thy power ex-
    pands?
There shall never be one lost good! What was, shall live as
  before;
  The evil is null, is naught, is silence implying sound;   70
What was good shall be good, with, for evil, so much good more;
  On the earth the broken arcs; in the heaven, a perfect round.

X

All we have willed or hoped or dreamed of good shall exist;
    Not its semblance, but itself; no beauty, nor good, nor power
Whose voice has gone forth, but each survives for the melodist
    When eternity affirms the conception of an hour.
The high that proved too high, the heroic for earth too hard,
    The passion that left the ground to lose itself in the sky,
Are music sent up to God by the lover and the bard;
    Enough that he heard it once: we shall hear it by-and-by. 80

XI

And what is our failure here but a triumph's evidence
    For the fulness of the days? Have we withered or agonized?
Why else was the pause prolonged but that singing might issue
    thence?
    Why rushed the discords in but that harmony should be
    prized?
Sorrow is hard to bear, and doubt is slow to clear,
    Each sufferer says his say, his scheme of the weal and woe:
But God has a few of us whom he whispers in the ear;
    The rest may reason and welcome: 'tis we musicians know.

XII

Well, it is earth with me; silence resumes her reign:
    I will be patient and proud, and soberly acquiesce. 90
Give me the keys. I feel for the common chord again,
    Sliding by semitones, till I sink to the minor,—yes,
And I blunt it into a ninth, and I stand on alien ground,
    Surveying awhile the heights I rolled from into the deep;
Which, hark, I have dared and done, for my resting-place is
    found,
    The C Major of this life: so, now I will try to sleep.

RABBI BEN EZRA

I

Grow old along with me!
The best is yet to be,
The last of life, for which the first was made:
Our times are in His hand
Who saith "A whole I planned,
Youth shows but half; trust God: see all nor be afraid!"

II

Not that, amassing flowers,
Youth sighed "Which rose make ours,
Which lily leave and then as best recall?"
Not that, admiring stars,   10
It yearned "Nor Jove, nor Mars;
Mine be some figured flame which blends, transcends them all!"

III

Not for such hopes and fears
Annulling youth's brief years,
Do I remonstrate: folly wide the mark!
Rather I prize the doubt
Low kinds exist without,
Finished and finite clods, untroubled by a spark.

IV

Poor vaunt of life indeed,
Were man but formed to feed   20
On joy, to solely seek and find and feast:
Such feasting ended, then
As sure an end to men;
Irks care the crop-full bird? Frets doubt the maw-crammed
        beast?

V

Rejoice we are allied
To That which doth provide

And not partake, effect and not receive!
    A spark disturbs our clod;
    Nearer we hold of God
Who gives, than of His tribes that take, I must believe.   30

VI

    Then, welcome each rebuff
    That turns earth's smoothness rough,
Each sting that bids nor sit nor stand but go!
    Be our joys three-parts pain!
    Strive, and hold cheap the strain;
Learn, nor account the pang; dare, never grudge the throe!

VII

    For thence,—a paradox
    Which comforts while it mocks,—
Shall life succeed in that it seems to fail:
    What I aspired to be,   40
    And was not, comforts me:
A brute I might have been, but would not sink i' the scale.

VIII

    What is he but a brute
    Whose flesh has soul to suit,
Whose spirit works lest arms and legs want play?
    To man, propose this test—
    Thy body at its best,
How far can that project thy soul on its lone way?

IX

    Yet gifts should prove their use:
    I own the Past profuse   50
Of power each side, perfection every turn:
    Eyes, ears took in their dole,
    Brain treasured up the whole;
uld not the heart beat once "How good to live and learn"?

X

Not once beat "Praise be Thine!
I see the whole design,
I, who saw power, see now love perfect too:
Perfect I call Thy plan:
Thanks that I was a man!
Maker, remake, complete,—I trust what Thou shalt do!"   60

XI

For pleasant is this flesh;
Our soul, in its rose-mesh
Pulled ever to the earth, still yearns for rest;
Would we some prize might hold
To match those manifold
Possessions of the brute,—gain most, as we did best!

XII

Let us not always say
"Spite of this flesh to-day
I strove, made head, gained ground upon the whole!"
As the bird wings and sings,   70
Let us cry "All good things
Are ours, nor soul helps flesh more, now, than flesh helps soul!"

XIII

Therefore I summon age
To grant youth's heritage,
Life's struggle having so far reached its term:
Thence shall I pass, approved
A man, for aye removed
From the developed brute; a god though in the germ.

XIV

And I shall thereupon
Take rest, ere I be gone   80
Once more on my adventure brave and new:
Fearless and unperplexed,

When I wage battle next,
What weapons to select, what armor to indue.

XV

Youth ended, I shall try
My gain or loss thereby;
Leave the fire ashes, what survives is gold:
And I shall weigh the same,
Give life its praise or blame:
Young, all lay in dispute; I shall know, being old.   90

XVI

For note, when evening shuts,
A certain moment cuts
The deed off, calls the glory from the gray:
A whisper from the west
Shoots—"Add this to the rest,
Take it and try its worth: here dies another day."

XVII

So, still within this life,
Though lifted o'er its strife,
Let me discern, compare, pronounce at last,
"This rage was right i' the main,   100
That acquiescence vain:
The Future I may face now I have proved the Past."

XVIII

For more is not reserved
To man, with soul just nerved
To act to-morrow what he learns to-day:
Here, work enough to watch
The Master work, and catch
ᵗints of the proper craft, tricks of the tool's true play.

XIX

Sʰ ᵗit was better, youth
ld strive, through acts uncouth,   110

Toward making, than repose on aught found made:
   So, better, age, exempt
   From strife, should know, than tempt
Further. Thou waitedest age: wait death nor be afraid!

XX

   Enough now, if the Right
   And Good and Infinite
Be named here, as thou callest thy hand thine own,
   With knowledge absolute,
   Subject to no dispute
From fools that crowded youth, nor let thee feel alone.   120

XXI

   Be there, for once and all,
   Severed great minds from small,
Announced to each his station in the Past!
   Was I, the world arraigned,
   Were they, my soul disdained,
Right? Let age speak the truth and give us peace at last!

XXII

   Now, who shall arbitrate?
   Ten men love what I hate,
Shun what I follow, slight what I receive;
   Ten, who in ears and eyes   130
   Match me: we all surmise,
They this thing, and I that: whom shall my soul believe?

XXIII

   Not on the vulgar mass
   Called "work," must sentence pass,
Things done, that took the eye and had the price;
   O'er which, from level stand,
   The low world laid its hand,
Found straightway to its mind, could value in a trice:

XXIV

But all, the world's coarse thumb
And finger failed to plumb,   140
So passed in making up the main account;
All instincts immature,
All purposes unsure,
That weighed not as his work, yet swelled the man's amount:

XXV

Thoughts hardly to be packed
Into a narrow act,
Fancies that broke through language and escaped;
All I could never be,
All, men ignored in me,
This, I was worth to God, whose wheel the pitcher shaped.   150

XXVI

Ay, note that Potter's wheel,
That metaphor! and feel
Why time spins fast, why passive lies our clay,—
Thou, to whom fools propound,
When the wine makes its round,
"Since life fleets, all is change; the Past gone, seize to-day!"

XXVII

Fool! All that is, at all,
Lasts ever, past recall;
Earth changes, but thy soul and God stand sure:
What entered into thee,   160
That was, is, and shall be:
Time's wheel runs back or stops: Potter and clay endure.

XXVIII

He fixed thee 'mid this dance
Of plastic circumstance,
This Present, thou, forsooth, wouldst fain arrest:

Machinery just meant
To give thy soul its bent,
Try thee and turn thee forth, sufficiently impressed.

XXIX

What though the earlier grooves
Which ran the laughing loves   170
Around thy base, no longer pause and press?
What though, about thy rim,
Skull-things in order grim
Grow out, in graver mood, obey the sterner stress?

XXX

Look not thou down but up!
To uses of a cup,
The festal board, lamp's flash and trumpet's peal,
The new wine's foaming flow,
The Master's lips a-glow!
Thou, heaven's consummate cup, what need'st thou with earth's
                    wheel?   180

XXXI

But I need, now as then,
Thee, God, who mouldest men;
And since, not even while the whirl was worst,
Did I,—to the wheel of life
With shapes and colors rife,
Bound dizzily,—mistake my end, to slake Thy thirst:

XXXII

So, take and use Thy work:
Amend what flaws may lurk,
What strain o' the stuff, what warpings past the aim!
My times be in Thy hand!   190
Perfect the cup as planned!
Let age approve of youth, and death complete the same!

A DEATH IN THE DESERT

[Supposed of Pamphylax the Antiochene:
It is a parchment, of my rolls the fifth,
Hath three skins glued together, is all Greek
And goeth from *Epsilon* down to *Mu:*
Lies second in the surnamed Chosen Chest,
Stained and conserved with juice of terebinth,
Covered with cloth of hair, and lettered *Xi,*
From Xanthus, my wife's uncle, now at peace:
Mu and *Epsilon* stand for my own name.
I may not write it, but I make a cross   10
To show I wait His coming, with the rest,
And leave off here: beginneth Pamphylax.]

I said, "If one should wet his lips with wine,
And slip the broadest plantain-leaf we find,
Or else the lappet of a linen robe,
Into the water-vessel, lay it right,
And cool his forehead just above the eyes,
The while a brother, kneeling either side,
Should chafe each hand and try to make it warm,—
He is not so far gone but he might speak."   20

This did not happen in the outer cave,
Nor in the secret chamber of the rock
Where, sixty days since the decree was out,
We had him, bedded on a camel-skin,
And waited for his dying all the while;
But in the midmost grotto: since noon's light
Reached there a little, and we would not lose
The last of what might happen on his face.

I at the head, and Xanthus at the feet,
With Valens and the Boy, had lifted him,   30
And brought him from the chamber in the depths,
And laid him in the light where we might see:
For certain smiles began about his mouth,
And his lids moved, presageful of the end.

Beyond, and half way up the mouth o' the cave,
The Bactrian convert, having his desire,
Kept watch, and made pretence to graze a goat
That gave us milk, on rags of various herb,
Plantain and quitch, the rocks' shade keeps alive:
So that if any thief or soldier passed,   40
(Because the persecution was aware)
Yielding the goat up promptly with his life,
Such man might pass on, joyful at a prize,
Nor care to pry into the cool o' the cave.
Outside was all noon and the burning blue.

"Here is wine," answered Xanthus,—dropped a drop;
I stooped and placed the lap of cloth aright,
Then chafed his right hand, and the Boy his left:
But Valens had bethought him, and produced
And broke a ball of nard, and made perfume.   50
Only, he did—not so much wake, as—turn
And smile a little, as a sleeper does
If any dear one call him, touch his face—
And smiles and loves, but will not be disturbed.
Then Xanthus said a prayer, but still he slept:
It is the Xanthus that escaped to Rome,
Was burned, and could not write the chronicle.

Then the Boy sprang up from his knees, and ran,
Stung by the splendor of a sudden thought,
And fetched the seventh plate of graven lead   60
Out of the secret chamber, found a place,
Pressing with finger on the deeper dints,
And spoke, as 't were his mouth proclaiming first,
"I am the Resurrection and the Life."

Whereat he opened his eyes wide at once,
And sat up of himself, and looked at us;
And thenceforth nobody pronounced a word:
Only, outside, the Bactrian cried his cry
Like the lone desert-bird that wears the ruff,
As signal we were safe, from time to time.   70

First he said, "If a friend declared to me,
This my son Valens, this my other son,
Were James and Peter,—nay, declared as well

This lad was very John,—I could believe!
—Could, for a moment, doubtlessly believe:
So is myself withdrawn into my depths,
The soul retreated from the perished brain
Whence it was wont to feel and use the world
Through these dull members, done with long ago.
Yet I myself remain; I feel myself: 80
And there is nothing lost. Let be, awhile!"

[This is the doctrine he was wont to teach,
How divers persons witness in each man,
Three souls which make up one soul: first, to wit,
A soul of each and all the bodily parts,
Seated therein, which works, and is what Does,
And has the use of earth, and ends the man
Downward: but, tending upward for advice,
Grows into, and again is grown into
By the next soul, which, seated in the brain,   90
Useth the first with its collected use,
And feeleth, thinketh, willeth,—is what Knows:
Which, duly tending upward in its turn,
Grows into, and again is grown into
By the last soul, that uses both the first,
Subsisting whether they assist or no,
And, constituting man's self, is what Is—
And leans upon the former, makes it play,
As that played off the first: and, tending up,
Holds, is upheld by, God, and ends the man   100
Upward in that dread point of intercourse,
Nor needs a place, for it returns to Him.
What Does, what Knows, what Is; three souls, one man.
I give the glossa of Theotypas.]

And then, "A stick, once fire from end to end;
Now, ashes save the tip that holds a spark!
Yet, blow the spark, it runs back, spreads itself
A little where the fire was: thus I urge
The soul that served me, till it task once more
What ashes of my brain have kept their shape,   110
And these make effort on the last o' the flesh,
Trying to taste again the truth of things—"
(He smiled)—"their very superficial truth:
As that ye are my sons, that it is long

Since James and Peter had release by death,
And I am only he, your brother John,
Who saw and heard, and could remember all.
Remember all! It is not much to say.
What if the truth broke on me from above
As once and oft-times? Such might hap again: 120
Doubtlessly He might stand in presence here,
With head wool-white, eyes flame, and feet like brass,
The sword and the seven stars, as I have seen—
I who now shudder only and surmise
'How did your brother bear that sight and live?'

"If I live yet, it is for good, more love
Through me to men: be naught but ashes here
That keep awhile my semblance, who was John,—
Still, when they scatter, there is left on earth
No one alive who knew (consider this!)   130
—Saw with his eyes and handled with his hands
That which was from the first, the Word of Life.
How will it be when none more saith 'I saw'?

"Such ever was love's way: to rise, it stoops.
Since I, whom Christ's mouth taught, was bidden teach,
I went, for many years, about the world,
Saying 'It was so; so I heard and saw,'
Speaking as the case asked: and men believed.
Afterward came the message to myself
In Patmos isle; I was not bidden teach,   140
But simply listen, take a book and write,
Nor set down other than the given word,
With nothing left to my arbitrament
To choose or change: I wrote, and men believed.
Then, for my time grew brief, no message more,
No call to write again, I found a way,
And, reasoning from my knowledge, merely taught
Men should, for love's sake, in love's strength believe;
Or I would pen a letter to a friend
And urge the same as friend, nor less nor more: 150
Friends said I reasoned rightly, and believed.
But at the last, why, I seemed left alive
Like a sea-jelly weak on Patmos strand,
To tell dry sea-beach gazers how I fared
When there was mid-sea, and the mighty things;

Left to repeat, 'I saw, I heard, I knew,'
And go all over the old ground again,
With Antichrist already in the world,
And many Antichrists, who answered prompt
'Am I not Jasper as thyself art John?   160
Nay, young, whereas through age thou mayest forget:
Wherefore, explain, or how shall we believe?'
I never thought to call down fire on such,
Or, as in wonderful and early days,
Pick up the scorpion, tread the serpent dumb;
But patient stated much of the Lord's life
Forgotten or misdelivered, and let it work:
Since much that at the first, in deed and word,
Lay simply and sufficiently exposed,
Had grown (or else my soul was grown to match,   170
Fed through such years, familiar with such light,
Guarded and guided still to see and speak)
Of new significance and fresh result;
What first were guessed as points, I now knew stars,
And named them in the Gospel I have writ.
For men said, 'It is getting long ago:
Where is the promise of His coming?'—asked
These young ones in their strength, as loth to wait,
Of me who, when their sires were born, was old.
I, for I loved them, answered, joyfully,   180
Since I was there, and helpful in my age;
And, in the main, I think such men believed.
Finally, thus endeavoring, I fell sick,
Ye brought me here, and I supposed the end,
And went to sleep with one thought that, at least,
Though the whole earth should lie in wickedness,
We had the truth, might leave the rest to God.
Yet now I wake in such decrepitude
As I had slidden down and fallen afar,
Past even the presence of my former self,   190
Grasping the while for stay at facts which snap,
Till I am found away from my own world,
Feeling for foot-hold through a blank profound,
Along with unborn people in strange lands,
Who say—I hear said or conceive they say—
'Was John at all, and did he say he saw?
Assure us, ere we ask what he might see!'

"And how shall I assure them? Can they share
—They, who have flesh, a veil of youth and strength
About each spirit, that needs must bide its time, 200
Living and learning still as years assist
Which wear the thickness thin, and let man see—
With me who hardly am withheld at all,
But shudderingly, scarce a shred between,
Lie bare to the universal prick of light?
Is it for nothing we grow old and weak,
We whom God loves? When pain ends, gain ends too.
To me, that story—ay, that Life and Death
Of which I wrote 'it was'—to me, it is;
—Is, here and now: I apprehend naught else. 210
Is not God now i' the world His power first made?
Is not His love at issue still with sin,
Visibly when a wrong is done on earth?
Love, wrong, and pain, what see I else around?
Yea, and the Resurrection and Uprise
To the right hand of the throne—what is it beside,
When such truth, breaking bounds, o'erfloods my soul,
And, as I saw the sin and death, even so
See I the need yet transiency of both,
The good and glory consummated thence? 220
I saw the power; I see the Love, once weak,
Resume the Power: and in this word 'I see,'
Lo, there is recognized the Spirit of both
That moving o'er the spirit of man, unblinds
His eye and bids him look. These are, I see;
But ye, the children, His beloved ones too,
Ye need,—as I should use an optic glass
I wondered at erewhile, somewhere i' the world,
It had been given a crafty smith to make;
A tube, he turned on objects brought too close, 230
Lying confusedly insubordinate
For the unassisted eye to master once:
Look through his tube, at distance now they lay,
Become succinct, distinct, so small, so clear!
Just thus, ye needs must apprehend what truth
I see, reduced to plain historic fact,
Diminished into clearness, proved a point
And far away: ye would withdraw your sense
From out eternity, strain it upon time,

Then stand before that fact, that Life and Death.   240
Stay there at gaze, till it dispart, dispread,
As though a star should open out, all sides,
Grow the world on you, as it is my world.

"For life, with all it yields of joy and woe,
And hope and fear,—believe the aged friend,—
Is just our chance o' the prize of learning love,
How love might be, hath been indeed, and is;
And that we hold thenceforth to the uttermost
Such prize despite the envy of the world,
And, having gained truth, keep truth: that is all.   250
But see the double way wherein we are led,
How the soul learns diversely from the flesh!
With flesh, that hath so little time to stay,
And yields mere basement for the soul's emprise,
Expect prompt teaching. Helpful was the light,
And warmth was cherishing and food was choice
To every man's flesh, thousand years ago,
As now to yours and mine; the body sprang
At once to the height, and stayed: but the soul,—no!
Since sages who, this noontide, meditate   260
In Rome or Athens, may descry some point
Of the eternal power, hid yestereve;
And, as thereby the power's whole mass extends,
So much extends the æther floating o'er,
The love that tops the night, the Christ in God.
Then, as new lessons shall be learned in these
Till earth's work stop and useless time run out,
So duly, daily, needs provision be
For keeping the soul's prowess possible,
Building new barriers as the old decay,   270
Saving us from evasion of life's proof,
Putting the question ever, 'Does God love,
And will ye hold that truth against the world?'
Ye know there needs no second proof with good
Gained for our flesh from any earthly source:
We might go freezing, ages,—give us fire,
Thereafter we judge fire at its full worth,
And guard it safe through every chance, ye know!
That fable of Prometheus and his theft,
How mortals gained Jove's fiery flower, grows old   280
(I have been used to hear the pagans own)

And out of mind; but fire, howe'er its birth,
Here is it, precious to the sophist now
Who laughs the myth of Æschylus to scorn,
As precious to those satyrs of his play,
Who touched it in gay wonder at the thing.
While were it so with the soul,—this gift of truth
Once grasped, were this our soul's gain safe, and sure
To prosper as the body's gain is wont,—
Why, man's probation would conclude, his earth   290
Crumble; for he both reasons and decides,
Weighs first, then chooses: will he give up fire
For gold or purple once he knows its worth?
Could he give Christ up were His worth as plain?
Therefore, I say, to test man, the proofs shift,
Nor may he grasp that fact like other fact,
And straightway in his life acknowledge it,
As, say, the indubitable bliss of fire.
Sigh ye, 'It had been easier once than now'?
To give you answer I am left alive;   300
Look at me who was present from the first!
Ye know what things I saw; then came a test,
My first, befitting me who so had seen:
'Forsake the Christ thou sawest transfigured, Him
Who trod the sea and brought the dead to life?
What should wring this from thee!'—ye laugh and ask.
What wrung it? Even a torchlight and a noise,
The sudden Roman faces, violent hands,
And fear of what the Jews might do! Just that,
And it is written, 'I forsook and fled:'   310
There was my trial, and it ended thus.
Ay, but my soul had gained its truth, could grow:
Another year or two,—what little child,
What tender woman that had seen no least
Of all my sights, but barely heard them told,
Who did not clasp the cross with a light laugh,
Or wrap the burning robe round, thanking God?
Well, was truth safe forever, then? Not so.
Already had begun the silent work
Whereby truth, deadened of its absolute blaze,   320
Might need love's eye to pierce the o'erstretched doubt.
Teachers were busy, whispering 'All is true
As the aged ones report; but youth can reach
Where age gropes dimly, weak with stir and strain,

And the full doctrine slumbers till to-day.'
Thus, what the Roman's lowered spear was found,
A bar to me who touched and handled truth,
Now proved the glozing of some new shrewd tongue,
This Ebion, this Cerinthus or their mates,
Till imminent was the outcry 'Save our Christ!'   330
Whereon I stated much of the Lord's life
Forgotten or misdelivered, and let it work.
Such work done, as it will be, what comes next?
What do I hear say, or conceive men say,
'Was John at all, and did he say he saw?
Assure us, ere we ask what he might see!'
Is this indeed a burthen for late days,
And may I help to bear it with you all,
Using my weakness which becomes your strength?
For if a babe were born inside this grot,   340
Grew to a boy here, heard us praise the sun,
Yet had but yon sole glimmer in light's place,—
One loving him and wishful he should learn,
Would much rejoice himself was blinded first
Month by month here, so made to understand
How eyes, born darkling, apprehend amiss:
I think I could explain to such a child
There was more glow outside than gleams he caught,
Ay, nor need urge 'I saw it, so believe!'
It is a heavy burthen you shall bear   350
In latter days, new lands, or old grown strange,
Left without me, which must be very soon.
What is the doubt, my brothers? Quick with it!
I see you stand conversing, each new face,
Either in fields, of yellow summer eves,
On islets yet unnamed amid the sea;
Or pace for shelter 'neath a portico
Out of the crowd in some enormous town
Where now the larks sing in a solitude;
Or muse upon blank heaps of stone and sand   360
Idly conjectured to be Ephesus:
And no one asks his fellow any more
'Where is the promise of His coming?' but
'Was he revealed in any of His lives,
As Power, as Love, as Influencing Soul?'

"Quick, for time presses, tell the whole mind out,

And let us ask and answer and be saved!
My book speaks on, because it cannot pass;
One listens quietly, nor scoffs but pleads
'Here is a tale of things done ages since;   370
What truth was ever told the second day?
Wonders, that would prove doctrine, go for naught.
Remains the doctrine, love; well, we must love,
And what we love most, power and love in one,
Let us acknowledge on the record here,
Accepting these in Christ: must Christ then be?
Has He been? Did not we ourselves make Him?
Our mind receives but what it holds, no more.
First of the love, then; we acknowledge Christ—
A proof we comprehend His love, a proof   380
We had such love already in ourselves,
Knew first what else we should not recognize.
'Tis mere projection from man's inmost mind,
And, what he loves, thus falls reflected back,
Becomes accounted somewhat out of him;
He throws it up in air, it drops down earth's,
With shape, name, story added, man's old way.
How prove you Christ came otherwise at least?
Next try the power: He made and rules the world:
Certes there is a world once made, now ruled,   390
Unless things have been ever as we see.
Our sires declared a charioteer's yoked steeds
Brought the sun up the east and down the west,
Which only of itself now rises, sets,
As if a hand impelled it and a will,—
Thus they long thought, they who had will and hands:
But the new question's whisper is distinct,
Wherefore must all force needs be like ourselves?
We have the hands, the will; what made and drives
The sun is force, is law, is named, not known,   400
While will and love we do know; marks of these,
Eye-witnesses attest, so books declare—
As that, to punish or reward our race,
The sun at undue times arose or set
Or else stood still: what do not men affirm?
But earth requires as urgently reward
Or punishment to-day as years ago,
And none expects the sun will interpose:
Therefore it was mere passion and mistake,

Or erring zeal for right, which changed the truth.   410
Go back, far, farther, to the birth of things;
Ever the will, the intelligence, the love,
Man's!—which he gives, supposing he but finds,
As late he gave head, body, hands and feet,
To help these in what forms he called his gods.
First, Jove's brow, Juno's eyes were swept away,
But Jove's wrath, Juno's pride continued long;
As last, will, power, and love discarded these,
So law in turn discards power, love, and will.
What proveth God is otherwise at least?   420
All else, projection from the mind of man!'

"Nay, do not give me wine, for I am strong,
But place my gospel where I put my hands.

"I say that man was made to grow, not stop;
That help, he needed once, and needs no more,
Having grown but an inch by, is withdrawn:
For he hath new needs, and new helps to these.
This imports solely, man should mount on each
New height in view; the help whereby he mounts,
The ladder-rung his foot has left, may fall,   430
Since all things suffer change save God the Truth.
Man apprehends Him newly at each stage
Whereat earth's ladder drops, its service done;
And nothing shall prove twice what once was proved.
You stick a garden-plot with ordered twigs
To show inside lie germs of herbs unborn,
And check the careless step would spoil their birth;
But when herbs wave, the guardian twigs may go,
Since should ye doubt of virtues, question kinds,
It is no longer for old twigs ye look,   440
Which proved once underneath lay store of seed,
But to the herb's self, by what light ye boast,
For what fruit's signs are. This book's fruit is plain,
Nor miracles need prove it any more.
Doth the fruit show? Then miracles bade 'ware
At first of root and stem, saved both till now
From trampling ox, rough boar and wanton goat.
What? Was man made a wheelwork to wind up,
And be discharged, and straight wound up anew?
No!—grown, his growth lasts; taught, he ne'er forgets: 450

May learn a thousand things, not twice the same.

"This might be pagan teaching: now hear mine.

"I say, that as the babe, you feed awhile,
Becomes a boy and fit to feed himself,
So, minds at first must be spoon-fed with truth:
When they can eat, babe's-nurture is withdrawn.
I fed the babe whether it would or no:
I bid the boy or feed himself or starve.
I cried once, 'That ye may believe in Christ,
Behold this blind man shall receive his sight!'   460
I cry now, 'Urgest thou, *for I am shrewd*
And smile at stories how John's word could cure—
Repeat that miracle and take my faith?'
I say, that miracle was duly wrought
When, save for it, no faith was possible.
Whether a change were wrought i' the shows o' the world,
Whether the change came from our minds which see
Of shows o' the world so much as and no more
Than God wills for His purpose,—(what do I
See now, suppose you, there where you see rock   470
Round us?)—I know not; such was the effect,
So faith grew, making void more miracles
Because too much: they would compel, not help.
I say, the acknowledgment of God in Christ
Accepted by thy reason, solves for thee
All questions in the earth and out of it,
And has so far advanced thee to be wise.
Wouldst thou unprove this to re-prove the proved?
In life's mere minute, with power to use that proof,
Leave knowledge and revert to how it sprung?   480
Thou hast it; use it and forthwith, or die!

"For I say, this is death and the sole death,
When a man's loss comes to him from his gain,
Darkness from light, from knowledge ignorance,
And lack of love from love made manifest;
A lamp's death when, replete with oil, it chokes;
A stomach's when, surcharged with food, it starves.
With ignorance was surety of a cure.
When man, appalled at nature, questioned first
'What if there lurk a might behind this might?'   490

He needed satisfaction God could give,
And did give, as ye have the written word:
But when he finds might still redouble might,
Yet asks, 'Since all is might, what use of will?'
—Will, the one source of might,—he being man
With a man's will and a man's might, to teach
In little how the two combine in large,—
That man has turned round on himself and stands,
Which in the course of nature is, to die.

"And when man questioned, 'What if there be love   500
Behind the will and might, as real as they?'—
He needed satisfaction God could give,
And did give, as ye have the written word:
But when, beholding that love everywhere,
He reasons, 'Since such love is everywhere,
And since ourselves can love and would be loved,
We ourselves make the love, and Christ was not,'—
How shall ye help this man who knows himself,
That he must love and would be loved again,
Yet, owning his own love that proveth Christ,   510
Rejecteth Christ through very need of Him?
The lamp o'erswims with oil, the stomach flags
Loaded with nurture, and that man's soul dies.

"If he rejoin, 'But this was all the while
A trick; the fault was, first of all, in thee,
Thy story of the places, names and dates,
Where, when and how the ultimate truth had rise,
—Thy prior truth, at last discovered none,
Whence now the second suffers detriment.
What good of giving knowledge if, because   520
O' the manner of the gift, its profit fail?
And why refuse what modicum of help
Had stopped the after-doubt, impossible
I' the face of truth—truth absolute, uniform?
Why must I hit of this and miss of that,
Distinguish just as I be weak or strong,
And not ask of thee and have answer prompt,
Was this once, was it not once?—then and now
And evermore, plain truth from man to man.
Is John's procedure just the heathen bard's?   530
Put question of his famous play again

How for the ephemerals' sake Jove's fire was filched,
And carried in a cane and brought to earth:
The fact is in the fable, cry the wise,
Mortals obtained the boon, so much is fact,
Though fire be spirit and produced on earth.
As with the Titan's, so now with thy tale:
Why breed in us perplexity, mistake,
Nor tell the whole truth in the proper words?'

"I answer, Have ye yet to argue out   540
The very primal thesis, plainest law,
—Man is not God but hath God's end to serve,
A master to obey, a course to take,
Somewhat to cast off, somewhat to become?
Grant this, then man must pass from old to new,
From vain to real, from mistake to fact,
From what once seemed good, to what now proves best.
How could man have progression otherwise?
Before the point was mooted 'What is God?'
No savage man inquired 'What am myself?'   550
Much less replied, 'First, last, and best of things.'
Man takes that title now if he believes
Might can exist with neither will nor love,
In God's case—what he names now Nature's Law—
While in himself he recognizes love
No less than might and will: and rightly takes.
Since if man prove the sole existent thing
Where these combine, whatever their degree,
However weak the might or will or love,
So they be found there, put in evidence,—   560
He is as surely higher in the scale
Than any might with neither love nor will,
As life, apparent in the poorest midge,
(When the faint dust-speck flits, ye guess its wing)
Is marvellous beyond dead Atlas' self—
Given to the nobler midge for resting-place!
Thus, man proves best and highest—God, in fine,
And thus the victory leads but to defeat,
The gain to loss, best rise to the worst fall,
His life becomes impossible, which is death.   570

"But if, appealing thence, he cower, avouch
He is mere man, and in humility

Neither may know God nor mistake himself;
I point to the immediate consequence
And say, by such confession straight he falls
Into man's place, a thing nor God nor beast,
Made to know that he can know and not more:
Lower than God who knows all and can all,
Higher than beasts which know and can so far
As each beast's limit, perfect to an end,   580
Nor conscious that they know, nor craving more;
While man knows partly but conceives beside,
Creeps ever on from fancies to the fact,
And in this striving, this converting air
Into a solid he may grasp and use,
Finds progress, man's distinctive mark alone,
Not God's, and not the beasts': God is, they are,
Man partly is and wholly hopes to be.
Such progress could no more attend his soul
Were all it struggles after found at first   590
And guesses changed to knowledge absolute,
Than motion wait his body, were all else
Than it the solid earth on every side,
Where now through space he moves from rest to rest.
Man, therefore, thus conditioned, must expect
He could not, what he knows now, know at first;
What he considers that he knows to-day,
Come but to-morrow, he will find misknown;
Getting increase of knowledge, since he learns
Because he lives, which is to be a man,   600
Set to instruct himself by his past self:
First, like the brute, obliged by facts to learn,
Next, as man may, obliged by his own mind,
Bent, habit, nature, knowledge turned to law.
God's gift was that man should conceive of truth
And yearn to gain it, catching at mistake,
As midway help till he reach fact indeed.
The statuary ere he mould a shape
Boasts a like gift, the shape's idea, and next
The aspiration to produce the same;   610
So, taking clay, he calls his shape thereout,
Cries ever 'Now I have the thing I see':
Yet all the while goes changing what was wrought,
From falsehood like the truth, to truth itself.
How were it had he cried 'I see no face,

No breast, no feet i' the ineffectual clay'?
Rather commend him that he clapped his hands,
And laughed 'It is my shape and lives again!'
Enjoyed the falsehood, touched it on to truth,
Until yourselves applaud the flesh indeed   620
In what is still flesh-imitating clay.
Right in you, right in him, such way be man's!
God only makes the live shape at a jet.
Will ye renounce this pact of creatureship?
The pattern on the Mount subsists no more,
Seemed awhile, then returned to nothingness;
But copies, Moses strove to make thereby,
Serve still and are replaced as time requires:
By these, make newest vessels, reach the type!
If ye demur, this judgment on your head,   630
Never to reach the ultimate, angels' law,
Indulging every instinct of the soul
There where law, life, joy, impulse are one thing!

"Such is the burthen of the latest time.
I have survived to hear it with my ears,
Answer it with my lips: does this suffice?
For if there be a further woe than such,
Wherein my brothers struggling need a hand,
So long as any pulse is left in mine,
May I be absent even longer yet,   640
Plucking the blind ones back from the abyss,
Though I should tarry a new hundred years!"
But he was dead; 'twas about noon, the day
Somewhat declining: we five buried him
That eve, and then, dividing, went five ways,
And I, disguised, returned to Ephesus.

By this, the cave's mouth must be filled with sand.
Valens is lost, I know not of his trace;
The Bactrian was but a wild childish man,
And could not write nor speak, but only loved: 650
So, lest the memory of this go quite,
Seeing that I to-morrow fight the beasts,
I tell the same to Phœbas, whom believe!
For many look again to find that face,
Beloved John's to whom I ministered,
Somewhere in life about the world; they err:

Either mistaking what was darkly spoke
At ending of his book, as he relates,
Or misconceiving somewhat of this speech
Scattered from mouth to mouth, as I suppose.   660
Believe ye will not see him any more
About the world with his divine regard!
For all was as I say, and now the man
Lies as he lay once, breast to breast with God.

———————

[Cerinthus read and mused; one added this:

"If Christ, as thou affirmest, be of men
Mere man, the first and best but nothing more,—
Account Him, for reward of what He was,
Now and forever, wretchedest of all.
For see; Himself conceived of life as love,   670
Conceived of love as what must enter in,
Fill up, make one with His each soul He loved:
Thus much for man's joy, all men's joy for Him.
Well, He is gone, thou sayest, to fit reward.
But by this time are many souls set free,
And very many still retained alive:
Nay, should His coming be delayed awhile,
Say, ten years longer (twelve years, some compute)
See if, for every finger of thy hands,
There be not found, that day the world shall end,   680
Hundreds of souls, each holding by Christ's word
That He will grow incorporate with all,
With me as Pamphylax, with him as John,
Groom for each bride! Can a mere man do this?
Yet Christ saith, this He lived and died to do.
Call Christ, then, the illimitable God,
Or lost!"

But 'twas Cerinthus that is lost.]

CALIBAN UPON SETEBOS; OR, NATURAL THEOLOGY IN THE ISLAND

"Thou thoughtest that I was altogether such a one as thyself."

['WILL sprawl, now that the heat of day is best,
Flat on his belly in the pit's much mire,

With elbows wide, fists clenched to prop his chin.
And, while he kicks both feet in the cool slush,
And feels about his spine small eft-things course,
Run in and out each arm, and make him laugh:
And while above his head a pompion-plant,
Coating the cave-top as a brow its eye,
Creeps down to touch and tickle hair and beard,
And now a flower drops with a bee inside,
And now a fruit to snap at, catch and crunch,— 10
He looks out o'er yon sea which sunbeams cross
And recross till they weave a spider-web
(Meshes of fire, some great fish breaks at times)
And talks to his own self, howe'er he please,
Touching that other, whom his dam called God.
Because to talk about Him, vexes—ha,
Could He but know! and time to vex is now,
When talk is safer than in winter-time.
Moreover Prosper and Miranda sleep 20
In confidence he drudges at their task,
And it is good to cheat the pair, and gibe,
Letting the rank tongue blossom into speech.]

Setebos, Setebos, and Setebos!
'Thinketh, He dwelleth i' the cold o' the moon.

'Thinketh He made it, with the sun to match,
But not the stars; the stars came otherwise;
Only made clouds, winds, meteors, such as that:
Also this isle, what lives and grows thereon,
And snaky sea which rounds and ends the same. 30

'Thinketh, it came of being ill at ease:
He hated that He cannot change His cold,
Nor cure its ache. 'Hath spied an icy fish
That longed to 'scape the rock-stream where she lived,
And thaw herself within the lukewarm brine
O' the lazy sea her stream thrusts far amid,
A crystal spike 'twixt two warm walls of wave;
Only, she ever sickened, found repulse
At the other kind of water, not her life,
(Green-dense and dim-delicious, bred o' the sun) 40
Flounced back from bliss she was not born to breathe,
And in her old bounds buried her despair,

Hating and loving warmth alike: so He.
'Thinketh, He made thereat the sun, this isle,
Trees and the fowls here, beast and creeping thing.
Yon otter, sleek-wet, black, lithe as a leech;
Yon auk, one fire-eye in a ball of foam,
That floats and feeds; a certain badger brown
He hath watched hunt with that slant white-wedge eye
By moonlight; and the pie with the long tongue   50
That pricks deep into oakwarts for a worm,
And says a plain word when she finds her prize,
But will not eat the ants; the ants themselves
That build a wall of seeds and settled stalks
About their hole—He made all these and more,
Made all we see, and us, in spite: how else?
He could not, Himself, make a second self
To be His mate; as well have made Himself:
He would not make what he mislikes or slights,
An eyesore to Him, or not worth His pains: 60
But did, in envy, listlessness or sport,
Make what Himself would fain, in a manner, be—
Weaker in most points, stronger in a few,
Worthy, and yet mere playthings all the while,
Things He admires and mocks too,—that is it.
Because, so brave, so better though they be,
It nothing skills if He begin to plague.
Look now, I melt a gourd-fruit into mash,
Add honeycomb and pods, I have perceived,
Which bite like finches when they bill and kiss,—   70
Then, when froth rises bladdery, drink up all,
Quick, quick, till maggots scamper through my brain;
Last, throw me on my back i' the seeded thyme,
And wanton, wishing I were born a bird.
Put case, unable to be what I wish,
I yet could make a live bird out of clay:
Would not I take clay, pinch my Caliban
Able to fly?—for, there, see, he hath wings,
And great comb like the hoopoe's to admire,
And there, a sting to do his foes offence,   80
There, and I will that he begin to live,
Fly to yon rock-top, nip me off the horns
Of grigs high up that make the merry din,
Saucy through their veined wings, and mind me not.
In which feat, if his leg snapped, brittle clay,

And he lay stupid-like,—why, I should laugh;
And if he, spying me, should fall to weep,
Beseech me to be good, repair his wrong,
Bid his poor leg smart less or grow again,—
Well, as the chance were, this might take or else   90
Not take my fancy: I might hear his cry,
And give the mankin three sound legs for one,
Or pluck the other off, leave him like an egg,
And lessoned he was mine and merely clay.
Were this no pleasure, lying in the thyme,
Drinking the mash, with brain become alive,
Making and marring clay at will? So He.

'Thinketh, such shows nor right nor wrong in Him,
Nor kind, nor cruel: He is strong and Lord.
'Am strong myself compared to yonder crabs   100
That march now from the mountain to the sea;
'Let twenty pass, and stone the twenty-first,
Loving not, hating not, just choosing so.
'Say, the first straggler that boasts purple spots
Shall join the file, one pincer twisted off;
'Say, this bruised fellow shall receive a worm,
And two worms he whose nippers end in red;
As it likes me each time, I do: so He.

Well then, 'supposeth He is good i' the main,
Placable if His mind and ways were guessed,   110
But rougher than His handiwork, be sure!
Oh, He hath made things worthier than Himself,
And envieth that, so helped, such things do more
Than He who made them! What consoles but this?
That they, unless through Him, do naught at all,
And must submit: what other use in things?
'Hath cut a pipe of pithless elder-joint
That, blown through, gives exact the scream o' the jay
When from her wing you twitch the feathers blue:
Sound this, and little birds that hate the jay   120
Flock within stone's throw, glad their foe is hurt:
Put case such pipe could prattle and boast forsooth
"I catch the birds, I am the crafty thing,
I make the cry my maker cannot make
With his great round mouth; he must blow through mine!"
Would not I smash it with my foot? So He.

But wherefore rough, why cold and ill at ease?
Aha, that is a question! Ask, for that,
What knows,—the something over Setebos
That made Him, or He, may be, found and fought,   130
Worsted, drove off and did to nothing, perchance.
There may be something quiet o'er His head,
Out of His reach, that feels nor joy nor grief,
Since both derive from weakness in some way.
I joy because the quails come; would not joy
Could I bring quails here when I have a mind:
This Quiet, all it hath a mind to, doth.
'Esteemeth stars the outposts of its couch,
But never spends much thought nor care that way.
It may look up, work up,—the worse for those   140
It works on! 'Careth but for Setebos
The many-handed as a cuttle-fish,
Who, making Himself feared through what He does,
Looks up, first, and perceives he cannot soar
To what is quiet and hath happy life;
Next looks down here, and out of very spite
Makes this a bauble-world to ape yon real,
These good things to match those as hips do grapes.
'Tis solace making baubles, ay, and sport.
Himself peeped late, eyed Prosper at his books   150
Careless and lofty, lord now of the isle:
Vexed, 'stitched a book of broad leaves, arrow-shaped,
Wrote thereon, he knows what, prodigious words;
Has peeled a wand and called it by a name;
Weareth at whiles for an enchanter's robe
The eyed skin of a supple oncelot;
And hath an ounce sleeker than youngling mole,
A four-legged serpent he makes cower and couch,
Now snarl, now hold its breath and mind his eye,
And saith she is Miranda and my wife: 160
'Keeps for his Ariel a tall pouch-bill crane
He bids go wade for fish and straight disgorge;
Also a sea-beast, lumpish, which he snared,
Blinded the eyes of, and brought somewhat tame,
And split its toe-webs, and now pens the drudge
In a hole o' the rock and calls him Caliban;
A bitter heart that bides its time and bites.
'Plays thus at being Prosper in a way,
Taketh his mirth with make-believes: so He.

His dam held that the Quiet made all things   170
Which Setebos vexed only: 'holds not so.
Who made them weak, meant weakness He might vex.
Had He meant other, while His hand was in,
Why not make horny eyes no thorn could prick,
Or plate my scalp with bone against the snow,
Or overscale my flesh 'neath joint and joint,
Like an orc's armor? Ay,—so spoil His sport!
He is the One now: only He doth all.
'Saith, He may like, perchance, what profits Him.
Ay, himself loves what does him good; but why?   180
'Gets good no otherwise. This blinded beast
Loves whoso places flesh-meat on his nose,
But, had he eyes, would want no help, but hate
Or love, just as it liked him: He hath eyes.
Also it pleaseth Setebos to work,
Use all His hands, and exercise much craft,
By no means for the love of what is worked.
'Tasteth, himself, no finer good i' the world
When all goes right, in this safe summer-time,
And he wants little, hungers, aches not much,   190
Than trying what to do with wit and strength.
'Falls to make something: 'piled yon pile of turfs,
And squared and stuck there squares of soft white chalk,
And, with a fish-tooth, scratched a moon on each,
And set up endwise certain spikes of tree,
And crowned the whole with a sloth's skull a-top,
Found dead i' the woods, too hard for one to kill.
No use at all i' the work, for work's sole sake;
'Shall some day knock it down again: so He.

'Saith He is terrible: watch His feats in proof!   200
One hurricane will spoil six good months' hope.
He hath a spite against me, that I know,
Just as He favors Prosper, who knows why?
So it is, all the same, as well I find.
'Wove wattles half the winter, fenced them firm
With stone and stake to stop she-tortoises
Crawling to lay their eggs here: well, one wave,
Feeling the foot of Him upon its neck,
Gaped as a snake does, lolled out its large tongue,
And licked the whole labor flat; so much for spite.   210
'Saw a ball flame down late (yonder it lies)

Where, half an hour before, I slept i' the shade:
Often they scatter sparkles: there is force!
'Dug up a newt He may have envied once
And turned to stone, shut up inside a stone.
Please Him and hinder this?—What Prosper does?
Aha, if He would tell me how! Not He!
There is the sport: discover how or die!
All need not die, for of the things o' the isle
Some flee afar, some dive, some run up trees;　　　　220
Those at His mercy,—why, they please Him most
When . . . when . . . well, never try the same way twice!
Repeat what act has pleased, He may grow wroth.
You must not know His ways, and play Him off,
Sure of the issue. 'Doth the like himself:
'Spareth a squirrel that it nothing fears
But steals the nut from underneath my thumb,
And when I threat, bites stoutly in defence:
'Spareth an urchin that contrariwise,
Curls up into a ball, pretending death　　　　　　230
For fright at my approach: the two ways please.
But what would move my choler more than this,
That either creature counted on its life
To-morrow and next day and all days to come,
Saying, forsooth, in the inmost of its heart,
"Because he did so yesterday with me,
And otherwise with such another brute,
So must he do henceforth and always."—Ay?
Would teach the reasoning couple what "must" means!
'Doth as he likes, or wherefore Lord? So He.　　　240

'Conceiveth all things will continue thus,
And we shall have to live in fear of Him
So long as He lives, keeps His strength: no change,
If He have done His best, make no new world
To please Him more, so leave off watching this,—
If He surprise not even the Quiet's self
Some strange day,—or, suppose, grow into it
As grubs grow butterflies: else, here are we,
And there is He, and nowhere help at all.

'Believeth with the life, the pain shall stop.　　　250
His dam held different, that after death
He both plagued enemies and feasted friends:

Idly! He doth His worst in this our life,
Giving just respite lest we die through pain,
Saving last pain for worst,—with which, an end.
Meanwhile, the best way to escape His ire
Is, not to seem too happy. 'Sees, himself,
Yonder two flies, with purple films and pink,
Bask on the pompion-bell above: kills both.
'Sees two black painful beetles roll their ball   260
On head and tail as if to save their lives:
Moves them the stick away they strive to clear.

Even so, 'would have Him misconceive, suppose
This Caliban strives hard and ails no less,
And always, above all else, envies Him;
Wherefore he mainly dances on dark nights,
Moans in the sun, gets under holes to laugh,
And never speaks his mind save housed as now:
Outside, 'groans, curses. If He caught me here,
O'erheard this speech, and asked "What chucklest at?"   270
'Would, to appease Him, cut a finger off,
Or of my three kid yearlings burn the best,
Or let the toothsome apples rot on tree,
Or push my tame beast for the orc to taste:
While myself lit a fire, and made a song
And sung it, *"What I hate, be consecrate*
To celebrate Thee and Thy state, no mate
For Thee; what see for envy in poor me?"
Hoping the while, since evils sometimes mend,
Warts rub away and sores are cured with slime,   280
That some strange day, will either the Quiet catch
And conquer Setebos, or likelier He
Decrepit may doze, doze, as good as die

———————

[What, what? A curtain o'er the world at once!
Crickets stop hissing; not a bird—or, yes,
There scuds His raven that has told Him all!
It was fool's play, this prattling! Ha! The wind
Shoulders the pillared dust, death's house o' the move,
And fast invading fires begin! White blaze—
A tree's head snaps—and there, there, there, there,
        there,   290
His thunder follows! Fool to gibe at Him!
Lo! 'Lieth flat and loveth Setebos!

'Maketh his teeth meet through his upper lip,
Will let those quails fly, will not eat this month
One little mess of whelks, so he may 'scape!]

CONFESSIONS

I

WHAT is he buzzing in my ears?
  "Now that I come to die,
Do I view the world as a vale of tears?"
  Ah, reverend sir, not I!

II

What I viewed there once, what I view again
  Where the physic bottles stand
On the table's edge,—is a suburb lane,
  With a wall to my bedside hand.

III

That lane sloped, much as the bottles do,
  From a house you could descry
O'er the garden-wall: is the curtain blue
  Or green to a healthy eye?

IV

To mine, it serves for the old June weather
  Blue above lane and wall;
And that farthest bottle labelled "Ether"
  Is the house o'ertopping all.

V

At a terrace, somewhere near the stopper,
  There watched for me, one June,
A girl: I know, sir, it's improper,
  My poor mind's out of tune.

VI

Only, there was a way . . . you crept
    Close by the side to dodge
Eyes in the house, two eyes except:
    They styled their house "The Lodge."

VII

What right had a lounger up their lane?
    But, by creeping very close,
With the good wall's help,—their eyes might strain
    And stretch themselves to Oes,

VIII

Yet never catch her and me together,
    As she left the attic, there,
By the rim of the bottle labelled "Ether,"
    And stole from stair to stair,

IX

And stood by the rose-wreathed gate. Alas,
    We loved, sir—used to meet:
How sad and bad and mad it was—
    But then, how it was sweet!

MAY AND DEATH

I

I wish that when you died last May,
    Charles, there had died along with you
Three parts of spring's delightful things;
    Ay, and, for me, the fourth part too.

II

A foolish thought, and worse, perhaps!
  There must be many a pair of friends
Who, arm in arm, deserve the warm
  Moon-births and the long evening-ends.

III

So, for their sake, be May still May!
  Let their new time, as mine of old,
Do all it did for me: I bid
  Sweet sights and sounds throng manifold.

IV

Only, one little sight, one plant,
  Woods have in May, that starts up green
Save a sole streak which, so to speak,
  Is spring's blood, spilt its leaves between,—

V

That, they might spare; a certain wood
  Might miss the plant; their loss were small:
But I,—whene'er the leaf grows there,
  Its drop comes from my heart, that's all.

PROSPICE

FEAR death?—to feel the fog in my throat,
  The mist in my face,
When the snows begin, and the blasts denote
  I am nearing the place,
The power of the night, the press of the storm,
  The post of the foe;
Where he stands, the Arch Fear in a visible form,
  Yet the strong man must go:
For the journey is done and the summit attained,
  And the barriers fall,   10

Though a battle's to fight ere the guerdon be gained,
    The reward of it all.
I was ever a fighter, so—one fight more,
    The best and the last!
I would hate that death bandaged my eyes, and forbore,
    And bade me creep past.
No! let me taste the whole of it, fare like my peers
    The heroes of old,
Bear the brunt, in a minute pay glad life's arrears
    Of pain, darkness and cold.   20
For sudden the worst turns the best to the brave,
    The black minute's at end,
And the elements' rage, the fiend-voices that rave,
    Shall dwindle, shall blend,
Shall change, shall become first a peace out of pain,
    Then a light, then thy breast,
O thou soul of my soul! I shall clasp thee again,
    And with God be the rest!

YOUTH AND ART

I

It ONCE might have been, once only:
    We lodged in a street together,
You, a sparrow on the housetop lonely,
    I, a lone she-bird of his feather.

II

Your trade was with sticks and clay,
    You thumbed, thrust, patted and polished,
Then laughed "They will see some day
    Smith made, and Gibson demolished."

III

My business was song, song, song;
    I chirped, cheeped, trilled and twittered,
"Kate Brown's on the boards ere long,
    And Grisi's existence embittered!"

IV

I earned no more by a warble
  Than you by a sketch in plaster;
You wanted a piece of marble,
  I needed a music-master.

V

We studied hard in our styles,
  Chipped each at a crust like Hindoos,
For air looked out on the tiles,
  For fun watched each other's windows.

VI

You lounged, like a boy of the South,
  Cap and blouse—nay, a bit of beard too;
Or you got it, rubbing your mouth
  With fingers the clay adhered to.

VII

And I—soon managed to find
  Weak points in the flower-fence facing,
Was forced to put up a blind
  And be safe in my corset-lacing.

VIII

No harm! It was not my fault
  If you never turned your eye's tail up,
As I shook upon E *in alt*,
  Or ran the chromatic scale up:

IX

For spring bade the sparrows pair,
  And the boys and girls gave guesses,
And stalls in our street looked rare
  With bulrush and watercresses.

X

Why did not you pinch a flower
   In a pellet of clay and fling it?
Why did not I put a power
   Of thanks in a look, or sing it?

XI

I did look, sharp as a lynx,
   (And yet the memory rankles)
When models arrived, some minx
   Tripped up-stairs, she and her ankles.

XII

But I think I gave you as good!
   "That foreign fellow,—who can know
How she pays, in a playful mood,
   For his tuning her that piano?"

XIII

Could you say so, and never say
   "Suppose we join hands and fortunes,
And I fetch her from over the way,
   Her, piano, and long tunes and short tunes"?

XIV

No, no: you would not be rash,
   Nor I rasher and something over:
You've to settle yet Gibson's hash,
   And Grisi yet lives in clover.

XV

But you meet the Prince at the Board,
   I'm queen myself at *bals-paré*,
I've married a rich old lord,
   And you're dubbed knight and an R. A.

XVI

Each life unfulfilled, you see;
    It hangs still, patchy and scrappy:
We have not sighed deep, laughed free,
    Starved, feasted, despaired,—been happy.

XVII

And nobody calls you a dunce,
    And people suppose me clever:
This could but have happened once,
    And we missed it, lost it forever.

A FACE

IF ONE could have that little head of hers
    Painted upon a background of pale gold,
Such as the Tuscan's early art prefers!
    No shade encroaching on the matchless mould
Of those two lips, which should be opening soft
    In the pure profile; not as when she laughs,
For that spoils all: but rather as if aloft
    Yon hyacinth, she loves so, leaned its staff's
Burthen of honey-colored buds to kiss
And capture 'twixt the lips apart for this.   10
Then her lithe neck, three fingers might surround,
How it should waver on the pale gold ground
Up to the fruit-shaped, perfect chin it lifts!
I know, Coreggio loves to mass, in rifts
Of heaven, his angel faces, orb on orb
Breaking its outline, burning shades absorb:
But these are only massed there, I should think,
    Waiting to see some wonder momently
    Grow out, stand full, fade slow against the sky
    (That's the pale ground you'd see this sweet face by),   20
    All heaven, meanwhile, condensed into one eye
Which fears to lose the wonder, should it wink.

A LIKENESS

SOME people hang portraits up
In a room where they dine or sup:
   And the wife clinks tea-things under,
And her cousin, he stirs his cup,
   Asks, "Who was the lady, I wonder?"
" 'Tis a daub John bought at a sale,"
   Quoth the wife,—looks black as thunder:
"What a shade beneath her nose!
Snuff-taking, I suppose,—"
Adds the cousin, while John's corns ail.   10

Or else, there's no wife in the case,
But the portrait's queen of the place,
   Alone 'mid the other spoils
   Of youth,—masks, gloves and foils,
And pipe-sticks, rose, cherry-tree, jasmine,
   And the long whip, the tandem-lasher,
And the cast from a fist ("not, alas! mine,
   But my master's, the Tipton Slasher"),
And the cards where pistol-balls mark ace,
And a satin shoe used for cigar-case,   20
And the chamois-horns ("shot in the Chablais")
   And prints—Rarey drumming on Cruiser,
   And Sayers, our champion, the bruiser,
And the little edition of Rabelais:
Where a friend, with both hands in his pockets,
   May saunter up close to examine it,
   And remark a good deal of Jane Lamb in it,
"But the eyes are half out of their sockets;
That hair's not so bad, where the gloss is,
But they've made the girl's nose a proboscis: 30
Jane Lamb, that we danced with at Vichy!
What, is not she Jane? Then, who is she?"

All that I own is a print,
An etching, a mezzotint;
   'Tis a study, a fancy, a fiction,
   Yet a fact (take my conviction)
Because it has more than a hint

   Of a certain face, I never
Saw elsewhere touch or trace of
In women I've seen the face of: 40
   Just an etching, and, so far, clever.

I keep my prints, an imbroglio,
Fifty in one portfolio.
When somebody tries my claret,
We turn round chairs to the fire,
Chirp over days in a garret,
   Chuckle o'er increase of salary,
Taste the good fruits of our leisure,
Talk about pencil and lyre,
   And the National Portrait Gallery: 50
Then I exhibit my treasure.
After we've turned over twenty,
   And the debt of wonder my crony owes
   Is paid to my Marc Antonios.
He stops me—"*Festina lentè!*
What's that sweet thing there, the etching?"
How my waistcoat-strings want stretching,
   How my cheeks grow red as tomatos,
How my heart leaps! But hearts, after leaps, ache.

"By the by, you must take, for a keepsake,   60
   That other, you praised, of Volpato's."
The fool! would he try a flight further and say—
He never saw, never before to-day,
What was able to take his breath away,
A face to lose youth for, to occupy age
With the dream of, meet death with,—why, I'll not engage
But that, half in a rapture and half in a rage,
I should toss him the thing's self—" 'Tis only a duplicate,
A thing of no value! Take it, I supplicate!"

MR. SLUDGE, "THE MEDIUM"

Now, don't, sir! Don't expose me! Just this once!
This was the first and only time, I'll swear,—
Look at me,—see, I kneel,—the only time,
I swear, I ever cheated,—yes, by the soul

Of Her who hears—(your sainted mother, sir!
All, except this last accident, was truth—
This little kind of slip!—and even this,
It was your own wine, sir, the good champagne,
(I took it for Catawba, you're so kind)
Which put the folly in my head!

           "Get up?"   1(
You still inflict on me that terrible face?
You show no mercy?—Not for Her dear sake,
The sainted spirit's, whose soft breath even now
Blows on my cheek—(don't you feel something, sir?)
You'll tell?

       Go tell, then! Who the devil cares
What such a rowdy chooses to . . .
                 Aie —aie—aie!
Please, sir! your thumbs are through my windpipe, sir!
Ch—ch!

       Well, sir, I hope you've done it now!
Oh Lord! I little thought, sir, yesterday,
When your departed mother spoke those words   2
Of peace through me, and moved you, sir, so much,
You gave me—(very kind it was of you)
These shirt-studs—(better take them back again,
Please, sir)—yes, little did I think so soon
A trifle of trick, all through a glass too much
Of his own champagne, would change my best of friends
Into an angry gentleman!

          Though, 'twas wrong.
I don't contest the point; your anger's just:
Whatever put such folly in my head,
I know 'twas wicked of me. There's a thick   30
Dusk undeveloped spirit (I've observed)
Owes me a grudge—a negro's, I should say,
Or else an Irish emigrant's; yourself
Explained the case so well last Sunday, sir,
When we had summoned Franklin to clear up
A point about those shares i' the telegraph:
Ay, and he swore . . . or might it be Tom Paine? . . .
Thumping the table close by where I crouched,

He'd do me soon a mischief: that's come true!
Why, now your face clears! I was sure it would!   40
Then, this one time . . . don't take your hand away,
Through yours I surely kiss your mother's hand . . .
You'll promise to forgive me?—or, at least,
Tell nobody of this? Consider, sir!
What harm can mercy do? Would but the shade
Of the venerable dead-one just vouchsafe
A rap or tip! What bit of paper's here?
Suppose we take a pencil, let her write,
Make the least sign, she urges on her child
Forgiveness? There now! Eh? Oh! 'Twas your foot,   50
And not a natural creak, sir?

                    Answer, then!
Once, twice, thrice . . . see, I'm waiting to say "thrice!"
All to no use! No sort of hope for me?
It's all to post to Greeley's newspaper?

What? If I told you all about the tricks?
Upon my soul!—the whole truth, and naught else,
And how there's been some falsehood—for your part,
Will you engage to pay my passage out,
And hold your tongue until I'm safe on board?
England's the place, not Boston—no offence!   60
I see what makes you hesitate: don't fear!
I mean to change my trade and cheat no more,
Yes, this time really it's upon my soul!
Be my salvation!—under Heaven, of course.
I'll tell some queer things. Sixty Vs must do.
A trifle, though, to start with! We'll refer
The question to this table?

                  How you're changed!
Then split the difference; thirty more, we'll say.
Ay, but you leave my presents! Else I'll swear
'Twas all through those: you wanted yours again,   70
So, picked a quarrel with me, to get them back!
Tread on a worm, it turns, sir! If I turn,
Your fault! 'Tis you'll have forced me! Who's obliged
To give up life yet try no self-defence?
At all events, I'll run the risk. Eh?

Done!

May I sit, sir? This dear old table, now!
Please, sir, a parting egg-nogg and cigar!
I've been so happy with you! Nice stuffed chairs,
And sympathetic sideboards; what an end
To all the instructive evenings! (It's alight.)   80
Well, nothing lasts, as Bacon came and said.
Here goes,—but keep your temper, or I'll scream!

Fol-lol-the-rido-liddle-iddle-ol!
You see, sir, it's your own fault more than mine;
It's all your fault, you curious gentlefolk!
You're prigs,—excuse me,—like to look so spry,
So clever, while you cling by half a claw
To the perch whereon you puff yourselves at roost,
Such piece of self-conceit as serves for perch
Because you chose it, so it must be safe.   90
Oh, otherwise you're sharp enough! You spy
Who slips, who slides, who holds by help of wing,
Wanting real foothold,—who can't keep upright
On the other perch, your neighbor chose, not you:
There's no outwitting you respecting him!
For instance, men love money—that, you know
And what men do to gain it: well, suppose
A poor lad, say a help's son in your house,
Listening at keyholes, hears the company
Talk grand of dollars, V-notes, and so forth,   100
How hard they are to get, how good to hold,
How much they buy,—if, suddenly, in pops he—
"I've got a V-note!"—what do you say to him?
What's your first word which follows your last kick?
"Where did you steal it, rascal?" That's because
He finds you, fain would fool you, off your perch,
Not on the special piece of nonsense, sir,
Elected your parade-ground: let him try
Lies to the end of the list,—"He picked it up,
His cousin died and left it him by will,   110
The President flung it to him, riding by,
An actress trucked it for a curl of his hair,
He dreamed of luck and found his shoe enriched,
He dug up clay, and out of clay made gold"—
How would you treat such possibilities?

Would not you, prompt, investigate the case
With cow-hide? "Lies, lies, lies," you'd shout: and why?
Which of the stories might not prove mere truth?
This last, perhaps, that clay was turned to coin!
Let's see, now, give him me to speak for him!   120
How many of your rare philosophers,
In plaguy books I've had to dip into,
Believed gold could be made thus, saw it made
And made it? Oh, with such philosophers
You're on your best behavior! While the lad—
With him, in a trice, you settle likelihoods,
Nor doubt a moment how he got his prize:
In his case, you hear, judge and execute,
All in a breath: so would most men of sense.

But let the same lad hear you talk as grand   130
At the same keyhole, you and company,
Of signs and wonders, the invisible world;
How wisdom scouts our vulgar unbelief
More than our vulgarest credulity;
How good men have desired to see a ghost,
What Johnson used to say, what Wesley did,
Mother Goose thought, and fiddle-diddle-dee:—
If he break in with, "Sir, *I* saw a ghost!"
Ah, the ways change! He finds you perched and prim;
It's a conceit of yours that ghosts may be: 140
There's no talk now of cow-hide. "Tell it out!
Don't fear us! Take your time and recollect!
Sit down first: try a glass of wine, my boy!
And, David, (is not that your Christian name?)
Of all things, should this happen twice—it may—
Be sure, while fresh in mind, you let us know!"
Does the boy blunder, blurt out this, blab that,
Break down in the other, as beginners will?
All's candor, all's considerateness—"No haste!
Pause and collect yourself! We understand!   150
That's the bad memory, or the natural shock,
Or the unexplained *phenomena!*"

               Egad,
The boy takes heart of grace; finds, never fear,
The readiest way to ope your own heart wide,
Show—what I call your peacock-perch, pet post

To strut, and spread the tail, and squawk upon!
"Just as you thought, much as you might expect!
There be more things in heaven and earth, Horatio," . . .
And so on. Shall not David take the hint,
Grow bolder, stroke you down at quickened rate?   160
If he ruffle a feather, it's "Gently, patiently!
Manifestations are so weak at first!
Doubting, moreover, kills them, cuts all short,
Cures with a vengeance!"

               There, sir, that's your style!
You and your boy—such pains bestowed on him,
Or any headpiece of the average worth,
To teach, say, Greek, would perfect him apace,
Make him a Person ("Porson?" thank you, sir!)
Much more, proficient in the art of lies.
You never leave the lesson! Fire alight,   170
Catch you permitting it to die! You've friends;
There's no withholding knowledge,—least from those
Apt to look elsewhere for their souls' supply:
Why should not you parade your lawful prize?
Who finds a picture, digs a medal up,
Hits on a first edition,—he henceforth
Gives it his name, grows notable: how much more,
Who ferrets out a "medium"? "David's yours,
You highly-favored man? Then, pity souls
Less privileged! Allow us share your luck!"   180
So, David holds the circle, rules the roost,
Narrates the vision, peeps in the glass ball,
Sets-to the spirit-writing, hears the raps,
As the case may be.

               Now mark! To be precise—
Though I say, "lies" all these, at this first stage,
'Tis just for science' sake: I call such grubs
By the name of what they'll turn to, dragonflies.
Strictly, it's what good people style untruth;
But yet, so far, not quite the full-grown thing:
It's fancying, fable-making, nonsense-work—   19
What never meant to be so very bad—
The knack of story-telling, brightening up
Each dull old bit of fact that drops its shine.
One does see somewhat when one shuts one's eyes,

If only spots and streaks; tables do tip
In the oddest way of themselves: and pens, good **Lord,**
Who knows if you drive them or they drive you?
'Tis but a foot in the water and out again;
Not that duck-under which decides your dive.
Note this, for it's important: listen why.   200

I'll prove, you push on David till he dives
And ends the shivering. Here's your circle, now:
Two-thirds of them, with heads like you their host,
Turn up their eyes, and cry, as you expect,
"Lord, who'd have thought it!" But there's always one
Looks wise, compassionately smiles, submits
"Of your veracity no kind of doubt,
But—do you feel so certain of that boy's?
Really, I wonder! I confess myself
More chary of my faith!" That's galling, sir!   210
What, he the investigator, he the sage,
When all's done? Then, you just have shut your eyes,
Opened your mouth, and gulped down David whole,
You! Terrible were such catastrophe!
So, evidence is redoubled, doubled again,
And doubled besides; once more, "He heard, we heard,
You and they heard, your mother and your wife,
Your children and the stranger in your gates:
Did they or did they not?" So much for him,
The black sheep, guest without the wedding-garb,   220
The doubting Thomas! Now's your turn to crow:
"He's kind to think you such a fool: Sludge cheats?
Leave you alone to take precautions!"

                                        Straight
The rest join chorus. Thomas stands abashed,
Sips silent some such beverage as this,
Considers if it be harder, shutting eyes
And gulping David in good fellowship,
Than going elsewhere, getting, in exchange,
With no egg-nogg to lubricate the food,
Some just as tough a morsel. Over the way,   230
Holds Captain Sparks his court: is it better there?
Have not you hunting-stories, scalping-scenes,
And Mexican War exploits to swallow plump

If you'd be free o' the stove-side, rocking-chair,
And trio of affable daughters?

                                    Doubt succumbs!
Victory! All your circle's yours again!
Out of the clubbing of submissive wits,
David's performance rounds, each chink gets patched,
Every protrusion of a point's filed fine,
All's fit to set a-rolling round the world,   240
And then return to David finally,
Lies seven-feet thick about his first half-inch.
Here's a choice birth o' the supernatural,
Poor David's pledged to! You've employed no tool
That laws exclaim at, save the devil's own,
Yet screwed him into henceforth gulling you
To the top o' your bent,—all out of one half-lie!

You hold, if there's one half or a hundredth part
Of a lie, that's his fault,—his be the penalty!
I dare say! You'd prove firmer in his place?   250
You'd find the courage,—that first flurry over,
That mild bit of romancing-work at end,—
To interpose with "It gets serious, this;
Must stop here. Sir, I saw no ghost at all.
Inform your friends I made . . . well, fools of them,
And found you ready-made. I've lived in clover
These three weeks: take it out in kicks of me!"
I doubt it. Ask your conscience! Let me know,
Twelve months hence, with how few embellishments
You've told almighty Boston of this passage   260
Of arms between us, your first taste o' the foil
From Sludge, who could not fence, sir! Sludge, your boy!
I lied, sir,—there! I got up from my gorge
On offal in the gutter, and preferred
Your canvas-backs: I took their carver's size,
Measured his modicum of intelligence,
Tickled him on the cockles of his heart
With a raven feather, and next week found myself
Sweet and clean, dining daintily, dizened smart,
Set on a stool buttressed by ladies' knees,   270
Every soft smiler calling me her pet,
Encouraging my story to uncoil

And creep out from its hole, inch after inch,
"How last night, I no sooner snug in bed,
Tucked up, just as they left me,—than came raps!
While a light whisked" . . . "Shaped somewhat like a star?"
"Well, like some sort of stars, ma'am."—"So we thought!
And any voice? Not yet? Try hard, next time,
If you can't hear a voice; we think you may:
At least, the Pennsylvanian 'mediums' did."   280
Oh, next time comes the voice! "Just as we hoped!"
Are not the hopers proud now, pleased, profuse
O' the natural acknowledgment?

                                        Of course!
So, off we push, illy-oh-yo, trim the boat,
On we sweep with a cataract ahead,
We're midway to the Horseshoe: stop, who can,
The dance of bubbles gay about our prow!
Experiences become worth waiting for,
Spirits now speak up, tell their inmost mind,
And compliment the "medium" properly,   290
Concern themselves about his Sunday coat,
See rings on his hand with pleasure. Ask yourself
How you'd receive a course of treats like these!
Why, take the quietest hack and stall him up,
Cram him with corn a month, then out with him
Among his mates on a bright April morn,
With the turf to tread; see if you find or no
A caper in him, if he bucks or bolts!
Much more a youth whose fancies sprout as rank
As toadstool-clump from melon-bed. 'Tis soon,   300
"Sirrah, you spirit, come, go, fetch and carry,
Read, write, rap, rub-a-dub, and hang yourself!"
I'm spared all further trouble; all's arranged;
Your circle does my business; I may rave
Like an epileptic dervish in the books,
Foam, fling myself at, rend my clothes to shreds;
No matter: lovers, friends and countrymen
Will lay down spiritual laws, read wrong things right
By the rule o' reverse. If Francis Verulam
Styles himself Bacon, spells the name beside   310
With a *y* and a *k*, says he drew breath in York,
Gave up the ghost in Wales when Cromwell reigned,
(As, sir, we somewhat fear he was apt to say,

Before I found the useful book that knows)
Why, what harm's done? The circle smiles apace,
"It was not Bacon, after all, you see!
We understand; the trick's but natural:
Such spirits' individuality
Is hard to put in evidence: they incline
To gibe and jeer, these undeveloped sorts.   320
You see, their world's much like a jail broke loose,
While this of ours remains shut, bolted, barred,
With a single window to it. Sludge, our friend,
Serves as this window, whether thin or thick,
Or stained or stainless; he's the medium-pane
Through which, to see us and be seen, they peep:
They crowd each other, hustle for a chance,
Tread on their neighbor's kibes, play tricks enough!
Does Bacon, tired of waiting, swerve aside?
Up in his place jumps Barnum—'I'm your man,   330
I'll answer you for Bacon!' Try once more!"

Or else it's—"What's a 'medium'? He's a means,
Good, bad, indifferent, still the only means
Spirits can speak by; he may misconceive,
Stutter and stammer,—he's their Sludge and drudge,
Take him or leave him; they must hold their peace,
Or else, put up with having knowledge strained
To half-expression through his ignorance.
Suppose, the spirit Beethoven wants to shed
New music he's brimful of; why, he turns   340
The handle of this organ, grinds with Sludge,
And what he poured in at the mouth o' the mill
As a Thirty-third Sonata, (fancy now!)
Comes from the hopper as bran-new Sludge, naught else,
The Shakers' Hymn in G, with a natural F,
Or the 'Stars and Stripes' set to consecutive fourths."

Sir, where's the scrape you did not help me through,
You that are wise? And for the fools, the folk
Who came to see,—the guests, (observe that word!)
Pray do you find guests criticize your wine,   350
Your furniture, your grammar, or your nose?
Then, why your "medium"? What's the difference?
Prove your madeira red-ink and gamboge,—
Your Sludge, a cheat—then, somebody's a goose

For vaunting both as genuine. "Guests!" Don't fear!
They'll make a wry face, nor too much of that,
And leave you in your glory.

                "No, sometimes
They doubt and say as much!" Ay, doubt they do!
And what's the consequence? "Of course they doubt"—
(You triumph) "that explains the hitch at once!   360
Doubt posed our 'medium,' puddled his pure mind;
He gave them back their rubbish: pitch chaff in,
Could flour come out o' the honest mill?" So, prompt
Applaud the faithful: cases flock in point,
"How, when a mocker willed a 'medium' once
Should name a spirit James whose name was George,
'James' cried the 'medium,'—'twas the test of truth!"
In short, a hit proves much, a miss proves more.
Does this convince? The better: does it fail?
Time for the double-shotted broadside, then—   370
The grand means, last resource. Look black and big!
"You style us idiots, therefore—why stop short?
Accomplices in rascality: this we hear
In our own house, from our invited guest
Found brave enough to outrage a poor boy
Exposed by our good faith! Have you been heard?
Now, then, hear us; one man's not quite worth twelve.
You see a cheat? Here's some twelve see an ass:
Excuse me if I calculate: good day!"
Out slinks the sceptic, all the laughs explode.   380
Sludge waves his hat in triumph!

                Or—he don't.
There's something in real truth (explain who can!)
One casts a wistful eye at, like the horse
Who mopes beneath stuffed hay-racks and won't munch
Because he spies a corn-bag: hang that truth,
It spoils all dainties proffered in its place!
I've felt at times when, cockered, cosseted
And coddled by the aforesaid company,
Bidden enjoy their bullying,—never fear,
But o'er their shoulders spit at the flying man,—   390
I've felt a child; only, a fractious child
That, dandled soft by nurse, aunt, grandmother,
Who keep him from the kennel, sun and wind,

Good fun and wholesome mud,—enjoined be sweet,
And comely and superior,—eyes askance
The ragged sons o' the gutter at their game,
Fain would be down with them i' the thick o' the filth,
Making dirt-pies, laughing free, speaking plain,
And calling granny the gray old cat she is.
I've felt a spite, I say, at you, at them,   400
Huggings and humbug—gnashed my teeth to mark
A decent dog pass! It's too bad, I say,
Ruining a soul so!

     But what's "so," what's fixed,
Where may one stop? Nowhere! The cheating's nursed
Out of the lying, softly and surely spun
To just your length, sir! I'd stop soon enough:
But you're for progress. "All old, nothing new?
Only the usual talking through the mouth,
Or writing by the hand? I own, I thought
This would develop, grow demonstrable,   410
Make doubt absurd, give figures we might see,
Flowers we might touch. There's no one doubts you, Sludge!
You dream the dreams, you see the spiritual sights,
The speeches come in your head, beyond dispute.
Still, for the sceptics' sake, to stop all mouths,
We want some outward manifestation!—well,
The Pennsylvanians gained such; why not Sludge?
He may improve with time!"

     Ay, that he may!
He sees his lot: there's no avoiding fate.
'Tis a trifle at first. "Eh, David? Did you hear?   420
You jogged the table, your foot caused the squeak,
This time you're . . . joking, are you not, my boy?"
"N-n-no!"—and I'm done for, bought and sold henceforth.
The old good easy jog-trot way, the . . . eh?
The . . . not so very false, as falsehood goes,
The spinning out and drawing fine, you know,—
Really mere novel-writing of a sort,
Acting, or improvising, make-believe,
Surely not downright cheatery,—any how,
'Tis done with and my lot cast; Cheat's my name: 430
The fatal dash of brandy in your tea
Has settled what you'll have the souchong's smack:

The caddy gives way to the dram-bottle.

Then, it's so cruel easy! Oh, those tricks
That can't be tricks, those feats by sleight of hand,
Clearly no common conjuror's!—no indeed!
A conjuror? Choose me any craft i' the world
A man puts hand to; and with six months' pains
I'll play you twenty tricks miraculous
To people untaught the trade: have you seen glass blown,   440
Pipes pierced? Why, just this biscuit that I chip,
Did you ever watch a baker toss one flat
To the oven? Try and do it! Take my word,
Practise but half as much, while limbs are lithe,
To turn, shove, tilt a table, crack your joints,
Manage your feet, dispose your hands aright,
Work wires that twitch the curtains, play the glove
At end o' your slipper,—then put out the lights
And . . . there, there, all you want you'll get, I hope!
I found it slip, easy as an old shoe.   450

Now, lights on table again! I've done my part,
You take my place while I give thanks and rest.
"Well, Judge Humgruffin, what's your verdict, sir?
You, hardest head in the United States,—
Did you detect a cheat here? Wait! Let's see!
Just an experiment first, for candor's sake!
I'll try and cheat you, Judge! The table tilts:
Is it I that move it? Write! I'll press your hand:
Cry when I push, or guide your pencil, Judge!"
Sludge still triumphant! "That a rap, indeed?   460
That, the real writing? Very like a whale!
Then, if, sir, you—a most distinguished man,
And, were the Judge not here, I'd say, . . . no matter!
Well, sir, if you fail, you can't take us in,—
There's little fear that Sludge will!"

                              Won't he, ma'am?
But what if our distinguished host, like Sludge,
Bade God bear witness that he played no trick,
While you believed that what produced the raps
Was just a certain child who died, you know,
And whose last breath you thought your lips had felt?   470
Eh? That's a capital point, ma'am: Sludge begins

At your entreaty with your dearest dead,
The little voice set lisping once again,
The tiny hand made feel for yours once more,
The poor lost image brought back, plain as dreams,
Which image, if a word had chanced recall,
The customary cloud would cross your eyes,
Your heart return the old tick, pay its pang!
A right mood for investigation, this!
One's at one's ease with Saul and Jonathan,   480
Pompey and Cæsar: but one's own lost child . . .
I wonder, when you heard the first clod drop
From the spadeful at the grave-side, felt you free
To investigate who twitched your funeral scarf
Or brushed your flounces? Then, it came of course
You should be stunned and stupid; then, (how else?)
Your breath stopped with your blood, your brain struck work.
But now, such causes fail of such effects,
All's changed,—the little voice begins afresh,
Yet you, calm, consequent, can test and try   490
And touch the truth. "Tests? Didn't the creature tell
Its nurse's name, and say it lived six years,
And rode a rocking-horse? Enough of tests!
Sludge never could learn that!"

                   He could not, eh?
You compliment him. "Could not?" Speak for yourself!
I'd like to know the man I ever saw
Once,—never mind where, how, why, when,—once saw,
Of whom I do not keep some matter in mind
He'd swear I "could not" know, sagacious soul!
What? Do you live in this world's blow of blacks,   500
Palaver, gossipry, a single hour
Nor find one smut has settled on your nose,
Of a smut's worth, no more, no less?—one fact
Out of the drift of facts, whereby you learn
What someone was, somewhere, somewhen, somewhy?
You don't tell folk—"See what has stuck to me!
Judge Humgruffin, our most distinguished man,
Your uncle was a tailor, and your wife
Thought to have married Miggs, missed him, hit you!"—
Do you, sir, though you see him twice a-week?   510
"No," you reply, "what use retailing it?
Why should I?" But, you see, one day you *should*,

Because one day there's much use,—when this fact
Brings you the Judge upon both gouty knees
Before the supernatural; proves that Sludge
Knows, as you say, a thing he "could not" know:
Will not Sludge thenceforth keep an outstretched face
The way the wind drives?

                 "Could not!" Look you now,
I'll tell you a story! There's a whiskered chap,
A foreigner, that teaches music here   520
And gets his bread,—knowing no better way:
He says, the fellow who informed of him
And made him fly his country and fall West
Was a hunchback cobbler, sat, stitched soles and sang,
In some outlandish place, the city Rome,
In a cellar by their Broadway, all day long;
Never asked questions, stopped to listen or look,
Nor lifted nose from lapstone; let the world
Roll round his three-legged stool, and news run in
The ears he hardly seemed to keep pricked up.   530
Well, that man went on Sundays, touched his pay,
And took his praise from government, you see;
For something like two dollars every week,
He'd engage tell you some one little thing
Of some one man, which led to many more,
(Because one truth leads right to the world's end)
And make you that man's master—when he dined
And on what dish, where walked to keep his health
And to what street. His trade was, throwing thus
His sense out, like an ant-eater's long tongue,   540
Soft, innocent, warm, moist, impassible,
And when 'twas crusted o'er with creatures—slick,
Their juice enriched his palate. "Could not Sludge!"

I'll go yet a step further, and maintain,
Once the imposture plunged its proper depth
I' the rotten of your natures, all of you,—
(If one's not mad nor drunk, and hardly then)
It's impossible to cheat—that's, be found out!
Go tell your brotherhood this first slip of mine,
All to-day's tale, how you detected Sludge,   550
Behaved unpleasantly, till he was fain confess,
And so has come to grief! You'll find, I think,

Why Sludge still snaps his fingers in your face.
There now, you've told them! What's their prompt reply?
"Sir, did that youth confess he had cheated me,
I'd disbelieve him. He may cheat at times;
That's in the 'medium'-nature, thus they're made,
Vain and vindictive, cowards, prone to scratch.
And so all cats are; still, a cat's the beast
You coax the strange electric sparks from out,   560
By rubbing back its fur; not so a dog,
Nor lion, nor lamb: 'tis the cat's nature, sir!
Why not the dog's? Ask God, who made them beasts!
D'ye think the sound, the nicely-balanced man
(Like me"—aside)—"like you yourself,"—(aloud)
"—He's stuff to make a 'medium'? Bless your soul,
'Tis these hysteric, hybrid half-and-halfs,
Equivocal, worthless vermin yield the fire!
We take such as we find them, 'ware their tricks,
Wanting their service. Sir, Sludge took in you—   570
How, I can't say, not being there to watch:
He was tried, was tempted by your easiness,—
He did not take in me!"

                    Thank you for Sludge!
I'm to be grateful to such patrons, eh,
When what you hear's my best word? 'Tis a challenge
"Snap at all strangers, half-tamed prairie-dog,
So you cower duly at your keeper's beck!
Cat, show what claws were made for, muffling them
Only to me! Cheat others if you can,
Me, if you dare!" And, my wise sir, I dared—   580
Did cheat you first, made you cheat others next,
And had the help o' your vaunted manliness
To bully the incredulous. You used me?
Have not I used you, taken full revenge,
Persuaded folk they knew not their own name,
And straight they'd own the error! Who was the fool
When, to an awe-struck wide-eyed open-mouthed
Circle of sages, Sludge would introduce
Milton composing baby-rhymes, and Locke
Reasoning in gibberish, Homer writing Greek   590
In naughts and crosses, Asaph setting psalms
To crotchet and quaver? I've made a spirit squeak
In sham voice for a minute, then outbroke

Bold in my own, defying the imbeciles—
Have copied some ghost's pothooks, half a page,
Then ended with my own scrawl undisguised.
"All right! The ghost was merely using Sludge,
Suiting itself from his imperfect stock!"
Don't talk of gratitude to me! For what?
For being treated as a showman's ape,   600
Encouraged to be wicked and make sport,
Fret or sulk, grin or whimper, any mood
So long as the ape be in it and no man—
Because a nut pays every mood alike.
Curse your superior, superintending sort,
Who, since you hate smoke, send up boys that climb
To cure your chimney, bid a "medium" lie
To sweep you truth down! Curse your women too,
Your insolent wives and daughters, that fire up
Or faint away if a male hand squeeze theirs,   310
Yet, to encourage Sludge, may play with Sludge
As only a "medium," only the kind of thing
They must humor, fondle . . . oh, to misconceive
Were too preposterous! But I've paid them out!
They've had their wish—called for the naked truth,
And in she tripped, sat down and bade them stare:
They had to blush a little and forgive!
"The fact is, children talk so; in next world
All our conventions are reversed,—perhaps
Made light of: something like old prints, my dear!   620
The Judge has one, he brought from Italy,
A metropolis in the background,—o'er a bridge,
A team of trotting roadsters,—cheerful groups
Of wayside travellers, peasants at their work,
And, full in front, quite unconcerned, why not?
Three nymphs conversing with a cavalier,
And never a rag among them: 'fine,' folk cry—
And heavenly manners seem not much unlike!
Let Sludge go on; we'll fancy it's in print!"
If such as came for wool, sir, went home shorn,   630
Where is the wrong I did them? 'Twas their choice;
They tried the adventure, ran the risk, tossed up
And lost, as some one's sure to do in games;
They fancied I was made to lose;—smoked glass
Useful to spy the sun through, spare their eyes:
And had I proved a red-hot iron plate

They thought to pierce, and, for their pains, grew blind,
Whose were the fault but theirs? While, as things go,
Their loss amounts to gain, the more's the shame!
They've had their peep into the spirit-world,   640
And all this world may know it! They've fed fat
Their self-conceit which else had starved: what chance
Save this, of cackling o'er a golden egg
And compassing distinction from the flock,
Friends of a feather? Well, they paid for it,
And not prodigiously; the price o' the play,
Not counting certain pleasant interludes,
Was scarce a vulgar play's worth. When you buy
The actor's talent, do you dare propose
For his soul beside? Whereas my soul you buy!   650
Sludge acts Macbeth, obliged to be Macbeth,
Or you'll not hear his first word! Just go through
That slight formality, swear himself's the Thane,
And thenceforth he may strut and fret his hour,
Spout, spawl, or spin his target, no one cares!
Why hadn't I leave to play tricks, Sludge as Sludge?
Enough of it all! I've wiped out scores with you—
Vented your fustian, let myself be streaked
Like tom-fool with your ochre and carmine,
Worn patchwork your respectable fingers sewed   660
To metamorphose somebody,—yes, I've earned
My wages, swallowed down my bread of shame,
And shake the crumbs off—where but in your face?

As for religion—why, I served it, sir!
I'll stick to that! With my *phenomena*
I laid the atheist sprawling on his back,
Propped up Saint Paul, or, at least, Swedenborg!
In fact, it's just the proper way to balk
These troublesome fellows—liars, one and all,
Are not these sceptics? Well, to baffle them,   670
No use in being squeamish: lie yourself!
Erect your buttress just as wide o' the line,
Your side, as they build up the wall on theirs;
Where both meet, midway in a point, is truth
High overhead: so, take your room, pile bricks,
Lie! Oh, there's titillation in all shame!
What snow may lose in white, snow gains in rose!
Miss Stokes turns—Rahab,—nor a bad exchange!

Glory be on her, for the good she wrought,
Breeding belief anew 'neath ribs of death,   680
Browbeating now the unabashed before,
Ridding us of their whole life's gathered straws
By a live coal from the altar! Why, of old,
Great men spent years and years in writing books
To prove we've souls, and hardly proved it then:
Miss Stokes with her live coal, for you and me!
Surely, to this good issue, all was fair—
Not only fondling Sludge, but, even suppose
He let escape some spice of knavery,—well,'
In wisely being blind to it! Don't you praise   690
Nelson for setting spy-glass to blind eye
And saying . . . what was it—that he could not see
The signal he was bothered with? Ay, indeed!

I'll go beyond: there's a real love of a lie,
Liars find ready-made for lies they make,
As hand for glove, or tongue for sugar-plum.
At best, 'tis never pure and full belief;
Those furthest in the quagmire,—don't suppose
They strayed there with no warning, got no chance
Of a filth-speck in their face, which they clenched teeth,   700
Bent brow against! Be sure they had their doubts,
And fears, and fairest challenges to try
The floor o' the seeming solid sand! But no!
Their faith was pledged, acquaintance too apprised,
All but the last step ventured, kerchiefs waved,
And Sludge called "pet": 'twas easier marching on
To the promised land; join those who, Thursday next,
Meant to meet Shakespeare; better follow Sludge—
Prudent, oh sure!—on the alert, how else?—
But making for the mid-bog, all the same!   730
To hear your outcries, one would think I caught
Miss Stokes by the scruff o' the neck, and pitched her flat,
Foolish-face-foremost! Hear these simpletons,
That's all I beg, before my work's begun,
Before I've touched them with my finger-tip!
Thus they await me (do but listen, now!)
It's reasoning, this is,—I can't imitate
The baby voice, though) "In so many tales
Must be some truth, truth though a pin-point big,
Yet, some: a single man's deceived, perhaps—   720

Hardly, a thousand: to suppose one cheat
Can gull all these, were more miraculous far
Than aught we should confess a miracle"—
And so on. Then the Judge sums up—(it's rare)
Bids you respect the authorities that leap
To the judgment-seat at once,—why don't you note
The limpid nature, the unblemished life,
The spotless honor, indisputable sense
Of the first upstart with his story? What—
Outrage a boy on whom you ne'er till now   730
Set eyes, because he finds raps trouble him?

Fools, these are: ay, and how of their opposites
Who never did, at bottom of their hearts,
Believe for a moment?—Men emasculate,
Blank of belief, who played, as eunuchs use,
With superstition safely,—cold of blood,
Who saw what made for them i' the mystery,
Took their occasion, and supported Sludge
—As proselytes? No, thank you, far too shrewd!
—But promisers of fair play, encouragers   740
O' the claimant; who in candor needs must hoist
Sludge up on Mars' Hill, get speech out of Sludge
To carry off, criticize, and cant about!
Didn't Athens treat Saint Paul so?—at any rate,
It's "a new thing" philosophy fumbles at.
Then there's the other picker-out of pearl
From dung-heaps,—ay, your literary man,
Who draws on his kid gloves to deal with Sludge
Daintily and discreetly,—shakes a dust
O' the doctrine, flavors thence, he well knows how,   750
The narrative or the novel,—half-believes,
All for the book's sake, and the public's stare,
And the cash that's God's sole solid in this world!
Look at him! Try to be too bold, too gross
For the master! Not you! He's the man for muck;
Shovel it forth, full-splash, he'll smooth your brown
Into artistic richness, never fear!
Find him the crude stuff; when you recognize
Your lie again, you'll doff your hat to it,
Dressed out for company! "For company,"   760
I say, since there's the relish of success:
Let all pay due respect, call the lie truth,

Save the soft silent smirking gentleman
Who ushered in the stranger: you must sigh
"How melancholy, he, the only one
Fails to perceive the bearing of the truth
Himself gave birth to!"—There's the triumph's smack!
That man would choose to see the whole world roll
I' the slime o' the slough, so he might touch the tip
Of his brush with what I call the best of browns—   770
Tint ghost-tales, spirit-stories, past the power
Of the outworn umber and bistre!

                              Yet I think
There's a more hateful form of foolery—
The social sage's, Solomon of saloons
And philosophic diner-out, the fribble
Who wants a doctrine for a chopping-block
To try the edge of his faculty upon,
Prove how much common sense he'll hack and hew
I' the critical minute 'twixt the soup and fish!
These were my patrons: these, and the like of them   780
Who, rising in my soul now, sicken it,—
These I have injured! Gratitude to these?
The gratitude, forsooth, of a prostitute
To the greenhorn and the bully—friends of hers,
From the wag that wants the queer jokes for his club,
To the snuff-box-decorator, honest man,
Who just was at his wits' end where to find
So genial a Pasiphae! All and each
Pay, compliment, protect from the police:
And how she hates them for their pains, like me!   790
So much for my remorse at thanklessness
Toward a deserving public!

                              But, for God?
Ay, that's a question! Well, sir, since you press—
(How you do tease the whole thing out of me!
I don't mean you, you know, when I say "them":
Hate you, indeed! But that Miss Stokes, that Judge!
Enough, enough—with sugar: thank you, sir!)
Now for it, then! Will you believe me, though?
You've heard what I confess; I don't unsay
A single word: I cheated when I could,   800
Rapped with my toe-joints, set sham hands at work,

Wrote down names weak in sympathetic ink,
Rubbed odic lights with ends of phosphor-match,
And all the rest; believe that: believe this,
By the same token, though it seem to set
The crooked straight again, unsay the said,
Stick up what I've knocked down; I can't help that
It's truth! I somehow vomit truth to-day.
This trade of mine—I don't know, can't be sure
But there was something in it, tricks and all!   810
Really, I want to light up my own mind.
They were tricks,—true, but what I mean to add
Is also true. First,—don't it strike you, sir?
Go back to the beginning,—the first fact
We're taught is, there's a world beside this world,
With spirits, not mankind, for tenantry;
That much within that world once sojourned here,
That all upon this world will visit there,
And therefore that we, bodily here below,
Must have exactly such an interest   820
In learning what may be the ways o' the world
Above us, as the disembodied folk
Have (by all analogic likelihood)
In watching how things go in the old home
With us, their sons, successors, and what not.
Oh yes, with added powers probably,
Fit for the novel state,—old loves grown pure,
Old interests understood aright,—they watch!
Eyes to see, ears to hear, and hands to help,
Proportionate to advancement: they're ahead,   830
That's all—do what we do, but noblier done—
Use plate, whereas we eat our meals off delf,
(To use a figure).

                Concede that, and I ask
Next what may be the mode of intercourse
Between us men here, and those once-men there?
First comes the Bible's speech; then, history
With the supernatural element,—you know—
All that we sucked in with our mothers' milk,
Grew up with, got inside of us at last,
Till it's found bone of bone and flesh of flesh.   840
See now, we start with the miraculous,
And know it used to be, at all events:

What's the first step we take, and can't but take,
In arguing from the known to the obscure?
Why this: "What was before, may be today.
Since Samuel's ghost appeared to Saul, of course
My brother's spirit may appear to me."
Go tell your teacher that! What's his reply?
What brings a shade of doubt for the first time
O'er his brow late so luminous with faith?   850
"Such things have been," says he, "and there's no doubt
Such things may be: but I advise mistrust
Of eyes, ears, stomach, and, more than all, your brain,
Unless it be of your great-grandmother,
Whenever they propose a ghost to you!"
The end is, there's a composition struck;
'Tis settled, we've some way of intercourse
Just as in Saul's time; only, different:
How, when and where, precisely,—find it out!
I want to know, then, what's so natural   860
As that a person born into this world
And seized on by such teaching, should begin
With firm expectancy and a frank look-out
For his own allotment, his especial share
I' the secret,—his particular ghost, in fine?
I mean, a person born to look that way,
Since natures differ: take the painter-sort.
One man lives fifty years in ignorance
Whether grass be green or red,—"No kind of eye
For color," say you; while another picks   870
And puts away even pebbles, when a child,
Because of bluish spots and pinky veins—
"Give him forthwith a paint-box!" Just the same
Was I born . . . "medium," you won't let me say,—
Well, seer of the supernatural
Everywhen, everyhow, and everywhere,—
Will that do?

          I and all such boys of course
Started with the same stock of Bible-truth;
Only,—what in the rest you style their sense,
Instinct, blind, reasoning but imperative,   880
This, betimes, taught them the old world had one law
And ours another: "New world, new laws," cried they:
"None but old laws, seen everywhere at work,"

Cried I, and by their help explained my life
The Jews' way, still a working way to me.
Ghosts made the noises, fairies waved the lights,
Or Santa Claus slid down on New Year's Eve
And stuffed with cakes the stocking at my bed,
Changed the worn shoes, rubbed clean the fingered slate
O' the sum that came to grief the day before.   890

This could not last long: soon enough I found
Who had worked wonders thus, and to what end:
But did I find all easy, like my mates?
Henceforth no supernatural any more?
Not a whit: what projects the billiard-balls?
"A cue," you answer: "Yes, a cue," said I;
"But what hand, off the cushion, moved the cue?
What unseen agency, outside the world,
Prompted its puppets to do this and that,
Put cakes and shoes and slates into their mind,   900
These mothers and aunts, nay even schoolmasters?"
Thus high I sprang, and there have settled since.
Just so I reason, in sober earnest still,
About the greater godsends, what you call
The serious gains and losses of my life.
What do I know or care about your world
Which either is or seems to be? This snap
O' my fingers, sir! My care is for myself;
Myself am whole and sole reality
Inside a raree-show and a market-mob   910
Gathered about it: that's the use of things.
'Tis easy saying they serve vast purposes,
Advantage their grand selves: be it true or false,
Each thing may have two uses. What's a star?
A world, or a world's sun: doesn't it serve
As taper also, time-piece, weather-glass,
And almanac? Are stars not set for signs
When we should shear our sheep, sow corn, prune trees?
The Bible says so.

                    Well, I add one use
To all the acknowledged uses, and declare   920
If I spy Charles's Wain at twelve to-night,
It warns me, "Go, nor lose another day,
And have your hair cut, Sludge!" You laugh: and why?

Were such a sign too hard for God to give?
No: but Sludge seems too little for such grace:
Thank you, sir! So you think, so does not Sludge!
When you and good men gape at Providence,
Go into history and bid us mark
Not merely powder-plots prevented, crowns
Kept on kings' heads by miracle enough,   930
But private mercies—oh, you've told me, sir,
Of such interpositions! How yourself
Once, missing on a memorable day
Your handkerchief—just setting out, you know,—
You must return to fetch it, lost the train,
And saved your precious self from what befell
The thirty-three whom Providence forgot.
You tell, and ask me what I think of this?
Well, sir, I think then, since you needs must know,
What matter had you and Boston city to boot   940
Sailed skyward, like burnt onion-peelings? Much
To you, no doubt: for me—undoubtedly
The cutting of my hair concerns me more,
Because, however sad the truth may seem,
Sludge is of all-importance to himself.
You set apart that day in every year
For special thanksgiving, were a heathen else:
Well, I who cannot boast the like escape,
Suppose I said "I don't thank Providence
For my part, owing it no gratitude"?   950
"Nay, but you owe as much"—you'd tutor me,
"You, every man alive, for blessings gained
In every hour o' the day, could you but know!
I saw my crowning mercy: all have such,
Could they but see!" Well, sir, why don't they see?
"Because they won't look,—or perhaps, they can't."
Then, sir, suppose I can, and will, and do
Look, microscopically as is right,
Into each hour with its infinitude
Of influences at work to profit Sludge?   960
For that's the case: I've sharpened up my sight
To spy a providence in the fire's going out,
The kettle's boiling, the dime's sticking fast
Despite the hole i' the pocket. Call such facts
Fancies, too petty a work for Providence,
And those same thanks which you exact from me

Prove too prodigious payment: thanks for what,
If nothing guards and guides us little men?
No, no, sir! You must put away your pride,
Resolve to let Sludge into partnership!   970
I live by signs and omens: looked at the roof
Where the pigeons settle—"If the further bird,
The white, takes wing first, I'll confess when thrashed;
Not, if the blue does"—so I said to myself
Last week, lest you should take me by surprise:
Off flapped the white,—and I'm confessing, sir!
Perhaps 'tis Providence's whim and way
With only me, i' the world: how can you tell?
"Because unlikely!" Was it likelier, now,
That this our one out of all worlds beside,   980
The what-d'you-call-'em millions, should be just
Precisely chosen to make Adam for,
And the rest o' the tale? Yet the tale's true, you know:
Such undeserving clod was graced so once;
Why not graced likewise undeserving Sludge?
Are we merit-mongers, flaunt we filthy rags?
All you can bring against my privilege
Is, that another way was taken with you,—
Which I don't question. It's pure grace, my luck:
I'm broken to the way of nods and winks,   990
And need no formal summoning. You've a help;
Holloa his name or whistle, clap your hands,
Stamp with your foot or pull the bell: all's one,
He understands you want him, here he comes.
Just so, I come at the knocking: you, sir, wait
The tongue o' the bell, nor stir before you catch
Reason's clear tingle, nature's clapper brisk,
Or that traditional peal was wont to cheer
Your mother's face turned heavenward: short of these
There's no authentic intimation, eh?   1000
Well, when you hear, you'll answer them, start up
And stride into the presence, top of toe,
And there find Sludge beforehand, Sludge that sprang
At noise o' the knuckle on the partition-wall!
I think myself the more religious man.
Religion's all or nothing; it's no mere smile
O' contentment, sigh of aspiration, sir—
No quality o' the finelier-tempered clay
Like its whiteness or its lightness; rather, stuff

O' the very stuff, life of life, and self of self.   1010
I tell you, men won't notice; when they do,
They'll understand. I notice nothing else:
I'm eyes, ears, mouth of me, one gaze and gape,
Nothing eludes me, everything's a hint,
Handle and help. It's all absurd, and yet
There's something in it all, I know: how much?
No answer! What does that prove? Man's still man,
Still meant for a poor blundering piece of work
When all's done; but, if somewhat's done, like this,
Or not done, is the case the same? Suppose   1020
I blunder in my guess at the true sense
O' the knuckle-summons, nine times out of ten,—
What if the tenth guess happen to be right?
If the tenth shovel-load of powdered quartz
Yield me the nugget? I gather, crush, sift all,
Pass o'er the failure, pounce on the success.
To give you a notion, now—(let who wins, laugh!)
When first I see a man, what do I first?
Why, count the letters which make up his name,
And as their number chances, even or odd,   1030
Arrive at my conclusion, trim my course:
Hiram H. Horsefall is your honored name,
And haven't I found a patron, sir, in you?
"Shall I cheat this stranger?" I take apple-pips,
Stick one in either canthus of my eye,
And if the left drops first—(your left, sir, stuck)
I'm warned, I let the trick alone this time.
You, sir, who smile, superior to such trash,
You judge of character by other rules:
Don't your rules sometimes fail you? Pray, what rule   1040
Have you judged Sludge by hitherto?

                        Oh, be sure,
You, everybody blunders, just as I,
In simpler things than these by far! For see:
I knew two farmers,—one, a wiseacre
Who studied seasons, rummaged almanacs,
Quoted the dew-point, registered the frost,
And then declared, for outcome of his pains,
Next summer must be dampish: 'twas a drought.
His neighbor prophesied such drought would fall,
Saved hay and corn, made cent. per cent. thereby,   1050

And proved a sage indeed: how came his lore?
Because one brindled heifer, late in March,
Stiffened her tail of evenings, and somehow
He got into his head that drought was meant!
I don't expect all men can do as much:
Such kissing goes by favor. You must take
A certain turn of mind for this,—a twist
I' the flesh, as well. Be lazily alive,
Open-mouthed, like my friend the ant-eater,
Letting all nature's loosely-guarded motes   1066
Settle and, slick, be swallowed! Think yourself
The one i' the world, the one for whom the world
Was made, expect it tickling at your mouth!
Then will the swarm of buzzing flies,
Clouds of coincidence, break egg-shell, thrive,
Breed, multiply, and bring you food enough.

I can't pretend to mind your smiling, sir!
Oh, what you mean is this! Such intimate way,
Close converse, frank exchange of offices,
Strict sympathy of the immeasurably great   1070
With the infinitely small, betokened here
By a course of signs and omens, raps and sparks,—
How does it suit the dread traditional text
O' the "Great and Terrible Name"? Shall the Heaven of Heavens
Stoop to such child's play?

                      Please, sir, go with me
A moment, and I'll try to answer you.
The "*Magnum et terribile*" (is that right?)
Well, folk began with this in the early day;
And all the acts they recognized in proof
Were thunders, lightnings, earthquakes, whirlwinds, dealt   1080
Indisputably on men whose death they caused.
There, and there only, folk saw Providence
At work,—and seeing it, 'twas right enough
All heads should tremble, hands wring hands amain,
And knees knock hard together at the breath
O' the Name's first letter; why, the Jews, I'm told,
Won't write it down, no, to this very hour,
Nor speak aloud: you know best if 't be so.
Each ague-fit of fear at end, they crept
(Because somehow people once born must live)   1090

Out of the sound, sight, swing and sway o' the Name,
Into a corner, the dark rest of the world,
And safe space where as yet no fear had reached;
'Twas there they looked about them, breathed again,
And felt indeed at home, as we might say.
The current o' common things, the daily life,
This had their due contempt; no Name pursued
Man from the mountain-top where fires abide,
To his particular mouse-hole at its foot
Where he ate, drank, digested, lived in short: 1100
Such was man's vulgar business, far too small
To be worth thunder: "small," folk kept on, "small,"
With much complacency in those great days!
A mote of sand, you know, a blade of grass—
What was so despicable as mere grass,
Except perhaps the life o' the worm or fly
Which fed there? These were "small" and men were great.
Well, sir, the old way's altered somewhat since,
And the world wears another aspect now:
Somebody turns our spy-glass round, or else   1110
Puts a new lens in it: grass, worm, fly grow big:
We find great things are made of little things,
And little things go lessening till at last
Comes God behind them. Talk of mountains now?
We talk of mould that heaps the mountain, mites
That throng the mould, and God that makes the mites.
The Name comes close behind a stomach-cyst,
The simplest of creations, just a sac
That's mouth, heart, legs and belly at once, yet lives
And feels, and could do neither, we conclude,   1120
If simplified still further one degree:
The small becomes the dreadful and immense!
Lightning, forsooth? No word more upon that!
A tin-foil bottle, a strip of greasy silk,
With a bit of wire and knob of brass, and there's
Your dollar's-worth of lightning! But the cyst—
The life of the least of the little things?

                         No, no!
Preachers and teachers try another tack,
Come near the truth this time: they put aside
Thunder and lightning: "That's mistake," they cry,   1130
"Thunderbolts fall for neither fright nor sport,

But do appreciable good, like tides,
Changes o' the wind, and other natural facts—
'Good' meaning good to man, his body or soul.
Mediate, immediate, all things minister
To man,—that's settled: be our future text
'We are His children!' " So, they now harangue
About the intention, the contrivance, all
That keeps up an incessant play of love,—
See the Bridgewater book.

      Amen to it!   1140
Well, sir, I put this question: I'm a child?
I lose no time, but take you at your word:
How shall I act a child's part properly?
Your sainted mother, sir,—used you to live
With such a thought as this a-worrying you?
"She has it in her power to throttle me,
Or stab or poison: she may turn me out,
Or lock me in,—nor stop at this to-day,
But cut me off to-morrow from the estate
I look for"—(long may you enjoy it, sir!) 1150
"In brief, she may unchild the child I am."
You never had such crotchets? Nor have I!
Who, frank confessing childship from the first,
Cannot both fear and take my ease at once,
So, don't fear,—know what might be, well enough,
But know too, child-like, that it will not be,
At least in my case, mine, the son and heir
O' the kingdom, as yourself proclaim my style.
But do you fancy I stop short at this?
Wonder if suit and service, son and heir 1160
Needs must expect, I dare pretend to find?
If, looking for signs proper to such an one,
I straight perceive them irresistible?
Concede that homage is a son's plain right,
And, never mind the nods and raps and winks,
'Tis the pure obvious supernatural
Steps forward, does its duty: why, of course!
I have presentiments; my dreams come true:
I fancy a friend stands whistling all in white
Blithe as a boblink, and he's dead I learn. 1170
I take dislike to a dog my favorite long,
And sell him; he goes mad next week and snaps.

I guess that stranger will turn up to-day
I have not seen these three years; there's his knock.
I wager "sixty peaches on that tree!"—
That I pick up a dollar in my walk,
That your wife's brother's cousin's name was George—
And win on all points. Oh, you wince at this?
You'd fain distinguish between gift and gift,
Washington's oracle and Sludge's itch   1180
O' the elbow when at whist he ought to trump?
With Sludge it's too absurd? *Fine, draw the line
Somewhere, but, sir, your somewhere is not mine!*

Bless us, I'm turning poet! It's time to end.
How you have drawn me out, sir! All I ask
Is—am I heir or not heir? If I'm he,
Then, sir, remember, that same personage
(To judge by what we read i' the newspaper)
Requires, beside one nobleman in gold
To carry up and down his coronet,   1190
Another servant, probably a duke,
To hold egg-nogg in readiness: why want
Attendance, sir, when helps in his father's house
Abound, I'd like to know?

                    Enough of talk!
My fault is that I tell too plain a truth.
Why, which of those who say they disbelieve,
Your clever people, but has dreamed his dream,
Caught his coincidence, stumbled on his fact
He can't explain, (he'll tell you smilingly)
Which he's too much of a philosopher   1200
To count as supernatural, indeed,
So calls a puzzle and problem, proud of it:
Bidding you still be on your guard, you know,
Because one fact don't make a system stand,
Nor prove this an occasional escape
Of spirit beneath the matter: that's the way!
Just so wild Indians picked up, piece by piece,
The fact in California, the fine gold
That underlay the gravel—hoarded these,
But never made a system stand, nor dug!   1210
So wise men hold out in each hollowed palm
A handful of experience, sparkling fact

They can't explain; and since their rest of life
Is all explainable, what proof in this?
Whereas I take the fact, the grain of gold,
And fling away the dirty rest of life,
And add this grain to the grain each fool has found
O' the million other such philosophers,—
Till I see gold, all gold and only gold,
Truth questionless though unexplainable,   1220
And the miraculous proved the commonplace!
The other fools believed in mud, no doubt—
Failed to know gold they saw: was that so strange?
Are all men born to play Bach's fiddle-fugues,
"Time" with the foil in carte, jump their own height,
Cut the mutton with the broadsword, skate a five,
Make the red hazard with the cue, clip nails
While swimming, in five minutes row a mile,
Pull themselves three feet up with the left arm,
Do sums of fifty figures in their head,   1230
And so on, by the scores of instances?
The Sludge with luck, who sees the spiritual facts
His fellows strive and fail to see, may rank
With these, and share the advantage.

                                      Ay, but share
The drawback! Think it over by yourself;
I have not heart, sir, and the fire's gone gray.
Defect somewhere compensates for success,
Everyone knows that. Oh, we're equals, sir!
The big-legged fellow has a little arm
And a less brain, though big legs win the race: 1240
Do you suppose I 'scape the common lot?
Say, I was born with flesh so sensitive,
Soul so alert, that, practice helping both,
I guess what's going on outside the veil,
Just as a prisoned crane feels pairing-time
In the islands where his kind are, so must fall
To capering by himself some shiny night,
As if your back-yard were a plot of spice—
Thus am I 'ware o' the spirit-world: while you,
Blind as a beetle that way,—for amends,   1250
Why, you can double your fist and floor me, sir!
Ride that hot hardmouthed horrid horse of yours,
Laugh while it lightens, play with the great dog,

Speak your mind though it vex some friend to hear,
Never brag, never bluster, never blush,—
In short, you've pluck, when I'm a coward—there!
I know it, I can't help it,—folly or no,
I'm paralyzed, my hand's no more a hand,
Nor my head a head, in danger: you can smile
And change the pipe in your cheek. Your gift's not mine.　　1260
Would you swap for mine? No! but you'd add my gift
To yours: I dare say! I too sigh at times,
Wish I were stouter, could tell truth nor flinch,
Keep cool when threatened, did not mind so much
Being dressed gayly, making strangers stare,
Eating nice things; when I'd amuse myself,
I shut my eyes and fancy in my brain
I'm—now the President, now Jenny Lind,
Now Emerson, now the Benicia Boy—
With all the civilized world a-wondering　　1270
And worshipping. I know it's folly and worse;
I feel such tricks sap, honeycomb the soul,
But I can't cure myself: despond, despair,
And then, hey, presto, there's a turn o' the wheel,
Under comes uppermost, fate makes full amends;
Sludge knows and sees and hears a hundred things
You all are blind to,—I've my taste of truth,
Likewise my touch of falsehood,—vice no doubt,
But you've your vices also: I'm content.
What, sir? You won't shake hands? "Because I cheat!"　　1280
"You've found me out in cheating!" That's enough
To make an apostle swear! Why, when I cheat,
Mean to cheat, do cheat, and am caught in the act,
Are you, or, rather, am I sure o' the fact?
(There's verse again, but I'm inspired somehow.)
Well then I'm not sure! I may be, perhaps,
Free as a babe from cheating: how it began,
My gift,—no matter; what 'tis got to be
In the end now, that's the question; answer that!
Had I seen, perhaps, what hand was holding mine,　　1290
Leading me whither, I had died of fright:
So, I was made believe I led myself.
If I should lay a six-inch plank from roof
To roof, you would not cross the street, one step,
Even at your mother's summons: but, being shrewd,
If I paste paper on each side the plank

And swear 'tis solid pavement, why, you'll cross
Humming a tune the while, in ignorance
Beacon Street stretches a hundred feet below:
I walked thus, took the paper-cheat for stone.   1300
Some impulse made me set a thing o' the move
Which, started once, ran really by itself;
Beer flows thus, suck the siphon; toss the kite,
It takes the wind and floats of its own force.
Don't let truth's lump rot stagnant for the lack
Of a timely helpful lie to leaven it!
Put a chalk-egg beneath the clucking hen,
She'll lay a real one, laudably deceived,
Daily for weeks to come. I've told my lie,
And seen truth follow, marvels none of mine;   1310
All was not cheating, sir, I'm positive!
I don't know if I move your hand sometimes
When the spontaneous writing spreads so far,
If my knee lifts the table all that height,
Why the inkstand don't fall off the desk a-tilt,
Why the accordion plays a prettier waltz
Than I can pick out on the piano-forte,
Why I speak so much more than I intend,
Describe so many things I never saw.
I tell you, sir, in one sense, I believe   1320
Nothing at all,—that everybody can,
Will, and does cheat: but in another sense
I'm ready to believe my very self—
That every cheat's inspired, and every lie
Quick with a germ of truth.

                    You ask perhaps
Why I should condescend to trick at all
If I know a way without it? This is why!
There's a strange secret sweet self-sacrifice
In any desecration of one's soul
To a worthy end,—isn't it Herodotus   1330
(I wish I could read Latin!) who describes
The single gift o' the land's virginity,
Demanded in those old Egyptian rites,
(I've but a hazy notion—help me, sir!)
For one purpose in the world, one day in a life,
One hour in a day—thereafter, purity,
And a veil thrown o'er the past for evermore!

Well, now, they understood a many things
Down by Nile city, or wherever it was!
I've always vowed, after the minute's lie,   1340
And the end's gain,—truth should be mine henceforth.
This goes to the root o' the matter, sir,—this plain
Plump fact: accept it and unlock with it
The wards of many a puzzle!

                              Or, finally,
Why should I set so fine a gloss on things?
What need I care? I cheat in self-defence,
And there's my answer to a world of cheats!
Cheat? To be sure, sir! What's the world worth else?
Who takes it as he finds, and thanks his stars?
Don't it want trimming, turning, furbishing up   1350
And polishing over? Your so-styled great men,
Do they accept one truth as truth is found,
Or try their skill at tinkering? What's your world!
Here are you born, who are, I'll say at once,
Of the luckiest kind, whether in head and heart,
Body and soul, or all that helps them both.
Well, now, look back: what faculty of yours
Came to its full, had ample justice done
By growing when rain fell, biding its time,
Solidifying growth when earth was dead,   1360
Spiring up, broadening wide, in seasons due?
Never! You shot up and frost nipped you off,
Settled to sleep when sunshine bade you sprout;
One faculty thwarted its fellow: at the end,
All you boast is "I had proved a topping tree
In other climes"—yet this was the right clime
Had you foreknown the seasons. Young, you've force
Wasted like well-streams: old,—oh, then indeed,
Behold a labyrinth of hydraulic pipes
Through which you'd play off wondrous waterwork;   1370
Only, no water's left to feed their play.
Young,—you've a hope, an aim, a love: it's tossed
And crossed and lost: you struggle on, some spark
Shut in your heart against the puffs around,
Through cold and pain; these in due time subside,
Now then for age's triumph, the hoarded light
You mean to loose on the altered face of things,—
Up with it on the tripod! It's extinct.

Spend your life's remnant asking, which was best,
Light smothered up that never peeped forth once,   1380
Or the cold cresset with full leave to shine?
Well, accept this too,—seek the fruit of it
Not in enjoyment, proved a dream on earth,
But knowledge, useful for a second chance,
Another life,—you've lost this world—you've gained
Its knowledge for the next. What knowledge, sir,
Except that you know nothing? Nay, you doubt
Whether 't were better have made you man or brute,
If aught be true, if good and evil clash.
No foul, no fair, no inside, no outside,   1390
There's your world!

           Give it me! I slap it brisk
With harlequin's pasteboard sceptre: what's it now?
Changed like a rock-flat, rough with rusty weed,
At first wash-over o' the returning wave!
All the dry dead impracticable stuff
Starts into life and light again; this world
Pervaded by the influx from the next.
I cheat, and what's the happy consequence?
You find full justice straightway dealt you out,
Each want supplied, each ignorance set at ease,   1400
Each folly fooled. No life-long labor now
As the price of worse than nothing! No mere film
Holding you chained in iron, as it seems,
Against the outstretch of your very arms
And legs i' the sunshine moralists forbid!
What would you have? Just speak and, there, you see!
You're supplemented, made a whole at last,
Bacon advises, Shakespeare writes you songs,
And Mary Queen of Scots embraces you.
Thus it goes on, not quite like life perhaps,   1410
But so near, that the very difference piques,
Shows that e'en better than this best will be—
This passing entertainment in a hut
Whose bare walls take your taste since, one stage more,
And you arrive at the palace: all half real,
And you, to suit it, less than real beside,
In a dream, lethargic kind of death in life,
That helps the interchange of natures, flesh
Transfused by souls, and such souls! Oh, 't is choice!

And if at whiles the bubble, blown too thin,   1420
Seem nigh on bursting,—if you nearly see
The real world through the false,—what *do* you see?
Is the old so ruined? You find you're in a flock
O' the youthful, earnest, passionate—genius, beauty,
Rank and wealth also, if you care for these:
And all depose their natural rights, hail you,
(That's me, sir) as their mate and yoke-fellow,
Participate in Sludgehood—nay, grow mine,
I veritably possess them—banish doubt,
And reticence and modesty alike!   1430
Why, here's the Golden Age, old Paradise
Or new Utopia! Here's true life indeed,
And the world well won now, mine for the first time!

And all this might be, may be, and with good help
Of a little lying shall be: so, Sludge lies!
Why, he's at worst your poet who sings how Greeks
That never were, in Troy which never was,
Did this or the other impossible great thing!
He's Lowell—it's a world (you smile applause),
Of his own invention—wondrous Longfellow,   1440
Surprising Hawthorne! Sludge does more than they,
And acts the books they write: the more his praise!

But why do I mount to poets? Take plain prose—
Dealers in common sense, set these at work,
What can they do without their helpful lies?
Each states the law and fact and face o' the thing
Just as he'd have them, finds what he thinks fit,
Is blind to what missuits him, just records
What makes his case out, quite ignores the rest.
It's a History of the World, the Lizard Age,   1450
The Early Indians, the Old Country War,
Jerome Napoleon, whatsoever you please,
All as the author wants it. Such a scribe
You pay and praise for putting life in stones,
Fire into fog, making the past your world.
There's plenty of "How did you contrive to grasp
The thread which led you through this labyrinth?
How build such solid fabric out of air?
How on so slight foundation found this tale,
Biography, narrative?" or, in other words,   1460

"How many lies did it require to make
The portly truth you here present us with?"
"Oh," quoth the penman, purring at your praise,
" 'T is fancy all; no particle of fact:
I was poor and threadbare when I wrote that book
'Bliss in the Golden City.' I, at Thebes?
We writers paint out of our heads, you see!"
"—Ah, the more wonderful the gift in you,
The more creativeness and godlike craft!"
But I, do I present you with my piece,   1470
It's "What, Sludge? When my sainted mother spoke
The verses Lady Jane Grey last composed
About the rosy bower in the seventh heaven
Where she and Queen Elizabeth keep house,—
You made the raps? 'T was your invention that?
Cur, slave and devil!"—eight fingers and two thumbs
Stuck in my throat!

              Well, if the marks seem gone,
'T is because stiffish cock-tail, taken in time,
Is better for a bruise than arnica.
There, sir! I bear no malice: 't isn't in me.   1480
I know I acted wrongly: still, I've tried
What I could say in my excuse,—to show
The devil's not all devil . . . I don't pretend,
He's angel, much less such a gentleman
As you, sir! And I've lost you, lost myself,
Lost all-l-l-l- . . .

              No—are you in earnest, sir?
O yours, sir, is an angel's part! I know
What prejudice prompts, and what's the common course
Men take to soothe their ruffled self-conceit:
Only you rise superior to it all!   1490
No, sir, it don't hurt much; it's speaking long
That makes me choke a little: the marks will go!
What? Twenty V-notes more, and outfit too,
And not a word to Greeley? One—one kiss
O' the hand that saves me! You'll not let me speak,
I well know, and I've lost the right, too true!
But I must say, sir, if She hears (she does)
Your sainted . . . Well, sir,—be it so! That's, I think,
My bed-room candle. Good-night! Bl-l-less you, sir!

R-r-r, you brute-beast and blackguard! Cowardly scamp!   1500
I only wish I dared burn down the house
And spoil your sniggering! Oh what, you're the man?
You're satisfied at last? You've found out Sludge?
We'll see that presently: my turn, sir, next!
I too can tell my story: brute,—do you hear?—
You throttled your sainted mother, that old hag,
In just such a fit of passion: no, it was . . .
To get this house of hers, and many a note
Like these . . . I'll pocket them, however . . . five,
Ten, fifteen . . . ay, you gave her throat the twist,   1510
Or else you poisoned her! Confound the cuss!
Where was my head? I ought to have prophesied
He'll die in a year and join her: that's the way.

I don't know where my head is: what had I done?
How did it all go? I said he poisoned her,
And hoped he'd have grace given him to repent,
Whereon he picked this quarrel, bullied me
And called me cheat: I thrashed him,—who could help?
He howled for mercy, prayed me on his knees
To cut and run and save him from disgrace: 1520
I do so, and once off, he slanders me.
An end of him! Begin elsewhere anew!
Boston's a hole, the herring-pond is wide,
V-notes are something, liberty still more.
Beside, is he the only fool in the world?

APPARENT FAILURE

"We shall soon lose a celebrated building."
PARIS NEWSPAPER

I

No, for I'll save it! Seven years since,
    I passed through Paris, stopped a day
To see the baptism of your Prince;
    Saw, made my bow, and went my way:
Walking the heat and headache off,
    I took the Seine-side, you surmise,

Thought of the Congress, Gortschakoff,
  Cavour's appeal and Buol's replies,
So sauntered till—what met my eyes?

II

Only the Doric little Morgue!
  The dead-house where you show your drowned:
Petrarch's Vaucluse makes proud the Sorgue,
  Your Morgue has made the Seine renowned.
One pays one's debt in such a case;
  I plucked up heart and entered,—stalked,
Keeping a tolerable face
  Compared with some whose cheeks were chalked:
Let them! No Briton's to be balked!

III

First came the silent gazers; next,
  A screen of glass, we're thankful for;
Last, the sight's self, the sermon's text,
  The three men who did most abhor
Their life in Paris yesterday,
  So killed themselves: and now, enthroned
Each on his copper couch, they lay
  Fronting me, waiting to be owned.
I thought, and think, their sin's atoned.

IV

Poor men, God made, and all for that!
  The reverence struck me; o'er each head
Religiously was hung its hat,
  Each coat dripped by the owner's bed,
Sacred from touch: each had his berth,
  His bounds, his proper place of rest,
Who last night tenanted on earth
  Some arch, where twelve such slept abreast,—
Unless the plain asphalt seemed best.

V

How did it happen, my poor boy?
  You wanted to be Buonaparte

And have the Tuileries for toy,
    And could not, so it broke your heart?
You, old one by his side, I judge,
    Were, red as blood, a socialist,
A leveller! Does the Empire grudge
    You've gained what no Republic missed?
Be quiet, and unclench your fist!

VI

And this—why, he was red in vain,
    Or black,—poor fellow that is blue!
What fancy was it turned your brain?
    Oh, women were the prize for you!
Money gets women, cards and dice
    Get money, and ill-luck gets just
The copper couch and one clear nice
    Cool squirt of water o'er your bust,
The right thing to extinguish lust!

VII

It's wiser being good than bad;
    It's safer being meek than fierce:
It's fitter being sane than mad.
    My own hope is, a sun will pierce
The thickest cloud earth ever stretched;
    That, after Last, returns the First,
Though a wide compass round be fetched;
    That what began best, can't end worst,
Nor what God blessed once, prove accurst.

EPILOGUE

FIRST SPEAKER, *as David*

I

On the first of the Feast of Feasts,
    The Dedication Day,
When the Levites joined the Priests
    At the Altar in robed array,
Gave signal to sound and say,—

II

When the thousands, rear and van,
   Swarming with one accord
Became as a single man
   (Look, gesture, thought and word)
In praising and thanking the Lord,—   10

III

When the singers lift up their voice,
   And the trumpets made endeavor,
Sounding, "In God rejoice!"
   Saying, "In Him rejoice
Whose mercy endureth forever!"—

IV

Then the Temple filled with a cloud,
   Even the House of the Lord;
Porch bent and pillar bowed:
   For the presence of the Lord,
In the glory of His cloud,   20
   Had filled the House of the Lord.

SECOND SPEAKER, *as Renan*

Gone now! All gone across the dark so far,
   Sharpening fast, shuddering ever, shutting still,
Dwindling into the distance, dies that star
   Which came, stood, opened once: We gazed our fill
With upturned faces on as real a Face
   That, stooping from grave music and mild fire,
Took in our homage, made a visible place
   Through many a depth of glory, gyre on gyre,
For the dim human tribute. Was this true?   30
   Could man indeed avail, mere praise of his,
To help by rapture God's own rapture too,
   Thrill with a heart's red tinge that pure pale bliss?
Why did it end? Who failed to beat the breast,
   And shriek, and throw the arms protesting wide,
When a first shadow showed the star addressed

Itself to motion, and on either side
The rims contracted as the rays retired;
  The music, like a fountain's sickening pulse,
Subsided on itself; awhile transpired   40
  .Some vestige of a Face no pangs convulse,
No prayers retard; then even this was gone,
  Lost in the night at last. We, lone and left
Silent through centuries, ever and anon
  Venture to probe again the vault bereft
Of all now save the lesser lights, a mist
  Of multitudinous points, yet suns, men say—
And this leaps ruby, this lurks amethyst,
  But where may hide what came and loved our clay?
How shall the sage detect in yon expanse   50
  The star which chose to stoop and stay for us?
Unroll the records! Hailed ye such advance
  Indeed, and did your hope evanish thus?
Watchers of twilight, is the worst averred?
  We shall not look up, know ourselves are seen,
Speak, and be sure that we again are heard,
  Acting or suffering, have the disk's serene
Reflect our life, absorb an earthly flame,
  Nor doubt that, were mankind inert and numb,
Its core had never crimsoned all the same,   60
  Nor, missing ours, its music fallen dumb?
Oh, dread succession to a dizzy post,
  Sad sway of sceptre whose mere touch appalls,
Ghastly dethronement, cursed by those the most
  On whose repugnant brow the crown next falls!

THIRD SPEAKER

I

Witless alike of will and way divine,
How heaven's high with earth's low should intertwine!
Friends, I have seen through your eyes: now use mine!

II

Take the least man of all mankind, as I;
Look at his head and heart, find how and why   70
He differs from his fellows utterly:

III

Then, like me, watch when nature by degrees
Grows alive round him, as in Arctic seas
(They said of old) the instinctive water flees

IV

Toward some elected point of central rock,
As though, for its sake only, roamed the flock
Of waves about the waste: awhile they mock

V

With radiance caught for the occasion,—hues
Of blackest hell now, now such reds and blues
As only heaven could fitly interfuse,— 80

VI

The mimic monarch of the whirlpool, king
O' the current for a minute: then they wring
Up by the roots and oversweep the thing,

VII

And hasten off, to play again elsewhere
The same part, choose another peak as bare,
They find and flatter, feast and finish there.

VIII

When you see what I tell you,—nature dance
About each man of us, retire, advance,
As though the pageant's end were to enhance

IX

His worth, and—once the life, his product, gained— 90
Roll away elsewhere, keep the strife sustained,
And show thus real, a thing the North but feigned—

X

When you acknowledge that one world could do
All the diverse work, old yet ever new,
Divide us, each from other, me from you,—

XI

Why, where's the need of Temple, when the walls
O' the world are that? What use of swells and falls
From Levites' choir, Priests' cries, and trumpet-calls?

XII

That one Face, far from vanish, rather grows,
Or decomposes but to recompose,   100
Become my universe that feels and knows.

From THE RING AND THE BOOK

[1868–69]

O LYRIC Love, half angel and half bird
And all a wonder and a wild desire,—
Boldest of hearts that ever braved the sun,
Took sanctuary within the holier blue,
And sang a kindred soul out to his face,—
Yet human at the red-ripe of the heart—
When the first summons from the darkling earth
Reached thee amid thy chambers, blanched their blue,
And bared them of the glory—to drop down,
To toil for man, to suffer or to die,—
This is the same voice: can thy soul know change?
Hail then, and hearken from the realms of help!
Never may I commence my song, my due
To God who best taught song by gift of thee,
Except with bent head and beseeching hand—
That still, despite the distance and the dark,
What was, again may be; some interchange
Of grace, some splendor once thy very thought,
Some benediction anciently thy smile:
—Never conclude, but raising hand and head
Thither where eyes, that cannot reach, yet yearn
For all hope, all sustainment, all reward,
Their utmost up and on,—so blessing back
In those thy realms of help, that heaven thy home,
Some whiteness which, I judge, thy face makes proud,
Some wanness where, I think, thy foot may fall!

[1876]

HOUSE

I

SHALL I sonnet-sing you about myself?
  Do I live in a house you would like to see?
Is it scant of gear, has it store of pelf?
  "Unlock my heart with a sonnet-key?"

II

Invite the world, as my betters have done?
  "Take notice: this building remains on view,
Its suites of reception every one,
  Its private apartment and bedroom too;

III

"For a ticket, apply to the Publisher."
  No: thanking the public, I must decline.
A peep through my window, if folk prefer;
  But, please you, no foot over threshold of mine!

IV

I have mixed with a crowd and heard free talk
  In a foreign land where an earthquake chanced:
And a house stood gaping, naught to balk
  Man's eye wherever he gazed or glanced.

V

The whole of the frontage shaven sheer,
  The inside gaped: exposed to day,
Right and wrong and common and queer,
  Bare, as the palm of your hand, it lay.

VI

The owner? Oh, he had been crushed, no doubt!
   "Odd tables and chairs for a man of wealth!
What a parcel of musty old books about!
   He smoked,—no wonder he lost his health!

VII

"I doubt if he bathed before he dressed.
   A brazier?—the pagan, he burned perfumes!
You see it is proved, what the neighbors guessed:
   His wife and himself had separate rooms."

VIII

Friends, the goodman of the house at least
   Kept house to himself till an earthquake came:
'T is the fall of its frontage permits you feast
   On the inside arrangement you praise or blame.

IX

Outside should suffice for evidence:
   And whoso desires to penetrate
Deeper, must dive by the spirit-sense—
   No optics like yours, at any rate!

X

"Hoity toity! A street to explore,
   Your house the exception! *With this same key
Shakespeare unlocked his heart,*' once more!"
   Did Shakespeare? If so, the less Shakespeare he!

SHOP

I

So, friend, your shop was all your house!
   Its front, astonishing the street,

Invited view from man and mouse
  To what diversity of treat
  Behind its glass—the single sheet!

II

What gimcracks, genuine Japanese:
  Gape-jaw and goggle-eye, the frog;
Dragons, owls, monkeys, beetles, geese;
  Some crush-nosed human-hearted dog:
  Queer names, too, such a catalogue!   10

III

I thought "And he who owns the wealth
  Which blocks the window's vastitude,
—Ah, could I peep at him by stealth
  Behind his ware, pass shop, intrude
On house itself, what scenes were viewed!

IV

"If wide and showy thus the shop,
  What must the habitation prove?
The true house with no name a-top—
  The mansion, distant one remove,
  Once get him off his traffic-groove!   20

V

"Pictures he likes, or books perhaps;
  And as for buying most and best,
Commend me to these City chaps!
  Or else he's social, takes his rest
  On Sundays, with a Lord for guest.

VI

"Some suburb-palace, parked about
  And gated grandly, built last year:
The four-mile walk to keep off gout;
  Or big seat sold by bankrupt peer:
  But then he takes the rail, that's clear.   30

VII

"Or, stop! I wager, taste selects
  Some out o' the way, some all-unknown
Retreat: the neighborhood suspects
  Little that he who rambles lone
  Makes Rothschild tremble on his throne!"

VIII

Nowise! Nor Mayfair residence
  Fit to receive and entertain,—
Nor Hampstead villa's kind defence
  From noise and crowd, from dust and drain,—
  Nor country-box was soul's domain!   40

IX

Nowise! At back of all that spread
  Of merchandise, woe's me, I find
A hole i' the wall where, heels by head,
  The owner couched, his ware behind,
  —In cupboard suited to his mind.

X

For why? He saw no use of life
  But, while he drove a roaring trade,
To chuckle "Customers are rife!"
  To chafe "So much hard cash outlaid
  Yet zero in my profits made!   50

XI

"This novelty costs pains, but—takes?
  Cumbers my counter! Stock no more!
This article, no such great shakes,
  Fizzes like wildfire? Underscore
  The cheap thing—thousands to the fore!"

XII

'Twas lodging best to live most nigh
    (Cramp, coffinlike as crib might be)
Receipt of Custom; ear and eye
    Wanted no outworld: "Hear and see
    The bustle in the shop!" quoth he.   60

XIII

My fancy of a merchant-prince
    Was different. Through his wares we groped
Our darkling way to—not to mince
    The matter—no black den where moped
    The master if we interloped!

XIV

Shop was shop only: household-stuff?
    What did he want with comforts there?
"Walls, ceiling, floor, stay blank and rough,
    So goods on sale show rich and rare!
    'Sell and scud home' be shop's affair!"   70

XV

What might he deal in? Gems, suppose!
    Since somehow business must be done
At cost of trouble,—see, he throws
    You choice of jewels, every one,
    Good, better, best, star, moon and sun!

XVI

Which lies within your power of purse?
    This ruby that would tip aright
Solomon's sceptre? Oh, your nurse
    Wants simply coral, the delight
Of teething baby,—stuff to bite!   80

XVII

Howe'er your choice fell, straight you took
    Your purchase, prompt your money rang
On counter,—scarce the man forsook
    His study of the "Times," just swang
    Till-ward his hand that stopped the clang,—

XVIII

Then off made buyer with a prize,
    Then seller to his "Times" returned;
And so did day wear, wear, till eyes
    Brightened apace, for rest was earned:
    He locked door long ere candle burned.   90

XIX

And whither went he? Ask himself,
    Not me! To change of scene, I think.
Once sold the ware and pursed the pelf,
    Chaffer was scarce his meat and drink,
    Nor all his music—money-chink.

XX

Because a man has shop to mind
    In time and place, since flesh must live,
Needs spirit lack all life behind,
    All stray thoughts, fancies fugitive,
    All loves except what trade can give?   100

XXI

I want to know a butcher paints,
    A baker rhymes for his pursuit,
Candlestick-maker much acquaints
    His soul with song, or, haply mute,
    Blows out his brains upon the flute!

XXII

But—shop each day and all day long!
   Friend, your good angel slept, your star
Suffered eclipse, fate did you wrong!
   From where these sorts of treasures are,
   There should our hearts be—Christ, how far!   110

PISGAH-SIGHTS 1

I

Over the ball of it,
   Peering and prying,
How I see all of it,
   Life there outlying!
Roughness and smoothness,
   Shine and defilement,
Grace and uncouthness:
   One reconcilement.

II

Orbed as appointed,
   Sister with brother
Joins, ne'er disjointed,
   One from the other.
All's lend-and-borrow;
   Good, see, wants evil,
Joy demands sorrow,
   Angel weds devil!

III

"Which things must—*why* be?"
   Vain our endeavor!
So shall things aye be
   As they were ever.
"Such things should *so* be!"
   Sage our desistence!

Rough-smooth let globe be,
Mixed—man's existence!

IV

Man—wise and foolish,
Lover and scorner,
Docile and mulish—
Keep each his corner!
Honey yet gall of it!
There's the life lying,
And I see all of it,
Only, I'm dying!

PISGAH-SIGHTS 2

I

COULD I but live again,
Twice my life over,
Would I once strive again?
Would not I cover
Quietly all of it—
Greed and ambition—
So, from the pall of it,
Pass to fruition?

II

"Soft!" I'd say, "Soul mine!
Three-score and ten years,
Let the blind mole mine
Digging out deniers!
Let the dazed hawk soar,
Claim the sun's rights too!
Turf 'tis thy walk's o'er,
Foliage thy flight's to."

III

Only a learner,
   Quick one or slow one,
Just a discerner,
   I would teach no one.
I am earth's native:
   No rearranging it!
I be creative,
   Chopping and changing it?

IV

March, men, my fellows!
   Those who, above me,
(Distance so mellows)
   Fancy you love me:
Those who, below me,
   (Distance makes great so).
Free to forego me,
   Fancy you hate so!

V

Praising, reviling,
   Worst head and best head
Past me defiling,
   Never arrested,
Wanters, abounders,
   March, in gay mixture,
Men, my surrounders!
   I am the fixture.

VI

So shall I fear thee,
   Mightiness yonder!
Mock-sun—more near thee,
   What is to wonder?
So shall I love thee,
   Down in the dark,—lest

Glowworm I prove thee,
Star that now sparklest!

FEARS AND SCRUPLES

I

HERE's my case. Of old I used to love him
This same unseen friend, before I knew:
Dream there was none like him, none above him,—
Wake to hope and trust my dream was true.

II

Loved I not his letters full of beauty?
Not his actions famous far and wide?
Absent, he would know I vowed him duty;
Present, he would find me at his side.

III

Pleasant fancy! for I had but letters,
Only knew of actions by hearsay:
He himself was busied with my betters;
What of that? My turn must come some day.

IV

"Some day" proving—no day! Here's the puzzle.
Passed and passed my turn is. Why complain?
He's so busied! If I could but muzzle
People's foolish mouths that give me pain!

V

"Letters?" (hear them!) "You a judge of writing?
Ask the experts!—How they shake the head
O'er these characters, your friend's inditing—
Call them forgery from A to Z!

VI

"Actions? Where's your certain proof" (they bother)
    "He, of all you find so great and good,
He, he only, claims this, that, the other
    Action—claimed by men, a multitude?"

VII

I can simply wish I might refute you,
    Wish my friend would,—by a word, a wink,—
Bid me stop that foolish mouth,—you brute you!
    He keeps absent,—why, I cannot think.

VIII

Never mind! Though foolishness may flout me,
    One thing's sure enough: 'tis neither frost,
No, nor fire, shall freeze or burn from out me
    Thanks for truth—though falsehood, gained—though lost.

IX

All my days, I'll go the softlier, sadlier,
    For that dream's sake! How forget the thrill
Through and through me as I thought "The gladlier
    Lives my friend because I love him still!"

X

Ah, but there's a menace some one utters!
    "What and if your friend at home play tricks?
Peep at hide-and-seek behind the shutters?
    Mean your eyes should pierce through solid bricks?

XI

"What and if he, frowning, wake you, dreamy?
    Lay on you the blame that bricks—conceal?
Say 'At least I saw who did not see me,
    Does see now, and presently shall feel'?"

XII

"Why, that makes your friend a monster!" say you:
   "Had his house no window? At first nod,
Would you not have hailed him?" Hush, I pray you!
   What if this friend happen to be—God?

APPEARANCES

I

And so you found that poor room dull,
   Dark, hardly to your taste, my dear?
Its features seemed unbeautiful:
   But this I know—'twas there, not here,
You plighted troth to me, the word
Which—ask that poor room how it heard.

II

And this rich room obtains your praise
   Unqualified,—so bright, so fair,
So all whereat perfection stays?
   Ay, but remember—here, not there,
The other word was spoken! Ask
This rich room how you dropped the mask!

ST. MARTIN'S SUMMER

I

No protesting, dearest!
   Hardly kisses even!
      Don't we both know how it ends?
How the greenest leaf turns serest,
   Bluest outbreak—blankest heaven,
      Lovers—friends?

II

You would build a mansion,
   I would weave a bower
      —Want the heart for enterprise.
Walls admit of no expansion: 10
   Trellis-work may haply flower
      Twice the size.

III

What makes glad Life's Winter?
   New buds, old blooms after.
      Sad the sighing "How suspect
Beams would ere mid-Autumn splinter,
   Rooftree scarce support a rafter,
      Walls lie wrecked?"

IV

You are young, my princess!
   I am hardly older: 20
      Yet—I steal a glance behind.
Dare I tell you what convinces
   Timid me that you, if bolder,
      Bold—are blind?

V

Where we plan our dwelling
   Glooms a graveyard surely!
      Headstone, footstone moss may drape,—
Name, date, violets hide from spelling,—
   But, though corpses rot obscurely,
      Ghosts escape. 30

VI

Ghosts! O breathing Beauty,
   Give my frank word pardon!
      What if I—somehow, somewhere—
Pledged my soul to endless duty

Many a time and oft? Be hard on
    Love—laid there?

VII

Nay, blame grief that's fickle,
    Time that proves a traitor,
        Chance, change, all that purpose warps,—
Death who spares to thrust the sickle   40
    Laid Love low, through flowers which later
        Shroud the corpse!

VIII

And you, my winsome lady,
    Whisper with like frankness!
        Lies nothing buried long ago?
Are yon—which shimmer mid the shady
    Where moss and violet run to rankness—
        Tombs or no?

IX

Who taxes you with murder?
    My hands are clean—or nearly!   50
        Love being mortal needs must pass.
Repentance? Nothing were absurder.
    Enough: we felt Love's loss severely;
        Though now—alas!

X

Love's corpse lies quiet therefore,
    Only Love's ghost plays truant,
        And warns us have in wholesome awe
Durable mansionry; that's wherefore
    I weave but trellis-work, pursuant
        —Life, to law.   60

XI

The solid, not the fragile,
    Tempts rain and hail and thunder.

If bower stand firm at Autumn's close,
Beyond my hope,—why, boughs were agile;
If bower fall flat, we scarce need wonder
        Wreathing—rose!

XII

So, truce to the protesting,
    So, muffled be the kisses!
        For, would we but avow the truth,
Sober is genuine joy. No jesting!   70
    Ask else Penelope, Ulysses—
        Old in youth!

XIII

For why should ghosts feel angered?
    Let all their interference
        Be faint march-music in the air!
"Up! Join the rear of us the vanguard!
    Up, lovers, dead to all appearance,
        Laggard pair!"

XIV

The while you clasp me closer,
    The while I press you deeper,   80
        As safe we chuckle,—under breath,
Yet all the slyer, the jocoser,—
    "So, life can boast its day, like leap-year,
        Stolen from death!"

XV

Ah me—the sudden terror!
    Hence quick—avaunt, avoid me,
        You cheat, the ghostly flesh-disguised!
Nay, all the ghosts in one! Strange error!
    So, 'twas Death's self that clipped and coyed me,
        Loved—and lied!   90

XVI

Ay, dead loves are the potent!
  Like any cloud they used you,
    Mere semblance you, but substance they!
Build we no mansion, weave we no tent!
  Mere flesh—their spirit interfused you!
    Hence, I say!

XVII

All theirs, none yours the glamour!
  Theirs each low word that won me,
    Soft look that found me Love's, and left
What else but you—the tears and clamor   100
  That's all your very own! Undone me—
    Ghost-bereft!

HERVÉ RIEL

I

On the sea and at the Hogue, sixteen hundred ninety-two,
  Did the English fight the French,—woe to France!
And, the thirty-first of May, helter-skelter through the blue,
Like a crowd of frightened porpoises a shoal of sharks pursue,
  Came crowding ship on ship to Saint-Malo on the Rance,
With the English fleet in view.

II

'Twas the squadron that escaped, with the victor in full chase;
  First and foremost of the drove, in his great ship, Damfreville;
    Close on him fled, great and small,
    Twenty-two good ships in all;   10
And they signalled to the place
"Help the winners of a race!
  Get us guidance, give us harbor, take us quick—or, quicker
    still,
  Here's the English can and will!"

III

Then the pilots of the place put out brisk and leapt on board;
    "Why, what hope or chance have ships like these to pass?"
      laughed they:
"Rocks to starboard, rocks to port, all the passage scarred and
    scored,—
Shall the 'Formidable' here, with her twelve and eighty guns,
    Think to make the river-mouth by the single narrow way,
Trust to enter—where 'tis ticklish for a craft of twenty tons,   20
    And with flow at full beside?
      Now, 'tis slackest ebb of tide.
    Reach the mooring? Rather say,
While rock stands or water runs,
    Not a ship will leave the bay!"

IV

Then was called a council straight.
Brief and bitter the debate:
"Here's the English at our heels; would you have them take in
    tow
All that's left us of the fleet, linked together stern and bow,
For a prize to Plymouth Sound?   30
Better run the ships aground!"
    (Ended Damfreville his speech).
"Not a minute more to wait!
    Let the Captains all and each
    Shove ashore, then blow up, burn the vessels on the beach!
France must undergo her fate.

V

"Give the word!" But no such word
Was ever spoke or heard;
    For up stood, for out stepped, for in struck amid all these
—A Captain? A Lieutenant? A Mate—first, second, third?   40
    No such man of mark, and meet
    With his betters to compete!
    But a simple Breton sailor pressed by Tourville for the fleet.
A poor coasting-pilot he, Hervé Riel the Croisickese.

VI

And "What mockery or malice have we here?" cries Hervé Riel:
   "Are you mad, you Malouins? Are you cowards, fools, or
     rogues?
Talk to me of rocks and shoals, me who took the soundings, tell
On my fingers every bank, every shallow, every swell
  'Twixt the offing here and Grève where the river disembogues?
Are you bought by English gold? Is it love the lying's for?   50
    Morn and eve, night and day,
    Have I piloted your bay,
Entered free and anchored fast at the foot of Solidor.
  Burn the fleet and ruin France? That were worse than fifty
     Hogues!
    Sirs, they know I speak the truth! Sirs, believe me there's a
     way!
Only let me lead the line,
  Have the biggest ship to steer,
  Get this 'Formidable' clear,
Make the others follow mine,
And I lead them, most and least, by a passage I know well,   60
  Right to Solidor past Grève,
    And there lay them safe and sound;
    And if one ship misbehave,—
    —Keel so much as grate the ground,
Why, I've nothing but my life,—here's my head!" cries Hervé
    Riel.

VII

Not a minute more to wait.
"Steer us in, then, small and great!
  Take the helm, lead the line, save the squadron!" cried its
    chief.
Captains, give the sailor place!
  He is Admiral, in brief.   70
Still the north-wind, by God's grace!
See the noble fellow's face
As the big ship, with a bound,
Clears the entry like a hound,
Keeps the passage, as its inch of way were the wide sea's
    profound!

See, safe thro' shoal and rock,
　　How they follow in a flock,
Not a ship that misbehaves, not a keel that grates the ground,
　　Not a spar that comes to grief!
The peril, see, is past. 80
All are harbored to the last,
And just as Hervé Riel hollas "Anchor!"—sure as fate,
Up the English come,—too late!

VIII

So, the storm subsides to calm:
　　They see the green trees wave
　　On the heights o'erlooking Grève.
Hearts that bled are stanched with balm.
"Just our rapture to enhance,
　　Let the English rake the bay,
Gnash their teeth and glare askance 90
　　As they cannonade away!
'Neath rampired Solidor pleasant riding on the Rance!"
How hope succeeds despair on each Captain's countenance!
Out burst all with one accord,
　　"This is Paradise for Hell!
　　　Let France, let France's King
　　　Thank the man that did the thing!"
What a shout, and all one word,
　　"Hervé Riel!"
As he stepped in front once more, 100
　　Not a symptom of surprise
　　In the frank blue Breton eyes,
Just the same man as before.

IX

Then said Damfreville, "My friend,
I must speak out at the end,
　　Though I find the speaking hard.
Praise is deeper than the lips:
You have saved the King his ships,
　　You must name your own reward.
Faith, our sun was near eclipse! 110
Demand whate'er you will,

France remains your debtor still.
Ask to heart's content and have! or my name's not Damfreville."

X

Then a beam of fun outbroke
On the bearded mouth that spoke,
As the honest heart laughed through
Those frank eyes of Breton blue:
"Since I needs must say my say,
 Since on board the duty's done,
  And from Malo Roads to Croisic Point, what is it but a
   run?—   120
Since 'tis ask and have, I may—
 Since the others go ashore—
Come! A good whole holiday!
 Leave to go and see my wife, whom I call the Belle Aurore!"
 That he asked and that he got,—nothing more.

XI

Name and deed alike are lost:
Not a pillar nor a post
 In his Croisic keeps alive the feat as it befell;
Not a head in white and black
On a single fishing-smack,   130
In memory of the man but for whom had gone to wrack
 All that France saved from the fight whence England bore
  the bell.
Go to Paris: rank on rank
 Search the heroes flung pell-mell
On the Louvre, face and flank!
 You shall look long enough ere you come to Hervé Riel.
So, for better and for worse,
Hervé Riel, accept my verse!
In my verse, Hervé Riel, do thou once more
Save the squadron, honor France, love thy wife the Belle
  Aurore!   140

A FORGIVENESS

I AM INDEED the personage you know.
As for my wife,—what happened long ago,—
You have a right to question me, as I
Am bound to answer.

              ("Son, a fit reply!"
The monk half spoke, half ground through his clenched teeth,
At the confession-grate I knelt beneath.)

Thus then all happened, Father! Power and place
I had as still I have. I ran life's race,
With the whole world to see, as only strains
His strength some athlete whose prodigious gains   10
Of good appall him: happy to excess,—
Work freely done should balance happiness
Fully enjoyed; and, since beneath my roof
Housed she who made home heaven, in heaven's behoof
I went forth every day, and all day long
Worked for the world. Look, how the laborer's song
Cheers him! Thus sang my soul, at each sharp throe
Of laboring flesh and blood—"She loves me so!"

One day, perhaps such song so knit the nerve
That work grew play and vanished. "I deserve   20
Haply my heaven an hour before the time!"
I laughed, as silverly the clockhouse-chime
Surprised me passing through the postern-gate
—Not the main entry where the menials wait
And wonder why the world's affairs allow
The master sudden leisure. That was how
I took the private garden-way for once.

Forth from the alcove, I saw start, ensconce
Himself behind the porphyry vase, a man.
My fancies in the natural order ran: 30
"A spy,—perhaps a foe in ambuscade,—
A thief,—more like, a sweetheart of some maid
Who pitched on the alcove for tryst perhaps."

"Stand there!" I bid.

           Whereat my man but wraps
His face the closelier with uplifted arm
Whereon the cloak lies, strikes in blind alarm
This and that pedestal as,—stretch and stoop,—
Now in, now out of sight, he thrids the group
Of statues, marble god and goddess ranged
Each side the pathway, till the gate's exchanged   40
For safety: one step thence, the street, you know!

Thus far I followed with my gaze. Then, slow,
Near on admiringly, I breathed again,
And—back to that last fancy of the train—
"A danger risked for hope of just a word
With—which of all my nest may be the bird
This poacher covets for her plumage, pray?
Carmen? Juana? Carmen seems too gay
For such adventure, while Juana's grave
—Would scorn the folly. I applaud the knave!   50
He had the eye, could single from my brood
His proper fledgeling!"

           As I turned, there stood
In face of me, my wife stone-still stone-white.
Whether one bound had brought her,—at first sight
Of what she judged the encounter, sure to be
Next moment, of the venturous man and me,—
Brought her to clutch and keep me from my prey:
Whether impelled because her death no day
Could come so absolutely opportune
As now at joy's height, like a year in June   60
Stayed at the fall of its first ripened rose:
Or whether hungry for my hate—who knows?—
Eager to end an irksome lie, and taste
Our tingling true relation, hate embraced
By hate one naked moment:—anyhow
There stone-still stone-white stood my wife, but now
The woman who made heaven within my house.
Ay, she who faced me was my very spouse
As well as love—you are to recollect!

"Stay!" she said. "Keep at least one soul unspecked 70
With crime, that's spotless hitherto—your own!
Kill me who court the blessing, who alone
Was, am, and shall be guilty, first to last!
The man lay helpless in the toils I cast
About him, helpless as the statue there
Against that strangling bell-flower's bondage: tear
Away and tread to dust the parasite,
But do the passive marble no despite!
I love him as I hate you. Kill me! Strike
At one blow both infinitudes alike 80
Out of existence—hate and love! Whence love?
That's safe inside my heart, nor will remove
For any searching of your steel, I think.
Whence hate? The secret lay on lip, at brink
Of speech, in one fierce tremble to escape,
At every form wherein your love took shape,
At each new provocation of your kiss.
Kill me!"

        We went in.

                Next day after this,
I felt as if the speech might come. I spoke—
Easily, after all.

                "The lifted cloak 90
Was screen sufficient: I concern myself
Hardly with laying hands on who for pelf—
Whate'er the ignoble kind—may prowl and brave
Cuffing and kicking proper to a knave
Detected by my household's vigilance.
Enough of such! As for my love-romance—
I, like our good Hidalgo, rub my eyes
And wake and wonder how the film could rise
Which changed for me a barber's basin straight
Into—Mambrino's helm? I hesitate 100
Nowise to say—God's sacramental cup!
Why should I blame the brass which, burnished up,
Will blaze, to all but me, as good as gold?
To me—a warning I was overbold
In judging metals. The Hidalgo waked

Only to die, if I remember,—staked
His life upon the basin's worth, and lost:
While I confess torpidity at most
In here and there a limb; but, lame and halt,
Still should I work on, still repair my fault   110
Ere I took rest in death,—no fear at all!
Now, work—no word before the curtain fall!"

The "curtain"? That of death on life, I meant:
My "word," permissible in death's event,
Would be—truth, soul to soul; for, otherwise,
Day by day, three years long, there had to rise
And, night by night, to fall upon our stage—
Ours, doomed to public play by heritage—
Another curtain, when the world, perforce
Our critical assembly, in due course   120
Came and went, witnessing, gave praise or blame
To art-mimetic. It had spoiled the game
If, suffered to set foot behind our scene,
The world had witnessed how stage-king and queen,
Gallant and lady, but a minute since
Enarming each the other, would evince
No sign of recognition as they took
His way and her way to whatever nook
Waited them in the darkness either side
Of that bright stage where lately groom and bride   130
Had fired the audience to a frenzy-fit
Of sympathetic rapture—every whit
Earned as the curtain fell on her and me,
—Actors. Three whole years, nothing was to see
But calm and concord; where a speech was due
There came the speech: when smiles were wanted too
Smiles were as ready. In a place like mine,
Where foreign and domestic cares combine,
There's audience every day and all day long;
But finally the last of the whole throng   140
Who linger lets one see his back. For her—
Why, liberty and liking: I aver,
Liking and liberty! For me—I breathed,
Let my face rest from every wrinkle wreathed
Smile-like about the mouth, unlearned my task
Of personation till next day bade mask,
And quietly betook me from that world

To the real world, not pageant; there unfurled
In work, its wings, my soul, the fretted power.
Three years I worked, each minute of each hour   150
Not claimed by acting:—work I may dispense
With talk about, since work in evidence,
Perhaps in history; who knows or cares?

After three years, this way, all unawares,
Our acting ended. She and I, at close
Of a loud night-feast, led, between two rows
Of bending male and female loyalty,
Our lord the king down staircase, while, held high
At arm's length did the twisted tapers' flare
Herald his passage from our palace, where   160
Such visiting left glory evermore.
Again the ascent in public, till at door
As we two stood by the saloon—now blank
And disencumbered of its guests—there sank
A whisper in my ear, so low and yet
So unmistakable!

                    "I half forget
The chamber you repair to, and I want
Occasion for one short word—if you grant
That grace—within a certain room you called
Our 'Study,' for you wrote there while I scrawled   170
Some paper full of faces for my sport.
That room I can remember. Just one short
Word with you there, for the remembrance' sake!"

"Follow me thither!" I replied.

                    We break
The gloom a little, as with guiding lamp
I lead the way, leave warmth and cheer, by damp
Blind disused serpentining ways afar
From where the habitable chambers are,—
Ascend, descend stairs tunnelled through the stone,—
Always in silence,—till I reach the lone   180
Chamber sepulchred for my very own
Out of the palace-quarry. When a boy,
Here was my fortress, stronghold from annoy,
Proof-positive of ownership; in youth

I garnered up my gleanings here—uncouth
But precious relics of vain hopes, vain fears;
Finally, this became in after years
My closet of entrenchment to withstand
Invasion of the foe on every hand—
The multifarious herd in bower and hall,   190
State-room,—rooms whatsoe'er the style, which call
On masters to be mindful that, before
Men, they must look like men and something more.
Here,—when our lord the king's bestowment ceased
To deck me on the day that, golden-fleeced,
I touched ambition's height,—'twas here, released
From glory (always symbolled by a chain!)
No sooner was I privileged to gain
My secret domicile than glad I flung
That last toy on the table—gazed where hung   200
On hook my father's gift, the arquebus—
And asked myself "Shall I envisage thus
The new prize and the old prize, when I reach
Another year's experience?—own that each
Equalled advantage—sportsman's—stateman's tool?
That brought me down an eagle, this—a fool!"

Into which room on entry, I set down
The lamp, and turning saw whose rustled gown
Had told me my wife followed, pace for pace.
Each of us looked the other in the face.   210
She spoke. "Since I could die now . . ."

                          (To explain
Why that first struck me, know—not once again
Since the adventure at the porphyry's edge
Three years before, which sundered like a wedge
Her soul from mine,—though daily, smile to smile,
We stood before the public,—all the while
Not once had I distinguished, in that face
I paid observance to, the faintest trace
Of feature more than requisite for eyes
To do their duty by and recognize: 220
So did I force mine to obey my will
And pry no further. There exists such skill,—
Those know who need it. What physician shrinks
From needful contact with a corpse? He drinks

No plague so long as thirst for knowledge—not
An idler impulse—prompts inquiry. What,
And will you disbelieve in power to bid
Our spirit back to bounds, as though we chid
A child from scrutiny that's just and right
In manhood? Sense, not soul, accomplished sight,   230
Reported daily she it was—not how
Nor why a change had come to cheek and brow.)

"Since I could die now of the truth concealed,
Yet dare not, must not die—so seems revealed
The Virgin's mind to me—for death means peace,
Wherein no lawful part have I, whose lease
Of life and punishment the truth avowed
May haply lengthen,—let me push the shroud
Away, that steals to muffle ere is just
My penance-fire in snow! I dare—I must   240
Live, by avowal of the truth—this truth—
I loved you! Thanks for the fresh serpent's tooth
That, by a prompt new pang more exquisite
Than all preceding torture, proves me right!
I loved you yet I lost you! May I go
Burn to the ashes, now my shame you know?"

I think there never was such—how express?—
Horror coquetting with voluptuousness,
As in those arms of Eastern workmanship—
Yataghan, kandjar, things that rend and rip,   250
Gash rough, slash smooth, help hate so many ways,
Yet ever keep a beauty that betrays
Love still at work with the artificer
Throughout his quaint devising. Why prefer,
Except for love's sake, that a blade should writhe
And bicker like a flame?—now play the scythe
As if some broad neck tempted,—now contract
And needle off into a fineness lacked
For just that puncture which the heart demands?
Then, such adornment! Wherefore need our hands   260
Enclose not ivory alone, nor gold
Roughened for use, but jewels? Nay, behold!
Fancy my favorite—which I seem to grasp
While I describe the luxury. No asp
Is diapered more delicate round throat

Than this below the handle! These denote
—These mazy lines meandering, to end
Only in flesh they open—what intend
They else but water-purlings—pale contrast
With the life-crimson where they blend at last?   270
And mark the handle's dim pellucid green,
Carved, the hard jadestone, as you pinch a bean,
Into a sort of parrot-bird! He pecks
A grape-bunch; his two eyes are ruby-specks
Pure from the mine: seen this way,—glassy blank,
But turn them,—lo the inmost fire, that shrank
From sparkling, sends a red dart right to aim!
Why did I choose such toys? Perhaps the game
Of peaceful men is warlike, just as men
War-wearied get amusement from that pen   280
And paper we grow sick of—statesfolk tired
Of merely (when such measures are required)
Dealing out doom to people by three words,
A signature and seal: we play with swords
Suggestive of quick process. That is how
I came to like the toys described you now,
Store of which glittered on the walls and strewed
The table, even, while my wife pursued
Her purpose to its ending. "Now you know
This shame, my three years' torture, let me go   290
Burn to the very ashes! You—I lost,
Yet you—I loved!"

        The thing I pity most
In men is—action prompted by surprise
Of anger: men? nay, bulls—whose onset lies
At instance of the firework and the goad!
Once the foe prostrate,—trampling once bestowed,—
Prompt follows placability, regret,
Atonement. Trust me, blood-warmth never yet
Betokened strong will! As no leap of pulse
Pricked me, that first time, so did none convulse   300
My veins at this occasion for resolve.
Had that devolved which did not then devolve
Upon me, I had done—what now to do
Was quietly apparent.

        "Tell me who
The man was, crouching by the porphyry vase!"

"No, never! All was folly in his case,
All guilt in mine. I tempted, he complied."

"And yet you loved me?"

                              "Loved you. Double-dyed
In folly and in guilt, I thought you gave
Your heart and soul away from me to slave   310
At statecraft. Since my right in you seemed lost,
I stung myself to teach you, to your cost,
What you rejected could be prized beyond
Life, heaven, by the first fool I threw a fond
Look on, a fatal word to."

                              "And you still
Love me? Do I conjecture well or ill?"

"Conjecture—well or ill! I had three years
To spend in learning you."

                              "We both are peers
In knowledge, therefore: since three years are spent
Ere thus much of yourself I learn—who went   320
Back to the house, that day, and brought my mind
To bear upon your action, uncombined
Motive from motive, till the dross, deprived
Of every purer particle, survived
At last in native simple hideousness,
Utter contemptibility, nor less
Nor more. Contemptibility—exempt
How could I, from its proper due—contempt?
I have too much despised you to divert
My life from its set course by help or hurt   330
Of your all-despicable life—perturb
The calm, I work in, by—men's mouths to curb,
Which at such news were clamorous enough—
Men's eyes to shut before my broidered stuff
With the huge hole there, my emblazoned wall
Blank where a scutcheon hung,—by, worse than all,
Each day's procession, my paraded life
Robbed and impoverished through the wanting wife
—Now that my life (which means—my work) was grown
Riches indeed! Once, just this worth alone   340

Seemed work to have, that profit gained thereby
Of good and praise would—how rewardingly!—
Fall at your feet,—a crown I hoped to cast
Before your love, my love should crown at last.
No love remaining to cast crown before,
My love stopped work now: but contempt the more
Impelled me task as ever head and hand,
Because the very fiends weave ropes of sand
Rather than taste pure hell in idleness.
Therefore I kept my memory down by stress   350
Of daily work. I had no mind to stay
For the world's wonder at the wife away.
Oh, it was easy all of it, believe,
For I despised you! But your words retrieve
Importantly the past. No hate assumed
The mask of love at any time! There gloomed
A moment when love took hate's semblance, urged
By causes you declare; but love's self purged
Away a fancied wrong I did both loves
—Yours and my own: by no hate's help, it proves,   360
Purgation was attempted. Then, you rise
High by how many a grade! I did despise—
I do but hate you. Let hate's punishment
Replace contempt's! First step to which ascent—
Write down your own words I re-utter you!
'I loved my husband and I hated—who
He was, I took up as my first chance, mere
Mud-ball to fling and make love foul with!' Here
Lies paper!"

         "Would my blood for ink suffice!"

"It may: this minion from a land of spice,   370
Silk, feather—every bird of jewelled breast—
This poignard's beauty, ne'er so lightly prest
Above your heart there . . ."

            "Thus?"

               "It flows, I see.
Dip there the point and write!"

                "Dictate to me!

Nay, I remember."

       And she wrote the words.
I read them. Then—"Since love, in you, affords
License for hate, in me, to quench (I say)
Contempt—why, hate itself has passed away
In vengeance—foreign to contempt. Depart
Peacefully to that death which Eastern art   380
Imbued this weapon with, if tales be true!
Love will succeed to hate. I pardon you—
Dead in our chamber!"

         True as truth the tale.
She died ere morning; then, I saw how pale
Her cheek was ere it wore day's paint-disguise,
And what a hollow darkened 'neath her eyes,
Now that I used my own. She sleeps, as erst
Beloved, in this your church: ay, yours!

         Immersed
In thought so deeply, Father? Sad, perhaps?
For whose sake, hers or mine or his who wraps   390
—Still plain I seem to see!—about his head
The idle cloak,—about his heart (instead
Of cuirass) some fond hope he may elude
My vengeance in the cloister's solitude?
Hardly, I think! As little helped his brow
The cloak then, Father—as your grate helps now!

FILIPPO BALDINUCCI ON THE PRIVILEGE OF BURIAL

A REMINISCENCE OF A.D. 1676

I

    "No, boy, we must not"—so began
      My Uncle (he's with God long since)
    A-petting me, the good old man!
      "We must not"—and he seemed to wince,
    And lost that laugh whereto had grown
      His chuckle at my piece of news,

How cleverly I aimed my stone—
   "I fear we must not pelt the Jews!

II

"When I was young indeed,—ah, faith
   Was young and strong in Florence too!   10
We Christians never dreamed of scathe
   Because we cursed or kicked the crew.
But now—well, well! The olive-crops
   Weighed double then, and Arno's pranks
Would always spare religious shops
   Whenever he o'erflowed his banks!

III

"I'll tell you"—and his eye regained
   Its twinkle—"tell you something choice!
Something may help you keep unstained
   Your honest zeal to stop the voice   20
Of unbelief with stone-throw—spite
   Of laws, which modern fools enact,
That we must suffer Jews in sight
   Go wholly unmolested! Fact!

IV

"There was, then, in my youth, and yet
   Is, by our San Frediano, just
Below the Blessed Olivet,
   A wayside ground wherein they thrust
Their dead,—these Jews,—the more our shame!
   Except that, so they will but die,   30
Christians perchance incur no blame
   In giving hogs a hoist to sty.

V

"There, anyhow, Jews stow away
   Their dead; and,—such their insolence,—
Slink at odd times to sing and pray
   As Christians do—all make-pretence!—

Which wickedness they perpetrate
  Because they think no Christians see.
They reckoned here, at any rate,
  Without their host: ha, ha, he, he!   40

VI

"For, what should join their plot of ground
  But a good Farmer's Christian field?
The Jews had hedged their corner round
  With bramble-bush to keep concealed
Their doings: for the public road
  Ran betwixt this their ground and that
The Farmer's, where he ploughed and sowed,
  Grew corn for barn and grapes for vat.

VII

"So, properly to guard his store
  And gall the unbelievers too,   50
He builds a shrine and, what is more,
  Procures a painter whom I knew,
One Buti (he's with God) to paint
  A holy picture there—no less
Than Virgin Mary free from taint
  Borne to the sky by angels: yes!

VIII

"Which shrine he fixed,—who says him nay?—
  A-facing with its picture-side
Not, as you'd think, the public way,
  But just where sought these hounds to hide   60
Their carrion from that very truth
  Of Mary's triumph: not a hound
Could act his mummeries uncouth
  But Mary shamed the pack all round!

IX

"Now, if it was amusing, judge!
  —To see the company arrive,

Each Jew intent to end his trudge
  And take his pleasure (though alive)
With all his Jewish kith and kin
  Below ground, have his venom out,   70
Sharpen his wits for next day's sin,
  Curse Christians, and so home, no doubt!

X

"Whereas, each phiz upturned beholds
  Mary, I warrant, soaring brave!
And in a trice, beneath the folds
  Of filthy garb which gowns each knave,
Down drops it—there to hide grimace,
  Contortion of the mouth and nose
At finding Mary in the place
  They'd keep for Pilate, I suppose!   80

XI

"At last, they will not brook—not they!—
  Longer such outrage on their tribe:
So, in some hole and corner, lay
  Their heads together—how to bribe
The meritorious Farmer's self
  To straight undo his work, restore
Their chance to meet and muse on pelf—
  Pretending sorrow, as before!

XII

"Forthwith, a posse, if you please,
  Of Rabbi This and Rabbi That   90
Almost go down upon their knees
  To get him lay the picture flat.
The spokesman, eighty years of age,
  Gray as a badger, with a goat's
Not only beard but bleat, 'gins wage
  War with our Mary. Thus he dotes:—

XIII

" 'Friends, grant a grace! How Hebrews toil
    Through life in Florence—why relate
To those who lay the burden, spoil
    Our paths of peace? We bear our fate.   100
But when with life the long toil ends,
    Why must you—the expression craves
Pardon, but truth compels me, friends!—
    Why must you plague us in our graves?

XIV

" 'Thoughtlessly plague, I would believe!
    For how can you—the lords of ease
By nurture, birthright—e'en conceive
    Our luxury to lie with trees
And turf,—the cricket and the bird
    Left for our last companionship: 110
No harsh deed, no unkindly word,
    No frowning brow nor scornful lip!

XV

" 'Death's luxury, we now rehearse
    While, living, through your streets we fare
And take your hatred: nothing worse
    Have we, once dead and safe, to bear!
So we refresh our souls, fulfil
    Our works, our daily tasks; and thus
Gather you grain—earth's harvest—still
    The wheat for you, the straw for us.   120

XVI

" ' "What flouting in a face, what harm,
    In just a lady born from bier
By boys' heads, wings for leg and arm?"
    You question. Friends, the harm is here—
That just when our last sigh is heaved,
    And we would fain thank God and you

For labor done and peace achieved,
  Back comes the Past in full review!

XVII

" 'At sight of just that simple flag,
  Starts the foe-feeling serpent-like   130
From slumber. Leave it lulled, nor drag—
  Though fangless—forth, what needs must strike
When stricken sore, though stroke be vain
  Against the mailed oppressor! Give
Play to our fancy that we gain
  Life's rights when once we cease to live!

XVIII

" 'Thus much to courtesy, to kind,
  To conscience! Now to Florence folk!
There's core beneath this apple-rind,
  Beneath this white-of-egg there's yolk!   140
Beneath this prayer to courtesy,
  Kind, conscience—there's a sum to pouch!
How many ducats down will buy
  Our shame's removal, sirs? Avouch!

XIX

" 'Removal, not destruction, sirs!
  Just turn your picture! Let it front
The public path! Or memory errs,
  Or that same public path is wont
To witness many a chance befall
  Of lust, theft, bloodshed—sins enough,   150
Wherein our Hebrew part is small.
  Convert yourselves!'—he cut up rough.

XX

"Look you, how soon a service paid
  Religion yields the servant fruit!
A prompt reply our Farmer made
  So following: 'Sirs, to grant your suit

Involves much danger! How? Transpose
　　Our Lady? Stop the chastisement,
All for your good, herself bestows?
　　What wonder if I grudge consent?　　160

XXI

" '—*Yet grant it: since, what cash I take*
　　Is so much saved from wicked use.
We know you! And, for Mary's sake,
　　A hundred ducats shall induce
Concession to your prayer. One day
　　Suffices: Master Buti's brush
Turns Mary round the other way,
　　And deluges your side with slush.

XXII

" '*Down with the ducats therefore!'* Dump,
　　Dump, dump it falls, each counted piece,　　170
Hard gold. Then out of door they stump,
　　These dogs, each brisk as with new lease
Of life, I warrant,—glad he'll die
　　Henceforward just as he may choose,
Be buried and in clover lie!
　　Well said Esaias—'*stiff-necked Jews!*'

XXIII

"Off posts without a minute's loss
　　Our Farmer, once the cash in poke
And summons Buti—ere its gloss
　　Have time to fade from off the joke—　　180
To chop and change his work, undo
　　The done side, make the side, now blank,
Recipient of our Lady—who,
　　Displaced thus, had these dogs to thank!

XXIV

"Now, boy, you're hardly to instruct
　　In technicalities of Art!

My nephew's childhood sure has sucked
   Along with mother's-milk some part
Of painter's-practice—learned, at least,
   How expeditiously is plied   190
A work in fresco—never ceased
   When once begun—a day, each side.

XXV

"So, Buti—(he's with God)—begins:
   First covers up the shrine all round
With hoarding; then, as like as twins,
   Paints, t'other side the burial-ground,
New Mary, every point the same;
   Next, sluices over, as agreed,
The old; and last—but, spoil the game
   By telling you? Not I, indeed!   200

XXVI

"Well, ere the week was half at end,
   Out came the object of this zeal,
This fine alacrity to spend
   Hard money for mere dead men's weal!
How think you? That old spokesman Jew
   Was High Priest, and he had a wife
As old, and she was dying too,
   And wished to end in peace her life!

XXVII

"And he must humor dying whims,
   And soothe her with the idle hope   210
They'd say their prayers and sing their hymns
   As if her husband were the Pope!
And she did die—believing just
   This privilege was purchased! Dead
In comfort through her foolish trust!
   'Stiff-necked ones,' well Esaias said!

XXVIII

"So, Sabbath morning, out of gate
   And on to way, what sees our arch

Good Farmer? Why, they hoist their freight—
   The corpse—on shoulder, and so, march!   220
'*Now for it, Buti!*' In the nick
   Of time 'tis pully-hauly, hence
With hoarding! O'er the wayside quick
   There's Mary plain in evidence!

XXIX

"And here's the convoy halting: right!
   O they are bent on howling psalms
And growling prayers, when opposite!
   And yet they glance, for all their qualms
Approve that promptitude of his,
   The Farmer's—duly at his post   230
To take due thanks from every phiz,
   Sour smirk—nay, surly smile almost!

XXX

"Then earthward drops each brow again;
   The solemn task's resumed; they reach
Their holy field—the unholy train:
   Enter its precinct, all and each,
Wrapt somehow in their godless rites;
   Till, rites at end, up-waking, lo
They lift their faces! What delights
   The mourners as they turn to go?   240

XXXI

"Ha, ha, he, he! On just the side
   They drew their purse-strings to make quit
Of Mary,—Christ the Crucified
   Fronted them now—these biters bit!
Never was such a hiss and snort,
   Such screwing nose and shooting lip!
Their purchase—honey in report—
   Proved gall and verjuice at first sip!

XXXII

"Out they break, on they bustle, where,
 A-top of wall, the Farmer waits   250
With Buti: never fun so rare!
 The Farmer has the best: he rates
The rascal, as the old High Priest
 Takes on himself to sermonize—
Nay, sneer *'We Jews supposed, at least,*
 Theft was a crime in Christian eyes!'

XXXIII

" *'Theft?'* cries the Farmer. *'Eat your words!*
 Show me what constitutes a breach
Of faith in aught was said or heard!
 I promised you in plainest speech   260
I'd take the thing you count disgrace
 And put it here—and here 'tis put!
Did you suppose I'd leave the place
 Blank, therefore, just your rage to glut?

XXXIV

" *'I guess you dared not stipulate*
 For such a damned impertinence!
So, quick, my graybeard, out of gate
 And in at Ghetto! Haste you hence!
As long as I have house and land,
 To spite you irreligious chaps   270
Here shall the Crucifixion stand—
 Unless you down with cash, perhaps?'

XXXV

"So snickered he and Buti both.
 The Jews said nothing, interchanged
A glance or two, renewed their oath
 To keep ears stopped and hearts estranged
From grace, for all our Church can do;
 Then off they scuttle: sullen jog

Homewards, against our Church to brew
   Fresh mischief in their synagogue.   280

XXXVI

"But next day—see what happened, boy!
   See why I bid you have a care
How you pelt Jews! The knaves employ
   Such methods of revenge, forbear
No outrage on our faith, when free
   To wreak their malice! Here they took
So base a method—plague o' me
   If I record it in my Book!

XXXVII

"For, next dav, while the Farmer sat
   Laughing with Buti, in his shop,   290
At their successful joke,—rat-tat,—
   Door opens, and they're like to drop
Down to the floor as in there stalks
   A six-feet-high herculean-built
Young he-Jew with a beard that balks
   Description. *'Help ere blood be spilt!'*

XXXVIII

—"Screamed Buti: for he recognized
   Whom but the son, no less no more,
Of that High Priest his work surprised
   So pleasantly the day before!   300
Son of the mother, then, whereof
   The bier he lent a shoulder to,
And made the moans about, dared scoff
   At sober Christian grief—the Jew!

XXXIX

" *'Sirs, I salute you! Never rise!*
   No apprehension!' (Buti, white
And trembling like a tub of size,
   Had tried to smuggle out of sight

The picture's self—the thing in oils,
    You know, from which a fresco's dashed   310
Which courage speeds while caution spoils)
    'Stay and be praised, sir, unabashed!

XL

" 'Praised,—ay, and paid too: for I come
    To buy that very work of yours.
My poor abode, which boasts—well, some
    Few specimens of Art, secures
Haply, a masterpiece indeed
    If I should find my humble means
Suffice the outlay. So, proceed!
    Propose—ere prudence intervenes!'   320

XLI

"On Buti, cowering like a child,
    These words descended from aloft,
In tone so ominously mild,
    With smile terrifically soft
To that degree—could Buti dare
    (Poor fellow) use his brains, think twice?
He asked, thus taken unaware,
    No more than just the proper price!

XLII

" 'Done!' cries the monster. 'I disburse
    Forthwith your moderate demand.   330
Count on my custom—if no worse
    Your future work be, understand,
Than this I carry off! No aid!
    My arm, sir, lacks nor bone nor thews:
The burden's easy, and we're made,
    Easy or hard, to bear—we Jews!'

XLIII

"Crossing himself at such escape,
    Buti by turns the money eyes

And, timidly, the stalwart shape
    Now moving doorwards; but, more wise,   340
The Farmer,—who, though dumb, this while
    Had watched advantage,—straight conceived
A reason for that tone and smile
    So mild and soft! The Jew—believed!

XLIV

"Mary in triumph borne to deck
    A Hebrew household! Pictured where
No one was used to bend the neck
    In praise or bow the knee in prayer!
Borne to that domicile by whom?
    The son of the High Priest! Through what?   350
An insult done his mother's tomb!
    Saul changed to Paul—the case came pat!

XLV

" *'Stay, dog Jew . . . gentle sir, that is!*
    Resolve me! Can it be, she crowned,—
Mary, by miracle,—Oh bliss!—
    My present to your burial ground?
Certain, a ray of light has burst
    Your veil of darkness! Had you else,
Only for Mary's sake, unpursed
    So much hard money? Tell—oh, tell's!'   360

XLVI

"Round—like a serpent that we took
    For worm and trod on—turns his bulk
About the Jew. First dreadful look
    Sends Buti in a trice to skulk
Out of sight somewhere, safe—alack!
    But our good Farmer faith made bold:
And firm (with Florence at his back)
    He stood, while gruff the gutturals rolled—

XLVII

" 'Ay, sir, a miracle was worked,
    By quite another power, I trow,   370
Than ever yet in canvas lurked,
    Or you would scarcely face me now!
A certain impulse did suggest
    A certain grasp with this right-hand,
Which probably had put to rest
    Our quarrel,—thus your throat once spanned!

XLVIII

" 'But I remembered me, subdued
    That impulse, and you face me still!
And soon a philosophic mood
    Succeeding (hear it, if you will!)   380
Has altogether changed my views
    Concerning Art. Blind prejudice!
Well may you Christians tax us Jews
    With scrupulosity too nice!

XLIX

" 'For, don't I see,—let's issue join!—
    Whenever I'm allowed pollute
(I—and my little bag of coin)
    Some Christian palace of repute,—
Don't I see stuck up everywhere
    Abundant proof that cultured taste   390
Has Beauty for its only care,
    And upon Truth no thought to waste?

L

" ' "Jew, since it must be, take in pledge
    Of payment"—so a Cardinal
Has sighed to me as if a wedge
    Entered his heart—"this best of all
My treasures!" Leda, Ganymede
    Or Antiope: swan, eagle, ape,

(Or what's the beast of what's the breed)
  And Jupiter in every shape!   400

LI

" 'Whereat if I presume to ask
  "But, Eminence, though Titian's whisk
Of brush have well performed its task,
  How comes it these false godships frisk
In presence of—what yonder frame
  Pretends to image? Surely, odd
It seems, you let confront The Name
  Each beast the heathen called his god!"

LII

" 'Benignant smiles me pity straight
  The Cardinal. " 'Tis truth, we prize!   410
Art's the sole question in debate!
  These subjects are so many lies.
We treat them with a proper scorn
  When we turn lies—called gods forsooth—
To lies' fit use, now Christ is born.
  Drawing and coloring are Truth.

LIII

" ' "Think you I honor lies so much
  As scruple to parade the charms
Of Leda—Titian, every touch—
  Because the thing within her arms   420
Means Jupiter who had the praise
  And prayer of a benighted world?
He would have mine too, if, in days
  Of light, I kept the canvas furled!"

LIV

" 'So ending, with some easy gibe.
  What power has logic! I, at once,
Acknowledged error in our tribe
  So squeamish that, when friends ensconce

A pretty picture in its niche
*   To do us honor, deck our graves,*   430
We fret and fume and have an itch
*   To strangle folk—ungrateful knaves!*

LV

" 'No, sir! Be sure that—what's its style,
*   Your picture?—shall possess ungrudged*
A place among my rank and file
*   Of Ledas and what not—be judged*
Just as a picture! and (because
*   I fear me much I scarce have bought*
A Titian) Master Buti's flaws
*   Found there, will have the laugh flaws ought!'*   440

LVI

"So, with a scowl, it darkens door—
    This bulk—no longer! Buti makes
Prompt glad re-entry; there's a score
    Of oaths, as the good Farmer wakes
From what must needs have been a trance,
    Or he had struck (he swears) to ground
The bold bad mouth that dared advance
    Such doctrine the reverse of sound!

LVII

"Was magic here? Most like! For, since,
    Somehow our city's faith grows still   450
More and more lukewarm, and our Prince
    Or loses heart or wants the will
To check increase of cold. 'Tis '*Live*
    And let live! Languidly repress
The Dissident! In short,—contrive
    Christians must bear with Jews: no less!'

LVIII

"The end seems, any Israelite
    Wants any picture,—pishes, poohs,

Purchases, hangs it full in sight
   In any chamber he may choose!
In Christ's crown, one more thorn we rue!
   In Mary's bosom, one more sword!
No, boy, you must not pelt a Jew!
   O Lord, how long? How long, O Lord?"

LA SAISIAZ

[1878]

I

GOOD, to forgive;
   Best, to forget!
   Living, we fret;
Dying, we live.
Fretless and free,
   Soul, clap thy pinion!
   Earth have dominion,
Body, o'er thee!

II

Wander at will,
   Day after day,—
   Wander away,
Wandering still—
Soul that canst soar!
   Body may slumber:
   Body shall cumber
Soul-flight no more.

III

Waft of soul's wing!
   What lies above?
   Sunshine and Love,
Skyblue and Spring!
Body hides—where?
   Ferns of all feather,
   Mosses and heather,
Yours be the care!

A. E. S. *September 14, 1877*

DARED and done: at last I stand upon the summit, Dear and
    True!
Singly dared and done; the climbing both of us were bound to
    do.
Petty feat and yet prodigious: every side my glance was bent
O'er the grandeur and the beauty lavished through the whole
    ascent.
Ledge by ledge, out broke new marvels, now minute and now
    immense:
Earth's most exquisite disclosure, heaven's own God in evidence!
And no berry in its hiding, no blue space in its outspread,
Pleaded to escape my footstep, challenged my emerging head,
(As I climbed or paused from climbing, now o'er-branched by
    shrub and tree,
Now built round by rock and boulder, now at just a turn
    set free,   10
Stationed face to face with—Nature? rather with Infinitude)
—No revealment of them all, as singly I my path pursued,
But a bitter touched its sweetness, for the thought stung "Even
    so
Both of us had loved and wondered just the same, five days ago!"
Five short days, sufficient hardly to entice, from out its den
Splintered in the slab, this pink perfection of the cyclamen;
Scarce enough to heal and coat with amber gum the sloe-tree's
    gash,
Bronze the clustered wilding apple, redden ripe the mountain-
    ash:
Yet of might to place between us—Oh the barrier! Yon Pro-
    found
Shrinks beside it, proves a pin-point: barrier this, without
    a bound!   20
Boundless though it be, I reach you: somehow seem to have you
    here
—Who are there. Yes, there you dwell now, plain the four low
    walls appear;
Those are vineyards they enclose from; and the little spire which
    points
—That's Collonge, henceforth your dwelling. All the same,
    howe'er disjoints

Past from present, no less certain you are here, not there: have
    dared,
Done the feat of mountain-climbing,—five days since, we both
    prepared
Daring, doing, arm in arm, if other help should haply fail.
For you asked, as forth we sallied to see sunset from the vale,
"Why not try for once the mountain,—take a foretaste, snatch
    by stealth
Sight and sound, some unconsidered fragment of the
    hoarded wealth?   30
Six weeks at its base, yet never once have we together won
Sight or sound by honest climbing: let us two have dared and
    done
Just so much of twilight journey as may prove to-morrow's jaunt
Not the only mode of wayfare—wheeled to reach the eagle's
    haunt!"
So, we turned from the low grass-path you were pleased to call
    "your own,"
Set our faces to the rose-bloom o'er the summit's front of stone
Where Salève obtains, from Jura and the sunken sun she hides,
Due return of blushing "Good Night," rosy as a borne-off bride's,
For his masculine "Good Morrow" when, with sunrise still in
    hold,
Gay he hails her, and, magnific, thrilled her black length
    burns to gold.   40
Up and up we went, how careless—nay, how joyous! All was
    new,
All was strange. "Call progress toilsome? that were just insulting
    you!
How the trees must temper noontide! Ah, the thicket's sudden
    break!
What will be the morning glory, when at dusk thus gleams the
    lake?
Light by light puts forth Geneva: what a land—and, of the land,
Can there be a lovelier station than this spot where now we
    stand?
Is it late, and wrong to linger? True, to-morrow makes amends.
Toilsome progress? child's play, call it—specially when one
    descends!
There, the dread descent is over—hardly our adventure, though!
Take the vale where late we left it, pace the grass-path,
    'mine,' you know!   50

Proud completion of achievement!" And we paced it, praising
    still
That soft tread on velvet verdure as it wound through hill and
    hill;
And at very end there met us, coming from Collonge, the pair
—All our people of the Chalet—two, enough and none to spare.
So, we made for home together, and we reached it as the stars
One by one came lamping—chiefly that prepotency of Mars—
And your last word was "I owe you this enjoyment!"—met with
    "Nay:
With yourself it rests to have a month of morrows like to-day!"
Then the meal, with talk and laughter, and the news of that rare
    nook
Yet untroubled by the tourist, touched on by no travel-book,   60
All the same—though latent—patent, hybrid birth of land and
    sea,
And (our travelled friend assured you)—if such miracle might
    be—
Comparable for completeness of both blessings—all around
Nature, and, inside her circle, safety from world's sight and
    sound—
Comparable to our Saisiaz. "Hold it fast and guard it well!
Go and see and vouch for certain, then come back and never tell
Living soul but us; and haply, prove our sky from cloud as clear,
There may we four meet, praise fortune just as now, another
    year!"

Thus you charged him on departure: not without the final charge
"Mind to-morrow's early meeting! We must leave our
    journey marge   70
Ample for the wayside wonders: there's the stoppage at the inn
Three-parts up the mountain, where the hardships of the track
    begin;
There's the convent worth a visit; but, the triumph crowning
    all—
There's Salève's own platform facing glory which strikes great-
    ness small,
—Blanc, supreme above his earth-brood, needles red and white
    and green,
Horns of silver, fangs of crystal set on edge in his demesne.
So, some three weeks since, we saw them: so, to-morrow we
    intend

You shall see them likewise; therefore Good Night till to-morrow,
    friend!"
Last, the nothings that extinguish embers of a vivid day:
"What might be the Marshal's next move, what Gambetta's
    counter-play?"   80
Till the landing on the staircase saw escape the latest spark:
"Sleep you well!" "Sleep but as well, you!"—lazy love quenched,
    all was dark.
Nothing dark next day at sundawn! Up I rose and forth I fared:
Took my plunge within the bath-pool, pacified the watch-dog
    scared,
Saw proceed the transmutation—Jura's black to one gold glow,
Trod your level path that let me drink the morning deep and
    slow,
Reached the little quarry—ravage recompensed by shrub and
    fern—
Till the overflowing ardors told me time was for return.
So, return I did, and gayly. But, for once, from no far mound
Waved salute a tall white figure. "Has her sleep been so pro-
    found?   90
Foresight, rather, prudent saving strength for day's expenditure!
Ay, the chamber-window's open: out and on the terrace, sure!"

No, the terrace showed no figure, tall, white, leaning through the
    wreaths,
Tangle-twine of leaf and bloom that intercept the air one
    breathes,
Interpose between one's love and Nature's loving, hill and dale
Down to where the blue lake's wrinkle marks the river's inrush
    pale
—Mazy Arve: whereon no vessel but goes sliding white and
    plain,
Not a steamboat pants from harbor but one hears pulsate amain,
Past the city's congregated peace of homes and pomp of spires
—Man's mild protest that there's something more than Nature,
    man requires,   100
And that, useful as is Nature to attract the tourist's foot,
Quiet slow sure money-making proves the matter's very root,—
Need for body,—while the spirit also needs a comfort reached
By no help of lake or mountain, but the texts whence Calvin
    preached.
"Here's the veil withdrawn from landscape: up to Jura and be-
    yond,

All awaits us ranged and ready; yet she violates the bond,
Neither leans nor looks nor listens: why is this?" A turn of eye
Took the whole sole answer, gave the undisputed reason "why!"

This dread way you had your summons! No premonitory touch,
As you talked and laughed ('tis told me) scarce a minute ere the
    clutch   110
Captured you in cold forever. Cold? nay, warm you were as life
When I raised you, while the others used, in passionate poor
    strife,
All the means that seemed to promise any aid, and all in vain.
Gone you were, and I shall never see that earnest face again
Grow transparent, grow transfigured with the sudden light that
    leapt,
At the first word's provocation, from the heart-deeps where it
    slept.

Therefore, paying piteous duty, what seemed You have we con-
    signed
Peacefully to—what I think were, of all earth-beds, to your
    mind
Most the choice for quiet, yonder: low walls stop the vines' ap-
    proach,
Lovingly Salève protects you; village-sports will ne'er en-
    croach   120
On the stranger lady's silence, whom friends bore so kind and
    well
Thither "just for love's sake,"—such their own word was: and
    who can tell?
You supposed that few or none had known and loved you in the
    world:
May be! flower that's full-blown tempts the butterfly, not flower
    that's furled.
But more learned sense unlocked you, loosed the sheath and let
    expand
Bud to bell and outspread flower-shape at the least warm touch
    of hand
—Maybe, throb of heart, beneath which,—quickening farther
    than it knew,—
Treasure oft was disembosomed, scent all strange and unguessed
    hue.
Disembosomed, re-embosomed,—must one memory suffice,

Prove I knew an Alpine-rose which all beside named Edel-
    weiss?   130

Rare thing, red or white, you rest now: two days slumbered
    through; and since
One day more will see me rid of this same scene whereat I wince,
Tetchy at all sights and sounds and pettish at each idle charm
Proffered me who pace now singly where we two went arm in
    arm,—
I have turned upon my weakness: asked "And what, forsooth,
    prevents
That, this latest day allowed me, I fulfill of her intents
One she had the most at heart—that we should thus again sur-
    vey
From Salève Mont Blanc together?" Therefore,—dared and done
    to-day
Climbing,—here I stand: but you—where?

                                    If a spirit of the place
Broke the silence, bade me question, promised answer,—what
    disgrace   140
Did I stipulate "Provided answer suit my hopes, not fears!"
Would I shrink to learn my life-time's limit—days, weeks,
    months or years?
Would I shirk assurance on each point whereat I can but guess—
"Does the soul survive the body? Is there God's self, no or yes?"
If I know my mood, 'twere constant—come in whatsoe'er un-
    couth
Shape it should, nay, formidable—so the answer were but truth.

Well, and wherefore shall it daunt me, when 'tis I myself am
    tasked,
When, by weakness weakness questioned, weakly answers—
    weakly asked?
Weakness never needs be falseness: truth is truth in each degree
—Thunderpealed by God to Nature, whispered by my soul to
    me.   150
Nay, the weakness turns to strength and triumphs in a truth
    beyond:
"Mine is but man's truest answer—how were it did God re-
    spond?"
I shall no more dare to mimic such response in futile speech,

Pass off human lisp as echo of the sphere-song out of reach,
Than,— because it well may happen yonder, where the far snows
    blanch
Mute Mont Blanc, that who stands near them sees and hears an
    avalanche,—
I shall pick a clod and throw,—cry "Such the sight and such the
    sound!
What though I nor see nor hear them? Others do, the proofs
    abound!"
Can I make my eye an eagle's, sharpen ear to recognize
Sound o'er league and league of silence? Can I know, who but
    surmise?   160
If I dared no self-deception when, a week since, I and you
Walked and talked along the grass-path, passing lightly in review
What seemed hits and what seemed misses in a certain fence-
    play,—strife
Sundry minds of mark engaged in "On the Soul and Future
    Life,"—
If I ventured estimating what was come of parried thrust,
Subtle stroke, and, rightly, wrongly, estimating could be just
—Just, though life so seemed abundant in the form which moved
    by mine,
I might well have played at feigning, fooling,—laughed "What
    need opine
Pleasure must succeed to pleasure, else past pleasure turns to
    pain,
And this first life claims a second, else I count its good no
    gain?"   170
Much less have I heart to palter when the matter to decide
Now becomes "Was ending ending once and always, when you
    died?"
Did the face, the form I lifted as it lay, reveal the loss
Not alone of life but soul? A tribute to yon flowers and moss,
What of you remains beside? A memory! Easy to attest
"Certainly from out the world that one believes who knew her
    best
Such was good in her, such fair, which fair and good were great
    perchance
Had but fortune favored, bidden each shy faculty advance;
After all—who knows another? Only as I know, I speak."
So much of you lives within me while I live my year or
    week.   180
Then my fellow takes the tale up, not unwilling to aver

Duly in his turn "I knew him best of all, as he knew her:
Such he was, and such he was not, and such other might have
    been
But that somehow every actor, somewhere in this earthly scene,
Fails." And so both memories dwindle, yours and mine together
    linked,
Till there is but left for comfort, when the last spark proves
    extinct,
This—that somewhere new existence led by men and women
    new
Possibly attains perfection coveted by me and you;
While ourselves, the only witness to what work our life evolved,
Only to ourselves proposing problems proper to be solved   190
By ourselves alone,—who working ne'er shall know if work bear
    fruit
Others reap and garner, heedless how produced by stalk and
    root,—
We who, darkling, timed the day's birth,—struggling, testified
    to peace,—
Earned, by dint of failure, triumph,—we, creative thought, must
    cease
In created word, thought's echo, due to impulse long since sped!
Why repine? There's ever some one lives although ourselves be
    dead!

Well, what signifies repugnance? Truth is truth howe'er it strike.
Fair or foul the lot apportioned life on earth, we bear alike.
Stalwart body idly yoked to stunted spirit, powers, that fain
Else would soar, condemned to grovel, groundlings through the
    fleshly chain,—   200
Help that hinders, hindrance proved but help disguised when all
    too late,—
Hindrance is the fact acknowledged, howsoe'er explained as
    Fate,
Fortune, Providence: we bear, own life a burthen more or less.
Life thus owned unhappy, is there supplemental happiness
Possible and probable in life to come? or must we count
Life a curse and not a blessing, summed-up in its whole amount,
Help and hindrance, joy and sorrow?

                Why should I want courage here?
I will ask and have an answer,—with no favor, with no fear,—
From myself. How much, how little, do I inwardly believe

True that controverted doctrine? Is it fact to which I cleave,   210
Is it fancy I but cherish, when I take upon my lips
Phrase the solemn Tuscan fashioned, and declare the soul's
     eclipse
Not the soul's extinction? take his "I believe and I declare—
Certain am I—from this life I pass into a better, there
Where that lady lives of whom enamored was my soul"—where
     this
Other lady, my companion dear and true, she also is?

I have , questioned and am answered. Question, answer pre-
     suppose
Two points: that the thing itself which questions, answers,—*is*,
     it knows;
As it also knows the thing perceived outside itself,—a force
Actual ere its own beginning, operative through its course,   220
Unaffected by its end,—that this thing likewise needs must be;
Call this—God, then, call that—soul, and both—the only facts
     for me.
Prove them facts? that they o'erpass my power of proving, proves
     them such:
Fact it is I know I know not something which is fact as much.
What before caused all the causes, what effect of all effects
Haply follows,—these are fancy. Ask the rush if it suspects
Whence and how the stream which floats it had a rise, and
     where and how
Falls or flows on still! What answer makes the rush except that
     now
Certainly it floats and is, and, no less certain than itself,
Is the everyway external stream that now through shoal and
     shelf
                                        230
Floats it onward, leaves it—may be—wrecked at last, or lands
     on shore
There to root again and grow and flourish stable evermore.
—May be! mere surmise not knowledge: much conjecture styled
     belief,
What the rush conceives the stream means through the voyage
     blind and brief.
Why, because I doubtless am, shall I as doubtless be? "Because
God seems good and wise." Yet under this our life's apparent
     laws
Reigns a wrong which, righted once, would give quite other
     laws to life.

"He seems potent." Potent here, then: why are right and wrong
     at strife?
Has in life the wrong the better? Happily life ends so soon!
Right predominates in life? Then why two lives and double
     boon?   240
"Anyhow, we want it: wherefore want?" Because, without the
     want,
Life, now human, would be brutish: just that hope, however
     scant,
Makes the actual life worth leading; take the hope therein away,
All we have to do is surely not endure another day.
This life has its hopes for this life, hopes that promise joy: life
     done—
Out of all the hopes, how many had complete fulfilment? none.
"But the soul is not the body:" and the breath is not the flute;
Both together make the music: either marred and all is mute.
Truce to such old sad contention whence, according as we shape
Most of hope or most of fear, we issue in a half-escape: 250
"We believe" is sighed. I take the cup of comfort proffered thus,
Taste and try each soft ingredient, sweet infusion, and discuss
What their blending may accomplish for the cure or doubt, till
     —slow,
Sorrowful, but how decided! needs must I o'erturn it—so!
Cause before, effect behind me—blanks! The midway point I
     am,
Caused, itself—itself efficient: in that narrow space must cram
All experience—out of which there crowds conjecture manifold,
But, as knowledge, this comes only—things may be as I behold,
Or may not be, but, without me and above me, things there are;
I myself am what I know not—ignorance which proves no
     bar   260
To the knowledge that I am, and, since I am, can recognize
What to me is pain and pleasure: this is sure, the rest—surmise.
If my fellows are or are not, what may please them and what
     pain,—
Mere surmise: my own experience—that is knowledge, once
     again!

I have lived, then, done and suffered, loved and hated, learnt
     and taught
This—there is no reconciling wisdom with a world distraught,
Goodness with triumphant evil, power with failure in the aim,

If—(to my own sense, remember! though none other feel the
    same!)—
If you bar me from assuming earth to be a pupil's place,
And life, time,—with all their chances, changes,—just probation-
    space,   270
Mine, for me. But those apparent other mortals—theirs, for
    them?
Knowledge stands on my experience: all outside its narrow hem,
Free surmise may sport and welcome! Pleasures, pains affect
    mankind
Just as they affect myself? Why, here's my neighbor color-blind,
Eyes like mine to all appearance: "green as grass" do I affirm?
"Red as grass" he contradicts me: which employs the proper
    term?
Were we two the earth's sole tenants, with no third for referee,
How should I distinguish? Just so, God must judge 'twixt man
    and me.
To each mortal peradventure earth becomes a new machine,
Pain and pleasure no more tally in our sense than red and
    green;   280
Still, without what seems such mortal's pleasure, pain, my life
    were lost
—Life, my whole sole chance to prove—although at man's
    apparent cost—
What is beauteous and what ugly, right to strive for, right to
    shun,
Fit to help and fit to hinder,—prove my forces every one,
Good and evil,—learn life's lesson, hate of evil, love of good,
As 'tis set me, understand so much as may be understood—
Solve the problem: "From thine apprehended scheme of things,
    deduce
Praise or blame of its contriver, shown a niggard or profuse
In each good or evil issue! nor miscalculate alike
Counting one the other in the final balance, which to strike,   290
Soul was born and life allotted: ay, the show of things unfurled
For thy summing-up and judgment,—thine, no other mortal's
    world!"
What though fancy scarce may grapple with the complex and
    immense
—"His own world for every mortal?" Postulate omnipotence!
Limit power, and simple grows the complex: shrunk to atom
    size,

That which loomed immense to fancy low before my reason
lies,—
I survey it and pronounce it work like other work: success
Here and there, the workman's glory,—here and there, his shame
no less,
Failure as conspicuous. Taunt not "Human work ape work
divine?"
As the power, expect performance! God's be God's as mine is
mine!   300
God whose power made man and made man's wants, and made,
to meet those wants,
Heaven and earth which, through the body, prove the spirit's
ministrants,
Excellently all,—did He lack power or was the will in fault
When He let blue heaven be shrouded o'er by vapors of the
vault,
Gay earth drop her garlands shrivelled at the first infecting
breath
Of the serpent pains which herald, swarming in, the dragon
death?
What, no way but this that man may learn and lay to heart how
rife
Life were with delights would only death allow their taste to
life?
Must the rose sigh "Pluck—I perish!" must the eye weep "Gaze
—I fade!"
—Every sweet warn " 'Ware my bitter!" every shine bid "Wait
my shade"?   310
Can we love but on condition, that the thing we love must die?
Needs there groan a world in anguish just to teach us sym-
pathy—
Multitudinously wretched that we, wretched too, may guess
What a preferable state were universal happiness?
Hardly do I so conceive the outcome of that power which went
To the making of the worm there in yon clod its tenement,
Any more than I distinguish aught of that which, wise and good,
Framed the leaf, its plain of pasture, dropped the dew, its fine-
less food.
Nay, were fancy fact, were earth and all it holds illusion mere,
Only a machine for teaching love and hate and hope and
fear   320
To myself. the sole existence, single truth mid falsehood,—well!

If the harsh throes of the prelude die not off into the swell
Of that perfect piece they sting me to become a-strain for,—if
Roughness of the long rock-clamber lead not to the last of cliff,
First of level country where is sward my pilgrim-foot can
    prize,—
Plainlier! if this life's conception new life fail to realize,—
Though earth burst and proved a bubble glassing hues of hell,
    one huge
Reflex of the devil's doings—God's work by no subterfuge—
(So death's kindly touch informed me as it broke the glamour,
    gave
Soul and body both release from life's long nightmare in the
    grave)   330
Still,—with no more Nature, no more Man as riddle to be read,
Only my own joys and sorrows now to reckon real instead,—
I must say—or choke in silence—"Howsoever came my fate,
Sorrow did and joy did nowise,—life well weighed,—prepon-
    derate."
By necessity ordained thus? I shall bear as best I can;
By a cause all-good, all-wise, all-potent? No, as I am man!
Such were God: and was it goodness that the good within my
    range
Or had evil in admixture or grew evil's self by change?
Wisdom—that becoming wise meant making slow and sure
    advance
From a knowledge proved in error to acknowledged igno-
    rance?   340
Power? 'tis just the main assumption reason most revolts at!
    power
Unavailing for bestowment on its creature of an hour,
Man, of so much proper action rightly aimed and reaching aim,
So much passion,—no defect there, no excess, but still the
    same,—
As what constitutes existence, pure perfection bright as brief
For yon worm, man's fellow-creature, on yon happier world—
    its leaf!
No, as I am man, I mourn the poverty I must impute:
Goodness, wisdom, power, all bounded, each a human attribute!

But, O world outspread beneath me! only for myself I speak,
Nowise dare to play the spokesman for my brothers strong and
    weak,   350
Full and empty, wise and foolish, good and bad, in every age,

Every clime, I turn my eyes from, as in one or other stage
Of a torture writhe they, Job-like couched on dung and crazed
   with blains
—Wherefore? whereto? ask the whirlwind what the dread voice
   thence explains!
I shall "vindicate no way of God's to man," nor stand apart,
"Laugh, be candid!" while I watch it traversing the human heart.
Traversed heart must tell its story uncommented on: no less
Mine results in "Only grant a second life, I acquiesce
In this present life as failure, count misfortune's worst assaults
Triumph, not defeat, assured that loss so much the more
   exalts   360
Gain about to be. For at what moment did I so advance
Near to knowledge as when frustrate of escape from ignorance?
Did not beauty prove most precious when its opposite obtained
Rule, and truth seem more than ever potent because falsehood
   reigned?
While for love—Oh how but, losing love, does whoso loves
   succeed
By the death-pang to the birth-throe—learning what is love
   indeed?
Only grant my soul may carry high through death her cup un-
   spilled,
Brimming though it be with knowledge, life's loss drop by drop
   distilled,
I shall boast it mine—the balsam, bless each kindly wrench that
   wrung
From life's tree its inmost virtue, tapped the root whence pleas-
   ure sprung,   370
Barked the bole, and broke the bough, and bruised the berry,
   left all grace
Ashes in death's stern alembic, loosed elixir in its place!

Witness, Dear and True, how little I was 'ware of—not your
   worth
—That I knew, my heart assures me—but of what a shade on
   earth
Would the passage from my presence of the tall white figure
   throw
O'er the ways we walked together! Somewhat narrow, some-
   what slow
Used to seem the ways, the walking: narrow ways are well to
   tread

When there's moss beneath the footstep, honeysuckle overhead:
Walking slow to beating bosom surest solace soonest gives,
Liberates the brain o'erloaded—best of all restoratives.　　380
Nay, do I forget the open vast where soon or late converged
Ways though winding?—world-wide heaven-high sea where music slept or surged
As the angel had ascendant, and Beethoven's Titan mace
Smote the immense to storm Mozart would by a finger's lifting chase?
Yes, I knew—but not with knowledge such as thrills me while I view
Yonder precinct which henceforward holds and hides the Dear and True.
Grant me (once again) assurance we shall each meet each some day,
Walk—but with how bold a footstep! on a way—but what a way!
—Worse were best, defeat were triumph, utter loss were utmost gain.
Can it be, and must, and will it?

　　　　　　　　　　　　　　Silence! Out of fact's domain,　　390
Just surmise prepared to mutter hope, and also fear—dispute
Fact's inexorable ruling "Outside fact, surmise be mute!"
Well!
　　　　Ay, well and best, if fact's self I may force the answer from!
'Tis surmise I stop the mouth of. Not above in yonder dome
All a rapture with its rose-glow,—not around, where pile and peak
Strainingly await the sun's fall,—not beneath, where crickets creak,
Birds assemble for their bed-time, soft the tree-top swell subsides,—
No, nor yet within my deepest sentient self the knowledge hides.
Aspiration, reminiscence, plausibilities of trust
—Now the ready "Man were wronged else," now the rash "and God unjust"—　　400
None of these I need. Take thou, my soul, thy solitary stand,
Umpire to the champions Fancy, Reason, as on either hand
Amicable war they wage and play the foe in thy behoof!
Fancy thrust and Reason parry! Thine the prize who stand aloof.

FANCY

I concede the thing refused: henceforth no certainty more plain
Than this mere surmise that after body dies soul lives again.
Two, the only facts acknowledged late, are now increased to
    three—
God is, and the soul is, and, as certain, after death shall be.
Put this third to use in life, the time for using fact!

REASON

                           I do:
Find it promises advantage, coupled with the other two.   410
Life to come will be improvement on the life that's now; destroy
Body's thwartings, there's no longer screen betwixt soul and
    soul's joy.
Why should we expect new hindrance, novel tether? In this first
Life, I see the good of evil, why our world began at worst:
Since time means amelioration, tardily enough displayed,
Yet a mainly onward moving, never wholly retrograde.
We know more though we know little, we grow stronger though
    still weak,
Partly see though all too purblind, stammer though we cannot
    speak.
There is no such grudge in God as scared the ancient Greek, no
    fresh
Substitute of trap for dragnet, once a breakage in the mesh.   420
Dragons were, and serpents are, and blind-worms will be: ne'er
    emerged
Any new-created python for man's plague since earth was
    purged.
Failing proof, then, of invented trouble to replace the old,
O'er this life the next presents advantage much and manifold:
Which advantage—in the absence of a fourth and farther fact
Now conceivably surmised, of harm to follow from the act—
I pronounce for man's obtaining at this moment. Why delay?
Is he happy? happiness will change: anticipate the day!
Is he sad? there's ready refuge: of all sadness death's prompt
    cure!
Is he both, in mingled measure? cease a burthen to endure!   430
Pains with sorry compensations, pleasures stinted in the dole,

Power that sinks and pettiness that soars, all halved and noth-
    ing whole,
Idle hopes that lure man onward, forced back by as idle fears—
What a load he stumbles under through his glad sad seventy
    years,
When a touch sets right the turmoil, lifts his spirit where, flesh-
    freed,
Knowledge shall be rightly named so, all that seems be truth
    indeed!
Grant his forces no accession, nay, no faculty's increase,
Only let what now exists continue, let him prove in peace
Power whereof the interrupted unperfected play enticed
Man through darkness, which to lighten any spark of hope suf-
    ficed,—   440
What shall then deter his dying out of darkness into light?
Death itself perchance, brief pain that's pang, condensed and
    infinite?
But at worst, he needs must brave it one day, while, at best, he
    laughs—
Drops a drop within his chalice, sleep not death his science
    quaffs!
Any moment claims more courage when, by crossing cold and
    gloom,
Manfully man quits discomfort, makes for the provided room
Where the old friends want their fellow, where the new ac-
    quaintance wait,
Probably for talk assembled, possibly to sup in state!
I affirm and re-affirm it therefore: only make as plain
As that man now lives, that, after dying, man will live
    again,—   450
Make as plain the absence, also, of a law to contravene
Voluntary passage from this life to that by change of scene,—
And I bid him—at suspicion of first cloud athwart his sky,
Flower's departure, frost's arrival—never hesitate, but die!

FANCY

Then I double my concession: grant, along with new life sure,
This same law found lacking now: ordain that, whether rich or
    poor
Present life is judged in aught man counts advantage—be it
    hope,
Be it fear that brightens, blackens most or least his horoscope,—

He, by absolute compulsion such as made him live at all,
Go on living to the fated end of life whate'er befall.   460
What though, as on earth he darkling grovels, man descry the
    sphere,
Next life's—call it, heaven of freedom, close above and crystal-
    clear?
He shall find—say, hell to punish who in aught curtails the term,
Fain would act the butterfly before he has played out the worm.
God, soul, earth, heaven, hell,—five facts now: what is to de-
    siderate?

REASON

Nothing! Henceforth man's existence bows to the monition "Wait!
Take the joys and bear the sorrows—neither with extreme con-
    cern!
Living here means nescience simply: 'tis next life that helps to
    learn.
Shut those eyes, next life will open,—stop those ears, next life
    will teach
Hearing's office,—close those lips, next life will give the power
    of speech!   470
Or, if action more amuse thee than the passive attitude,
Bravely bustle through thy being, busy thee for ill or good,
Reap this life's success or failure! Soon shall things be unper-
    plexed
And the right and wrong, now tangled, lie unravelled in the next."

FANCY

Not so fast! Still more concession! not alone do I declare
Life must needs be borne,—I also will that man become aware
Life has worth incalculable, every moment that he spends
So much gain or loss for that next life which on this life depends.
Good, done here, be there rewarded,—evil, worked here, there
    amerced!
Six facts now, and all established, plain to man the last as
    first.   480

REASON

There was good and evil, then, defined to man by this decree?
Was—for at its promulgation both alike have ceased to be.
Prior to this last announcement "Certainly as God exists,

As He made man's soul, as soul is quenchless by the deathly
    mists,
Yet is, all the same, forbidden premature escape from time
To eternity's provided purer air and brighter clime,—
Just so certainly depends it on the use to which man turns
Earth, the good or evil done there, whether after death he earns
Life eternal,—heaven, the phrase be, or eternal death,—say, hell.
As his deeds, so proves his portion, doing ill or doing well!"   490
—Prior to this last announcement, earth was man's probation-
    place:
Liberty of doing evil gave his doing good a grace;
Once lay down the law, with Nature's simple "Such effects suc-
    ceed
Causes such, and heaven or hell depends upon man's earthly
    deed
Just as surely as depends the straight or else the crooked line
On his making point meet point or with or else without incline,"—
Thenceforth neither good nor evil does man, doing what he must.
Lay but down that law as stringent "Wouldst thou live again, be
    just!"
As this other "Wouldst thou live now, regularly draw thy breath!
For, suspend the operation, straight law's breach results in
    death—"   500
And (provided always, man, addressed this mode, be sound and
    sane)
Prompt and absolute obedience, never doubt, will law obtain!
Tell not me "Look round us! nothing each side but acknowledged
    law,
Now styled God's—now, Nature's edict!" Where's obedience
    without flaw
Paid to either? What's the adage rife in man's mouth? Why, "The
    best
I both see and praise, the worst I follow"—which, despite pro-
    fessed
Seeing, praising, all the same he follows, since he disbelieves
In the heart of him that edict which for truth his head receives.
There's evading and persuading and much making law amends
Somehow, there's the nice distinction 'twixt fast foes and
    faulty friends,   510
—Any consequence except inevitable death when "Die,
Whoso breaks our law!" they publish, God and Nature equally.
Law that's kept or broken—subject to man's will and pleasure!
    Whence?

How comes law to bear eluding? Not because of impotence:
Certain laws exist already which to hear means to obey;
Therefore not without a purpose these man must, while those
　　man may
Keep and, for the keeping, haply gain approval and reward.
Break through this last superstructure, all is empty air—no
　　sward
Firm like my first fact to stand on "God there is, and soul there
　　is,"
And soul's earthly life-allotment: wherein, by hypothesis,　520
Soul is bound to pass probation, prove its powers, and exercise
Sense and thought on fact, and then, from fact educing fit sur-
　　mise,
Ask itself, and of itself have solely answer, "Does the scope
Earth affords of fact to judge by warrant future fear or hope?"

Thus have we come back full circle: fancy's footsteps one by one
Go their round conducting reason to the point where they begun,
Left where we were left so lately, Dear and True! When, half a
　　week
Since, we walked and talked and thus I told you, how suffused
　　a cheek
You had turned me had I sudden brought the blush into the
　　smile
By some word like "Idly argued! you know better all the
　　while!"　530
Now, from me—Oh not a blush but, how much more, a joyous
　　glow,
Laugh triumphant, would it strike did your "Yes, better I do
　　know"
Break, my warrant for assurance! which assurance may not be
If, supplanting hope, assurance needs must change this life to me.
So, I hope—no more than hope, but hope—no less than hope,
　　because
I can fathom, by no plumb-line sunk in life's apparent laws,
How I may in any instance fix where change should meetly fall
Nor involve, by one revisal, abrogation of them all:
—Which again involves as utter change in life thus law-released,
Whence the good of goodness vanished when the ill of evil
　　ceased.　540
Whereas, life and laws apparent re-instated,—all we know,
All we know not,—o'er our heaven again cloud closes, until,
　　lo—

Hope the arrowy, just as constant, comes to pierce its gloom, compelled
By a power and by a purpose which, if no one else beheld,
I behold in life, so—hope!

                     Sad summing-up of all to say!
Athanasius contra mundum, why should he hope more than they?
So are men made notwithstanding, such magnetic virtue darts
From each head their fancy haloes to their unresisting hearts!

Here I stand, methinks a stone's throw from yon village I this morn
Traversed for the sake of looking one last look at its forlorn   550
Tenement's ignoble fortune: through a crevice, plain its floor
Piled with provender for cattle, while a dung-heap blocked the door.
In that squalid Bossex, under that obscene red roof, arose,
Like a fiery flying serpent from its egg, a soul—Rousseau's.
Turn thence! Is it Diodati joins the glimmer of the lake?
There I plucked a leaf, one week since,—ivy, plucked for Byron's sake.
Famed unfortunates! And yet, because of that phosphoric fame
Swathing blackness' self with brightness till putridity looked flame,
All the world was witched: and wherefore? what could lie beneath, allure
Heart of man to let corruption serve man's head as cynosure?   560
Was the magic in the dictum "All that's good is gone and past;
Bad and worse still grows the present, and the worst of all comes last:
Which believe—for I believe it?" So preached one his gospel-news;
While melodious moaned the other "Dying day with dolphin-hues!
Storm, for loveliness and darkness like a woman's eye! Ye mounts
Where I climb to 'scape my fellow, and thou sea wherein he counts
Not one inch of vile dominion! What were your especial worth
Failed ye to enforce the maxim 'Of all objects found on earth
Man is meanest, much too honored when compared with—what by odds
Beats him—any dog: so, let him go a-howling to his gods!'   570

Which believe—for I believe it!" such the comfort man received

Sadly since perforce he must: for why? the famous bard believed!

Fame! Then, give me fame, a moment! As I gather at a glance

Human glory after glory vivifying yon expanse,

Let me grasp them all together, hold on high and brandish well

Beacon-like above the rapt world ready, whether heaven or hell

Send the dazzling summons earthward, to submit itself the
    same,

Take on trust the hope or else despair flashed full on face by—
    Fame!

Thanks, thou pine-tree of Makistos, wide thy giant torch I wave!

Know ye whence I plucked the pillar, late with sky for archi-
    trave?   580

This the trunk, the central solid Knowledge, kindled core, began

Tugging earth-deeps, trying heaven-heights, rooted yonder at
    Lausanne.

This which flits and spits, the aspic,—sparkles in and out the
    boughs

Now, and now condensed, the python, coiling round and round
    allows

Scarce the bole its due effulgence, dulled by flake on flake of
    Wit—

Laughter so bejewels Learning,—what but Ferney nourished it?

Nay, nor fear—since every resin feeds the flame—that I dispense

With yon Bossex terebinth-tree's all-explosive Eloquence:

No, be sure! nor, any more than thy resplendency, Jean-Jacques,

Dare I want thine, Diodati! What though monkeys and ma-
    caques   590

Gibber "Byron"? Byron's ivy rears a branch beyond the crew,

Green forever, no deciduous trash macaques and monkeys chew!

As Rousseau, then, eloquent, as Byron prime in poet's power,—

Detonations, fulgurations, smiles—the rainbow, tears—the
    shower,—

Lo, I lift the coruscating marvel—Fame! and, famed, declare

—Learned for the nonce as Gibbon, witty as wit's self Vol-
    taire . . .

O the sorriest of conclusions to whatever man of sense

Mid the millions stands the unit, takes no flare for evidence!

Yet the millions have their portion, live their calm or troublous
    day,

Find significance in fireworks: so, by help of mine, they
    may   600

Confidently lay to heart and lock in head their life long—this:

"He there with the brand flamboyant, broad o'er night's forlorn
　　abyss,
Crowned by prose and verse; and wielding, with Wit's bauble,
　　Learning's rod . . .
Well? Why, he at least believed in Soul, was very sure of God."

So the poor smile played, that evening: pallid smile long since
　　extinct
Here in London's mid-November! Not so loosely thoughts were
　　linked,
Six weeks since as I, descending in the sunset from Salève,
Found the chain, I seemed to forge there, flawless till it reached
　　your grave,—
Not so filmy was the texture, but I bore it in my breast
Safe thus far. And since I found a something in me would not
　　rest
Till I, link by link, unravelled any tangle of the chain, 610
—Here it lies, for much or little! I have lived all o'er again
That last pregnant hour: I saved it, just as I could save a root
Disinterred for re-interment when the time best helps to shoot.
Life is stocked with germs of torpid life; but may I never wake
Those of mine whose resurrection could not be without earth-
　　quake!
Rest all such, unraised forever! Be this, sad yet sweet, the sole
Memory evoked from slumber! Least part this: then what the
　　whole?

From DRAMATIC IDYLS [FIRST SERIES]

[1879]

PHEIDIPPIDES

Χαίρετε, νικῶμεν

First I salute this soil of the blessed, river and rock!
Gods of my birthplace, dæmons and heroes, honor to all!
Then I name thee, claim thee for our patron, co-equal in praise
--Ay, with Zeus the Defender, with Her of the ægis and spear!
Also, ye of the bow and the buskin, praised be your peer,
Now, henceforth and forever,—O latest to whom I upraise
Hand and heart and voice! For Athens, leave pasture and flock!
Present to help, potent to save, Pan—patron I call!

Archons of Athens, topped by the tettix, see, I return!
See, 'tis myself here standing alive, no spectre that speaks!   10
Crowned with the myrtle, did you command me, Athens and you,
"Run, Pheidippides, run and race, reach Sparta for aid!
Persia has come, we are here, where is She?" Your command I
    obeyed,
Ran and raced: like stubble, some field which a fire runs through,
Was the space between city and city: two days, two nights did
    I burn
Over the hills, under the dales, down pits and up peaks.
Into their midst I broke: breath served but for "Persia has come!
Persia bids Athens proffer slaves'-tribute, water and earth
Razed to the ground is Eretria—but Athens, shall Athens sink,
Drop into dust and die—the flower of Hellas utterly die,   20
Die, with the wide world spitting at Sparta, the stupid, the
    stander-by?
Answer me quick, what help, what hand do you stretch o'er
    destruction's brink?
How,—when? No care for my limbs!—there's lightning in all
    and some—
Fresh and fit your message to bear, once lips give it birth!"
O my Athens—Sparta love thee? Did Sparta respond?
Every face of her leered in a furrow of envy, mistrust,
Malice,—each eye of her gave me its glitter of gratified hate!
Gravely they turned to take counsel, to cast for excuses. I stood

Quivering,—the limbs of me fretting as fire frets, an inch from
    dry wood:
"Persia has come, Athens asks aid, and still they debate?   30
Thunder, thou Zeus! Athené, are Spartans a quarry beyond
Swing of thy spear? Phoibos and Artemis, clang them 'Ye must'!"

No bolt launched from Olumpos! Lo, their answer at last!
"Has Persia come,—does Athens ask aid,—may Sparta befriend?
Nowise precipitate judgment—too weighty the issue at stake!
Count we no time lost time which lags through respect to the
    Gods!
Ponder that precept of old, 'No warfare, whatever the odds
In your favor, so long as the moon, half-orbed, is unable to take
Full-circle her state in the sky!' Already she rounds to it fast:
Athens must wait, patient as we—who judgment suspend."   40

Athens,—except for that sparkle,—thy name, I had mouldered
    to ash!
That sent a blaze through my blood; off, off and away was I back,
—Not one word to waste, one look to lose on the false and the
    vile!
Yet "O Gods of my land!" I cried, as each hillock and plain,
Wood and stream, I knew, I named, rushing past them again,
"Have ye kept faith, proved mindful of honors we paid you
    erewhile?
Vain was the filleted victim, the fulsome libation! Too rash
Love in its choice, paid you so largely service so slack!

"Oak and olive and bay,—I bid you cease to enwreathe
Brows made bold by your leaf! Fade at the Persian's foot,   50
You that, our patrons were pledged, should never adorn a
    slave!
Rather I hail thee, Parnes,—trust to thy wild waste tract!
Treeless, herbless, lifeless mountain! What matter if slacked
My speed may hardly be, for homage to crag and to cave
No deity deigns to drape with verdure? at least I can breathe,
Fear in thee no fraud from the blind, no lie from the mute!"

Such my cry as, rapid, I ran over Parnes' ridge;
Gully and gap I clambered and cleared till, sudden, a bar
Jutted, a stoppage of stone against me, blocking the way.
Right! for I minded the hollow to traverse, the fissure
    across: 60

"Where I could enter, there I depart by! Night in the fosse?
Athens to aid? Though the dive were through Erebos, thus I
    obey—
Out of the day dive, into the day as bravely arise! No bridge
Better!"—when—ha! what was it I came on, of wonders that are?

There, in the cool of a cleft, sat he—majestical Pan!
Ivy drooped wanton, kissed his head, moss cushioned his hoof:
All the great God was good in the eyes grave-kindly—the curl
Carved on the bearded cheek, amused at a mortal's awe,
As, under the human trunk, the goat thighs grand I saw.
"Halt, Pheidippides!"—halt I did, my brain of a whirl: 70
"Hither to me! Why pale in my presence?" he gracious began:
"How is it,—Athens, only in Hellas, holds me aloof?

"Athens, she only, rears me no fane, makes me no feast!
Wherefore? Than I what godship to Athens more helpful of old?
Ay, and still, and forever her friend! Test Pan, trust me!
Go, bid Athens take heart, laugh Persia to scorn, have faith
In the temples and tombs! Go, say to Athens, 'The Goat-God
    saith:
When Persia—so much as strews not the soil—is cast in the sea,
Then praise Pan who fought in the ranks with your most and
    least,
Goat-thigh to greaved-thigh, made one cause with the free and
    the bold!'   80

"Say Pan saith: 'Let this, foreshowing the place, be the pledge!' "
(Gay, the liberal hand held out this herbage I bear
—Fennel—I grasped it a-tremble with dew—whatever it bode)
"While, as for thee . . ." But enough! He was gone. If I ran
    hitherto—
Be sure that, the rest of my journey, I ran no longer, but flew.
Parnes to Athens—earth no more, the air was my road:
Here am I back. Praise Pan, we stand no more on the razor's
    edge!
Pan for Athens, Pan for me! I too have a guerdon rare!

Then spoke Miltiades. "And thee, best runner of Greece,
Whose limbs did duty indeed,—what gift is promised
    thyself?   90
Tell us straightway,—Athens the mother demands of her son!"

Rosily blushed the youth: he paused: but, lifting at length
His eyes from the ground, it seemed as he gathered the rest of
    his strength
Into the utterance—"Pan spoke thus: 'For what thou hast done
Count on a worthy reward! Henceforth be allowed thee release
From the racer's toil, no vulgar reward in praise or in pelf!'

"I am bold to believe, Pan means reward the most to my mind!
Fight I shall, with our foremost, wherever this fennel may
    grow,—
Pound—Pan helping us—Persia to dust, and, under the deep,
Whelm her away forever; and then,—no Athens to save,—   100
Marry a certain maid, I know keeps faith to the brave,—
Hie to my house and home: and, when my children shall creep
Close to my knees,—recount how the God was awful yet kind,
Promised their sire reward to the full—rewarding him—so!"

Unforeseeing one! Yes, he fought on the Marathon day:
So, when Persia was dust, all cried "To Akropolis!
Run, Pheidippides, one race more! the meed is thy due!
'Athens is saved, thank Pan,' go shout!" He flung down his shield,
Ran like fire once more: and the space 'twixt the Fennel-field
And Athens was stubble again, a field which a fire runs
    through,   110
Till in he broke: "Rejoice, we conquer!" Like wine through clay,
Joy in his blood bursting his heart, he died—the bliss!

So, to this day, when friend meets friend, the word of salute
Is still "Rejoice!"—his word which brought rejoicing indeed.
So is Pheidippides happy forever,—the noble strong man
Who could race like a God, bear the face of a God, whom a
    God loved so well;   •
He saw the land saved he had helped to save, and was suffered
    to tell
Such tidings, yet never decline, but, gloriously as he began,
So to end gloriously—once to shout, thereafter be mute:
"Athens is saved!"—Pheidippides dies in the shout for
    his meed.   120

IVÀN IVÀNOVITCH

"THEY tell me, your carpenters," quoth I to my friend the Russ,
"Make a simple hatchet serve as a tool-box serves with us.
Arm but each man with his axe, 'tis a hammer and saw and plane
And chisel, and—what know I else? We should imitate in vain
The mastery wherewithal, by a flourish of just the adze,
He cleaves, clamps, dovetails in,—no need of our nails and
        brads,—
The manageable pine: 'tis said he could shave himself
With the axe,—so all adroit, now a giant and now an elf,
Does he work and play at once!"
                              Quoth my friend the Russ to me,
"Ay, that and more beside on occasion! It scarce may be   10
You never heard tell a tale told children, time out of mind,
By father and mother and nurse, for a moral that's behind,
Which children quickly seize. If the incident happened at all,
We place it in Peter's time when hearts were great not small,
Germanized, Frenchified. I wager 'tis old to you
As the story of Adam and Eve, and possibly quite as true."

In the deep of our land, 'tis said, a village from out the woods
Emerged on the great main-road 'twixt two great solitudes.
Through forestry right and left, black verst and verst of pine,
From village to village runs the road's long wide bare line.   20
Clearance and clearance break the else-unconquered growth
Of pine and all that breeds and broods there, leaving loth
Man's inch of masterdom,—spot of life, spirt of fire,—
To star the dark and dread, lest right and rule expire
Throughout the monstrous wild, a-hungered to resume
Its ancient sway, suck back the world into its womb:
Defrauded by man's craft which clove from North to South
This highway broad and straight e'en from the Neva's mouth
To Moscow's gates of gold. So, spot of life and spirt
Of fire aforesaid, burn, each village death-begirt   30
By wall and wall of pine—unprobed undreamed abyss.

Early one winter morn, in such a village as this,
Snow-whitened everywhere except the middle road

Ice-roughed by track of sledge, there worked by his abode
Ivàn Ivànovitch, the carpenter, employed
On a huge shipmast trunk; his axe now trimmed and toyed
With branch and twig, and now some chop athwart the bole
Changed bole to billets, bared at once the sap and soul.
About him, watched the work his neighbors sheepskin-clad;
Each bearded mouth puffed steam, each gray eye
     twinkled glad   40
To see the sturdy arm which, never stopping play,
Proved strong man's blood still boils, freeze winter as he may.
Sudden, a burst of bells. Out of the road, on edge
Of the hamlet—horse's hoofs galloping. "How, a sledge?
What's here?" cried all as—in, up to the open space,
Workyard and market-ground, folk's common meeting-place,—
Stumbled on, till he fell, in one last bound for life,
A horse: and, at his heels, a sledge held—"Dmìtri's wife!
Back without Dmìtri too! and children—where are they?
Only a frozen corpse!"

                They drew it forth: then—"Nay,   50
Not dead, though like to die! Gone hence a month ago:
Home again, this rough jaunt—alone through night and snow—
What can the cause be? Hark—Droug, old horse, how he groans:
His day's done! Chafe away, keep chafing, for she moans:
She's coming to! Give here: see, mother-kin, your friends!
Cheer up, all safe at home! Warm inside makes amends
For outside cold,—sup quick! Don't look as we were bears!
What is it startles you? What strange adventure stares
Up at us in your face? You know friends—which is which?
I'm Vàssili, he's Sergeì, Ivàn Ivànovitch . . ."   60

At the word, the woman's eyes, slow-wandering till they neared
The blue eyes o'er the bush of honey-colored beard,
Took in full light and sense and—torn to rags, some dream
Which hid the naked truth—O loud and long the scream
She gave, as if all power of voice within her throat
Poured itself wild away to waste in one dread note!
Then followed gasps and sobs, and then the steady flow
Of kindly tears: the brain was saved, a man might know.
Down fell her face upon the good friend's propping knee;
His broad hands smoothed her head, as fain to brush it free   70
From fancies, swarms that stung like bees unhived. He soothed—

"Loukèria, Loùscha!"—still he, fondling, smoothed and smoothed.
At last her lips formed speech.

                "Ivàn, dear—you indeed!
You, just the same dear you! While I . . . O intercede,
Sweet Mother, with thy Son Almighty—let his might
Bring yesterday once more, undo all done last night!
But this time yesterday, Ivàn, I sat like you,
A child on either knee, and, dearer than the two,
A babe inside my arms, close to my heart—that's lost
In morsels o'er the snow! Father, Son, Holy Ghost,   80
Cannot you bring again my blessed yesterday?"

When no more tears would flow, she told her tale: this way.

"Maybe, a month ago,—was it not?—news came here,
They wanted, deeper down, good workmen fit to rear
A church and roof it in. 'We'll go,' my husband said:
'None understands like me to melt and mould their lead.'
So, friends here helped us off—Ivàn, dear, you the first!
How gay we jingled forth, all five—(my heart will burst)—
While Dmìtri shook the reins, urged Droug upon his track!

"Well, soon the month ran out, we just were coming back,   90
When yesterday—behold, the village was on fire!
Fire ran from house to house. What help, as, nigh and nigher,
The flames came furious? 'Haste,' cried Dmìtri, 'men must do
The little good man may: to sledge and in with you,
You and our three! We check the fire by laying flat
Each building in its path,—I needs must stay for that,—
But you . . . no time for talk! Wrap round you every rug,
Cover the couple close,—you'll have the babe to hug.
No care to guide old Droug, he knows his way, by guess,
Once start him on the road: but chirrup, none the less!   100
The snow lies glib as glass and hard as steel, and soon
You'll have rise, fine and full, a marvel of a moon.
Hold straight up, all the same, this lighted twist of pitch!
Once home and with our friend Ivàn Ivànovitch,
All's safe: I have my pay in pouch, all's right with me,
So I but find as safe you and our precious three!
Off, Droug!'—because the flames had reached us, and the men
Shouted 'But lend a hand, Dmìtri—as good as ten!'

"So, in we bundled—I, and those God gave me once;
Old Droug, that's stiff at first, seemed youthful for the
nonce: 110
He understood the case, galloping straight ahead.
Out came the moon: my twist soon dwindled, feebly red
In that unnatural day—yes, daylight, bred between
Moon-light and snow-light, lamped those grotto-depths which
screen
Such devils from God's eye. Ah, pines, how straight you grow
Nor bend one pitying branch, true breed of brutal snow!
Some undergrowth had served to keep the devils blind
While we escaped outside their border!

                                        "Was that—wind?
Anyhow, Droug starts, stops, back go his ears, he snuffs,
Snorts,—never such a snort! then plunges, knows the
sough's   120
Only the wind: yet, no—our breath goes up too straight!
Still the low sound,—less low, loud, louder, at a rate
There's no mistaking more! Shall I lean out—look—learn
The truth whatever it be? Pad, pad! At last, I turn—
" 'Tis the regular pad of the wolves in pursuit of the life in the
sledge!
An army they are: close-packed they press like the thrust of a
wedge:
They increase as they hunt: for I see, through the pine-trunks
ranged each side,
Slip forth new fiend and fiend, make wider and still more wide
The four-footed steady advance. The foremost—none may pass:
They are elders and lead the line, eye and eye—green-glowing
brass!   130
But a long way distant still. Droug, save us! He does his best:
Yet they gain on us, gain, till they reach,—one reaches . . .
How utter the rest?
O that Satan-faced first of the band! How he lolls out the length
of his tongue,
How he laughs and lets gleam his white teeth! He is on me, his
paws pry among
The wraps and the rugs! O my pair, my twin-pigeons, lie still and
seem dead!
Stepàn, he shall never have you for a meal,—here's your mother
instead!

No, he will not be counselled—must cry, poor Stiòpka, so foolish!
    though first
Of my boy-brood, he was not the best: nay, neighbors have
    called him the worst:
He was puny, an undersized slip,—a darling to me, all the same!
But little there was to be praised in the boy, and a plenty to
    blame.   140
I loved him with heart and soul, yes—but, deal him a blow
    for a fault,
He would sulk for whole days. 'Foolish boy! lie still or the villain
    will vault,
Will snatch you from over my head!' No use! he cries, screams,
    —who can hold
Fast a boy in a frenzy of fear! It follows—as I foretold!
The Satan-face snatched and snapped: I tugged, I tore—and
    then
His brother too needs must shriek! If one must go, 'tis men
The Tsar needs, so we hear, not ailing boys! Perhaps
My hands relaxed their grasp, got tangled in the wraps:
God, he was gone! I looked: there tumbled the cursed crew,
Each fighting for a share: too busy to pursue!   150
That's so far gain at least: Droug, gallop another verst
Or two, or three—God send we beat them, arrive the first!
A mother who boasts two boys was ever accounted rich:
Some have not a boy: some have, but lose him,—God knows
    which
Is worse: how pitiful to see your weakling pine
And pale and pass away! Strong brats, this pair of mine!

"O misery! for while I settle to what near seems
Content, I am 'ware again of the tramp, and again there gleams—
Point and point—the line, eyes, levelled green brassy fire!
So soon is resumed your chase? Will nothing appease, naught
    tire   160
The furies? And yet I think—I am certain the race is slack,
And the numbers are nothing like. Not a quarter of the pack!
Feasters and those full-fed are staying behind . . . Ah why?
We'll sorrow for that too soon! Now,—gallop, reach home, and
    die,
Nor ever again leave house, to trust our life in the trap
For life—we call a sledge! Teriòscha, in my lap!
Yes, I'll lie down upon you, tight-tie you with the strings

Here—of my heart! No fear, this time, your mother flings . . .
Flings? I flung? Never! but think!—a woman, after all
Contending with a wolf! Save you I must and shall,   170
Terentìi!
        "How now? What, you still head the race,
Your eyes and tongue and teeth crave fresh food, Satan-face?
There and there! Plain I struck green fire out! Flash again?
All a poor fist can do to damage eyes proves vain!
My fist—why not crunch that? He is wanton for . . . O God,
Why give this wolf his taste? Common wolves scrape and prod
The earth till out they scratch some corpse—mere putrid flesh!
Why must this glutton leave the faded, choose the fresh?
Terentìi—God, feel!—his neck keeps fast thy bag
Of holy things, saints' bones, this Satan-face will drag   180
Forth, and devour along with him, our Pope declared
The relics were to save from danger!

                        "Spurned, not spared!
'Twas through my arms, crossed arms, he—nuzzling now with
    snout,
Now ripping, tooth and claw—plucked, pulled Terentìi out,
A prize indeed! I saw—how could I else but see?—
My precious one—I bit to hold back—pulled from me!
Up came the others, fell to dancing—did the imps!—
Skipped as they scampered round. There's one is gray, and
    limps:
Who knows but old bad Màrpha,—she always owed me spite
And envied me my births,—skulks out of doors at night   190
And turns into a wolf, and joins the sisterhood,
And laps the youthful life, then slinks from out the wood,
Squats down at door by dawn, spins there demure as erst
—No strength, old crone,—not she!—to crawl forth half a verst!

'Well, I escaped with one: 'twixt one and none there lies
The space 'twixt heaven and hell. And see, a rose-light dyes
The endmost snow: 'tis dawn, 'tis day, 'tis safe at home!
We have outwitted you! Ay, monsters, snarl and foam,
Fight each the other fiend, disputing for a share,—
Forgetful, in your greed, our finest off we bear,   200
Tough Droug and I,—my babe, my boy that shall be man,
My man that shall be more, do all a hunter can
To trace and follow and find and catch and crucify
Wolves, wolfkins, all your crew! A thousand deaths shall die

The whimperingest cub that ever squeezed the teat!
'Take that!' we'll stab you with,—'the tenderness we met
When, wretches, you danced round—not this, thank God—not
   this!
Hellhounds, we balk you!'

                  "But—Ah, God above!—Bliss, bliss—
Not the band, no! And yet—yes, for Droug knows him! One—
This only of them all has said 'She saves a son!'   210
His fellows disbelieve such luck: but he believes,
He lets them pick the bones, laugh at him in their sleeves:
He's off and after us,—one speck, one spot, one ball
Grows bigger, bound on bound,—one wolf as good as all!
Oh but I know the trick! Have at the snaky tongue!
That's the right way with wolves! Go, tell your mates I wrung
The panting morsel out, left you to howl your worst!
Now for it—now! Ah me! I know him—thrice-accurst
Satan-face,—him to the end my foe!

                  "All fight's in vain:
This time the green brass points pierce to my very brain. 220
I fall—fall as I ought—quite on the babe I guard:
I overspread with flesh the whole of him. Too hard
To die this way, torn piecemeal? Move hence? Not I—one inch!
Gnaw through me, through and through: flat thus I lie nor flinch!
O God, the feel of the fang furrowing my shoulder!—see!
It grinds—it grates the bone. O Kirill under me,
Could I do more? Beside he knew wolf's way to win:
I clung, closed round like wax: yet in he wedged and in,
Past my neck, past my breasts, my heart, until . . . how feels
The onion-bulb your knife parts, pushing through its peels, 230
Till out you scoop its clove wherein lie stalk and leaf
And bloom and seed unborn?

                  "That slew me: yes, in brief,
I died then, dead I lay doubtlessly till Droug stopped
Here, I suppose. I come to life, I find me propped
Thus—how or when or why,—I now not. Tell me, friends,
All was a dream: laugh quick and say the nightmare ends!
Soon I shall find my house: 'tis over there: in proof,
Save for that chimney heaped with snow, you'd see the roof
Which holds my three—my two—my one—not one?

"Life's mixed
With misery, yet we live—must live. The Satan fixed   240
His face on mine so fast, I took its print as pitch
Takes what it cools beneath. Ivàn Ivànovitch,
'Tis you unharden me, you thaw, disperse the thing!
Only keep looking kind, the horror will not cling.
Your face smooths fast away each print of Satan. Tears
—What good they do! Life's sweet, and all its after-years,
Ivàn Ivànovitch, I owe you! Yours am I!
May God reward you, dear!"

                         Down she sank. Solemnly
Ivàn rose, raised his axe,—for fitly, as she knelt,
Her head lay: well-apart, each side, her arms hung,—
    dealt   250
Lightning-swift thunder-strong one blow—no need of more!
Headless she knelt on still: that pine was sound at core
(Neighbors were used to say)—cast-iron-kernelled—which
Taxed for a second stroke Ivàn Ivànovitch.

The man was scant of words as strokes. "It had to be:
I could no other: God it was bade 'Act for me!' "
Then stooping, peering round—what is it now he lacks?
A proper strip of bark wherewith to wipe his axe.
Which done, he turns, goes in, closes the door behind.
The others mute remain, watching the blood-snake wind   260
Into a hiding-place among the splinter-heaps.

At length, still mute, all move: one lifts,—from where it steeps
Redder each ruddy rag of pine,—the head: two more
Take up the dripping body: then, mute still as before,
Move in a sort of march, march on till marching ends
Opposite to the church; where halting,—who suspends,
By its long hair, the thing, deposits in its place
The piteous head: once more the body shows no trace
Of harm done: there lies whole the Loùscha, maid and wife
And mother, loved until this latest of her life.   270
Then all sit on the bank of snow which bounds a space
Kept free before the porch for judgment: just the place!

Presently all the souls, man, woman, child, which make
The village up, are found assembling for the sake
Of what is to be done. The very Jews are there:
A Gipsy-troop, though bound with horses for the Fair,

Squats with the rest. Each heart with its conception seethes
And simmers, but no tongue speaks: one may say,—none
    breathes.

Anon from out the church totters the Pope—the priest—
Hardly alive, so old, a hundred years at least.   280
With him, the Commune's head, a hoary senior too,
Stàrosta, that's his style,—like Equity Judge with you,—
Natural Jurisconsult: then, fenced about with furs,
Pomeschìk,—Lord of the Land, who wields—and none demurs—
A power of life and death. They stoop, survey the corpse.

Then, straightened on his staff, the Stàrosta—the thorpe's
Sagaciousest old man—hears what you just have heard,
From Droug's first inrush, all, up to Ivàn's last word
"God bade me act for him: I dared not disobey!"

Silence—the Pomeschìk broke with "A wild wrong way   290
Of righting wrong—if wrong there were, such wrath to rouse!
Why was not law observed? What article allows
Whoso may please to play the judge, and, judgment dealt,
Play executioner, as promptly as we pelt
To death, without appeal, the vermin whose sole fault
Has been—it dared to leave the darkness of its vault,
Intrude upon our day! Too sudden and too rash!
What was this woman's crime? Suppose the church should crash
Down where I stand, your lord: bound are my serfs to dare
Their utmost that I 'scape: yet, if the crashing scare   300
My children,—as you are,—if sons fly, one and all,
Leave father to his fate,—poor cowards though I call
The runaways, I pause before I claim their life
Because they prized it more than mine. I would each wife
Died for her husband's sake, each son to save his sire:
'Tis glory, I applaud—scarce duty, I require.
Ivàn Ivànovitch has done a deed that's named
Murder by law and me: who doubts, may speak unblamed!"

All turned to the old Pope. "Ay, children, I am old—
How old, myself have got to know no longer. Rolled   310
Quite round, my orb of life, from infancy to age,
Seems passing back again to youth. A certain stage
At least I reach, or dream I reach, where I discern
Truer truths, laws behold more lawlike than we learn

When first we set our foot to tread the course I trod
With man to guide my steps: who leads me now is God.
'Your young men shall see visions:' and in my youth I saw
And paid obedience to man's visionary law:
'Your old men shall dream dreams:' and, in my age, a hand
Conducts me through the cloud round law to where I
    stand   320
Firm on its base,—know cause, who, before, knew effect.

"The world lies under me: and nowhere I detect
So great a gift as this—God's own—of human life.
'Shall the dead praise thee?' No! 'The whole live world is rife,
God, with thy glory,' rather! Life then, God's best of gifts,
For what shall man exchange? For life—when so he shifts
The weight and turns the scale, lets life for life restore
God's balance, sacrifice the less to gain the more,
Substitute—for low life, another's or his own—
Life large and liker God's who gave it: thus alone   330
May life extinguish life that life may trulier be!
How low this law descends on earth, is not for me
To trace: complexed becomes the simple, intricate
The plain, when I pursue law's winding. 'Tis the straight
Outflow of law I know and name: to law, the fount
Fresh from God's footstool, friends, follow while I remount.

"A mother bears a child: perfection is complete
So far in such a birth. Enabled to repeat
The miracle of life,—herself was born so just
A type of womankind, that God sees fit to trust   340
Her with the holy task of giving life in turn.
Crowned by this crowning pride,—how say you, should she spurn
Regality—discrowned, unchilded, by her choice
Of barrenness exchanged for fruit which made rejoice
Creation, though life's self were lost in giving birth
To life more fresh and fit to glorify God's earth?
How say you, should the hand God trusted with life's torch
Kindled to light the world—aware of sparks that scorch,
Let fall the same? Forsooth, her flesh a fire-flake stings:
The mother drops the child! Among what monstrous things   350
Shall she be classed? Because of motherhood, each male
Yields to his partner place, sinks proudly in the scale:
His strength owned weakness, wit—folly, and courage—fear,
Beside the female proved male's mistress—only here.

The fox-dam, hunger-pined, will slay the felon sire
Who dares assault her whelp: the beaver, stretched on fire,
Will die without a groan: no pang avails to wrest
Her young from where they hide—her sanctuary breast.
What's here then? Answer me, thou dead one, as, I trow,
Standing at God's own bar, he bids thee answer now!   360
Thrice crowned wast thou—each crown of pride, a child—thy
      charge!
Where are they? Lost? Enough: no need that thou enlarge
On how or why the loss: life left to utter 'lost'
Condemns itself beyond appeal. The soldier's post
Guards from the foe's attack the camp he sentinels:
That he no traitor proved, this and this only tells—
Over the corpse of him trod foe to foe's success.
Yet—one by one thy crowns torn from thee—thou no less
To scare the world, shame God,—livedst! I hold He saw
The unexampled sin, ordained the novel law,   370
Whereof first instrument was first intelligence
Found loyal here. I hold that, failing human sense,
The very earth had oped, sky fallen, to efface
Humanity's new wrong, motherhood's first disgrace.
Earth oped not, neither fell the sky, for prompt was found
A man and man enough, head-sober and heart-sound,
Ready to hear God's voice, resolute to obey.
Ivàn Ivànovitch, I hold, has done, this day,
No otherwise than did, in ages long ago,
Moses when he made known the purport of that flow   380
Of fire athwart the law's twain-tables! I proclaim
Ivàn Ivànovitch God's servant!"

                              At which name
Uprose that creepy whisper from out the crowd, is wont
To swell and surge and sink when fellow-men confront
A punishment that falls on fellow flesh and blood,
Appallingly beheld—shudderingly understood,
No less, to be the right, the just, the merciful.
"God's servant!" hissed the crowd.

                              When that Amen grew dull
And died away and left acquittal plain adjudged,
"Amen!" last sighed the lord. "There's none shall say
      I grudged   390
Escape from punishment in such a novel case.

Deferring to old age and holy life,—be grace
Granted! say I. No less, scruples might shake a sense
Firmer than I boast mine. Law's law, and evidence
Of breach therein lies plain,—blood-red-bright,—all may see!
Yet all absolve the deed: absolved the deed must be!

"And next—as mercy rules the hour—methinks 'twere well
You signify forthwith its sentence, and dispel
The doubts and fears, I judge, which busy now the head
Law puts a halter round—a halo—you, instead!   400
Ivàn Ivànovitch—what think you he expects
Will follow from his feat? Go, tell him—law protects
Murder, for once: no need he longer keep behind
The Sacred Pictures—where skulks Innocence enshrined,
Or I missay! Go, some! You others, haste and hide
The dismal object there: get done, whate'er betide!"

So, while the youngsters raised the corpse, the elders trooped
Silently to the house: where halting, some one stooped,
Listened beside the door; all there was silent too.
Then they held counsel; then pushed door and, passing
          through,   410
Stood in the murderer's presence.

                              Ivàn Ivànovitch
Knelt, building on the floor that Kremlin rare and rich
He deftly cut and carved on lazy winter nights.
Some five young faces watched, breathlessly, as, to rights,
Piece upon piece, he reared the fabric nigh complete.
Stèscha, Ivàn's old mother, sat spinning by the heat
Of the oven where his wife Kàtia stood baking bread.
Ivàn's self, as he turned his honey-colored head,
Was just in act to drop, 'twixt fir-cones,—each a dome,—
The scooped-out yellow gourd presumably the home   420
Of Kolokol the Big: the bell, therein to hitch,
—An acorn-cup—was ready: Ivàn Ivànovitch
Turned with it in his mouth.

                              They told him he was free
As air to walk abroad. "How otherwise?" asked he.

TRAY

Sing me a hero! Quench my thirst
Of soul, ye bards!
                Quoth Bard the first:
"Sir Olaf, the good knight, did don
His helm and eke his habergeon . . ."
Sir Olaf and his bard——!

"That sin-scathed brow" (quoth Bard the second)
"That eye wide ope as though Fate beckoned
My hero to some steep, beneath
Which precipice smiled tempting death" . . .
You too without your host have reckoned!   10

"A beggar-child" (let's hear this third!)
"Sat on a quay's edge: like a bird
Sang to herself at careless play,
And fell into the stream. 'Dismay!
Help, you the standers-by!' None stirred.

"Bystanders reason, think of wives
And children ere they risk their lives.
Over the balustrade has bounced
A mere instinctive dog, and pounced
Plumb on the prize. 'How well he dives!   20

" 'Up he comes with the child, see, tight
In mouth, alive too, clutched from quite
A depth of ten feet—twelve, I bet!
Good dog! What, off again? There's yet
Another child to save? All right!

" 'How strange we saw no other fall!
It's instinct in the animal.
Good dog! But he's a long while under:
If he got drowned I should not wonder—
Strong current, that against the wall!   30

" 'Here he comes, holds in mouth this time
—What may the thing be? Well, that's prime!

Now, did you ever? Reason reigns
In man alone, since all Tray's pains
Have fished—the child's doll from the slime!'

"And so, amid the laughter gay,
Trotted my hero off,—old Tray,
Till somebody, prerogatived
With reason, reasoned: 'Why he dived,
His brain would show us, I should say.   40

" 'John, go and catch—or, if needs be,
Purchase—that animal for me!
By vivisection, at expense
Of half-an-hour and eighteenpence,
How brain secretes dog's soul, we'll see!' "

[1880]

ECHETLOS

Here is a story shall stir you! Stand up, Greeks dead and gone,
Who breasted, beat Barbarians, stemmed Persia rolling on,
Did the deed and saved the world, for the day was Marathon!
No man but did his manliest, kept rank and fought away
In his tribe and file: up, back, out, down—was the spear-arm
    play:
Like a wind-whipt branchy wood, all spear-arms a-swing that
    day!

But one man kept no rank and his sole arm plied no spear,
As a flashing came and went, and a form i' the van, the rear,   •
Brightened the battle up, for he blazed now there, now here.

Nor helmed nor shielded, he! but, a goat-skin all his wear,   10
Like a tiller of the soil, with a clown's limbs broad and bare,
Went he ploughing on and on: he pushed with a ploughman's
    share.

Did the weak mid-line give way, as tunnies on whom the shark
Precipitates his bulk? Did the right-wing halt when, stark
On his heap of slain lay stretched Kallimachos Polemarch?

Did the steady phalanx falter? To the rescue, at the need,
The clown was ploughing Persia, clearing Greek earth of weed,
As he routed through the Sakian and rooted up the Mede.

But the deed done, battle won,—nowhere to be descried
On the meadow, by the stream, at the marsh,—look far and
    wide   20
From the foot of the mountain, no, to the last blood-plashed
    seaside,—

Not anywhere on view blazed the large limbs thonged and
    brown,
Shearing and clearing still with the share before which—down
To the dust went Persia's pomp, as he ploughed for Greece, that
    clown!

How spake the Oracle? "Care for no name at all!
Say but just this: 'We praise one helpful whom we call
The Holder of the Ploughshare.' The great deed ne'er grows
    small."

Not the great name! Sing—woe for the great name Míltiadés
And its end at Paros isle! Woe for Themistokles
—Satrap in Sardis court! Name not the clown like these!   30

CLIVE

I AND Clive were friends—and why not? Friends! I think you
    laugh, my lad.
Clive it was gave England India, while your father gives—egad,
England nothing but the graceless boy who lures him on to
    speak—
"Well, Sir, you and Clive were comrades—" with a tongue thrust
    in your cheek!
Very true: in my eyes, all the world's eyes, Clive was man,
I was, am and ever shall be—mouse, nay, mouse of all its clan
Sorriest sample, if you take the kitchen's estimate for fame;
While the man Clive—he fought Plassy, spoiled the clever
    foreign game,
Conquered and annexed and Englished!

                    Never mind! As o'er my punch
(You away) I sit of evenings,—silence, save for biscuit-
    crunch,   10
Black, unbroken,—thought grows busy, thrids each pathway of
    old years,
Notes this forthright, that meander, till the long-past life appears
Like an outspread map of country plodded through, each mile
    and rood,
Once, and well remembered still: I'm startled in my solitude
Ever and anon by—what's the sudden mocking light that breaks
On me as I slap the table till no rummer-glass but shakes
While I ask—aloud, I do believe, God help me!—"Was it thus?
Can it be that so I faltered, stopped when just one step for us—"
(Us,—you were not born, I grant, but surely some day born
    would be)

"—One bold step had gained a province" (figurative talk, you
see) 20
"Got no end of wealth and honor,—yet I stood stock still no
less?"
—"For I was not Clive," you comment: but it needs no Clive
to guess
Wealth were handy, honor ticklish, did no writing on the wall
Warn me "Trespasser, 'ware man-traps!" Him who braves that
notice—call
Hero! none of such heroics suit myself who read plain words,
Doff my hat, and leap no barrier. Scripture says the land's the
Lord's:
Louts then—what avail the thousand, noisy in a smock-frocked
ring,
All-agog to have me trespass, clear the fence, be Clive their king?
Higher warrant must you show me ere I set one foot before
T' other in that dark direction, though I stand for evermore 3c
Poor as Job and meek as Moses. Evermore? No! By-and-by
Job grows rich and Moses valiant, Clive turns out less wise than
I.
Don't object "Why call him friend, then?" Power is power, my
boy, and still
Marks a man,—God's gift magnific, exercised for good or ill.
You've your boot now on my hearth-rug, tread what was a tiger's
skin:
Rarely such a royal monster as I lodged the bullet in!
True, he murdered half a village, so his own death came to pass;
Still, for size and beauty, cunning, courage—ah, the brute he
was!
Why, that Clive,—that youth, that greenhorn, that quill-driving
clerk, in fine,—
He sustained a seige in Arcot. . . . But the world knows! Pass
the wine. 40

Where did I break off at? How bring Clive in? Oh, you men-
tioned "fear"!
Just so: and, said I, that minds me of a story you shall hear.

We were friends then, Clive and I: so, when the clouds, about
the orb
Late supreme, encroaching slowly, surely, threatened to absorb
Ray by ray its noontide brilliance,—friendship might, with
steadier eye

Drawing near, bear what had burned else, now no blaze—all
    majesty.

Too much bee's-wing floats my figure? Well, suppose a castle's
    new:

None presume to climb its ramparts, none find foothold sure for
    shoe

'Twixt those squares and squares of granite plating the im-
    pervious pile

As his scale-mail's warty iron cuirasses a crocodile.   50

Reels that castle thunder-smitten, storm-dismantled? From with-
    out

Scrambling up by crack and crevice, every cockney prates about

Towers—the heap he kicks now! turrets—just the measure of his
    cane!

Will that do? Observe moreover—(same similitude again)—

Such a castle seldom crumbles by sheer stress of cannonade:

'Tis when foes are foiled and fighting's finished that vile rams
    invade,

Grass o'ergrows, o'ergrows till night-birds congregating find no
    holes

Fit to build in like the topmost sockets made for banner-poles.

So Clive crumbled slow in London—crashed at last.

                                A week before,

Dining with him,—after trying churchyard-chat of days of
    yore,—   60

Both of us stopped, tired as tombstones, head-piece, foot-piece,
    when they lean

Each to other, drowsed in fog-smoke, o'er a coffined Past be-
    tween.

As I saw his head sink heavy, guessed the soul's extinguishment

By the glazing eyeball, noticed how the furtive fingers went

Where a drug-box skulked behind the honest liquor,—"One more
    throw

Try for Clive!" thought I: "Let's venture some good rattling
    question!" So—

"Come, Clive, tell us"—out I blurted—"what to tell in turn,
    years hence,

When my boy—suppose I have one—asks me on what evidence

I maintain my friend of Plassy proved a warrior every whit

Worth your Alexanders, Cæsars, Marlboroughs and—what said
    Pitt?—   70

Frederick the Fierce himself! Clive told me once"—I want to
say—
"Which feat out of all those famous doings bore the bell away
—In his own calm estimation, mark you, not the mob's rough
guess—
Which stood foremost as evincing what Clive called coura-
geousness!
Come! what moment of the minute, what speck-centre in the
wide
Circle of the action saw your mortal fairly deified?
(Let alone that filthy sleep-stuff, swallow bold this wholesome
Port!)
If a friend has leave to question,—when were you most brave,
in short?"

Up he arched his brows o' the instant—formidably Clive again.
"When was I most brave? I'd answer, were the instance half as
plain   80
As another instance that's a brain-lodged crystal—curse it!—
here
Freezing when my memory touches—ugh!—the time I felt most
fear.
Ugh! I cannot say for certain if I showed fear—anyhow,
Fear I felt, and, very likely, shuddered, since I shiver now."

"Fear!" smiled I. "Well, that's the rarer: that's a specimen to
seek,
Ticket up in one's museum, *Mind-Freaks, Lord Clive's Fear,
Unique!*"
Down his brows dropped. On the table painfully he pored as
though
Tracing, in the stains and streaks there, thoughts encrusted long
ago.
When he spoke 'twas like a lawyer reading word by word some
will,
Some blind jungle of a statement,—beating on and on until   90
Out there leaps fierce life to fight with.

                                    "This fell in my factor-days.
Desk-drudge, slaving at St. David's, one must game, or drink, or
craze.
I chose gaming: and,—because your high-flown gamesters
hardly take

Umbrage at a factor's elbow if the factor pays his stake,—
I was winked at in a circle where the company was choice,
Captain This and Major That, men high of color, loud of voice,
Yet indulgent, condescending to the modest juvenile
Who not merely risked but lost his hard-earned guineas with a
    smile.

"Down I sat to cards, one evening,—had for my antagonist
Somebody whose name's a secret—you'll know why—so, if you
    list,   100
Call him Cock o' the Walk, my scarlet son of Mars from head to
    heel!
Play commenced: and, whether Cocky fancied that a clerk must
    feel
Quite sufficient honor came of bending over one green baize,
I the scribe with him the warrior,—guessed no penman dared
    to raise
Shadow of objection should the honor stay but playing end
More or less abruptly,—whether disinclined he grew to spend
Practice strictly scientific on a booby born to stare
At—not ask of—lace-and-ruffles if the hand they hide plays
    fair,—
Anyhow, I marked a movement when he bade me 'Cut!'

                                           "I rose.
'Such the new manœuvre, Captain? I'm a novice: knowledge
    grows.   110
What, you force a card, you cheat, Sir?'

                            "Never did a thunder-clap
Cause emotion, startle Thyrsis locked with Chloe in his lap,
As my word and gesture (down I flung my cards to join the
    pack)
Fired the man of arms, whose visage, simply red before, turned
    black.

"When he found his voice, he stammered 'That expression once
    again!'

" 'Well, you forced a card and cheated!'

                             " 'Possibly a factor's brain,

Busied with his all-important balance of accounts, may deem
Weighing words superfluous trouble: *cheat* to clerkly ears may
    seem
Just the joke for friends to venture: but we are not friends, you
    see!
When a gentleman is joked with,—if he's good at repartee,   120
He rejoins, as do I—Sirrah, on your knees, withdraw in full!
Beg my pardon, or be sure a kindly bullet through your skull
Lets in light and teaches manners to what brain it finds! Choose
    quick—
Have your life snuffed out or, kneeling, pray me trim yon candle-
    wick!'

" 'Well, you cheated!'
               "Then outbroke a howl from all the friends around.
To his feet sprang each in fury, fists were clenched and teeth
    were ground.
'End it! no time like the present! Captain, yours were our disgrace!
No delay, begin and finish! Stand back, leave the pair a space!
Let civilians be instructed: henceforth simply ply the pen,
Fly the sword! This clerk's no swordsman? Suit him with a
    pistol, then!   130
Even odds! A dozen paces 'twixt the most and least expert
Make a dwarf a giant's equal: nay, the dwarf, if he's alert,
Likelier hits the broader target!'

                        "Up we stood accordingly.
As they handed me the weapon, such was my soul's thirst to
    try
Then and there conclusions with this bully, tread on and stamp
    out
Every spark of his existence, that,—crept close to, curled about
By that toying tempting teasing fool-forefinger's middle joint,—
Don't you guess?—the trigger yielded. Gone my chance! and at
    the point
Of such prime success moreover: scarce an inch above his head
Went my ball to hit the wainscot. He was living, I was
    dead.   140

"Up he marched in flaming triumph—'twas his right, mind!—up,
    within
Just an arm's length. 'Now, my clerkling,' chuckled Cocky with
    a grin

As the levelled piece quite touched me, 'Now, Sir Counting-
        House, repeat
That expression which I told you proved bad manners! Did I
        cheat?'

" 'Cheat you did, you knew you cheated, and, this moment,
        know as well.
As for me, my homely breeding bids you—fire and go to Hell!'

"Twice the muzzle touched my forehead. Heavy barrel, flurried
        wrist,
Either spoils a steady lifting. Thrice: then, 'Laugh at Hell who
        list,
I can't! God's no fable either. Did this boy's eye wink once? No!
There's no standing him and Hell and God all three against me,
        —so,   150
I did cheat!'

        "And down he threw the pistol, out rushed—by the door
Possibly, but, as for knowledge if by chimney, roof or floor,
He effected disappearance—I'll engage no glance was sent
That way by a single starer, such a blank astonishment
Swallowed up their senses: as for speaking—mute they stood
        as mice.

"Mute not long, though! Such reaction, such a hubbub in a
        trice!
'Rogue and rascal! Who'd have thought it? What's to be expected
        next,
When His Majesty's Commission serves a sharper as pretext
For . . . But where's the need of wasting time now? Naught
        requires delay:
Punishment the Service cries for: let disgrace be wiped
        away   160
Publicly, in good broad daylight! Resignation? No, indeed
Drum and fife must play the Rogue's March, rank and file be
        free to speed
Tardy marching on the rogue's part by appliance in the rear
—Kicks administered shall right this wronged civilian,—never
        fear,
Mister Clive, for—though a clerk—you bore yourself—suppose
        we say—
Just as would beseem a soldier!'

"'Gentlemen, attention—pray!
First, one word!'

                    "I passed each speaker severally in review.
When I had precise their number, names and styles, and fully
    knew
Over whom my supervision thenceforth must extend,—why,
    then——

" 'Some five minutes since, my life lay—as you all saw, gentle-
    men—   170
At the mercy of your friend there. Not a single voice was raised
In arrest of judgment, not one tongue—before my powder
    blazed—
Ventured "Can it be the youngster blundered, really seemed to
    mark
Some irregular proceeding? We conjecture in the dark,
Guess at random,—still, for sake of fair play—what if for a freak,
In a fit of absence,—such things have been!—if our friend proved
    weak
—What's the phrase?—corrected fortune! Look into the case,
    at least!"
Who dared interpose between the altar's victim and the priest?
Yet he spared me! You eleven! Whosoever, all or each,
To the disadvantage of the man who spared me, utters
    speech   180
—To his face, behind his back,—that speaker has to do with
    me:
Me who promise, if positions change and mine the chance
    should be,
Not to imitate your friend and waive advantage!'

                                              "Twenty-five
Years ago this matter happened: and 'tis certain," added Clive,
"Never, to my knowledge, did Sir Cocky have a single breath
Breathed against him: lips were closed throughout his life, or
    since his death,
For if he be dead or living I can tell no more than you.
All I know is—Cocky had one chance more; how he used it,—
    grew
Out of such unlucky habits, or relapsed, and back again
Brought the late-ejected devil with a score more in his
    train,—   190

That's for you to judge. Reprieval I procured, at any rate.
Ugh—the memory of that minute's fear makes goose-flesh rise!
    Why prate
Longer? You've my story, there's your instance: fear I did, you
    see!"

"Well"—I hardly kept from laughing—"if I see it, thanks must
    be
Wholly to your Lordship's candor. Not that—in a common
    case—
When a bully caught at cheating thrusts a pistol in one's face,
I should underrate, believe me, such a trial to the nerve!
'Tis no joke, at one-and-twenty, for a youth to stand nor swerve.
Fear I naturally look for—unless, of all men alive,
I am forced to make exception when I come to Robert Clive.   200
Since at Arcot, Plassy, elsewhere, he and death—the whole
    world knows—
Came to somewhat closer quarters."

                       Quarters? Had we come to blows,
Clive and I, you had not wondered—up he sprang so, out he
    rapped
Such a round of oaths—no matter! I'll endeavor to adapt
To our modern usage words he—well, 'twas friendly license—
    flung
At me like so many fire-balls, fast as he could wag his tongue.

"You—a soldier? You—at Plassy? Yours the faculty to nick
Instantaneously occasion when your foe, if lightning-quick,
—At his mercy, at his malice,—has you, through some stupid
    inch
Undefended in your bulwark? Thus laid open,—not to
    flinch   210
—That needs courage, you'll concede me. Then, look here!
    Suppose the man,
Checking his advance, his weapon still extended, not a span
Distant from my temple,—curse him!—quietly had bade me
    'There!
Keep your life, calumniator!—worthless life I freely spare:
Mine you freely would have taken—murdered me and my good
    fame
Both at once—and all the better! Go, and thank your own bad
    aim

Which permits me to forgive you!' What if, with such words
    as these,
He had cast away his weapon? How should I have borne me,
    please?
Nay, I'll spare you pains and tell you. This, and only this, re-
    mained—
Pick his weapon up and use it on myself. I so had gained   220
Sleep the earlier, leaving England probably to pay on still
Rent and taxes for half India, tenant at the Frenchman's will."

"Such the turn," said I, "the matter takes with you? Then I
    abate
—No, by not one jot nor tittle,—of your act my estimate.
Fear—I wish I could detect there: courage fronts me, plain
    enough—
Call it desperation, madness—never mind! for here's in rough
Why, had mine been such a trial, fear had overcome disgrace.
True, disgrace were hard to bear: but such a rush against God's
    face
—None of that for me, Lord Plassy, since I go to church at times,
Say the creed my mother taught me! Many years in foreign
    climes   230
Rub some marks away—not all, though! We poor sinners reach
    life's brink,
Overlook what rolls beneath it, recklessly enough, but think
There's advantage in what's left us—ground to stand on, time
    to call
'Lord, have mercy!' ere we topple over—do not leap, that's all!"

Oh, he made no answer,—re-absorbed into his cloud. I caught
Something like "Yes—courage: only fools will call it fear."

                            If aught
Comfort you, my great unhappy hero Clive, in that I heard,
Next week, how your own hand dealt you doom, and uttered
    just the word
"Fearfully courageous!"—this, be sure, and nothing else I
    groaned.
I'm no Clive, nor parson either: Clive's worst deed—we'll hope
    condoned.   240

MULEYKEH

IF A stranger passed the tent of Hóseyn, he cried "A churl's!"
Or haply "God help the man who has neither salt nor bread!"
—"Nay," would a friend exclaim, "he needs nor pity nor scorn
More than who spends small thought on the shore-sand, picking
    pearls,
—Holds but in light esteem the seed-sort, bears instead
On his breast a moon-like prize, some orb which of night makes
    morn.

"What if no flocks and herds enrich the son of Sinán?
They went when his tribe was mulct, ten thousand camels the
    due,
Blood-value paid perforce for a murder done of old.
'God gave them, let them go! But never since time began,   10
Muléykeh, peerless mare, owned master the match of you,
And you are my prize, my Pearl: I laugh at men's land and gold!'

"So in the pride of his soul laughs Hóseyn—and right, I say.
Do the ten steeds run a race of glory? Outstripping all,
Ever Muléykeh stands first steed at the victor's staff.
Who started, the owner's hope, gets shamed and named, that
    day.
'Silence,' or, last but one, is 'The Cuffed,' as we use to call
Whom the paddock's lord thrusts forth. Right, Hóseyn, I say, to
    laugh!"

"Boasts he Muléykeh the Pearl?" the stranger replies: "Be sure
On him I waste nor scorn nor pity, but lavish both   20
On Duhl the son of Sheybán, who withers away in heart
For envy of Hóseyn's luck. Such sickness admits no cure.
A certain poet has sung, and sealed the same with an oath,
'For the vulgar—flocks and herds! The Pearl is a prize apart.'"

Lo, Duhl the son of Sheybán comes riding to Hóseyn's tent,
And he casts his saddle down, and enters and "Peace!" bids he.
"You are poor, I know the cause: my plenty shall mend the
    wrong.

'Tis said of your Pearl—the price of a hundred camels spent
In her purchase were scarce ill paid: such prudence is far from
    me
Who proffer a thousand. Speak! Long parley may last too
    long."   30

Said Hóseyn "You feed young beasts a many, of famous breed,
Slit-eared, unblemished, fat, true offspring of Múzennem:
There stumbles no weak-eyed she in the line as it climbs the hill.
But I love Múleykeh's face: her forefront whitens indeed
Like a yellowish wave's cream-crest. Your camels—go gaze on
    them!
Her fetlock is foam-splashed too. Myself am the richer still."

A year goes by: lo, back to the tent again rides Duhl.
"You are open-hearted, ay—moist-handed, a very prince.
Why should I speak of sale? Be the mare your simple gift!
My son is pined to death for her beauty: my wife prompts
    'Fool,   40
Beg for his sake the Pearl! Be God the rewarder, since
God pays debts seven for one: who squanders on Him shows
    thrift.' "

Said Hóseyn "God gives each man one life, like a lamp, then
    gives
That lamp due measure of oil: lamp lighted—hold high, wave
    wide
Its comfort for others to share! once quench it, what help is left?
The oil of your lamp is your son: I shine while Muléykeh lives.
Would I beg your son to cheer my dark if Muléykeh died?
It is life against life: what good avails to the life-bereft?"

Another year, and—hist! What craft is it Duhl designs?
He alights not at the door of the tent as he did last time,   50
But, creeping behind, he gropes his stealthy way by the trench
Half-round till he finds the flap in the folding, for night combines
With the robber—and such is he: Duhl, covetous up to crime,
Must wring from Hóseyn's grasp the Pearl, by whatever the
    wrench.

"He was hunger-bitten, I heard: I tempted with half my store,
And a gibe was all my thanks. Is he generous like Spring dew?
Account the fault to me who chaffered with such an one!

He has killed, to feast chance comers, the creature he rode: nay,
    more—
For a couple of singing-girls his robe has he torn in two:
I will beg! Yet I nowise gained by the tale of my wife and
    son.   60

"I swear by the Holy House, my head will I never wash
Till I filch his Pearl away. Fair dealing I tried, then guile,
And now I resort to force. He said we must live or die:
Let him die, then,—let me live! Be bold—but not too rash!
I have found me a peeping-place: breast, bury your breathing
    while
I explore for myself! Now, breathe! He deceived me not, the
    spy!

"As he said—there lies in peace Hóseyn—how happy! Beside
Stands tethered the Pearl: thrice winds her headstall about his
    wrist:
'Tis therefore he sleeps so sound—the moon through the roof
    reveals.
And, loose on his left, stands too that other, known far and
    wide,   70
Buhéyseh, her sister born: fleet is she yet ever missed
The winning tail's fire-flash a-stream past the thunderous heels.

"No less she stands saddled and bridled, this second, in case some
    thief
Should enter and seize and fly with the first, as I mean to do.
What then? The Pearl is the Pearl: once mount her we both
    escape."
Through the skirt-fold in glides Duhl,—so a serpent disturbs no
    leaf
In a bush as he parts the twigs entwining a nest: clean through,
He is noiselessly at his work: as he planned, he performs the rape.

He has set the tent-door wide, has buckled the girth, has clipped
The headstall away from the wrist he leaves thrice bound as
    before,   80
He springs on the Pearl, is launched on the desert like bolt from
    bow.
Up starts our plundered man: from his breast though the heart
    be ripped,

Yet his mind has the mastery: behold, in a minute more,
He is out and off and away on Buhéyseh, whose worth we know!

And Hóseyn—his blood turns flame, he has learned long since
    to ride,
And Buhéyseh does her part,—they gain—they are gaining fast
On the fugitive pair, and Duhl has Ed-Dárraj to cross and quit,
And to reach the ridge El-Sabán,—no safety till that be spied!
And Buhéyseh is, bound by bound, but a horse-length off at last,
For the Pearl has missed the tap of the heel, the touch of the
    bit.   90

She shortens her stride, she chafes at her rider the strange and
    queer:
Buhéyseh is mad with hope—beat sister she shall and must
Though Duhl, of the hand and heel so clumsy, she has to
    thank.
She is near now, nose by tail—they are neck by croup—joy!
    fear!
What folly makes Hóseyn shout "Dog Duhl, Damned son of the
    Dust,
Touch the right ear and press with your foot my Pearl's left
    flank!"

And Duhl was wise at the word, and Muléykeh as prompt per-
    ceived
Who was urging redoubled pace, and to hear him was to obey,
And a leap indeed gave she, and evanished for evermore.
And Hóseyn looked one long last look as who, all bereaved,   100
Looks, fain to follow the dead so far as the living may:
Then he turned Buhéyseh's neck slow homeward, weeping sore.

And, lo, in the sunrise, still sat Hóseyn upon the ground
Weeping: and neighbors came, the tribesmen of Bénu-Asád
In the vale of green Er-Rass, and they questioned him of his
    grief;
And he told from first to last how, serpent-like, Duhl had wound
His way to the nest, and how Duhl rode like an ape, so bad!
And how Buhéyseh did wonders, yet Pearl remained with the
    thief.

And they jeered him, one and all: "Poor Hóseyn is crazed past
    hope!

How else had he wrought himself his ruin, in fortune's spite?   110
To have simply held the tongue were a task for a boy or girl,
And here were Muléykeh again, the eyed like an antelope,
The child of his heart by day, the wife of his breast by night!"—
"And the beaten in speed!" wept Hóseyn: "You never have loved
     my Pearl."

PAN AND LUNA

Si credere dignum est.—Georgic. *iii. 390.*

O WORTHY of belief I hold it was,
Virgil, your legend in those strange three lines!
No question, that adventure came to pass
One black night in Arcadia: yes, the pines,
Mountains and valleys mingling made one mass
Of black with void black heaven: the earth's confines,
The sky's embrace,—below, above, around,
All hardened into black without a bound.

Fill up a swart stone chalice to the brim
With fresh-squeezed yet fast-thickening poppy-juice: 10
See how the sluggish jelly, late a-swim,
Turns marble to the touch of who would loose
The solid smooth, grown jet from rim to rim,
By turning round the bowl! So night can fuse
Earth with her all-comprising sky. No less,
Light, the least spark, shows air and emptiness.

And thus it proved when—diving into space,
Stript of all vapor, from each web of mist
Utterly film-free—entered on her race
The naked Moon, full-orbed antagonist   20
Of night and dark, night's dowry: peak to base,
Upstarted mountains, and each valley, kissed
To sudden life, lay silver-bright: in air
Flew she revealed, Maid-Moon with limbs all bare.

Still as she fled, each depth—where refuge seemed—
Opening a lone pale chamber, left distinct
Those limbs: mid still-retreating blue, she teemed
Herself with whiteness,—virginal, uncinct

By any halo save what finely gleamed
To outline not disguise her: heaven was linked   30
In one accord with earth to quaff the joy,
Drain beauty to the dregs without alloy.

Whereof she grew aware. What help? When, lo,
A succorable cloud with sleep lay dense:
Some pine-tree-top had caught it sailing slow,
And tethered for a prize: in evidence
Captive lay fleece on fleece of piled-up snow
Drowsily patient: flake-heaped how or whence,
The structure of that succorable cloud,
What matter? Shamed she plunged into its shroud.   40

Orbed—so the woman-figure poets call
Because of rounds on rounds—that apple-shaped
Head which its hair binds close into a ball
Each side the curving ears—that pure undraped
Pout of the sister paps—that . . . Once for all,
Say—her consummate circle thus escaped
With its innumerous circlets, sank absorbed,
Safe in the cloud—O naked Moon full-orbed!

But what means this? The downy swathes combine,
Conglobe, the smothery coy-caressing stuff   50
Curdles about her! Vain each twist and twine
Those lithe limbs try, encroached on by a fluff
Fitting as close as fits the dented spine
Its flexile ivory outside-flesh: enough!
The plumy drifts contract, condense, constringe,
Till she is swallowed by the feathery springe.

As when a pearl slips lost in the thin foam
Churned on a sea-shore, and, o'er-frothed, conceits
Herself safe-housed in Amphitrite's dome,—
If, through the bladdery wave-worked yeast, she meets   60
What most she loathes and leaps from,—elf from gnome
No gladlier,—finds that safest of retreats
Bubble about a treacherous hand wide ope
To grasp her—(divers who pick pearls so grope)—

So lay this Maid-Moon clasped around and caught
By rough red Pan, the god of all that tract:

He it was schemed the snare thus subtly wrought
With simulated earth-breath,—wool-tufts packed
Into a billowy wrappage. Sheep far-sought
For spotless shearings yield such: take the fact   70
As learned Virgil gives it,—how the brèed
Whitens itself forever: yes, indeed!

If one forefather ram, though pure as chalk
From tinge on fleece, should still display a tongue
Black 'neath the beast's moist palate, prompt men balk
The propagating plague: he gets no young:
They rather slay him,—sell his hide to calk
Ships with, first steeped in pitch,—nor hands are wrung
In sorrow for his fate: protected thus,
The purity we love is gained for us.   80

So did Girl-moon, by just her attribute
Of unmatched modesty betrayed, lie trapped,
Bruised to the breast of Pan, half-god half-brute,
Raked by his bristly boar-sward while he lapped
—Never say, kissed her! that were to pollute
Love's language—which moreover proves unapt
To tell how she recoiled—as who finds thorns
Where she sought flowers—when, feeling, she touched—horns!

Then—does the legend say?—first moon-eclipse
Happened, first swooning-fit which puzzled sore   90
The early sages? Is that why she dips
Into the dark, a minute and no more,
Only so long as serves her while she rips
The cloud's womb through and, faultless as before,
Pursues her way? No lesson for a maid
Left she, a maid herself thus trapped, betrayed?

Ha, Virgil? Tell the rest, you! "To the deep
Of his domain the wildwood, Pan forthwith
Called her, and so she followed"—in her sleep,
Surely?—"by no means spurning him." The myth   100
Explain who may! Let all else go, I keep
—As of a ruin just a monolith—
Thus much, one verse of five words, each a boon:
Arcadia, night, a cloud, Pan, and the moon.

"Touch him ne'er so lightly, into song he broke:
Soil so quick-receptive,—not one feather-seed,
Not one flower-dust fell but straight its fall awoke
Vitalizing virtue: song would song succeed
Sudden as spontaneous—prove a poet-soul!"

                                        Indeed?
Rock's the song-soil rather, surface hard and bare:
Sun and dew their mildness, storm and frost their rage
Vainly both expend,—few flowers awaken there:
Quiet in its cleft broods—what the after age
Knows and names a pine, a nation's heritage.   110

From JOCOSERIA

[1883]

PROLOGUE

WANTING is—what?
Summer redundant,
Blueness abundant,
—Where is the blot?
Beamy the world, yet a blank all the same,
—Framework which waits for a picture to frame:
What of the leafage, what of the flower?
Roses embowering with naught they embower!
Come then, complete incompletion, O comer,
Pant through the blueness, perfect the summer!
Breathe but one breath
Rose-beauty above,
And all that was death
Grows life, grows love,
Grows love!

CRISTINA AND MONALDESCHI

AH, BUT how each loved each, Marquis!
Here's the gallery they trod
Both together, he her god,
She his idol,—lend your rod,
Chamberlain!—ay, there they are—*"Quis
Separabit?"*—plain those two
Touching words come into view,
Apposite for me and you:

Since they witness to incessant
Love like ours: King Francis, he—
Diane the adored one, she—
Prototypes of you and me.
Everywhere is carved her Crescent
With his Salamander-sign—

675

Flame-fed creature: flame benign
To itself or, if malign,

Only to the meddling curious,
    —So, be warned, Sir! Where's my head?
    How it wanders! What I said
    Merely meant—the creature, fed   20
Thus on flame, was scarce injurious
    Save to fools who woke its ire,
    Thinking fit to play with fire.
    'Tis the Crescent you admire?

Then, be Diane! I'll be Francis.
    Crescents change,—true!—wax and wane.
    Woman-like: male hearts retain
    Heat nor, once warm, cool again.
So, we figure—such our chance is—
    I as man and you as . . . What?   30
    Take offence? My Love forgot
    He plays woman, I do not?

I—the woman? See my habit,
    Ask my people! Anyhow,
    Be we what we may, one vow
    Binds us, male or female. Now,—
Stand, Sir! Read! "*Quis separabit?*"
    Half a mile of pictured way
    Past these palace-walls to-day
    Traversed, this I came to say.   40

You must needs begin to love me;
    First I hated, then, at best,
    —Have it so!—I acquiesced;
    Pure compassion did the rest.
From below thus raised above me,
    Would you, step by step, descend,
    Pity me, become my friend,
    Like me, like less, loathe at end?

That's the ladder's round you rose by!
    That—my own foot kicked away,   50
    Having raised you: let it stay,
    Serve you for retreating? Nay.

Close to me you climbed: as close by,
　　Keep your station, though the peak
　　Reached proves somewhat bare and bleak!
　　Woman's strong if man is weak.

Keep here, loving me forever!
　　Love's look, gesture, speech, I claim;
　　Act love, lie love, all the same—
　　Play as earnest were our game!　　　　　　　　60
Lonely I stood long: 'twas clever
　　When you climbed, before men's eyes,
　　Spurned the earth and scaled the skies,
　　Gained my peak and grasped your prize.

Here you stood, then, to men's wonder;
　　Here you tire of standing? Kneel!
　　Cure what giddiness you feel,
　　This way! Do your senses reel?
Not unlikely! What rolls under?
　　Yawning death in yon abyss　　　　　　　　　70
　　Where the waters whirl and hiss
　　Round more frightful peaks than this.

Should my buffet dash you thither . . .
　　But be sage! No watery grave
　　Needs await you: seeming brave
　　Kneel on safe, dear timid slave!
You surmised, when you climbed hither,
　　Just as easy were retreat
　　Should you tire, conceive unmeet
　　Longer patience at my feet?　　　　　　　　80

Me as standing, you as stooping,—
　　Who arranged for each the pose?
　　Lest men think us friends turned foes,
　　Keep the attitude you chose!
Men are used to this same grouping—
　　I and you like statues seen.
　　You and I, no third between,
　　Kneel and stand! That makes the scene.

Mar it—and one buffet . . . Pardon!
　　Needless warmth—wise words in waste!　　　　90

'Twas prostration that replaced
 Kneeling, then? A proof of taste.
Crouch, not kneel, while I mount guard on
 Prostrate love—become no waif,
 No estray to waves that chafe
 Disappointed—love's so safe!

Waves that chafe? The idlest fancy!
 Peaks that scare? I think we know
 Walls enclose our sculpture: so
 Grouped, we pose in Fontainebleau. 100
Up now! Wherefore hesitancy?
 Arm in arm and cheek by cheek,
 Laugh with me at waves and peak!
 Silent still? Why, pictures speak.

See, where Juno strikes Ixion,
 Primatice speaks plainly! Pooh—
 Rather, Florentine Le Roux!
 I've lost head for who is who—
So it swims and wanders! Fie on
 What still proves me female! Here, 110
 By the staircase!—for we near
 That dark "Gallery of the Deer."

Look me in the eyes once! Steady!
 Are you faithful now as erst
 On that eve when we two first
 Vowed at Avon, blessed and cursed
Faith and falsehood? Pale already?
 Forward! Must my hand compel
 Entrance—this way? Exit—well,
 Somehow, somewhere. Who can tell? 120

What if to the self-same place in
 Rustic Avon, at the door
 Of the village church once more,
 Where a tombstone paves the floor
By that holy-water basin
 You appealed to—"As, below,
 This stone hides its corpse, e'en so
 I your secrets hide"? What ho!

Friends, my four! You, Priest, confess him!
   I have judged the culprit there: 130
   Execute my sentence! Care
   For no mail such cowards wear!
Done, Priest? Then, absolve and bless him!
   Now—you three, stab thick and fast,
   Deep and deeper! Dead at last?
   Thanks, friends—Father, thanks! Aghast?

What one word of his confession
   Would you tell me, though I lured
   With that royal crown abjured
   Just because its bars immured   140
Love too much? Love burst compression,
   Fled free, finally confessed
   All its secrets to that breast
   Whence . . . let Avon tell the rest!

ADAM, LILITH, AND EVE

ONE day it thundered and lightened.
Two women, fairly frightened,
Sank to their knees, transformed, transfixed,
At the feet of the man who sat betwixt;
And "Mercy!" cried each—"if I tell the truth
Of a passage in my youth!"

Said This: "Do you mind the morning
I met your love with scorning?
As the worst of the venom left my lips,
I thought 'If, despite this lie, he strips
The mask from my soul with a kiss—I crawl
His slave,—soul, body and all!'"

Said That: "We stood to be married;
The priest, or some one, tarried;
'If Paradise-door prove locked?' smiled you.
I thought, as I nodded, smiling too,
'Did one, that's away, arrive—nor late
Nor soon should unlock Hell's gate!'"

It ceased to lighten and thunder.
Up started both in wonder,
Looked round and saw that the sky was clear,
Then laughed "Confess you believed us, Dear!"
"I saw through the joke!" the man replied.
They re-seated themselves beside.

NEVER THE TIME AND THE PLACE

NEVER the time and the place
 And the loved one all together!
This path—how soft to pace!
 This May—what magic weather!
Where is the loved one's face?
In a dream that loved one's face meets mine,
 But the house is narrow, the place is bleak
Where, outside, rain and wind combine
 With a furtive ear, if I strive to speak,
 With a hostile eye at my flushing cheek,   10
With a malice that marks each word, each sign!
O enemy sly and serpentine,
 Uncoil thee from the waking man!
   Do I hold the Past
   Thus firm and fast
 Yet doubt if the Future hold I can?
This path so soft to pace shall lead
Thro' the magic of May to herself indeed!
Or narrow if needs the house must be.
Outside are the storms and strangers: we—   20
Oh, close, safe, warm sleep I and she,
 —I and she!

THE NAMES

[1884]

SHAKESPEARE!—to such name's sounding, what succeeds
　　Fitly as silence? Falter forth the spell,—
　　Act follows word, the speaker knows full well,
Nor tampers with its magic more than needs.
Two names there are: That which the Hebrew reads
　　With his soul only: if from lips it fell,
　　Echo, back thundered by earth, heaven and hell,
Would own, "Thou didst create us!" Naught impedes
We voice the other name, man's most of might,
　　Awesomely, lovingly: let awe and love
Mutely await their working, leave to sight
　　All of the issue as—below—above—
　　Shakespeare's creation rises: one remove,
Though dread—this finite from that infinite.

March 12, 1884.

WHY I AM A LIBERAL

[1885]

"WHY?" Because all I haply can and do,
　　All that I am now, all I hope to be,—
　　Whence comes it save from fortune setting free
Body and soul the purpose to pursue,
God traced for both? If fetters, not a few,
　　Of prejudice, convention, fall from me,
　　These shall I bid men—each in his degree
Also God-guided—bear, and gayly too?

But little do or can the best of us:
　　That little is achieved through Liberty.
Who, then, dares hold, emancipated thus,
　　His fellow shall continue bound? Not I,
Who live, love, labor freely, nor discuss
　　A brother's right to freedom. That is "Why."

From PARLEYINGS WITH CERTAIN PEOPLE OF IMPORTANCE IN THEIR DAY

[1887]

WITH DANIEL BARTOLI

I

Don, the divinest women that have walked
Our world were scarce those saints of whom we talked.
My saint, for instance—worship if you will!
'Tis pity poets need historians' skill:
What legendary's worth a chronicle?

II

Come, now! A great lord once upon a time
Visited—oh a king, of kings the prime,
To sign a treaty such as never was:
For the king's minister had brought to pass
That this same duke—so style him—must engage   10
Two of his dukedoms as an heritage
After his death to this exorbitant
Craver of kingship. "Let who lacks go scant,
Who owns much, give the more to!" Why rebuke?
So bids the devil, so obeys the duke.

III

Now, as it happened, at his sister's house
—Duchess herself—indeed the very spouse
Of the king's uncle,—while the deed of gift
Whereby our duke should cut his rights adrift
Was drawing, getting ripe to sign and seal—   20
What does the frozen heart but uncongeal
And, shaming his transcendent kin and kith,
Whom do the duke's eyes make acquaintance with?
A girl. "What, sister, may this wonder be?"
"Nobody! Good as beautiful is she,
With gifts that match her goodness, no faint flaw

683

I' the white: she were the pearl you think you saw,
But that she is—what corresponds to white?
Some other stone, the true pearl's opposite,
As cheap as pearls are costly. She's—now, guess   30
Her parentage! Once—twice—thrice? Foiled, confess!
Drugs, duke, her father deals in—faugh, the scents!—
Manna and senna—such medicaments
For payment he compounds you. Stay—stay—stay!
I'll have no rude speech wrong her! Whither away,
The hot-head? Ah, the scapegrace! She deserves
Respect—compassion, rather! Right it serves
My folly, trusting secrets to a fool!
Already at it, is he? She keeps cool—
Helped by her fan's spread. Well, our state atones   40
For thus much license, and words break no bones!"
(Hearts, though, sometimes.)

IV

                    Next morn 'twas "Reason, rate,
Rave, sister, on till doomsday! Sure as fate,
I wed that woman—what a woman is
Now that I know, who never knew till this!"
So swore the duke. "I wed her: once again—
Rave, rate, and reason—spend your breath in vain!"

V

At once was made a contract firm and fast,
Published the banns were, only marriage, last,
Required completion when the Church's rite   50
Should bless and bid depart, make happy quite
The coupled man and wife for evermore:
Which rite was soon to follow. Just before—
All things at all but end—the folk o' the bride
Flocked to a summons. Pomp the duke defied:
"Of ceremony—so much as empowers,
Naught that exceeds, suits best a tie like ours—"
He smiled—"all else were mere futility.
We vow, God hears us: God and you and I—
Let the world keep at distance! This is why   60
We choose the simplest forms that serve to bind
Lover and lover of the human kind,

No care of what degree—of kings or clowns—
Come blood and breeding. Courtly smiles and frowns
Miss of their mark, would idly soothe or strike
My style and yours—in one style merged alike—
God's man and woman merely. Long ago
'Twas rounded in my ears 'Duke, wherefore slow
To use a privilege? Needs must one who reigns
Pay reigning's due: since statecraft so ordains—   70
Wed for the commonweal's sake! law prescribes
One wife: but to submission license bribes
Unruly nature: mistresses accept
—Well, at discretion!' Prove I so inept
A scholar, thus instructed? Dearest, be
Wife and all mistresses in one to me,
Now, henceforth, and forever!" So smiled he.

VI

Good: but the minister, the crafty one,
Got ear of what was doing—all but done—
Not sooner, though, than the king's very self,   80
Warned by the sister on how sheer a shelf
Royalty's ship was like to split. "I bar
The abomination! Mix with muck my star?
Shall earth behold prodigiously enorbed
An upstart marsh-born meteor sun-absorbed?
Nuptial me no such nuptials!" "Past dispute,
Majesty speaks with wisdom absolute,"
Admired the minister: "yet, all the same,
I would we may not—while we play his game,
The ducal meteor's—also lose our own,   90
The solar monarch's: we relieve your throne
Of an ungracious presence, like enough:
Balked of his project he departs in huff,
And so cuts short—dare I remind the king?—
Our not so unsuccessful bargaining.
The contract for eventual heritage
Happens to *pari passu* reach the stage
Attained by just this other contract,—each
Unfixed by signature though fast in speech.
Off goes the duke in dudgeon—off withal   100
Go with him his two dukedoms past recall.
You save a fool from tasting folly's fruit,

Obtain small thanks thereby, and lose to boot
Sagacity's reward. The jest is grim:
The man will mulct you—for amercing him?
Nay, for . . . permit a poor similitude!
A witless wight in some fantastic mood
Would drown himself: you plunge into the wave,
Pluck forth the undeserving: he, you save,
Pulls you clean under also for your pains.   110
Sire, little need that I should tax my brains
To help your inspiration!" "Let him sink!
Always contriving"—hints the royal wink—
"To keep ourselves dry while we claim his clothes."

VII

Next day, the appointed day for plighting troths
At eve,—so little time to lose, you see,
Before the Church should weld indissolubly
Bond into bond, wed these who, side by side,
Sit each by other, bold groom, blushing bride,—
At the preliminary banquet, graced   120
By all the lady's kinsfolk come in haste
To share her triumph,—lo, a thunderclap!
"Who importunes now?" "Such is my mishap—
In the king's name! No need that any stir
Except this lady!" bids the minister:
"With her I claim a word apart, no more:
For who gainsays—a guard is at the door.
Hold, duke! Submit you, lady, as I bow
To him whose mouthpiece speaks his pleasure now!
It well may happen I no whit arrest   130
Your marriage: be it so,—we hope the best!
By your leave, gentles! Lady, pray you, hence!
Duke, with my soul and body's deference!"

VIII

Doors shut, mouth opens and persuasion flows
Copiously forth. "What flesh shall dare oppose
The king's command? The matter in debate
—How plain it is! Yourself shall arbitrate,
Determine. Since the duke affects to rate
His prize in you beyond all goods of earth,

Accounts as naught old gains of rank and birth,   140
Ancestral obligation, recent fame,
(We know his feats)—nay, ventures to disclaim
Our will and pleasure almost—by report—
Waives in your favor dukeliness, in short,—
We— ('tis the king speaks)—who might forthwith stay
Such suicidal purpose, brush away
A bad example shame would else record,—
Lean to indulgence rather. At his word
We take the duke: allow him to complete
The cession of his dukedoms, leave our feet   150
Their footstool when his own head, safe in vault,
Sleeps sound. Nay, would the duke repair his fault
Handsomely, and our forfeited esteem
Recover,—what if wisely he redeem
The past,—in earnest of good faith, at once
Give us such jurisdiction for the nonce
As may suffice—present occasion slip—
And constitute our actual ownership?
Concede this—straightway be the marriage blessed
By warrant of this paper! Things at rest,   160
This paper duly signed, down drops the bar,
To-morrow you become—from what you are,
The druggist's daughter—not the duke's mere spouse,
But the king's own adopted: heart and house
Open to you—the idol of a court
'Which heaven might copy'—sing our poet-sort.
In this emergency, on you depends
The issue: plead what bliss the king intends!
Should the duke frown, should arguments and prayers,
Nay, tears if need be, prove in vain,—who cares?   170
We leave the duke to his obduracy,
Companionless,—you, madam, follow me
Without, where divers of the body-guard
Wait signal to enforce the king's award
Of strict seclusion: over you at least
Vibratingly the sceptre threats increased
Precipitation! How avert its crash?"

IX

"Re-enter, sir! A hand that's calm, not rash,
Averts it!" quietly the lady said.
"Yourself shall witness."

           At the table's head   180
Where, mid the hushed guests, still the duke sat glued
In blank bewilderment, his spouse pursued
Her speech to end—syllabled quietude.

X

"Duke, I, your duchess of a day, could take
The hand you proffered me for love's sole sake,
Conscious my love matched yours; as you, myself
Would waive, when need were, all but love—from pelf
To potency. What fortune brings about
Haply in some far future, finds me out,
Faces me on a sudden here and now.   190
The better! Read—if beating heart allow—
Read this, and bid me rend to rags the shame!
I and your conscience—hear and grant our claim!
Never dare alienate God's gift you hold
Simply in trust for him! Choose muck for gold?
Could you so stumble in your choice, cajoled
By what I count my least of worthiness
—The youth, the beauty,—you renounce them—yes,
With all that's most too: love as well you lose,
Slain by what slays in you the honor! Choose!   200
Dear—yet my husband—dare I love you yet?"

XI

How the duke's wrath o'erboiled,—words, words and yet
More words,—I spare you such fool's fever-fret.
They were not of one sort at all, one size,
As souls go—he and she. 'Tis said, the eyes
Of all the lookers-on let tears fall fast.
The minister was mollified at last:
"Take a day,—two days even, ere through pride
You perish,—two days' counsel—then decide!"

XII

—"If I shall save his honor and my soul?   210
Husband,—this one last time,—you tear the scroll?
Farewell, duke! Sir, I follow in your train!"

XIII

So she went forth: they never met again,
The duke and she. The world paid compliment
(Is it worth noting?) when, next day, she sent
Certain gifts back—"jewelry fit to deck
Whom you call wife." I know not round what neck
They took to sparkling, in good time—weeks thence.

XIV

Of all which was the pleasant consequence,
So much and no more—that a fervid youth,   220
Big-hearted boy,—but ten years old, in truth,—
Laid this to heart and loved, as boyhood can,
The unduchessed lady: boy and lad grew man:
He loved as man perchance may: did meanwhile
Good soldier-service, managed to beguile
The years, no few, until he found a chance:
Then, as at trumpet-summons to advance,
Outbroke the love that stood at arms so long,
Brooked no withstanding longer. They were wed.
Whereon from camp and court alike he fled,   230
Renounced the sun-king, dropped off into night,
Evermore lost, a ruined satellite:
And, oh, the exquisite deliciousness
That lapped him in obscurity! You guess
Such joy is fugitive: she died full soon.
He did his best to die—as sun, so moon
Left him, turned dusk to darkness absolute.
Failing of death—why, saintship seemed to suit:
Yes, your sort, Don! He trembled on the verge
Of monkhood: trick of cowl and taste of scourge   240
He tried: then, kicked not at the pricks perverse,
But took again, for better or for worse,

The old way in the world, and, much the same
Man o' the outside, fairly played life's game.

XV

"Now, Saint Scholastica, what time she fared
In Paynimrie, behold, a lion glared
Right in her path! Her waist she promptly strips
Of girdle, binds his teeth within his lips,
And, leashed all lamblike, to the Soldan's court
Leads him." Ay, many a legend of the sort   250
Do you praiseworthily authenticate:
Spare me the rest. This much of no debate
Admits: my lady flourished in grand days
When to be duchess was to dance the hays
Up, down, across the heaven amid its host:
While to be hailed the sun's own self almost—
So close the kinship—was—was—

                                        Saint, for this,
Be yours the feet I stoop to—kneel and kiss!
So human? Then the mouth too, if you will!
Thanks to no legend but a chronicle.   260

XVI

One leans to like the duke, too: up we'll patch
Some sort of saintship for him—not to match
Hers—but man's best and woman's worst amount
So nearly to the same thing, that we count
In man a miracle of faithfulness
If, while unfaithful somewhat, he lays stress
On the main fact that love, when love indeed,
Is wholly solely love from first to last—
Truth—all the rest a lie. Too likely, fast
Enough that necklace went to grace the throat   270
—Let's say, of such a dancer as makes doat
The senses when the soul is satisfied—
Trogalia, say the Greeks—a sweetmeat tried
Approvingly by sated tongue and teeth,
Once body's proper meal consigned beneath
Such unconsidered munching.

XVII

Fancy's flight
Makes me a listener when, some sleepless night,
The duke reviewed his memories, and aghast
Found that the Present intercepts the Past
With such effect as when a cloud enwraps   280
The moon and, moon-suffused, plays moon perhaps
To who walks under, till comes, late or soon,
A stumble: up he looks, and lo, the moon
Calm, clear, convincingly herself once more!
How could he 'scape the cloud that thrust between
Him and effulgence? Speak, fool—duke, I mean!

XVIII

"Who bade you come, brisk-marching bold she-shape,
    A terror with those black-balled worlds of eyes,
That black hair bristling solid-built from nape
    To crown it coils about? O dread surmise!   29(
Take, tread on, trample under past escape
    Your capture, spoil and trophy! Do—devise
Insults for one who, fallen once, ne'er shall rise!

"Mock on, triumphant o'er the prostrate shame!
    Laugh 'Here lies he among the false to Love—
Love's loyal liegeman once: the very same
    Who, scorning his weak fellows, towered above
Inconstancy: yet why his faith defame?
    Our eagle's victor was at least no dove,
No dwarfish knight picked up our giant's glove—   30(

" 'When, putting prowess to the proof, faith urged
    Her champion to the challenge: had it chanced
That merely virtue, wisdom, beauty—merged
    All in one woman—merely these advanced
Their claim to conquest,—hardly had he purged
    His mind of memories, dearnesses enhanced
Rather than harmed by death, nor, disentranced,

" 'Promptly had he abjured the old pretence
    To prove his kind's superior—first to last

Display erect on his heart's eminence   310
    An altar to the never-dying Past.
For such feat faith might boast fit play of fence
    And easily disarm the iconoclast
Called virtue, wisdom, beauty: impudence

" 'Fought in their stead, and how could faith but fall?
    There came a bold she-shape brisk-marching, bent
No inch of her imperious stature, tall
    As some war-engine from whose top was sent
One shattering volley out of eye's black ball,
    And prone lay faith's defender!' Mockery spent?   320
Malice discharged in full? In that event,

"My queenly impudence, I cover close,
    I wrap me round with love of your black hair,
Black eyes, black every wicked inch of those
    Limbs' war-tower tallness: so much truth lives there
'Neath the dead heap of lies. And yet—who knows?
    What if such things are? No less, such things were.
Then was the man your match whom now you dare

"Treat as existent still. A second truth!
    They held—this heap of lies you rightly scorn—   330
A man who had approved himself in youth
    More than a match for—you? for sea-foam-born
Venus herself: you conquer him forsooth?
    'Tis me his ghost: he died since left and lorn,
As needs must Samson when his hair is shorn.

"Some day, and soon, be sure himself will rise,
    Called into life by her who long ago
Left his soul whiling time in flesh-disguise.
    Ghosts tired of waiting can play tricks, you know!
Tread, trample me—such sport we ghosts devise,   340
    Waiting the morn-star's re-appearance—though
You think we vanish scared by the cock's crow."

From ASOLANDO

[1889]

PROLOGUE

"THE Poet's age is sad: for why?
   In youth, the natural world could show
No common object but his eye
   At once involved with alien glow—
His own soul's iris-bow.

"And now a flower is just a flower:
   Man, bird, beast are but beast, bird, man—
Simply themselves, uncinct by dower
   Of dyes which, when life's day began,
Round each in glory ran."   10

Friend, did you need an optic glass,
   Which were your choice? A lens to drape
In ruby, emerald, chrysopras,
   Each object—or reveal its shape
Clear outlined, past escape,

The naked very thing?—so clear
   That, when you had the chance to gaze,
You found its inmost self appear
   Through outer seeming—truth ablaze,
Not falsehood's fancy-haze?   20

How many a year, my Asolo,
   Since—one step just from sea to land—
I found you, loved yet feared you so—
   For natural objects seemed to stand
Palpably fire-clothed! No—

No mastery of mine o'er these!
   Terror with beauty, like the Bush
Burning but unconsumed. Bend knees,
   Drop eyes to earthward! Language? Tush!
Silence 'tis awe decrees.   30

And now? The lambent flame is—where?
　Lost from the naked world: earth, sky,
Hill, vale, tree, flower,—Italia's rare
　O'er-running beauty crowds the eye—
But flame? The Bush is bare.

Hill, vale, tree, flower—they stand distinct,
　Nature to know and name. What then?
A Voice spoke thence which straight unlinked
　Fancy from fact: see, all's in ken:
Has once my eyelid winked?　　　　　　40

No, for the purged ear apprehends
　Earth's import, not the eye late dazed:
The Voice said "Call my works thy friends!
　At Nature dost thou shrink amazed?
God is it who transcends."

ASOLO: *Sept. 6, 1889.*

DUBIETY

I WILL be happy if but for once:
　Only help me, Autumn weather,
Me and my cares to screen, ensconce
　In luxury's sofa-lap of leather!

Sleep? Nay, comfort—with just a cloud
　Suffusing day too clear and bright:
Eve's essence, the single drop allowed
　To sully, like milk, Noon's water-white.

Let gauziness shade, not shroud,—adjust,
　Dim and not deaden,—somehow sheathe　　10
Aught sharp in the rough world's busy thrust,
　If it reach me through dreaming's vapor-wreath.

Be life so, all things ever the same!
　For, what has disarmed the world? Outside,
Quiet and peace: inside, nor blame
　Nor want, nor wish whate'er betide.

What is it like that has happened before?
　　A dream? No dream, more real by much.
A vision? But fanciful days of yore
　　Brought many: mere musing seems not such.　　　20

Perhaps but a memory, after all!
　　—Of what came once when a woman leant
To feel for my brow where her kiss might fall.
　　Truth ever, truth only the excellent!

NOW

Out of your whole life give but a moment!
All of your life that has gone before,
All to come after it,—so you ignore,
So you make perfect the present,—condense,
In a rapture of rage, for perfection's endowment,
Thought and feeling and soul and sense—
Merged in a moment which gives me at last
You around me for once, you beneath me, above me—
Me—sure that despite of time future, time past,—
This tick of our life-time's one moment you love me!　　10
How long such suspension may linger? Ah, Sweet—
The moment eternal—just that and no more—
When ecstasy's utmost we clutch at the core
While cheeks burn, arms open, eyes shut and lips meet!

HUMILITY

　　What girl but, having gathered flowers,
　　Stript the beds and spoilt the bowers,
　　From the lapful light she carries
　　Drops a careless bud?—nor tarries
　　To regain the waif and stray:
　　"Store enough for home"—she'll say.

　　So say I too: give your lover
　　Heaps of loving—under, over,

Whelm him—make the one the wealthy!
Am I all so poor who—stealthy
Work it was!—picked up what fell:
Not the worst bud—who can tell?

POETICS

"So SAY the foolish!" Say the foolish so, Love?
　"Flower she is, my rose"—or else "My very swan is she"—
Or perhaps "Yon maid-moon, blessing earth below, Love,
　That art thou!"—to them, belike: no such vain words from me.

"Hush, rose, blush! no balm like breath," I chide it:
　"Bend thy neck its best, swan,—hers the whiter curve!"
Be the moon the moon: my Love I place beside it;
　What is she? Her human self,—no lower word will serve.

SUMMUM BONUM

ALL the breath and the bloom of the year in the bag of one bee:
　All the wonder and wealth of the mine in the heart of one
　　gem:
In the core of one pearl all the shade and the shine of the sea:
　Breath and bloom, shade and shine,—wonder, wealth, and—
　　how far above them—
　　　Truth, that's brighter than gem,
　　　Trust, that's purer than pearl,—
Brightest truth, purest trust in the universe—all were for me
　In the kiss of one girl.

A PEARL, A GIRL

A SIMPLE ring with a single stone
　To the vulgar eye no stone of price:
Whisper the right word, that alone—
　Forth starts a sprite, like fire from ice,
And lo, you are lord (says an Eastern scroll)

Of heaven and earth, lord whole and sole
   Through the power in a pearl.

A woman ('tis I this time that say)
   With little the world counts worthy praise
Utter the true word—out and away
   Escapes her soul: I am wrapt in blaze,
Creation's lord, of heaven and earth
Lord whole and sole—by a minute's birth—
   Through the love in a girl!

SPECULATIVE

OTHERS may need new life in Heaven—
   Man, Nature, Art—made new, assume!
Man with new mind old sense to leaven,
   Nature—new light to clear old gloom,
Art that breaks bounds, gets soaring-room.

I shall pray: "Fugitive as precious—
   Minutes which passed,—return, remain!
Let earth's old life once more enmesh us,
   You with old pleasure, me—old pain,
So we but meet nor part again!"

BAD DREAMS   1

LAST night I saw you in my sleep:
   And how your charm of face was changed!
I asked "Some love, some faith you keep?"
   You answered "Faith gone, love estranged."

Whereat I woke—a twofold bliss:
   Waking was one, but next there came
This other: "Though I felt, for this,
   My heart break, I loved on the same."

BAD DREAMS   2

You in the flesh and here—
   Your very self! Now, wait!
One word! May I hope or fear?
   Must I speak in love or hate?
Stay while I ruminate!

The fact and each circumstance
   Dare you disown? Not you!
That vast dome, that huge dance,
   And the gloom which overgrew
A—possibly festive crew!   10

For why should men dance at all—
   Why women—a crowd of both—
Unless they are gay? Strange ball—
   Hands and feet plighting troth,
Yet partners enforced and loth!

Of who danced there, no shape
   Did I recognize: thwart, perverse,
Each grasped each, past escape
   In a whirl or weary or worse:
Man's sneer met woman's curse,   20

While he and she toiled as if
   Their guardian set galley-slaves
To supple chained limbs grown stiff:
   Unmanacled trulls and knaves—
The lash for who misbehaves!

And a gloom was, all the while,
   Deeper and deeper yet
O'ergrowing the rank and file
   Of that army of haters—set
To mimic love's fever-fret.   30

By the wall-side close I crept,
   Avoiding the livid maze,
And, safely so far, outstepped

On a chamber—a chapel, says
  My memory or betrays—

Closet-like, kept aloof
    From unseemly witnessing
What sport made floor and roof
    Of the Devil's palace ring
While his Damned amused their king.   40

Ay, for a low lamp burned,
    And a silence lay about
What I, in the midst, discerned
    Though dimly till, past doubt,
'Twas a sort of throne stood out—

High seat with steps, at least:
    And the topmost step was filled
By—whom? What vestured priest?
    A stranger to me,—his guild,
His cult, unreconciled   50

To my knowledge how guild and cult
    Are clothed in this world of ours:
I pondered, but no result
    Came to—unless that Giaours
So worship the Lower Powers.

When suddenly who entered?
    Who knelt—did you guess I saw?
Who—raising that face where centred
    Allegiance to love and law
So lately—off-casting awe,   60

Down-treading reserve, away
    Thrusting respect . . . but mine
Stands firm—firm still shall stay!
    Ask Satan! for I decline
To tell—what I saw, in fine!

Yet here in the flesh you come—
    Your same self, form and face,—

In the eyes, mirth still at home!
  On the lips, that commonplace
Perfection of honest grace!   70

Yet your errand is—needs must be
  To palliate—well, explain,
Expurgate in some degree
  Your soul of its ugly stain.
Oh, you—the good in grain—

How was it your white took tinge?
  "A mere dream"—never object!
Sleep leaves a door on hinge
  Whence soul, ere our flesh suspect,
Is off and away: detect   80

Her vagaries when loose, who can!
  Be she pranksome, be she prude,
Disguise with the day began:
  With the night—ah, what ensued
From draughts of a drink hell-brewed?

Then She: "What a queer wild dream!
  And perhaps the best fun is—
Myself had its fellow—I seem
  Scarce awake from yet. 'Twas this—
Shall I tell you? First, a kiss!   90

' For the fault was just your own,—
  'Tis myself expect apology:
You warned me to let alone
  (Since our studies were mere philology)
That ticklish (you said) Anthology.

"So, I dreamed that I passed *exam*
  Till a question posed me sore:
'Who translated this epigram
  By—an author we best ignore?'
And I answered 'Hannah More'!"   100

BAD DREAMS 3

THIS was my dream: I saw a Forest
  Old as the earth, no track nor trace
Of unmade man. Thou, Soul, explorest—
  Though in a trembling rapture—space
Immeasurable! Shrubs, turned trees,
Trees that touch heaven, support its frieze
Studded with sun and moon and star:
While—oh, the enormous growths that bar
Mine eye from penetrating past
  Their tangled twine where lurks—nay, lives   10
Royally lone, some brute-type cast
  I' the rough, time cancels, man forgives.

On, Soul! I saw a lucid City
  Of architectural device
Every way perfect. Pause for pity,
  Lightning! nor leave a cicatrice
On those bright marbles, dome and spire.
Structures palatial,—streets which mire
Dares not defile, paved all too fine
For human footstep's smirch, not thine—   20
Proud solitary traverser,
  My Soul, of silent lengths of way—
With what ecstatic dread, aver,
  Lest life start sanctioned by thy stay!

Ah, but the last sight was the hideous!
  A City, yes,—a Forest, true,—
But each devouring each. Perfidious
  Snake-plants had strangled what I knew
Was a pavilion once: each oak
Held on his horns some spoil he broke   30
By surreptitiously beneath
Upthrusting: pavements, as with teeth,
Griped huge weed widening crack and split
  In squares and circles stone-work erst.
Oh, Nature—good! Oh, Art—no whit
  Less worthy! Both in one—accurst!

WHICH?

So, the three Court-ladies began
　　Their trial of who judged best
In esteeming the love of a man:
Who preferred with most reason was thereby confessed
Boy-Cupid's exemplary catcher and cager;
An Abbé crossed legs to decide on the wager.

First the Duchesse: "Mine for me—
　　Who were it but God's for Him,
And the King's for—who but he?
Both faithful and loyal, one grace more shall brim　　10
His cup with perfection: a lady's true lover,
He holds—save his God and his king—none above her."

"I require"—outspoke the Marquise—
　　"Pure thoughts, ay, but also fine deeds:
Play the paladin must he, to please
My whim, and—to prove my knight's service exceeds
Your saint's and your loyalist's praying and kneeling—
Show wounds, each wide mouth to my mercy appealing."

Then the Comtesse: "My choice be a wretch,
　　Mere losel in body and soul,　　　　　　　　20
Thrice accurst! What care I, so he stretch
Arms to me his sole saviour, love's ultimate goal,
Out of earth and men's noise—names of 'infidel,' 'traitor,'
Cast up at him? Crown me, crown's adjudicator!"

And the Abbé uncrossed his legs,
　　Took snuff, a reflective pinch,
Broke silence: "The question begs
Much pondering ere I pronounce. Shall I flinch?
The love which to one and one only has reference
Seems terribly like what perhaps gains God's preference."　　30

THE POPE AND THE NET

WHAT, he on whom our voices unanimously ran,
Made Pope at our last Conclave? Full low his life began:
His father earned the daily bread as just a fisherman.

So much the more his boy minds book, gives proof of mother-
    wit,
Becomes first Deacon, and then Priest, then Bishop: see him sit
No less than Cardinal ere long, while no one cries "Unfit!"

But some one smirks, some other smiles, jogs elbow and nods
    head:
Each winks at each: "I'-faith, a rise! Saint Peter's net, instead
Of sword and keys, is come in vogue!" You think he blushes red?

Not he, of humble holy heart! "Unworthy me!" he sighs: 10
"From fisher's drudge to Church's prince—it is indeed a rise:
So, here's my way to keep the fact forever in my eyes!"

And straightway in his palace-hall, where commonly is set
Some coat-of-arms, some portraiture ancestral, lo, we met
His mean estate's reminder in his fisher-father's net!

Which step conciliates all and some, stops cavil in a trice:
"The humble holy heart that holds of new-born pride no spice!
He's just the saint to choose for Pope!" Each adds " 'Tis my
    advice."

So, Pope he was: and when we flocked—its sacred slipper on—
To kiss his foot, we lifted eyes, alack the thing was gone—   20
That guarantee of lowlihead,—eclipsed that star which shone!

Each eyed his fellow, one and all kept silence. I cried "Pish!
I'll make me spokesman for the rest, express the common wish.
Why, Father, is the net removed?" "Son, it hath caught the
    fish."

THE BEAN-FEAST

He was the man—Pope Sixtus, that Fifth, that swineherd's son:
He knew the right thing, did it, and thanked God when 'twas
    done:
But of all he had to thank for, my fancy somehow leans
To thinking, what most moved him was a certain meal on beans.

For one day, as his wont was, in just enough disguise
As he went exploring wickedness,—to see with his own eyes
If law had due observance in the city's entrail dark
As well as where, i' the open, crime stood an obvious mark,—

He chanced, in a blind alley, on a tumble-down once house
Now hovel, vilest structure in Rome the ruinous: 10
And, as his tact impelled him, Sixtus adventured bold,
To learn how lowliest subjects bore hunger, toil, and cold.

There sat they at high-supper—man and wife, lad and lass,
Poor as you please but cleanly all and care-free: pain that was
—Forgotten, pain as sure to be let bide aloof its time,—
Mightily munched the brave ones—what mattered gloom or
    grime?

Said Sixtus "Feast, my children! who works hard needs eat well.
I'm just a supervisor, would hear what you can tell.
Do any wrongs want righting? The Father tries his best,
But, since he's only mortal, sends such as I to test   20
The truth of all that's told him—how folk like you may fare:
Come!—only don't stop eating—when mouth has words to
    spare—

"You"—smiled he—"play the spokesman, bellwether of the
    flock!
Are times good, masters gentle? Your grievances unlock!
How of your work and wages?—pleasures, if such may be—
Pains, as such are for certain." Thus smiling questioned he.

But somehow, spite of smiling, awe stole upon the group—
An inexpressible surmise: why should a priest thus stoop—

Pry into what concerned folk? Each visage fell. Aware,
Cries Sixtus interposing: "Nay, children, have no care!   30

"Fear nothing! Who employs me requires the plain truth. Pelf
Beguiles who should inform me: so, I inform myself.
See!" And he threw his hood back, let the close vesture ope,
Showed face, and where on tippet the cross lay: 'twas the Pope.

Imagine the joyful wonder! "How shall the like of us—
Poor souls—requite such blessing of our rude bean-feast?"
          "Thus—
Thus amply!" laughed Pope Sixtus. "I early rise, sleep late:
Who works may eat: they tempt me, your beans there: spare
          a plate!"

Down sat he on the door-step: 'twas they this time said grace:
He ate up the last mouthful, wiped lips, and then, with face   40
Turned heavenward, broke forth thankful: "Not now, that earth
          obeys
Thy word in mine, that through me the peoples know Thy
          ways—
But that Thy care extendeth to Nature's homely wants,
And, while man's mind is strengthened, Thy goodness nowise
          scants
Man's body of its comfort,—that I whom kings and queens
Crouch to, pick crumbs from off my table, relish beans!
The thunders I but seem to launch, there plain Thy hand all see:
That I have appetite, digest, and thrive—that boon's for me."

"IMPERANTE AUGUSTO NATUS EST——"

WHAT it was struck the terror into me?
This, Publius: closer! while we wait our turn
I'll tell you. Water's warm (they ring inside)
At the eighth hour, till when no use to bathe.

Here in the vestibule where now we sit,
One scarce stood yesterday, the throng was such
Of loyal gapers, folk all eye and ear
While Lucius Varius Rufus in their midst

Read out that long-planned late-completed piece,
His Panegyric on the Emperor.   10
"Nobody like him" little Flaccus laughed
"At leading forth an Epos with due pomp!
Only, when godlike Cæsar swells the theme,
How should mere mortals hope to praise aright?
Tell me, thou offshoot of Etruscan kings!"
Whereat Mæcenas smiling sighed assent.

I paid my quadrans, left the Thermæ's roar
Of rapture as the poet asked "What place
Among the godships Jove, for Cæsar's sake,
Would bid its actual occupant vacate   20
In favor of the new divinity?"
And got the expected answer "Yield thine own!"—
Jove thus dethroned, I somehow wanted air,
And found myself a-pacing street and street,
Letting the sunset, rosy over Rome,
Clear my head dizzy with the hubbub—say
As if thought's dance therein had kicked up dust
By trampling on all else: the world lay prone,
As—poet-propped, in brave hexameters—
Their subject triumphed up from man to God.   30
Caius Octavius Cæsar the August—
Where was escape from his prepotency?
I judge I may have passed—how many piles
Of structure dropt like doles from his free hand
To Rome on every side? Why, right and left,
For temples you've the Thundering Jupiter,
Avenging Mars, Apollo Palatine:
How count Piazza, Forum—there's a third
All but completed. You've the Theatre
Named of Marcellus—all his work, such work!—   40
One thought still ending, dominating all—
With warrant Varius sang "Be Cæsar God!"
By what a hold arrests he Fortune's wheel,
Obtaining and retaining heaven and earth
Through Fortune, if you like, but favor—no!
For the great deeds flashed by me, fast and thick
As stars which storm the sky on autumn nights—
Those conquests! but peace crowned them,—so, of peace!
Count up his titles only—these, in few—
Ten years Triumvir, Consul thirteen times,   50

There's Heine, where the big books block the shelf:
Don't skip a word, thumb well the Lexicon!"

I thumbed well and skipped nowise till I learned
Who was who, what was what, from Homer's tongue,
And there an end of learning. Had you asked   50
The all-accomplished scholar, twelve years old,
"Who was it wrote the Iliad?"—what a laugh!
"Why, Homer, all the world knows: of his life
Doubtless some facts exist: it's everywhere:
We have not settled, though, his place of birth:
He begged, for certain, and was blind beside:
Seven cities claimed him—Scio, with best right,
Thinks Byron. What he wrote? Those Hymns we have.
Then there's the 'Battle of the Frogs and Mice,'
That's all—unless they dig 'Margites' up   60
(I'd like that) nothing more remains to know."

Thus did youth spend a comfortable time;
Until—"What's this the Germans say is fact
That Wolf found out first? It's unpleasant work
Their chop and change, unsettling one's belief:
All the same, while we live, we learn, that's sure."
So, I bent brow o'er *Prolegomena*.
And, after Wolf, a dozen of his like
Proved there was never any Troy at all,
Neither Besiegers nor Besieged,—nay, worse,—   70
No actual Homer, no authentic text,
No warrant for the fiction I, as fact,
Had treasured in my heart and soul so long—
Ay, mark you! and as fact held still, still hold,
Spite of new knowledge, in my heart of hearts
And soul of souls, fact's essence freed and fixed
From accidental fancy's guardian sheath.
Assuredly thenceforward—thank my stars!—
However it got there, deprive who could—
Wring from the shrine my precious tenantry,   80
Helen, Ulysses, Hector and his Spouse,
Achilles and his Friend?—though Wolf—ah, Wolf!
Why must he needs come doubting, spoil a dream?
But then "No dream's worth waking"—Browning says:
And here's the reason why I tell thus much
I, now mature man, you anticipate,

May blame my Father justifiably
For letting me dream out my nonage thus,
And only by such slow and sure degrees
Permitting me to sift the grain from chaff,   90
Get truth and falsehood known and named as such.
Why did he ever let me dream at all,
Not bid me taste the story in its strength?
Suppose my childhood was scarce qualified
To rightly understand mythology,
Silence at least was in his power to keep:
I might have—somehow—correspondingly—
Well, who knows by what method, gained my gains,
Been taught, by forthrights not meanderings,
My aim should be to loathe, like Peleus' son,   100
A lie as Hell's Gate, love my wedded wife,
Like Hector, and so on with all the rest.
Could not I have excogitated this
Without believing such men really were?
That is—he might have put into my hand
The "Ethics"? In translation, if you please,
Exact, no pretty lying that improves,
To suit the modern taste: no more, no less—
The "Ethics": 'tis a treatise I find hard
To read aright now that my hair is gray,   110
And I can manage the original.
At five years old—how ill had fared its leaves!
Now, growing double o'er the Stagirite,
At least I soil no page with bread and milk,
Nor crumple, dogsear and deface—boys' way.

REPHAN

[Suggested by a very early recollection of a prose story by the noble
woman and imaginative writer, Jane Taylor, of Norwich.—R. B.]

    How I lived, ere my human life began
    In this world of yours,—like you, made man,—
    When my home was the Star of my God Rephan?

    Come then around me, close about,
    World-weary earth-born ones! Darkest doubt
    Or deepest despondency keeps you out?

Nowise! Before a word I speak,
Let my circle embrace your worn, your weak,
Brow-furrowed old age, youth's hollow cheek—

Diseased in the body, sick in soul,   10
Pinched poverty, satiate wealth,—your whole
Array of despairs! Have I read the roll?

All here? Attend, perpend! O Star
Of my God Rephan, what wonders are
In thy brilliance fugitive, faint and far!

Far from me, native to thy realm,
Who shared its perfections which o'erwhelm
Mind to conceive. Let drift the helm,

Let drive the sail, dare unconfined
Embark for the vastitude, O Mind,   20
Of an absolute bliss! Leave earth behind!

Here, by extremes, at a mean you guess:
There, all's at most—not more, not less:
Nowhere deficiency nor excess.

No want—whatever should be, is now:
No growth—that's change, and change comes—how
To royalty born with crown on brow?

Nothing begins—so needs to end:
Where fell it short at first? Extend
Only the same, no change can mend!   30

I use your language: mine—no word
Of its wealth would help who spoke, who heard,
To a gleam of intelligence. None preferred,

None felt distaste when better and worse
Were uncontrastable: bless or curse
What—in that uniform universe?

Can your world's phrase, your sense of things
Forth-figure the Star of my God? No springs,
No winters throughout its space. Time brings

No hope, no fear: as to-day, shall be   40
To-morrow: advance or retreat need we
At our stand-still through eternity?

All happy: needs must we so have been,
Since who could be otherwise? All serene:
What dark was to banish, what light to screen?

Earth's rose is a bud that's checked or grows
As beams may encourage or blasts oppose:
Our lives leapt forth, each a full-orbed rose—

Each rose sole rose in a sphere that spread
Above and below and around—rose-red: 50
No fellowship, each for itself instead.

One better than I—would prove I lacked
Somewhat: one worse were a jarring fact
Disturbing my faultlessly exact.

How did it come to pass there lurked
Somehow a seed of change that worked
Obscure in my heart till perfection irked?—

Till out of its peace at length grew strife—
Hopes, fears, loves, hates,—obscurely rife,—
My life grown a-tremble to turn your life?   60

Was it Thou, above all lights that are,
Prime Potency, did Thy hand unbar
The prison-gate of Rephan my Star?

In me did such potency wake a pulse
Could trouble tranquillity that lulls
Not lashes inertion till throes convulse

Soul's quietude into discontent?
As when the completed rose bursts, rent
By ardors till forth from its orb are sent

New petals that mar—unmake the disk—   70
Spoil rondure: what in it ran brave risk,
Changed apathy's calm to strife, bright, brisk,

Pushed simple to compound, sprang and spread
Till, fresh-formed, facetted, floretted,
The flower that slept woke a star instead?

No mimic of Star Rephan! How long
I stagnated there where weak and strong,
The wise and the foolish, right and wrong,

Are merged alike in a neutral Best,
Can I tell? No more than at whose behest   8
The passion arose in my passive breast,

And I yearned for no sameness but difference
In thing and thing, that should shock my sense
With a want of worth in them all, and thence

Startle me up, by an Infinite
Discovered above and below me—height
And depth alike to attract my flight,

Repel my descent: by hate taught love.
Oh, gain were indeed to see above
Supremacy ever—to move, remove,   90

Not reach—aspire yet never attain
To the object aimed at! Scarce in vain,—
As each stage I left nor touched again.

To suffer, did pangs bring the loved one bliss,
Wring knowledge from ignorance,—just for this—
To add one drop to a love-abyss!

Enough: for you doubt, you hope, O men,
You fear, you agonize, die: what then?
Is an end to your life's work out of ken?

Have you no assurance that, earth at end,   100
Wrong will prove right? Who made shall mend
In the higher sphere to which yearnings tend?

Why should I speak? You divine the test.
When the trouble grew in my pregnant breast
A voice said "So wouldst thou strive, not rest?

"Burn and not smoulder, win by worth,
Not rest content with a wealth that's dearth?
Thou art past Rephan, thy place be Earth!"

REVERIE

I KNOW there shall dawn a day
 —Is it here on homely earth?
Is it yonder, worlds away,
 Where the strange and new have birth,
That Power comes full in play?

Is it here, with grass about,
 Under befriending trees,
When shy buds venture out,
 And the air by mild degrees
Puts winter's death past doubt?   10

Is it up amid whirl and roar
 Of the elemental flame
Which star-flecks heaven's dark floor,
 That, new yet still the same,
Full in play comes Power once more?

Somewhere, below, above,
 Shall a day dawn—this I know—
When Power, which vainly strove
 My weakness to o'erthrow,
Shall triumph. I breathe, I move,   20

I truly am, at last!
 For a veil is rent between
Me and the truth which passed
 Fitful, half-guessed, half-seen,
Grasped at—not gained, held fast.

I for my race and me
 Shall apprehend life's law:
In the legend of man shall see
 Writ large what small I saw
In my life's tale: both agree.   30

As the record from youth to age
    Of my own, the single soul—
So the world's wide book: one page
    Deciphered explains the whole
Of our common heritage.

How but from near to far
    Should knowledge proceed, increase?
Try the clod ere test the star!
    Bring our inside strife to peace
Ere we wage, on the outside, war!   40

So, my annals thus begin:
    With body, to life awoke
Soul, the immortal twin
    Of body which bore soul's yoke
Since mortal and not akin.

By means of the flesh, grown fit,
    Mind, in surview of things,
Now soared, anon alit
    To treasure its gatherings
From the ranged expanse—to-wit,   50

Nature,—earth's, heaven's wide show
    Which taught all hope, all fear:
Acquainted with joy and woe,
    I could say "Thus much is clear,
Doubt annulled thus much: I know.

"All is effect of cause:
    As it would, has willed and done
Power: and my mind's applause
    Goes, passing laws each one,
To Omnipotence, lord of laws."   60

Head praises, but heart refrains
    From loving's acknowledgment.
Whole losses outweigh half-gains:
    Earth's good is with evil blent:
Good struggles but evil reigns.

Yet since Earth's good proved good—
   Incontrovertibly
Worth loving—I understood
   How evil—did mind descry
Power's object to end pursued—   70

Were haply as cloud across
   Good's orb, no orb itself:
Mere mind—were it found at loss
   Did it play the tricksy elf
And from life's gold purge the dross?

Power is known infinite:
   Good struggles to be—at best
Seems—scanned by the human sight,
   Tried by the senses' test—
Good palpably: but with right   80

Therefore to mind's award
   Of loving, as power claims praise?
Power—which finds naught too hard,
   Fulfilling itself all ways
Unchecked, unchanged: while barred,

Baffled, what good began
   Ends evil on every side.
To Power submissive man
   Breathes "E'en as Thou art, abide!"
While to good "Late-found, long-sought,   90

"Would Power to a plenitude
   But liberate, but enlarge
Good's strait confine,—renewed
   Were ever the heart's discharge
Of loving!" Else doubts intrude.

For you dominate, stars all!
   For a sense informs you—brute,
Bird, worm, fly, great and small,
   Each with your attribute
Or low or majestical!   100

Thou earth that embosomest
  Offspring of land and sea—
How thy hills first sank to rest,
  How thy vales bred herb and tree
Which dizen thy mother-breast—

Do I ask? "Be ignorant
  Ever!" the answer clangs:
Whereas if I plead world's want,
  Soul's sorrows and body's pangs,
Play the human applicant,—   110

Is a remedy far to seek?
  I question and find response:
I—all men, strong or weak,
  Conceive and declare at once
For each want its cure. "Power, speak!

"Stop change, avert decay,
  Fix life fast, banish death,
Eclipse from the star bid stay,
  Abridge of no moment's breath
One creature! Hence, Night, hail, Day!"   120

What need to confess again
  No problem this to solve
By impotence? Power, once plain
  Proved Power,—let on Power devolve
Good's right to co-equal reign!

Past mind's conception—Power!
  Do I seek how star, earth, beast,
Bird, worm, fly, gained their dower
  For life's use, most and least?
Back from the search I cower.   130

Do I seek what heals all harm,
  Nay, hinders the harm at first,
Saves earth? Speak, Power, the charm!
  Keep the life there unamerced
By chance, change, death's alarm!

As promptly as mind conceives,
    Let Power in its turn declare
Some law which wrong retrieves,
    Abolishes everywhere
What thwarts, what irks, what grieves!   140

Never to be! and yet
    How easy it seems—to sense
Like man's—if somehow met
    Power with its match—immense
Love, limitless, unbeset

By hindrance on every side!
    Conjectured, nowise known,
Such may be: could man confide
    Such would match—were Love but shown
Stript of the veils that hide—   150

Power's self now manifest!
    So reads my record: thine,
O world, how runs it? Guessed
    Were the purport of that prime line,
Prophetic of all the rest!

"In a beginning God
    Made heaven and earth." Forth flashed
Knowledge: from star to clod
    Man knew things: doubt abashed
Closed its long period.   160

Knowledge obtained Power praise.
    Had Good been manifest,
Broke out in cloudless blaze,
    Unchequered as unrepressed,
In all things Good at best—

Then praise—all praise, no blame—
    Had hailed the perfection. No!
As Power's display, the same
    Be Good's—praise forth shall flow
Unisonous in acclaim!   170

Even as the world its life,
   So have I lived my own—
Power seen with Love at strife,
   That sure, this dimly shown,
—Good rare and evil rife.

Whereof the effect be—faith
   That, some far day, were found
Ripeness in things now rathe,
   Wrong righted, each chain unbound,
Renewal born out of scathe.   18^

Why faith—but to lift the load,
   To leaven the lump, where lies
Mind prostrate through knowledge owed
   To the loveless Power it tries
To withstand, how vain! In flowed

Ever resistless fact:
   No more than the passive clay
Disputes the potter's act,
   Could the whelmed mind disobey
Knowledge the cataract.   190

But, perfect in every part,
   Has the potter's moulded shape,
Leap of man's quickened heart,
   Throe of his thought's escape,
Stings of his soul which dart

Through the barrier of flesh, till keen
   She climbs from the calm and clear,
Through turbidity all between,
   From the known to the unknown here,
Heaven's "Shall be," from Earth's "Has been"?   200

Then life is—to wake not sleep,
   Rise and not rest, but press
From earth's level where blindly creep
   Things perfected, more or less,
To the heaven's height, far and steep,

Where, amid what strifes and storms
   May wait the adventurous quest,
Power is Love—transports, transforms
   Who aspired from worst to best,
Sought the soul's world, spurned the worms'.   210

I have faith such end shall be:
   From the first, Power was—I knew.
Life has made clear to me
   That, strive but for closer view,
Love were as plain to see.

When see? When there dawns a day,
   If not on the homely earth,
Then yonder, worlds away,
   Where the strange and new have birth,
And Power comes full in play.   220

EPILOGUE

AT THE midnight in the silence of the sleep-time,
   When you set your fancies free,
Will they pass to where—by death, fools think, imprisoned—
Low he lies who once so loved you, whom you loved so,
        —Pity me?

Oh to love so, be so loved, yet so mistaken!
   What had I on earth to do
With the slothful, with the mawkish, the unmanly?
Like the aimless, helpless, hopeless, did I drivel
        —Being—who?

One who never turned his back but marched breast forward,
   Never doubted clouds would break,
Never dreamed, though right were worsted, wrong would
   triumph,
Held we fall to rise, are baffled to fight better,
        Sleep to wake.

No, at noonday in the bustle of man's work-time
   Greet the unseen with a cheer!
Bid him forward, breast and back as either should be,
"Strive and thrive!" cry "Speed,—fight on, fare ever
      There as here!"

INDEX OF TITLES

The Best of the World's Best Books
COMPLETE LIST OF TITLES IN
THE MODERN LIBRARY
For convenience in ordering use number at right of title

MODERN LIBRARY GIANTS

A series of full-sized library editions of books that formerly were available only in cumbersome and expensive sets.
THE MODERN LIBRARY GIANTS REPRESENT A
SELECTION OF THE WORLD'S GREATEST BOOKS

These volumes contain from 600 to 1,400 pages each
